The Winshaw Legacy

The Winshaw Legacy

or

What a Carve Up!

Jonathan Coe

ALFRED A. KNOPF NEW YORK

1995

THIS IS A BORZOI BOOK
PUBLISHED BY ALFRED A. KNOPF, INC.

Copyright © 1994 by Jonathan Coe

Library of Congress Cataloging-in-Publication Data

Coe, Jonathan.
The Winshaw legacy or What a carve up! /
Jonathan Coe. — 1st ed.
p. cm.
ISBN 0-679-43385-6
1. Family—England—Fiction. 2. Biographers—Fiction.
I. Title.
PR6053.O26 1995
823'.914—dc20 94-12842
CIP

Manufactured in the United States of America
FIRST AMERICAN EDITION

For 1994, Janine

Contents

Prologue

1942–1961

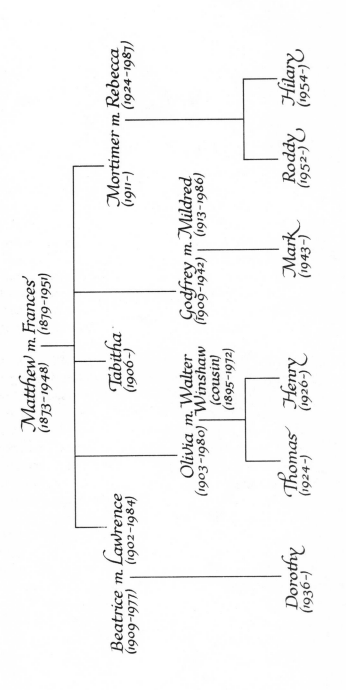

Matthew m. Frances
(1873–1948) (1879–1951)

Beatrice m. Lawrence
(1909–1977) (1902–1984)

Tabitha
(1906–)

Mortimer m. Rebecca
(1911–) (1924–1987)

Olivia m. Walter
(1903–1980) Winshaw
(cousin)
(1895–1972)

Godfrey m. Mildred
(1909–1942) (1913–1986)

Dorothy
(1936–)

Thomas
(1924–)

Henry
(1926–)

Mark
(1943–)

Roddy
(1952–)

Hilary
(1954–)

I

Tragedy had struck the Winshaws twice before, but never on such a terrible scale.

The first of these incidents takes us back to the night of November 30th 1942, when Godfrey Winshaw, then only in his thirty-third year, was shot down by German anti-aircraft fire as he flew a top-secret mission over Berlin. The news, which was relayed to Winshaw Towers in the early hours of the morning, was enough to drive his elder sister Tabitha clean out of her wits, where she remains to this day. Such was the violence of her distraction, in fact, that it was deemed impossible for her even to attend the memorial service which was held in her brother's honour.

It is a curious irony that this same Tabitha Winshaw, today aged eighty-one and no more in possession of her thinking faculties than she has been for the last forty-five years, should be the patron and sponsor of the book which you, my friendly readers, now hold in your hands. The task of writing with any objectivity about her condition becomes somewhat problematic. Yet the facts must be stated, and the facts are these: that from the very moment she heard of Godfrey's tragic demise, Tabitha has been in the grip of a grotesque delusion. In a word, it has been her belief (if such it can be called) that he was not brought down by German gunfire at all, but that the killing was the work of his own brother, Lawrence.

I have no wish to dwell unnecessarily on the pitiful infirmities which fate has chosen to visit upon a poor and weak-minded woman, but this matter must be explained insofar as it has a material bearing on the subsequent history of the Winshaw family, and it must, therefore, be put into some sort of context. I shall at least endeavour to be brief. The reader should know, then, that

Tabitha was thirty-six years old when Godfrey died, and that she was still living the life of a spinster, never having shown the slightest inclination towards matrimony. In this regard it had already been noticed by several members of her family that her attitude towards the male sex was characterized at best by indifference and at worst by aversion: the lack of interest with which she received the approaches of her occasional suitors was matched only by her passionate attachment and devotion to Godfrey – who was, as the few reports and surviving photographs testify, by far the gayest, most handsome, most dynamic and generally prepossessing of the five brothers and sisters. Knowing the strength of Tabitha's feelings, the family had fallen prey to a certain anxiety when Godfrey announced his engagement in the summer of 1940: but in place of the violent jealousy which some had feared, a warm and respectful friendship grew up between sister and prospective sister-in-law, and the marriage of Godfrey Winshaw to Mildred, née Ashby, passed off most successfully in December of that year.

Instead, Tabitha continued to reserve the sharpest edge of her animosity for her eldest brother Lawrence. The origins of the ill-feeling which subsisted between these unhappy siblings are not easy to trace. Most probably they had to do with temperamental differences. Like his father Matthew, Lawrence was a reserved and sometimes impatient man, who pursued his extensive national and international business interests with a single-minded determination which many construed as ruthlessness. That realm of feminine softness and delicate feeling in which Tabitha moved was thoroughly alien to him: he considered her flighty, over-sensitive, neurotic and – in a turn of phrase which can now be seen as sadly prophetic – 'a bit soft in the head'. (Nor, it has to be admitted, was he entirely alone in this view.) In short, they did their best to keep out of each other's way; and the wisdom of this policy can be judged from the appalling events which followed upon Godfrey's death.

Immediately before setting off on his fatal mission, Godfrey had been enjoying a few days' rest in the tranquil atmosphere of Winshaw Towers. Mildred, of course, was with him: she was at this stage several months pregnant with their first and only child (a son, as it was to turn out), and it was presumably the prospect of seeing these, her favourite members of the family, which induced Tabitha to forsake the comfort of her own substantial residence and cross the threshold of her hated brother's home. Although Matthew Winshaw and his wife were still alive and in good health, they were by now effectively consigned to a set of chambers in a self-contained wing, and Lawrence had established himself as master of the house. It would be stretching a point, all the same, to say that he and his wife Beatrice made good hosts. Lawrence, as usual, was preoccupied with his business activities, which required him to spend long hours on the telephone in the privacy of his office, and even, on one occasion, to make an overnight trip to London (for which he departed without making any kind of apology or explanation to his guests). Meanwhile Beatrice made no pretence of welcoming her husband's relatives, and would leave them unattended for the better part of each day while she retired to her bedroom on the pretext of a recurrent migraine. Thus Godfrey, Mildred and Tabitha, perhaps as they themselves would have wished, were thrown back on their own devices, and passed several pleasant days in each other's company, wandering through the gardens and amusing themselves in the vast drawing, sitting, dining and reception rooms of Winshaw Towers.

In the afternoon on which Godfrey was to leave for the airfield at Hucknall on the first leg of his mission – something of which his wife and sister had only an inkling – he had a long and private interview with Lawrence in the brown study. No details of their discussion will ever be known. Following his departure, both women became uneasy: Mildred with the natural anxiety of a wife and mother-to-be whose husband has set out upon an errand of some importance and uncertain outcome, Tabitha with a more violent and uncontrolled agitation which manifested itself in a worsening of her hostility towards Lawrence.

Her irrationality in this respect was already evident from a foolish misunderstanding which had arisen only a few days earlier. Bursting into her brother's office late in the evening, she had surprised him during one of his business conversations and snatched away the scrap of paper upon which – in her version of events – he had been transcribing secret instructions over the telephone. She even went so far as to claim that Lawrence had been 'looking guilty' when she interrupted him, and that he had attempted to seize the piece of paper back from her by force. With pathetic obstinacy, however, she clung on to it and subsequently stored it away among her personal documents. Later, when she made her fantastic accusation against Lawrence, she threatened to bring it forward as 'evidence'. Fortunately the excellent Dr Quince, trusted physician to the Winshaws for several decades, had by that stage made his diagnosis – the effect of which was to determine that no statements made by Tabitha thereafter would be received with anything other than the deepest scepticism. History, incidentally, seems to have vindicated the good doctor's judgment, because when certain of Tabitha's relics recently came into the hands of the present writer, the contended scrap of paper was found to be among them. Now yellowed with age, it turned out to contain nothing more remarkable than Lawrence's scribbled note to the butler, asking for a light supper to be sent up to his room.

Tabitha's condition deteriorated still further after Godfrey had left, and on the night that he flew his final mission a peculiar incident took place, both more serious and more ludicrous than any that had gone before. This grew out of another of Tabitha's delusions, to the effect that her brother was holding secret meetings with Nazi spies in his bedroom. Time and again she claimed to have stood outside his locked bedroom door and caught the distant murmur of voices talking in clipped, authoritative German. Finally, when not even Mildred was able to take this allegation seriously, she attempted to make a desperate proof. Having pilfered the key (the only key) to Lawrence's bedroom earlier that afternoon, she waited until such time as she was convinced that he was engaged in one of his sinister conferences, then locked the door from the outside and ran downstairs, shouting at the top of her voice that she had captured her brother in the very act of betraying his country. The butler, the maids, the kitchen staff, the chauffeur, the valet, the bootboy and all the domestics immediately came to her aid, followed closely by Mildred and Beatrice; and the entire company, now gathered in the Great Hall, was about to climb the staircase to investigate when Lawrence himself emerged, cue in hand, from the billiard room where he had been passing the hours after dinner in a few solitary frames. Needless to say, his bedroom was found empty; but this demonstration did not satisfy Tabitha, who continued to scream at her brother, accusing him of every manner of trickery and under-handedness, until finally she was restrained and carried to her room in the West Wing, where a sedative was administered by the ever-resourceful Nurse Gannet.

Such was the atmosphere at Winshaw Towers on that dreadful evening, as the deathly silence of nightfall spread itself over the venerable old seat; a silence which was to be broken at three o'clock in the morning by the ringing of the telephone, and with it the news of Godfrey's terrible fate.

*

No bodies were ever recovered from that wreckage; neither Godfrey nor his co-pilot was ever to be accorded the honour of a Christian burial. Two weeks later, however, a small memorial service was held at the Winshaws' private chapel. His parents sat stone-faced and ashen throughout the proceedings. His younger brother Mortimer, his sister Olivia and her husband Walter had all travelled to Yorkshire to pay their respects: only Tabitha was absent, for as soon as she heard the news, she had thrown herself into a frenzy. Among the instruments of violence with which she had attacked Lawrence were candlesticks, golf umbrellas, butter knives, razor blades, riding crops, a loofah, a mashie, a niblick, an Afghan battle horn of considerable archaeological interest, a chamber-pot and a bazooka. The very next day, Dr Quince signed the papers which authorized her immediate confinement in a nearby asylum.

She was not to step outside the walls of this establishment for another nineteen years. During that time she rarely attempted to communicate with other members of the family, or expressed any interest in receiving them as visitors. Her mind (or what few, pitiable shreds and tatters of it remained) continued to dwell inflexibly on the circumstances surrounding her brother's death, and she became an obsessive reader of books, journals and periodicals concerned with the conduct of the war, the history of the Royal Air Force, and all matters even remotely connected with aviation. (During this period, for instance, her name appears on the regular subscribers' lists of such magazines as *Professional Pilot*, *Flypast*, *Jane's Military Review* and *Cockpit Quarterly*.) And so there she remained, prudently left to the care of a trained and dedicated staff, until September 16th 1961, when she was granted a temporary release at the request of her brother Mortimer: a decision, however compassionately taken, which in itself would soon come to be regarded as unfortunate.

Death visited Winshaw Towers again that night.

2

Sitting at the bay window of their bedroom, looking out over the East Terrace and the bleak sprawl of the moors which rolled towards the horizon, Rebecca felt Mortimer's hand rest gently against her shoulder.

'It'll be all right,' he said.

'I know.'

He squeezed her and went over to the mirror, where he made small adjustments to his tie and cummerbund.

'It's really very nice of Lawrence. In fact they're all being very nice. I've never known my family be so nice to each other.'

It was Mortimer's fiftieth birthday and to honour the occasion Lawrence had organized a small but lavish dinner, to which the entire family – even the outcast Tabitha – was invited. It would be the first time that Rebecca, thirteen years her husband's junior and still possessed of a childlike, rather vulnerable beauty, had met them all at one sitting.

'They're not monsters, you know. Not really.' Mortimer rotated his left cuff-link through fifteen degrees, squinting at the angle critically. 'I mean, you like Mildred, don't you?'

'But she's not really family.' Rebecca continued to stare out of the window. 'Poor Milly. It's such a shame she never remarried. I'm afraid Mark's turned into an awful handful.'

'He's just got in with a boisterous set, that's all. Happened to me when I was at school. Oxford'll soon knock that out of him.'

Rebecca turned her head: an impatient gesture.

'You're always making excuses for them. I know they all hate me. They've never forgiven us for not inviting them to the wedding.'

'Well that was my decision, not yours. I didn't want them all there, gawping at you.'

'Well there you are: it's quite obvious that you don't like them yourself, and there must be a rea– '

There was a discreet knock on the door, and the butler's gaunt, solemn figure took a few deferential steps into the room.

'Drinks are now being served, sir. In the ante-drawing room.'

'Thank you, Pyles.' He had turned on his heels and was about to leave when Mortimer detained him. 'Oh, Pyles?'

'Sir?'

'If you could just look in and check on the children. We left them in the nursery. They were with Nurse Gannet, but you know how she . . . dozes, sometimes.'

'Very good, sir.' He paused and added, before withdrawing: 'And may I offer you, sir, on behalf of all the staff, our warmest congratulations, and many happy returns of the day.'

'Thank you. That's very kind.'

'Our pleasure, sir.'

He made a silent exit. Mortimer walked over to the window and stood behind his wife, whose gaze remained fixed on the pitiless landscape.

'Well, we'd better be getting downstairs.'

Rebecca did not move.

'The kids'll be fine. He'll keep an eye on them. He's an absolute brick, really.'

'I hope they don't break anything. Their games always seem so violent, and then we'd never hear the end of it from Lawrence.'

'It's Roddy who's the little devil. He goads Hilary on. She's a sweet little thing.'

'They're both as bad as each other.'

Mortimer began stroking her neck. He could feel her nervousness.

'Darling, you're shivering.'

'I don't know what it is.' He sat beside her and impulsively she nestled against his shoulder, like a bird seeking refuge. 'I'm all of a flutter. I can hardly bear to face them.'

'If it's Tabitha you're worried about –'

'Not just Tabitha –'

'– then you've nothing to be afraid of. She's changed completely in the last couple of years. She and Lawrence even talked for a little while this afternoon. I honestly think she's forgotten that whole business about Godfrey: she doesn't even remember who he was. She's been writing these nice letters to Lawrence from the – from the home, and he's said the whole thing's forgiven and forgotten as far as he's concerned, so I don't think there'll be any trouble from that quarter tonight. The doctors say she's more or less back to normal.'

Mortimer heard the hollowness of these words and hated himself for it. Only that afternoon he had seen evidence of his sister's continued eccentricity, when he had surprised her in the course of a walk around the wildest and most far-flung reaches of the grounds. He had been emerging from the hounds' graveyard and was about to strike out in the direction of the croquet lawn when he caught what seemed to be a glimpse of Tabitha crouched in one of the densest areas of shrubbery. As he approached, without making a sound for fear of alarming her, he was dismayed to find that she was muttering to herself. His heart sank: it seemed that he had, after all, been too optimistic about her condition, and perhaps too precipitate in suggesting that she should be allowed to attend the family party. Unable to make out anything intelligible from her broken mumbles and whispers, he had coughed politely, whereupon Tabitha gave a little scream of shock, there was a violent rustling from the bushes, and she burst out a few seconds later, nervously brushing the twigs and thorns from her clothing and almost speechless with confusion.

'I – Morty, I had no idea, I – I was just . . .'

'I didn't mean to surprise you, Tabs. It's just –'

'Not at all, I was – I was out for a walk, and I saw – I thought I'd explore . . . Heavens, what must you think of me? I'm mortified. Morty-fied, in front of Morty . . .'

Her voice died, and she coughed: a high, anxious cough. To ward off a heavy silence, Mortimer said:

'Magnificent, isn't it? This garden. I don't know how they keep it so well.' He took a deep breath. 'That jasmine. Just smell it.'

Tabitha didn't reply. Her brother took her by the arm and walked her back towards the terrace.

He had not mentioned this incident to Rebecca.

'It's not just Tabitha. It's this whole house.' Rebecca turned towards him and for the first time that evening looked deep into his eyes. 'If we ever came to live here, darling, I should die. I'm sure I would.' She shuddered. 'There's something about this place.'

'Why on earth should we come to live here? What a silly thing to say.'

'Who else is going to take it over when Lawrence is gone? He's got no sons to leave it to; and you're his only brother, now.'

Mortimer gave an irritable laugh; it was clear he wanted the subject dropped. 'I very much doubt if I shall outlive Lawrence. He's got a good many more years in him yet.'

'I dare say you're right,' said Rebecca, after a while. She took a long, last look at the moors, then gathered up her pearls from the dresser and fastened them carefully. Outside the dogs were howling for their supper.

*

Poised in the doorway leading from the Great Hall, her own small hand folded tightly in Mortimer's, Rebecca found herself confronted by a roomful of Winshaws. There were no more than a dozen of them, but to her it seemed like a vast, numberless throng, whose braying and mewling voices merged into a single unintelligible clamour. Within seconds she and her husband had been pounced upon, separated, absorbed into the crowd, patted and touched and kissed, welcomed and congratulated, plied with drink, their news solicited, their health inquired after. Rebecca could not distinguish half of the faces; she didn't even know who she was talking to, some of the time, and her recollection of each conversation would forever afterwards be hazy and unfocused.

For our part, meanwhile, we should seize the opportunity offered by this gathering to become more closely acquainted with four particular members of the family.

*

Here, for one, is Thomas Winshaw: thirty-seven, unmarried, and still having to justify himself to his mother Olivia, in whose eyes all his glittering success in the financial world counts for nothing beside his continued failure to start a family of his own. Now she listens tight-lipped as he tries to put a favourable gloss on a new development in his career which clearly strikes her as more frivolous than most.

'Mother, you can get an extremely high return from investing in films these days. You've only got to be involved with one really big hit, you see, and you're sitting on an absolute fortune. Enough to compensate for a dozen failures.'

'If you were just in it for the money you'd have my blessing, you know you would,' says Olivia. Her Yorkshire accent is thicker than her brothers' and sister's, but her mouth has the same downward, humourless turn. 'The Lord knows, you've shown yourself clever enough where that's concerned. But Henry's told me what your real motives are, so don't try to deny it. Actresses. That's what you're after. You like being able to tell them you can get them a job in the pictures.'

'You do talk nonsense sometimes, Mother. You should listen to yourself.'

'I just don't want any member of this family making a fool of himself, that's all. They're no better than whores, most of those women, and you'll only end up catching something nasty.'

But Thomas, who feels for his mother no more or less than he feels for most people – namely, such contempt that he seldom considers them worth arguing with – merely smiles. Something about her last remark seems to amuse him, and his eyes take on a cold glaze of private reminiscence. He is thinking, in fact, that his mother is quite wide of the mark: for his interest in young actresses, strong as it is, does not extend to physical contact. His real interest is in watching, not touching, and so for Thomas the principal benefit of his new-found role in the film industry lies in the excuse it gives him to visit the studios whenever he wants. Thus he is able to turn up during the filming of scenes which, on the screen, will simply offer innocent titillation, but which in the actual making provide perfect opportunities for the serious voyeur. Bedroom scenes; bathroom scenes; sunbathing scenes; scenes involving missing bikini tops and vanishing soap suds and falling towels. He has friends, spies, minions among the cast and camera crew to alert him in advance whenever such a scene is about to be shot. He has even persuaded editors to give him access to discarded footage, sequences which turned out to be too revealing for inclusion in the final cut. (For Thomas has started out by investing in comedies, modestly budgeted, reliably popular entertainments starring the likes of Sid James, Kenneth Connor, Jimmy Edwards and Wilfrid Hyde-White.) From these, he likes to clip his favourite images and turn them into slides which he will project on to the wall of his office in Cheapside late at night, long after his employees have gone home. So much cleaner, so much more personal, so much less risky than the tedious business of inviting actresses back to his house, making them absurd promises, all that fumbling and coercion. Thomas is annoyed with Henry, then, not so much for giving away secrets to his mother, as for implying that his own motives could be quite so commonplace and demeaning.

'You shouldn't take notice of anything that Henry tells you, you know,' he now says, with a chilly smile. 'After all, he is a politician.'

*

And here is Henry, Thomas's younger brother, already recognized as one of the most ambitious Labour MPs of his generation. Their relationship goes beyond the ordinary ties of blood and extends to a number of common business interests, for Henry has a seat on the board of several companies generously supported by Thomas's bank. Should anyone have the temerity to suggest a conflict of loyalty between these activities and the socialist ideals which he professes so loudly in the House of Commons, Henry has a variety of well-rehearsed answers. He is used to dealing with naïve questions, which is why he is able to laugh airily as his young cousin Mark shoots him a teasing glance and says:

'So, I take it you'll be travelling back to London first thing tomorrow morning, in time for the demonstration? We all know that you Labour bods are in cahoots with CND.'

'Some of my colleagues will undoubtedly be attending. You

won't find me there. There are no votes in the nuclear issue, for one thing. Most of the people in this country recognize the unilateralists for what they are: a bunch of cranks.' He pauses to allow one of the under-footmen to refill their glasses of champagne. 'Do you know the best bit of news I've heard all month?'

'Bertrand Russell getting seven days in the slammer?'

'That did bring a smile to my face, I must say. But I was thinking more about Khrushchev. I suppose you've heard that he's started testing H-bombs again, out in the Arctic or somewhere?'

'Really?'

'Ask Thomas what that did to shares in the munitions companies a couple of days later. Through the roof, they went. Through the bloody roof. We made a few hundred grand overnight. I'm telling you, earlier this year, with Gagarin coming over and everyone talking about a bit of a thaw, things were beginning to look a bit shaky. I didn't like the look of it at all. Thank God it turned out to be a flash in the pan. First the Wall goes up, and now the Russkies start letting off fireworks again. Looks like we're back in business.' He drains his glass and pats his cousin affectionately. 'Of course, I can talk to you like this, because you're family.'

*

Mark Winshaw digests this information in silence. Perhaps because he never knew his own father, Godfrey, he has always regarded his cousins as paternal figures and looked to them for guidance. (His mother has attempted to offer him guidance too, of course, has tried to inculcate her own values and codes of conduct, but he has, from an early age, made a point of ignoring her.) He has already learned a great deal from Thomas and Henry, about how to make money, and how the divisions and conflicts between lesser, weaker-minded men can be exploited for personal gain. He will be going up to Oxford in a few weeks' time, and has just spent the summer working in a minor administrative capacity at the office of Thomas's bank in Cheapside.

'It was so kind of you to give him that job,' Mildred now says to Thomas. 'I do hope he wasn't a nuisance or anything.'

Mark's expression is one of undiluted hatred, but his glance goes unnoticed, and he says nothing.

'Not at all,' Thomas answers. 'He was very useful to have around. In fact he made quite an impression on my colleagues. Quite an impression.'

'Really? In what way?'

Thomas proceeds to tell the story of a discussion which took place between senior members of the bank over lunch in the City one Friday afternoon: a lunch to which Mark had been invited. The conversation had turned to the recent resignation of one of the partners over the role taken by the bank in the Kuwait crisis. Thomas feels called upon to explain the details of this crisis to Mildred, assuming that, as a woman, she won't know anything about it. He therefore tells her how Kuwait was declared an independent Sheikdom in June, and how, only one week later, Brigadier-General Kassem had announced his intention of absorbing it into his own country, claiming that according to historical precedent it had always been an 'integral part of Iraq'. He reminds her that Kuwait had appealed to the British government for military support, which had been promised by both the Foreign Secretary, Lord Home, and the Lord Privy Seal, Edward Heath; and that, since the first week of July, more than six thousand British troops had been moved to Kuwait from Kenya, Aden, Cyprus, the United Kingdom and Germany, establishing a sixty-mile defence line only five miles from the border in readiness for an Iraqi attack.

'The thing is,' says Thomas, 'that this junior partner fellow, Pemberton-Oakes, couldn't stomach the fact that we were still lending enormous sums of money to the Iraqis to help them keep their army going. He said that they were the enemy, and we were more or less at war with them, so we shouldn't be giving them any help at all. He said it was Kuwait we should be dealing with as a matter of principle – I think that was the word he used – even though their borrowing requirements were pretty negligible and the bank wouldn't get much out of it in the long run. Well, there we all were, with people chipping in on both sides, putting the alternative points of view, when somebody had the bright idea of asking young Mark what he thought.'

'And what did he think?' asks Mildred, with a resigned note to her voice.

Thomas chuckles. 'He said it was perfectly obvious, as far as he could see. He said we should be lending money to both sides, of course, and if war broke out we should lend them even more, so they could be kept at it for as long as possible, using up more and more equipment and losing more and more men and getting more and more heavily in our debt. You should have seen their faces! Well, it was probably what they'd all been thinking, you see, but he was the only one who had the nerve to come right out with it.' He turns to Mark, whose face has remained, throughout this conversation, a perfect blank. 'You'll go a long way in the banking business, Mark, old boy. A long way.'

Mark smiles. 'Oh, I don't think banking is for me, to be honest. I intend to be more in the thick of things. But thanks for giving me the opportunity, all the same. I certainly learned a thing or two.'

He turns and crosses the room, conscious that his mother's eyes have never left him.

*

Mortimer now approaches Dorothy Winshaw, the stolid, ruddy-faced daughter of Lawrence and Beatrice, who is standing alone in a corner of the room, her lips set in their usual petulant, ferocious pout.

'Well, well,' says Mortimer, straining to inject a note of cheerfulness into his voice. 'And how's my favourite niece?' (Dorothy is, by the way, his only niece, so his use of this epithet is a touch disingenuous.) 'Not long now before the happy event. A bit of excitement in the air, I dare say?'

'I suppose so,' says Dorothy, sounding anything but excited. Mortimer's reference is to the fact that she will shortly, at the age of twenty-five, be married off to George Brunwin, one of the county's most successful and well-liked farmers.

'Oh, come on,' says Mortimer. 'Surely you must be feeling a little . . . well . . .'

'I feel exactly what you would expect in any woman,' Dorothy cuts in, 'who knows that she is about to marry one of the biggest fools in the world.'

Mortimer looks around to see whether her fiancé, who has also been invited to the party, might have heard this remark. Dorothy doesn't seem to care.

'What on earth can you mean?'

'I mean that if he doesn't grow up, soon, and join the rest of us in the twentieth century, he and I aren't going to have a penny between us in five years' time.'

'But Brunwin's is one of the best-run farms for miles around. That's common knowledge.'

Dorothy snorts. 'Just because he went to agricultural college twenty years ago, that doesn't mean that George has a clue what's going on in the modern world. He doesn't even know what a conversion rate is, for God's sake.'

'A conversion rate?'

'The ratio,' Dorothy explains patiently, as if to a dim-witted farmhand, 'of how much food you put *in* to an animal, compared to what you get *out* of it in the end, by way of meat. Really, all you have to do is read a few issues of *Farming Express*, and it all becomes perfectly clear. You've heard of Henry Saglio, I suppose?'

'Politician, isn't he?'

'Henry Saglio is an American chicken farmer who's been promising great things for the British housewife. He's managed to breed a new strain of broiler which grows to three and a half pounds in nine weeks, with a feed conversion rate of 2.3. He uses the most up-to-date and intensive methods.' Dorothy is growing animated; more animated than Mortimer has ever seen her in his life. Her eyes are aglow. 'And here's George, the bloody simpleton, still letting his chickens scratch around in the open air as if they were household pets. Not to mention his veal calves, which are allowed to sleep on straw and get more exercise than his blasted dogs do, probably. And he wonders why he doesn't get good white meat out of them!'

'Well, I don't know . . .' says Mortimer. 'Perhaps he has other things to think about. Other priorities.'

'Other priorities?'

'You know, the . . . welfare of the animals. The atmosphere of the farm.'

'*Atmosphere?*'

'Sometimes there can be more to life than making a profit, Dorothy.'

She stares at him. Perhaps it is her fury at finding herself addressed in a tone which she remembers from many years ago – the tone which an adult would adopt towards a trusting child – which provokes the insolence of her reply.

'You know, Daddy always said that you and Aunt Tabitha were the odd ones of the family.'

She puts down her glass, pushes past her uncle and moves quickly to join in a conversation on the other side of the room.

*

Meanwhile, up in the nursery, there are two more Winshaws with a part to play in the family's history. Roddy and Hilary, aged nine and seven, have tired of the rocking-horse, the model railway, the table-tennis set, the dolls and the puppets. They have even tired of their attempts to rouse Nurse Gannet by tickling her softly under the nose with a feather. (The feather in question having previously belonged to a sparrow which Roddy shot down with his airgun earlier that afternoon.) They are on the point of abandoning the nursery altogether and going downstairs to eavesdrop on the party – although, to tell the truth, the thought of walking down those long, dimly lit corridors and staircases frightens them somewhat – when Roddy has a flash of inspiration.

'I know!' he says, seizing upon a little pedal car and squeezing himself with difficulty into the driver's seat. 'I'll be Yuri Gagarin, and this is my space-car, and I've just landed on Mars.'

For like every other boy of his age, Roddy worships the young cosmonaut. Earlier in the year he was even taken to see him when he visited the Earl's Court exhibition, and Mortimer had held him aloft so that he could actually shake hands with the man who had voyaged among the stars. Now, crammed awkwardly into the undersized car, he starts to pedal with all his might while making guttural engine noises. 'Gagarin to Mission Control. Gagarin to Mission Control. Are you reading me?'

'Well who am I supposed to be then?' says Hilary.

'You can be Laika, the Russian space dog.'

'But she's dead. She died in her rocket. Uncle Henry told me.'

'Well just pretend.'

So Hilary starts scampering around on all fours, barking madly, sniffing at the Martian rocks and scratching in the dust. She keeps it up for about two minutes.

'This is really boring.'

'Shut up. This is Major Gagarin to Mission Control. I have safely landed on Mars and am now looking for signs of intelligent life. All I can see so far are some – hey, what's that?'

A bright object on the nursery floor has caught his eye, and he pedals towards it as fast as he can: but Hilary gets there first.

'A half-crown!'

She covers the coin with her hand and her eyes shine with triumph. Then Major Gagarin steps out of his space-car and stands over her.

'I saw it first. Give me that.'

'Not on your life.'

Slowly but purposefully, Roddy places his right foot over Hilary's hand and begins to press down.

'Give it to me!'

'No!'

Her voice rises to a scream as Roddy increases the pressure, until there is a sudden crack: the sound of bones crushing and splintering. Hilary howls as her brother lifts his foot and picks up the coin with calm satisfaction. There is blood on the nursery floor. Hilary sees this and her screams get shriller and wilder until they are loud enough to wake even Nurse Gannet from her cocoa-induced stupor.

*

Downstairs, the dinner party is by now well advanced. The guests have whetted their appetite with a light soup (Stilton and steamed pumpkin) and have made short work of their trout (poached in dry Martini with a nettle sauce). While waiting for the third course to arrive, Lawrence, who is seated at the head of the table, excuses himself and leaves the room; on his return, he stops to have a few words with Mortimer, the guest of honour, who is seated at the centre. Lawrence's intention is to make a discreet inquiry into the condition of their sister.

'How d'you reckon the old loony's bearing up?' he whispers.

Mortimer winces, and his reply has a reproving tone: 'If you're referring to Tabitha, then you'll find that she's behaving herself perfectly. Just as I said she would.'

'I saw you both having a bit of a chinwag this afternoon on the croquet lawn. You looked rather serious, that's all. There wasn't anything up, was there?'

'Of course not. We'd just been for a walk together.' Mortimer sees an opportunity to change the subject at this point. 'The gardens are looking magnificent, by the way. Especially your jasmine: the scent was quite overpowering. Wouldn't mind learning your secret, one of these days.'

Lawrence laughs cruelly. 'Sometimes I think you're as bats as she is, old boy. There's no jasmine in our garden, I can vouch for it. Not even a sprig!' He glances up and notices a huge silver tureen being carried in at the far end of the dining room. 'Hello, here comes the next course.'

*

Midway through her saddle of curried hare, Rebecca hears a diffident cough at her side.

'What is it, Pyles?'

'A word in private, if I may, Mrs Winshaw. It's a matter of some urgency.'

They withdraw into the transverse corridor and when Rebecca returns, a minute later, her face is pale.

'It's the children,' she tells her husband. 'There's been some silly accident in the nursery. Hilary's hurt her hand. I'm going to have to take her to the hospital.'

Mortimer half-rises from his seat in panic.

'Is it serious?'

'I don't think so. She's just a bit upset.'

'I'll come with you.'

'No, you'll have to stay here. I doubt if I'll be much more than an hour. You stay and enjoy your party.'

*

But Mortimer does not enjoy his party. The only aspect of it which he was enjoying in the first place was the company of Rebecca, upon whom he has come to depend more and more in the last few years as a means of shielding himself from his hated family. Now, in her absence, he is forced to spend most of the evening in conversation with his sister Olivia; dry, sour-faced Olivia, who is so implacably loyal to the Winshaw pedigree that she even married one of her own cousins, and who now drones on remorselessly about the management of her estate and her husband's impending knighthood for services to industry and the political future of her son Henry who has at least been clever enough to see that it's the Labour Party which offers him the best prospect of a cabinet position by the age of forty. Mortimer nods tiredly throughout her monologue, and takes an occasional glance at the other faces around the table: Dorothy shovelling food into her mouth; her sheep-faced fiancé sitting morosely beside her; Mark's ratty, calculating eyes maintaining their restless vigil; sweet, bewildered Mildred telling some shy anecdote to Thomas, who listens with all the frosty indifference of a merchant banker about to withhold a loan from a small businessman. And there, of course, is Tabitha, sitting erect at the table and not saying a word to anyone. He notices that she consults her pocket watch every few minutes, and that more than once she asks one of the footmen to check the time on the grandfather clock in the hallway. Otherwise, she sits perfectly still and keeps her eyes fixed upon Lawrence. It's almost as if she is waiting for something to happen.

*

Rebecca returns from the hospital just as coffee is about to be served. She slips in beside her husband and squeezes his hand.

'She'll be fine,' she says. 'Nurse Gannet is just putting her to bed.'

Lawrence stands up, raps on the table with his dessertspoon and proposes a toast.

'To Mortimer!' he says. 'Health and happiness on his fiftieth birthday.'

Muted echoes of 'Mortimer' and 'Health and happiness' resound throughout the room as the guests drain off whatever is left in their glasses. Then there is a loud and contented sigh, and somebody says:

'Well! It *has* been a most pleasant evening.'

All heads turn. Tabitha has spoken.

'It's so nice to get out and about. You've no idea. Only – ' Tabitha frowns, and her face assumes a lost, downcast expression. 'Only . . . I was just thinking how nice it would have been, if Godfrey could have been here tonight.'

There is a long pause; broken eventually by Lawrence, who says, with an attempt at jovial sincerity: 'Quite so. Quite so.'

'He was *so* fond of Mortimer. Morty was most definitely his favourite brother. He told me so, many times. He much preferred Mortimer to Lawrence. He was quite decided about it.' She frowns again, and looks around the table: 'I wonder why?'

Nobody answers. Nobody meets her eye.

'I suppose it's because . . . I *suppose* it's because he knew – that Mortimer had no intention of killing him.'

She watches her relatives' faces, as if looking for confirmation. Their silence is horror-struck and absolute.

Tabitha lays her napkin down on the table, pushes her chair back and rises painfully to her feet.

'Well, it's time I was getting to bed. Up Wood Hill to Blanket Fair, as Nanny used to say to me.' She walks towards the dining-room door, and it becomes hard to tell whether she is still talking to the guests or merely to herself. 'Up the long and winding stairs; up the stairs, to say my prayers.' She turns, and there can be no doubt that her next question is addressed to her brother.

'Do you still say your prayers, Lawrence?'

He doesn't answer.

'I should say them tonight, if I were you.'

*

Drained of feeling, Rebecca lay back against the thick bank of pillows. Slowly she stretched her legs apart and massaged her thigh, easing the soreness. Beside her, his head weighing heavy upon her shoulder, Mortimer was already sinking into sleep. It had taken him almost forty minutes to reach his climax. It took longer every time; and although he was on the whole a gentle and considerate lover, Rebecca was beginning to find these marathon sessions something of a trial. Her back ached and her mouth was dry, but she did not reach out for the bedside glass of water in case she disturbed her husband.

He started to mumble something drowsy and incoherent. She stroked his thinning hair.

'. . . what I'd do without you . . . so lovely . . . make everything all right . . . bearable . . .'

'There, there,' she whispered. 'We'll be going home tomorrow. It's over.'

'. . . hate them all . . . what I'd do if you weren't here to . . . make things better . . . feel like killing them sometimes . . . kill them all . . .'

Rebecca hoped that Hilary was managing to get some sleep. Three of her fingers had been broken. She didn't believe that story about it being an accident, didn't believe it for a moment. There was nothing she wouldn't put past Roddy, these days. Like those photographs she'd caught him with: which had turned out to be a present from Thomas, damn him . . .

Half an hour later, at a quarter to two in the morning, Mortimer was snoring rhythmically and Rebecca was still wide awake. That was when she thought she heard the footsteps in the corridor, stealing past their bedroom door.

Then the noises started. Crashes and banging and the unmistakable sounds of a fight. Two men fighting, using all their strength on each other, grabbing whatever weapons came to hand. Grunting with the exertion, shouting and calling each other names. She barely had time to slip into her dressing-gown and turn on the bedroom light when she heard a long and terrible cry, far louder than the rest. Lights were going on all over Winshaw Towers by now and she could hear people running in the direction of the disturbance. But Rebecca stayed where she was, paralysed with fear. She had recognized that cry, even though she had never heard anything like it before. It was the sound of a man dying.

*

Two days later, the following story appeared in the local newspaper:

Attempted Burglary at Winshaw Towers

Lawrence Winshaw in fight to the death with intruder

THERE WERE dramatic scenes at Winshaw Towers on Saturday night when a family celebration was tragically disrupted.

Fourteen guests had gathered to mark the fiftieth birthday of Mortimer Winshaw, younger brother of Lawrence – who is now the owner of the 300-year-old mansion. But soon after they had gone to bed, a man broke into the house in a daring burglary attempt which was shortly to cost him his life.

The intruder seems to have entered the house through the library window, which is normally kept securely locked. He then forced his way into Lawrence Winshaw's bedroom, where a violent altercation ensued. Finally, acting entirely in his own defence, Mr Winshaw got the better of his assailant and dealt him a fatal blow to the skull with the copper-headed backscratcher which he always keeps by his bedside. Death was instantaneous.

Police have not yet been able to identify the attacker, who does not appear to have been a local man, but they are satisfied that burglary was the motive behind the break-in. There is no question, a spokesman added, of charges being preferred against Mr Winshaw, who is said to be in a state of deep shock following the incident.

The investigation will continue and readers of this newspaper can expect to be brought up to date with every development.

*

On Sunday morning, the day after his birthday party, Mortimer found his loyalties divided. Family sentiment, or what little residue of it continued to lurk inside him, insisted that he should stay with his brother and help him to recover from his ordeal; but at the same time, Rebecca's anxiety to leave Winshaw Towers and return to their Mayfair apartment as soon as possible could not be disguised. It was not, in the end, a difficult decision to make. He could never deny his wife anything; and besides, there remained a whole army of relatives who could safely be trusted with the task of helping Lawrence to recuperate. By eleven o'clock their cases were gathered in the hall waiting to be carried out to the silver Bentley, and Mortimer was preparing to pay his final respects to Tabitha, who had yet to emerge from her room after learning of last night's shocking events.

Mortimer caught sight of Pyles at the far end of the hallway, and beckoned him over.

'Has Dr Quince been in to see Miss Tabitha this morning?' he asked.

'Yes, sir. He visited her quite early, at about nine o'clock.'

'I see. I don't suppose . . . I hope nobody in the servants' quarters is thinking that she might be in any way connected with . . . what happened.'

'I wouldn't know what the other servants are thinking, sir.'

'No, of course not. Well, if you'll see to it that our cases are taken out, Pyles, I think I'll go and have a quick word with her myself.'

'Very good, sir. Except that – I think she has another visitor with her at the moment.'

'Another visitor?'

'A gentleman called about ten minutes ago, sir, inquiring after Miss Tabitha. Burrows dealt with the matter and I'm afraid to say that he showed him up to her room.'

'I see. I think I'd better go and investigate this.'

Mortimer rapidly climbed the several sets of stairs leading to his sister's chambers, then paused outside her door. He could hear no voices issuing from within: not until he knocked and, after a substantial pause, heard Tabitha's cracked, expressionless cry of 'Enter'.

'I just came to say goodbye,' he explained, finding that she was alone after all.

'Goodbye,' said Tabitha. She was knitting something large, purple and shapeless, and a copy of *Spitfire!* magazine was propped open on the desk beside her.

'We must see more of each other in future,' he went on, nervously. 'You'll come to visit us in London, perhaps?'

'I doubt it,' said Tabitha. 'The doctor was here again this morning, and I know what that means. They're going to try to blame me for what happened last night, and have me put away again.' She laughed, and shrugged her bony shoulders. 'Well, what if they do. I've missed my chance, now.'

'Missed your . . .?' Mortimer began, but checked himself. Instead he walked to the window, and tried to adopt a casual tone as he said: 'Well, of course, there are some . . . circumstances which take some accounting for. The library window, for instance. Pyles swears that he locked it as usual, and yet this man, this burglar, whoever he was, doesn't seem to have forced it in any way. I don't suppose you'd happen to know anything . . .'

He tailed off.

'Now look what you've made me do with your chatter,' said Tabitha. 'I've dropped a stitch.'

Mortimer could see that he was wasting his time.

'Well, I'll be off,' he said.

'Have a nice journey,' Tabitha answered, without looking up.

Mortimer paused in the doorway.

'By the way,' he said, 'who was your visitor?'

She stared at him blankly.

'Visitor?'

'Pyles said that someone had called on you a few minutes ago.'

'No, he was mistaken. Quite mistaken.'

'I see.' Mortimer took a deep breath and was about to leave, when something detained him; he turned back with a frown. 'Am I just imagining this,' he said, 'or is there a peculiar smell in here?'

'It's jasmine,' said Tabitha, beaming at him for the first time. 'Isn't it lovely?'

3

Yuri was my one and only hero at this time. My parents would save every photograph from the magazines and newspapers, and I fixed them to the wall of my bedroom with drawing-pins. That wall has been re-papered now, but for many years after the pictures came down you could still see the pin marks, dotted into a random and fantastic pattern like so many stars. I knew that he had visited London recently: I had watched the scenes on television as he drove through streets lined with welcoming crowds. I had heard of his appearance at the Earl's Court exhibition, and the knowledge that he had shaken hands with hundreds of lucky children turned me hot with envy. Yet it had never occurred to me to ask my parents to take me there. A trip to London for my family would have been as bold and far-fetched a proposition as a trip to the moon itself.

For my ninth birthday, however, my father proposed, if not a trip to the moon, then at least a tentative shot into the stratosphere in the form of a day's outing to Weston-super-Mare. I was promised a visit to the newly opened model railway and aquarium, and, if the weather was fine, a swim in the open-air pool. It was mid September: September 17th 1961, to be precise. My grandparents were invited on this trip, as well – by which I mean my mother's parents, because we had nothing to do with my father's; had not even heard from them, in fact, for as long as I could remember, although I knew they were still alive. Perhaps my father himself secretly kept in contact; but I doubt it. It was never easy to know what he was feeling, and I couldn't say, even now, whether or not he missed them very much. He got on passably well with Grandma and Grandpa, in any case, and over the years had built up a quiet defensive wall against Grandpa's genial but consistent teasing. I think it was my mother who invited them along with us that day, probably without consulting him. All the same, there was no hint of a quarrel. My parents never quarrelled. He simply muttered something to the effect that he hoped they would sit in the back.

But it was the women who sat in the back, of course, with me sandwiched in between. Grandpa sat in the passenger seat with a road atlas open on his knees and that distant, facetious smile which clearly announced that my father was in for a hard time. They had already been arguing about which car they should take. My grandparents' Volkswagen was old and unreliable but Grandpa never missed an opportunity to pour scorn on the British models which my father, who worked for a local engineering firm, had a small hand in designing and bought out of loyalty both to his employers and to his country.

'Fingers crossed,' said Grandpa, as my father reached for the ignition key. And when the car started first time: 'Wonders will never cease.'

I had been given a travelling chess set for my birthday, so Grandma and I played a few games to while away the journey. Neither of us understood the rules at all, but we didn't like to admit this to each other and managed to get by with an improvisation that was something like a cross between draughts and table football. My mother, withdrawn and reflective as ever, merely stared out of the window: or perhaps she was listening to the conversation from the front of the car.

'What's the matter?' Grandpa was saying. 'Are you trying to save petrol or something?'

My father took no notice of this.

'You can do fifty miles along here, you know,' he went on. 'It's a fifty-mile limit.'

'We don't want to get there too early. We're in no hurry.'

'Mind you, I suppose this old crock soon starts to rattle if you try going above forty-five. We want to get there in one piece, after all. Hang on, though, I think that bicycle behind us wants to overtake.'

'Look, Michael, cows!' said my mother, by way of diversion.

'Where?'

'In the field.'

'The boy's seen cows before,' said Grandpa. 'Leave him be. Can anybody hear a rattle?'

Nobody could hear a rattle.

'I'm sure I can hear a rattle. Sounds like one of the fittings or something, coming loose.' He turned to my father. 'Which bit of this car was it that you designed, Ted? The ashtrays, wasn't it?'

'The steering column,' said my father.

'Look, Michael, sheep!'

We parked at the sea front. The wisps of cloud streaking the sky made me think of candy floss, setting in motion a train of thought which led inevitably to a booth by the pier, where my grandparents bought me a huge pink ball of the glutinous ambrosia, and a stick of rock which I put by for later. Normally my father would have said something about the adverse effects – dental and psychological – of granting me such favours, but because it was my birthday he let it pass. I sat on a low wall overlooking the sea and gobbled the candy floss down, savouring the delicious tension between its unthinkable sweetness and the slightly prickly texture, until I got about three quarters of the way through and started to feel sick. It was quiet on the sea front. Cocooned in my own happiness, I wasn't paying much attention to the passers-by, but I have a hazy impression of respectful couples walking arm in arm, and of a few older people striding past more purposefully, dressed for church.

'I hope it wasn't a mistake,' whispered my mother, 'coming on a Sunday. It would be awful if nothing was open.'

Grandpa treated my father to one of his more eloquent winks: in a moment it combined malicious sympathy with the amused recognition of a familiar situation.

'Looks like she's dropped you in it again,' he said.

'Well, birthday boy,' said my mother, wiping my lips with a tissue. 'Where do you want to start?'

We went to the aquarium first. It was probably a very good aquarium, but I have only the palest recollection: strange to think that my family schemed so hard to provide these entertainments, and yet it's their own unplanned words, their own thoughtless gestures and inflections, which have clung to my memory like flies caught on flypaper. I do know, anyway, that the sky was already starting to cloud over as we came out, and that a vigorous sea breeze made it difficult for my mother to enjoy the picnic which we shared on the Beach Lawns, our deck-chairs clustered in a semi-circle: I can still see her bounding off in pursuit of stray paper bags, struggling to distribute the sandwiches amid the wilful flap of their greaseproof wrapping. There were plenty left over, and she ended up offering them to the man who came to ask for money for our deck-chairs. (In common with all of their generation, my parents had the gift of getting into conversation with strangers without apparent difficulty. It was a gift I assumed I would one day grow into – once the shynesses of childhood and adolescence were behind me, perhaps – but it never happened, and I realize now that the easy sociability which they seemed to enjoy wherever they went had more to do with the times than with any special maturity of temperament.)

'Good bit of ham, this,' said the man, after taking an experimental bite. 'Mind you, I like a bit of mustard on it myself.'

'So do we,' said Grandpa. 'But his nibs won't have it.'

'She spoils him,' said Grandma, smiling in my direction. 'Spoils him something rotten.'

I pretended not to hear, and stared so hard at the last piece of my mother's chocolate cake that she handed it to me without a word, putting a warning finger to her mouth in a mock display of conspiracy. It was my third piece. She never used ordinary cake-making chocolate: only real Dairy Milk.

It was getting to the point where I didn't feel I could wait much longer for the promised swim, but she told me I would have to let my food settle first. Hoping to walk off my impatience, my father took me out to the sea, which was at low tide, with a grey expanse of muddy sand stretched almost to the horizon and a few dogged toddlers trotting out like fledgling explorers, a shrimping net in one hand and a reluctant parent in the other. We wandered pointlessly for about half an hour, and then at last we were allowed to go to the swimming-pool. It wasn't very crowded. There were a few people lying or sitting on deck-chairs and sunloungers next to the water: the minority who had chosen to swim were doing so very vigorously, with much splashing and shouting. There was a confusion of different musics. Watery orchestral pieces leaked out over a tannoy system, but they were in competition with a number of transistor radios, playing everything from Cliff Richard to Kenny Ball and his Jazzmen. The water shimmered and sparkled irresistibly. I couldn't understand why people preferred to lie flat on their backs listening to the radio when faced with the prospect of such liquid happiness. My father and I emerged from the changing cubicles together: I thought he looked easily the strongest and most handsome man at the poolside that afternoon, but to my memory's eye our thin white bodies now seem equally childlike and vulnerable. I ran ahead of him and stood at the water's edge, relishing a tiny but priceless moment of expectancy. After that I jumped; and after that, screamed.

The pool was not heated. Why had we thought that it would be? A bolt of ice shot through me and at once I was numb with shock, but my first response – not only to the physical sensation but to the higher agony of pleasure anticipated and then denied – was to burst into tears. How long this continued I don't know. My father must have lifted me from the water; my mother must have run down from the spectators' gallery where she had been sitting with Grandma and Grandpa. Her arms were around me, everybody's eyes were upon me, and still I was inconsolable. They told me afterwards that it felt as though I would never stop crying. But somehow they got me changed, dressed and shepherded into an outside world which was by now dark with the threat of heavy rain.

'It's a disgrace,' Grandma was saying. She had given one of the pool attendants a piece of her mind, not something to be wished upon anybody. 'There ought to be a notice. Or a chart, telling you what the temperature is. We ought to write a letter.'

'Poor little lamb,' said my mother. I was still snivelling a little bit. 'Ted, why don't you run back to the car and fetch the umbrellas? Otherwise we're all going to catch our deaths. We'll wait for you here.'

'Here' was a bus shelter near the sea front. The four of us sat there listening to the rain hammering on the glass roof. Grandpa muttered 'Dear heart alive', and this – a sure sign that the day was, in his estimation, taking a nose dive into disaster – was the cue for me to resume my wailing with twice the energy. When my father returned. carrying two umbrellas and a tightly folded plastic headscarf, my mother looked at him with silent panic; but he had clearly been giving the situation some thought and his resourceful suggestion was, 'Perhaps there's something on at the cinema.'

The nearest and biggest was the Odeon, which was showing a film called *The Naked Edge* with Gary Cooper and Deborah Kerr. My parents took one look at this and hurried on, although I lingered yearningly, catching the exotic scent of forbidden pleasures in the title, and intrigued by a card which the cinema manager had placed in a prominent position beneath the poster: NO ONE, BUT NO ONE, WILL BE ADMITTED TO THE THEATRE DURING THE LAST THIRTEEN MINUTES OF THIS FILM. FLASHING RED LIGHT WILL WARN YOU. Grandpa took me roughly by the hand and dragged me away.

'What about this one?' said my father.

We stood in front of a smaller and less imposing building which announced itself as 'Weston's Only Independent Cinema'. My mother and Grandma bent down to peer closely at the lobby cards. Grandma's lips formed into a doubtful pucker and a gentle frown creased my mother's brow.

'Do you think it looks suitable?'

'Sid James and Kenneth Connor. Should be funny.'

Grandpa said this but his real attention, I noticed, was on a picture of a beautiful blonde actress called Shirley Eaton, who was the third star of the film.

'Certificate U,' my father pointed out.

Then I shouted, 'Mum! Mum!'

Her eyes followed my pointing finger. I had found a notice which announced that the supporting film told the story of the Russian space programme, and was called *With Gagarin to the Stars*. Furthermore, the notice boasted, it was 'in COLOUR', although I for one didn't need this extra inducement. I launched into a routine of wide-eyed supplication, sensing even as I began that it wasn't really necessary, because my parents had already made up their minds. We joined the queue to buy tickets. When the woman at the ticket desk took a dubious look at me from her lofty enclosure, my hand gripping anxiously on to my father's, she said, 'Are you sure he's old enough?', and suddenly I experienced the same plummeting misery, the same emotional nausea that I had felt the second I jumped into the unheated swimming-pool. But Grandpa wasn't having any of this. 'Just sell us the tickets, woman,' he said, 'and mind your own business.' Someone in the queue behind us giggled. Then we were filing into the dark, musky auditorium and I was sinking deeper and deeper into my seat in a heaven of contentment, Grandma to the left of me, my father to the right.

Six years later, Yuri would be dead, his MiG-15 diving inexplicably out of low cloud and crashing to the ground during an approach to landing. I was old enough by then to have imbibed some of the prevailing distrust of all things Russian, to take notice of the dark mutterings about the KGB and the displeasure my hero may have incurred in his own country for having so charmed the cheering Westerners. Perhaps Yuri really had condemned himself the day he shook hands with all those children at Earl's Court; and yet it had been them that I wished dead at the time. Whatever the explanation, I can no longer recapture or even imagine the state of innocence in which I must have sat through that afternoon's artless, stentorian celebration of his achievement. I wish that I could. I wish that he had remained an object of unthinking adoration, instead of becoming another of adulthood's ubiquitous, insoluble mysteries: a story without a proper ending. I was soon to find out about those.

SUNDAY, 17th SEPTEMBER AND WEEK
Children Under 16 Admitted on Sunday in Care of Guardian
Sunday Doors Open at 4.15 p.m.   Weekday Doors Open at 1.30 p.m.

Sidney JAMES Shirley EATON Kenneth CONNOR
in

WHAT A CARVE UP !

Showing Weekdays at : 3.00 - 5.53 - 8.45 (U)

— ALSO —

WITH GAGARIN TO THE STARS

The Official Russian Film in COLOUR,
with Commentary by BOB DANVERS-WALKER
Showing Weekdays at : 1.40 - 4.30 - 7.25 (U)

---

*

Just as the lights were going down for the second time, and the censor's certificate appeared on the screen to announce the beginning of the main feature, my mother leaned over and started whispering across the top of my head.

'Ted, it's nearly six o'clock.'

'What about it?'

'Well, how long's this film going to go on?'

'I don't know. About ninety minutes, I suppose.'

'Well then we've got to drive all the way back. It'll be hours past his bedtime.'

'It won't matter just this once. It is his birthday, after all.'

The credits had started and my eyes were fixed on the screen. The film was in black and white and the music, although it was not without a certain jokiness, somehow filled me with foreboding.

'And then there's dinner,' my mother whispered. 'What are we going to do about dinner?'

'Oh, I don't know. Stop somewhere on the way back.'

'But then we'll be even later.'

'Just sit back and enjoy it, can't you?'

But I noticed that for the next few minutes, my mother kept leaning towards the light in order to sneak regular glances at her watch. After that I don't know what she was doing, because I was too busy concentrating on the film.

It told the story of a nervous, mild-mannered man (played by Kenneth Connor) who was startled in his flat late one night by the arrival of a sinister solicitor. The solicitor had come to tell him that his rich uncle had recently died, and that he was required to travel immediately up to Yorkshire, where the reading of the will was to take place at the family home, Blackshaw Towers. Kenneth went up to Yorkshire by train in the company of his friend, a worldly bookmaker (played by Sidney James), and found that Blackshaw Towers was situated on a remote edge of the moors far from the nearest village. Failing to find a taxi, they accepted a lift in a hearse, which left them stranded on the moors in the middle of a dense fog.

When they finally arrived at the house, they could hear the distant howling of dogs.

Sidney said: 'Not exactly a holiday camp, is it?'

Kenneth said: 'There's something creepy about this place.'

The rest of the audience seemed to be finding it funny, but by now I was thoroughly scared. I had never been taken to see anything like this before: although it wasn't strictly a horror film, the detail was very convincing, and the gloomy atmosphere, dramatic music and perpetual sense that something terrible was about to happen all combined to torment me with a strange mixture of fear and exhilaration. Part of me wanted nothing more than to run out of the cinema into what was left of the daylight; but another part of me was determined to stay until I found out where it was all leading.

Kenneth and Sidney crept into the hallway of Blackshaw Towers, and found that the house was just as eerie as it had looked from the outside. They were met by a gaunt and forbidding butler called Fisk, who led them upstairs and showed them to their rooms. Much to his dismay, Kenneth found himself not only being taken to the East Wing, far away from his friend, but being required to sleep in the very room where his late uncle had died. Soft, unsettling organ music could be heard in the corridor. They went downstairs again and were introduced to the other members of Kenneth's family: his cousins Guy, Janet and Malcolm, his Uncle Edward, and his mad Aunt Emily, for whom time seemed to have stood still ever since the First World War. Just before the solicitor began reading the will, another woman appeared: a young, blonde and beautiful woman played by the actress Shirley Eaton. She was there because she had nursed Kenneth's uncle during his final illness. There weren't enough chairs for everybody to sit around the table, so Kenneth had to balance on Shirley's knee. He seemed quite pleased about this.

The will was read and it transpired that none of the relatives had been left anything at all: they had been made the victims of a practical joke. They argued with each other bitterly as they began getting ready for bed. Then, suddenly, all the lights in the house went off. By now there was a terrible storm raging outside and Fisk suggested that the generator must have broken down. Kenneth and Sidney volunteered to go with him and investigate. When they reached the shed which housed the generator they found that the machinery had been smashed to pieces. They started going back towards the house, but were amazed to find Uncle Edward sitting on a deck-chair in the middle of the lawn, drenched by the pouring rain.

Sidney said: 'What's he sitting out there for?'

Kenneth laughed and said: 'It's unbelievable. He'll catch his death of – death of –'

He gave a violent sneeze, and Uncle Edward fell stiffly off the deck-chair. He was dead.

Kenneth said: 'Sid . . . is he?'

Sidney said: 'Well if he ain't, he's a very heavy sleeper.'

There was a terrific thunderclap, and my mother leaned across to my father. She whispered: 'Ted, come on, let's go.'

My father was laughing. He said: 'What for?'

My mother said: 'It's not suitable.'

Kenneth said: 'Well I mean, we can't leave him round here, can we? Look, let's put him in the potting shed – it's over there somewhere.'

There was more audience laughter as Kenneth, Sid and the butler attempted to pick up Uncle Edward's corpulent body.

Sidney said: 'Look, it'd be easier to bring the potting shed over to him.'

Even Grandma laughed at that. But my mother just looked at her watch again and my father, perhaps imagining that I might be frightened, ruffled my hair and laid his arm close by, so that I could take hold of it and lean against him.

Kenneth and Sid went back inside and told the rest of the family that Uncle Edward had been killed. Sid tried to telephone the police, only to discover that the line had been cut off. Kenneth said that he was going home, but the solicitor pointed out that the moors were impassable in this weather, and that if he were to leave now, he would be the first to come under suspicion for Edward's murder. He recommended that everyone should go to bed at once and lock their doors.

Fisk said: 'It's only the start of it. There'll be another one yet, mark my words.'

Sidney said: 'Good-night, laughing boy.'

Kenneth and Sidney went back upstairs, but then, left to his own devices, Kenneth found it easy to get lost in the rambling old house. He opened the door to what he thought was his bedroom and discovered that it was already occupied by Shirley, wearing only her slip and about to put on a nightgown.

Kenneth said: 'I say, what are you doing in my room?'

Shirley said: 'This isn't your room. I mean, that isn't your luggage, is it?'

She clutched the nightgown modestly to her bosom.

Kenneth said: 'Oh, blimey. No. Wait a minute, that's not my bed, either. I must have got lost. I'm sorry. I'll – I'll push off.'

He started to leave, but paused after only a few steps. He turned and saw that Shirley was still holding on to her nightgown, unsure of his intentions.

My mother stirred uneasily in her chair.

Kenneth said: 'Miss, you don't happen to know where my bedroom is, do you?'

Shirley shook her head sadly and said: 'No, I'm afraid I don't.'

Kenneth said: 'Oh,' and paused. 'I'm sorry. I'll go now.'

Shirley hesitated, a resolve forming within her: 'No. Hang on.' She gestured with her hand, urgently. 'Turn your back a minute.'

Kenneth turned, and found himself staring into a mirror in which he could see his own reflection, and beyond that, Shirley's. Her back was to him, and she was wriggling out of her slip, pulling it over her head.

He said: 'J– just a minute, miss.'

My mother tried to get my father's attention.

Kenneth hastily lowered the mirror, which was on a hinge.

Shirley turned to him and said: 'You're sweet.' She finished pulling her slip over her head, and started to unfasten her bra.

My mother said: 'Come on. We're going. It's far too late already.'

But Grandpa and my father were both staring goggle-eyed at the screen as the beautiful Shirley Eaton took her bra off with her back to the camera, while Kenneth heroically tried to stop himself from peeping into the mirror which would have yielded a precious glimpse of her body. I was staring at her too, I suppose, and thinking that I had never seen anyone so lovely, and from that moment it was no longer Kenneth she spoke to but me, my own nine-year-old self, because I was now the person who had lost his way in the corridor, and, yes, it was me that I saw on the screen, sharing a room with the most beautiful woman in the world, trapped in that old dark house in that terrible storm in that shabby little cinema in my bedroom that night and in my dreams forever afterwards. It was me.

Shirley emerged from behind my head, her body swathed in the knee-length gown, and said: 'You can turn round now.'

My mother stood up, and the woman behind her said: 'For Heaven's sake sit down, can't you.'

On the screen, I turned and looked at her. I said: 'Cor. Very provoking.'

Shirley brushed back her hair, embarrassed.

My mother grabbed my hand and pulled me out of my seat. I let out a little howl of protest.

The woman behind us said: 'Sssh!'

Grandpa said: 'What are you doing?'

My mother said: 'We're leaving is what we're doing. And you're coming too, unless you want to walk all the way back to Birmingham.'

'But the film hasn't finished yet.'

Shirley and I were sitting on the double bed together. She said: 'I've a proposal to make.'

Grandma said: 'Come on then, if we're going. We've got to stop somewhere for dinner, I suppose.'

On the screen, I said: 'Oh?'

Off the screen, I said: 'Mum, I want to stay and see the end.'

'Well you can't.'

My father said: 'Oh well. Looks like we've been given our marching orders.'

Grandpa said: 'I'm staying put. I'm enjoying this.'

The woman behind us said: 'Look, I'm going to call the management in a minute.'

Shirley moved closer towards me. She said: 'Why don't you stay here tonight? I don't fancy spending the night alone, and we'd be company for each other.'

My mother grabbed me underneath the armpits and lifted me out of my seat, and for the second time that day I burst into tears: partly out of real distress and partly, no doubt, because of the sheer indignity of it. I hadn't been picked up like that since I was tiny. She pushed past the other people in the row and started carrying me down the steps towards the exit.

On the screen I seemed to be uncertain how to respond to Shirley's offer. I mumbled something but in the confusion I couldn't hear what it was. I could see Grandma and my father following us into the aisle and Grandpa rising reluctantly from his seat. As my mother pushed open the door which led to the chill concrete stairs and the salty air, I turned and caught a last glimpse of the screen. I was leaving the room but Shirley didn't

know this because she had her back to me and was fiddling with
the bed.

Shirley said: 'I'll be quite all right on the –' She turned, and
stopped. She saw that I had gone.

'– chair.'

The door closed and my family were clattering down the
stairway. I shouted, 'Let me down. Let me *down*!', and when my
mother put me down I immediately tried to run back up the stairs
into the cinema, but my father caught me and said, 'Where do
you think you're going?', and then I knew that it was all over. I
pummelled him with my fists and even tried to scratch his cheek
with my fingernails. For the first and only time in his life my
father swore and smacked me, hard, across the face. After that,
we were all very quiet.

*

In the car going home, I pretend to be asleep, but in reality my
eyelids are not properly closed and I can see the light from the
amber roadlamps flashing across my mother's face. Light, shadow.
Light, shadow.

Grandpa says, 'Now we'll never know what happened,' and
from the back of the car Grandma says, 'Oh do shut up,' and she
pokes him in the shoulder.

I am no longer crying, no longer even sulking. As for Yuri, he
has been quite forgotten and I can barely even call to mind the
film which so excited me a couple of hours ago. All I can think of
is the fearsome atmosphere of Blackshaw Towers, and the inexplicable scene in the bedroom where this beautiful, beautiful woman
asks Kenneth to spend the night with her, and he runs away when
she isn't looking.

But why did he run away? Out of fear?

I look at my mother and I'm on the point of asking her if she
understands why Kenneth ran away instead of spending the night
with a woman who would have made him feel safe and happy.
But I know that she wouldn't really answer. She would just say
that it was a silly film and it's been a long day and I should go to
sleep and forget about it. She doesn't realize that I can never

forget about it. And it's in this private knowledge that I lie back and pretend to be asleep, with my head on her lap and my eyelids half-closed so that I can just make out the light from the amber roadlamps flashing across her face. Light, shadow. Light, shadow. Light, shadow.

PART ONE

*

LONDON

August 1990

Kenneth said: 'Miss, you don't happen to know where my bedroom is, do you?'

Shirley shook her head sadly and said: 'No, I'm afraid I don't.'

Kenneth said: 'Oh,' and paused. 'I'm sorry. I'll go now.'

Shirley hesitated, a resolve forming within her: 'No. Hang on.' She gestured with her hand, urgently. 'Turn your back a minute.'

Kenneth turned, and found himself staring into a mirror in which he could see his own reflection, and beyond that, Shirley's. Her back was to him, and she was wriggling out of her slip, pulling it over her head.

He said: 'J– just a minute, miss.'

My hand, resting between my legs, stirred.

Kenneth hastily lowered the mirror, which was on a hinge.

Shirley turned to him and said: 'You're sweet.' She finished pulling her slip over her head, and started to unfasten her bra.

My hand began to move, lazily stroking the coarse denim.

Shirley disappeared behind Kenneth's head.

Kenneth said: 'Well, a – a handsome face isn't everything, you know.'

Continuing to hold down the mirror, he tried not to look in it but couldn't resist taking occasional glimpses. With every glimpse, his face registered physical pain. Shirley put on her nightgown.

Kenneth said: 'All that glitters is not gold.'

She emerged from behind his head, her body swathed in the knee-length gown, and said: 'You can turn round now.'

He turned and looked at her. He seemed pleased.

'Cor. Very provoking.'

Shirley brushed back her hair, embarrassed.

My hand came to rest. I reached for the pause button, but thought better of it.

Kenneth began to pace the room, and said, with a show of bravado: 'Well, I suppose you must be rather scared, with all the things that have been going on here tonight.'

Shirley said: 'Oh, not really.' She sat down on the double bed, with its heavy oak frame.

Kenneth moved rapidly towards her. He said: 'Well, I am.'

Shirley said: 'I've an idea.' She leaned forward.

Kenneth turned and began pacing again. As if to himself, he said: 'Yes, I've got one or two myself.'

Shirley said: 'Come and sit here.' She patted the space next to her on the bed. 'Come on.' An orchestra started playing, but neither of them took any notice. Kenneth sat down beside her. She said: 'I've a proposal to make.'

Kenneth said: 'Oh?'

Shirley moved closer towards him. She said: 'Why don't you stay here tonight? I don't fancy spending the night alone, and we'd be company for each other.'

As Shirley said this, Kenneth turned towards her and leaned closer. For a moment they seemed on the point of kissing.

I watched.

Kenneth turned away. He said: 'Yes, it's – quite a good plan, miss, but, well . . .' He got up and began pacing again. '. . . I – we don't know each other really very well . . .'

He made for the door. Shirley seemed to say something, but it couldn't be heard, and then she started turning down the sheets on the bed and fluffing up the pillows. As she did this, she was seen in reflection again, this time in a full-length mirror opposite the bed. She didn't notice that Kenneth had reached the door. He turned to take a final look at her and then quickly sneaked out.

Still fussing over the bed, Shirley said: 'I'll be quite all right on the –' She turned, and stopped. She saw that Kenneth had gone.

'– chair.'

I pressed the rewind button.

For a moment Shirley froze: her mouth was open and her whole body shuddered. Then she turned, smoothed down the bed, Kenneth walked backwards into the room, Shirley seemed to say something, sat down on the bed, Kenneth seemed to say something, sat down beside her, they seemed to talk, he got up and paced backwards, moved rapidly away from her, she got up, Kenneth paced and talked, she fiddled with her hair, he looked away from her, she hid behind his head, began to take off her nightgown, Kenneth's face contorted repeatedly and he lifted the mirror up and down, Shirley put her bra back on, emerged from behind his head, started to pull her slip back over her head, said something, Kenneth hastily lifted the mirror, said something, glanced in the mirror, and Shirley began to wriggle back into her slip.

I pressed the pause button.

Kenneth's face and the back of Shirley's body were reflected in the mirror. They shuddered. I pressed the pause button again. They moved slightly. I pressed it again and again. They began to move in jerky stages. Shirley moved her arms. And again. And again. She was wriggling. She was taking off her slip. She was pulling it over her head. Kenneth was watching. He knew he shouldn't watch. The slip was nearly off. Shirley's arms were above her head.

My hand, resting between my legs, stirred.

Kenneth mouthed something, very slowly. He lowered the mirror, out of his range of vision. He continued to hold it down so that he couldn't look into it.

Shirley turned to him, and mouthed something. There were only two words but it seemed to take a long time. Then she continued to pull her slip over her head. She finished pulling it off in seven jerky stages. She put her hands behind her back. Her fingers worked at the clasp of her bra.

My hand began to move, stroking the coarse denim.

Shirley turned. She took the beginnings of a step. She disappeared behind Kenneth's head.

Kenneth began to mouth something.

Somebody knocked at the door.

I said, 'Oh shit!', and leapt out of my chair. I turned off the tape. The screen changed from monochrome to colour and the volume came back: a male voice, very deep and loud. There was a man on the screen. He had his arms around a child. Some documentary. I turned the volume down on the television and checked that my trousers were buttoned up. I looked around at

49

my flat. It was very untidy. I decided that it was too late to do anything about that, and went to answer the knock. Who could it be, at nine-fifteen on a Thursday evening?

I opened the door a few inches. It was a woman.

*

She had piercing and very intelligent blue eyes, eyes which would certainly have held mine in a strong and steady gaze had I not deliberately avoided them, preferring instead to take in the details of her pale, slightly mottled complexion and rich coppery hair. She smiled at me, not fulsomely, just enough to offer a hint of nice even teeth, and to make me feel that I had to smile back however difficult this might prove to be. I managed to produce what I think must have looked like a sort of sinister half-grin. It was exciting and unusual to find this person standing on my doorstep, but my pleasure was tempered not only by the awkward timing of the interruption but by an uneasy, insistent sense that I had seen the woman somewhere before: that I might, in fact, have been expected to recognize her and even remember her name. In her left hand she was holding a sheet of A4 paper, folded down the middle; her right hand dangled restlessly at her side, as if she was trying to find a pocket in which to hide it.

'Hello,' she said.

'Hello.'

'I'm not disturbing you, am I?'

'Not at all. I was just watching the television.'

'It's just that – Well, I know we don't know each other very well or anything, but I thought I might ask you a favour. If that's all right.'

'Sounds fine. Would you like to come in?'

'Thanks.'

As she crossed the threshold to my flat I tried to remember how long it had been since I last had a visitor of any description. Probably not since my mother came down: two, maybe three years. That would also have been the last time I had dusted or vacuumed. What on earth did she mean, anyway, 'We don't know each other very well'? It seemed an eccentric thing to say.

'Can I take your coat?' I asked.

She stared at me: then I noticed that she wasn't wearing a coat, just jeans and a cotton blouse. I found this a little puzzling, but managed to hide the fact by joining in her nervous laughter. It was hot outside, after all, and still fairly light.

'So,' I said, once we had both sat down. 'How can I help?'

'Well, it's like this.' And then just as she started to explain, my attention was caught by the liver spots on the back of her hand, and I found myself trying to guess how old she was, because her face, and especially her eyes, still had this questioning, fresh, youthful quality, and going by that alone I would have said that she was in her early thirties at the most, and yet now I was beginning to wonder if she wasn't nearer my age, or even older, early to mid forties perhaps, and as I was trying to reach a decision on this I realized that she had finished talking and was waiting for me to answer and I hadn't been listening to a word she'd said.

There was a long and difficult pause. I got up, put my hands in my pockets and walked over to the window. There was nothing for it but to turn round after a few seconds and say, as politely as I could: 'Do you think you could run that by me again?'

She was taken aback but did her best to hide it. 'Sure,' she said, and then started explaining the whole thing again, only this time, now that I had come over to the window, I found that I was facing the television and couldn't help staring at the swarthy, dark-haired, smiling gentleman on the screen, who had his arm around this little boy, and seemed to be trying so hard to be liked by this kid who was standing rigidly to attention and staring into space and almost pulling away from the avuncular figure next to him, with the permanent smile and the thick black moustache. And there was something so compelling about this scene, something so charged and unnatural, that it made me forget I was supposed to be listening to the woman until she had almost finished, and then I realized that I still didn't have a clue what she was talking about.

There was another pause, longer and more difficult than the first. I thought out my next move carefully before making it: a pensive, nonchalant stroll across to the other side of the room, and then a casual lowering of my buttocks on to the edge of the dining table, so that I was leaning back slightly as I faced her. At which point I said: 'Do you think you could see your way clear to repeating that, by any chance?'

She regarded me intently for a few seconds. 'I hope you don't mind me asking this, Michael,' she said, 'but are you feeling all right?'

It was a fair question, by anybody's standards: but I didn't have it in me to give an honest answer.

'It's my powers of concentration,' I said. 'They're not what they used to be. Too much television, I expect. If you could just . . . one more time . . . I'm listening this time. Really, I am.'

It was touch and go for a while. I wouldn't have been at all surprised if she had simply got up and left the room. She looked at her sheet of A4 paper and seemed to be wondering whether to drop the subject altogether, to jack in the clearly thankless task of trying to get me to listen to a few simple words of English. But then, after taking a deep breath, she started speaking again: slow, loud, deliberate. It was obvious that this was my last chance.

And I would have listened at this point, I really would, for my curiosity was aroused, apart from anything else, but my brain was spinning, all my senses were in a whirl, because she had used my name, she had actually called me by my first name, Michael, she had said, 'I hope you don't mind me asking this, Michael,' and I can't tell you how long it was since anybody had called me by my name, it can't have happened since my mother came down – two, maybe three years – and the funny thing about it was that if she knew my name, then in all probability I knew hers, or I had known it once, or I was expected to know it, we must have been introduced at one time or another, and I was so busy trying to put a name to her face, and to put her face into a context where I may have seen it before, that I completely forgot to pay any attention to her slow, loud, deliberate speech, so that as soon as she finished I knew we were in for something more, something much more and something much much worse than just another long and difficult pause.

'You haven't been listening to a word of this, have you?'

I shook my head.

'I get the sense,' she said, rising quickly to her feet, 'that I'm wasting my time here.'

She stared at me accusingly; and not having much to lose any more, I stared back.

'Can I ask you something?'

She shrugged. 'Why not?'

'Who are you?'

Her eyes widened, and it felt as though she had taken a step away from me, although as far as I could see she didn't actually move.

'I'm sorry?'

'I don't know who you are.'

She gave a mirthless, incredulous smile.

'I'm Fiona.'

'Fiona.' The name dropped into my mind with a heavy thud: there were no echoes. 'Should I know you?'

'I'm your neighbour,' said Fiona. 'I live just across the hall from you. I introduced myself to you just a few weeks ago. We pass on the stairs . . . three or four times a week. You say hello.'

I blinked, and came a little closer, gazing rudely into her face. I steeled myself to make an enormous effort of memory. Fiona . . . I still couldn't remember having heard the name, not recently, and if it seemed that something about her was starting to take on a distant familiarity, the origins of this feeling were obscure, and tasted less of day-to-day encounters on the staircase than the sensation, perhaps, of being presented with a photograph of a long-dead ancestor, in whose sepia features it might just be possible to detect the ghost of a family resemblance. Fiona . . .

'When you introduced yourself to me,' I asked, 'did I say anything?'

'Not much, no. I thought you were rather unfriendly. But then I don't tend to give up very easily: so I've kept trying.'

'Thank you,' I said, and sat down in an armchair. 'Thank you.'

Fiona was left standing by the door. 'I'll go then, shall I?'

'No – please – if you could just bear with me a little longer. We might get somewhere. Please, sit down.'

Fiona hesitated, and before coming to sit down on the sofa opposite me, she opened the door to the landing outside and left it ajar. I pretended not to have noticed this. She perched on the edge of the sofa, her back arched and her hands folded unhappily in her lap.

'What were you saying just now?' I asked.

'You want me to go through all that again?'

'Just briefly. In a couple of words.'

'I was asking you to sponsor me. I'm doing a sponsored bike ride, for the hospital.' She passed me the sheet of A4 paper, roughly half of which was covered with signatures.

A few lines at the top of the paper explained the nature of the event, and what the money was being raised for. I read them quickly and said, 'Forty miles sounds an awful long way. You must be very fit.'

'Well, I've never done anything quite like this before. I thought it would get me out and about.'

I folded the paper in two, laid it aside and thought for a moment. I could feel a new energy rising in me and the temptation to laugh, odd though it would have seemed, was quite powerful. 'Do you know what the funny thing is?' I said. 'Shall I tell you the really funny thing?'

'Please do.'

'This is the longest conversation I've had – the most I've talked to someone – for something like two years. More than two years, I think. The longest.'

Fiona laughed in disbelief. 'But we've barely spoken.'

'None the less.'

She laughed again. 'But that's ridiculous. Have you been on a desert island or something?'

'No. I've been right here.'

A confused shake of the head. 'Well how come?'

'I don't know: I just didn't want to. It hasn't been a conscious decision or anything, it's just that the occasion's never arisen. It's easy, you'd be surprised. I suppose in the old days you'd have to have talked to someone: going into shops and things. But now you can do all your shopping in the supermarket, and you can do all your banking by machine, and that's about it.'

A thought occurred to me, and I got up to lift the receiver on the telephone. It was still connected.

'Does my voice sound strange to you? How does it sound?'

'It sounds fine. Quite normal.'

'What about this flat? Does it smell?'

'It's a bit . . . close, yes.'

I picked up the remote control for the television and was about to switch off. The young boy with the locked, expressionless eyes, his back as tense and rigid as Fiona's when she had sat down on my sofa, was no longer on the screen: but the avuncular man with the big grin and the heavy black moustache was still stomping around, this time in full military uniform and surrounded by men of the same age and nationality and bearing. I watched him for a few seconds and felt another memory beginning to recover its shape.

'I know who that is,' I said, pointing and clicking my finger. 'It's – whatsisname – President of Iraq . . .'

'Michael, everyone knows who that is. It's Saddam Hussein.'

'That's right. Saddam.' Then, before turning the television off, I asked: 'Who was that boy with him? The one he was trying to put his arms around?'

'Haven't you been watching the news? That was one of the hostages. He's been parading them on television, as if they were cattle or something.'

This made little sense to me, but I could tell it was not the moment for elaborate explanations. I switched the television off and said – listening with interest to my own voice – 'I'm sorry, you must think I'm being very rude. Would you like a drink? I've got wine and orange juice and beer and lemonade, and even a bit of whisky, I think.'

Fiona hesitated.

'We can leave the door open if you like. I don't mind about that at all.'

And then she smiled, and sat back on the sofa, and crossed her legs, saying, 'Well, why not. That would be very nice.'

'Wine?'

'I think orange juice, please. I can't seem to shake off this dreadful sore throat.'

*

My little kitchen had always been the cleanest room in the flat. I never dusted or used a vacuum cleaner because dust is not easily visible to the casual observer, it's possible to turn a blind eye to it, yet I could not tolerate the sight of smudges and splashes of dried food caked to my brilliant white surfaces. When I withdrew into the kitchen, therefore, and turned on the two 100-watt spotlights which sent their beams of pure brightness fearlessly exploring every gleaming angle and corner, it restored my self-confidence. The night was slowly darkening, and from the kitchen sink the first thing I could see was my own reflected face, hovering like a spectre outside my fifth-floor window. This was the face that Fiona had been addressing for the last few minutes. I took a good look at it and tried to imagine how it would have appeared to her. The eyes were puffy from lack of sleep and bloodshot from too much glassy staring at the television screen; deeply scored lines were beginning to appear around the corners of the mouth, although these were partially obscured by two days' worth of stubble; the jaw-line was still reasonably firm, but another three or four years would probably see the onset of a double chin; the hair, once tawny, was now streaked with grey and stood desperately in need of cutting and re-styling; there were the shreds of a parting, so tentative and wasted that the onlooker might easily have been forgiven for not noticing that it was there at all. It wasn't a friendly face: the eyes, a deep, velvety blue, might once have suggested wells of possibility but now seemed guarded, fenced off. But at the same time it was honest. It was a face you could trust.

And if you looked beyond the face, what did you see? I peered out into the twilight. Nothing much. A few scattered lights had been turned on across the courtyard, and the gentle babble of televisions and stereo systems drifted over from open windows. It was a muggy August evening, entirely typical of a summer which seemed to be taking a malicious pleasure in testing Londoners to the limit, drenching them day and night in dense city heat. Looking down, I noticed the movement of a shadow in the gardens. Two shadows, one very small. An old woman walking her dog, probably struggling to keep up as it zig-zagged from bush to bush, its nerves stretched and tingling with the excitement of secret, nocturnal pleasures. I listened to its intermittent rustles and scuffles, the only distinct sounds to be made out, apart from the occasional siren, above London's buried monotonous hum.

Turning away from the window, I fetched a carton of orange juice from the fridge and cracked three or four ice cubes into a tumbler. I poured the juice over the blocks of ice, enjoying their dull music as they clinked together and rose to the top of the glass. Then I poured myself a glass of beer and took the drinks into the sitting room.

As I paused on the threshold, I tried to look at the room with the same objectivity I had brought to the reflection of my own face: wanting to imagine the impression it would have made on Fiona. She was watching me, now, so I didn't have as much time, but some quick observations presented themselves: the fact that the curtains, which had come with the flat, and the pictures, which had been bought many years ago, reflected nothing of my present taste; the fact that so many of the surfaces – the table, the window-sills, the top of the television, the mantelpiece – were stacked with papers and magazines and videotapes rather than the few well-chosen ornaments which might have given the room form and personality; the fact that the bookshelves, which I had put up myself, also many years ago, had been largely cleared of books (now jumbled into a tower of cardboard boxes in the spare bedroom) and were scattered, instead, with still more videotapes, piled both horizontally and vertically, some pre-recorded and some filled with scraps of films and programmes taped off the television. It was a room, I thought, which presented an aspect not dissimilar to the face reflected in the kitchen window: it had the potential to be welcoming but for the moment seemed to have transformed itself, through a mixture of carelessness and disuse, into something ungainly and almost eerily neutral.

The first thing Fiona said about the flat, after we had been talking a little while, was that she felt it needed some pot plants. She sang the praises of cyclamen and hibiscus. She waxed lyrical about the merits of cineraria and asparagus fern. She had gone crazy on cineraria recently, she said. It would never have occurred to me to buy myself a pot plant and I tried to imagine what it would be like to share this room with a living, growing organism

as well as my stale litter of films and magazines. I poured myself
another beer and fetched her some more orange juice and this
time she asked me to put some vodka in it. I could tell she was a
warm and friendly woman because when I came to sit next to her
on the sofa in order to fill out her sponsorship form, she was
quite happy to let our legs come into occasional contact: there
was no shrinking away, and as I wrote down the amount and
signed my name I could feel our thighs touching, and I wondered
how this had happened, if in fact it was Fiona who had edged
closer to me. And soon it became clear that she was in no great
hurry to leave, that she was for some reason enjoying talking to
me – I who had so little to give in return – and I could only
conclude from this that she must in some brave, quiet, reckless
way have been a little desperate for companionship, because
although I was a poor companion that evening, and although my
behaviour must certainly have frightened her to start with, still
she persisted, and grew more and more relaxed, and more and more
talkative. I can't remember how long she stayed, or what it was we
talked about, but I can remember enjoying it, at first, this unaccustomed business of talking, and it must have been quite a while,
several drinks later, before I began to feel tired again and uneasy. I
don't know why this should have happened, because I was still
enjoying myself, but I had this sudden and intense craving to be on
my own. Fiona carried on talking, I may even have been answering
back, but my attention had started to wander and she only regained
it by saying something which surprised me very much.

'You can't switch me off,' she said.

'Pardon?'

'You can't switch me off.'

She nodded at my hands. I had gone back to the armchair
opposite her and without realizing it I had picked up the remote
control for the video. It was pointed in her direction and my
finger had strayed to the pause button.

'I think I'd better go,' she said, and stood up.

As she made for the door, sponsorship form in hand, I made a
sudden bid to save the situation by blurting out: 'I think I'll get
myself one of those plants. It'll make quite a difference.'

She turned. 'There's a little nursery on my way home from work,' she said softly. 'I'll get one for you if you like. I'll bring it round tomorrow.'

'Thanks. That's very kind.'

And then she was gone. For a few seconds after the door had closed behind her I experienced a peculiar sensation: a feeling of loneliness. But this loneliness was mingled with relief and before long the relief had taken over, swamping me and calming me and guiding me gently back to the armchair and to my two friends, my trusted companions, the remote control units for the television and the video, resting one on each arm. I switched the machines on and pressed play, and Kenneth said:

'Well, a – a handsome face isn't everything, you know.'

*

I woke up the next morning with a sense that something subtly momentous had happened. The event, whatever it was, would clearly not bear analysis at this stage, but in the meantime I was anxious to take advantage of its most immediate symptom, which was a surge of mental and physical energy unprecedented in my recent experience. A handful of disagreeable tasks had been gathered, cloudy and lowering, on my mental horizon for some months now, but today it felt as though their weight had been lifted and they lay before me, unthreatening, inviting even, like a set of stepping stones which would lead me to a brighter future. I wasted no time lying around in bed. I got up and showered, made myself some breakfast, washed up and then began to hoover the whole of the flat. After that I went round with a duster, creaming off layers of dust so thick that I had to shake the cloth out of the window with every wipe. Then, tiring a little, I did a bit of desultory tidying and re-organizing. I was anxious, among other to make sure that certain papers were still to be found where I had left them many months ago, because I intended to re-acquaint myself with these and to start work on them again in the afternoon. They turned up after a search of perhaps thirty minutes, and I dropped them in a single pile on my freshly cleared desk.

This was without doubt an extraordinary day and to prove

it I now did yet another extraordinary thing. I went for a walk.

My flat was at the rear of a large mansion block which fronted on to Battersea Park. Although this had been one of my main reasons for buying it, some seven or eight years ago, I rarely took advantage of the location. Circumstances sometimes obliged me to walk through the park, it's true, but this was not the same as choosing to do so for the purposes of pleasure or meditation, and I would take absolutely no notice of my surroundings on these occasions. As it happens, I hadn't intended to take much notice of them today, either, because when I set out on my walk I did so primarily in the hope that it would enable me to reach a certain decision, the taking of which, like so much else in my life, I had now been deferring for far too long. But it seemed that in my newly wakened state I was also less than usually capable of ignoring the world around me, and I found that I was beginning to warm to this park, which had never before struck me as being one of London's most attractive. The grass was parched, the flowerbeds cracked and grey in the sun, but none the less their colours astounded me. It felt as though I were seeing them for the first time. Beneath a sky of impossibly pale blue, hordes of lunchtime sunbathers were surrendering themselves to the glare; occasional bits of clothing in garish primary colours shielded their pinkening bodies, while their heads throbbed to the beat of the sun and the deadening pulse of their ghetto-blasters and personal stereos. (There was a confusion of different musics.) The bins were overflowing with bottles, cans and the discarded wrappings of pre-packed sandwiches. The mood seemed to be one of festivity, with just a distant hint of tension and resentment – perhaps because the heat verged, as usual, on the unbearable, or simply because we all knew in our hearts that this was not the best place to be trying to enjoy it. I wondered how many other people were wishing that they could have been in the countryside; the real countryside, of which this park was in fact little more than a scurrilous parody. In the north-western corner, not far from the river, there was an attempt at a walled garden, and as I sat there for a few minutes it reminded me of the garden at the back of Mr Nuttall's farm, where I used to play with Joan. But here, instead of that enchanted silence which we had taken so much for granted, I heard the rattling of lorries and the thunder of passing aeroplanes, and there were no sparrows or starlings to watch us from the trees, just strutting city pigeons and fat black rooks the size of small chickens.

As for that decision, it was arrived at soon enough. Earlier in the week I had received a bank statement, and this morning I had opened it to discover, not very much to my surprise, that I was heavily overdrawn. In which case, something would have to be done about the pile of manuscript now lying on my desk. With luck – perhaps with the aid of a miracle – there might just be money to be raised on it: but I would have to read it through as quickly as possible, so that I could decide how to approach the relevant publishers.

I started on this task as soon as I got back to the flat, and had managed to read about seventy pages when Fiona called by in the early evening. She brought two large paper carrier bags, one of which had foliage spilling over the top.

'Gosh,' she said. 'You look different.'

(I remember these rather absurd exclamations of hers, now. 'Gosh' was one; 'Crikey', another.)

'Do I?' I said.

'I caught you on a bad night, didn't I? Last evening, I mean.'

'Maybe. I'm feeling more . . . with it, tonight.'

She put the carrier bags down on the floor, saying: 'I brought these round right away. They need re-potting. If I can leave them here, I'll just go and freshen up and things, and then I'll come and give you a hand.'

When she had gone I took a peek inside the bags. There were plants in one and a couple of fair-sized earthenware pots and saucers in the other, along with some bits of shopping, and a newspaper. It was a long time since I had looked at this particular tabloid, but remembering that today was a Friday I took it out of the bag and thumbed rapidly to a page near the middle. When I found what I was looking for I smiled a private smile, and started to read through it: without much interest at first, but then, after a few lines, I frowned and something chimed within my memory. I went into my spare bedroom, the one I used as a study (the one I never went into), and came back with a large box file full of news-paper clippings. I was looking through these when Fiona returned.

She took her bags through into the kitchen and set about re-potting the plants. I could hear the noise of things being moved about and taps being turned on and off. At one point she said: 'I must say your kitchen's awfully clean.'

'I'll come and help in a minute,' I said. 'I really appreciate this, you know. I must reimburse you.'

'Don't be silly.'

'Ha!'

I had found the cutting, which I pulled out of the box with this small cry of triumph. It was a vindication of my powers of recall, apart from anything else. I laid out today's paper on the dining table, opened at the appropriate page, placed the cutting next to it and read both items again carefully. My frown deepened. When Fiona came in carrying one of the plants, she said: 'I wouldn't mind a drink.'

'Sorry. Of course. Only I was just looking at this column. What do you make of it?'

When she saw that I was looking at her newspaper, Fiona became defensive: 'I didn't buy that, you know. I found it on the tube.' She glanced at the identical pictures of Hilary Winshaw which headed each page, and grimaced. 'That dreadful woman. I hope you're not going to tell me you're a fan.'

'Not at all. But I do have a professional interest. Read them while I get you something, and let me know what you think.'

The column had been running for more than six years now and still bore the title PLAIN COMMON SENSE. The photograph at the top hadn't changed, either. It was here, every Friday, that the great television mogul and media personality could be found airing her views on any topic which happened to seize her wandering fancy, holding forth with equal conviction on issues ranging from the welfare state and the international situation to the length of hemline sported by members of the royal family on recent social outings. Countless thousands of readers seemed to have been charmed, over the years, by her endearing habit of professing almost total ignorance of any subject which she chose to discuss – her speciality in this regard being a willingness to put forward the most strident opinions relating to controversial books and films while cheerfully admitting that she had been unable to find the time to read or see them. Another winning feature was her way of making the reader feel generously included within her circle of intimates, by being prepared to write at extraordinary length about the minutiae of her domestic arrangements, in tones which would rise to a pitch of righteous indignation whenever she described the vagaries of the successive builders, plumbers and decorators who seemed to be in permanent attendance at her enormous Chelsea home. It's an interesting but little known fact that for pouring out this torrent of nonsense, Ms Winshaw was paid a yearly fee equivalent to six times the salary of a qualified school-teacher and eight times that of a staff nurse in the National Health Service. I've got proof of that, as well.

The two items which I'd chosen for comparison found Hilary in a political frame of mind. Although they were separated by roughly four years, I present them here as Fiona and I read them that day: side by side.

A NEWSLETTER reaches my desk today from a group who call themselves the Supporters of Democracy in Iraq – or SODI for short.

They claim that President Saddam Hussein is a brutal dictator who maintains his power through torture and intimidation.

Well, I've got some words of advice for this silly bunch of SODIs: *check your facts!*

Who is responsible for the social welfare programmes which have brought such massive improvements in housing,

It's not often that a television programme can make me feel physically sick, but last night was an exception.

Can there be anyone in the country whose stomach did not turn over, as we watched Saddam Hussein on the *Nine O'Clock News*, parading the so-called 'hostages' he is wickedly proposing to use as a human shield?

This was one image that will stay with me for the rest of my life: the spectacle of a defenceless and clearly terrified child being mauled and education and medical services throughout Iraq?

Who has recently given the Iraqis pension rights and a minimum wage?

Who has installed new and more efficient irrigation and drainage systems, made generous loans to local farmers, and promised 'health for all' by the year 2000?

Who has no less a figure than President Reagan ordered to be removed from the list of political leaders accused of supporting terrorism?

And who else, out of all the Middle Eastern leaders, has put his moolah where his mouth is and called on so many *British* builders and industrialists to help with the rebuilding of his country?

That's right – it's 'brutal', 'torturing' Saddam Hussein.

Come off it, SODI! It's those barking Ayatollahs you should be complaining about. Life in Iraq may not be perfect, but it's better now than it has been for a long, long time.

So lay off Saddam. I say he's a man we can do business with.

pawed by one of the most vicious and ruthless dictators to hold power anywhere in the world today.

If any good at all can come from such a revolting display, it will be to make the so-called 'peace' lobby come to their senses and realize that we can't just sit back and allow this Mad Dog of the Middle East to get away scot-free with his terrible crimes.

It's not just the invasion of Kuwait I'm talking about. The whole eleven-year presidency of Saddam Hussein is one long, sickening history of torture, brutality, intimidation and murder. Anyone who doesn't believe me should take a look at some of the information leaflets published by SODI (Supporters of Democracy in Iraq).

There can be no doubt about it: the time for moral fudging is over; the time for action is here.

Let us pray that President Bush and Mrs Thatcher understand that. And let us pray, too, that the brave, plucky little boy we saw on our television screens last night will live to forget his meeting with the evil Butcher of Baghdad.

Fiona finished reading and looked at me for a few seconds.
'I'm not sure that I understand,' she said.

Hilary

In the summer of 1969, shortly before they went up to Oxford together, Hugo Beamish invited his best friend Roddy Winshaw to stay with his family for a few weeks. They lived in a huge, cluttered, slightly dirty house in North West London. Roddy's sister Hilary was invited too. She was fifteen.

Hilary found the whole thing excruciatingly tedious. It was perhaps marginally better than spending the summer in Tuscany with her parents (again!), but Hugo's mother and father turned out to be almost as dull – she was a writer, he worked at the BBC – while his sister, Alicia, was nothing but a crashing bore with buck teeth and terrible spots.

Alan Beamish was a kindly man who noticed quickly enough that Hilary wasn't enjoying herself. One night as they all sat around the dinner table, with Roddy and Hugo loudly discussing their respective career options, he watched her pushing a mound of tepid pasta around her plate and asked a sudden question:

'And what do you see yourself doing in ten years' time, I wonder?'

'Oh, I don't know.' Hilary hadn't given this matter much thought, taking it for granted (rightly, of course) that something glamorous and well-paid would sooner or later fall into her lap. Besides, she hated the idea of sharing her aspirations with these people. 'I thought I might go into television,' she improvised, lazily.

'Well you know of course that Alan is a producer,' said Mrs Beamish.

Hilary didn't know this. She had got him down as a company accountant or at best some sort of engineer. Even so, she was not in the least impressed: but from that moment on, Alan, for his part, chose to take Hilary under his wing.

'Do you know the secret of success in the television business?' he asked her, late one afternoon. 'It's very simple. You have to watch it, that's all. You have to watch it all the time.'

Hilary nodded. She never watched television. She knew she was too good for it.

'Now I'll tell you what we're going to do,' said Alan.

What they were going to do, it transpired – much to Hilary's horror – was to sit down in front of the television and take in an entire evening's viewing, with Alan talking her through every programme, explaining how it was made, how much it cost, why it had been scheduled at a certain time, and where its target audience lay.

'Scheduling is everything,' he said. 'A programme stands or falls by its scheduling. Understand that, and you'll already have a march on all the other bright young graduates you'll be competing with.'

They started off with the news on BBC1 at ten to six, followed by a magazine programme called *Town and Around*. Then they switched channels to ITV and watched *The Saint*, with Roger Moore.

'This is the kind of show the independent companies do best,' said Alan. 'Very sellable abroad: even to America. High production values, lots of location work. Snappy direction, too. It's all a bit shallow, for my liking, but I wouldn't knock it.'

Hilary yawned. At seven twenty-five they watched something about a Scottish doctor and his housemaid, which all seemed very slow and provincial to her. Alan explained that this was one of the most popular programmes on television. Hilary had never heard of it.

'They'll be discussing this storyline in every pub, office and factory in Britain tomorrow,' he said. 'That's the great thing about television: it's one of the fibres that holds the country together. It collapses class distinctions and helps create a sense of national identity.'

He was equally lyrical about the next two programmes: a documentary called *The Rise and Fall of the Third Reich*, and another news bulletin at nine o'clock, this one lasting a quarter of an hour.

'The BBC is respected the world over for the quality and fair-mindedness of its news coverage. Thanks to the World Service, you can tune in a radio almost anywhere on the globe and be sure to hear impartial, authoritative bulletins, mixed in with lighter programmes which maintain the highest standards in music and entertainment. It's one of our greatest post-war achievements.'

Until now Hilary had merely been bored, but at this point things started to go rapidly downhill. She was made to sit through a dreadful comedy show called *Nearest and Dearest*, full of coarse jokes which had the studio audience screeching with vulgar laughter, and then they saw a thing called *It's a Knockout*, which featured a series of witless outdoor games. She began to squirm with rage and embarrassment. Unconsciously, she channelled her agitation through her fingertips by reaching across to a fruit bowl next to the sofa and plucking off grape after grape: she would peel each one with her tapered fingernail before popping it into her mouth. A little pile of the skins started to form on her lap.

'This isn't my sort of show at all,' said Alan. 'But I don't look down on it. You have to make things which appeal to everyone. Everyone's entitled to their bit of fun.'

They finished off by turning over to BBC2 and watching a series called *Ooh La La!*, adapted from the farces of Georges Feydeau. This one starred Donald Sinden and Barbara Windsor. Hilary fell asleep halfway through, and woke up just in time to catch the end of an astronomy programme presented by a peculiar man in an ill-fitting suit.

'So there you have it,' said Alan proudly. 'News, entertainment, comedy, documentary and classical drama in equal measure. There's no other country in the world which could offer you an experience like that.' With his gentle, melodious voice and greying bushes of hair he was beginning to look and sound, to Hilary, like the worst sort of parish priest. 'And it's all in the hands of people like you. Talented youngsters whose task in the years to come will be to carry the tradition forward.'

At the end of the holiday, Roddy and Hilary took the train back to their parents' current home in Sussex.

'I thought old Mr Beamish was a bit of a sweetie, actually,' said Roddy, taking out a cigarette. 'And yet Henry told me that he's frightfully left wing.' He lit up. 'Hasn't rubbed off on Hugo, thank God. Anyway, you'd never guess it, would you?'

Hilary stared out of the window.

*

From THE 10 MOST LIKELY: *colour feature in* Tatler, *October 1976*

> Lovely Hilary Winshaw is a recent Cambridge graduate who intends to make quite a splash in her new job at —— Television, where she will be training as a producer. Hilary already has strong views about the work which lies ahead of her. 'I think of television as one of the fibres which holds the country together,' she says. 'It's brilliant at collapsing distinctions and building a sense of identity. And that's definitely a tradition I hope to encourage and foster.'
>
> In this picture Hilary is all ready to keep the winter cold at bay with a Royal Samink cape from Furs Renée, 39 Dover St, W1 (£3,460), sweater with roll-neck in camel cashmere by Pringle, 28 Old Bond St, W1 (£52.50), gloves in camel wool, medium-length from Herbert Johnson Ladies Shop, 80 Grosvenor St, W1 (£14.95), and boots in beige leather, mid calf, with stacked heels, from Midas at 36 Hans Crescent, SW1 (£129).

*

—— *Television plc. Extract from minutes of Executive Board Meeting, 14 November 1983. Confidential.*

... It was reiterated at this point that nobody undervalued Ms Winshaw's contribution to the company's programming successes over the last seven years. However, Mr Fisher insisted that her decision to purchase TMT, the American production company, for £120 million in 1981, had never been offered to the board for proper scrutiny. He asked for clarification on four points:

i) was she aware that, at the time of purchase, TMT was running up losses of $32 million a year?

ii) was she aware that her weekly flights to Hollywood, the purchase of her flat in Los Angeles, and the running expenses of her three company cars had all been cited as major contributing factors in the assessment, by independent management consultants Webster Hadfield, that the company's costs were currently 40% too high?

iii) was she aware that her policy of purchasing low-cost drama from TMT, and then insisting that it be re-edited by the addition of previously deleted sequences (in order to expand the running time – often by as much as thirty minutes – and thereby increase the cost-effectiveness of the purchase) had significantly influenced the IBA's recent judgment that the company was failing to meet acceptable quality thresholds?

iv) was the doubling of her salary to £210,000 p.a., agreed upon by the board in February 1982, a fair and accurate reflection of her increased workload since the acquisition of TMT?

Mr Gardner remarked at this point that he would have thought twice about accepting this job if he had known that he was joining a sinking ship, and asked whose idea it had been to employ this bloody woman in the first place.

Mr Fisher replied that Ms Winshaw had joined the company on the recommendation of Mr Alan Beamish, the distinguished producer, formerly of the BBC.

Mrs Rawson requested, on a point of order, that Ms Winshaw stop playing with the grapes as somebody might want to eat them and there was no longer scope for waste in any area of the company's activities . . .

At 4.37 p.m. it was agreed by a vote of 11–1 that Ms Winshaw's contract should be terminated forthwith, and that she should be compensated with a lump sum which took realistic account of the present state of the company finances.

The meeting adjourned at 4.41 p.m.

*

From the Guardian, *Diary, 26 November 1983*

RAISED eyebrows all round at the news of Hilary Winshaw's recent departure from —— Television. It's not so much the fact that she was ousted (most observers had been predicting that for some time) as the size of the pay-off: a cool £320,000, if rumours are to be believed. Not a bad reward for reducing this once-profitable outfit to a condition of near-bankruptcy in a couple of years.

Could such unprecedented generosity have anything to do with her cousin Thomas Winshaw, chairman of Stewards, the merchant bank which has a hefty stake in the company? And could it be true that the multi-talented Ms Winshaw is about to land herself a plum job as columnist on a certain daily newspaper whose proprietor also just happens to be one of Stewards' most valuable clients? Watch, as they say, this space . . .

*

Hilary's reputation had preceded her, and she found that on her first day she did not receive much of a welcome from her new colleagues. Well, she thought: fuck them. She was only going to be coming in one or two days a week. If that.

She had her own desk with her name on it in a far corner of the open-plan office. All it contained, so far, was a typewriter and a pile of the day's other newspapers. It had been decided that the title of her column would be PLAIN COMMON SENSE. She had to fill up most of a tabloid page, leading off with a longish opinionated piece and following it with two or three more personal, gossipy items.

It was March 1984. She picked up the first newspaper that came to hand and glanced over the headlines. Then, after a couple of minutes, she put it down and began to type.

Underneath the headline THE POLITICS OF GREED, she wrote:

> Most of us, still tightening our belts in the wake of the recession, would agree that this is not the time to

start banging on the government's door and asking for more money.

And most of us, with images of the dreadful 'Winter of Discontent' still fresh in our minds, would agree that another wave of strikes is the last thing the country needs.

But we would have reckoned without neo-Marxist Arthur Scargill and his greedy National Union of Mineworkers.

Already Mr Scargill is threatening 'industrial action' – which of course means *inaction*, in anybody else's books – if he and his comrades aren't showered with yet another round of pay rises and perks.

Well I say, Shame on you, Mr Scargill! Just when we are all pulling together to put this country back on its feet again, who are you to take us back into the Dark Ages of industrial unrest?

How dare you put selfish greed before the national interest!

Hilary looked at her watch. Her first piece had taken slightly less than twelve minutes to write: not bad for a beginner. She took it along to the deputy editor, who began by crossing out her headline, then slid the sheet of paper back across his desk after a few moments' bored scrutiny.

'They're not asking for more money,' he said.

'I'm sorry?'

'The miners. That's not why they're striking.'

Hilary's brow puckered. 'Are you sure?'

'Quite sure.'

'But I thought all strikes were about asking for more money.'

'Well, this one's about pit closures. The NCB is planning to close twenty pits this year. They're striking because they don't want to lose their jobs.'

Still looking doubtful, Hilary picked up the piece of paper.

'I suppose I might have to change one or two things, then.'

'One or two.'

Back at her desk, she read through several of the newspapers more thoroughly. This took her nearly half an hour. Then, having mastered her brief, she typed out her second draft – this time, in just under seven and a half minutes.

> **THEY SAY that if there's one thing the Scots know, it's how to look after their money.** And Ian McGregor, chairman of the National Coal Board, is, if nothing else, a shrewd auld Scot with a lifetime's business experience behind him.
>
> Mr Arthur Scargill, however, comes from quite a different background: a lifelong union agitator, a known Marxist and an all-round troublemaker with the glint of battle in his beady little eye.
>
> So I put this question to you: which of these two figures would you rather trust with the future of the British mining industry?
>
> For this is the point about the miners' dispute. For all Mr Scargill's scaremongering rhetoric about jobs, families and what he likes to call 'the community', the argument isn't really about any of these things. It's about efficiency. If something isn't paying its way, you close it down. It's one of the first – and simplest – lessons that any businessman learns.
>
> Unfortunately Mr Scargill, bless him, doesn't seem to have learned it yet.
>
> *Which is why, when it comes to the industry's purse-strings, I for one would rather have canny Mr Mc-Gregor in control any day – the noo!*

The deputy editor read it through twice and then looked up with the ghost of a smile.

He said: 'I think you may turn out to be rather good at this.'

*

Hilary's appointment had been made against the better judgment of the editor, Peter Eaves, who for several weeks ignored her completely. One Monday evening, however, they both happened to be in the office at the same time. Hilary was writing up an interview with an old Cambridge friend, an actress who had just published a book about her collection of teddy bears, while Peter and his deputy were trying out various lay-outs for the next day's front page. As she walked past on her way to the coffee machine, she stopped to take a critical glance.

'That wouldn't make me want to buy the paper,' she said.

They took no notice.

'I mean, it's boring. Who wants to read another union story?'

News had just come in of a surprise verdict from the High Court. Back in March, the Foreign Secretary Geoffrey Howe had ordered civil servants at GCHQ in Cheltenham to give up their union membership, arguing that it presented a conflict with the national interest. The unions had tried to overturn the ban by bringing an action in the High Court, and today, much to everyone's surprise, the judge had ruled in their favour. He said that the government's actions had been 'contrary to natural justice'. The provisional front page juxtaposed pictures of Mrs Thatcher and Mr Justice Glidewell, beneath the banner headline NOT NATURAL, and, in smaller type, ELATED STAFF HAIL LEGAL VICTORY.

'I think you'll find,' said Peter, in measured tones, 'that this is a major news story. Spare us your thoughts on the subject, will you?'

'I'm serious,' said Hilary. 'Who wants to read about a bunch of civil servants and whether they can join a union or not? I mean, big deal. On top of that, why should we run a story that's damaging to the government?'

'I don't care who we damage,' said Peter, 'as long as it sells papers.'

'Well you're not going to sell many like that.' She looked at her watch. 'I can get you a better front page in twenty minutes. Maybe less.'

'I beg your pardon?'

'I'll write it *and* give you the picture.'

Hilary went back to her desk and dialled the home number of her Cambridge friend. Among the subjects they had discussed after their interview was a mutual acquaintance – another actress – who had just given birth to her third child. Her body was no longer looking its best, but this had not prevented her, apparently, from doing nude scenes for a television film to be broadcast in a few months' time. Hilary's friend, who happened to be living with the film's editor, had mentioned in passing that she had access to some of the footage, which made for interesting viewing.

'Listen, be a darling, would you, and bike some stills over?' said Hilary. 'We'll have a bit of fun.'

In the meantime she sat down and typed:

IT'S BOOBS AT TEN!

Saucy BBC bosses have got a raunchy treat in store for us this autumn, with a hot new play so sexy that it won't be screened until well after the nine o'clock watershed.

The torrid drama stars —— ——, whose three young children will certainly be in for a surprise when they see their Mum cavorting in an outrageous three-in-a-bed romp with American heartthrob —— ——

It didn't take long to make up the rest. Hilary's story dominated the next day's front page, with the High Court's decision relegated to a small paragraph in the bottom corner.

Later that evening, Peter Eaves took her out to dinner.

*

From 'Jennifer's Diary', Harpers & Queen, December 1984

PRETTY WEDDING

On Saturday afternoon I went to St Paul's, Knightsbridge, for the marriage of Peter Eaves, the well-known newspaper editor, to Hilary Winshaw, daughter of Mr and Mrs Mortimer Winshaw. The bride looked most attractive in a lovely parchment colour silk dress, with a pearl and diamond tiara holding her tulle veil in place. Her attendants wore very pretty peach silk dresses . . .

The reception was held at the Savoy hotel, and came to a most spectacular conclusion. The guests were all led out on to the riverside terrace, where the groom surprised his bride with a lovely present: her own private seaplane, a four-seater, tied up in an enormous pink ribbon. The happy couple stepped inside and took off along the Thames to start their honeymoon in tremendous style.

*

So the government has published its White Paper on the future of television, and already those moaning minnies in the broadcasting establishment are up in arms!

They would have us believe that deregulation would bring us American-style television (not that there's anything wrong with that). But the plain fact is that there's one word which terrifies this posse of Hampstead liberals more than any other.

That word is 'choice'.

And the reason they don't like it? Because they know that, given the opportunity, very few of us would 'choose' to watch the dreary round of high-brow drama and leftwing agitprop that they would like to inflict on us.

When will these self-appointed nannies of the broadcasting mafia realize that what the British people want, at the end of the day, is a bit of relaxation and a bit of fun: not to be 'educated' by some bearded prig of a critic introducing three hours of one-legged mime from Bulgaria.

Roll on, deregulation, I say, if it means more power to the viewer's elbow and more of our favourite shows with the likes of Brucie, Noel and Tarby.* (*NB subs please check these names)

Meanwhile, next time you find that the only things on the telly are one of those boring documentaries about Peruvian peasants, or some incomprehensibly 'arty' film (with subtitles, of course), remember that there's always one 'choice' they can't take away from us.

The choice to reach for that 'off' button and head down to the nearest video store!

– 'Plain Common Sense', November 1988

*

'What the hell are you watching now?'

'Bit late, aren't you?'

'I've been working, actually.'

'Oh, spare me.'

'I'm sorry?'

'You are *so* fucking transparent, darling.'

'What is this rubbish, anyway?'

'I don't know, some game show. One of those hearty, down-to-earth pieces of entertainment you've been extolling in your column lately.'

'I don't know how you can watch this crap. No wonder you're so in tune with the brain-dead morons who read your paper. You're not much better yourself.'

'Do I detect a little post-coital tetchiness, by any chance?'

'Oh, for God's sake.'

'I don't know why you keep shagging Nigel if it just puts you in a bad mood.'

'It gives you a thrill to think that, does it?'

'It gives everyone on the paper a thrill, I should imagine, since you're not exactly discreet about it.'

'Well, that's just marvellous, coming from you. I suppose getting blow-jobs from a temp, in your own office – *with the bloody door open* – I suppose that counts as discretion, does it?'

'Look, do me a favour, will you? Just fuck off and die.'

*

From Hello! *magazine, March 1990*

HILARY WINSHAW AND SIR PETER EAVES

Husband-and-wife team are so happy with baby Josephine
but 'our love for each other didn't need strengthening'

Maternal love shines out of Hilary Winshaw's eyes as she lifts her giggling, one-month-old daughter Josephine high in the air in the conservatory of the happy couple's lovely South Kensington home. They've waited a long time for their first child – Hilary and Sir Peter were married almost six years ago, when they met on the newspaper which he continues to edit and for which she still writes a popular weekly column – but, as Hilary told *Hello!* in this exclusive interview, Josephine was well worth waiting for!

Tell us, Hilary, how did you feel when you first saw your baby daughter?

Well, exhausted, for one thing! I suppose by most people's standards it was an easy labour but I certainly don't intend to go through it again in a hurry! But one glimpse of Josephine and it all seemed worthwhile. It was an amazing feeling.

Had you begun to despair of ever having a child?

One never quite gives up hope, I suppose. We'd never been to see doctors or anything, which was perhaps silly of us. But when you're with someone who feels so right for you, when two people are as happy together as Peter and I have been, then you can't help believing that your dream will come true in the end, no matter what. We're both a bit starry-eyed that way.

And has Josephine brought you even closer together?

She has, yes, inevitably. I only hesitate to say this because to be honest with you I find it hard to see how we *could* have been closer. Our love for each other really didn't need strengthening.

The baby seems to have your eyes, and I think I can even make out a bit of the Winshaw nose, there! Can you see much of Sir Peter in her?

Not yet, really, no. I think babies often grow into a resemblance with the parent. I'm sure that's what will happen.

Does this mean you'll have to take a break from your column for a while?

I don't think so. Obviously I want to spend as much time with Josephine as possible – and, of course, Peter was able to offer me pretty good terms for maternity leave. It does help if your husband is also your boss! But I'd be loath to let my readers down. They're so loyal, and they've all been so kind, sending cards and so on. It really restores your faith in people.

I must say, as an avid reader of the column, that it's something of a surprise not to find the builders here!
I know – I do tend to go on about it, don't I? But we've had to have such a lot done recently. This conservatory's new, for instance, and so is the whole of the extension with the swimming-pool. It took even longer than expected because the neighbours were so beastly about it. They even took us to court over the noise, would you believe. Anyway they've moved now, so that's all been amicably resolved.

And now I believe we're about to discover yet another side to your talents.
Yes, I'm currently working on my first novel. Several publishers have been bidding for it and I'm pleased to say it's coming out next spring.

Can you tell us about the subject?
Well actually I haven't started writing it yet, but I know it's going to be very exciting, with plenty of glamour and romance I hope. Of course the nicest thing is that I can write at home – we've put in this dear little study overlooking the garden – so I don't have to be away from Josephine. Which is just as well, because right now I don't think I could bear to be parted from her for a moment!

*

Hilary stared malevolently at her daughter, watching her face crumple as she gathered breath for another scream.

'*Now* what's the matter with it?' she said.

'Just wind, I think,' said the nanny.

Hilary fanned herself with the menu.

'Well can't you take it outside for a while? It's showing us up in front of everybody.'

Once they'd gone, she turned to her companion.

'I'm sorry, Simon, you were saying?'

'I was saying we must think of a title. A single word, preferably. Lust, or Revenge, or Desire, or something.'

'Well, can't we leave that to their marketing people? I'm going to have enough trouble writing the bloody thing.'

Simon nodded. He was a tall and handsome man whose slightly vague exterior masked a sharp business sense. He had come highly recommended: Hilary had chosen him to be her agent from a shortlist of seven or eight.

'Look, I'm sorry the auction was a bit disappointing,' he said. 'But publishers are really playing safe at the moment. A few years ago six figures would have been no problem at all. Anyway, you didn't do too badly. I read recently that the same people paid some new writer seven hundred and fifty quid for his first novel.'

'Couldn't you have pushed a *little* bit harder, though?'

'There was no point. Once they'd gone up to eighty-five thousand they weren't going to budge. I could tell.'

'Oh well. I'm sure you did your best.'

They ordered oysters followed by fresh lobster. Just as the waitress was leaving, Simon said: 'Shouldn't we order something for – what's her name – Maria?'

'Who?'

'Your nanny.'

'Oh, yes. I suppose we should.'

Hilary called the waitress back and ordered a hamburger.

'What does Josephine eat?' asked Simon.

'Oh, some vile muck you have to get in little bottles from the supermarket. It goes in one end and comes out of the other about ten minutes later looking exactly the same. It really is the most disgusting business. And it screams *all* the time. Honestly, if I'm *ever* going to get this book started, I'm going to have to go away for a few weeks. I don't mind where – maybe Bali again, or one of the Barrier Reef islands – any old dump, really. But I can't get a *thing* done with that blasted baby around. Honestly, I just can't.'

Simon laid a sympathetic hand on her arm.

Over coffee, he said: 'Once you've got this novel under your belt, why not do a book about motherhood? Terribly popular these days.'

*

Hilary disliked most women, regarding them as competitors rather than allies, and so she always felt at home in the Heartland Club, the stodgy, calcified and male-dominated establishment where her cousin Henry liked to conduct most of his informal business.

Henry had broken with the Labour Party shortly before the second general election of 1974, and although he had never officially joined the Conservatives, he had, throughout the 1980s, been among their most loyal and outspoken supporters. During this period he became a familiar public figure, his bushy white hair and bulldog features (always rendered a little rakish by a trademark spotted bow-tie) forever cropping up on television discussion programmes, where he would take full advantage of his freedom from party loyalties by slavishly toeing the line of whichever cynical new shift in policy the present administration happened to be trying out at the time. It was partly for these appearances, but also – and more importantly – for the decade of legwork he had put in on a succession of policy-making committees, that he was rewarded with a peerage in the 1990 honours' list. The notepaper upon which Hilary had been summoned to her latest audience was proudly headed with his new title: Lord Winshaw of Micklethorpe.

'Ever think of going back into television?' he asked her, pouring two brandies from a crystal decanter.

'Of course, I'd love to,' said Hilary. 'I was bloody good at it, apart from anything else.'

'Well, I hear there's a vacancy coming up soon at one of the ITV companies. I'll look into it for you, if you like.'

'In return for which . . .?' said Hilary archly, as they sat down on opposite sides of the empty fireplace. It was a hot evening in late July.

'Oh, nothing much. We just wondered if you and your fellow scribes could start putting a bit more heat on the BBC. There's a general feeling that they've gone way out of control.'

'What did you have in mind: features? Or just the column?'

'A bit of both, I would have thought. I really think that something pretty urgent has to be done, because as you know the situation now is completely unacceptable. The place is overrun with Marxists. They're making absolutely no secret of it. I don't know if you've seen the *Nine O'Clock News* recently, but there's no longer even a pretence of impartiality. Particularly on the Health Service: the way they've reported our reforms has been deplorable. Quite deplorable. There are homes up and down the country which are being invaded – quite literally invaded every night – by a torrent of anti-government lies and propaganda. It's intolerable.' He raised a brandy glass to his bilious face and took a lengthy gulp, which seemed to cheer him up. 'By the way,' he said, 'the PM loved your front page on Tuesday.'

'What, LOONY LABOUR LESBIANS BAN KIDS' CLASSICS?'

'That's the one. Laughed like a drain, she did. God knows, we all need a bit of light relief these days.' His face clouded over again. 'There's talk of another leadership challenge, you know. Heseltine might make his move. Madness. Utter madness.'

'This vacancy you were talking about . . .' Hilary prompted.

'Oh, that.' Henry mentioned the name of one of the larger independent companies. 'You know there's been a reshuffle there and they've got a new MD. Luckily we were able to get one of our own men in. Comes from a financial background, so not only is he good with figures but best of all he knows absolutely sweet FA about the business. One of his first jobs is going to be to get rid of that clapped-out old pinko Beamish.'

'So they'll be looking for a new head of current affairs.'

'Absolutely.'

Hilary digested this news.

'He gave me my first break, you know. Back in the mid seventies.'

'Quite.' Henry drained his glass and reached for the decanter. 'But then not even your worst enemies,' he said drily, 'could accuse you of being the sentimental type.'

*

When Hilary turned up for her meeting with Alan Beamish she was shown – as arranged – not into his office but into an impersonal interview room with a view over the main entrance.

'I'm sorry about this,' he said. 'It's a blasted nuisance. They're repainting my ceiling, or something. I wouldn't mind but I was only told about it this morning. Can I get you a coffee?'

He hadn't changed much. His hair may have been greyer, his movements slower, and his resemblance to an elderly parish priest even more pronounced: but otherwise, it seemed to Hilary that the dreadful evening he had inflicted on her during that long school holiday might have been yesterday rather than twenty years ago.

'I was more than a little surprised to get your call,' he said. 'To be honest, I don't really see that you and I have got very much to discuss.'

'Well, for instance: I might have come to ask you to apologize for calling me a barbarian in your little diatribe for the *Independent*.'

Alan had recently published an article about the decline of public service broadcasting called 'The Barbarians at the Gate', in which Hilary had been held up (rather to her delight, it must be said) as an example of everything he hated about the present cultural climate.

'I meant every word,' he said. 'And you know very well that you give as good as you get. You've devoted plenty of column inches to attacking me over the years – as a type, if not by name.'

'Do you ever regret giving me so much help,' Hilary asked, 'when you see what a Fury you unleashed upon the world?'

'You would have got there sooner or later.'

Hilary took her coffee cup and sat on the window-sill. The sun was shining brightly.

'Your new boss can't have been too delighted with that piece,' she said.

'He hasn't mentioned it.'

'How have things been since he took over?'

'Difficult, if you must know,' said Alan. 'Bloody awful, in fact.'

'Oh? In what way?'

'No money for programmes. No enthusiasm for programmes, either: at least not the sort I want to make. I mean, you wouldn't *believe* their attitude over this Kuwaiti thing. I've been telling them for months we should be doing a programme on Saddam and his military build-up. We're in this bloody ridiculous situation whereby we've spent the last few years selling him these weapons, and now we're turning round and calling him the Beast of Babel because he's actually using them. You'd have thought there'd be something to be said on that subject. I mean, just in the last few weeks I've been having talks with an independent film-maker who's been working on a documentary about all this for years, purely off his own bat. Showed me some superb footage. But the people upstairs won't commit themselves to it. They don't want to know.'

'That's too bad.'

Alan glanced at his watch.

'Look, Hilary, I'm sure you didn't come all the way here just to look at the view of our forecourt, beautiful though it is. Would you mind coming to the point?'

'That photo that went with your article,' she said absently. 'Was it taken in your office?'

'Yes, it was.'

'Was that a Bridget Riley hanging on the wall?'

'That's right.'

'You bought it off my brother, didn't you?'

'Yes, I did.'

'Lots of green and black rectangles, all on a slant.'

'That's the one. Why do you ask?'

'Well, it's just that there seem to be two men outside, loading it into the back of a van.'

'What the —'

Alan leapt to his feet and came to the window. He looked down and saw a removal van parked by the steps, with the contents of his office stacked on the sunbaked tarmac: his books, his swivel chair, his plants, stationery and paintings. Hilary smiled.

'We thought this would be the kindest way to tell you. It's best to get these things over with quickly.'

Somehow, he managed to say: 'We?'

'Is there anything I should know about the job before you go?' When no answer was forthcoming, she opened her briefcase and said, 'Well look, here's your P45, and I've even written down the address of your nearest DSS office. It's open till three-thirty today, so you've got plenty of time.' She offered him the piece of paper, but he didn't take it. Laying it down on the window-sill, her smile broadened, and she shook her head. 'The barbarians aren't at the gate any more, Alan. Unfortunately, you left the gate swinging wide open. So we wandered right inside, and now we've got all the best seats and our feet are up on the table. And we intend to stay here for a long, long time.'

Hilary snapped her briefcase shut and made for the door.

'Now: how do I get to your office from here?'

September 1990

It was purely by chance that I found myself writing a book about the Winshaws. The story of how it all came about is quite complicated and can probably wait. Sufficient to say that if it had not been for an entirely accidental meeting on a railway journey from London to Sheffield in the month of June, 1982, I would never have become their official historian and my life would have taken a very different turn. An amusing vindication, when you think about it, of the theories outlined in my first novel, *Accidents Will Happen*. But I doubt if many people remember that far back.

The 1980s were not a good time for me, on the whole. Perhaps it had been a mistake to accept the Winshaw commission in the first place; perhaps I should have carried on writing fiction in the hope that one day I would be able to make a living at it. After all, my second novel had attracted a certain amount of attention, and there had at least been a few isolated moments of glory – such as the week when I'd been featured in a regular Sunday newspaper article, usually devoted to vastly more famous writers, entitled 'The First Story I Ever Wrote'. (You had to supply a sample of something you had written when you were very young, along with a photograph of yourself as a child. The overall effect was rather cute. I've still got the cutting somewhere.) But my financial situation remained desperate – the general public persisting in a steely indifference to the products of my imagination – and so I had sound economic reasons for trying my luck with Tabitha Winshaw and her peculiarly generous offer.

The terms of this offer were as follows. It seemed that in the seclusion of her long-term inmate's quarters at the Hatchjaw-Bassett Institute for the Actively Insane, Miss Winshaw, then aged seventy-six and by all accounts madder than ever, had taken it into her sad, confused head that the time was ripe for the history of her glorious family to be laid before the world. In the face of implacable opposition from her relatives, and drawing only upon her own far from inconsiderable resources, she had set up a trust fund for this purpose and enlisted the services of the Peacock Press, a discreetly operated private concern which specialized in the publication (for a small fee) of military memoirs, family chronicles and the reminiscences of minor public figures. They, for their part, were entrusted with the task of finding a suitable writer, of proven experience and ability, who was to be paid an annual, five-figure salary throughout the entire period of research and composition, conditional upon a progress report – or a 'significant portion' of completed manuscript – being presented to the publishers and forwarded for Tabitha's inspection every year. Otherwise, it seemed that time and money were no object. She wanted the best, the most thorough, the most honest and most up-to-date history that it was possible to compile. There was no deadline for final submission.

The story of how I came to be offered this job is, as I mentioned, a long and complicated one, and must wait its turn; but once the offer was made, I had little hesitation in accepting it. The prospect of a regular income was itself too much to resist, but I was also, if truth be told, in no hurry to start writing another work of fiction. So it seemed like the perfect arrangement. I bought my flat in Battersea (property was cheaper in those days) and set to work with some eagerness. Inspired by the very novelty of the enterprise, I wrote the first two thirds of the book in a couple of years, delving deep into the Winshaws' early history and recording everything that I found there with absolute candour: for it was quite obvious to me, from the very beginning, that I was essentially dealing with a family of criminals, whose wealth and prestige were founded upon every manner of swindling, forgery, larceny, robbery, thievery, trickery, jiggery-pokery, hanky-panky, plundering, looting, sacking, misappropriation, spoliation and embezzlement. Not that the Winshaws' activities were *openly* criminal, or indeed ever recognized as such by polite society: in fact, as far as I could determine, there was only one convicted felon in the family. (I refer, of course, to Matthew's great uncle, Joshua Winshaw, universally acknowledged as the most brilliant pickpocket and burglar of his time – the most celebrated of his achievements being, as you will scarcely need to be reminded, his audacious visit to the country home of a rival family, the Kenways of Britteridge: where, during the course of a public guided tour in the company of seventeen tourists, he succeeded – quite unnoticed – in pilfering a Louis XV grandfather clock worth tens of thousands of pounds.) But because every penny of the Winshaw fortune – dating right back to the seventeenth century, when Alexander Winshaw first made it his business to corner a lucrative portion of the burgeoning slave trade – could be said to have derived, by some route or other, from the shameless exploitation of persons weaker than themselves, I felt that the word 'criminal' fitted the bill well enough, and that I was performing a useful service by bringing this fact to the attention of the public, while staying scrupulously within the bounds of my commission.

There came a point, however, somewhere in the mid 1980s, when I realized that I had lost nearly all enthusiasm for the project. For one thing there was my father's death. I hadn't been in close contact with my parents for a number of years, but the days of my childhood – a calm, happy and untroubled childhood – had formed bonds of empathy and affection between us which made the fact of our physical separation irrelevant. My father was only sixty-one when he died and his loss affected me deeply. I spent several months in the Midlands, doing whatever I could to comfort my mother, and when I returned to London and the Winshaws it was with unmistakable feelings of distaste.

In another two or three years' time I was to abandon work on the book altogether, but before that happened a significant change had taken place in the nature of my research. I had by now reached the final chapters, in which I was to have the honour and the duty of celebrating the achievements of those members of the family who still had the good fortune to be with us: and it was here that I began to meet with serious opposition, not only from my own conscience, but from the Winshaws themselves. Some of them, it grieves me to say, became unaccountably shy in the face of my inquiries, and even began to show a scarcely befitting modesty when I invited them to discuss the details of their glittering careers. Thus it became something of a pattern for my interviews to break up amid scenes of what can only be described as unpleasantness. Thomas Winshaw threw me out on to the street when I asked him to disclose the precise nature of his involvement with the Westland Helicopters incident which had resulted in the resignation of two cabinet ministers in 1986. Henry Winshaw attempted to throw my manuscript on to the fire at the Heartland Club, when he discovered that it drew attention to some minor discrepancies between the socialist programme upon which he had first risen to power, and his subsequent role (for which he will perhaps be better remembered) as a prominent spokesman for the extreme right and, above all, one of the key figures behind the clandestine dismantling of the National Health Service. And I sometimes wonder, even now, whether it was entirely by coincidence that I happened to be assaulted in the street late one night as I walked back to my flat, only two days after a meeting with Mark Winshaw during which I had pressed him – perhaps a little too forcibly – for further information about his post as 'sales co-ordinator' for the Vanguard Import and Export Company, and the real reasons for his frequent visits to the Middle East throughout the bloodiest years of the Iraq–Iran war.

The more I saw of these wretched, lying, thieving, self-advancing Winshaws, the less I liked them, and the more difficult it became for me to preserve the tone of the official historian. And the less I was able to get access to solid and demonstrable facts, the more I had to bring my imagination to bear on the narrative, fleshing out incidents of which I had been able to learn only the shadowy outline, speculating on matters of psychological motivation, even inventing conversations. (Yes, inventing: I won't fight shy of the word, even if I'd fought shy of the thing itself for nearly five years by then.) And so, out of my loathing for these people came a rebirth of my literary personality, and out of this rebirth came a change of perspective, a change of emphasis, an irreversible change in the whole character of the work. It began to take on the aspect of a voyage of discovery, a dogged, fearless expedition into the darkest corners and most secret recesses of the family history. Which meant, as I soon came to realize only too well, that I would never be able to rest, would never consider my journey at an end, until I had uncovered the answer to one fundamental question: was Tabitha Winshaw really mad, or was there a vestige of truth in her belief that Lawrence had, in some devious and obscure way, been responsible for his brother's death?

Not surprisingly, this was another subject on which the family was reluctant to give me anything in the way of concrete information. Early in 1987, I was lucky enough to be granted an interview with Mortimer and Rebecca at a hotel in Belgravia. I found them by far the most approachable and helpful of the Winshaws, and this in spite of Rebecca's serious ill-health: it is largely to them that I owe what little knowledge I have of the events surrounding Mortimer's fiftieth birthday party. Lawrence had died a couple of years earlier and they now, as Rebecca had once fearfully predicted, found themselves in possession of Winshaw Towers, although they spent as little time there as possible. In any case, she too passed away within a few months of my visit; and shortly afterwards Mortimer returned, a broken man, to live out his last days in the family seat which he had always so heartily detested.

My investigations became ever more sporadic and desultory, until one day they stopped altogether. I forget the exact date, but it was on the same day that my mother came down to stay with me. She arrived one evening and we went out for a meal at a Chinese restaurant in Battersea and then she drove straight back home again the same night. After that I didn't go out or talk to anyone for two, perhaps three years.

*

On Saturday morning I settled down to continue work on the manuscript. As I suspected, it was in a serious mess. Parts of it read like a novel and parts of it read like a history, while in the closing pages it assumed a tone of hostility towards the family which was quite unnerving. Worse still, it didn't even have a proper ending, but simply broke off with the most tantalizing abruptness. When I finally rose from my desk, then, late in the afternoon of that hot, sweaty, summer Saturday, the obstacles which stood between me and the book's completion had at least taken on a certain starkness and clarity. I would have to decide once and for all whether to present it as a work of fact or fiction, and I would have to renew my efforts to delve into the mystery of Tabitha's illness.

On Monday morning, I took three decisive steps:

– I made two copies of the manuscript, and sent one of them to the editor who had once been responsible for publishing my novels.

– I sent another copy to the Peacock Press, in the hope that it would either earn me another instalment of salary (which I hadn't been paid for three years) or alternatively so horrify Tabitha, when she saw it, that she would cancel our arrangement and release me from the contract altogether.

– I placed the following advertisement in the personal columns of the major newspapers:

> **INFORMATION WANTED** Writer, compiling official records of the Winshaws of Yorkshire, seeks information on all aspects of the family history. In particular, would like to hear from anyone (witnesses, former servants, concerned parties, etc.) who can shed light on the events of September 16, 1961, and related incidents.
> SERIOUS RESPONDENTS ONLY, please contact Mr M. Owen, c/o The Peacock Press, Vanity House, 116 Providence Street, London W7.

And that, for the time being, was all I could do. My burst of energy had in any case turned out to be temporary, and I spent the next few days mostly slumped in front of the television, sometimes watching Kenneth Connor scuttle in fear from the beautiful Shirley Eaton, sometimes watching the news. I became familiar with the face of Saddam Hussein, and started to learn why he had recently become so famous: how he had announced his intention of absorbing Kuwait into his own country, claiming that according to historical precedent it had always been an 'integral part of Iraq'; and how Kuwait had appealed to the United Nations for military support, which had been promised by both the American President, Mr Bush, and his friend the British Prime Minister, Mrs Thatcher. I learned of the British and American hostages or 'guests' who were being detained in hotels in Iraq and Kuwait. I saw frequent re-runs of the scene where Saddam Hussein brought these hostages before the television cameras and put his arms around the flinching, unwilling child.

Fiona dropped by two or three times. We drank cool drinks together and talked, but something about my manner must have put her off, because she usually left to go to bed early. She told me she was having trouble getting to sleep.

Sometimes, lying hotly awake at night, I could hear her dry, irritable cough. The walls in our building were not thick.

2

At first there was little sign that my strategy would bear fruit. But then suddenly, after two or three weeks, I got telephone calls from both publishers and managed to fix up two appointments for the same day: the Peacock Press in the afternoon, and, in the morning, the rather more prestigious firm which had once been pleased to consider me one of their most promising young writers. (Long years ago.) It was a small but well-respected imprint which had run its business, for most of the century, from a Georgian terrace in Camden, although recently it had been swallowed up by an American conglomerate and relocated to the seventh floor of a tower block near Victoria. Something like half of the personnel had survived the change: among them the fiction editor, a forty-year-old Oxford graduate called Patrick Mills. I arranged to meet him shortly before lunch, at around eleven-thirty.

It should have been a simple enough journey. First of all I had to walk to the tube station, which meant going through the park, across the Albert Bridge, past the fortress-like homes of the super-rich on Cheyne Walk, up Royal Hospital Road and into Sloane Square. I stopped only once, to get myself some chocolate (a Marathon and a Twix, if memory serves). It was another viciously hot morning, and there was no escaping the palls of thick black smog which issued from the backsides of cars, trucks, lorries and buses, hanging heavy in the air and all but forcing me to hold my breath whenever I had to cross the road at a busy junction. But then, when I arrived at the station and rode down on the escalator, as soon as the platform came into view I could see that it was absolutely packed. There was some fault with the service and there couldn't have been a train for about fifteen minutes. Even though the line at Sloane Square isn't deep, the steady downward motion of the escalator made me feel like Orpheus descending to the underworld, confronted by this throng of pale and sad-looking people, the sunlight which I'd just left behind already a distant memory.

... *perque leves populos simulacraque functa sepulchro* ...

Four minutes later a District Line train arrived, every inch of every carriage filled with sweating, hunched, compacted bodies. I didn't even try to get on, but in the pandemonium of people fighting past each other I managed to manoeuvre my way to the front of the platform in readiness for the next train. It came after a couple of minutes, a Circle Line train this time, just as full as the last one. When the doors opened and a few red-faced passengers had forced their way out through the waiting crowd, I squeezed inside and took my first mouthful of the foul, stagnant air: you could tell, just from that one taste, that it had already been in and out of the lungs of every person in the carriage, a hundred times or more. More people piled in behind me and I found myself squashed between this young, gangly office worker – he had a single-breasted suit and a pasty complexion – and the glass partition which separated us from the seated passengers. Normally I would have preferred to stand with my nose up against the partition, but when I tried it that way I found there was a huge slimy patch, exactly at face-level, an accumulation of sweat and grease off the back of the earlier passengers' heads where they had been rubbing up against the glass, so I had no choice but to turn round and stare eyeball-to-eyeball at this corporate lawyer or swaps dealer or whatever he was. We were pushed up even closer after the doors closed, on the third or fourth attempt, because the people who had been standing half in and half out of the train now had to cram themselves inside with the rest of us, and from then on his pallid, pimply skin was almost touching mine, and we were breathing hot breath into each other's faces. The train shunted into motion and half the people who were standing lost their balance, including a builder's labourer who was pressed against my left shoulder and was wearing nothing on top except a pale blue vest. He apologized for nearly falling on top of me and then he reached up to hang on to one of the roof-straps, so I suddenly found that my nose was right inside his moist, gingery armpit. As unobtrusively as I could I put my fingers up to my nostrils and started breathing through my mouth. But I consoled myself, thinking, Never mind, I'm only going as far as Victoria, one stop, that's all it is, it'll be over in a couple of minutes.

But the train was already slowing down, and when it finally came to a standstill in the pitch dark of the tunnel I reckoned that it had only travelled three or four hundred yards. As soon as it stopped you could feel the atmosphere grow tense. We can't have been there for more than a minute, perhaps, or a minute and a half, but already it seemed like an eternity, and when the train started crawling forward there was visible relief on all our faces. But it turned out to be short-lived. After only a few seconds the brakes came on again, and this time, as the train shuddered to a decisive halt, it was with a terrible sense of finality. At once everything seemed very quiet, except for the hiss of a personal stereo further up the carriage, which grew louder as the passenger in question took her headphones off to listen for announcements. In no time at all the air had grown unbearably warm and clammy: I could feel the uneaten chocolate bars turning to liquid in my pocket. We looked around anxiously at each other – some passengers raising despairing eyebrows, others tutting or swearing under their breath – and anyone who was carrying a newspaper or a business document started using it as a fan.

I tried to look on the bright side. If I were to faint – which seemed entirely possible – then there was no chance of falling over and sustaining an injury, because there was nowhere to fall. Similarly, there was little danger of death by hypothermia. It was true that the charms of my neighbour's armpit might begin to pall after an hour or two: but then again perhaps, like a mature cheese, it would improve upon acquaintance. I looked around at the other passengers and wondered who would be the first to crack. There were several possible candidates: a rather frail and wizened old man who was clinging weakly to a pole; a slightly plump woman who for some reason was wearing a thick woollen jumper and had already gone purple in the face; and a tall, asthmatic guy with an earring and a Rolex who was taking regular gulps from his inhaler. I shifted my weight, closed my eyes and counted to one hundred very slowly. In the process, I noticed the level of noise in the carriage increasing perceptibly: people were beginning to talk to one another, and the woman in the woollen jumper had started moaning softly to herself, saying Oh God Oh God Oh God Oh God – when suddenly, the lights in the carriage went out, and we were thrown into total darkness. A few feet away from me a woman let out a little scream, and there was a fresh round of exclamations and complaints. It was a scary feeling, not only being immobilized but now completely unable to see, although at least I had the compensation that I was no longer required to stare at City Slicker's blackheads. But I could sense fear, now, fear all around me whereas before there had only been boredom and discomfort. There was desperation in the air, and before it proved contagious I decided to beat a retreat, as far as possible, into the privacy of my own mind. To start with, I tried telling myself that the situation could be worse: but there were surprisingly few scenarios which bore this out – a rat on the loose in the carriage, perhaps, or a busker spontaneously whipping out his guitar and treating us all to a few rousing choruses of 'Imagine'. No, I would have to try harder than that. Next I attempted to construct an erotic fantasy, based on the premise that the body I was pressed up against belonged not to some spotty stockbroker but to Kathleen Turner, wearing a thin, almost transparent silk blouse and an unbelievably short, unbelievably tight mini-skirt. I imagined the firm, ample contours of her chest and buttocks, the look of hooded, unwilling desire in her eyes, her pelvis beginning unconsciously to grind against mine – and all at once, to my horror, I was getting an erection, and my whole body went taut with panic as I tried to pull away from the businessman whose crotch was already in direct contact with mine. But it didn't work: in fact, unless I was very much mistaken, now *he* was getting an erection, which either meant that he was trying the same trick as me, or I was giving out the wrong signals and was about to find myself in very serious trouble.

Just at that moment, thank God, the lights flickered back on, and a muted cheer went up around the carriage. The speaker system also crackled into life, and we heard the laconic drawl of a London Underground guard who, without actually apologizing for the delay, explained that the train was experiencing 'operating difficulties' which would be rectified as soon as possible. It wasn't the most satisfying of explanations, but at least we no longer felt quite so irredeemably alone and abandoned, and now as long as nobody tried leading us into prayer or starting a singalong to keep our spirits up, I felt that I could cope with a few more minutes. The guy with the inhaler was looking worse and worse, though. I'm sorry, he said, as his breathing began to get faster and more frantic, I don't think I can take much more of this, and the man next to him started making reassuring noises but I could sense the silent resentment of the other passengers at the thought that they might soon have to deal with the problem of someone fainting or having a fit or something. At the same time I could also sense something else, something quite different: a strong, sickly, meaty sort of smell which was now beginning to establish itself above the competing bouquets of sweat and body odour. Its source quickly became apparent as the lanky businessman next to me squeezed open his briefcase and took out a paper bag with the logo of a well-known fast food chain on it. I watched him in amazement and thought, He isn't going to do this, he can't be going to do this, but yes, with the merest grunt of apology – 'It'll go cold otherwise' – he opened his gaping jaws and crammed in a great big mouthful of this damp, lukewarm cheeseburger and started chomping on it greedily, every chew making a sound like wet fish being slapped together and a steady dribble of mayonnaise appearing at the corners of his mouth. There was no question of being able to look away or block my ears: I could see every shred of lettuce and knob of gristle being caught between his teeth, could hear whenever the gummy mixture of cheese and masticated bread got stuck to the roof of his mouth and had to be dislodged with a probing tongue. Then things started to go a bit hazy, the carriage was getting darker and the floor was giving way beneath my feet and I could hear someone say, Watch out, he's going!, and the last thing I can remember thinking was, Poor guy, it's no wonder, with asthma like that: and then nothing, no memory at all of what happened next, just blackness and emptiness for I don't know how long.

*

'You look a bit done in,' said Patrick, once we'd sat down.

'Well, it's just that I haven't been out much lately. I'd forgotten what it's like.'

Apparently the train had started up again just two or three minutes after I'd fainted, and then the businessman, the asthmatic and the woman in the woollen jumper had between them taken me to a First Aid room at Victoria station, where I slowly recovered with the help of a lie-down and a strong cup of tea. It was nearly midday by the time I arrived at Patrick's office.

'Bit of a sticky journey, I suppose, on a day like this?' He nodded sympathetically. 'You could probably do with a drink.'

'I could, now that you mention it.'

'Me too. Unfortunately my budget doesn't run to that sort of thing any more. I can get you a glass of water if you like.'

Patrick looked even more depressed than I remembered him from our last meeting, and his new surroundings were made to match. It was a tiny office, done out in an impersonal beige, with a smoked-glass window offering a partial view of a car park and a brick wall. I had expected there to be posters advertising the latest books but the walls were in fact quite bare, apart from a large and glossy calendar supplied by a rival firm, which hung in the dead centre of one wall directly behind Patrick's head. His face had always been long and lugubrious, but I'd never seen his eyes looking so sleepy before, or his lips set in such a resigned, melancholy pucker. For all that, I think he was quite pleased to see me, and as he fetched two plastic beakers full of water and set them down on his desk, he managed to summon the ghost of a smile.

'Well, Michael,' he said, settling into his chair, 'to say that you've been keeping a low profile these last few years would be putting it mildly.'

'Well, I've been working,' I lied. 'As you can see.'

We both looked at my typescript, which lay on the desk between us.

'Have you read it?' I asked.

'Oh, yes, I've read it,' said Patrick. 'I've read it all right.'

He fell silent.

'And . . .?'

'Tell me something, Michael: can you remember when we last saw each other?'

I could, as it happened. But before I had the chance to answer, he said:

'I'll tell you. It was April the 14th, 1982.'

'Eight years ago,' I said. 'Fancy that.'

'Eight years, five months, seven days. That's a long time, in anybody's book.'

'It certainly is.'

'We'd just published your second novel. You were getting excellent reviews.'

'Was I?'

'Magazine profiles. Newspaper interviews.'

'But no sales.'

'Oh, but the sales would have come, Michael. The sales would have come. If only you'd –'

'– stuck at it.'

'Stuck at it, exactly.' He took a long sip from his beaker of water. 'Not long after that, you wrote me a letter. I don't suppose you can remember what you said in that letter?'

I remembered only too well. But before I could get a word in, he said:

'You told me that you wouldn't be writing any more novels for a while, because you'd been commissioned to write an important non-fiction book, by another publisher. A rival publisher. Whose name, I think it's true to say, you never disclosed.'

I nodded, waiting to see what he was driving at.

'I wrote you two or three letters subsequently. You never replied.'

'Well, you know how it is, when you're . . . wrapped up in something.'

'I could have pushed it. I could have chivvied you along. I could have come down on you like a ton of bricks. But I chose not to. I decided to wait in the background, and see what developed. It's one of the most important parts of my job, you see, being prepared to just wait in the background, and see what develops. There are times when you can tell you need to do something like that, simply by instinct. Especially when you're dealing with a writer you've taken a personal interest in. One that you feel close to.'

He fell silent and gave me what can only have been intended as a meaningful look. Not knowing what it meant, I ignored it and shifted slightly in my chair.

'I felt very close to you, back then, Michael. I discovered you. I pulled you out of the slush pile. In fact – and correct me if I'm being fanciful here – you would have had grounds, in those days, for looking on me not just as your editor, but as your friend.'

I felt no inclination to correct him on that point, but couldn't make up my mind whether to nod or shake my head, and so did neither.

'Michael,' he said, leaning forward, 'allow me one favour.'

'You've got it.'

'Allow me, for one moment, to speak as your friend, and not as your editor.'

I shrugged. 'Feel free.'

'OK, then. Speaking as your friend, and not as your editor – and I hope you won't take this the wrong way – may I just say – in a spirit of constructive criticism, and personal interest – that you look fucking terrible.'

I stared back at him.

'Michael, you look as though you've aged about twenty years.'

I struggled for words. 'What . . . Are you saying that I look old?'

'The thing is that you always used to look so young. Back then, you always looked ten years younger than you really were, and now you look ten years older than you really are.'

I thought about this for a moment, and wondered whether to point out that in that case, allowing for the eight years which had gone by in the meantime, I should really have been looking as though I'd aged about thirty years. But instead I just sat there, my mouth opening and shutting like a land-locked fish.

'So what happened?' said Patrick. 'What's been going on?'

'Well, I don't know . . . I don't really know where to begin.'
Patrick got up at this point, but I carried on talking. 'The 1980s
weren't a good time for me, on the whole. I suppose they weren't
for a lot of people.' He had opened a cupboard, and seemed to be
staring at the inside of the door. 'My father died a few years ago,
and that hit me quite hard, and then – well, as you probably
know, ever since I split up with Verity, I haven't had much –'

'Do I look older?' Patrick asked suddenly. I realized that he
was peering into a mirror.

'What? No, not really.'

'I feel it.' He sat down again, with an exaggerated flop. 'It
suddenly seems all such a long time ago, you showing up in my
office, full of youthful promise.'

'Well, as I was saying, so much has happened since then: first
there was my father dying, which was all a bit of a blow, and
then –'

'I hate this job, you know. I really hate what it's become.'

'I'm sorry to hear that.' I waited for him to elaborate, but there was
just a heavy pause. 'Anyway, and then, as you know, since Verity and
I broke up, I haven't been all that successful when it comes to –'

'I mean, it's just not the same job any more. The whole
business has changed out of all recognition. We get all our
instructions from America and nobody pays the slightest bit of
attention to anything I say at editorial meetings. Nobody gives a
tinker's fuck about fiction any more, not *real* fiction, and the only
kind of . . . values anybody seems to care about are the ones that
can be added up on a balance sheet.' He poured himself another
beakerful and took a deep swig, as if it was neat whisky. 'Now,
here – *here's* something that'll make you laugh. This'll really
crease you up, this will. I read a new novel the other day, in
typescript. Do you want to guess who it was by?'

'All right, tell me.'

'A friend of yours. Someone you know a lot about.'

'I give up.'

'Hilary Winshaw.'

Once again I found myself at a loss for words.

'Oh yes, they're all at it now, you know. It's not enough to be stinking rich, land yourself one of the most powerful jobs in television and have two million readers paying good money every week to find out about the dry rot in your skirting-board: these people want fucking immortality! They want their names in the British Library catalogue, they want their six presentation copies, they want to be able to slot that handsome hardback volume between the Shakespeare and the Tolstoy on their living-room bookshelf. And they're going to get it. They're going to get it because people like me know only too well that even if we decide we've found the new Dostoevsky, we're still not going to sell half as many copies as we would of any old crap written by some bloke who reads the weather on the fucking *television!*'

His voice rose almost to a shout on the last word. Then he sat back and ran his hands through his hair.

'So what's it like then, her book?' I asked, after he had had time to calm down a bit.

'Oh, it's the usual sort of rubbish. Lots of media people being dynamic and ruthless. Sex every forty pages. Cheap tricks, mechanical plot, lousy dialogue, could have been written by a computer. Probably was written by a computer. Empty, hollow, materialistic, meretricious. Enough to make any civilized person heave, really.' He stared ruefully into space. 'And the worst of it is they didn't even accept my bid. Somebody tipped me by ten grand. Bastards. I just know it's going to be the hit of the spring season.'

There appeared to be no easy way of breaking the ensuing silence. Patrick's eyes were popped out like a frog's as he looked straight past me, and he seemed to have completely forgotten that I was in the room.

'Look,' I said at last, making a big show of glancing at my watch. 'I really have to go and keep another appointment quite soon. If you could just give me a few pointers about the stuff I sent you . . .'

Patrick's eyes slowly turned in my direction and came into focus. A dreamy, rueful grin spread over his face. I don't think he had heard me.

'Then again, maybe none of this matters,' he said. 'Maybe there are more important things going on in the world and my little problems don't count for much at all. Perhaps we'll be at war soon, anyway.'

'At war?'

'Well, it's beginning to look that way, isn't it? Britain and France sending more troops to Saudi Arabia. On Sunday we expel all those people from the Iraqi Embassy. And now the Ayatollah's joining in and calling for a holy war against the United States.' He shuddered. 'I'm telling you, the implications of this situation look pretty grim from where I'm sitting.'

'You mean that as soon as the fighting starts, Israel is going to get involved and before we know it relationships in the Middle East will be even worse. And then if the United Nations breaks up under the strain, the whole Cold War situation is wide open again and we could be looking at the possibility of a limited nuclear war?'

Patrick's glance expressed pity at my naïvety.

'That's hardly my point,' he said. 'The thing is that if we don't get a biography of Saddam Hussein into the shops in the next three or four months, we're going to get crapped on by every publisher in town.' He looked up at me with a sudden desperate gleam in his eye. 'Maybe you could do one for us. What do you say? Six weeks' research, six weeks' writing. Twenty thousand upfront if we keep all the overseas and serial rights.'

'Patrick, I can't believe I'm hearing this.' I got up, paced the room a couple of times and then looked him square in the face. 'I can't believe you're the same person I had all those discussions with eight years ago. All that stuff about the – permanence of great literature; the need to look beyond the horizons of the merely contemporary. I mean, what's the business doing to you these days?'

I could see that I'd caught his attention at last and, from the way his face was rapidly falling, that my message had a chance of getting through. So I decided to press the point home.

'You used to have such faith in literature, Patrick. I've never known faith like it. I used to sit in this chair listening to you talk and it was like a – like a revelation. You taught me about the eternal verities. The values which transcend generations and centuries, and which are encoded in the great imaginative works of every culture.' I couldn't keep this bullshit up for much longer, that was for sure. 'You taught me to forget about every-day truths, ephemeral truths, truths that seem significant one day and irrelevant the next. You made me see that there's a higher truth than any of that. *Fiction*, Patrick.' I thumped the manuscript which was still lying on his desk. 'Fiction – that's what's important. That's what you and I believed in once, and that's what I've returned to now. I thought you of all people would understand that.'

He was silent for a little while, and when he spoke again, his voice quivered with emotion.

'You're right, Michael. I'm sorry, really I am. You came here to get my opinion about something you've written, something you feel very deeply about, and all I can talk about is my own problems.' He waved me back to my chair. 'Come on, sit down. Let's talk about your book.'

Determined to retain my advantage, I held my hand up in a gesture of deprecation and said: 'Perhaps it's not such a good time. I have this other appointment, and you maybe need a little longer to think before you can reach a decision, so why don't we –'

'I've already reached a decision about your book, Michael.'

I sat down immediately. 'You have?'

'Oh yes. I wouldn't have called you in here if I hadn't.'

Neither of us spoke for a few seconds. Then I said: 'Well?'

Patrick leaned back in his chair and smiled teasingly. 'I think you'd better tell me a little bit about it first. The background. Why you've written a book about the Winshaws. Why you've written a book about them which seems to have started out as a history and turned into a novel. What on earth gave you the idea?'

I answered these questions truthfully, precisely and at some length. After which, neither of us spoke for a few seconds. Then I said: 'Well?'

'Well ... I hardly need to tell you that we have a serious problem with this book, Michael. It's flagrantly libellous.'

'That's not a problem,' I said. 'I'll change everything: names, locations, timings, the lot. This is just a beginning, you see, it's just a basis. I can cover my tracks, make the whole thing practically unrecognizable. This is just the start.'

'Hmm.' Patrick put his forefingers together and laid them thoughtfully against his mouth. 'Well, what does that leave us with, exactly? That leaves us with a book which is scurrilous, scandal-seeking, vindictive in tone, obviously written out of feelings of malice and even, in parts – if you don't mind me saying this – a little shallow.'

I breathed a sigh of relief. 'So you'll publish it?'

'I think so. Subject to your carrying out the necessary revisions, and, of course, providing it with some sort of ending.'

'Absolutely. I'm working on that at the moment, and I expect to come up with something ... soon. Very soon.' In my exhilaration I felt a sudden rush of warmth towards Patrick. 'You know, I was sure that this book was perfect for the market right now, but I can't tell you how much I needed to hear you say this. I was worried, you know, with it being so different from my other novels – '

'Oh, not that different,' he said, with a wave of his hand.

'You don't think so?'

'There's a definite stylistic link between this stuff and your last book, for instance. I could recognize your voice immediately. In many ways, this has the same strengths, and the ...'

'... and the what?' I asked, after he'd tailed off.

'Pardon?'

'You were about to say something. The same strengths, and ...?'

'Oh, it doesn't matter. Really.'

'The same weaknesses, that's what you were about to say. Isn't it? The same strengths, and the same weaknesses.'

'Well yes, if you must know.'

'And what does that mean?'

'Oh, we don't want to bother about that now.'

'Come on, Patrick, tell me.'

'Well . . .' He got up and walked to the window. The car park and the brick wall didn't seem to inspire him. 'I don't suppose you can remember, can you, what we talked about the last time we met? That last conversation we had, all those years ago?'

I remembered it vividly.

'Not offhand, no.'

'We talked a lot about your work. We talked a lot about your previous work, and your future work, and your work in progress, and I ventured to make a small criticism which seemed to upset you, to a certain extent. I don't suppose you can remember what it was?'

I could almost remember his exact words.

'Can't put my finger on it, I'm afraid.'

'I suggested . . . well I suggested, to be frank, that there was a certain element of passion lacking from your writing. You don't remember that?'

'Doesn't ring a bell.'

'Not that this suggestion in itself would have caused you to take offence. But I did also go on to suggest – and here I really was being a bit presumptuous, I suppose – that the explanation for this might lie in the fact that there was also a certain element of passion lacking in – well, how shall I put this? – your life. For want of a better word.' He watched me carefully: carefully enough to be able to say, 'You do remember, don't you?'

I stared back at him until my indignation got the better of me. 'I don't know how you can say that,' I spluttered. 'This book is full of passion. Full of anger, anyway. If it communicates anything at all, it's how much I hate these people, how *evil* they are, how much they've spoiled everything, with their vested interests and their influence and their privilege and their stranglehold on all the centres of power; how they've got us all cornered, how they've pretty well carved up the whole bloody country between them. You don't know what it was like, Patrick, having to surround myself with that family for so many years; day after day with no one but the Winshaws for company. Why do you think the book turned out like that? Because writing it all down, trying to put

down the *truth* about them, was the only thing that stopped me
from wanting to kill them. Which somebody should do one of
these days, incidentally.'

'All right then, let me put it another –'

'So how you can say there's no *passion* in it beats me, I must
say.'

'Well, perhaps "passion" is the wrong word.' He hesitated, but
only for a second. 'In fact it wasn't even the word that I used
when we first had this conversation. To be absolutely blunt,
Michael, I pointed out that there was an absence of *sex* in your
work – sex was the very word I used, now I come to think of it –
and I then went on to speculate whether this might mean – *might*
mean, I go no further than that – that there was also, and equally,
a parallel and . . . concomitant absence of . . . sex . . . in your . . .
Let me put this another way: there's no *sexual dimension* to your
writing at the moment, Michael, and I only wondered if this
might possibly be because there is no – or at least not much –
sexual dimension to your . . . to your life. As it stands.'

'I see.' I stood up. 'Patrick, I'm disappointed. I didn't think you
were the kind of editor who told authors to put sex in their books
just to help the sales along.'

'No, that's not what I'm saying. Not what I'm saying at all. I'm
saying that there's a crucial aspect of your characters' experience
which is simply not finding expression here. You're avoiding it.
You're pussyfooting around it. If I didn't know you better, I'd say
you were afraid of it.'

'I'm not staying here to listen to any more of this,' I said,
making for the door.

'Michael?'

I turned.

'I'll get a contract in the post for you tonight.'

'Thank you,' I said, and was about to leave, when something
made me stop and say: 'You hit a bit of a nerve, you know, when
you went on about . . . an element, being lacking in my life.'

'I know.'

'Good sex scenes are very difficult to write, anyway.'

'I know.'

'Thanks, all the same.' Another afterthought. 'We must have lunch together soon, like in the old days.'

'The firm won't let me buy lunch for authors any more,' said Patrick. 'But still, if you know somewhere cheap, we could always go Dutch.'

He was pouring himself more water as I left.

3

My meeting with Patrick had gone on for much longer than I'd
expected, and I was almost late arriving at Vanity House. I'd
been hoping to have a meal somewhere on the way, but there
wasn't time, so I had to make do with some more chocolate
instead. I tried one of these new bars called Twirls: spirals of
flaky chocolate covered in a rich, creamy, succulent coat. Not
bad, as a matter of fact, although they did have a bit of nerve
describing it as 'new', since it clearly owed a large conceptual
debt to the Ripple. This one seemed firmer, somehow, though:
chunkier and more substantial. I'd bought a packet of Maltesers
as well but didn't feel like opening it.

I was looking forward to visiting the Peacock Press, and partly
for a reason which will perhaps seem foolish. The first person I
had ever spoken to there – the person who had actually approached me with the idea for the Winshaw book – was a woman
called Alice Hastings, and we had, I thought, struck up an
immediate rapport. I might as well add that she was also young
and very beautiful, and not a small part of the attraction of the
whole project lay in the opportunities it promised for further
meetings with her. But this was not to be. After that initial
encounter, I was passed on to the attention of one Mrs Tonks, a
plain-speaking and by no means unfriendly woman of late middle
age who subsequently assumed complete responsibility for overseeing the progress of the book. She took her duties seriously and
did her best to make me feel well looked after: every Christmas, for
instance, she would send me a parcel of her favourite books from
the year's catalogue, wrapped up in gift paper. This was how my
library came to be adorned with such choice items as *Great
Plumbers of Albania, 300 Years of Halitosis*, the Reverend J.W.
Pottage's pioneering study, *So You Think You Know about*

Plinths?, and a frankly unforgettable memoir – although its author's name escapes me – entitled A *Life in Packaging – Fragments of an Autobiography: Volume IX – The Styrofoam Years*. Much as I appreciated this generosity, it was no substitute for seeing Alice again, and on the rare occasions (no more than three or four) when I had visited the office in person, I had always made a point of asking after her. As luck would have it, though, she had always been out at lunch, or away on holiday, or busy dealing with an author. And yet even now, absurdly, eight years since I had last seen her, I felt a sweet ache of sexual nostalgia as I entered the building, and the thought that I might glimpse her again or even exchange a few words with her put a tiny spring in my step and a flourish in the movement of my wrist as I pressed the lift button for the ninth floor.

Today, in any case, even the unassuming efficiency of Mrs Tonks offered a cheering prospect: doing business with her would be a blissfully uncomplicated affair after my dealings with Patrick. That at least was my expectation, as I stood peering into the mirror and wiping a smudge of chocolate from my lower lip, while the lift carried me smoothly upwards.

I caught a sense that something different was in the air, however, when Mrs Tonks, instead of keeping me waiting in the reception area, hurried out to see me as soon as she heard that I'd arrived. Her stout, businesslike face wore more than its habitual flush, and her fingers fiddled nervously with the heavy wooden beads which hung low over her pendulous bosom.

'Mr Owen,' she said. 'I've been trying to telephone you all morning. I was hoping to save you a journey.'

'You didn't manage to look at the manuscript?' I asked, following her into a large, comfortable office, handsomely decked out with bonsai trees and modern abstracts.

'I was intending to read it today, before you came in,' she said, waving me to a chair, 'but circumstances didn't permit. The fact is, we're in disarray. There's been a little upset. Not to keep you in suspense any longer, we were burgled last night.'

I can never think of anything intelligent to say in response to such statements. My reply was something like, 'How awful'. Followed by: 'I hope you didn't lose anything valuable.'

'Nothing was stolen at all,' said Mrs Tonks. 'Except your manuscript.'

That shut me up.

'It was in the top drawer of my desk,' she continued. 'It doesn't seem to have taken long for the thief to find it. We haven't notified the police yet: I wanted to talk to you first. Mr Owen, is there any reason why this should have happened now, so soon after we received it? Have you done anything recently which might have alerted someone to the fact that you'd resumed work on this book?'

I thought for a moment and said, 'Yes.' Pacing the room angrily (the anger directed at myself) I explained about the newspaper advertisement. 'It was meant as a declaration of war, as much as anything else. A coded challenge. Well, someone's obviously taken me up on it.'

'You shouldn't have done that,' said Mrs Tonks. 'Not given them our address, without consulting us first. Anyway, that leaves the field wide open. It could have been anyone.'

'No, I don't think so,' I said, as a suspicion began to take shape within me. 'There are certain members of the family who've already expressed an interest in suppressing this book, and I wouldn't be at all surprised –'

Mrs Tonks wasn't listening.

'I think we're going to have to bring Mr McGanny in on this,' she said. 'Come with me, will you?'

She led me out into reception and for a few moments disappeared into another office, leaving me alone with the secretary. Lulled by the gentle tapping of her computer keyboard, I drifted off into some random speculations as to which of the Winshaws might have pilfered my manuscript (or more probably hired someone else to do it). The obvious candidate was Henry: after all, he had already attempted to burn the thing once. But then none of the others could be entirely ruled out. Whoever was behind it, their objective was unlikely to be the suppression of the book: they would surely have anticipated my taking several copies, so the intention presumably was just to find out how far my investigations had proceeded. I decided not to worry about this until I was in possession of a few more facts. The time was ripe to ask another, more urgent question.

I wandered over to the secretary's desk and said, with affected carelessness: 'I don't suppose . . . Miss Hastings wouldn't be here this afternoon, by any chance, would she?'

She stared back at me, her eyes bored, without expression.

'I'm only temporary,' she said.

Just then Mrs Tonks re-emerged and beckoned me to follow her. I had never met Mr McGanny, the managing director of the Press, and wasn't sure what to expect. The sumptuousness of his office took me by surprise, for one thing: it boasted leather arm-chairs and a huge picture window fronting on to the local park. As for the man himself, I placed him somewhere in his mid fifties: his face made me think of a horse – thoroughbred, perhaps, but slightly on the lean and cunning side – and instead of the Scottish brogue which I'd been anticipating, he spoke in the suave drawl of the Oxbridge- and public-school-educated Englishman.

'Sit down, Owen, sit down.' He faced me across the desk. Mrs Tonks stood by the window. 'This is serious news about the Winshaw book. What do you make of it?'

'I think my line of inquiry has started to prove a little too con-troversial for certain members of the family. I think they may have wanted a foretaste of exactly what I was proposing to write.'

'Hmm. Well, it's a damned underhand way of going about it, that's all I can say.' He leaned forward. 'I'll be frank with you, Owen. I don't approve of controversy.'

'I see.'

'But there are two sides to every coin. I didn't commission you to write this book, and I don't give a damn what you put in it. That's Miss Winshaw's business. It's down to her what goes in and what comes out, and it seems to me that this arrangement gives you a pretty free hand, since we all know, and there's not much point beating around the bush here, that she's one or two fly-leaves short of a folio. To put it mildly.'

'Quite.'

'Now I'll be frank with you, Owen. My understanding is that through her solicitors, Miss Winshaw has fixed up a pretty cosy financial arrangement on your behalf.'

'You could say that.'

'And there's no harm in letting you know that she's done very much the same for yours truly. By which I mean the firm.' He coughed. 'So the fact of the matter is that there's no hurry for you to get this book finished. No hurry at all. The longer the better, one might say.' He coughed again. 'And by the same token, I would hope that there's no question of you dropping it at any point, just because of a bit of intimidation from various interested –'

A buzzer sounded on his desk.

'Yes?' he said, jabbing at a button.

The secretary's voice: 'I finally got through to Wing Commander Fortescue, sir. He says he's sure he put the cheque in the mail last week.'

'Hm! Send him the usual letter. And don't disturb me again unless it's urgent.'

'Also, sir, your daughter phoned.'

'I see – cancelling dinner, I suppose. Some new boyfriend she'd rather be seeing instead.'

'Not exactly: she said her audition this afternoon was called off so she's coming to meet you early. She's on her way now.'

'Oh. All right then, thank you.'

Mr McGanny thought for a few seconds, then rose abruptly.

'Well, Owen, I think I've said all I needed to say at this juncture. We're both busy men. As indeed is Mrs Tonks. No point in hanging around when there's work to be done.'

'I'll see you to the lift,' said Mrs Tonks, coming forward and taking my arm.

'Good to meet you at last, Owen,' said Mr McGanny as she propelled me towards the door. 'Head down and pecker up, eh?'

I was out of his office before I had time to reply.

'How are you getting home?' asked Mrs Tonks, who surprised me somewhat by travelling down with me in the lift. 'Taking a cab?'

'Well, I hadn't really thought –'

'I'll call you one,' she said; and sure enough, she accompanied me out on to the street and had hailed a taxi in less than a minute.

'Really, there was no need,' I said, opening the door and half-expecting her to follow me inside.

'Don't mention it. We like to pamper our authors. Especially' (with a simper) 'the important ones.'

The cab moved off and stopped at a set of traffic lights almost immediately. As we waited, I noticed a taxi pass us in the opposite direction and pull up outside the main entrance to Vanity House. A woman got out and I turned to watch, assuming that it would be Mr McGanny's daughter and stirred by an idle curiosity to see what she looked like. But no; much to my surprise and – irrationally – my delight, it turned out to be none other than Alice Hastings.

'Alice!' I called out of the window. 'Alice, hello!'

She was bending down to pay the driver and didn't hear me: then the lights changed and my taxi pulled away. I had to be content with the knowledge that she was at least still working for the company, and that she hadn't, from what I could see, changed very much in the years since our meeting.

Not many minutes had gone by when the driver pulled back the partition and said, 'Excuse me, mate, but you wouldn't happen to know anybody who might be following you, would you?'

'Following me? Why?'

'There's this blue Citroen 2CV. Couple of cars behind us.'

I turned to have a look.

'It's difficult to tell in this kind of traffic, of course, but he's still with us after a couple of short cuts I know, so I just wondered . . .'

'It's not impossible,' I said, straining to get a look at the driver.

'Well, I'll speed up a bit and see what happens.' He didn't speak again until we had nearly reached Battersea. 'No, we've lost him. I must've been imagining it.'

I breathed a quiet sigh of relief and sank back in my seat. It had been a long day. I wanted nothing more, now, than to spend the evening alone in my flat with the television and the video recorder. I'd had enough of people for a while. They were exhausting. I didn't even want to see Fiona when I got home.

The taxi driver was counting out my change and handing it through the window when a blue Citroen 2CV chugged noisily by, gathering speed as it passed us.

'Well, bugger me sideways,' he said, staring after it. 'We *were* being followed. You want to watch out, mate: I think somebody's on your case.'

'You might be right,' I murmured, as the car disappeared around the corner of my mansion block. 'You might very well be right.'

And yet at the same time, I couldn't help thinking – a battered old Citroen 2CV? Would even Henry Winshaw be that devious?

Henry

November 21st 1942

Sixteen today! Mater and Pater gave me this smashing leather-bound notebook in which I shall record all my most secret thoughts from now on.[1] Also, of course, another £200 in the old savings account, although I can't touch that for another five years, more's the pity!

In the afternoon they threw me a really super tea party. Binko, Puffy, Meatball and Squidge were all there, as well as one or two representatives of the fairer sex, such as the exquisite Wendy Carpenter, who didn't speak to me much, alas.[2] Thomas was aloof and snooty, as usual. But the real surprise was when Uncle Godfrey turned up out of the blue. Apparently he's on leave at the moment, staying up at Winshaw Towers, and he drove all the way over just to look in on yours truly! He was wearing his full RAF kit and looked tremendously dashing. He came up to my bedroom to have a look at my model Spitfires and we got embroiled in a pretty deep conversation, all about El Alamein and how it's provided just the fillip which was needed for everyone's morale. He was saying that the chaps are already looking forward to how much better things are going to be after the war, and started waxing rather lyrical about something called the Beaveredge (?) Report, which apparently says that

1. *Editor's Note* [1995]: Henry Winshaw remained true to this resolve and has, indeed, some claim to be considered one of the country's most prolific political diarists. The task of editing his journals – which run to some four million words in total – has proved an enormous one, but it is hoped that the first volume at least will be ready for publication early next year. In the meantime these few short extracts must serve by way of an appetizer.

2. This reticence, it seems, was later surmounted: Ms Carpenter married Henry Winshaw in the spring of 1953.

everyone is going to have a better standard of living from now on, even the working classes and people like that.[1] When he left he slipped a fiver into my pocket without saying a word. He really is about as decent an uncle as any cove could possibly want.

December 15th 1942

The worst day of my life so far, ever, definitely. Frightful scenes up at Winshaw Towers as we came to pay tribute to poor Uncle Godfrey. Nobody can really believe that he's gone: less than a month since he came to my birthday party.[2] The memorial service was bad enough, what with Granny and Gramps looking so wretched, and the chapel being so freezing, with the wind howling outside and all that. But the night before, we stayed in the house itself, where there was the most terrible how-do-you-do. Poor Aunty Tabs has been driven completely bats by the news, and has started accusing Uncle Lawrence of murdering his own brother! She physically attacked him in the hallway as he was coming down for dinner: tried to bash him over the head with a croquet mallet. Apparently this was about the sixth time this has happened. They tried not to let me see what was going on but while we were all having dinner some doctors arrived and I could hear poor old Aunty screaming as they took her to the front door. Then I heard this van driving off and that's the last we all saw of her. Mater says she has been taken somewhere where she'll be 'well looked after'. I do hope she recovers soon.

Mind you, I certainly know how she feels. The service certainly brought a lump to the old throat, and for the rest of the afternoon I was in a pretty sombre mood, full of deepish thoughts about the

1. *Social Insurance and Allied Services* by William Henry Beveridge (1879–1963) became the blueprint for Britain's post-war welfare legislation and, in particular, laid the theoretical groundwork for the establishment of the National Health Service (see below, *passim*).

2. Godfrey Winshaw (born 1909) had been shot down by the Germans over Berlin on November 30th 1942. For a thorough, if rather speculative, account of the family crisis which followed, see Michael Owen, *The Winshaw Legacy: A Family Chronicle* (Peacock Press, 1991).

futility of war and all that sort of racket. As Pater drove us home I started writing this sort of poem in my head:

In Memory of Uncle Godfrey

Weep, yea weep, ye men of War,
For one among you is no more.
The wind that howls round chapel walls,
Each drop of rain, each leaf that falls –
In mourning, all, for Matthew's son,
So cruelly killed by filthy Hun.
Though fight we must – and not give in –
What bitter joy, if yet we win!
We used to call him 'Uncle God',
But now he lies 'neath Yorkshire's sod,
Never to share in victor's mirth –
Just pushing daisies through the earth.[1]

When Pater came up to say good-night I told him I didn't think I could bear to go to war, the whole idea was just too dreadful. I don't know what I shall do when my call-up papers come. But he told me not to worry about that and said something mysterious about wheels within wheels. Not exactly sure what he meant, but went to bed feeling oddly comforted.

November 12th 1946

After a decidedly sticky tutorial with Prof Goodman, my new – though in fact rather decrepit – Probability Tutor, went for a walk around Magdalen gardens. Oxford looking very beautiful this autumn evening. Am beginning to feel more at home here. After that, finally decided to attend a meeting of the Conservative Association. Pater will be very pleased. (Must write and tell him about it.)

---

1. This last couplet makes little sense, unfortunately, since Godfrey Winshaw's body was never recovered from Germany. The impressionable young Henry's excess of grief would seem to have blinded him to this detail.

And now, dear Diary, I am about to trust you with some top secret information: for the truth of the matter is, I THINK I AM IN LOVE. Yes! For the very first time! The President of the Association is a girl from Somerville called Margaret Roberts and I have to say that she is an absolute pip![1] An utterly gorgeous head of nut-brown hair – I just wanted to bury myself in it. Most of the time all I could do was stare at her but afterwards I did pluck up the nerve to go up and say how much I'd enjoyed the meeting. She thanked me and said she hoped I'd come again. Just try stopping me!

She made the most brilliant speech. Everything she said was true. It was all true. I've never heard it put so clearly before.

My heart and mind are yours, Margaret, to do with what you will.

February 11th 1948

Uncle Lawrence visited today. This is good news, because we're only halfway through term and I'm already running out of cash, and you can always rely on the old boy to slip you something on his way out. Gillam was in my rooms when he arrived, at about 12.30, so he came out to lunch with us too. I thought this might cause fireworks, because he and Uncle were bound to get on to politics sooner or later: it was all quite good-natured, however. Gillam is all for Labour – we've always tried to keep off the subject, for the most part, but privately I think that most of what he talks is a lot of rot. Anyway, Uncle soon sniffed him out for a hardened Bevanite,[2] and began ribbing him about this and that. He asked him what he thought of the idea of a National Health Service and of course Gillam went into raptures about it. But then Uncle said, In that case, why do you think all the doctors are opposing it? – because apparently only yesterday the British

1. Margaret Hilda Roberts (born Grantham, Lincs., October 13th 1925), later Margaret Thatcher, later Baroness Thatcher of Kesteven, became President of the OUCA in the autumn of 1946.

2. Aneurin 'Nye' Bevan (1897–1960), Labour MP for Ebbw Vale who in 1946 obtained passage of the National Health Service Act. Biography: *Aneurin Bevan*, by Michael Foot (2 vols., London, 1962 and 1973).

Medical Association voted (again) not to cooperate with the whole thing. Gillam said something feeble about the forces of reaction having to be resisted, and then Uncle pulled the rug out from under his feet again by saying that actually, as a business-man, he thought the idea of having a centralized Health Service made a lot of sense, because ultimately it could be run as a business, with shareholders and a board of directors and a chief executive, and that was the way to make sure it was efficient, to run it along business lines, i.e. with a view to making a profit. All of this was absolute anathema to Gillam, of course. But Uncle was in full swing by now, and started saying that in fact the Health Service, if properly managed, could turn out to be the most profitable business of all time, because health care was like prostitution, it was something for which the demand could never dry up: it was inexhaustible. He said that if someone could get himself appointed manager of a privatized Health Service, he would soon be just about the richest and most powerful man in the country. Gillam argued that this would never happen, because the commodity involved – human life – could not be quantified. Quality of life, he said, was not something you could put a price on, and added, In spite of anything Winshaw might say to the contrary. This was a rather flattering allusion to a short paper which I gave to the Pythagorean Society last year, under the title 'Quality is Quantifiable' – in which I argued (rather frivolously, it has to be said) that there was no condition – spiritual, metaphysical, psychological or emotional – which could not be expressed mathematically, by some sort of formula. (This paper seems to have made a bit of a splash: Gillam told Uncle, in passing, that its title invariably comes up in conversation whenever my name is mentioned.)

After lunch Uncle and I took tea together in my rooms. I congratulated him on ribbing Gillam so successfully but he assured me that it had all been perfectly serious, and I would do well to remember what he'd said about the Health Service. He asked me what I was planning to do when I left Oxford and I said I hadn't decided, it was probably either industry or politics. When I said politics he asked which side, and I said I didn't know, and he said it didn't make much difference at the moment, they were both too far to the Left, it was a reaction against Hitler. Then he said there were several companies he could find me a position with, if I wanted: there was no point in starting at the bottom, I might as well go straight on to the board. So I thanked him for that and said I would bear it in mind. I'd never cared much for Uncle Lawrence before now, but he really does seem a very decent sort. As he left he gave me eighty pounds in ten pound notes, which should see me through the next few weeks nicely.[1]

*

BBC TRANSCRIPTION SERVICE
PROGRAMME TITLE: 'Matters of Moment'
TX: 18 July 1958
PRESENTER: Alan Beamish[2]

BEAMISH: . . . We move on now to a new feature which we have called 'Backbencher', and which we hope will soon establish itself as a regular item on the programme. If we want to know the Prime Minister's views on any particular issue, or – em – the views of the Leader of the Opposition, for instance, then we all know where to look. We can find them in the newspapers, or we can hear them on the wireless. But what of the – em – ordinary, working Member of Parliament, the backbencher, the

1. There arises a regrettable lacuna in the diaries at this point. Either Winshaw kept no records at all for the years 1949–59, or – as is more likely – the relevant volumes have been irretrievably lost. Whatever the explanation, we are lacking any account of his rapid rise to industrial prominence after graduating from Oxford, his selection as a Labour candidate in 1952, his marriage the following year, or his election to Parliament in 1955 (on the occasion, ironically, of a disastrous nationwide defeat for Labour). In my trawl for any kind of documentation which would provide a flavour of the young MP's political acumen, I have been able to unearth only the following transcript from the BBC archives.
2. Alan Beamish (1926–): distinguished broadcaster who began his career as a BBC political correspondent, and then went on to make his name as an innovative producer throughout the Sixties and Seventies while continuing to make occasional appearances before the camera. After an unhappy period with independent television he retired abruptly in 1990.

man *you* have elected to best represent the interests of your own local community? What does he think of the larger – em – political questions of the day? To help us find out, I have pleasure in welcoming to the studio our first guest in this series, Henry – em – Winshaw, the Labour member for Frithville and Ropsley. Mr Winshaw, good evening.

WINSHAW: Good evening. Now, what this government fails to understand –

BEAMISH: Just a moment, Mr Winshaw. If I might just leap in with a little – em – biographical information, so that our viewers at home might know something of the background . . .

WINSHAW: Oh, yes, certainly. By all means.

BEAMISH: Now, you were born in Yorkshire, I believe, and took a degree in Mathematics from – em – Oxford University. In the years since leaving university, I understand that you worked in industry and held the post of Executive Chairman on the board of Lambert and Cox at the time when you put yourself forward for candidacy in the Labour Party.

WINSHAW: That's correct, yes.

BEAMISH: You were elected to Parliament in 1955 but have retained your position with Lambert, and in addition you've continued to serve as an active – em – board member with Spraggon Textiles and Daintry Ltd.

WINSHAW: Well, I believe it's very important to maintain contact with the manufacturing – erm – process, at – erm – at grass-roots level, as it were.

BEAMISH: Naturally, with your close interest in – em – matters industrial, you must have strong views on Mr Amory's[1] recent decision to relax the credit squeeze.

WINSHAW: I certainly do. And what this government simply fails to understand is that –

BEAMISH: But before we come on to that topic I thought we should perhaps consider things in a more – em – global perspective, because after all only one issue has been dominating

---

1. Derick Heathcoat Amory (1899–1981), later first Viscount Amory, Conservative MP for Tiverton and Chancellor of the Exchequer from 1958 to 1960.

proceedings in the Commons for the last few days, and that of course is the revolution in – em – Iraq.[1] You must have been following the debates with interest.

WINSHAW: Ah. Well I haven't been in the House this week, nearly as much – erm – nearly as much as one would wish. Business commitments have – I mean *constituency* business, of course – have been very – erm – very pressing . . .

BEAMISH: But, for instance, what sort of impact do you, personally, think that Brigadier-General Kassem's uprising will have on the balance of power?

WINSHAW: Well . . . well, the whole Middle East situation, as you know, is very delicate.

BEAMISH: Absolutely. But I think it's true to say that this was an especially bloodthirsty coup, even by the standards of the region.

WINSHAW: Quite.

BEAMISH: Do you foresee that Mr Macmillan[2] will face any problems in recognizing the new government?

WINSHAW: Oh, I'm sure he'd . . . know them if he saw them. I gather he's pretty well acquainted with that part of the world.

BEAMISH: No, my point, Mr Winshaw – my point is that there is concern, in some quarters, about the effect that the violent imposition of a new, left-wing regime will have on our trading prospects with Iraq. And indeed on our relations generally.

WINSHAW: Well, I personally don't have any relations in Iraq, but anybody who does would be well advised, I would have thought, to get them flown home at once. It sounds absolutely ghastly out there at the moment.

---

1. In the early morning of July 14th, an announcement from Baghdad Radio stated that Iraq had been 'liberated from the domination of a corrupt group installed by imperialism'. King Faisal, the Crown Prince Abdul Ilah and General Nuri es-Said had all been assassinated in the military coup, and a Republican regime was proclaimed. At the request of King Hussein, British paratroops were then sent out to Jordan to safeguard the area.

2. Harold Macmillan (1894–1984), later Earl of Stockton. Conservative MP for Bromley and Prime Minister from 1957 to 1963.

BEAMISH: Let me put it another way. There's been considerable disquiet in the House over Mr Macmillan's decision to send British troops into the area. Do you think we could now be faced with another Suez?

WINSHAW: No, I don't, and I'll tell you why. The Suez, you see, is a canal: a very large canal, as I understand it, running through Egypt. Now there are no canals in Iraq. Absolutely none at all. This is the essential factor which has been overlooked by people who have tried to make this point. So I really don't think the comparison stands up to scrutiny.

BEAMISH: Finally, Mr Winshaw, do you see any irony in the fact that this coup – so hostile, potentially, to our national interests – has been carried out by an army trained and equipped by the British? Traditionally, the British and Iraqi governments have cooperated very closely in this area. Do you think their military ties will now be a thing of the past?

WINSHAW: Well, I very much hope not. I've always thought that the Iraqi military tie is an extremely attractive one, and I know there are many British officers who wear it with pride. So it would be a sad day for our country if that were to happen.

BEAMISH: Well, I see now that we're out of time, and all that remains for me to say is – Henry Winshaw, thank you very much for being our guest on the programme. And now over to Alastair for our location report.

WINSHAW: Is there a bar in here?

BEAMISH: We're still on air, I think.

*

February 5th 1960

The shock of my life. Not having much to do this morning, wandered into the House at around eleven. The agenda wasn't promising: second reading of the Public Bodies (Admission of the Press to Meetings) Bill. This was to be the maiden speech of the new Member for Finchley, one Margaret Thatcher: and blow me if she didn't turn out to be the self-same Margaret Roberts who knocked me for six at the Conservative Association back in Oxford! Fifteen years ago, for Heaven's sake! She made the most magnificent début – everyone was congratulating her in the most effusive terms – although to my shame I have to say that I only took in about half of it. While she was speaking the years just seemed to slip away, and by the end I was probably staring at her open-mouthed across the benches like some sex-starved pubescent. That hair! Those eyes! That voice!

Afterwards I approached her in the Corridor to see if she remembered me. I think she did: she wasn't just saying it. She's married, now, of course (to an entrepreneur of some sort), with children (twins).[1] What pride, what wonderful pride that man must feel. She was rushing off to meet him, and we spoke for only a few minutes. Then I dined alone in the Members' Room, and then back to digs. Telephoned Wendy, but didn't have much to say. She sounded drunk.

What a millstone she's become. Even the name – Wendy Winshaw – even that sounds absurd. Daren't take her out in public with me any more. Now 3 years and 247 days since last coitus. (With her, that is.)

Asked Margaret what she thought about Macmillan and his winds of change.[2] She didn't give much away, but I suspect we think alike. Neither of us can afford to declare our hands at this stage.

I feel, just as I did all those years ago – tho' perhaps now with more reason – that our destinies are inextricably bound together.

1. Margaret Roberts had married Dennis Thatcher, then Managing Director of the Atlas Preservative Co., in December 1951. Their son Mark and daughter Carol were born two years later. (Atlas itself was sold to Castrol Oil for £560,000 in 1965.)

2. On February 3rd Macmillan had proudly told the South African parliament in Cape Town that 'a wind of change is blowing through the continent'. Certain elements within his own party considered his position on this issue to be dangerously progressive.

September 20th 1961

Impertinent telephone call this afternoon from the Whip, who has somehow caught wind of our little *contretemps* up at Winshaw Towers over the weekend.[1] Don't ask me how – the thing was in the local paper, but Lawrence will already have seen to it that it doesn't get any further. Damn this wretched family of mine! If ever they turn out to be a liability . . . Well, they can expect no loyalty from me.

Anyway, he wanted to know about Tabitha and her illness and whether we had any other mental cases locked away in the attic at all. I did my best to play it all down, but he didn't seem entirely convinced. If it gets back to Gaitskell[2] (as I'm sure it will) – what will that do to my cabinet prospects?

July 14th 1962

Much righteous indignation in the newspapers over Macmillan's reshuffle. I must say that sacking seven ministers in one night seems pretty good going to me. For my own part – not that I'm allowed to say this to anyone, of course – I admire (and am pleasantly surprised by) his guts. We could do with the same ruthlessness in our own party, frankly, to get rid of some of the spineless Yes-Men who have allowed the Communists to get a foothold – those ructions at Glasgow merely being the most public example.[3] I'd hoped, to be honest, that most of that nonsense would have died with Bevan. What place is there for me if the party drifts further and further to the Left? There's talk of

---

1. On September 16th an intruder had broken into the family residence under rather mysterious circumstances, and met his death while launching a violent attack on Lawrence Winshaw. The incident aroused little comment at the time, although a characteristically overheated version of it can be found in Owen, *op. cit.*

2. Hugh Todd Naylor Gaitskell (b. 1906), MP for South Leeds and leader of the Labour Party from 1955 until his sudden death in 1963.

3. Gaitskell's speech in Glasgow on May 6th had been disrupted by supporters of unilateralism, leading to allegations of Trotskyist infiltration of Labour's youth section.

Wilson becoming the next leader, which would be nothing short of disastrous. The man hates and despises me, for one thing. Never says hello at Conference or in the House. Seven bloody years I've sat on these benches and I'm damned if it's not going to pay off in the end.[1]

November 8th 1967

Brief but humiliating conversation with Richard Crossman[2] in the Tea Room this afternoon. Ostensibly he stopped by to congratulate me on my appointment, but there was an element of mockery there. I could hear it. Bastard. Well, Parliamentary Under-Secretary: it's a step nearer to the front bench, isn't it? There's no point in fooling myself, though. The fact is that if I was with the Other Side I'd be near the top of the shadow team by now. I'm batting for the wrong eleven, and it's getting more and more obvious. Wilson and his pack of cronies don't have the faintest idea what a man of ability looks like. No *vision*, any of them.

Nothing but gloom on the financial front, too. Under this blinkered administration it's becoming impossible for businesses to forge ahead – like trying to run through treacle. Profits down 16% at Amalgamated, 38% at Evergreen. Dorothy seems to be doing well, however, so her offer of a non-executive position starts to look more and more attractive. Should I resign at the next election and get out of this rat race altogether?

Of course, there's no guarantee that I'd get back in, in any case. Very much a moot point at the moment. Wendy's little appearance in the local rag won't have helped at all. Stupid bitch:

1. Harold Wilson (1916–), later Baron Wilson of Rievaulx, did indeed become party leader on February 14th 1963. It's possible, however, that Winshaw may have overestimated the extent of his animosity. I have been able to find only one instance of Wilson referring to him in print, during an interview for *The Times* in November 1965. Winshaw's name was mentioned in connection with the abolition of the death penalty (which he opposed), and the then Prime Minister is reported to have asked: 'Who?'

2. Richard Howard Stafford Crossman (1907–74), Labour MP for Coventry East, was at this time Leader of the House of Commons. Curiously his own copious diaries contain no reference at all to this conversation.

with that much inside her, she was lucky not to have crashed the thing. Could have been killed.

(Dangerous line of thinking, Winshaw. Very dangerous.)

June 19th 1970

Well, we deserved to lose.[1] Now the country will get the most hardline government it will have known since the war, and a good thing too. People need shaking out of their swinish complacency.

Margaret has her cabinet post at last: Education. She will be wonderful, I just know she will.

Keith Joseph[2] in charge of Health. He's a bit of an unknown quantity to me. Hasn't made a big impression. All I've noticed is a slightly manic gleam in his eye, which I find a trifle disconcerting.

My majority down to 1,500. Amazes me that it's as big as that, frankly – but these people would probably vote for a tailor's dummy if it wore a badge with 'Labour' written on it. What a dismal farce it all is.

March 27th 1973

Debate on Joseph's NHS reforms[3] dragged on for another day. The usual people making the usual footling objections. Our Man making a poor job of his speech. Didn't stay to hear the whole thing – dropped in and out during the course of the day. The Bill isn't all it should be, but a step in the right direction: more efficient management structure, more externals (or 'generalists' as he calls them) on the various boards – business people, I assume that means. I think this may be it – the beginning of the asset-

---

1. Confounding the opinion polls, the Conservatives had just won an overall majority of 31 seats in the Commons, with 46.4% of the national vote. Edward Heath (1916–) became Prime Minister.

2. Keith Sinjohn Joseph (1918–), later Baron Joseph of Portsoken. Secretary of State for Social Services (1970–74) and subsequently for Industry (1970–81) and Education and Science (1981–86).

3. The National Health Service Reorganization Act (1973), which was finally passed on its third reading in the Commons on June 19th by a majority of 11.

stripping process. So I must start looking for ways to make my move.

Voting, finally, at about 10.15. Did my duty, as per usual. But will try to buttonhole Sir Keith some time over the next few days and let him know where my allegiances really lie. He looks the sort of chap who can keep a secret.

July 3rd 1974

Forgot to mention it at the time, but Wendy died last week. Came as no surprise to anyone, really – least of all me. 20 aspirin and a big tumbler-full of Scotch. Never did anything by halves, that woman.

Funeral this morning, so whizzed up the motorway and made it just in time. Fairly low-key affair – no family, thank God. Back to London in time to hear Castle's statement on the nurses' strike.[1] Confirmed my worst fears – she wants to phase private beds out of the Health Service altogether. Lunacy. Am beginning to see our election victory (if you can call it that) for what it was: a national disaster. This cannot go on. Wilson can't govern for long without a majority and when he announces the next polling date, I shall stand down. Please God let it be soon.

October 7th–10th 1975

Attended the Conservative Conference in my new capacity as journalist. The editor wants 8–900 words a day, my brief being to decide whether Margaret's election[2] means a break with old-style Conservatism once and for all. He thought it would be interesting to have someone write about it from a Left perspec-

---

1. Barbara Anne Castle (1910–), later Baroness Castle of Blackburn: Labour MP for Blackburn and at this time Secretary of State for Social Services. The strike mentioned here was threatened by paramedical staff at Charing Cross Hospital, who were refusing to serve forty penthouse suites set aside for private patients.

2. Margaret Thatcher had defeated Edward Heath in a leadership ballot and on February 10th 1975 was elected the first woman leader of a major British political party.

tive, although he may get a surprise when he reads what I have to say.[1]

Everyone here is remarking on the contrast with last week's Labour bash in Blackpool. Apparently it was a shambles – the party is tearing itself apart and Wilson has been warning of extremists in the constituency parties, although I could have told him about that ages ago. The Marxists have been worming their way inside for years. It was there for anyone with eyes to see.

The highlight of this week has been Joseph's magnificent speech. He said there was no such thing as the 'middle ground' and the only possible consensus had to be based upon the market economy. Some of the delegates looked a bit stunned, but give them a few years and they'll see how right he is.

It's just beginning. I can feel it. Can it really have taken so long to get this far?

November 18th 1977

The Party held me down and kept me back for twenty years. Twenty wasted years. Nothing could give me greater pleasure than to see it unravelling before my eyes. The leadership election was a joke, and now we have a new tenant at Number Ten who can only be described as a political dwarf, with no idea how to govern, and no mandate from the people.[2] Every vote has to be fought to the death, and he will have to spend most of his time trying to appease the Liberals.

Reg Prentice[3] has announced his defection to the Tories. Fool. Real power lies in the media, and in backroom policy-making: if he hasn't worked that out after all those years in Parliament, he's

1. He probably did. The article in question was entitled 'The Dawn of a Golden Age' and contained little evidence of socialist bias.

2. Winshaw's reference is to James Callaghan (1912–), later Baron Callaghan of Cardiff. His opponents in the leadership contest had been Michael Foot and Denis Healey.

3. Reginald Ernest Prentice (1912–), later Baron Prentice of Daventry, justified his sudden change of political allegiance in an ingenious volume called *Right Turn* (1978). He subsequently became Social Security Minister for two years in Mrs Thatcher's first government.

more of a sap than I thought he was. It's perfectly obvious that Margaret is going to be PM in a year or two, and the important thing now is to start getting the legislation in place. They will have to move fast once they get there.

Work on an NHS bill is progressing. I've managed to convince them that the first thing to do is reverse the policy of phasing out private beds. More radical measures will have to wait, but not for long. We need to get a few business types in, to do a major report and show that the present system is nothing but a shambles. If someone from a supermarket chain, for instance, were to come in and see how it operates at the moment . . . he'd probably have a fit.

Here's a thought: why not suggest Lawrence? I think he's still got his wits about him (just about), and he could certainly be relied upon to come to the right conclusions. Worth a try, anyway.

I see her now, and talk to her, more than ever before. Such happy days.

June 23rd 1982

Very agreeable lunch with Thomas in the private dining room at Stewards.[1] Extremely fine port – must encourage the Club to buy some, to replace the raspberry syrup they serve at the moment. Pheasant a little overcooked. Nearly lost a tooth on the gunshot.

Thomas has agreed to help us out with the flogging-off of Telecom.[2] Took a little persuading at first, but I convinced him that if he and the bank were going to prosper under Margaret's government then they were going to have to be a little more robust in their business practices. It helped, of course, when I told him the kind of fees he could expect to collect. Also predicted that there was going to be any number of these sell-offs over the

---

1. Respected and powerful merchant bank with which Thomas Winshaw (1924–91) was long associated, first as director and later as Chairman.

2. The Telecommunications Bill for the privatizing of British Telecom was introduced into the Commons in November 1982; it was not actually passed until April 12th 1984, after Mrs Thatcher had won her second term.

next few years, and if Stewards wanted a good slice of the action they should get in early. He asked me what else was going to come up in the near future and I told him that it was basically the lot: steel, gas, BP, BR, electricity, water, you name it. Not sure that he believed me about the last two. Just wait and see, I said.

This was the longest chat we've had, I think, for about thirty years. Stayed till about 5, talking about this and that. He showed off his new toy, a machine that plays back films on what looks like a silver gramophone record, with which he seemed inordinately pleased. I couldn't really see it catching on, but didn't say so. He'd seen my latest appearance on the box, and told me that I'd done very well. Asked him if he'd noticed I hadn't answered any of the questions, and he said no, not really. Must tell this to the PR people: they'll be very pleased. They've been training us all quite intensively over the last few weeks and I must say it seems to be paying off. I timed the interview on playback last night and was impressed to find that only 23 seconds after being asked about the *Belgrano*, I was already talking about Militant infiltration of the Labour Party. Sometimes I surprise even myself.

June 18th 1984

Reforms progressing, although not as speedily as I'd hoped. Everybody on the committee seems to have a full calendar, and today was only the second time we'd managed to get together since the review was announced. Still, the Griffiths[1] report gives us plenty to go on, and is a firm nudge in the right direction, since it deals something of a death blow to the whole idea of 'consensus' management. One lady committee member (of pinkish hue, I suspect) queried this but I shut her up by quoting Margaret's definition of consensus as 'the process of abandoning all beliefs, principles, values and policies' and 'something in which no one believes and to which no one objects'. Point made, I think.

---

1. Sir (Ernest) Roy Griffiths (1926–), Managing Director of Sainsbury's plc, was Chairman of the Management Inquiry into the NHS which published its report in 1983. It was highly critical of the 'lack of a clearly defined general management function' in the Health Service.

What we'll now end up recommending – if I have anything to do with it – is the introduction of general managers at every level on *performance-related pay*. That's the crucial thing. We've got to squash this dewy-eyed belief that people can be motivated by anything other than money. If I'm going to end up running this show, after all, I need people underneath me who I can be sure are going to give of their best.

Went upstairs to the TV room at the Club for the *Nine O'Clock News* this evening and saw extraordinary scenes at some pit or other.[1] A whole gang of thuggish-looking miners were mounting a murderous, unprovoked assault – throwing stones, some of them – on policemen who were armed only with truncheons and riot gear. When the police tried to ride through, some of these hooligans blatantly obstructed them, actually trying to trip up the horses by getting in the way. What will Kinnock[2] have to say about that, I wonder?

October 29th 1985

Over to Shepherd's Bush this evening to appear on *Newsnight*, where it turned out that the guest presenter was none other than my old enemy Beamish. Contemplated walking off at that point, since it's well known that the man is practically a Communist and has no business chairing a supposedly impartial discussion programme. Anyway, I managed to come off very well from the whole thing. To present the 'other point of view' they wheeled out some pig-ugly female doctor with NHS specs and a bleeding heart, who whined and moaned a lot about 'goodwill' and 'chronic underfunding' before I put her in her place by quoting a few simple facts. Thought I'd heard the last of her, after that, but she came up to me afterwards in hospitality and claimed that her father had known me at Oxford. Gillam was the name, apparently. Meant nothing to me, I must say – in fact this sounded

1. The confrontation between miners and police took place at Orgreave and was the most violent of the year-long strike.

2. Neil Kinnock (1942–): former leader of the Labour Party, now one of Britain's two Commissioners to the European Community in Brussels.

suspiciously like a chat-up line, and since she didn't look quite such a Gorgon away from the studio lights, I asked if she fancied a quick one to show there were no hard feelings. Nothing doing, needless to say. She took the hump and stormed off. (Did look a bit dyke-ish, now I come to think of it. Just my luck.)[1]

*

From A Pox on the Box: Memoirs of a Disillusioned Broadcaster, *by Alan Beamish (Cape, 1993)*

... I can even pinpoint the incident which first convinced me that the quality of public debate in this country had entered into precipitous decline. It was in October 1985, during one of my occasional stints as presenter of *Newsnight*: the guest was Henry Winshaw (or Lord Winshaw, as we all had to get used to calling him for a year or two prior to his death) and the subject was the NHS.

This, you will recall, was at the high tide of Thatcherism, and the last few months had seen a series of aggressive measures which had left the more liberal wing of the electorate feeling punch-drunk and disoriented: a radical cutting-back of the Welfare State announced in June, the GLC abolished in July, the BBC forced to abandon a documentary featuring interviews with Sinn Fein leaders, and, most recently, Mrs Thatcher's implacable opposition to sanctions against South Africa, which left her isolated at the Commonwealth Prime Ministers' conference. At the same time, the question of the Health Service continued to bubble away in the background. A fundamental policy review had been set in motion, and there was mounting unrest within the medical profession about dwindling resources and 'privatization by the back door'. We decided it would be instructive to invite one of the architects of the NHS reforms on to the programme and confront him with someone working at the front line of medical practice in a London hospital.

For this purpose we brought in a junior doctor called Jane Gillam, who had recently taken part in a Radio 4 phone-in and impressed everyone with her commitment and grasp of detail. I remember her

---

1. Dr Jane Gillam, to whom Winshaw is referring here, left the medical profession in 1991 and has since become well known as a freelance journalist writing widely on health issues. For a different account of her television appearance with Henry Winshaw, see the following extract.

as a tall woman, whose jet-black hair was cut in a bob and whose small, gold-rimmed glasses framed a pair of striking and combative brown eyes: and yet it was obvious from the beginning that she was going to be no match for Winshaw. Long gone were the days when I had interviewed him for the old 'Backbencher' slot and inadvertently exposed his hazy grasp of foreign policy. It was impossible, now, to connect that nervous, fresh-faced MP with the puffy, glowering old firebrand who stared at me across the table, thumping it with his fist and barking like a rabid dog as he answered Dr Gillam's questions. Or rather, failed to answer them: for Winshaw's mode of political debate, by this stage in his career, had long since parted company with rational discourse and tended to consist entirely of statistics diluted with the occasional gobbet of scattergun abuse. And so, consulting a transcript of that discussion, I find that when Dr Gillam first raised the subject of deliberate underfunding as a prelude to privatization, his answer was:

'17,000,000 over 5 years 12.3% of GDP 4% more than the EEC 35% up on the USSR 34,000 GPs for every HAS × 19.24 in real terms 9,586 for every FHSA seasonally adjusted 12,900,000 + 54.67 @ 19% incl VAT rising to 47% depending on IPR by the IHSM £4.52p NHS safe in our hands.'

In response to which, Dr Gillam said:

'I don't dispute the truth of your figures, but neither do I dispute the truth of what I see every day with my own eyes. And the problem is that these two truths contradict each other. Every day I see staff working longer hours, under greater stress, for less reward, and I see patients waiting a longer time, for worse treatment, under worse conditions. These are facts, I'm afraid. They can't be argued away.'

And Winshaw's second answer to Dr Gillam was:

'16%! 16.5%! Rising to 17.5% under a DMU with 54,000 extra for PAYE and SERPS! 64% PRP as promised in the CIPs and £38,000 = \$45,000 + ¥93,000,000 divided by $\sqrt{451}$ to the power of 68.7 recurring! 45% IPR, 73% NUT, 85.999% CFC and $9\frac{1}{2}$ weeks more than under the last Labour government.'

In response to which, Dr Gillam said:

'My point really is that you can't make the NHS more efficient by making it more geared to costs. If you do that, you're effectively trimming its resources, because the NHS runs on goodwill, on the goodwill of its staff, and under the right conditions, this goodwill is potentially infinite. But if you continue to erode it, as you're doing at the moment, and replace it with a finite range of financial incentives, then eventually you will end up with a more expensive NHS, a less efficient NHS, an NHS which is always going to be a millstone round the government's neck.'

And Winshaw's third and final answer to Dr Gillam was:

'60 CMOs, 47 DHAs, 32 TQMs, 947 NAHATs, 96% over 4 years, 37.2 in 11 months, 78.224 × 295 ÷ 13¼ + 63.5374628374, leaving £89,000,000 for the DTI, the DMU, the DSS, the KLF, the ERM and the AEGWU's NHSTA. 43% up, 64% down, 23.6% way over the top and 100–1 bar. And that's all I have to say on the matter.'

After that, he left the studio with the victorious air of a man who has finally conquered the medium. And I suppose, in a way, that he had.

*

October 6th 1987

At long last, another full meeting of the Review Board – the first since Margaret's victory in June.[1] The first White Paper[2] is finished and work will be starting on a second and third.[3]

The next reforms will be much further-reaching. We're getting to the heart of the matter, at last. To remind everyone where our priorities lie, I've had a large notice pinned to the wall: it says

FREEDOM

COMPETITION

CHOICE

I've also decided to take a strong line with the word 'hospital'. This word is no longer permitted at discussions: from now on, we call them 'provider units'. This is because their sole purpose, in future, will be to provide services which will be *purchased* from them by Health Authorities and fundholding GPs through

---

1. Mrs Thatcher's government was returned for a third term on June 11th 1987, with an overall majority of 101 seats and 42.2% of the national vote.

2. *Promoting Better Health* (1987).

3. *Working for Patients* and *Caring for People* (both 1989).

negotiated contracts. The hospital becomes a shop, the operation becomes a piece of merchandise, and normal business practices prevail: pile 'em high and sell 'em cheap. The beautiful simplicity of this idea astounds me.

Also on the agenda today was income generation. I see no reason at all why provider units shouldn't impose car-parking charges, for instance, on visitors. Also, they should be encouraged to rent out their premises for retail developments. There's no point in all those closed wards standing empty when they could be turned into shops selling flowers, or grapes, or all those other things people feel like buying when visiting a sick relative. Hamburgers, and so on. Little knick-knacks and souvenirs.

Towards the end of the meeting somebody brought up the subject of Quality Adjusted Life Years. This is one of my own personal favourites, I must say. The idea is that you take the cost of an operation and then calculate not just how many years' life it saves, but what the *quality* of the life is. You simply put a figure on it. Then you can work out the cost-effectiveness of each operation: and so something basic like a hip replacement will come out at around £700 per QALY, while a heart transplant is more like £5,000 and a full hospital haemodialysis will cost a cool £14,000 per QALY.

I've been arguing it all my life: quality is quantifiable!

Most of the Board, nevertheless, don't think the public is ready for this concept just yet, and they may be right. But it can't be long now. We're all feeling tremendously buoyant after the election result. The sell-offs have been proceeding at an amazing rate – Aerospace, Sealink, Vickers shipyards, British Gas last year, British Airways in May. Surely the day for the NHS can't be far off.

Such a shame Lawrence never lived to see it happen. But I shall do his memory proud.

We must never forget that we owe it all to Margaret. If ambition turns to reality, it will be thanks to her, and her alone. She is magnificent, unstoppable. I've never known such resolution in a woman, such backbone. She cuts her opponents down as if they were so many weeds blocking her path. Knocks them aside with a flick of her finger. She looked so beautiful in victory. How can I ever repay her – how can any of us even begin to repay her – for all that she's done?

November 18th 1990

The call came through at about 9 p.m. Nothing had been decided yet, but they were starting to canvass opinion among the faithful. I was one of the first to be asked. The poll findings are grim: she gets more and more unpopular. In fact it's gone beyond unpopularity, now. The plain truth of the matter is that with Margaret as leader, the party is unelectable.

'Dump the bitch,' I said. 'And fast.'

Nothing must be allowed to stop us.[1]

---

1. Margaret Thatcher was deposed as leader of the Conservatives on November 22nd 1990. Her successor, John Major, led the party into its unprecedented fourth election victory in 1992, thereby ensuring continuity in health policy. But this was a triumph, of course, which Henry Winshaw would never live to see.

October 1990

I

'The fact is,' said Fiona, 'that I don't really trust my GP. From what I can see, most of his energy these days goes into balancing his budget and trying to keep his costs down. I didn't get the sense that I was being taken very seriously.'

I did my best to concentrate while she was telling me this, but couldn't help keeping a watchful eye on the other diners as the restaurant started to fill up. It was beginning to dawn on me that I was underdressed. Hardly any of the men were wearing ties, but everything about their clothes looked expensive, and Fiona herself seemed to have been much more successful in judging the mood: she wore a collarless, herringbone-patterned jacket over a black cotton T-shirt, and cream linen trousers, cut a little bit short to show off her ankles. I hoped she hadn't noticed the worn patches on my jeans, or the chocolate stains which had been ingrained on my jumper for longer than I cared to remember.

'I mean, it's not as if I'm some flappy little thing who comes running into his surgery every time I get a cold,' she continued. 'And this has been going on for nearly two months now, this flu or whatever it is. I can't just keep taking days off work all the time.'

'Well, Saturday's probably his busiest day. He was bound to be rushed.'

'I think I deserved more than just a pat on the head and a few antibiotics, that's all.' She bit into a prawn cracker and sipped some wine: an attempt, it seemed, to wash the irritation away. 'Anyway.' She looked up and smiled. 'Anyway, this is very nice of you, Michael. Very nice, and quite unexpected.'

If there was an irony intended, it managed to pass me by. I still couldn't quite get over my amazement at the thought that I was actually sitting with another person – a woman, no less – at a table for two in a restaurant. I suppose part of me, the most vocal and persuasive part, had simply given up believing that such a thing might happen: and yet it could hardly have been easier to accomplish. I'd spent the previous evening slumped in front of the television, almost mad with boredom even though my intentions had been admirable enough. Over the last few years I'd accumulated a pile of unwatched videos, and it had been my hope that this time I'd find the stamina to get through at least one of them. But it seemed that optimism had got the better of me again. I watched the first half of Cocteau's *Orphée*, the first thirty minutes of Ray's *Pather Panchali*, the first ten minutes of Mizoguchi's *Ugetsu Monogatari*, the opening credits of Tarkovsky's *Solaris* and the trailers at the beginning of Wenders' *The American Friend*. After that I gave up, and sat in front of a silent screen, steadily making my way down a bottle of supermarket wine. This continued until about two o'clock in the morning. In the old days I would have just poured myself a final glass and gone to bed, but now I realized that this wasn't good enough. Fiona had called by a couple of hours earlier and I hadn't even answered when she knocked; she would have seen the light under my door and must have known that I was ignoring her. And now suddenly, sitting by myself with only the television's dumb flickering to combat the darkness, it seemed ridiculous to me that I should prefer these blank, unresponsive images to the company of an attractive and intelligent woman. It was anger, above all, which drove me to perform an impetuous and selfish act. I went directly on to the landing and rang the bell to Fiona's flat.

She answered after a minute or two, wearing a light, Japanese-style dressing-gown. An expanse of freckled breastbone was exposed, sheened thinly with sweat although I for one thought the temperature had dropped quite sharply this evening.

'Michael?' she said.

'I've been really unfriendly these last few weeks,' I blurted out. 'I came to apologize.'

She looked puzzled, of course, but managed to take it in her stride.

'That's not necessary.'

'There are some things – possibly there are some things you ought to know about me,' I said. 'Things I'd like to tell you.'

'Well, that's wonderful, Michael. I certainly look forward to that.' She was humouring me, I could tell. 'But it is the middle of the night.'

'I didn't mean now. I thought maybe . . . over dinner.'

That seemed to surprise her more than anything. 'Are you asking me out?'

'I suppose I am.'

'When?'

'Tomorrow night?'

'OK. Where?'

This put me in a corner, because I only knew one local restaurant and didn't want to go back there. But there wasn't much choice.

'The Mandarin? Nine o'clock?'

'I look forward to it.'

'Fine: well, we could either get a taxi from here, say ten minutes beforehand, or actually it's not very far to walk, and then we could maybe stop on the way . . .'

I realized that I was talking to a closed door, and went back to my flat.

Now Fiona was spreading plum sauce over a pancake with the back of her spoon, and filling it with thin strips of duck and cucumber. Her fingers worked neatly.

'So, Michael, what are these revelations about yourself that you've been bursting to tell me? I'm agog.'

I smiled. I had been nervous all day, thinking how peculiar it would be to share a meal with someone again, but now I was beginning to feel quietly euphoric. 'There are no revelations,' I said.

'So last night – that was just a subtle way of getting to see me in my dressing-gown, was it?'

'It was just an impulse, that's all. It had only just occurred to me how strange my behaviour must seem. You know – the way I keep myself to myself, how I barely answer you sometimes, all the time I spend watching things on the television: you must wonder what on earth's going on.'

'Not really,' said Fiona, biting into her folded pancake. 'You're hiding from the world because it frightens you. I frighten you. You've probably never learned to form real relationships with people. Did you think I wouldn't be able to see that?'

Wrongfooted, I tried to bite into my pancake, but I hadn't folded it properly and the contents spilled out just as I was about to put it into my mouth.

'You have to work at these things, that's the point,' said Fiona. 'If it's depression we're talking about then let me tell you, I've been there. But, you know . . . Take that bike ride I went on the other week. Agony, it was. Complete bloody agony. But at least I met some people, went for a drink afterwards, got a couple of dinner invitations out of it. It may not sound like very much, but after a while you realize . . . there's nothing worse than being on your own. Nothing.' She sat back and wiped her fingers on her napkin. 'Well, it's just a thought. Perhaps we shouldn't get heavy this early in the evening.'

I wiped my fingers too. Huge amounts of plum sauce seemed to come off and smudge the napkin with great brown patches.

'You made a good choice here,' said Fiona, glancing around the restaurant. It had a comfortable atmosphere, somehow intimate and convivial at the same time. 'Have you been here before?'

'No, no. I just read about it somewhere.'

But this, of course, was a lie, since we were in the very place where my mother and I had had the last, explosive argument from which our relationship was yet to recover. I had vowed never to come back here, fearing that someone on the staff might recognize me and make some embarrassing reference – for we had created quite a scene at the time – but now, finding myself both calmed and exhilarated by Fiona's company, this anxiety seemed preposterous. It was after all one of the most popular restaurants in the area, and when I thought of all the thousands of customers who must have come and gone during the last two or three years . . . Really, I was flattering myself to suppose that anybody might have found the incident at all memorable.

A waiter came to clear our plates. 'Good evening, sir,' he said with a slight bow. 'How nice that you come back again after all this time. Your mother is well?'

I sat speechless for a while after he had gone, unable to meet Fiona's eyes which were laughing even as her mouth remained politely quizzical. Then I admitted: 'Well, yes, I did come here with my mother once. We had a terrible row and . . . well, it's not something I really wanted to talk about.'

'I thought that was the whole point of this evening,' she said. 'To tell me things.'

'Yes, it is. And I will. It's just that there are certain things, certain areas . . .' This was coming out badly, and it was clear that if I was to regain her confidence, a major gesture was called for. 'Come on, you can ask me anything. Anything at all. Ask me a question.'

'All right then: when did you get divorced?'

I put my wineglass down in mid-sip, spilling some on the table. 'How did you know about that?'

'It was on the cover of that book you showed me.'

And yes, it was true: I'd wasted no time in trying to impress Fiona by showing her a copy of my first novel, the dustjacket of which did indeed contain this little nugget of personal information. (Which had been Patrick's idea: he said that it made me sound more interesting.)

'That would have been in 1974, believe it or not,' I said. I could hardly believe it myself.

Fiona raised her eyebrows. 'What was her name?'

'Verity. We met at school.'

'You must have married very young.'

'We were both nineteen. Neither of us had been out with anyone before. We didn't know what we were doing, really.'

'Are you bitter about it?'

'I suppose not. I just look on it as my misspent youth: genuinely misspent – not taking drugs and sleeping with lots of different people, which would probably have been good fun, but this . . . perverse drive towards conformity.'

'I've never liked the name Verity,' said Fiona decisively. 'I knew someone called Verity at college. She was prissy. Set a great value on telling the truth but I don't think she ever told it to herself. If you see what I mean.'

'You think names are important, then?'

'Some names. Some people grow to resemble their names, like owners and their dogs. They can't help it.'

'I came across a curious one today. Findlay. Findlay Onyx.'

I had to pronounce the two halves quite distinctly before Fiona could be sure what I was saying. Then I explained to her how the name had come to my attention.

Earlier in the day I'd gone out to the newspaper library in Colindale to chase up further reports concerning the death at Winshaw Towers on the night of Mortimer's fiftieth birthday. You may remember that the local newspaper had promised to keep its readers informed of every development. I had naïvely expected from this that there would be a series of stories dealing with the subsequent investigation in some detail. But, needless to say, I had reckoned without the fact that the Winshaws happened to own the newspaper in question, and that Lawrence Winshaw was Grand Master of the lodge which also numbered several representatives of the constabulary among its most influential members. Such an investigation had either not been reported, or, more likely, had never been undertaken at all. There was only one item of interest, a brief sequel to the report which I had already seen, and that was more cryptic than enlightening. It said that no further information had come to light, but that police were anxious to interview a private detective who was known to operate in the area – the aforementioned Mr Onyx. It seemed that someone answering to the description of the dead man (who had still not been identified) had been seen dining with the detective at a restaurant in Scarborough on the evening of the burglary attempt; furthermore, according to a local solicitor who had been acting as proxy for Tabitha Winshaw, Mr Onyx was known to have visited her at the Hatchjaw-Bassett Institute on at least three separate occasions earlier in the month, presumably on business. For good measure the report added that he was also wanted for questioning on three counts of gross indecency under Section 13 of the Sexual Offences Act (1956). After that, there was no further mention of the mysterious incident. The lead item in the next edition concerned an unprecedentedly large aubergine which had been grown by a local gardener.

'So, that would appear to be that,' I said, as we were served with a plate of steaming king prawns, heavy with ginger and garlic. 'This guy was nearly sixty, it said, so there's not much chance of him still being around. Which means the trail has more or less gone cold.'

'Becoming quite the little detective yourself, aren't you?' said Fiona, spooning out a modest portion. 'Is there any point to all this, though? I mean, does it really matter what happened thirty years ago?'

'Somebody thinks so, obviously, if they're prepared to break in to my publishers and follow my taxi home.'

'But that was more than a month ago now.'

I shrugged. 'I still reckon I'm on to something. It's just a question of where to start looking next.'

'Perhaps I could help you,' said Fiona.

'Help me? How?'

'I'm used to doing research. That's what my job is, really. I write abstracts of articles from the scientific press, and then they're indexed and put into this huge reference book which usually winds up in university libraries. The name Winshaw comes up quite often – you'd be surprised. Thomas, for instance, he's still involved with quite a few of the big petrochemical firms. And then of course there's Dorothy Brunwin – wasn't she a Winshaw, originally? Every year there's a whole stack of pieces about some wonderful innovation she's thought up, some new way of processing various disgusting parts of a chicken's anatomy and passing it off as meat. We go back all the way to the 1950s, so I could check out all the contemporary references – you never know, there might be a clue buried in there somewhere.'

'Thanks. That would help,' I said, and then added (equally insincerely): 'Sounds like interesting work. Have you been doing it for long?'

'I started . . . just under two years ago. It was a few weeks before my divorce finally came through.' She caught my eye and smiled. 'Oh yes, you're not the only one to have screwed up on that front.'

'Well, that's a relief, in a way.'

'Did you and Verity have children?'

'We *were* children: we didn't need to have any. What about you?'

'*He* had children. He had three daughters, from his first marriage, but he wasn't allowed access to them. Understandably, I suppose. He was a manic-depressive and a born-again Christian.'

I didn't know quite how to react to this. A large chunk of beef covered in oyster sauce fell from my chopsticks and landed on my shirt, and that distracted us for a while. Then I said: 'Of course, I don't know you very well, but somehow he doesn't sound like your type.'

'True: you don't know me very well. Oh, he was my type all right. You see, unfortunately I'm one of those people . . . I have a giving nature.'

'I'd noticed.'

'The way I showered you with pot plants, for instance.'

'The way you give money to beggars – even when they don't really want it.'

This was a reference to an old man who had approached Fiona as we were walking to the restaurant. Although he had merely asked her for the time, immediately she had taken twenty pence out from her purse and pressed it into his palm. He seemed more taken aback than pleased, and it was left to me to tell him that it was actually a quarter to nine – for which he thanked me as he went on his way.

'Quite,' she said. 'I take pity on people.'

'Even when they don't really want it?'

'But nobody really wants it, do they? However desperate their case is. That's what you find out, in the end.' She sighed and stroked her wineglass pensively. 'I won't be marrying out of pity again, that's for sure.'

'His case sounds pretty desperate, anyway.'

'Well, he and his wife had both been devout evangelicals for a while. They had these two kids and then she had an incredible job giving birth to the next one. The upshot was that she lost her religion – with a vengeance – and walked out on him, taking these three daughters with her. Faith, Hope and Brenda.'

'How long did it last?'

'What, him and me? Five years, nearly.'

'Quite a while.'

'Quite a while.' She took the last shred of green pepper from her bowl and popped it in her mouth. 'There are even moments – moments of great weakness, I have to say – when I miss him a little bit.'

'Oh?'

'Well, it's nice just to have somebody there, sometimes, isn't it. He was quite helpful when my mother died, for instance. Quite kind.'

'What about your father: is he . . . still . . .?'

'Alive? I've no idea. He ran off when I was ten.'

'Brothers and sisters?'

She shook her head. 'I'm an only child. Just like you.'

After that we found ourselves staring in silence at the debris of our meal. Fiona had replaced her chopsticks tidily on their cradle and, apart from a few stray grains of rice, her half of the table-cloth remained spotless. Mine looked as though it had recently been used by Jackson Pollock to form the basis of a particularly brutal composition fashioned entirely out of authentic Chinese foodstuffs. We ordered a pot of tea and a bowl of lychees.

'Well,' said Fiona. 'I wouldn't exactly say that you'd opened up to me this evening, after all those promises. I wouldn't say that your soul had been laid naked before me across the dinner table. All I've found out is that you got married at a ridiculously young age and that most of the time you'd rather watch films than talk to people.'

'I don't just watch films,' I said, after a short pause during which I had the sensation of standing poised to dive into uncertain waters. 'I obsess over them.'

She waited for me to clarify this.

'Well, just one film, actually. And you've probably never heard of it.'

I told her the title and she shook her head.

'I was taken to see it by my parents when I was only small. We left the cinema in the middle and ever since then I've had this strange feeling that it's – that it's never really finished, I suppose. That I've been . . . inhabiting it.'

'What's it about?'

'Oh, it's a silly film. All about this wealthy family who turn up at a big country house for the reading of a will, and get bumped off one by one. It's meant to be funny, of course, but I didn't see it like that at the time. It scared me to death, and I fell wildly in love with the heroine, who was played by Shirley Eaton – do you remember her?'

'Vaguely. Didn't she come to a nasty end in a James Bond film, once?'

'In *Goldfinger*, yes. She gets covered in gold paint and suffocates. But in this other film she has a scene with Kenneth Connor, where she invites him to stay the night in her room, and he's very attracted to her and she's obviously very kind and sensible as well as being beautiful, so it would be the best thing from every point of view, but he can't bring himself to do it. There are all these terrible things going on in the house, this homicidal maniac wandering around the place, and yet he finds all of that less frightening than the thought of being alone with this wonderful woman for a whole night. And I've never forgotten that scene: it's been with me for the last thirty years. For some reason.'

'Well, that's not hard to understand either, is it?' said Fiona. 'It's the story of your life, that's why you've never forgotten it.' She took the last lychee out of the bowl. 'Do you mind if I have this? They're so refreshing.'

'Go ahead. My tastebuds are crying out for some chocolate, anyway.' I signalled for the bill. 'Maybe there'll be a shop open on the way home.'

*

Outside, it became clear that the heatwave was now on the wane, and I noticed that Fiona was even shivering slightly as we walked back to our mansion block. We stopped at a late-night news-agent's, where I bought an Aero and a white Toblerone: I offered her half of the Aero and was quite relieved when she didn't take it. There was a light mist in the air as we turned off Battersea Bridge Road and began cutting up some side streets. This was a quiet, poorly lit area, the houses squat and mournful, the front gardens neglected, with few signs of life at this time of night except for the occasional cat bolting across the road at our approach. No doubt it was the effect of the alcohol and my excitement at the success, as I saw it, of the whole evening, but the atmosphere suddenly felt heady, pregnant with the certainty of similar, even better times to come, and I was filled with a wild optimism which had to be given voice, however obliquely.

'I hope we can do this again soon,' I stammered. 'I haven't enjoyed myself this much since . . . well, within living memory, let's say.'

'Yes, it's been nice. Very nice.' But there was something tenta-tive about Fiona's agreement, and it didn't surprise me to hear a qualifying note enter her voice. 'Only, I don't want you to think . . . Look, I don't really know how to put this.'

'Go on,' I said, when she faltered.

'Well, I'm just not in the business of rescuing people any more. That's all. I just want you to understand that.'

We walked on in silence. After a while she added: 'Not that I really think you need rescuing. Maybe shaking up a little.'

'That's fair enough,' I said, and then asked an obvious question: 'Are you in the business of shaking people up?'

She smiled at that. 'Possibly. Just possibly.'

I could sense the imminence of one of those critical, life-chang-ing moments: one of those turning points where you must either seize the fleeting opportunity presented to you or watch helplessly as it slips from your grasp and recedes into invisibility. So I knew, apart from anything else, that I had to keep talking, even though I had nothing much left to say.

'You know, I've always thought of luck as a negative thing; I've always felt that if luck has any kind of part in shaping our lives then everything must be somehow arbitrary and senseless. It never really occurred to me that luck can also bring happiness. I mean it's only because of luck that I met you in the first place, it's only because of luck that we live in the same building, and now here we are, two people –'

Fiona stopped, and brought me to a halt with her arm. Very gently she laid a finger to my lips and said, 'Ssh.' I was astonished by the intimacy of the gesture. Then she slid her hand into mine so that our fingers locked, and we walked on. Her body leaned into me. After only a few paces, she leaned even closer, until I could feel the brush of her lips against my ear. I steeled myself deliciously for her words.

'I think we're being followed,' she whispered. 'Listen.'

Stunned into silence, I let her hand drop and strained to catch a hint of anything untoward above the noise of our own irregular footsteps. And yes, there was something: a pursuing echo, some way behind us. Furthermore, when we stopped, it continued for a second or two and then paused abruptly; when we started again, it followed. Our movements were being shadowed with some accuracy.

'I think you're right,' I said. It was one of my less helpful remarks.

'Of course I'm right. Women develop a sense for it. You have to.'

'Keep walking,' I said. 'I'm going to turn round and have a look.'

But by now the mist was thickening, and I couldn't see more than about twenty yards back. It was impossible to be sure whether there was any movement behind the grey curtain of shifting fog. The footsteps were still with us, though, as audible as ever, and I started to propel Fiona forward by the elbow until our pace had almost doubled. We were not far from home, and I hit upon the idea of taking a few sudden detours in order to throw the stalker off our trail.

'What are you doing?' she hissed, after I had guided her into an unexpected right turn.

'Keep walking and stick close to me,' I said. 'We'll soon have him confused.'

I took another right and then a left and then doubled back

down a footpath which led between a row of three-storey terraces. Then we crossed the road a couple of times and cut through a small alleyway which brought us out nearly at the edge of Battersea Park. We stopped and listened. There was the usual traffic noise, and the distant sounds of a party just beginning to warm up a few streets away. But no more footsteps. We sighed with relief and Fiona let go of my hand, as if only just realizing that she had been clasping it for the last ten minutes.

'I think we've lost him,' she said.

'If there was anyone.'

'There was. I know there was.'

We walked the rest of the way down the main road, a small unfamiliar distance having opened up between us. There was a short pathway leading up to our entrance porch, lined raggedly with laurel bushes, and it was here, just before unlocking the door, that I had been hoping to offer Fiona a first tentative kiss. But the mood was no longer right. She was still looking tense, her handbag held tightly to her chest within folded arms, and I was so flustered that I worked stupidly at the lock for what seemed like an age before noticing that I had taken out the wrong key. Then, when I had finally got the door open and was about to step inside, Fiona let out a sudden cry – somewhere between a gasp and a scream – and leapt in before me, grabbing my arm so as to drag me with her and slamming the door which she then stood against, breathing heavily.

'What is it? What's the matter?'

'He was out there – I could see him. His face in the bushes.'

'Who?'

'For God's sake, I don't know who. He was crouched there, peering at us.'

I made for the door handle.

'This is ridiculous. I'm going to take a look.'

'No – Michael. Please, no.' She stopped me with a cautioning hand. 'I saw his face quite clearly, and . . . and I recognized him.'

'Recognized him? – Well who is it?'

'I'm not sure. I didn't actually recognize him, but . . . I've seen his face before. I'm sure I have. Michael, I don't think it's you he's following. I think it must be me.'

I shook myself free and said, 'Well, we can soon settle this.' I opened the door and slipped outside; Fiona followed as far as the step.

It was cold by now and very quiet. Thin lines of mist hung in the air and coiled strangely around the white glow of the street lamps. I walked up and down the pathway, across the lawns, and looked both ways along the street. Nothing. Then I checked the bushes, pushing my face between branches, cracking twigs and making sudden thrusts into every leafy opening. Again, nothing.

Except that . . .

'Fiona, come here a minute.'

'Not on your life.'

'Look, there's nobody here. I just want to see if you notice anything.'

She squatted down beside me.

'Is this the bush where you saw him?'

'I think so.'

'Breathe in deeply.'

We inhaled together: two long, exploratory sniffs.

'That's odd,' she said, after a moment's thought; and I knew what was coming next. 'There's no jasmine round here, is there?'

2

Fiona and I watched *Orphée* together one evening, two or three days after our dinner at the Mandarin. She had recovered from her fright soon enough, and now I was the one who was having trouble sleeping. The last few hours before dawn would find me wide awake, listening tiredly to the fitful lull which, in London anyway, is the closest you ever get to silence.

... *La silence va plus vite à reculons. Trois fois* ...

My thoughts would be dizzy and incoherent, a pointless rehearsal of half-remembered conversations, unpleasant memories and wasteful anxieties. Once your mind is locked into such a pattern, it soon becomes obvious that the only way to break free is by getting out of bed: and yet this is the very last thing you feel capable of doing. It was only when the dry, acid tang in my mouth became too strong to bear that I would find the impetus to go out into the kitchen for a glass of water; after that, I might be assured of some sleep at last, because the circle would have been broken.

... *Un seul verre d'eau éclair le monde. Deux fois* ...

I had an alarm clock which was set for nine o'clock, but invariably I would wake before then. Struggling for consciousness, the first noise I recognized would not be the rumble of traffic or the passing aeroplanes, but the song of a persevering robin as he greeted the feeble daylight from the treetops beneath my bedroom window.

... *L'oiseau chante avec ses doigts. Une fois* ...

Then I would lie in bed, half-asleep, half-awake, listening for the postman's footsteps on the staircase. For some reason I have never lost faith, not since I was a young child, in the power of letters to transform my existence. The mere sight of an envelope lying on my doormat can still flood me with anticipation, however transitory. Brown envelopes rarely do this, it has to be said; window envelopes, never. But then there is the white, handwritten envelope, that glorious rectangle of pure possibility which has even shown itself, on some occasions, to be nothing less than the threshold of a new world. And this morning, while I gazed with heavy, expectant eyes into the hallway through the half-open door of my bedroom, just such an envelope slid noiselessly into my flat, carrying with it the potential to transport me, not only onward into an unsuspected future but at the same time backward, back to a moment in my childhood more than thirty years ago, when letters first started to play an important part in my life.

*

Messrs Bulb, Plugg and Sockitt,
Electricians since 1945 (or a ¼ to 8),
24 Cable Crescent,
Meterborough.

26 July 1960

Dear Mr Owen,

We must apologize for the delay in connecting the electricity supply to your new home, viz. the second cowshed on the left on Mr Nuttall's farm.

The truth is that we have been somewhat amp-ered in our attempts by the failure of our latest recruit, a bright spark if ever I saw one, to turn up for work. As a result, we realize that you have now been without electricity for several weeks, through no volt of your own.

Watt are we going to do about it, you ask? Rest assured, Mr Owen, that your supply will be connected a.s.a.p.,* and in the meantime please accept this small gift as a token of our goodwill – a month's supply of current buns (enclosed).

Yours sincerely,

A. Daptor
(Head of Complaints).

*(after several appalling procrastinations)

Once upon a time, a short walk from my parents' house along quiet roads would bring you to the edge of a wood. We lived at the point where Birmingham's outermost suburbs began to shade into countryside, in a placid, respectable backwater, slightly grander and more gentrified than my father could really afford, and every weekend, usually on a Sunday afternoon, the three of us would set off for this wood on one of those long, mildly resented walks which have since become the nucleus of my earliest and happiest memories. There were various routes available, each given its own functional (but at the time intensely romantic and evocative) designation: 'the glade'; 'the ponds'; 'the dangerous way'. But I had a personal favourite which, though we must have taken it more often than any other, never failed to exert its pull of (even then) nostalgic glamour. This was known simply as 'the farm'.

You came upon it suddenly. The walk took you around the periphery of the wood, along a path which was broad and well-established but never seemed to be much used: in my memory's version of events, at any rate, this vision of heaven was always offered to us in utter seclusion and privacy. For heaven it was: looming into view just when you least expected it, after a series of turns, dips and rises which seemed to be leading you ever deeper into the dark heart of the forest, a nest of redbricked barns and outhouses and, at their centre, an ivy-covered farmhouse of impossible charm. An orchard flanked one side of the house, its trees dappled with yellowing fruit, and we would later discover that behind it, screened from view, was a tiny walled garden, divided up into orderly chessboard squares by gravelled paths and miniature box hedgerows. Best of all, near to the wire fence which marked the boundary between public land and property, there was a little muddied pool where ducks swam and the occasional waddling goose came to drink. On subsequent visits we never failed to bring a brown paper bag filled with stale bread which I would throw at the water or sometimes, in a fit of daring, dangle through the wire until the geese approached and snapped it from my outstretched fingers.

'This must be the farm you can see from the road,' said my

father, the first time we chanced upon it. 'The one I go past when I'm driving to work.'

'I wonder if they have a shop,' said my mother. 'I bet it would be cheaper than in the village.'

After that she started using the farm to buy all her eggs and vegetables, and before long this arrangement began to take on a social as well as practical aspect. Showing once again her aptitude for striking up friendships with relative strangers, my mother lost no time in gaining the confidence of Mrs Nuttall, the farmer's wife, whose lengthy, colourful monologues on the pains and pleasures of the bucolic life meant that a good half hour had to be set aside even for something as seemingly uncomplicated as the purchase of a few potatoes. To offset my boredom on these occasions I was introduced to a farmhand called Harry, who would let me follow him around as he went about his duties, sometimes even allowing me to feed the pigs, or to sit aloft on the driver's seat of a combine harvester. And over the next few months Harry's guided tours seemed to get longer, more frequent and more elaborate, until I became a familiar figure on the farm, well known to everyone who worked there including Mr Nuttall himself. It was round about this time, too, that my parents decided I was old enough to ride my bicycle unaccompanied along the local roads, and after that I became an even more regular visitor. Sometimes my mother would make me up packets of sandwiches, and I would eat them sitting in the orchard, or by the duckpond, before setting off to explore the buildings by myself; always remembering to take a look at the calves – my favourites among the animals – and to climb the bales of hay stacked at the back of the largest barn, where there was usually any number of lean, sleepy tabby cats to be found. I would lie on the hay beside them, puzzling over the deep mystery of their purr, hypnotized by the impenetrable half-smile which always made me envy them their dreams.

*

I was in love, at this time, with a girl called Susan Clement, who had the desk next to me at school. Her hair was long and blonde, her eyes were pale blue and I think, in retrospect, that she was fond of me too, but I was never to know for sure because although I passed many weeks, perhaps even months, consumed with longing for her, it would have been easier for me to fly to the moon than to find the right words in which to express my feelings. But I remember vividly the night I woke up to find that she was in bed beside me. The sensation at first was not entirely unfamiliar, for I had shared a bed with Joan earlier that year, when our families went on a camping holiday together: but I had never wanted to touch or be touched by her; had shrunk from the idea, in fact. And yet with Susan, the first thing I knew – almost fainting with the joy of it, the amazing, palpable reality – was that she was touching me, that I was touching her, that we were dovetailed, entangled, coiled like dreamy snakes. It seemed that every part of my body was being touched by every part of her body, that from now on the entire world was to be apprehended only through touch, so that in the musty warmth of my bed, the curtained darkness of my bedroom, we could not but find ourselves starting to writhe gently, every movement, every tiny adjustment creating new waves of pleasure, until finally we were rocking back and forth, cradle-like, and then I couldn't stand it any longer and had to stop. And no sooner had I stopped than I awoke, alone and desolate.

This is my earliest memory of sex and one of only three dreams from my childhood that I can now recall with any accuracy.

*

Joan lived a few doors down the road from us. It was when our respective mothers had been pregnant that they first became friendly with one another, so we could truly claim to have grown up together. We went to the same school, and even at this age had the reputation of being slightly on the intellectual side, which was another factor in determining the closeness of our relationship. By now not only had I made up my mind, somehow or other, that I was destined to be a writer, but my first book had already appeared, in a limited edition of one – designed, illustrated and handwritten by myself. In a narrative peppered with cheerful anachronisms, it told of several episodes from the casebook of a

Victorian detective; my hero being modelled, without much regard for the restrictions laid down by copyright law, on a character from one of the many comics which formed the backbone of my reading matter during this period. Joan had literary aspirations as well: she wrote historical romances, usually concerning one or other of the wives of Henry VIII. But in my opinion – not that I would ever have been so blunt as to tell her this – her work was immature. The characterizations were thin, compared with my own, and her spelling wasn't up to much. None the less, we enjoyed showing each other our stories.

Joan and I would often ride out to Mr. Nuttall's farm together. It was a short ride, not much more than ten minutes, and contained a fabulous stretch of road – downhill but not too steep, just enough to get a bit of speed up, take your feet off the pedals and coast forward with the wind skimming your face and rushing through your ears, sweet tears of excitement welling at the corner of each eye. Of course, riding back was a different matter. We usually had to get off and push. Being conscientious children – unnaturally so, I would think now – we knew that our parents would begin to worry about us if we were gone for more than a couple of hours, which meant that our visits at first tended to be breathless, episodic affairs. We'd take books and pens and paper and things to eat, but usually, through lack of industry, would end up spending most of our time with Harry and the animals. That's my recollection, anyway, of how things were in the spring and early summer of 1960: before Joan and I took the momentous step of setting up house together.

A word of explanation, at this point. For some weeks now I had been keeping my eye on a cowshed which stood empty in one of the outbuildings and which was, as far as I could see, going begging. I nagged my mother about this with some persistence, until finally she caved in and made a polite inquiry as to whether it would be possible for me to use it. 'He's writing a book,' she explained with reluctant pride, 'and needs somewhere where he can get peace and quiet.' Clearly Mrs Nuttall was quick to pass this information on to her husband, who was so impressed that he took personal responsibility for the matter: and when I next rode down to the farm and opened the heavy, rust-hinged door on to the cowshed's dark interior, I found that my new retreat had been supplied with a desk (actually, I think, an obsolete workbench) and a little wooden chair, and that the naked bulb which hung by a wire from the roofbeams was now tastefully veiled with a faded green lampshade. And that was just the start. As the summer went on I moved all my favourite books and ornaments out of my bedroom and into this gloomy haven; Mrs Nuttall provided me with two vases and a regular supply of irises and chrysanthemums; and Harry even managed to fix up a makeshift hammock, attached to the wall in a corner of the shed by two sturdy nails which were presumed (rather cavalierly, if you ask me) to be capable of bearing the weight of my recumbent body. I had, in short, acquired a new home, and it seemed to me that no happiness could be more complete.

But I was soon to find out that it could. One morning, early in the school holidays, I arrived at the shed to discover that a white envelope had been pushed underneath the door. It was addressed to me, in my father's handwriting. It was my first letter.

*

The Nuttall Farm Residents' Association,
Poultry Place,
Much Clucking in the Yard,
Cropshire.

19 July 1960

Dear Mr Owen,

May I just say, on behalf of all my fellow-residents, how delighted we are that you have decided to take up the tenancy of Mr Nuttall's vacant cowshed.

This news has caused general rejoicing all over the farm. Some of the animals have even come out in goose-pimples, and can't wait to come and have a gander at your new house, while the cows are simply over the moon. As for the horses, they, of course, are especially pleased to have acquired a new neigh-bour.

You may find at first that some of the smaller birds have a

tendency to grouse, or even snipe. But you must bear in mind that many of these animals, far from being as educated as yourself, can only be described as pig-ignorant. In short, I hope that you won't be cowed by any of the remarks you may have herd.

Don't hesitate to drop round for a chat whenever you like, as my wives and I are always happy to receive visitors. We get sick and tired of being cooped up in here, as the atmosphere is positively fowl.

Yours sincerely,

Bertie Rooster
(Cock of the Walk).

*

The next dream that I remember is the briefest of the three, but was so vivid and frightening that it had me screaming at the top of my voice until my father came running from his bedroom to quieten me. When he asked me what was wrong, all I could say was that I'd had a nightmare, in which a man had been bending over my bed, staring into my face so intently that I was sure he was going to kill me. My father sat down beside me and stroked my hair. After a while I must have fallen asleep again.

There was one other thing I might have told him – except that I didn't really grasp it myself at the time – to explain why the dream had been so terrifying. The truth is that I had recognized the man bending over the bed. I had recognized him because it was me. It was me, as an older man, staring back at my own young self, and my face was now ravaged with age and grooved like an ancient carving with the traces of pain.

*

Photography was one of my father's hobbies. He had a little, leather-cased box camera and a home-made flash unit, and in lieu of a darkroom he would cover up the bathroom windows with black paper and fill the bath with developing fluid until one day he miscalculated and burned off all the enamel and my mother forbade him to use it ever again. Before that happened, though, he came down to Mr Nuttall's farm to make a photographic record of Joan and me at the height of our domestic bliss.

Yes, we were now living together. Or at least, writing together – for I had warily agreed to embark upon a collaboration, in which my Victorian detective was to be transported back to the Tudor period in order to solve a murder mystery at the behest of Henry VIII himself. (This whole scenario, I seem to recall, was largely inspired by *The Time Machine*, which my father had been reading aloud to me at bedtime.) For this purpose another chair had been obtained from Mrs Nuttall, and we now sat opposite each other, writing alternate chapters and passing them back and forth along the workbench, in between breaks for refreshment and inspirational walks around the miniature garden. Needless to say, the venture was not a success: we never finished our story, and when we found ourselves reminiscing about it more than twenty years later, neither of us could remember what had become of the manuscript.

None the less, it was during our brief period of creative partnership that my father took his photograph. It caught us in characteristic poses: Joan sitting eager and upright, a trusting, toothy grin lighting up her face, while I half turned away from the camera, a pencil held to my lips, my head inclined at an introspective angle. My father made two prints from the negative, and gave us one each. For many years, she told me, Joan kept her copy in a secret drawer, where it occupied a special place even among her most prized possessions. But I chose to have it on show in my bedroom; and before very long, as so often happens with these childish treasures, it was lost.

*

Barkers Bank Ltd,
The Counting House,
Lucre Lane,
Shillingham.

23 July 1960

Dear Mr Owen,

We were most interested to hear that you have recently received a rise in your pocket money to the tune of 6d a week. With your weekly income now totalling 3s, we thought you might like to hear of some of our new savings opportunities.

May we recommend, for instance, our Bonanza Budget account? This package combines minimum investment with maximum growth. In fact one of our customers, who only opened his account last month, has already shot up to more than 6' 6".

Failing that, as a farm-dweller you may like to consider our Piggy Bank Special. We supply the pig, you supply the cash – and you might end up saving more than your bacon! At the end of the year, you could find yourself with a lump sum of more than £1 1s (or a 'guinea pig', as we like to call it) simply by depositing sixpence a week: we wouldn't suggest anything rasher.

Incidentally, as one of our most valued customers, you are now entitled to join the bank's social club, which meets every Tuesday at 'The Quids Inn' for an evening of capital entertainment and first-class cuisine: whether your taste runs to bags of dough, some royal mint or just the occasional bit of lolly, we'd be glad to have you along.

Yours in the pink,

Midas Touch,
(Manager).

*

There is one other dream that I can remember clearly, and it dates from several years later, when I was fifteen. On Wednesday March 27th 1968, in the early hours of the morning, I dreamed that I was flying in a small jet plane which suddenly and for no apparent reason began to plummet to the earth. I can still hear the quiet hum of the engine turned to a throaty splutter, and see the wall of dense grey cloud appear out of nowhere. The window shatters loudly and in an instant there are shards of glass hurling themselves at me, spearing my arms and shoulders, and now there is a mighty rush of air, throwing me backwards into bruising collision with the fusilage, and now we plunge, hurtling down-wards at unthinkable speed, and I am hollow, my body is an empty shell, my mouth is open and everything that was inside me has been left way behind, way up in the sky, and the noise is deafening, the terrible whine of engine and airstream, and yet above it all I can still hear myself talking, for I am repeating a phrase, either to myself or to some absent listener, evenly and without emphasis, I repeat the words: 'I'm going down. I'm going down. I'm going down.' And then there is the final scream of metal, the piercing laceration as sections of the fuselage start to tear themselves apart, until at once the whole plane breaks up and shoots off in a million different directions, and I am in freefall, diving, unshackled, nothing but blue sky between me and the earth which I can see clearly now, rising up to meet me, the coasts of continents, islands, big rivers, big surfaces of water. I am no longer in pain, I am no longer afraid, I have already forgotten what it means to feel these things: I merely notice that the shadow of the earth has begun to swallow the delicate blue of the sky, and this transition from the blue to the black is very gradual and lovely.

Then I wake up, not shaking or sweating or shouting for my father, but registering, with a sense of anti-climax, even regret, the fact of my familiar shadowed bedroom and the unresponding night outside. I turn over and lie awake for a few minutes before falling again, this time into a dreamless and pellucid sleep.

It was two days later, over breakfast on the Friday morning, that my father passed me his copy of *The Times* and I learned that Yuri Gagarin was dead, and his co-pilot too, their two-seat jet trainer having crashed at Kirzhatsk just as I was having my dream. The last that anyone had heard from Yuri was the calm announcement 'I'm going down' as he tried to steer his aircraft away from a populated area. I didn't believe it at first, not until I saw a photograph in the next day's paper which showed the building where his ashes had been put on display, the Central House of the Soviet Army; and coiled around it, threading through the blackened streets, a queue of mourners six deep and three miles long.

*

. . . Si vous dormez, si vous rêvez, acceptez vos rêves. C'est le rôle du dormeur . . .

The envelope dropped to the floor. Immediately, roused by its arrival as nothing else could have roused me, I swung my legs out of bed and rushed into the hallway to retrieve it. It bore a first-class stamp and was addressed to 'M Owen, Esq' in elegant, spidery handwriting. Too impatient to go into the kitchen for a knife, I opened it roughly with my thumb, then took it into the sitting room and began to read the following communication, my astonishment mounting with every sentence:

Dear Mr Owen,

This brief, too hastily written notelet is by way of apology, and by way of a proposal.

Apologies first. I have, let me be the first to admit it, been the perpetrator of several crimes, against your property, and against your person. My only excuse – my only claim, in fact, upon your mercy and forgiveness – is that I have always acted out of motives of humanity. For many years now, I have been deeply interested in the case of Miss Tabitha Winshaw, whose long and unwarranted confinement I regard as one of the most shocking injustices I have ever encountered in my professional career. Accordingly, when I learned, through your advertisement in *The Times*, that you were engaged on an investigation into circumstances not wholly unrelated to this matter, my curiosity was at once excited.

You must pardon the eccentricities, Mr Owen (or may I call you Michael, for I must admit to feeling, having read your two excellent novels, that we are already the oldest and dearest of friends) – you must pardon the eccentricities, as I said, of a wayward old man, who, rather than approaching you direct, preferred to sound out the territory in advance, according to his own tried and tested methods. I must confess that it was I, Michael, who broke into the office of your remarkable publishers, and pilfered your manuscript; it was I who followed your taxi home the very next day; it was I, wishing to make personal contact with you, in order to assure you of the honesty of my intentions, who approached you outside a restaurant in Battersea, and was privileged – if somewhat surprised – to receive a gift of twenty pence from your charming companion (a cheque for which sum you will find enclosed with this letter); and it was I, you will have guessed by now, who followed you both home from the restaurant, my aged legs struggling to keep pace, and finally, through a sad miscalculation on my part, gave said companion a most regrettable shock at the very moment – if my reading of the situation is to be trusted – that you might have been about to progress to terms of the most delightful intimacy.

Can you forgive such a sorry record of reprehensible behaviour? I can only hope that my present candour, at least, will be partial atonement.

Now, Michael, for the proposal. It seems clear to me that, as independent operators, we have both proceeded as far as we can with our inquiries. The time has come for us to join forces. Let me assure you that I have in my possession a great deal of information which would be of assistance to you in your work, and that I am willing to share it all. For my own part, in return, I request sight of only one item: namely, a scrap of paper mentioned in the early stages of your fascinating history, a message jotted down by Lawrence Winshaw, which you describe – with an elegance and concision entirely characteristic, if I may say so, of the whole narrative – as a 'scribbled note to the butler, asking for a light supper to be sent up to his room'. I believe that this scrap of paper – which I once made my own unsuccessful efforts to retrieve, but which now seems, through some obscure caprice of Fate, to have fallen into your possession – will be of vital importance in establishing Miss Winshaw's sanity and innocence; that it must contain, in short, some coded meaning or clue which may well have proved elusive – you won't take this the wrong way, I trust – to someone who is perhaps lacking in my wide and varied experience of these matters.

We must meet, Michael. There are no two ways about it. We must arrange a rendezvous, and there is no time to be lost. Might I make an impish little suggestion, as to an appropriate venue? I notice that on Thursday next the Narcissus Gallery in Cork Street (prop. Roderick Winshaw, as you will certainly be aware) is holding a preview of – true to form – some doubtless vapid new paintings by a young member of the minor aristocracy. I think we can be confident that the lure of such an occasion to London's *cognoscenti* will not be so overpowering that two strangers would fail to recognize each other in the assembled throng. I will be there at seven-thirty sharp. I look forward to the pleasure of your company, and, more tremblingly, to the beginnings of what I trust will be a fertile and cordial professional association.

The letter ended with a simple 'Most sincerely', and was signed, with a flourish:

Findlay Onyx

(Detective)

Roddy

Phoebe stood in a corner of the gallery, where she had been standing for the last quarter of an hour. Her wineglass was sticky in her hand, the wine itself warm and no longer palatable. So far not one person had stopped to talk to her, or even acknowledged her presence. She felt invisible.

Three of the guests were known to her, nevertheless. She recognized Michael, for one, even though they had only met once, more than eight years ago, when he was just about to start work on his Winshaw biography. How grey his hair was looking now. He probably didn't remember her, and besides, he seemed to be deep in conversation with a white-haired and very loquacious pensioner who had done nothing but make rude comments about the paintings ever since he arrived. And then there was Hilary: well, that was all right. They had nothing to say to each other anyway.

But finally, of course, there was Roddy himself. She had caught his guilty eye more than once and seen him turn away in panic, so he clearly had no intention of making his peace. That was hardly surprising: her only real reason for coming to the opening in the first place was to cause him embarrassment. But it had been naïve of her to think that it would work. She was the one who felt embarrassed, by now, as she watched him moving easily among his friends and colleagues, chatting, gossiping. All of them, she was sure, would know exactly who she was, and be fully informed as to the nature of her distant, presumptuous connection with the gallery. Her cheeks started to burn at the very thought. But she would hang on. She would cope. She would just grip her glass more tightly, and stand firm.

This evening, after all, could threaten nothing to compare with the tidal waves of humiliation which had crashed over her when she had first walked through these doors, more than a year ago.

*

Phoebe had always painted, ever since she could remember, and her talent had been obvious from an early age to everyone but herself. With every school report, her art teacher's praises had scaled new heights of rapture; but they had rarely been echoed by his colleagues, who found her academic performances on the whole disappointing. When she left school she didn't have the nerve to apply to art college, and had begun to train as a nurse instead. A few years later her friends managed to persuade her that this had been a mistake, and she went on to study for three years at Sheffield, where her style underwent some rapid changes. All at once, an infinity of unsuspected freedoms had been laid before her: in the space of a few hungry, incredulous weeks she discovered fauvism and cubism, the futurists and the abstract expressionists. Already skilled in landscape and portraiture, she began to produce dense, cluttered canvases, packed with incongruous detail and imbued with a fascination for physical minutiae which drew her towards unlikely sources, including medical textbooks and books of zoological and entomological drawings. She was also starting to read widely for the first time, and in a Penguin edition of Ovid she found the inspiration for her first series of major paintings, all dealing with themes of flux, instability and the continuity of the human and animal worlds. Without realizing it – for she allowed nothing to complicate her exhilaration during this period – she was edging on to dangerous territory: she was heading for that unfashionable cusp between the abstract and the figurative; between decoration and accessibility. She was about to become unsellable.

But even before she was in a position to make this discovery, there were setbacks: a crisis of confidence, the abandonment of her course at the end of its second year, a return to full-time nursing. She didn't paint for several years. When she took it up again, it was with renewed passion and urgency. She rented a shared studio in Leeds (where she now lived) and spent every spare waking moment there. Small exhibitions followed, in libraries and adult education centres, and there were occasional commissions, none of them very challenging or imaginative. But locally, at least, she had begun to acquire a sort of reputation.

One of her old tutors at Sheffield, with whom she kept sporadically in touch, invited her out for a drink and suggested that it was time to start showing her work to some London galleries. To make the process simpler, he offered her a personal introduction: she had his permission to approach the Narcissus Gallery in Cork Street, and to mention his name. Phoebe thanked him cautiously, for she was a little doubtful about this proposal. Her tutor's much-vaunted influence with Roderick Winshaw had been something of a standing joke among her fellow students, who had never been able to find much evidence for it. He and Roddy had been at school together, it was true, but there was nothing to suggest that they had ever been close, or that the great art dealer had done anything to keep up the friendship in the intervening years. (When once invited, for instance, to give a guest lecture at the college, he forgot all about it and never showed up.) None the less, this was a real opportunity, and kindly offered, and it was not to be turned down lightly. Phoebe phoned the gallery next morning, spoke to a cheery and helpful receptionist, and made an appointment to come down the following week. She spent the next few days preparing her slides.

*

When she closed the glass door of the gallery behind her, Phoebe found that London's demented clamour was silenced in an instant, and she had entered a haven: hushed, clinical and exclusive. She proceeded on tiptoe. It was a simple, rectangular space, with a desk at the far end, occupied by a blonde and stunningly beautiful woman who looked about five years younger than Phoebe and who smiled Hello in a distinctly threatening manner as soon as she came in. Phoebe mumbled some sort of reply and then for a few seconds, too scared to advance any further, lingered to look at the paintings on the walls. This was encouraging: they were dreadful. But something occurred to her, all the same, as she took a deep breath and dragged her resisting feet towards the desk under the receptionist's insolent scrutiny. This morning, right up until the moment she had to leave for her train, she had been busy rearranging her selection of slides: but she now realized that this time could have been spent much more usefully. She should have been deciding what to wear.

'Can I help you?' said the woman.

'My name's Phoebe Barton. I've come to show you some of my work. I think you were expecting me.'

Phoebe sat down, although she hadn't actually been invited to do so.

'You mean you have an appointment?' said the woman, glancing through the blank pages of her desk diary.

'Yes.'

'When did you make it?'

'Last week.'

She tutted. 'I was away last week. You would have spoken to Marcia, our temp. She doesn't actually have the authority to make appointments.'

'But we fixed up a time and everything.'

'I'm sorry, but there's no record of it here. You haven't come far, have you? I mean, I'd hate to think you'd dragged yourself in from miles away, like Chiswick or somewhere.'

'I've come down from Leeds,' said Phoebe.

'Ah.' The woman nodded. 'Yes, of course. That accent.' She closed the diary and sighed heavily. 'Oh, well, I suppose now that you've come all this way . . . You've brought some slides, I take it?'

Phoebe took out the viewing sheet and was on the point of handing it over, when she said: 'I was supposed to be showing these to Mr Winshaw, you see. He's a friend of my old tutor, and I was told that –'

'Roddy's in a meeting at the moment,' said the woman. She took the slides, held them up to the light, and glanced over them for perhaps half a minute. 'No, these won't be any good to us, I'm afraid.'

She handed them back.

Phoebe could feel herself shrivelling. Already she despised this woman, but she knew her own utter powerlessness.

'But you've hardly seen them.'

'I'm sorry. They're not what we're looking for at all at the moment.'

'Well, what are you looking for?'

'Perhaps you might care to try some of the smaller galleries,' she said, dodging this question with an icy smile. 'Some of them do rent out space to amateur painters. I don't know what sort of prices they charge.'

Just then a tall, well-built man in his late thirties emerged from an open doorway at the back of the gallery and strolled over.

'Everything all right here, Lucinda?' he said. He affected to ignore Phoebe, but she could tell that she was being quietly examined and evaluated.

'There's been a small misunderstanding, I think. This lady, Miss Barker, was under the impression that she'd made an appointment to see you, and she's brought along some of her sketches.'

'That's quite all right. I was expecting Miss Barton,' he said, and held out his hand, which Phoebe shook. 'Roderick Winshaw. Now why don't you bring those things through here, and I can have a proper look at them.' He turned to the receptionist. 'That'll be all, Lucy. You can go to lunch.'

Inside his office, Roddy gave the transparencies an even more cursory inspection. He had already decided what he wanted from this tantalizing new arrival.

'Harry's told me about your work,' he lied, after a brief struggle to remember the first name of the old acquaintance he had done everything in his power to avoid for the last twenty years. 'But I'm glad to have the opportunity to meet you in person. Establishing a rapport is very important.'

As part of the process of establishing this rapport, he invited Phoebe out to lunch. She did her best to pretend that she knew her way around the menu, and managed to refrain from commenting on the prices, which at first she thought were misprinted. He was paying, after all.

'In today's market, you see,' said Roddy, his mouth full of

smoked salmon blinis, 'it's naïve to suppose that you can promote an artist's work in isolation from his personality. There has to be an image, something you can market through the newspapers and magazines. It doesn't matter how wonderful the pictures are: if you've got nothing interesting to say about yourself when the woman from the *Independent* comes round for an interview, then you're in trouble.'

Phoebe listened in silence. For all his avowed interest in her personality, this seemed to be what he wanted.

'It's also important, of course, that you photograph well.' He smirked. 'I can't imagine that you'd have any problems in that department.'

Roddy seemed strangely restless. Although he was obviously trying to impress Phoebe with his charm and attentiveness, the restaurant appeared to be full of people he knew, and he spent much of the time looking over her shoulder to make sure that he made eye contact with the more important diners. Whenever she raised the subject of painting, which she assumed was at least one interest that they had in common, he would immediately start talking about something completely different.

Roddy called for the bill after about forty minutes, before they'd had time for either dessert or coffee. He had another appointment at two o'clock.

'Bloody nuisance, really. Some journalist doing a feature on promising young artists: wants me to give him a few names, I suppose. I wouldn't bother, only you have to cooperate with these people or the gallery never gets good write-ups. You can't think of anybody, can you?'

Phoebe shook her head.

'Look, I'm sorry this has been such a rush,' said Roddy, lowering his gaze and modulating his tone to one of bashful sincerity. 'I feel that I've hardly got to know you.'

She thought this a ridiculous remark, given that they had run out of things to say to each other after about five minutes, but found herself saying, 'Yes, that's true.'

'Where are you staying in London?' he asked.

'I'm going home tonight,' said Phoebe.

'Is that really necessary? I was just thinking that you could stay at my flat if you liked. There's plenty of room.'

'That's very kind of you,' said Phoebe, immediately suspicious. 'But I have to be at work tomorrow.'

'Of course. But look, we must meet again soon. I want to have a really good look at these pictures of yours. You must talk me through them.'

'Well, I don't come down very often, what with work, and the train fare . . .'

'Yes, I can see, it must be very difficult for you. But I do find myself in Leeds occasionally. My family have got a place up in that part of the world.' He looked at his watch. 'Damn this meeting. I'll tell you what, though – why don't you pop round to my flat now? It's only just round the corner, and I could come and join you in about an hour or so. We could – sort of, pick up where we left off, and there'd be plenty of time for you to catch a train this evening.'

Phoebe stood up. 'Nice try. If rather lacking in subtlety.' She put her bag over her shoulder and said: 'If I'd known that was the sort of rapport you had in mind, I could have saved you the cost of an expensive meal. Could I have my slides back now, please?'

'I'll put them in the post, if you really want me to,' said Roddy, and he watched, fascinated, as she turned on her heel and marched wordlessly out of the restaurant. This was going to be more fun than he'd thought.

*

'He was a creep,' Phoebe told her flatmate, Kim, over a disconsolate cup of coffee in their kitchen that evening.

'Aren't they all,' said Kim. 'The question is, was he a good-looking creep?'

'That's hardly relevant,' said Phoebe. (To her own annoyance, she had found him rather handsome, although much too aware of it for his own good.)

She thought no more about Roddy until the weekend, when there was an excited phone call from her father, who asked if she'd seen Saturday's *Times*. Phoebe went out and bought it, and found that she was mentioned as one of a handful of young painters whose careers looked likely to blossom in the coming decade.

'I'm very wary of making prophecies: history can so easily prove you wrong,' says top London dealer Roderick Winshaw, 'but of all the new artists I've seen recently, I've been most impressed by Phoebe Barton, a young woman from Leeds who promises great things for the future.'

Kim thought that she should telephone Roddy and thank him, but Phoebe, who was trying hard to conceal her pleasure, didn't bother, even though the first thing she said to him when he phoned a few nights later was, 'I saw what you said in the paper. It was very nice of you.'

'Oh, that thing,' said Roddy dismissively. 'I wouldn't set too much store by that. I've had a few inquiries about you since it came out, but it's early days yet.'

Phoebe's heart was racing. 'Inquiries?' she said.

'The reason I was phoning,' said Roddy, 'was to find out if you were doing anything this weekend. I'm going up to the old family seat and I wondered if you might care to join me: then we could have a good look at your work. I thought I might pick you up in Leeds on the Saturday afternoon, and we'd drive up from there.'

Phoebe thought about this. A whole weekend alone with Roderick Winshaw? Just having lunch with him had been bad enough. It was a terrible idea.

'Fine,' she said. 'That would be lovely.'

2

Roddy took one look at the council estate and decided there was no way he was going to park the Mercedes Sports on it. He didn't much like leaving it parked on the hillside, either, outside what seemed to be some sort of school or community centre: the two young thugs who watched him getting out and locking the doors looked as though they'd cheerfully smash the windows or let the tyres down the minute his back was turned. He hoped Phoebe would be ready and he wouldn't have to hang around in this godforsaken spot a minute longer than necessary.

Outside the front door of her tower block he pressed a button and announced himself over the intercom system. There was no reply, only the abrupt sound of the door buzzing open. Roddy took a last look at the estate – kids playing noisily in a sunbaked recreation area, young mothers pushing prams up the hill from the centre of town, weighed down by bags of shopping – and then stepped into the hallway. It was damp and evil-smelling, and the lift looked especially gruesome; but walking all the way up to the eleventh floor would have meant arriving bedraggled and out of breath, and he was determined to make the best possible impression. So he gritted his teeth, blocked his nose and was relieved to find the ride relatively quick and painless. Next he had to negotiate a gloomy corridor, lit only by a series of feeble 40-watt bulbs which gave no hint of the brilliant Saturday afternoon sunshine he had left behind; but just as he was on the point of getting lost, the door to one of the flats opened and Phoebe herself appeared, beckoning. At once his spirits rose: against these surroundings she looked more ravishing than ever, and the doubts he had been entertaining all day on the drive up from London evaporated in a haze of desire.

'Come on in,' she said. 'I'm almost ready. Kim's just made a pot of tea.'

Roddy followed her inside and was surprised to find himself being led into a light and spacious sitting room. A young man in T-shirt and frayed jeans was slumped on the sofa watching television, flicking channels between *Grandstand* and a black-and-white comedy film on BBC2. He didn't look up.

'This is Darren,' said Phoebe. 'Darren, this is Roderick Winshaw.'

'Pleased to meet you,' said Roddy.

Darren grunted.

'He's driven all the way up from London,' said Phoebe, reaching for the off button on the television. 'I'm sure he'd like to relax.'

'Oy, I'm watching that!'

The television stayed on, and Phoebe retreated to her room to finish packing. Roddy drifted into the kitchen, where a tidy, sandy-haired woman was pouring out four cups of tea.

'You must be Roddy,' she said, and handed him a cup. 'I'm Kim. Phoebe and I share this flat together. For our sins.' She giggled. 'Do you take sugar?'

Roddy shook his head.

'We're all so excited that she's finally got someone important on her side,' said Kim, helping herself to three spoonfuls. 'It's just the break she needs.'

'Well, I certainly intend to . . . do whatever I can,' said Roddy, thrown off balance.

Phoebe reappeared from her bedroom, carrying a large folio under her arm. 'Will there be room for this in the car?'

Roddy drew in his breath. 'Might be a bit of a squash.'

'Well . . .' Phoebe looked doubtful. 'You did say you wanted to see them. That's why you came, isn't it?'

'I thought they were all on slides.'

'Not all of them.' She brightened. 'We could look at them now, if you like. It would only take an hour or two.'

This, of course, was the last thing he wanted.

'Actually I'm sure it'll fit in. We'll just have to put the seats forward a bit.'

'Thanks.' Phoebe flashed him a smile. 'I'll get my bag.'

Darren shuffled in from the sitting room. 'Where's my tea?'

'I thought you were going to Sainsbury's,' said Kim, spooning sugar into his cup.

'It doesn't close till six.'

'Yes, but there won't be any stuff left by then.'

'The rugby starts in a minute.'

'Darren, what are your weights doing in my room?' Phoebe was standing in the hallway, ready to leave.

'There's more space for them there. Why, are they in the way?'

'Of course they're in the bloody way. I want them *out* when I get back, OK?'

'Fine, if you want to make a big deal out of it.'

'Well, thanks for the tea,' said Roddy, who hadn't drunk any. 'We seem to be off.'

'Nice jacket,' said Darren, as Roddy brushed past him in the kitchen doorway. 'Looks like it's from Next or somewhere, is it?'

The jacket in question, a sporty, cream linen number, had been tailor-made and had cost more than five hundred pounds.

'It's from Charles of Jermyn Street,' said Roddy.

'Oh. Yes, I thought so. I thought it was probably one of those places.'

Phoebe blew him a contemptuous kiss, and said: 'Goodbye, Kim. I'll give you a call when I'm coming back.'

'All right, take care. Have a good time, and don't do anything . . . don't do anything you'll regret.'

Roddy, fortunately, was out of earshot.

*

'He's an idiot, that guy,' said Phoebe, as they drove up the A1 towards Thirsk. 'And he's round at the flat all the time nowadays. It's really beginning to depress me.'

'Your flatmate seemed very nice.'

'Don't you think it's upsetting, though, when your friends choose totally unsuitable partners?'

Roddy accelerated to within ten feet of the car in front and flashed his headlights impatiently. So far he had been averaging about ninety-five miles an hour.

'I know what you mean, actually,' he said. 'Take this friend of mine. He was engaged to this woman for two years – cousin of the Duchess of —, as it happens. Not much of a looker but she had the most fabulous contacts. He was hoping to get into opera, you see. Anyway, suddenly, without a word of warning, he breaks the whole thing off and shacks up with this complete stranger: a primary school teacher, if you please. Nobody, but *nobody* had ever heard of her. Next thing you know, they're married. Come to think of it they seem very happy, but I still think he should have bitten the bullet and stuck with Mariella. Probably be running the ENO by now. D'you get my point?'

'I don't think we're talking about quite the same thing,' said Phoebe.

They drove in silence for several minutes.

'Seems pretty similar to me,' said Roddy.

*

It was getting on for six o'clock when they drove through Helmsley and then struck out in the direction of the North York Moors. The sunshine was still bright and Phoebe found that the moors themselves, which she had visited many times before and had always considered overpoweringly bleak, today seemed cheery and welcoming.

'You're so lucky,' she said, 'having a home out here. It must have been a wonderful place to grow up.'

'Oh, I didn't spend much time here when I was a kid. Thank God. This is the dreariest place on earth, if you ask me. Never come here now if I can avoid it.'

'So who lives in the house at the moment?'

'No one, really. There's a minimal staff – a couple of cooks and gardeners, and this old butler who's been with the family for about five hundred years, and that's about it. So the place is pretty much empty.' He took out another cigarette for himself and gave it Phoebe to light. 'Oh, apart from my father, of course.'

'I didn't realize he was still alive.'

Roddy smiled. 'Well, as far as anyone can tell.'

Not knowing quite what to make of this, Phoebe said: 'Do you know that John Bellany portrait of his father? I love that painting:

it's so rich and detailed – it tells you so much about the man, and at the same time it's done with such warmth and affection. It positively glows.'

'I know his work, yes. I'm not sure I'd recommend it to anyone as an investment these days. Look,' he said, fixing Phoebe with a half-humorous, half-admonitory stare, 'I hope you're not going to want to talk about painting all weekend. I get enough of that down in London.'

'What else are we here to talk about?'

'Anything.'

'"I live and breathe art",' said Phoebe. '"What other people refer to as 'the real world' has always seemed pale and insipid by comparison".'

'Well, that's as may be. Personally I find that sort of attitude rather affected.'

'Yes, but I didn't say it: you did. *Observer* magazine, April 1987.'

'Ah. Well, that's the sort of thing you're expected to say to journalists, in my line of business. You're supposed to take it with a pinch of salt.' Still puffing away on his cigarette, an edgier, more dangerous tone entering his voice, he said: 'Do you know what I'd planned to be doing this evening? I'd been invited to dinner with the Marquis of ——, at his flat in Knightsbridge. Also on the guest list were one of the most powerful theatrical producers in London, a member of the royal family, and an incredibly beautiful American actress, currently starring in a film being screened all over the country, who was flying over from Hollywood especially for the occasion.'

'And what am I supposed to say to that? You must obviously be bored with these people, if you'd rather spend the time up here with me, in the back of beyond.'

'Not necessarily. I look on this as a working weekend. After all, my livelihood depends on the cultivation of talented young people: and I do regard you as talented.' The compliment, he thought, was well calculated, and gave him the courage to add: 'What I'm saying, my dear, is that I'm expecting something a little more exciting from this weekend than a few hours in the drawing room discussing the influence of Velazquez on Francis Bacon.' And then, before Phoebe could reply, he caught sight of something on the distant horizon. 'Hello, there it is. The beloved homestead.'

*

Phoebe's first impression of Winshaw Towers was not encouraging. Perched almost on the crest of a vast, forbidding ridge, it cast deep dark shadows over the grounds beneath it. The gardens were not yet visible; but she could already make out a dense area of woodland which screened off the approach to the house, and at the foot of the hill lay a large expanse of dismal and featureless water. As for the mad conglomeration of gothic, neo-gothic, sub-gothic and pseudo-gothic towers which gave the house its name, they resembled nothing so much as a giant black hand, gnarled and deformed: its fingers clawed at the heavens, as if to snatch down the setting sun which shone like a burnished penny and would soon, it seemed, have descended inexorably into its grasp.

'Not exactly a holiday camp, is it?' said Roddy.

'Aren't there any other houses around here?'

'There's a little village about five miles away, on the other side of the hill. That's about it.'

'Why would anyone want to live in such a lonely spot?'

'God knows. The main body of the house was built in 1625, so they say. It didn't come into my family for another fifty years or so. One of my ancestors, Alexander, bought it up – for reasons best known to himself – and then started adding to it, which is why there's hardly any of the original brickwork left. Now this trumped-up duckpond' – he gestured out of the window, for the road was now running parallel to the water's edge – 'goes by the name of Cavendish Tarn. It isn't really a tarn, of course, because it's man-made. Cavendish Winshaw was my great-great-uncle, and he had the whole thing dug out and filled with water about a hundred and twenty years ago. I think he must have envisaged hours of happy pleasure-boating and trout-fishing. Well, just look at it! You'd catch your death of pneumonia if you tried to stay out there for more than five minutes. I've always suspected that

Cavendish – and Alexander too, if it comes to that – must have belonged to the . . . well, the eccentric side of the family.'

'And what does that mean, exactly?'

'Oh, didn't you know? The Winshaws have a long and honourable history of insanity. It continues right up to the present day, as a matter of fact.'

'How fascinating,' said Phoebe. 'Somebody should write a book about you all.' There was a knowing, mischievous undertone to this remark which a more alert listener than Roddy might have registered.

'Somebody *was* writing a book about us, now you come to mention it,' he said blithely. 'I even met up with him once: gave him an interview a few years ago. Inquisitive sort, I must say. Anyway, all that's gone very quiet. Good job too.'

They had arrived at the main driveway. He swung the car in and they were at once plunged into a dark tunnel of foliage. In days long past, perhaps, it might have been broad enough to admit a fair-sized vehicle, but now their windscreen and roof were under constant attack from vines, ivy, creepers and overhanging branches of every description. And when they finally emerged into what was left of the daylight, the same neglect was evident on every side: the lawns were overgrown and choked with weeds, the location of paths and flowerbeds could only be guessed at, and most of the outbuildings seemed in a state of near-collapse, with cracked windows, crumbling masonry and doors hanging off rusty hinges. Roddy seemed impervious to all of this: he drove with inscrutable single-mindedness right up to the front door, and the car pulled to a halt on the pebbled forecourt.

They got out of the car and Phoebe looked around her, silenced by awe but also by a strange, unaccustomed apprehension. She realized, now, that Roddy had managed to lure her into a situation of peculiar loneliness and vulnerability, and she began to shiver. And then, while he was taking their cases out of the boot, she glanced up at the second storey and a movement behind one of the mullioned windows caught her eye. She saw it for only a brief moment: a pale, drawn and crooked face, surmounted by a wild tangle of grey hair, staring down at the new arrivals with a look of lunatic malevolence which was enough to freeze the blood.

*

Roddy sank down on to the bed and dabbed with a silk handkerchief at his now beetroot-coloured face.

'Phew. I wasn't expecting that, I must say.'

'Well, I did offer to carry them for you,' said Phoebe, walking over to the bay window.

A prolonged bout of bell-ringing and hammering on the front door had failed to produce any response, so Roddy had been obliged to use his own keys, and had then insisted on taking both their cases upstairs himself, with Phoebe's folio wedged precariously beneath his arm. She had followed him in silence, amazed at the atmosphere of gloom and decay which permeated the whole house. The tapestries which hung from the walls were threadbare and tattered; the heavy velvet curtains on the landings were already drawn, admitting nothing of the dying sunlight; two suits of armour, standing precariously to attention in opposite alcoves, seemed about to fall apart from rust; and even the heads of the various unfortunate species of wildlife which had ended their days adorning the walls wore expressions of the utmost despondency.

'Pyles is around, but he's sure to be dead drunk by now,' Roddy explained, between gasps for breath. 'Here, let's see if this does the trick.'

He took hold of a bell-rope hanging above the bed and pulled on it violently six or seven times. From the distant bowels of the house they could hear a far-off ringing. 'That ought to do it,' he said, panting heavily and lying flat out on the bed, and after about five minutes the approach of footsteps along the corridor could be heard: their tread irregular and unbelievably slow, with one step much heavier than the other. As they came closer, they were accompanied by a dreadful wheezing. Then the footsteps came to an abrupt stop outside their door, the wheezing continued, and a few seconds later there was a loud knock.

'Come in!' said Roddy, and the door creaked open to reveal a shabby, cadaverous figure whose eyes, set off by thick, beetling brows, flickered suspiciously about the room before coming to rest on Phoebe, seated at the bay window, who stared back in astonishment. The smell of alcohol overwhelmed her: she thought she would get drunk just by breathing.

'Young Master Winshaw,' the butler rasped, his voice hoarse and expressionless, his gaze still fixed on the female visitor. 'What a pleasure to have you with us again.'

'You got my message, I take it.'

'I did, sir. Your room was prepared this morning. However, I was not aware – that is, I do not recall being informed – that you would be bringing a . . .' (he coughed a dry cough, and moistened his lips) '. . . companion.'

Roddy sat up. 'This is Miss Barton, Pyles, a young artist who I hope to be representing in a professional capacity in the very near future. She'll be staying a day or two. I thought this room might be the most comfortable for her.'

'As you wish, sir. I'll go down and tell Cook that we shall be four for dinner.'

'Four? Why, who else is coming?'

'I received a telephone call earlier this afternoon, sir, from Miss Hilary. She's flying up this evening, it seems, and she also intends to bring a . . .' (clearing his throat once again, and licking the cracked corners of his mouth) '. . . companion.'

'I see.' Roddy seemed none too pleased with this information. 'Well in that case surely we shall be five for dinner? I assume my father will be eating with us.'

'I'm afraid not, sir. Your father suffered a slight misfortune this afternoon, and has already retired. The doctor has advised him not to exert himself any further today.'

'Misfortune? What sort of misfortune?'

'A most regrettable accident, sir. My fault entirely. I was taking him out for his afternoon constitutional, when I – most carelessly – lost control of his chair, and sent it hurtling down a slope, where it crashed. Crashed into the hen coop.'

'My God – was there . . . was there any injury?'

'A chicken was decapitated, sir.'

Roddy eyed him narrowly, as if trying to decide whether this was a joke. 'All right, Pyles,' he said at last. 'I'm sure Miss Barton would like to freshen up after her journey. You may tell Cook that we shall be four for dinner.'

'Very good, sir,' he said, shambling towards the door.

'What are we having, anyway?'

'Chicken,' said Pyles, without turning round.

Phoebe and Roddy were alone again. There was a difficult pause, and then Roddy said, with an awkward laugh: 'He should really be put out to grass. Mind you, I don't know who else they could find to look after a place like this.'

'Should I go and see your father, do you think? There might be something I could do.'

'No, no, the doctor will have seen to all that. Best not to get involved.'

'Your butler seems to have a dreadful limp.'

'Yes, poor soul.' He got up from the bed and began to pace the room aimlessly. 'That goes back about ten or fifteen years, when my uncle, Lawrence, still lived here. They were having a lot of trouble with poachers at the time and some man traps were put down. Seems that old Pyles got caught in one – late in the evening, as I understand it. Poor devil, they didn't find him till the morning. The pain must have been shocking. That's when he turned to drink, apparently. They even say that it . . . you know, turned his head a bit. Made him a bit strange – mentally, I mean.'

Phoebe said nothing.

'Well, I did warn you what this place was like.'

'Am I expected to dress for dinner?' she asked.

'Good Lord, no. Not on my account: and certainly not on account of my dear sister and her so-called companion. Which reminds me, I'd better go down and put the landing lights on for them. Pyles is bound to forget. Why don't I come back up for you in about ten minutes or so, and we could perhaps do a quick guided tour before it gets dark?'

'What about your father?'

Roddy's smile was a perfect blank.

'What about him?'

It was dusk. Roddy and Phoebe stood on the terrace overlooking Cavendish Tarn, drinking a Château-Lafite 1970, newly brought up from the cellar. They had been on a cursory tour of the house, during which Roddy had proved himself wearily knowledgeable on the subject of Ionic columns and basket arches, and Phoebe had done her dutiful best to admire the brick diapers and the flush quoins and the close carving on the spandrels. Now it appeared that Roddy had other things on his mind. While Phoebe stared out at the two parallel rows of landing lights which stretched across the lake and seemed to converge only at its furthest shore, Roddy's eyes were turned intently on her profile. She knew that he was about to say something unwelcome, and steeled herself for it.

'You're very beautiful,' he said at last.

'I don't really see,' she answered – slowly, and not without a smile – 'what that's got to do with anything.'

'It's why you're here, and we both know it,' said Roddy. He shifted a few inches closer. 'There's a cousin of mine called Thomas. A fair bit older than me – getting on for seventy, now, I should think. He's quite big in the city. When he was younger – back in the late fifties, early sixties – he lent money to some film companies and got to know a few people in the business. Used to hang around the studios, and so on.'

'Is there a point to all this?'

'Hang on, I'm just coming to it. You see, I was only about eight or nine at the time, and Thomas – well, Thomas was, you know . . . a bit of a lad. A bit of an old rake. He used to bring me these photographs.'

'Photographs?'

'Pretty run of the mill stuff, most of them. Scenes from nudist films that he'd been involved with, that sort of thing. But there was one photograph – just an ordinary portrait shot, head and shoulders – of an actress: she was called Shirley Eaton. And I was really smitten with it for a while. Used to sleep with it under my pillow, if you can believe that. Of course, I was very young. But the funny thing is –'

'– that I look exactly like her?'

'Well, you do, actually.' He frowned. 'Why, has somebody told you that before?'

'No, but I could see it coming. And now I'm to have the honour of helping you to live out your childhood fantasies, I suppose.' Roddy didn't answer that, and she continued to stare ahead, relishing the silence, until she noticed a red light winking in the night sky. 'Look, there's something up there.'

'Sister dearest, I expect.' He left his wineglass on the balustrade, and said: 'Come on, let's get down to the jetty and give her a proper welcome.'

The descent to the lake involved crossing three more lawns – all of them thick with wild, unkempt grass – linked steeply by walkways which had to be negotiated with care, for many of the slabs were loose, or concealed cracks which were big enough to trap the unwary foot. Finally, a set of rotting wooden steps led down to the water itself. They arrived just in time to see the plane skim down on to the tarn's moonlit surface, and then taxi towards them, sending out shockwaves of foam as it came to a graceful if noisy halt at the edge of the jetty. Seconds later a door opened and the ash-blonde tresses of Britain's most highly paid columnist popped into view.

'Roddy?' she said, peering out into the semi-dark. 'You couldn't be a love and take this case for me, could you?'

She handed him her case and squeezed herself through the doorway, to be followed by a square-shouldered, chisel-jawed, very bronzed and muscular figure who leapt out behind her and swung the door shut in one lithe, athletic movement.

'Have you met Conrad, my pilot?'

'A pleasure,' said Roddy, shaking his hand and almost getting his fingers broken in the process.

'And I don't believe . . .' Hilary prompted, having glimpsed Phoebe lurking in the shadows.

'Phoebe Barton,' said Roddy, as she stepped forward shyly. 'Phoebe is my guest this weekend. She's a most gifted young painter.'

'Of course.' Hilary appraised her coolly. 'They always are. Is this your first time at the house of horrors, my dear?'

Phoebe had the sense that a clever answer was expected of her; but all she could manage was: 'Yes.'

'In that case, welcome,' said Hilary, leading the way up the steps, 'to Baskerville Hall. Come on, everybody, I'm famished. We had the most loathsome flight.'

3

The dining table could comfortably have seated twenty. The four of them huddled together at one end, and beneath the arches of that cavernous, overblown chamber, their voices sounded puny and faint. Not that Phoebe and Conrad had much to say in any case: for the first twenty minutes or so, brother and sister conducted an exclusive and (despite all the disparaging remarks Roddy had been making about Hilary before her arrival) affectionate conversation which consisted entirely of salacious gossip about mutual friends. Phoebe occasionally read the review pages of the national papers and watched arts programmes on the television, so she recognized most of the names as belonging to that small, self-elected and mutually supporting circle which seemed – for better or worse – to be at the heart of what passed for cultural life down in London. What she couldn't quite understand was the odd, persistent note of reverence which underpinned even the sleaziest or most trivial of the anecdotes: the sense that Roddy and Hilary did, in fact, ascribe real importance to everything said and done by these people; that they did believe them, at heart, to be something like colossi bestriding the national stage, even though Phoebe could easily have gone through the entire roster of her friends, colleagues, neighbours and patients and not found a single person in whom their names would have produced even the dimmest flicker of recognition. None the less, the flow of private jokes and inside stories showed no sign of abating until Roddy moved things on to an altogether more personal level, by asking after the health of his brother-in-law.

'Oh, Peter's on some freebie in Barbados. Won't be back until Tuesday.'

'Didn't you want to go with him?'

'I wasn't asked, dear. He's gone with that bitch of a Features Editor.'

Roddy smiled. 'Well, you always said you wanted an open marriage.'

'Interesting little phrase, isn't it, though: "open" marriage? Makes it sound like a drain, or a sewer. Quite appropriate in our case, really.' Absently, she wiped the lipstick traces from the rim of her wineglass. 'Actually he's not such a bad old sod. He got me that Matisse for my birthday.'

Phoebe could not contain her astonishment. 'You *own* a Matisse?'

Hilary looked up sharply, and said, 'Good God, she talks.' Then, turning back to her brother: 'The trouble is that it clashes horribly with the green in the music room. We're going to have to redecorate the whole bloody thing again.'

'On the subject of presents,' said Roddy, 'you realize it was father's birthday two weeks ago?'

'Oh, shit. I forgot all about it. How about you?'

'Slipped my mind completely.'

'Why isn't he eating with us, anyway?'

'Had a bit of an accident this afternoon, it seems. His wheel-chair got out of control.'

'Pyles again?'

'Naturally.'

'Oh well.' She giggled. 'Perhaps we should slip him a few quid and make sure he does the job properly next time. I suppose I'd better go up and see the old misery at some point tomorrow.' She pushed aside her plate of half-eaten food and noticed that Conrad was still struggling with his. 'You don't have to finish it, darling. We won't be offended.'

'It's delicious,' said Conrad.

'No, it isn't delicious,' she said, like a grown-up talking to a retarded child. 'It's shit.'

'Oh.' He put down his fork. 'I don't know much about food,' he confessed, to the company in general.

'Conrad's American,' said Hilary, as if this explained everything.

'Do you own many famous paintings?' Phoebe asked.

'She has something of a one-track mind, doesn't she?' Hilary aimed this remark at no one in particular, and then put a finger

to her chin, affecting an attempt at recollection. 'Well, let me see
. . . There's that Klee, and one or two Picassos, and some Turner
drawings . . . Plus a few hideous eyesores by protégés of my
brother . . .'

'Why did you buy them,' Phoebe asked, 'if you think they're
hideous?'

'Well, I'm an innocent in these matters, you see. Roddy tells me
that they're good, and I believe him. We're all at his mercy.' She
thought about this for a moment and leaned forward. 'Except for
you, of course. After all, you're a professional. You must have an
opinion about the artists he represents.'

'All I know is what I saw in the gallery last week.'

'And?'

'And . . .' Phoebe glanced at Roddy, then plunged on. 'I thought
it was dreadful. Elementary stuff that wouldn't even have been
given a pass at any decent art school. Wispy pastels and those
terrible would-be naïve landscapes – except that they weren't
even . . . *clean* enough to be called naïve – which looked as
though they'd been knocked off by some pampered socialite's
daughter to pass the time between garden parties. The photographs of the artist were nice, though. I'm sure she went down a
storm at the private view.'

'Hermione happens to be very talented,' said Roddy indignantly. 'And yes, it's true that I did know her brother at Trinity,
but not everybody that I represent comes from that kind of
background, or has to be introduced to me personally. I do go
round all the art schools, you know, looking for new work. I've
just taken this chap on, and he lives in Brixton. Thoroughly
working class. It's pretty dangerous stuff, too: pretty ground-
breaking. He takes these enormous canvases and holds them at a
sort of angle and then he tips these big cans of paint over them so
that it all runs –'

Phoebe tutted impatiently. 'That sort of stunt was interesting
for about five minutes in the sixties. You're so easily taken in,
you people.'

'Forthright little thing, isn't she?' said Hilary.

'Well, it matters, you see. Because this is how reputations get inflated and mediocre work gets promoted, and then even when a good painter *does* manage to slip through the net you've already pushed the prices up so high that the smaller galleries can't afford to buy them and it all ends up going into private collections. So what you're doing, in effect, is robbing the country of its own culture. It's as simple as that.' She sipped her wine, somewhat abashed.

'I wonder how long she's been working on that little speech?' Hilary asked.

'Well, it's a point of view,' said Roddy, 'and she's entitled to it.' He turned to Conrad, hoping to lighten the atmosphere. 'What do you make of all this?'

'I don't know much about art.'

'Have another drink, dear,' said Hilary, refilling his glass. 'You're doing just fine.'

'I'm not trying to start an argument, or anything,' said Phoebe, who was growing more wary of Hilary by the minute, 'but I always had the impression that you agreed with me on this. I thought you dismissed the whole business of collecting modern art as so much snobbery.'

Hilary's eyes widened, and for several seconds she didn't answer. Her left hand groped towards a bowl of fruit between the two silver candelabra, and she broke off a small cluster of grapes, one of which she then began to peel slowly, sliding her long fingernail between the skin and the purple flesh.

'Have we met before?' she asked suddenly.

'No,' said Phoebe. 'No, I don't think so. Why?'

'I'd just like to know,' she said, finishing one grape and starting on another, 'what makes you think you have any kind of insight into my personal opinions.'

'I'll tell you what,' said Roddy, keeping a close watch on his sister's fingers. 'Why don't we all go into the smoking room and make ourselves comfortable, if we're going to chat away like this?'

'I'm only going by what I read in your column once,' said Phoebe. 'I remember when somebody – some businessman or other – had just paid hundreds and thousands of pounds for a

Rothko to go in his private collection, and you went on about what a waste of money it was and how it could all have gone into building schools and hospitals.'

There was a pause, before Hilary said, 'She really does come out with the most remarkable things,' in a slightly strangled voice. Then, turning back to Phoebe: 'It's only a bit of junk for the newspapers, you know. I don't write it on tablets of stone. Besides, that column has literally millions of readers. You don't think I'd share my *beliefs* – anything that was actually *mine* – with all those people, do you?'

'I thought that was the whole point.'

'There's this thing called the real world,' said Hilary. 'Have you heard of it?' She didn't wait for the answer. 'You see, we can't all decide that we want to be artists, sitting up in some lofty enclosure, knocking off the occasional painting whenever the fancy takes us. Some of us have to work to order, and meet deadlines, and little, unimportant things like that. Perhaps what you really need is a lesson in how it feels to be stuck in front of a keyboard with five hundred words to write and the subs expecting it in thirty minutes.'

'I don't paint for a living,' said Phoebe. 'I'm a health visitor. Ask anyone who works in my profession and you'll find that they know all about pressure.'

'I'll give you an example of *pressure*.' Hilary was on to her fourth grape by now. 'Pressure is being holed up in some hotel in the middle of Kent with three colleagues and a fax machine, knowing that you've got to put together an autumn schedule by Thursday morning.'

'Possibly,' said Phoebe. 'But you might just as well say that pressure is having twenty pounds in your purse and wondering how you're going to make it last until the end of the week. Or finding that you're pregnant again two days after your husband has lost his job. That's the sort of problem I come across most days, and these people don't even have the consolation of feeling that the decisions they have to make are in any way glamorous, or make any kind of difference to people's lives other than their own.'

A smile spread itself across Hilary's face, and she turned to her brother. 'Oh, darling, she's priceless. I really must congratulate you. How *did* you find her? You realize what you've got here, don't you? I do believe you've managed to track down a *bona fide*, old-fashioned, dyed-in-the-wool, head-in-the-clouds *socialist*. They're *terribly* rare, you know. And now, clever old you, you've managed to catch this creature and transport her all the way up here. I mean, whatever next? Are you hoping that she'll mate in captivity?'

Roddy jumped to his feet.

'All right, Hilary: that's enough. Just leave her alone.'

'It's a bit late to come over all chivalrous, isn't it?'

'You're being offensive.'

'She won't go to bed with you, you know. I would have thought that was pretty obvious.'

Roddy turned to their guests. 'I must apologize for my sister. She's clearly had a very hard week. All the same, that doesn't excuse her manners. I think you'll agree they've been appalling.'

'I don't know much about manners,' said Conrad.

Hilary put her arm around him and kissed him on the cheek. 'Conrad doesn't know much about anything,' she said, 'except for flying, and fucking.' She got up, and, taking his hand, pulled him gently with her. 'I think it's about time I put his second area of expertise to the test. Good-night to you both.' And to Phoebe she added: 'It's been an education, my dear. I wouldn't have missed it for the world.'

Once they had left, Roddy and Phoebe sat in silence for some time.

'That was nice of you,' she said finally. 'Thanks.'

He glanced at her: perhaps on the look-out for irony.

'Pardon?'

'Sticking up for me. You didn't have to do that.'

'Well, you know . . . She was way out of line.'

'She doesn't seem to have a very high opinion of your motives for bringing me here.'

Roddy gave an apologetic shrug, and said: 'Perhaps she's right.'

'So what's the deal?'

'The deal?'

'I sleep with you, and I get – what? A mixed show? A show of my own? Written about in the newspapers? Introduced to lots of wealthy and influential people?'

'I think you're jumping the gun a bit.'

'And do we do it just the once, or is this going to be a regular thing?'

Roddy walked over to the fireplace, where the two bars of an electric fire were doing their feeble best to make an impact on the room's deathly chill. He seemed about to embark upon a speech.

'You're quite right, of course.' The words came with some difficulty. 'Clearly I wanted to sleep with you – I mean, what man in his right mind wouldn't? – and I knew that the only way I was going to . . . persuade you, was by offering to help with your career. Which I'm certainly in a position to do. But the thing is' – he laughed awkwardly, running a hand through his hair – 'I mean, it galls me to admit that anything my sister might say could have any influence, but – hearing her ranting on like that, it has made me realize that my assumptions, my *pre*sumptions, even, have been decidedly . . . Well, the whole business suddenly seems dreadfully cheap. And I feel that I owe you an apology. I really am very sorry: for bringing you here under . . . false pretences.'

'You must think I'm very innocent,' said Phoebe, joining him at the fireplace, 'if you expected me to come up here without suspecting anything.'

'So why did you come?'

'Well, that's a good question. Let me tell you two things.' She leaned back against the mantelpiece, only occasionally turning to meet his eye. 'First of all, although I do genuinely believe that you know hardly anything about art, that the power you wield is unhealthy, and that your business practices probably stink to high heaven, I don't find you totally unattractive.'

Roddy snorted. 'Well, that's something, I suppose.'

'Secondly.' Phoebe hesitated, her eyes closed, and then took a breath. 'I've never really been brave enough to say this to anyone before, but – You see, over the years, I have, with great difficulty, built up a certain . . . faith in myself. In my painting, I mean. In fact, it's got to the point where I think it's probably quite good.' She smiled. 'That must sound very arrogant.'

'Not at all.'

'It wasn't always like this. There was a time when I didn't have any faith in myself at all. It's quite . . . painful to talk about, but – well, it happened when I was a student. I'd given up nursing for a while to go to art college, and I was living with some people in this house – we were sharing it – when someone came and stayed with us for a few days. A visitor. And one day I was out shopping, and I came back to find that he was in my room, looking at this painting that was only half-finished. Less than half-finished, really. And it was as if . . . as if he'd seen me naked, I suppose. And not just that, but he started trying to talk about the painting, and it was obvious that it meant something completely different to him, that I was completely failing to communicate anything through it, in fact, and I . . . It was very strange. A few days later he left without saying anything. Didn't say goodbye to any of us. He left us all feeling . . . empty, somehow, and I couldn't bear the thought of looking at those paintings again – of anyone looking at them. The upshot was that I asked the landlady if we could have a bonfire in the back yard, and I burnt everything I'd done. Every painting, every drawing. I dropped out of college and went back into nursing full time. And that was that for a while. I didn't paint at all. Not that I wasn't thinking about it. I still used to visit galleries, and read all the magazines and everything. There was this sort of – empty space, inside me, where I used to paint, and I was looking for something to fill it: some*one*, I should say, because I was longing just to find a picture – any picture – which would leap out at me and suddenly . . . *connect*. Do you know that feeling? You must do: coming across an artist whose work speaks to you so directly, it's as if you both understand the same private language – somehow confirming everything you've ever thought and at the same time saying something completely new.' Roddy was mute, incomprehending. 'You don't, do you? Well, anyway. It never happened, needless to say. But what did happen was that a couple of years later I got a parcel in the post, from one of my old lecturers at the college. They'd been having some sort of clear-out, and they'd found some sketches of mine, apparently, which they wanted to return. So I unpacked these things and started looking at them again. Funnily enough, there was an early version of the painting which had caused so much trouble in the first place, the one this man had completely misunderstood. And seeing it again – seeing all of them again, really – I realized how wrong he'd been: how wrong *I'd* been, to over-react like that. Because I *knew*, as soon as I saw them after all this time I knew that they were good. I knew that I'd been on to something. I knew that there was no one else around who was – I won't say better than me, I don't have that much of an ego – but who was really working in the same field, or attempting anything at all similar . . . It just gave me my confidence back, somehow, made me feel that I'd actually been doing something at least as worthwhile as all the other painters who were getting bought and sold and commissioned and exhibited. And I've never really lost that feeling. I do feel that I . . . that I *deserve*. So what you should know, I suppose, is that I'm pretty determined. I don't think there's anything, now, anything in the world that matters to me as much as finding some kind of audience for my work.'

She took a few sips from her glass and brushed a strand of hair back from her brow. Roddy didn't speak for some time.

'What we should probably do,' he said at last, 'is take a look through the pictures tomorrow and see what we can arrange.' Phoebe nodded. 'Right now, I think we'd better go to bed.' She looked up, questioning. 'Separately,' he explained.

'All right.'

Together they climbed the Great Staircase, and at the entrance to the East Corridor, they kissed a formal good-night.

4

Phoebe felt tiny in the four-poster. Her mattress was soft and full of lumps, and although she had intended to lie to the side of the bed nearest the window, she found herself rolled by the weight of her own body into a deep valley at the centre. The bed creaked whenever she moved: but then the whole house seemed to be forever creaking, or groaning, or whispering, or rustling, as if never for a moment at ease with itself, and in an effort to close her ears to this disquieting soundtrack, she tried to focus her mind on the day's strange events. She was pleased, on the whole, with the way things had worked out with Roddy. Even before arriving at Winshaw Towers, she had taken the reluctant decision to sleep with him if he made this his absolute precondition for promoting her work, but she was glad that she hadn't been obliged to go through with it. Instead, something much better, and much more unexpected, was starting to emerge from their weekend together: a sense of mutual understanding. She even realized – very much to her own surprise – that she was beginning to trust him. And in the warm glow of this realization, she permitted herself a fantasy: the same fantasy to which all artists, however good their intentions, however unflinching their principles, have recourse from time to time. It was a fantasy of success; of recognition, and acclaim. Phoebe's ambitions were too modest to encompass worldwide celebrity, or serious wealth, but she did dream – as she often had before – of having her work seen and appreciated by other painters; of touching the lives and colouring the perceptions of a few members of the public; of being exhibited, perhaps, in her home town, so that she might give something back to the people with whom she had grown up, repay her parents for the faith and patience which they had vouched her and which had been so valuable during her worst moments of self-doubt. At the thought that some – or even all – of this might now, possibly, miraculously, be about to happen, she stretched her legs beneath the grey, musty sheets and added a whole new chorus of delicious creaks to the furtive stirrings of the house itself.

But all at once she was aware of another noise, too. It was coming from the direction of the door, which she had taken the precaution of locking before getting into bed. She sat up cautiously and reached out for the table lamp, which cast a murky, ineffectual glow over the room. She looked towards the door. Suddenly feeling like the leading lady in some low-budget and none too original horror film, she realized that the handle was turning. There was someone out in the corridor, trying to get in.

Phoebe swung her legs out of bed and tiptoed towards the door. She was wearing a thick, striped cotton nightshirt which buttoned up at the front and reached down almost to her knees.

'Who is it?' she asked, in a brave, slightly quavering voice, after the handle had been tried a few more times.

'Phoebe? Are you awake?' It was Roddy's voice: a loud whisper.

She sighed with exasperation. 'Well of course I'm awake,' she said, unlocking the door and holding it ajar. 'If I wasn't before I certainly am now.'

'Can I come in?'

'I suppose so.'

She opened the door and Roddy, who was wearing a satin kimono, slid inside and sat down on the bed.

'What is it?'

'Come and sit down a minute.'

She sat beside him.

'I couldn't sleep,' he said.

No further explanation seemed to be forthcoming.

'So?'

'So I thought I'd come and see how you were.'

'Well, I'm fine. I mean, I haven't contracted any life-threatening diseases in the last half hour or anything.'

'No, but I mean – I came to check that you weren't too upset.'

'Upset?'

'By my sister, and . . . oh, I don't know, by everything. I thought it might all have been a bit much for you.'

'That's very nice of you, but I'm fine. Really. I'm quite a tough little cookie, you know.' She smiled. 'Are you *sure* that's the reason you came?'

'Of course it is. Well, pretty much.' He sidled closer towards her. 'I was lying in bed, if you must know, thinking about that story you told me. About you burning all your paintings. I was thinking that – well, correct me if I'm wrong here – but that's not the sort of story you would have told to just anybody. It occurred to me that possibly' (he put his arm around her shoulder) 'you must have begun to like me a little bit.'

'Possibly,' said Phoebe, pulling fractionally away from him.

'There's a feeling between us, isn't there?' said Roddy. 'I'm not just imagining it. We started something down there.'

'Possibly,' Phoebe repeated. Her voice was toneless. She had begun to feel strangely removed from the situation, and hardly noticed, at first, when Roddy kissed her softly on the mouth. She noticed the second kiss, though: the feel of his tongue slipping between her moist lips. She pushed him away gently and said: 'Look, I'm not sure this is such a good idea.'

'No? I'll tell you what is a good idea, though. November the 13th.'

'November the 13th?' she said, dimly aware that he was starting to unbutton her nightshirt. 'What about it?'

'The opening night of your show, of course.' He undid the last three buttons.

Phoebe laughed. 'Are you serious?'

'Of course I am.' He pulled the nightshirt back over her shoulders. Her skin, in the weak glow of the table lamp, was golden and flawless: ochre, almost. 'I've been looking in my diary. It's the earliest we can manage.'

'But you haven't even seen the pictures yet,' said Phoebe, as his finger began to trace a line from her neck across her collarbone and beyond.

'It'll mean a bit of reshuffling,' said Roddy, kissing her again on her lips, which were wide with astonishment. 'But who cares.' He drew her nightshirt further open and brushed his hand across her breast.

Phoebe felt herself being pushed back on to the pillows. There were fingers stroking the inside of her thigh. Her head was swimming. November the 13th was only six weeks away. Did she have enough pictures for a major exhibition? Ones that she was really happy with? Was there time to finish the two large canvases which stood half-completed in her studio? The rush of excitement made her weak and dizzy. Her mind was so busy racing over the possibilities that it seemed the easiest thing in the world to let Roddy lie on top of her, his kimono thrown aside to reveal strong forearms and a hairless chest, his knees pushing their way between her legs, his tongue working assiduously at her nipple, until the impulse to resist asserted itself again and her whole body tautened.

'Look, Roddy – we have to talk about this.'

'I know. There are hundreds of things we have to talk about. Prices, for instance.'

In spite of herself she responded to the movement of his hand, and stretched her legs even further apart. '. . . Prices?' she said, with an effort.

'We've got to get them as high as possible. I've got Japanese clients who'll pay thirty or forty thousand for a big canvas. Seven by nine, something like that. Abstracts, landscapes, minimalism, anything: they don't care. Does that feel nice, by the way?'

'Thirty or forty . . .? But I've never painted anything that . . . Yes, yes it does, it feels very nice.'

'Stay there a minute.'

He rolled off and took something from a drawer in the bedside table. Phoebe could hear the sound of a packet being opened and rubber being unfurled.

'We'll have to take the show to New York, of course,' said Roddy, sitting with his back towards her, his fingers working with a dexterity born of long practice, 'after it's been in London a few weeks. I've got a sort of twinning arrangement with a gallery over there, so I don't anticipate any problems.' He replaced the packet and lay on his back. 'Well, what do you think?'

'I think you're mad,' said Phoebe, giggling joyfully. Accepting the invitation in his eyes, she raised herself and knelt over him, her hair brushing his face. 'And I don't think I should be doing this.'

But she did.

Roddy fell asleep soon afterwards. He slept on his side, facing the wall, taking up three quarters of the bed. Phoebe dozed more fitfully, her mind still dancing to the tune of his promises, awash with visions of the glories soon to come. At one point she was awoken by voices coming from the grounds outside her window. Pulling back the curtains she saw two figures wielding mallets and chasing each other across the floodlit lawn. Hilary's piercing cackle merged with the more apologetic laughter of Conrad as he explained that 'I don't know much about croquet'. They both appeared to be naked.

Phoebe returned to bed, tried to get Roddy to move, failed, and then had little option other than to lie up against his back. For a while she tried putting her arm across his shoulder: but she might as well have been hugging a block of marble.

*

She woke to the sound of loud groans coming from a distant room. She was alone in the bed, and the weather was grey and drizzly. She guessed it was between nine and ten in the morning. Hastily pulling a blouse and trousers over her nightshirt, and slipping shoes on to her bare feet, Phoebe went out into the corridor to investigate. Pyles was limping by, carrying a tray which contained the congealed remains of an uneaten breakfast.

'Good morning, Miss Barton,' he said coldly.

'Is anything the matter?' she asked. 'It sounds as though somebody might be in pain.'

'Mr Winshaw, I fear, is suffering the consequences of my carelessness yesterday. The bruising is worse than we thought.'

'Has someone sent for the doctor?'

'The doctor, as I understand it, prefers not to be disturbed on a Sunday.'

'Then I'll attend to him.'

This suggestion met with stunned silence.

'I *am* a qualified nurse, you know.'

'I scarcely think that would be appropriate,' the butler murmured. 'Too bad.'

She hurried off down the corridor, paused outside the room from which the groans were issuing, then knocked and walked briskly in. Mortimer Winshaw – whose pale and crooked face she had glimpsed behind his bedroom window when she arrived yesterday – was sitting up in bed, his hands clutching the blankets and his teeth clenched in pain. He opened his eyes when Phoebe came in, gasped, and pulled the bedclothes up to his chin, as if modesty demanded the concealment of his egg-stained pyjamas.

'Who are you?' he said.

'My name's Phoebe,' she answered. 'I'm a friend of your son's.' Mortimer gave a snort of indignation. 'I'm also a nurse. I could hear you from my room and thought I might be able to do something to help. You must be very uncomfortable.'

'How do I know you're a real nurse?' he said, after a pause.

'Well, you'll just have to trust me.'

She met his gaze.

'Where does it hurt?'

'All down here.' Mortimer drew the bedclothes back and pulled down his pyjama bottoms. His right thigh was severely bruised and swollen. 'That clumsy oaf of a butler. He was probably trying to kill me.'

Phoebe inspected the bruise, then pulled off his pyjama bottoms altogether.

'Let me know if this hurts.'

She raised his leg and tested the range of movement of the hip.

'Of course it damn well hurts,' said Mortimer.

'Well, there's nothing broken, anyway. You could probably do with some painkillers.'

'There are pills in the chest over there. Hundreds of 'em.'

She made him take two Coproxamol, with a glass of water.

'We'll make up an ice pack in a minute. That should help it go down. Do you mind if I take this dressing off?'

His shin was loosely bound with a yellowing bandage which should clearly have been changed some time ago. Underneath was a nasty leg ulcer.

'What's my treacherous little runt of a son doing bringing nurses up here, anyway?' he said, as she unwound the dressing.

'I paint as well,' Phoebe explained.

'Ah. Any good at it?'

'That's not really for me to say.'

She fetched cotton wool from the chest, water from the basin in an adjoining washroom, and began to clean up the ulcer.

'You have a delicate touch,' said Mortimer. 'Painting and nursing. Well, well. Both of them rather demanding vocations, I would have thought. Do you have your own studio?'

'Not my own, no. I share with another woman.'

'Doesn't sound very satisfactory.'

'I manage.' She took a strip of clean bandage and began to wind it around the scrawny, brittle shin. 'When was this dressing last changed?'

'Doctor comes about twice a week.'

'It should be changed daily. How long have you been in the wheelchair?'

'A year or so. It started with osteoarthritis: then these ulcers.' He watched her working for a few minutes, and said: 'Pretty, aren't you?' Phoebe smiled. 'Makes a change to see a young woman about the place.'

'Apart from your daughter, you mean.'

'What, Hilary? Don't tell me she's here as well.'

'You didn't know?'

Mortimer went tight-lipped. 'Let me give you a warning about my family,' he said eventually, 'in case you hadn't worked it out already. They're the meanest, greediest, cruellest bunch of back-stabbing penny-pinching bastards who ever crawled across the face of the earth. And I include my own offspring in that statement.'

Phoebe, who was on the point of tying up the bandage, stopped to look at him in surprise.

'There's only ever been two nice members of my family: Godfrey, my brother, who died in the war, and my sister Tabitha, who they've managed to shut up in a loony bin for the last half a century.'

For some reason she very much didn't want to hear this. 'I'll go and get that ice pack,' she said, standing.

'Before you go,' said Mortimer, as she made for the door, 'how much do they pay you?'

'Pardon?'

'At the hospital, or wherever it is you work.'

'Oh. Not much. Not much at all, really.'

'Come and work for me,' he said. 'I'll give you a proper wage.' He thought for a moment, and named a five-figure sum. 'They don't look after me here. There's no one to talk to. And you could paint. Nobody uses half of these rooms. You could have your own studio: a really big one.'

Phoebe laughed. 'That's very sweet of you,' she said. 'And the funny thing is that if you'd asked me yesterday I probably would have accepted. But it looks as though I'm going to be giving up nursing for good.'

Mortimer chuckled and said unkindly: 'I wouldn't bank on it.' But she had gone by then.

*

Her ministrations complete, Phoebe washed, dressed and arrived in the dining room just in time to see Pyles clearing away the plates and tureens.

'I was hoping for some breakfast,' she said.

'Breakfast has been served,' he answered, without looking up. 'You're too late.'

'I could do myself some toast: if there's a toaster somewhere I could use.'

He stared at her as if she were a madwoman.

'I'm afraid that won't be possible,' he said. 'There are cold kidneys left. That's all. And some sweetbreads.'

'Never mind. Do you happen to know where Roddy is at the moment?'

'Young Master Winshaw, so far as I am aware, is in the library annexe. Miss Hilary likewise.'

He gave Phoebe a series of elaborate directions which, followed to the letter, eventually brought her out in some sort of laundry in the basement. Undaunted, she went back upstairs and wandered the corridors for about ten minutes until she heard the laughing voices of brother and sister behind a half-closed door. Pushing it open, she found herself in a wide room which seemed both chilly and airless. Roddy and Hilary had her folio open on a table and were flicking rapidly through it, barely glancing at one picture before taking up the next. Hilary looked up and stopped in mid-cackle when she saw Phoebe standing in the doorway.

'Well, well,' she said. 'It's Florence Nightingale herself. Pyles has been telling us about your little mission of mercy.'

'Do you want me to talk you through any of those?' Phoebe asked, ignoring her and walking straight up to Roddy.

'Perhaps I should leave you two lovebirds to plan your glittering future together,' said Hilary. 'Cocktails on the terrace in half an hour, anyone?'

'Make it a quarter,' said Roddy. 'This won't take long.'

Hilary closed the door behind her and he resumed his desultory browsing. Watching him, Phoebe began to quiver with anxiety. She didn't know which was more worrying – his silence on the subject of the paintings or his failure, so far at least, to make the smallest acknowledgement of anything that had happened between them during the night. She stood beside him and briefly laid a hand on his arm but he was unresponsive. After that Phoebe went and stood over by the window. About three minutes later he snapped the folio shut. One picture – a simple watercolour of snow-covered rooftops, part of a commission which she had reluctantly accepted to design Christmas cards for a local firm – lay on the table. Roddy picked it up, carried it over to the wall and tried holding it at different heights. Then he put it back on the table.

'Fifty for that one,' he said.

Phoebe didn't understand.

'I'm sorry?'

'Frankly, that's more than it's worth. But I'm feeling generous this morning. You can take it or leave it.'

'You're offering to *buy* that painting . . . for fifty pounds?'

'Yes. It would cover that damp patch rather well, don't you think?'

'But what about the others?'

'The others? Well, to be honest, I was hoping to find something a little more exciting. I don't really see anything here that would justify an investment.'

Phoebe thought about this for a moment.

'You bastard,' she said.

'There's no need to take it personally,' said Roddy. 'Tastes differ, the world over. It's all subjective in the long run.'

'After everything you said last night.'

'But I'd hardly seen any of your work last night. As you were at pains to point out yourself.'

She frowned and said hollowly: 'Is this some sort of joke?'

'My dear,' he said, 'the Narcissus Gallery has an international reputation. I think you're the one who must be joking, if you suppose that any of these . . . studenty daubs are ever likely to find a place in it.'

'I see.' She looked out of the window, which was thick with dust. 'Wasn't it rather a lot of trouble to go to, just for a quick fuck? I mean, I don't know what your standards are, in this area, but I didn't think it was anything special.'

'Well, of course, I've also had the pleasure of your company for the weekend. That's not to be discounted. You'll stay for some lunch, I hope?'

Phoebe drew in her breath sharply and advanced towards him. 'You slimy little piece of shit. Phone for a taxi. Now.'

'As you wish. I'll tell him to wait at the bottom of the drive, shall I?'

Those were the last words he spoke to her. He closed the door behind him and left her alone, dumbfounded, dwarfed by the dimensions of the enormous room. But for the next few hours she managed to bottle up her rage and remained steel-eyed and silent. She said nothing to the driver who took her all the way to York station, keeping up an unbroken stream of small talk which to her racing mind was so much meaningless noise, like radio static. She said nothing to the other passengers on the train, or on the bus which took her back to the flat. It wasn't until she returned to her bedroom and found, not only that it was still cluttered with Darren's bodybuilding equipment but that there had been an accident with one of his dumb-bells, smashing the glass on her prized Kandinsky print, that she collapsed heavily on to the bed and gave herself over to tears: tears which were brief, cleansing and salty with hate.

Later that week, she phoned Mortimer and told him that she'd reconsidered his offer. He was so pleased that he raised her salary another two thousand on the spot.

*

Now, more than a year later, standing in a corner of the gallery, her wineglass sticky in her hand, the wine itself warm and no longer palatable, she saw no reason to regret her decision. She was glad to have escaped the increasingly difficult atmosphere in the flat; and although Mortimer had turned out to be a demanding patient (prone to exaggerate his ailments wildly) and a disagreeable companion (incapable of concentrating for long on any subject other than his obsessive, almost murderous hatred for his family), she only had to be with him for a few hours every day. The rest of the time she was free to do her own work, and had been given a large, well-lit room on the second floor to use as a studio. It was a solitary existence, but she was allowed to have friends to stay, and to take the occasional weekend off. She missed the self-respect and the sense of usefulness she had felt as a health visitor, but consoled herself with the thought that it would not be long before she went back to it. Not that she had any intention of deserting Mortimer, who had come to depend on her more and more. But it was obvious, now, that his next serious illness would be his last.

So far as she knew, Roddy himself had no idea that she had taken this job: he hadn't been up to Winshaw Towers once since their weekend together. When Mortimer's birthday came round again, Roddy had discharged his filial duty by sending him a card and an invitation to the gallery's latest private view, in the full knowledge that his wheelchair-bound father would not be able to attend. Mortimer had passed the invitation over to Phoebe with a grim smile, and given her permission to attend if she wanted to. And so here she was.

Now, sick of being ignored by the other guests, she was on the point of going over and reintroducing herself to Michael when she saw that he and his companion were putting on their coats and preparing to go. Leaving her half-empty glass on a table top, she pushed through the crowd and followed them outside. They were already halfway down the street, deep in conversation; there was no point running after them. She watched as they disappeared round a corner, then shivered and buttoned up her jacket. November was beginning to bite. She looked at her watch and saw that she still had time to catch the last train to York.

November 1990

'Let us leave this sordid gathering,' said Findlay, taking me by the arm. He gestured at the pictures. 'These gewgaws, these baubles, these gaudy trinkets of a decayed society, let us affront our eyes with them no more. The stench of ill-gotten affluence and self-satisfaction overpowers me. I can't stomach the company of these people a moment longer. Some fresh air, for pity's sake.'

With this he propelled me towards the door, and out into the fresh, wintry Piccadilly night. As soon as we were outside he leaned heavily against the wall, the back of one hand pressed to his forehead while the other fanned his drawn and pallid face.

'That family,' he moaned. 'I can't be in their presence for more than a few minutes without feeling physically sickened. Nauseous.'

'There were only two of them,' I pointed out.

'It's a good thing: otherwise I might have been recognized. Some of the Winshaws have got memories which go back a long way. It's because they've got such dreadful secrets to hide.'

Only Roddy and Hilary had attended the private view, and neither of them – despite having met me on a number of occasions – had stooped to acknowledge my presence. At any other time I might have made a point of forcing myself on their attention, but tonight I was too busy taking the measure of my new acquaintance. He was a small man, his shoulders stooped and his body tightened in the grip of his ninety-odd years; but the gusto with which he wielded his gold-topped cane, and his spectacular head of white, sculpted hair managed to give the lie to his age. It was also impossible not to notice, at the very first, the overwhelming scent of jasmine in which (as he later explained) he was wont to douse himself before stepping out of doors, so that at least one of the riddles which had been haunting me these last few weeks was now finally laid to rest.

'Now, Mr Owen –' he began.

'Michael, please.'

'Michael. We must proceed with our business. I can feel myself recovering. The strength seeps back into my feeble bones. I can almost walk. Where's it to be?'

'I really don't mind.'

'There are a number of pubs round here, of course, where gentlemen of my own persuasion like to congregate. But perhaps this isn't the right time. We don't want to be distracted, after all. Privacy is of the utmost importance. I have a car parked a few streets away, provided the boys in blue haven't removed it by force. I'm no great admirer of the police, we've been at logger-heads for many years; it's one of the things you'll soon find out about me. My flat is in Islington. Twenty minutes' drive, or thereabouts. How does that suit you?'

'Sounds fine.'

'I hope you've brought the necessary documentation,' he said, as we began walking along Cork Street.

He was referring to the yellowed scrap of paper, the note scribbled nearly fifty years ago by Lawrence Winshaw which his sister Tabitha, in her simplicity, had believed to provide certain proof of his guilt, but I must say that his insistence on this point struck me as rather brazen. Here was a man who had recently stolen my manuscript from the publisher's office, followed me home twice and almost scared Fiona to death. To be sure, his letter had been apologetic enough, but still it didn't seem to me that he was in much of a position to dictate terms.

'I've brought it,' I said. 'I haven't decided yet whether I'm going to show it to you.'

'Come, come, Michael,' said Findlay, patting me reprovingly on the leg with his cane. 'We're in this together. We both have the same objective – to arrive at the truth: and we'll get there quicker if we cooperate. So, my methods are a little irregular. They always have been. You can't change the habits of a lifetime: and a lifetime is almost how long I've been working on this case.'

'Surely there've been others in between?'

'Oh, a little debt-collecting here, a little divorce work there. Nothing worthy the name of detection. My career, you see, has been a little – how shall I put this – sporadic. My professional activities have frequently had to be suspended for reasons of . . . well, pleasure.'

'Pleasure?'

'Her Majesty's pleasure, to be precise. The jug. The slammer. I've spent a goodly part of my life in prison, Michael: in fact, believe it or not, I had a two-month suspended sentence handed down to me only this year. I am, as the saying goes, on a bender.' He gave a mirthless laugh. 'An ironic turn of phrase, when you consider that all this persecution, this hounding that I have been subject to all my life, is what I have to pay for the sake of a few happy moments snatched every now and again in the darkness of a public toilet or the waiting room of a suburban railway station. Can you believe this society of ours would be so cruel? To punish a man for the most natural of cravings, for indulging his forlorn, lonely need to find companionship with the occasional passing stranger. It's not our fault if it can't always take place behind closed doors; if the arrangements sometimes have to be a little on the ad hoc side. We didn't choose to be driven into this corner, after all.' His tone, which had been edging its way towards anger, suddenly quietened. 'Anyway, this is all by the by. No, this has not been my only case for the last thirty years, to answer your question, but it's the only one which I haven't brought to a successful conclusion. Not that I don't have my suspicions, my own personal theories. But what we are lacking is proof.'

'I see. And what exactly are these personal theories of yours?'

'Well, that's going to take a little while to explain. Let's wait until we get to the car, at least. Do you work out, Michael? Attend a gym, or anything like that?'

'No. Why do you ask?'

'It's just that you have unusually firm buttocks. For a writer, that is. It was the first thing I noticed about you.'

'Thank you,' I said – for want of anything better.

'If you find that my hand strays in that direction at any point during the evening, feel free to say something about it. I'm an incorrigible groper these days, I'm afraid. The older I get, the less control I seem to have over this wretched libido of mine. You mustn't hold an old man's weaknesses against him.'

'Of course not.'

'I knew you'd understand. Here we are: it's the blue Citroen 2CV.'

It took us a while to get settled in the car. Findlay's ancient joints groaned loudly as he lowered himself into the driver's seat, and then, while struggling to find a suitable resting place for his cane, he dropped the car keys which I had to retrieve, contorting myself and almost pulling a muscle in my effort to reach down behind the gear lever. Once the engine had started, on the fourth attempt, Findlay tried to get the car moving with the handbrake on and the gears still in neutral. I sat back and resigned myself to a bumpy ride.

'The news that you were writing this book came as a great surprise to me,' said Findlay, as we headed for Oxford Street. 'It delights me to say that I'd hardly given that appalling family any thought for about ten years. May I ask what could possibly have induced such a charming and – if you don't mind me saying so – handsome young man as yourself to get involved with that shabby crew?'

I told him the story of Tabitha and how I came to be offered her peculiar commission.

'Curious,' he said. 'Very curious. There must be some new scheme behind all this. I wonder what she's up to. Have you been in communication with her solicitor?'

'Solicitor?'

'Think about it, dear boy. A woman confined to an insane asylum is scarcely in a position to go around setting up trust funds all of her own accord. She'd need a responsible agent to act on her behalf – just as she did thirty years ago, when she decided to engage the services of a private detective. I suspect that she continues to deal through the same fellow – if he's still alive, that is. His name was Proudfoot: a local man, unscrupulous enough to be swayed by the thought of all that money lying around in high-interest accounts.'

'And he was the one who first approached you: that was how you came to be involved with the Winshaws?'

'Well, where shall I begin?' We were waiting at a red traffic light, and Findlay showed every sign of sinking into a deep reverie. Fortunately the angry horn of a car behind us startled him out of it. 'It all seems such a long time ago, now. I imagine myself almost as a young man. Ridiculous. I was already in my late fifties. Thinking about retirement. Planning long days of sunlit debauchery in Turkey or Morocco or somewhere. Well, look what happened to *that* idea . . . London was about as far south as I ever got.

'Anyway, there I was, my business pretty well established in Scarborough, ticking over nicely, money coming in – the only cloud on the horizon, as usual, being the tendency of the local police to pounce on me whenever I got involved in a little bit of harmless naughtiness. Things were getting worse on that front, now I come to think of it, because for some years I'd had the benefit of a mutually satisfying arrangement with a certain detective sergeant, who sadly had just been transferred to the North West. He was a beauty: Herbert, I think his name was . . . Six foot five of solid muscle and a bottom like a ripened peach . . .' He sighed and fell momentarily silent. 'I'm sorry, I seem to have lost my drift.'

'Business was ticking over nicely.'

'Precisely. And then one afternoon . . . early in 1961, it would have been . . . this solicitor fellow, Proudfoot, turned up. As soon as he mentioned the name of Tabitha Winshaw, I knew that something special had arrived on my doorstep. Everybody knew about the Winshaws and their mad old sister, you see. It was the stuff of local legend. And now here was this slovenly, rather repulsive character – with whom, I'm pleased to say, my further dealings were kept to a minimum – bearing a message from the woman herself. Word of my reputation had reached her, it seemed, and she had a job for me. Quite a simple, innocuous little job it sounded at first. I'm sorry, are you ticklish?'

'A little,' I said. 'Besides, you should really keep both hands on the wheel while you're driving.'

'You're quite right, of course. Now, you're aware, I think, that when Godfrey's plane was shot down, he wasn't the only person in it? There was a co-pilot. And apparently Tabitha had been brooding about this, and had decided that she wanted to trace this unfortunate man's family and to make them some sort of financial reparation, by way of atonement, as she saw it, for the treachery carried out by her brother. So my job was to find them.'

'Which you did?'

'In those days, Michael, I was at the peak of my powers. Mental and physical. Such a task really presented no challenge to a man of my experience and abilities: it was the work of only a few days. But then I went one better, and managed to present Tabitha with rather more than she'd bargained for. I found the man himself.'

I stared at him in surprise. 'You mean the co-pilot?'

'Oh, yes. I found him alive and well and living in Birkenhead, and with a most fascinating story to tell. His name was Farringdon. John Farringdon. And this was the man that Lawrence Winshaw bludgeoned to death in the manner so vividly described in your manuscript.'

It took me a few seconds to take this in. 'But how did he survive the crash?'

'Parachuted to safety at the last moment.'

'Does this mean . . . did it mean that Godfrey was still alive?'

'Sadly, no. I did entertain some hopes, for a while. It would have been a tremendous coup on my part. But Mr Farringdon was quite adamant on that point. He himself had seen Godfrey consumed by the flames.'

'So how on earth did you find this man?'

'Well, it seems that he'd been picked up by the Germans and was imprisoned for the rest of the war. Then, when it was over, he returned home – anxious to be reunited with his family – but discovered that he had been reported dead, and that his mother had never survived the news. She'd died within a week of hearing it, and his father had remarried little more than a year later. And so he couldn't bring himself to do it. To render all that grief . . .

senseless. He kept the truth to himself, moved to a new town, took Farringdon as his new name, and began a long, lonely and restless existence, trying to build up some sort of life on these ruined foundations. There was one member of his family, a distant cousin, whom he had to take into his confidence when he needed to retrieve some personal documents; and that was the person who started me off on my search. He never came right out with it, but he wanted me to know, I'm sure. There were one or two carefully dropped hints – enough to send me off to Germany, to pick up the beginnings of the trail.' He sighed again. 'Ah, that was a happy time. Tabitha was paying my expenses. It was spring in the Rhine Valley. I struck up an all-too-brief friendship with a cowherd called Fritz: a vision of bronzed loveliness, fresh from the sunkissed slopes of the German Alps. I've been a pushover for anything in *lederhosen* ever since.' We had reached Islington by now, and he turned off into a side street. 'You must indulge an old man in his foolish reminiscences, Michael. The best years of my life are behind me, now. Only memories remain.' He pulled over to the side of the road, about two feet from the kerb, the back end of the car sticking out alarmingly into the flow of traffic. 'Well, here we are.'

We had arrived outside a small terraced house in one of Islington's less fashionable byways. Findlay led me inside, up several flights of uncarpeted stairs until we reached the attic floor, where he threw open the door on to a room which caused me to gasp in sudden astonishment: for it was a perfect replica, as far as I could see, of the apartment described by Conan Doyle in *The Sign of Four*, when Sherlock Holmes first encounters the mysterious Thaddeus Sholto. The richest and glossiest of curtains and tapestries did indeed drape the walls, looped back here and there to expose some richly mounted painting or Oriental vase. The carpet, too, was of amber and black, so soft and so thick that the foot sank pleasantly into it, as into a bed of moss. There were even two great tiger-skins thrown athwart it, increasing the suggestion of Eastern luxury, and a huge hookah standing upon a mat in the corner. To complete the *hommage*, a lamp in the fashion of a silver dove was hung from an almost invisible golden wire in the centre of the room: as it burned it filled the air with a subtle and aromatic odour.

'Welcome to my little nest, Michael,' said Findlay, shrugging off the raincoat which he had slung across his shoulders. 'You'll excuse all this kitsch, this ersatz Orientalism. I was brought up by uncouth parents, in surroundings of meanness and austerity. My life ever since has been an attempt to cast all that aside. But I have never been a wealthy man. What you see here is an expression of my personality. Voluptuousness on a low budget. Spread yourself out on the Ottoman while I go and make us some tea. Does Lapsang suit?'

The Ottoman turned out, on closer inspection, to be an MFI sofa-bed swathed in threadbare pseudo-Turkish blankets, but it was comfortable enough. Findlay's tiny kitchen led off from the sitting room, so it was easy to continue our conversation as he busied himself with the kettle and the teapot.

'This is a wonderful flat,' I said. 'Have you been here long?'

'I moved down in the early sixties – almost immediately after my brush with the Winshaws. Partly to escape the attentions of the police, as I said: but there were larger reasons as well. After so many years, the narrowness, the insularity, the petty pride of provincial life had become more than could be borne by a man of my temperament. Oh, but this whole area was different then: it had a bit of style, before the brokers and the management consultants and all the other capitalist lackeys moved in. It used to be Bohemian, vibrant, thrilling. Painters, poets, actors, artists, philosophers, faggots, dykes, dancers; even the odd detective. Orton and Halliwell lived just around the corner, you know. Joe used to come round occasionally, but I can't say I ever took to the man. It was over before you started with him. There wasn't a shred of affection in it. Still, it was a terrible end they both came to, you wouldn't wish that upon anybody. I was able to help the authorities in clearing up one or two small details, as it happens, although my name doesn't appear in any of the official accounts.'

Interesting though I found these recollections, I was anxious to get back to the matter in hand. 'You were telling me about Farringdon, the co-pilot,' I prompted.

'A dangerous man, Michael. A desperate man.' Findlay emerged from the kitchen and handed me a cracked bone-china cup filled with steaming tea. 'Not a vicious man, by any means. Capable of strong feelings and great personal loyalty, I would have said. But a man embittered; destroyed by circumstance. He had never managed to settle; had drifted around the country for years, taking factory jobs, casual jobs, edging closer and closer to the world where private enterprise starts shading into crime. Getting by pretty well on a combination of versatility and personal charm. Because he was indeed charming: and handsome, in a chiselled sort of way. His eyes were like blue velvet, I remember, and he had the longest and most luxuriant of eyelashes: not unlike your own, if you'll permit me a small compliment.'

I looked away, bashful.

'I might almost have been tempted to try my luck, but his inclinations lay only too clearly in the opposite direction. A breeder, through and through. He claimed to have conquered a few hearts in his time, and it was easy enough to believe. To sum up, a charismatic rogue: not by any means an uncommon type, in the post-war period, although he had more excuse than most for going to the bad.'

'And what did you tell him, exactly?'

'Well, first of all I told him that I was acting on behalf of the family of the late Godfrey Winshaw. That in itself had an extraordinary effect. He immediately became very passionate and animated. It was clear that Godfrey had inspired him with feelings of the most devoted friendship.'

'As he seems to have done with everybody: Tabitha being the most extreme example.'

'Quite. So this naturally brought us on to the subject of the plane crash, and raised the tricky question of whether I should tell him about Tabitha and her eccentric theory. As things turned out, it could scarcely be avoided, because Farringdon himself was in no doubt about the matter. He was convinced that the Germans had been tipped off. He said that their plane had been intercepted well before it reached its destination, and well before it could have been picked up by radar, in normal circumstances. Somehow

or other, the enemy had been forewarned of their mission.'
Findlay drained his teacup and stared thoughtfully at the leaves,
as if they could offer a reading of the past. 'I could tell at once
that there hadn't been a single day in the last eighteen years of
this man's life when he hadn't thought about this incident,
puzzled over it, agonized and baffled. Wondering who the traitor
might have been. Wondering what he would do to the villain if
fate ever sent him his way.' He put the cup down and shook his
head. 'A dangerous man, Michael. A desperate man.'

Findlay stood by the window and drew the heavy, slightly
moth-eaten curtains, after taking a final look outside at an
evening which had now turned rainy and cold.

'It's getting very late,' he said. 'Perhaps you'n care to stay the
night, and we could continue this story in the morning. Sadly this
is a small flat and there is only the one bed, but –'

'It's only twenty to nine,' I pointed out.

Findlay smiled apologetically and sat down opposite me with a
crestfallen air. 'It's no use, I know. You see through the wiles of a
lonely and pathetic old man. I disgust you, of course. Try not to
make it obvious, Michael. That's all that I ask.'

'It's not that at all –'

'Please, no kind words. You've come to carry out a simple
business transaction, I realize that. Information is all that you want
from me. Once you have it, I can be discarded, like a used rag.'

'Far from it, I –'

'To resume.' He waved me into silence with an imperious
hand. 'I had no intention of letting the odious lawyer share in my
glory, and so on my return to Yorkshire I requested an immediate
interview with Tabitha in person: which was duly arranged. The
asylum could only be reached, I discovered, by means of a long
drive over the moors, and my first sight of it filled me with gloom
and trepidation. Probably there is only one more bleak and
desolate spot in the entire area. I refer, of course, to Winshaw
Towers itself.

'I was shown into Tabitha's private apartment, which was at
the top of one of the highest towers in the building. My impression, I can assure you, was not one of talking to a madwoman.

Certainly her room seemed to be in a severe state of disarray. It was scarcely possible to move for all the piles of magazines, all those dreadful titles to do with aviation and bomber jets and military history. But the woman herself seemed to be quite *compos mentis*. To be brief, I told her of my discovery, and she reacted quite calmly. She said that she needed a little time to digest the information, and asked if I would mind amusing myself for half an hour or so, by walking in the grounds. At the end of this period I came back to her room and she handed me a letter, addressed to Mr Farringdon. That was that. I didn't inquire after its contents; merely put it in the post when I got back to town.

'I got to know that journey pretty well: I must have done it four or five times after that, because very soon after I had posted the letter, Farringdon himself arrived in Scarborough. This would have been in September. It seemed that Tabitha had asked to see him, and that I had been trusted with the task of escorting him out to the Institute. They had several long interviews over the next few days. Whatever they discussed, it was kept a close secret, even from myself. Each time, I waited on a bench in the gardens, overlooking the moors, and read some pages of Proust – I think I must have got through most of the first two volumes – and every day when we drove home, my passenger would sit in grim and impenetrable silence, or chat idly about some wholly unrelated topic. It wasn't until our very last visit that I was re-admitted into Tabitha's presence, and for once it was Farringdon who had to suffer this inglorious banishment.

'"Mr Onyx," she said, "you have shown yourself to be a man of integrity. The time has come when I must trust you with some secrets regarding my family which I feel sure you will keep to yourself." I can't do the voice, I'm afraid. Mimicry has never been one of my talents. "In a few days' time, thanks to the good offices of my brother Mortimer, I shall be released from this confinement for the first time in nearly twenty years." I remember congratulating her in some awkward phrase or other, but she was having none of that. "It will only be temporary, I'm sure. My brother Lawrence persists in the most implacable opposition to any suggestion that I should be set completely at liberty. That is because he is a liar and a murderer." "Strong words," I said. "Nothing but the truth," she answered. "You see, I have written evidence of his perfidy, and it is now my intention to put this evidence into your hands for safe-keeping." I asked her what form this evidence took, and she told me about the note, whose nature, I believe, is already well known to you. It was her hope that this note was still to be found in the guest room where she had always stayed when visiting Winshaw Towers, in the pocket of a cardigan which she had last seen in the bottom drawer of the wardrobe. She proposed to retrieve it as soon as possible and pass it over to me: and to this end we agreed to meet on the afternoon of Mortimer's birthday party, at the very edge of the grounds, near a spot which was consecrated, believe it or not, for the burial of various dogs which had had the misfortune to live out their miserable lives as part of the Winshaw family.'

'Of course – and Tabitha met you there, all right, but you were interrupted by Mortimer, and he thought that she was jabbering away to herself in the bushes.'

'Precisely. Luckily he didn't notice my presence, although the scent of this cheap but rather exotic perfume to which I've always been partial – excessively partial, it has been argued – could hardly fail to escape his attention. In any case, it made no difference, because Tabitha and I had already concluded our business – without any success at all, I'm afraid to say. The note was nowhere to be found in her room, and she hadn't had the time to look for it anywhere else. Besides, the house is enormous. It might have taken days, even weeks. However' – and here he favoured me with a rather frosty smile – 'it appears that you succeeded where even I, the fabled, the infamous, the redoubtable Findlay Onyx drew the most unequivocal of blanks. I wonder if you'd care to tell me how you managed it.'

'Well, there's hardly anything to say, really. I certainly can't take any credit. Not long after Godfrey's death, when Tabitha had first been sent away, it seems that Lawrence found the clothes which had been left in her room, and had them put in a trunk and taken up to one of the attics. Then after he'd died, and Mortimer and Rebecca moved into the house, they went through them all and came upon the note – which Mortimer recognized immediately, of course. He could still remember all the fuss there'd been about it at the time. As far as he was concerned, anyway, it was of little more than curiosity value, so when I met him a few years ago and we talked about the book I was writing, he let me have it. Simple as that.'

Findlay sighed with admiration.

'Remarkable, Michael, remarkable. The economy of your methods astounds me. I can only hope that you don't consider me, in the light of such glaring disparity, to be an entirely unworthy recipient of your confidences. In other words, perhaps the moment has come, at long last, for you to share with me the contents of this enigmatic memorandum.'

'But you haven't finished the story yet. What about later that night, when –'

'Patience, Michael. A little patience, please. I've satisfied your curiosity on a number of points: surely I'm entitled to the same – or equivalent – satisfactions in return?'

I conceded this with a slow nod.

'Fair enough. It's in my wallet, in my coat pocket. I'll just go and get it.'

'You're a gentleman, Michael. One of the old school.'

'Thank you.'

'There's just one thing, before you do.'

'Yes?' I paused in the act of getting up.

'I suppose a quick hand-job's out of the question?'

'I'm afraid so. Another cup of tea would be nice, though.'

Findlay retreated, abashed, into the kitchen, and once I had retrieved my wallet I went after him.

'I don't know what you're expecting from this,' I said, taking out the tiny, tightly folded scrap of paper and smoothing it out on the kitchen table. 'As I say in the book, it's only a little message that Lawrence wrote, asking for some supper to be sent up to his room. It doesn't prove anything at all: except that Tabitha's mad, possibly.'

'I think I'll be the judge of that, if you don't mind,' said Findlay. He took a pair of bifocals from the pocket of his shirt and stooped down to inspect the crucial piece of evidence which had eluded him for almost thirty years. It shames me to admit that I felt a mean glow of satisfaction as I saw the sudden disappointment cloud his face.

'Oh,' he said.

'I did tell you.'

Lawrence's note consisted of only three words, scrawled in tiny capitals. They were BISCUIT, CHEESE and CELERY.

The kettle started to whistle. Findlay turned off the gas and filled the teapot, then bent over the table again. He stared at the message for almost a minute: turned it over, turned it upside down, held it to the light, sniffed it, scratched his head and read it a few times more.

'Is that all there is?' he said finally.

'That's it.'

'Well then, that settles it. She's as mad as a hatter.'

He finished making the tea and we trooped back into the sitting room, where we sat for some time in a silence which was on my part expectant, on Findlay's angry and thoughtful. He got up once to take another look at the note, which was still in the kitchen, and came back carrying it but without saying a word. After a while he laid it on the table beside him with a grunt, and said: 'Well, you'll be wanting to hear the rest of it, I suppose.'

'If you wouldn't mind.'

'There isn't much to tell. I'd arranged to dine with Farringdon that night. Scarborough was not famed for its cuisine, even then, but there was a small Italian place which I'd been known to use in the past – for the purposes of seduction, Michael, I'll be perfectly frank with you – and it was there that he and I shared a few bottles of Chianti, even as the Winshaws were sitting down to their wretched family dinner.' He shook his head sadly. 'That was to be his last meal. I had no idea, at that stage. Didn't even know that he and Tabitha had hatched any kind of plot together. Of course, I can see it all, in retrospect. The years of smouldering resentment; abstract hopes of vengeance suddenly made concrete; those long, secret talks in her room which must have driven him to a murdero s frenzy. I can only speculate about the bonds formed, the vows taken, the oaths sworn, between those ill-fated partners in crime. He was in a sombre mood, as you can imagine, and not much given to talk – which I, fool that I was, put down to travel fatigue. He'd been down to Birkenhead for a few days, you see, and had only come back up again that afternoon. I couldn't quite see the purpose of this trip at the time, but towards the end of the evening he was good enough to explain.

'Just as we were about to leave the restaurant, he drew my attention to a large manila envelope he'd brought along with him. It was to retrieve this, apparently, that he'd made his journey home. "Mr Onyx, I've a favour to ask of you," he said. "I want you to look after this, just for a few hours. And promise me, that if I don't meet you at your office at nine o'clock tomorrow morning, you'll deliver it into Miss Winshaw's hands as soon as possible." This seemed an extraordinary request, and I told him so: but he absolutely refused to divulge the undertaking which was to occupy him at this peculiar hour of the night. "At least tell me what's in here," I pleaded, reasonably enough, I think you'll agree. And after a few moments' hesitation, he answered: "My life." Rather dramatic, wouldn't you say? I tried to lighten the atmosphere somewhat by saying that if the contents of this envelope repre- sented his life, then there didn't seem to be much of it. He laughed bitterly at that. "Of course there isn't much of it. This is what I've been reduced to, thanks to one man's treachery: a few documents; some souvenirs of the old RAF days; a single photograph, the only trace of myself I've managed to leave behind these last twenty years. I want her to have them, anyway. She isn't mad, Mr Onyx, I know that for a fact. They've got no right to lock her up in that place. But there's been a terrible injustice done, and whatever happens to me, she's the person to keep the memory of it alive."

'Well, I took the envelope and we said good-night. I knew now that something deadly was afoot, but it was no part of my job to stand in the way of – fate, destiny, call it what you will. I could see that the events to which I had involuntarily become witness had to be played out to their conclusion. And so we went our separate ways: I to bed, and Farringdon, as I afterwards dis- covered, first of all to steal a motor car from some luckless citizen–

not a difficult task, for a man of his experience – and then to drive out to Winshaw Towers, there to gain entry through the library window which Tabitha, I surmise, would have opened for him, and to make his calamitous attempt on Lawrence's life.'

I brooded on this. 'From the way you've described him, I wouldn't have thought he'd have much trouble polishing off a weedy little man like Lawrence.'

'Maybe so. But Lawrence had made many enemies over the years, and had probably found it worth his while to learn how to defend himself against them. Besides, I suspect he was ready for trouble that night: he knew something was up. Farringdon's best bet would have been to surprise him, if possible, but I'd wager he couldn't resist having a few words with him first. Those wasted moments might have been critical.'

'And then I suppose when he failed to show up in your office the next morning, you drove straight out to the house?'

'You anticipate me superbly, Michael. Your prognostic powers defy belief. I was there shortly after ten. You probably know that although it can be seen from a great distance across the moors, Winshaw Towers is approached by a heavily wooded drive, and it was easy enough to conceal my car at some distance from the house itself and to arrive on foot without attracting any notice. In those days – and who knows, he may be there still – the premises were patrolled by an exceptionally lugubrious and unprepossessing butler by the name of Pyles, and I knew that, even with things being in such an obvious state of confusion, my chances of getting past him were not good at all. So I waited my moment, until I saw him disappear off in the direction of the outhouses on some errand or other, and then had no difficulty bluffing my way past some halfwit of an under-footman. I claimed to be a colleague of Dr Quince's, I seem to remember.'

'The family doctor.'

'That's right: some quack physician they used to slip a bribe to every three or four years to make sure that Tabitha remained safely under lock and key. I'd passed his car on the road a few miles back, so I knew that he'd already paid a visit. I said that I'd been asked to give a second opinion.

'How to convey an impression of Tabitha's state of mind that morning? She told me what had happened, quite calmly, without any apparent shock or agitation: but beneath her composure I caught glimpses of such despondency, such disappointment ... Her last hope dashed, her one taste of freedom squandered, forfeited ... I am anything but a man of sentiment, Michael: womanly feelings are entirely foreign to me, and yet that morning, absurd though it sounds, my heart almost broke. I handed her Farringdon's envelope; she put it away in her writing case without opening it; and just then Mortimer knocked at the door, come to say his farewells. I had but a few moments to conceal myself: just time to leap into her dressing room and close the door, while Tabitha picked up her knitting and resumed her habitual air of abstraction. Their conversation was brief. When it was safe for me to emerge, she and I exchanged only a few more words. She had a considerable sum of money in her purse, I remember, and she insisted on paying me in full for my services. Then I took my leave. I slipped out through a back doorway and took a circuitous route to the car; and that was the end of my dealings with Tabitha Winshaw. I have not seen her since.'

Findlay stared into space. A mood of profound melancholy seemed to have come over him, and for the moment I could think of nothing to say.

'It was a glorious morning,' he continued suddenly. 'Bright sunshine. Deep blue skies. The leaves just turning to gold. Do you know that part of the world at all, Michael? I miss it sometimes, even now. Winshaw Towers is on the edge of Spaunton Moor, and since I couldn't face going back to town, I drove to a quiet spot and walked for several hours, thinking back over the last few curious weeks, wondering what it all meant and where it left me. The seeds of my decision to come down to London were sown that day, I think. It was a Sunday, but there weren't many walkers: I had the place more or less to myself, and the sun shone kindly on my schemes and resolutions.'

'You were lucky,' I said. 'I remember that Sunday, too, but it poured with rain. At least where I was.'

'Come come, Michael, you romanticize,' said Findlay, chuckling incredulously. 'You were only a young boy at the time. How can your memory possibly distinguish one such day from any other?'

'I remember it vividly. It was my ninth birthday, and my parents took me to Weston-super-Mare, and it rained in the afternoon so we went to the cinema.' This information didn't appear to mean much to Findlay, and since we were now both in danger of sinking into a nostalgic torpor, I decided that a rapid change of tone was called for. 'Anyway – what do you want to do about this note? Hang on to it?'

He read the message again and then handed it over. 'No, Michael. This is of no further use to me. I've committed it to memory, in any case.'

'Aren't you going to perform tests on it, or something? Look for invisible ink?'

'What colourful ideas you entertain when it comes to the detective's art,' said Findlay. 'My own procedures seem very prosaic in comparison. I must be a disappointment to you.'

His sarcasm was mischievous rather than icy, so I tried to enter into the spirit.

'It's true,' I said. 'I was brought up on a diet of Hercule Poirot and Sherlock Holmes. I even used to write detective stories once, when I was very little. I was rather hoping that you'd give it a cool, expert glance, and then look at me through half-closed lids and say something impressive like, "Singular, Mr Owen. Very singular".'

He smiled. 'Well, all is not lost, Michael. We still have work we can do together, avenues to explore, and besides . . .' He tailed off suddenly, and a transient gleam seemed to flicker in his eye. '. . . and besides . . . You know, you may actually have a point there.'

'I may? What point?'

'Well it *is* singular, isn't it? That's the strange thing about it.'

'I'm afraid I don't follow.'

'The word "biscuit", Michael. Surely it ought to be in the plural. *One* biscuit, to be taken with some cheese and a stick of celery? It doesn't sound very substantial, does it, even for a snack?'

I cast around for an explanation, and said rather lamely: 'Well, this was during the war. Perhaps with rationing, and so on . . .'

Findlay shook his head. 'Something tells me,' he said, 'that wartime economies would not have impinged very seriously on the Winshaw ménage. They have never struck me as being among nature's belt-tighteners. No, this is beginning to look more interesting than I'd supposed. A little further thought may be called for.'

'And there's another mystery, too, don't forget.'

Findlay waited for me to explain.

'Don't you remember? All that business about Tabitha thinking that she could hear German voices coming from Lawrence's bedroom, and how she locked him in there but it turned out that he'd been in the billiard room all along.'

'Well, of course, there's a perfectly plausible explanation for that. But we'd have to visit the house itself to put it to the test. In the meantime, I thought we might try approaching the problem from the other end.'

'Meaning?'

'Meaning that there's one part of this story, one component, which sticks out like the proverbial sore thumb. One player who sits so uneasily with the others that you wonder whether he hasn't wandered in from a different drama altogether. My reference, Michael, is to yourself.'

'Me? What have I got to do with it? I just drifted into this whole business. It could have been anybody.'

'It *could* have been anybody, naturally. But it wasn't. It was you. Now there may even be a reason for this, and it may be possible to find out what it is. Tell me, Michael, don't you think it's about time that you met Tabitha Winshaw? She may not be around for much longer, after all.'

'I know, I've been putting it off. Also I've always had the sense, somehow, that the publishers have wanted to discourage it.'

'Ah, yes, your inscrutable publishers. Quite an outfit, I must say. I was most impressed by their offices, or what I could see of them, on my brief and unofficial visit. I even helped myself to one of their brochures, you'll be shocked to hear.' Reaching over to his desk, he brandished a glossy, expensively printed catalogue and flicked through its pages. 'The list is certainly eclectic,' he murmured. 'Take this, for instance: *Dropping in on Jerry: A Light-Hearted Account of the Dresden Bombings*, by Wing Commander "Bullseye" Fortescue, v.c. Sounds hysterical, I must say. This one caught my eye: *A Lutheran Approach to the Films of Martin and Lewis*. Or, better still, *The A–Z of Plinths*, by the Reverend J. W. Pottage – "an invaluable reference companion", it says here, "to his earlier groundbreaking work". Well, well. Quite a cornucopia, isn't it?'

'You don't have to tell me,' I said. 'I get sent a parcel of the things for Christmas every year.'

'Well, that in itself is rather generous, don't you think? There seems to be no shortage of money in their line of business. This fellow who runs it – McGanny, isn't it? – must be something of a shrewd operator. I've a feeling that it might be worth looking a little more closely into his affairs.'

I was disappointed by this proposed line of inquiry, and couldn't hold back from saying so. 'How's that going to help us find out what Lawrence was up to in 1942?'

'Perhaps it won't, Michael. But perhaps that isn't the real mystery in any case.'

'What are you suggesting, exactly?'

Findlay got up from his armchair and sat beside me. 'I'm suggesting,' he said, laying a claw-like hand on my thigh, 'that the real mystery is you. And I intend to get to the bottom of it.'

*

Kenneth said: 'Miss, you don't happen to know where my bedroom is, do you?'

Shirley shook her head sadly and said: 'No, I'm afraid I don't.'

Kenneth said: 'Oh,' and paused. 'I'm sorry. I'll go now.'

I thought about Findlay's description of me: 'one player who sits so uneasily with the others that you wonder whether he hasn't wandered in from a different drama altogether'. It seemed oddly perceptive, suddenly exact about the way I tended to feel when contemplating the Winshaws. This evening, for instance . . .

Shirley hesitated, a resolve forming within her: 'No. Hang on.' She gestured with her hand, urgently. 'Turn your back a minute.'

Kenneth turned, and found himself staring into a mirror in which he could see his own reflection, and beyond that, Shirley's. Her back was to him, and she was wriggling out of her slip, pulling it over her head.

. . . leaving Findlay's flat, catching the Number 19 bus, feeling the characteristic lowering of the spirits as I returned to South West London; arriving home. All this mundanity, my too familiar surroundings, made his narrative and the mad, gothic horrors towards which it gestured seem like a grotesque fantasy . . .

He said: 'J– just a minute, miss.'

Kenneth hastily lowered the mirror, which was on a hinge.

Shirley turned to him and said: 'You're sweet.' She finished pulling her slip over her head, and started to unfasten her bra.

. . . Did they have the same worries that I had, these absurd people? Did they have the sort of feelings I would even understand? It wasn't enough to say that they came from a different walk of life. It was more extreme, more final than that: they belonged to a different *genre* of existence altogether. One which actually horrified me . . .

Shirley disappeared behind Kenneth's head.

Kenneth said: 'Well, a – a handsome face isn't everything, you know.'

Continuing to hold down the mirror, he tried not to look in it, but couldn't resist taking occasional glimpses. With every glimpse, his face registered physical pain. Shirley put on her nightgown.

. . . and one which over the last few years had almost caused me to lose, I now realized, any sense of life as it ought to be lived. Had almost killed me off, in fact, or at least put me to sleep: bringing on a paralysis from which I might never have recovered if it had not been for that knock on my door: if Fiona had not appeared, to unfreeze the frame . . .

Kenneth said: 'All that glitters is not gold.'

She emerged from behind his head, her body swathed in the knee-length gown, and said: 'You can turn round now.'

He turned and looked at her. He seemed pleased.

'Cor. Very provoking.'

I turned off the television. Kenneth and Shirley dwindled to a pinpoint of light and I went into the kitchen to pour myself another drink.

Every time I went in there, now, and saw my reflection in the window, it reminded me of the night she had first come round, asking for my name on her sponsorship form and having to repeat herself again and again to make me understand.

And here was the reflection again. But if you looked beyond it, what did you see? Nothing much. Dreamer though I was, I did not have the power of Cocteau's Orpheus, who could pass through liquefying mirrors into unimagined worlds. No, I was more like Kenneth Connor – and always would be – forcing myself not to look in the mirror at a gorgeous, terrifying reality disclosing itself only a few inches behind my back.

Except that last night I had seen a new reflection: only briefly, because I had had to close my eyes to the beauty of it, and yet it had been so vivid, so real, that I looked for traces even now, scarcely believing that the window itself could have no memory.

... *Les miroirs feraient bien de réfléchir davantage. Trois fois* ...

Fiona had called round with a small fuchsia cutting which she proposed to add to the ever-expanding forest of greenery which now covered most of the available surfaces in my flat. She was wearing an old jumper and a pair of jeans and she didn't want to stay for a drink or a chat: she wanted to get to bed, even though it was only about eight o'clock. It had been a long day at work, apparently, and her temperature was up again. In spite of this she seemed to be finding excuses for not leaving right away, making a point of checking up on the condition of all the plants even though I could sense that her mind wasn't really on it. It felt as though there was something she wanted to say, something important. And then when we got into the kitchen, where the lights were bright, and I was asking her if she was sure she didn't want a beer or a gin and tonic or a vodka and orange or something, she suddenly leaned back against the fridge and asked if I would do her a favour.

I said yes, of course I would.

She said: 'Do you think you could feel my throat?'

I said: 'Your throat?'

She tilted her head back and looked at the ceiling and said: 'Just touch it. Touch it and tell me what you think.'

If this was the beginning, I thought, if this was how the whole business was going to start up again, then it wasn't what I'd been expecting. Not at all. Any sense of control over the situation had drained out of me: I felt as though I was plunging to earth, and I walked towards her with the tread of a sleepwalker, my fingertips outstretched until they came into contact with the pale skin at the base of her neck. From there I traced a slow line, sensing a film of fine, downy hair as I touched the soft ridges of her throat. Fiona remained perfectly still, and perfectly quiet.

'Like that?' I said.

'Again. To the left.'

And this time I came upon it almost at once: a small obstruction, a ball of hardness about the size of an olive lodged well beneath her skin. I stroked it, then pinched it gently between forefinger and thumb.

'Does that hurt?'

'No.'

'What is it?'

'I don't know.'

'What did the doctor say?'

'Nothing. He didn't seem very interested.'

I took my hand away and stepped back, searching her blue-green eyes for clues. They stared back neutrally.

'Have you always had it?'

'No. I noticed it a few weeks ago.'

'Is it growing?'

'Hard to say.'

'You should go back to the doctor.'

'He didn't think it was important.'

I had nothing else to say: just stood there, as if rooted to the spot. Fiona watched me for a moment and then folded her arms and hunched her shoulders, withdrawing into herself.

'I really am tired,' she said. 'I must go.'

'OK.'

But before she went I put my hand against her neck again and we slid into an embrace which was clumsy at first, but it didn't matter, we persisted, and by the end we were clasping each other tightly: I clung to her silence and, closing my eyes to our reflection in the kitchen window, pictured a knot, made from the threads of her wordless fears and my famished longing, which would hold fast against the very worst that the future might throw at us.

Dorothy

To hug someone, and to be hugged, now and again, in return: this is important. George Brunwin had never been hugged by his wife, and it was many years since he had taken a mistress. None the less, he regularly enjoyed long, rapt, tender embraces, stolen, more often than not, in darkened corners of the farm which he had once been pleased to call his own. The latest willing object of his advances was a veal calf called Herbert.

Contrary to local rumour, however, George had never had sex with an animal.

Although he probably never rationalized it to himself, it was one of his more deeply rooted beliefs that the life unvisited by physical affection was scarcely worth living. His mother had been a great one for touching, cuddling, swaddling and coddling; for ruffling of hair, patting of bottoms and dandling on the knee. Even his father had not been averse to the occasional firm handshake or manly embrace. George had grown up in the assumption that these delightful collisions, these outbursts of spontaneous, loose-limbed intimacy were the very stuff of loving relationships. Furthermore, the rhythm of life on his father's farm was dictated, to a large extent, by the reproductive cycles of the animals, and George had proved perhaps more than usually sensitive to these, for he developed a healthy sexual appetite at an early age. In the light of which, he could hardly have found a less suitable partner (not that he was ever given much choice in the matter) than Dorothy Winshaw, to whom he was married in the spring of 1962.

They had spent their honeymoon at a hotel in the Lake District, with a view over Derwent Water: and it was in this same hotel, twenty years later, that George found himself drinking, alone, one clammy evening in June. Clouded as it was by alcohol, his mind still carried an unpleasantly vivid memory of their wedding night. While she had not exactly fought him off, Dorothy's stolid passivity had itself been resistance enough, and there was also – to add to the humiliation – a discernibly bored and mocking aspect to it. Despite all that George could provide in the way of foreplay, his questioning fingertips had met with nothing but tight dryness. To have proceeded further in these circumstances would have been to commit rape (for which he hadn't the physical strength, apart from anything else). Three or four more attempts had followed, over the ensuing weeks, and after that the subject – like George's hopes – was never raised again. Looking back on those days now, through his alcoholic fog, he found it absurd, laughable, that he should ever have expected the marriage to be consummated. There had been, between Dorothy and himself, an absolute physical incompatibility. Sexual union between them would have been as impossible as it had recently become for the misshapen turkeys which his wife was now obliged to propagate through artificial insemination: their meat-yielding breasts so horribly enlarged through years of chemical injections and selective breeding that their sex organs could not even make contact.

Why did George not hate his wife? Was it because she had enriched him (financially) beyond his wildest expectations? Did he even take a certain reluctant pride in the fact that she had built up what used to be a quiet, old-fashioned, modestly run family farm into one of the biggest agrichemical empires in the country? Or had the hate merely been washed away, over the years, by the tides of whisky to which he surrendered daily and with fewer and fewer pretensions to secrecy? He and Dorothy now lived very separate lives, at any rate. Every working day she would drive into town, where a bleak scrub of land in one of the outermost suburbs was dominated by a huge four-storey complex of offices and laboratories: the world headquarters of Brunwin Holdings PLC. George himself had not set foot there for more than fifteen years. With no head for business, no understanding of science and nothing but disdain for the boys' game of stockmarket snakes and ladders which seemed to preoccupy most of the directors, he chose to retreat, instead, into a fantasy version of happier times. There was a small redbricked cowshed which had somehow managed to survive Dorothy's expansion programme (she had demolished most of the original buildings and replaced them with row upon row of massive broiler-sheds and controlled environment houses in dull grey steel), and it was here that he spent most of every day, his only companions being his whisky bottle and whichever of the sicker, more enfeebled farm animals he had managed to rescue from their confinement in the hope of restoring them to health: chickens, for instance, whose legs could no longer support their over-developed bodies, or cattle with dipped backs and distorted hips from carelessly prescribed growth hormones. For a long time, the existence of this gloomy haven was unknown to Dorothy, who could rarely be bothered to inspect her own premises: but when, by chance, it was finally discovered, she could not conceal her furious contempt for her husband's sentimentality.

'His leg was broken,' said George, blocking the doorway of the cowshed while Herbert shrank in a corner. 'I couldn't bear to see him loaded on to a lorry with the others.'

'I'll break your bloody legs if you don't leave my stock alone,' shouted Dorothy. 'I could report you to the bloody police for what I caught you doing.'

'I was petting him, that's all.'

'God Almighty! And have you done what I asked you to do: have you spoken to the cook about dinner on Friday night?'

He stared back blankly. 'What dinner on Friday night?'

'The dinner we're giving for Thomas and Henry and the people from Nutrilite.' Dorothy habitually carried a riding crop: she now whacked it across her own thighs in exasperation. 'You don't even remember, do you? You can't remember a bloody thing about anything. You're just a useless, dried-out, washed-up old piss artist. God Almighty!'

She stormed off to the farmhouse; and all at once, as he watched her receding figure, George felt abruptly, overwhelmingly sober.

He asked himself a sudden question: Why did I marry this woman?

Then he went to the Lake District to think it through.

*

He had started drinking to combat the loneliness. Not the loneliness he had sometimes felt when he ran the farm by himself, and would often spend whole days in the proud, kingly solitude of the moors, with only sheep and cattle for company. This was the loneliness, rather, of spartan hotel rooms in central London: late in the evening, with the prospect of a sleepless night ahead, and nothing better to occupy the mind than a Gideon bible and the latest issue of *Poultry News*. George spent many nights like this, shortly after his marriage to Dorothy, because she had persuaded him that it was in his interest to join the council of the National Farmers' Union. He served on it for little more than a year, and discovered in the process that he had no talent for lobbying or committee work, and that he had nothing in common with the other members, none of whom shared his enthusiasm for the day-to-day running of farms. (He got the impression that most of them had joined the council to get away from it.) And when he gave up this position and Dorothy herself took his place, she made it clear that she didn't trust him, by this stage, to look after the farm in her absence. Without bothering to consult her husband she advertised for a full-time manager, and George found that he had effectively been made redundant.

Meanwhile, Dorothy got to work. Taking full advantage of her cousin Henry's parliamentary contacts (on both sides of the House), she soon became a practised winer and diner of all the most influential figures from the Treasury and the Ministry of Agriculture. At exclusive restaurants and lavish dinner parties, she would convince civil servants and MPs of the necessity for ever more extravagant subsidies being paid out to farmers who wished to convert to the new intensive methods: it was through her efforts (and the efforts of others like her) that the government began to step up its provision of grants and tax allowances to help with the laying down of concrete, the putting up of buildings, and the purchase of fittings and equipment. Smaller farmers who resisted these incentives soon found themselves unable to match the prices being offered to the consumer by their highly subsidized competitors.

And as soon as they heard the news that large amounts of

public money were being channelled into intensive farming, the financial institutions began to move in. Dorothy had a head start on her rivals in this respect, since Thomas Winshaw was by now well on his way to becoming one of the most powerful members of the banking establishment. When he learned of the direction government policy was taking, he began to invest heavily in agricultural land, and was more than happy to offer Dorothy substantial loans – with land as security – for her various expansion programmes (the size of the debt obliging her, every year, to force higher and higher yields out of her soil and stock). From the outset, her aim was to guarantee profits by controlling every stage of production. She began by buying up all the smaller farms in the county and putting them under contract. Then, once she had established her stranglehold on most of the egg, chicken, bacon and vegetable supplies to the North East of England, she started to expand her sphere of operations. A series of specialist divisions was set up: Easilay Eggs (slogan: 'The Yolk's on Us, Folks!'), Porkers, the bacon curers ('If It's Porker, It Must Be a Corker'), Green Shoots vegetable products ('Are you getting enough, Missus?') and Pluckalot Chickens ('They Keep on Cluckin' and We Keep on Pluckin'!'). The Brunwin insignia was reserved for what was, in terms of profits, the jewel in the corporate crown: the frozen dinner and instant pudding division, for which the slogan was simply 'They're Brunwin Fantastic!' Each of these companies was served by hundreds of contracted farmers up and down the country, whose task – if they were to stand any chance of making a livelihood – was to use every growth-inducing antibiotic and every yield-increasing pesticide known to man in order to meet the ever more stringent production quotas laid down by Dorothy from her head office at Brunwin Holdings. These farmers were also obliged to place all their orders for feed with a company called Nutrilite (a division of Brunwin Holdings) and to supplement it with chemical additives obtained from another company called Kemmilite (a division of Brunwin Holdings). In this way, internal costs were kept down to an absolute minimum.

Dorothy's empire had taken a long time to build. By the time of George's trip to the Lake District, however, it was enjoying its heyday. For instance, figures for this period show that Easilay were now supplying the nation with more than 22 million eggs a week, while the annual turnover of Pluckalot was more than 55 million. That's chickens, of course: not pounds.

*

One afternoon when I was about twenty, Verity and I had a quarrel at my parents' house, and when it was over I went out for a walk to calm myself down. She had been having fun, as usual, at the expense of my aspirations as a writer, and I was riddled with righteous self-pity as I stormed off down a lane in the direction of the wood which I used to explore on my Sunday walks as a child. No doubt there was a semi-conscious intention behind this. I wanted to revisit the site of those happy occasions (and, of course, the scene of my first literary endeavours) because I felt that it would somehow restore a sense of myself as a uniquely precious and sentient being, a storehouse of aesthetically charged memories. And so I headed for what used to be Mr Nuttall's farm, which I hadn't visited for more than ten years.

At first, when I came to the barbed wire fence and the unfamiliar buildings, I thought that my memory was playing tricks, and had brought me to the wrong place. I seemed to be looking at some sort of factory. All I could see was a row of long, utilitarian wooden sheds, each with a giant metal canister at the end, supported on poles and ranged oppressively against the cloudy afternoon sky. Puzzled, I wriggled my way beneath the fence and went to take a closer look. The sheds had no windows: but by climbing up the side of one of the canisters, I could peer in through a gap between the wooden boards.

For a few seconds my eyes met with nothing but blackness, and I was overwhelmed by an atmosphere of dusty humidity, the air heavy with the smell of ammonia. Then, gradually, some shapes began to emerge from the gloom. But what I saw is difficult to explain, because it made no sense, and continues to make no sense, even now. I felt as though I was looking at a scene in a film, sprung from the fantastic imagination of some surrealist director. I was looking at what I can only describe as a sea of chickens. I was looking down what seemed to be a long, wide, dark tunnel, the floor covered with chickens as far as the eye could see. God knows how many birds were in that shed – thousands, or perhaps even tens of thousands. There was no movement at all: they were packed in too tightly to turn or to move around, and I was aware only of a great stillness. This was finally shattered, I don't know how many minutes later, by the sound of a door opening and the appearance of a little rectangle of light at the far end of the tunnel. Two figures were framed in the doorway, and there was a sudden bustle and flapping of feathers.

'This is it,' said one of the men.

'Blimey,' said the other. Their voices travelled boomingly.

'Let's throw some light on the subject,' said the first man, and switched on a torch.

'You certainly pack them in here, don't you?'

'We do our best.' I took this man to be the owner. It was not Mr Nuttall, but I could remember my mother telling me that the farm had changed hands quite recently.

'Feels warm enough in here to me, I must say.'

'No, we need to keep it much warmer than this.'

'When do you reckon it broke down, then?'

'Some time last night.'

'And your lighting's gone as well, has it?'

'No, no, it's supposed to be dark. These birds are six weeks old, you see. They'd fight in these conditions if we gave them any light.'

'Well, all I can do really is to check your circuit. More often than not you'll find it's the earthing system that's at fault.'

'Yes, but I only had a new one put in last year. Had a whole new system put in, you see, because the old one was completely useless. We had an absolute disaster one night. All the ventilators shut down. I came in in the morning and there were nine thousand dead birds on the floor. Nine bloody thousand. Took

*four of us all morning to clear them out. We were shovelling
them out with a spade.'*

'Well, where can I get at it, anyway?'

'At the back of the shed, near the big hopper.'

There was a short silence. Then the second man said: 'Yes, but
how do I get there?'

'You walk it, of course. How do you think?'

'I can't get through there. There's no room. Not with all these
birds.'

'They won't hurt you.'

'What about me hurting them?'

'No, that's all right. I mean, don't tread on too many if you
can help it. But there's always a few dead 'uns in there anyway. I
wouldn't worry about it.'

'You must be bloody joking, mate.'

*The second man turned and left the doorway. I could see the
farmer pursuing him.*

'Where are you going?'

'No way am I going to trample through a flock of bloody
chickens just to check your circuit.'

'Look, how else are you going to . . .'

*The voices faded out of earshot. I climbed down from my
perch on the canister and dusted off my clothing. As I made
my way back to the fence at the edge of the wood I saw a van
coming up the driveway and pulling to a halt. On the side of the
van was a logo which said* PLUCKALOT CHICKENS – A DIVISION
OF THE BRUNWIN GROUP. *The name at that time was not familiar
to me.*

*

Dorothy was a great believer in research and development, and
over the years the Brunwin Group built up a reputation for
technological innovation, particularly in chicken farming. These
were some of the problems she set out to solve:

1. AGGRESSION: Dorothy's broilers, just before going to
the slaughter at seven weeks old (roughly one fiftieth of the

way through their natural lifespan) were typically allotted a space of half a square foot per bird. Feather-pecking and cannibalism were common among birds held in such confinement.

SOLUTION: After experimenting with special red-tinted spectacles clipped on to the beak (so that, by neutralizing the colour, the bird would be prevented from pecking at the red combs of its fellows), Dorothy replaced these with blinkers which simply blocked off the vision to either side. When this also proved too cumbersome, she applied herself to finding the most effective method of de-beaking. At first it was done with a blow-torch, then with a soldering iron. Finally her designers came up with a small guillotine equipped with hot blades. It was reasonably efficient, except that if the blades were too hot they caused blisters in the mouth; also, since it was necessary to de-beak about fifteen birds a minute, perfect accuracy was not always possible and there were many cases of burned nostrils and facial mutilations. The damaged nerves of the beak stumps had a habit of growing back, turning in upon themselves and forming chronic pain-inducing neuromas. As a last resort, Dorothy arranged for soothing music to be piped into the battery cages and broiler-houses. Manuel and His Music of the Mountains was especially popular.

2. **SECOND PERIOD EGG-PRODUCTION:** For many years, the battery hens were sent to the slaughterhouse at the end of one laying period, after about fifteen months: but Dorothy believed it ought to be possible to hurry them through into a second year of laying.

SOLUTION: Force moulting. She discovered that she could hurry chickens through their moulting period, during which they did not lay eggs, by causing them severe shock through abrupt changes in the lighting pattern or a rigorous programme of food and water deprivation.

3. **MALE CHICKS:** Males born into an egg-laying flock are not genetically bred to fatten up for human consumption, and

have, consequently, no economic value. Clearly they must be destroyed – on the day of birth, if possible – but how?

SOLUTION: For a while Dorothy experimented with a special mill which was capable of mincing 1,000 chicks to pulp every two minutes. The resulting mush could be used either for feed or manure. However, the mills were expensive to install. Decompression through oxygen withdrawal was one possible alternative, as was gassing with chloroform or carbon dioxide. But nothing could really be cheaper, it was finally decided, than good old-fashioned suffocation. The simplest method was to pack thousands of chicks on top of each other and tie them together in sacks. The birds would either suffocate slowly or be crushed to death.

4. STUNNING PRIOR TO SLAUGHTER: Before settling for the standard method of a water bath charged with low-level electric current, Dorothy had tried to patent a form of small gas chamber through which the chickens would pass before being hoisted on to the conveyor belt. It was found, however, that the frantic flapping of wings inside the chamber was causing a loss of roughly $\frac{1}{8}$lb of gas per bird, and so the system was rejected on economic grounds.

Dorothy had always found that cost-effective methods of slaughter were hard to come by. The electrical stunning equipment installed in her abattoirs was both expensive and slow (if used with care, that is). In this respect, at least, she was something of a traditionalist, and privately believed that there was really nothing to beat a well-aimed blow with a poleaxe for stunning pigs and cattle. She also continued to provide specialist services for ritual slaughter, even though many Jews and Moslems had begun to oppose the practice: the market was still there, she argued, and had to be catered for. It was in the business of slaughter, all the same, that she felt her competitors continued to run at a slight advantage, mainly because this was the area which had been most glaringly neglected by George before she assumed overall management. She was amazed to discover that he had almost no personal experience of killing: she once found him weeping openly as he struggled to finish off a cow which was sick with mastitis. His sledgehammer, aimed at the centre of the skull, had gone wide of the mark and crashed through the animal's eye. As it thrashed around in agony, George had just stood there, quivering and numb. It was left to Dorothy to fetch a clamp, secure the bloody, squealing creature by the nostrils and knock it dead with one almighty swing of the hammer. 'Men!' she had muttered, in a scornful tone of voice, and had gone inside to change her clothes before settling down for a pre-dinner gin and tonic.

*

One evening when I was about twenty-four, I went to see a programme of French films presented by the university film society. The first to be shown was Le Sang des Bêtes, *Georges Franju's short documentary about a Parisian slaughterhouse. By the time it was over, the theatre was half empty.*

It was the usual film society audience: hardened connoisseurs of the horror film, in many cases, for whom it was fashionable to admire low-budget movies about American teenagers being dismembered by psychopaths, or science-fiction nightmares full of bloodthirsty special effects. What was it about this film, then, so gentle and melancholy in some respects, that caused women to scream with revulsion, and men to rush for the exits?

I have never seen it since, but many of the details have stayed with me. The beautiful white carthorse keeling over as a spike is plunged into its neck, bringing forth fountains of blood; calves juddering after their throats have been cut, the violent jerking of their heads sending pans of hot blood crashing over and skimming across the floor; rows of headless sheep, their legs still kicking furiously; cows having long steel spikes banged through their skulls into their brains. And then, by way of counterpoint, the girl's voice introducing us to the sad suburbs of Paris – les terrains vagues, jardins des enfants pauvres . . . à la limite de la vie des camions et des trains . . . *The workmen singing Trenet's* 'La Mer' *as they chop up the bodies –* 'ses blancs moutons, avec les anges si pures' . . . *A flock of sheep, bleating like hostages as they are led to the slaughterhouse by the decoy*, le traître, *who knows the way and knows that his own life will be spared:* les autres suivent comme des hommes ... *The workmen whistling, laughing and joking* avec le simple bonne humeur des tueurs, *wielding their hammers, knives, axes and cleavers* sans colère, sans haine ... *without anger, without hate.*

I could not forget this film, and over the next few weeks, during bored moments in the university library, I would look through catalogues of film books and magazines to see if anything had been written about it: hoping, perhaps, that the poleaxe of academic criticism would deal a death blow to the images which continued to twitch horribly in my memory. It didn't happen that way: for instead, after a good deal of searching I came upon a long and brilliant essay by a writer who seemed to have unlocked the secret of its dreadful truthfulness. When I finished reading it I opened my exercise book and copied down these words:

> It's a reminder that what is inevitable may also be spiritually
> unendurable, that what is justifiable may be atrocious ...
> that, like our Mad Mother Nature, our Mad Father Society
> is an organization of deaths as well as of lives ...

*

'So,' said Henry, 'what's new down on the farm?'

'The usual,' said Dorothy. 'Business isn't bad, although it would be a lot better if we didn't have to spend half our time fending off the environmental cranks. These are rather good, aren't they?'

'These' were the fresh quail's eggs, wrapped in roasted green and red peppers, which constituted their hors d'oeuvre. Henry and Dorothy were having supper together in a private dining room at the Heartland Club.

'That was partly what I wanted to talk to you about,' Dorothy continued. 'We've been getting some scare stories from the States. You've heard of a drug called sulphadimidine?'

'Can't say I have. What does it do?'

'Well, as far as pig farming's concerned, it's invaluable. Absolutely invaluable. As you know, we've made enormous advances in production levels over the last twenty years, but there have been one or two adverse side-effects. Respiratory diseases, for one thing: but sulphadimidine can help with some of the worst of these, you see.'

'So where's the problem?'

'Oh, the Americans have been testing it on rats and they reckon it causes cancer. Now apparently they're going to legislate.'

'Hm. And are there other drugs you can use?'

'Nothing as effective. I mean, we could probably cut down on these diseases by stocking less intensively, but . . .'

'Oh, but that's absurd. There's no point interfering with anything which helps you to stay competitive. I'll have a word with the minister about it. I'm sure he'll see your point of view. Tests on rats don't prove anything, anyway. And besides, we have a long and honourable history of ignoring the recommendations of our independent advisers.'

The main course consisted of glazed loin of pork, with garlic potatoes. The meat (like the quail's eggs) was Dorothy's own: her chauffeur had brought it down in an ice-box in the back of the car that afternoon, and she had given the chef detailed instructions on how to prepare it. She kept a small herd of free-range porkers in an enclosure at the back of the farmhouse, for her personal use. Like Hilary (who never watched her own television programmes), Dorothy had no intention of ever consuming the products which she was happy to foist upon an uncomplaining public.

'These environmentalists get up our nose just as much as yours,' said Henry, tucking in with gusto. 'They've wrecked the veal trade, for instance.'

This was true: Britain's largest retail producers of veal had recently scrapped their narrow crates and gone back to straw-yards. In response to public pressure, the managing director had admitted that the intensive system had been 'morally repugnant'.

'Well, I shall carry on using crates,' said Dorothy. 'We can still export them, after all. Besides, there's so much stupid sentimentality about veal calves. They really are the most filthy creatures. If you don't give them anything to drink for a few days, do you know what they do? They start drinking their own urine.'

Henry shook his head incredulously over the vagaries of the

animal kingdom, and refilled their glasses of Sauterne. Meanwhile Dorothy was cutting the fat off her meat and carefully pushing it to one side of the plate. 'We've got to watch out for the lobbyists, anyway. I've a suspicion they're going to get more and more vocal.'

'You've got nothing to worry about,' said Henry. 'The newspapers are never going to run stories about anything as boring as food production, and even if they did, the public wouldn't be interested, because they're stupid. You know that as well as I do. On top of which, most of the data's protected by the Official Secrets Act. Absurd, but true. And anyway, whenever one of these boffins in white coats starts popping up with some crackpot report, what's to stop you getting your own people to produce a set of figures which prove the exact opposite?'

Dorothy smiled. 'You're right, of course. One's inclined to forget that not everyone's as sceptical as you . . .'

'It surprises me to hear you say that,' said Henry, leaning back and loosening his belt with a pleasurable grimace. 'I'm not a sceptic by nature. If anything I'm an idealist. And besides, I happen to believe most of what the nutritionists are saying at the moment. The difference is that I tend to be heartened rather than alarmed by the social implications.'

'Meaning?'

Henry paused, absently wiping gravy from his plate with a finger. 'Put it this way: did you know that over the next five years we were planning to scrap free school meals for more than half a million children?'

'Not calculated to be a very popular move, I wouldn't have thought.'

'Well, there'll be an outcry, of course, but then it'll die down and something else will come along for people to get annoyed about. The important thing is that we save ourselves a lot of money, and meanwhile a whole generation of children from working-class or low-income families will be eating nothing but crisps and chocolate every day. Which means, in the end, that they'll grow up physically weaker and mentally slower.' Dorothy raised an eyebrow at this assertion. 'Oh, yes,' he assured her. 'A diet high in sugars leads to retarded brain growth. Our chaps have proved it.' He smiled. 'As every general knows, the secret of winning any war is to demoralize the enemy.'

The meal concluded with apple-quince bread pudding, smothered in a honey and ginger sauce. The apples, as usual, were from Dorothy's orchard.

*

Ingredients: Modified starch, dried glucose syrup, salt; flavour enhancers monosodium glutamate, sodium 5-ribonucleotide; dextrose, vegetable fat, tomato powder, hydrolysed vegetable protein, yeast extract, dried oxtail, onion powder, spices, flavouring; colours E150, E124, E102; caseinate, acidity regulator E460; emulsifiers E471, E472(b); antioxidant E320.

Once when I was about twenty-five, I came home to visit my parents for the weekend. There were many such weekends during my time at university, but this one stands out because it was then, for the first time, that I noticed how drastically their eating habits had changed since I was a child. It started, probably, when I was eleven and they decided to send me to a fee-paying school. From then on they never seemed to have enough money. My father's rises in salary were small and infrequent, and I think he continued to wish that they had bought a house in a less expensive area. My mother, at this point, went from part-time to full-time teaching. And yet it was a point of honour with her that there should be a hot meal on the table for us every evening. Increasingly, these meals were starting to come from packets, and in the mid 1970s this process was accelerated when they bought a small deep-freeze which was kept in the garage. My father, far from complaining, had developed quite a taste for this sort of food, partly because it bore a resemblance to the lunches which he enjoyed with his colleagues at the office canteen every day. I remember coming home that weekend and finding that the deep-freeze was stacked with more than twenty cartons of one of the Brunwin Group's more lethal inventions: hamburger fritters with chips. All you had to do was shove the whole tray in the oven, and voilà, you had an appetizing meal on your plate in about twenty minutes. He explained that this came in very useful on the two evenings a week when he had to cook for himself, when my mother was working late at the school, supervising extra games. I said that it didn't sound very balanced to me, and he explained that he supplemented it with two more Brunwin delicacies, viz. a powdered soup for starters, and then a strawberry or chocolate flavoured instant whip for pudding.

Ingredients: Sugar, hydrogenated vegetable oil, modified starch; emulsifiers E477, E322; flavourings, lactose, caseinate, fumaric acid; gelling agents E339, E450a; whey powder, stabilizer E440a; colours E110, E160a; antioxidant E320.

All those years, I see now, my father was clogging his arteries up with saturated fats. He would die of a heart attack, not long after his sixty-first birthday.

Does this mean that Dorothy killed my father?

*

Dorothy's record of success in pig management was just as impressive. These are only a few of the difficulties she was able to surmount:

1. **CLUMSINESS:** As soon as she started taking her sows off the earth, away from straw and into concrete stalls, she found that their chain of instinct would be upset: they would become clumsy and often lie on their own piglets while suckling.
   SOLUTION: To fit a farrowing rail, allowing piglets access to the teat without getting close enough to be crushed.

2. **CANNIBALISM:** Denied the opportunity to exercise their rooting instincts, the sows started to eat their own piglets.
   SOLUTION: To fit them into closely confined farrowing crates where they could neither move nor turn around, their movements usually restricted by a device known as the 'iron maiden'. The piglets would then be lured away from their mothers with

an infra-red light. This would reduce the weaning period to two or three weeks, instead of the more usual eight.

3. DISEASE: Unfortunately the piglets treated in this way became subject to severe pulmonary diseases which could only be partially halted by antibiotics and rigid temperature controls.
SOLUTION: Embryotomy. It was discovered that living piglets could be cut from the womb of their dead mother in aseptic conditions in order to establish what was to become known as a 'minimal disease herd'.

4. TAIL-BITING AND BOAR-TAINT: Weaned piglets moved into densely stocked pens soon develop aggressive behaviour, of which tail-biting is the most obvious example. 'Boar-taint' is the strong, unpalatable taste which is alleged by some butchers (notably the supermarket chains) to be found in meat from male pigs.
SOLUTIONS: Tail-docking and castration. Preferably to be done with a blunt instrument, as the crushing action helps to reduce bleeding.

5. DEFORMITY: Dorothy once conducted a survey of 2,000 of her pigs kept on concrete floors, and found that 86 per cent suffered from lameness or serious damage to their hoof horns.
SOLUTION: None. As she once drily remarked to a journalist from *Farmers' Weekly*, 'I don't get paid for producing animals with good posture.'

*

One evening when I was about thirty-seven, I came home to my flat carrying a small plastic bag, half filled with provisions from the local supermarket. I had a pint of milk, some cans of soft drinks, a packet of chocolate biscuits, four Mars bars, a loaf of bread, and one serving of the Brunwin Group's 'Heat'n'Eat' Bangers and Mash, which I put in the oven at once, before transferring my other purchases to the fridge or the food cupboards.

Twenty-five minutes later, when it was time to turn the oven off, I fished the packet out of the waste bin to check that I had followed the instructions correctly: and that was when it happened. It was, I suppose, a sort of epiphany. You have to remember that at this stage I hadn't spoken to anyone for more than a year: I may have been going mad, but I don't think so. I didn't start laughing hysterically, or anything like that. None the less, I experienced what you might call a rare moment of lucidity: a flash of insight, very subtle and fleeting, but enough to produce a lasting change, if not in my life, then at least in my diet from that time onward.

It wasn't so much the picture on the front, although that in itself might have given me pause for thought. A family of four were shown gathered around the dinner table: the healthy, white-teethed paterfamilias, two ruddy-cheeked children beaming with anticipation, and their young, pretty mother, her face lit by an almost beatific glow as she laid the last helping of Bangers and Mash before her husband, as if this meal, the final, crowning triumph to a day of honest toil and wifely achievement, offered the ultimate confirmation of her own self-worth. Such fantasies are thrust upon us every day, and I've become immune to them. But on the back of the packet was a photograph I was not prepared for. It was captioned 'serving suggestion'. It showed a portion of Bangers and Mash on a plate. The Bangers took up one half of the plate, and the Mash took up the other. The plate was on a table, and there was a knife and a fork on either side. And that was it.

I stared at this photograph for some time, while a nasty suspicion began to creep over me. All at once I had the feeling that someone, somewhere, was enjoying a monstrous joke at my expense. And not just at my expense, but at all our expenses. I suddenly took this photograph to be an insult aimed both at myself and at the world in general. I pulled the plastic tray out of the oven and threw it into the bin. It was the last Brunwin meal I ever bought.

I remember being hungry that night.

*

On his way back from the Lake District, only ten miles or so from the farm, George stopped his car by the side of the road and stood for a while at a gate, looking out over the moors. He was reasonably sober, and had no hangover (he never got hangovers these days), but still managed to feel weighed down by a curious heaviness, a sense of foreboding. As usual, he was nervous about seeing his wife again; and to make matters worse, they would be entertaining her insufferable cousins Thomas and Henry the next evening, along with a couple of senior managers from Nutrilite, the Brunwin animal-feed supplier. He was supposed to have discussed a provisional menu with the cook, but had forgotten all about it. Dorothy would probably be furious.

He had been away for three days: three wasted days, because he had come to no important decision regarding his marriage, even though — now he came to think of it — that had been the purpose of the trip, originally. He knew, at least, that he would never be able to leave Dorothy and live with the knowledge that she retained control of the farm; and in that case, it seemed there was nothing for it but to carry on as before. There were always the animals, of course. Pathetic though it might seem, he did not feel that he was completely wasting his life as long as he was able to bring some kind of comfort to the creatures who had suffered the worst of his wife's abuses. He was already looking forward to seeing them again, to revisiting the cowshed and drinking their health from the whisky bottle he kept hidden behind the loose bricks in the wall.

It was late in the afternoon when he arrived home. Dorothy's car was parked in the yard but he was able to sneak round to the kitchens without being seen. The cook was sitting at a table with her feet up, reading a magazine. She did not give a guilty start and resume working when George appeared: it had long been the case (although he never noticed it) that he had absolutely no authority over his staff.

He asked if everything was in order for the dinner tomorrow night, and she told him that it was all under control, that they would be having veal, and that Dorothy herself had chosen the calf and carried out the slaughter less than an hour ago.

George felt suddenly sick. He ran to the cowshed and kicked open the door.

Herbert was not yet dead. He was hanging by his legs from a beam, and blood was dripping from the thinnest of cuts in his neck into a bucket on the floor, now three quarters full. His eyes were milky, pale and sightless. Otherwise, the cowshed was empty.

Beginning to whimper, George ran back to the farmhouse and found Dorothy in her office, tapping away at a computer keyboard.

'Hello, darling,' she said. 'Home already?'

When George didn't answer, she said: 'I'm sorry about your little friend, darling, but he was really the leanest and best-looking of the bunch. It had to be him.'

She swung around in her chair, looked at him, sighed, and left the room. A minute or two later she came back, carrying a shotgun.

'For God's sake,' she said, handing him the gun. 'Finish him off if you want to. He won't taste as good, but who cares? Anything to spare your feelings.'

George took the gun and left. Dorothy went back to her keyboard, and listened out for the shot. In fact there were two, a few seconds apart.

'Idiot,' she muttered. 'He can't even hit a calf from three feet away.'

She was never able to establish, with absolute certainty, which of her farmworkers fed the story to the *News of the World*. She ended up sacking a troublesome middle-aged labourer called Harold, but that was very much by way of killing two birds with one stone, because his lungs were giving out from inhaling too much crop spray and he wasn't much use to her any more. It was unlikely to have been him, on the whole. In any case it was only a small story, tucked away on page nine: a few lurid, joky paragraphs under the headline KINKY FARMER IN CALF-LOVE SUICIDE PACT. Her PR people assured her that no one would take it very seriously, and indeed the whole incident was all but forgotten after a few months.

This would have been in June, 1982.

June 1982

I

The word existed, I knew. I just couldn't think of it.

. . . panache . . . polish . . . style . . .

My aim was to catch the 3.35 train, but this review had taken longer than expected, and now I was running late. Clumsily I stuffed five days' worth of clothes into a holdall, along with a couple of books and my writing pad. I'd been hoping to phone the copy through to the newspaper before I left, but there wasn't time now. It would have to be done when I got to Sheffield. It was always the same: always those last couple of sentences, the even-handed summation, the ironic parting shot, which took such a disproportionate toll on one's time and effort.

I scribbled a note to my flatmate, locked all the doors, and then, bag in hand, climbed the wrought-iron stairs which led up to street level. It was a hot, windless summer day, but because I hadn't stepped out of the flat for more than forty-eight hours – the time it had taken to read the book and formulate my responses to it – the sunlight and the fresh air seemed immediately invigorating. Our basement flat was in a side street not far from the Earl's Court Road, just a few minutes' walk from the tube station. It was a lively area, a little overcrowded, a little seedy; its restless bustle and activity could sometimes be overwhelming, but this afternoon it really lifted my spirits. Suddenly I began to feel, for the very first time, that I might be setting out on a great adventure.

Getting from Earl's Court to St Pancras required a tedious journey of twenty minutes on the Piccadilly Line. As usual I had a book open in my hands, but I couldn't concentrate on it. Currents of anxiety and anticipation shivered through me. It would be strange to see Joan again: at least, not just to see her (I did that nearly every Christmas, when we both went home to visit our parents) but to spend time with her, to become reacquainted. On the telephone she had sounded friendly, confident, authoritative. The invitation to come and visit had been thrown off easily, almost as an afterthought, and it occurred to me now that she probably saw nothing very significant in it – just another house guest to be fleetingly accommodated within what sounded like a busy working schedule – whereas for me it was a development of enormous import and promise: a chance to rediscover the youthful and optimistic self which I had somehow mislaid during that absurd marriage, and to which Joan was now, in effect, the only surviving witness.

These were my thoughts as I travelled towards King's Cross; or some of them, anyway. Much of the journey, to be honest, was spent looking at the women in my carriage. Not only had I been divorced for eight years, but I hadn't made love to a woman for more than nine, and I had in the meantime become an inveterate starer, appraiser, sizer-up of possibilities, my every glance heavy with that furtive intensity which is the hallmark of the truly desperate (and dangerous) male. It quickly became obvious that there were only two serious objects of interest on this occasion. There was one sitting further down my row of seats, next to the doors – small, composed, expensively dressed: the classic, Grace Kelly-style icy blonde. She'd got on at Knightsbridge. And then down at the other end of the carriage was a taller and more ascetic-looking brunette: I'd noticed her on the platform at Earl's Court, but then, as now, it was hard to make out her features behind the curtain of fine dark hair and the newspaper in which she was clearly absorbed. I looked at the blonde again, a risky, sidelong gaze which – unless I was imagining it – she caught and held for a fragile moment, her eyes responding without encourage-ment but also without rebuke. At once I launched into a fantasy, my favourite fantasy: the one in which it turned out, miraculously, that she was getting out at the same stop, continuing on to the same station, catching the same train, travelling to the same town – a series of coincidences which would bring us together while usefully absolving me from the need to take events into my own hands. And so the closer we came to King's Cross, the more I willed her to stay on the train. At every stop I felt the onset of a hollow, tightening dread, and the prospect of falling into conversation with her started to seem more and more desirable, just as her face and figure appeared to take on an extra degree of almost-perfection. Leicester Square. Covent Garden. Holborn. I was sure she was going to get out at Holborn, but no, if anything she seemed to be settling even more comfortably into her seat, her very posture now assuming an air of seductive languor (we were the only passengers left in our half of the carriage and I was getting thoroughly carried away by this stage). Just two more stops. If only . . . If only . . . And then we were pulling into King's Cross, and as I looked at her, unashamedly now, it was suddenly obvious that she had no intention of getting out even here: I was the one who was about to shatter the fantasy, and to make matters worse I stole a final glance, just before the doors opened, and she looked back with a light of lazy inquiry in her eye, unmistakable and transfixing. As I stepped down on to the platform my limbs were leaden; cords of feeling bound me to the train, prohibiting, elastic. It pulled away; I turned, failed to glimpse her; and for the next few minutes, as I made my way to St Pancras, bought my ticket and killed time at the newsagent's kiosk, there was a deadness in my stomach, the bruised sense of having somehow survived yet another in a sequence of tiny tragedies which threatened endless, daily repetition.

Sitting in a carriage of the Sheffield train, waiting for it to shift into motion, I brooded on this humiliating incident and cursed the ill-luck – if that's what it was – which had stamped me forever as a man of imagination rather than action: condemned, like Orpheus, to roam an underworld of fantasies, when my hero Yuri would not have hesitated to plunge boldly towards the stars. A few well-chosen words, that was all it need have taken, and yet I couldn't even think of them: me, a published writer, for God's sake. Instead I was stuck here dreaming up scenarios of ever-spiralling ridiculousness: the latest of which involved the object of my attraction suddenly realizing that she had missed her stop, leaping out at Caledonian Road, hailing a taxi and arriving just in time to jump on my train as it pulled away from the platform. Pathetic. I closed my eyes and tried to think of something else. Something useful, for once. The word: that was what I should be concentrating on, the elusive word . . . It was vital that I should have that final sentence sorted out before arriving in Sheffield.

. . . the necessary *grace* . . . necessary *zest* . . . *esprit* . . .

This stratagem proved surprisingly successful. I became so preoccupied that I never heard the guard's whistle blow; barely noticed the train starting to move; was only dimly aware of the door to my carriage sliding open to admit a breathless, flustered figure who collapsed into a seat just a few rows away from me. It wasn't until we were speeding through the outskirts of London that I registered her presence, looked up, and recognized her as the dark-haired woman from my tube journey. The inevitable thrill of excitement lasted only a fraction of an instant. It was superseded by something much more powerful: a fantastic emotional shockwave, compounded of delight, confusion and, at first, stubborn disbelief. For how could it possibly be true that she appeared to be reading – no, not her newspaper, but a slim, hardback novel with my photograph on the cover?

*

It's every author's dream, I suppose. And since it happens rarely enough even in the life of the literary celebrity, imagine how much more precious it would seem to the young, unknown writer like myself, hungry for any kind of evidence that his work has impinged on the consciousness of the public. The brief, respectful reviews I'd received in the papers and the literary journals – which I'd learned, in some cases, almost off by heart – paled into insignificance in the face of this sudden hint that the wider world might be hiding something else altogether, something unsuspected, alive and arbitrary: a readership. That was my first feeling. And then, of course, came the realization that I had finally been presented with the longed-for opportunity, the foolproof excuse, the perfect doorway into conversation: for it would surely be impolite *not* to introduce myself in these circumstances. The only question was how, and when, to make my move.

I was determined to be subtle about it. It wouldn't do simply to blunder up, sit down opposite her and say something crass like 'I see you're reading one of my books' – or, even worse, 'I admire a woman with good taste in literature'. Far better to arrange it so that *she* made the discovery. Well, that shouldn't be difficult. After a few minutes' hesitation I got up and moved to a seat just across the central aisle from hers, taking my luggage with me. This in itself was enough to make her look up and watch me with surprise; perhaps even annoyance. I said, 'Just trying to get out of the sunlight' – a meaningless remark, given that my new seat was just as much in the sunlight as the old one. She said nothing; just smiled half-heartedly and returned to the book. I could see that she was on about page fifty, roughly a quarter of the way through: only a few pages from what was (or so I had thought when writing it) the most riotously funny scene in the whole novel. I sat back and kept a discreet watch on her from the corner of my eye; taking care, at the same time, to ensure that she had a good view – should she care to glance up – of my profile, seen from much the same angle as had been chosen by the studio photographer whose services I had myself engaged at considerable personal expense. Ten or twelve pages went by, in as many minutes, without producing anything in the way of visible amusement: not even the distant echo of a smile, let alone those helpless spasms of laughter I had fondly imagined the passage provoking in its readers. What on earth was the matter with her? In hardback, my novels sold a pitiful number of copies – five or six hundred, or something – so how had this one managed to fall into the hands of someone so obviously unattuned to its tone and methods? Looking closely at her face for the first time, I noticed the lack of humour in her eyes and the line of her mouth, and the traces of a solemn pucker which had creased her brow into a permanent frown. She read on. I waited another five minutes or more, with growing impatience. I shifted ostentatiously in my seat, even got up twice to take unnecessary items out of my holdall in the luggage rack above me; and finally I was reduced to the expedient of feigning a loud coughing fit, which went on until she looked across at me with wary expectancy, and said:

'I'm sorry, are you trying to attract my attention?'

'No, no, not at all,' I said, conscious of a furious blush starting to inflame my cheek.

'Would you like a cough sweet?'

'No, I'm fine. Really.'

She returned to the book without another word, and I sank back into baffled silence, scarcely able to credit how difficult this was proving. The situation had gone beyond embarrassment into the realm of helpless stupidity. My only remaining option was to say: 'Actually, I *was* trying to get your attention.'

She looked up and waited for me to explain.

'It's just . . . that book you're reading.'

'What about it?'

'Well, don't you notice anything about the photograph on the back?'

She turned it over. 'No, I don't see . . .' And then, looking from me to the photograph, from the photograph to me, she broke into an incredulous smile. 'Well, I'll be . . .' It lit up her whole face, this smile; changed everything at once, so that she was suddenly welcoming and radiant. Then it turned to laughter. 'And you just sitting there . . . I mean, this is incredible. I'm a *huge* fan of yours, you know. I've read all your books.'

'Both of them,' I corrected.

'Both of them, absolutely. Well, I mean, I've read the first one, and now I'm reading this. And enjoying it hugely.'

'Do you mind if . . .?' I gestured at the seat opposite her.

'Do I *mind*? How could I possibly . . . I mean, this is so extraordinary. It's – well, it's every reader's dream, really, isn't it?'

'And every writer's,' I said, moving across to her table.

For a while we just smiled at each other, shyly, uncertain how to start.

'I was watching you, just now,' I said. 'You were reading that big scene, weren't you – at the wedding?'

'The wedding, yes, absolutely. It's such a marvellous chapter, too – so moving.'

'Mm: do you think so? I was really hoping that it would be funny, you see.'

'Oh, but it is. I mean, it's, er, moving . . . and funny. That's what's so terribly clever about it.'

'You didn't seem to be laughing much, that's all.'

'No, I was; I was laughing on the inside, really. I never laugh aloud at books. It's just a thing with me.'

'Well, you've made my day, anyway.' That smile again; and a captivating lightness when she tossed back her hair. 'I'd introduce myself, of course, except that you already know who I am.'

She took the hint. 'Oh, I'm sorry, I should have told you before. My name's Alice. Alice Hastings.'

*

The train was approaching Bedford. Alice and I had been talking for perhaps half an hour; I'd been up to the buffet car and treated her to a sandwich and a cup of coffee; we'd exchanged views on the Falklands War and the merits of various contemporary authors, finding ourselves in agreement in both instances. She had a lovely, rather equine face, a long, graceful neck and her voice was full, fruity, deep. It felt wonderful to be enjoying female company again. The last few years had been so desolate in that respect: that hopeless marriage to Verity, then the decision to go to university in the mid 1970s, where I found, despite my official designation as a 'mature' student, that my fellow undergraduates all seemed to have such a gift for slipping in and out of physical relationships that I, by comparison, ended up feeling like a gawky adolescent. Perhaps that's why the writer's life had always seemed so attractive: the refuge it offered for the socially backward, the gleaming legitimacy it conferred upon solitude. Patrick had hinted as much when he made that crack about there being no 'sexual dimension' to my work; but I pushed that recollection aside. I still burned from that conversation, couldn't imagine when I would next feel equal to the task of facing him again.

'So, where are you heading for, anyway?' Alice asked; and when I told her, 'Do you have family there?'

'No, I'm going to see a friend. She's been living there a few years now. She's a social worker.'

'I see. This is – this is a girlfriend, then, is it?'

'No, no, not at all. Absolutely not. No, Joan and I go . . . way back. I mean —' It suddenly occurred to me that there was a quick and easy way of filling her in on the situation. 'Did you see that feature on me a couple of months ago, in one of the Sunday supplements: "The First Story I Ever Wrote"?'

'Yes, I did. I adored it, too: that terribly funny spoof you wrote on detective stories when you were twelve or something. You must have been such a precocious little thing.'

'I was eight,' I said gravely. 'And it was meant to be perfectly serious. Anyway, Joan was — well, I suppose my best friend in those days. She lived almost next door, and we used to go and play together on this farm: and that photograph which they used in the magazine, the one of me sitting at a desk and looking very serious and intellectual, that was taken in this cowshed where we had a sort of den. I knew it would be the perfect one for them to use — you know, they'd just have to cut it in half so she wasn't actually in it — but I lost my copy years and years ago. I phoned up my parents and they had no idea where it was, either, so in the end I phoned Joan on the off chance that she might still have one. Which she did, much to my amazement: seems that she's hung on to it all this time. And so she sent it down, and — well, it was sort of nice to have made contact again, because we hadn't really had much to say to each other since . . . I don't know, since my rather short-lived marriage, I suppose, and after that we had a few more phone calls and then she asked me if I wanted to come up and stay for a few days and I thought — well, why not? So here I am.'

Alice smiled. 'Sounds like she's a bit stuck on you.'

'Who, Joan? No. We hardly know each other, really. We were just kids.'

'I don't know, though: keeping your photograph all those years. And now that you've had books published and everything you might seem very glamorous to her.'

'No, I mean, all this is really just for . . . you know, old times' sake.'

Despite all that I was doing to play things down, I could see that the subject of Joan was starting to make Alice uncomfortable. A twinge of incipient jealousy, perhaps? Already? That was how I chose to interpret it, at any rate, in my treacherous exhilaration, and my suspicion was merely confirmed when she glanced at her watch and changed the subject with shameless abruptness.

'Do you make much money from writing, Michael?'

This might well have been an impertinent question; but if Alice had taken a risk, it was a well-judged one: I would have told her anything by now.

'Not a lot, no. That's not why you do it, really.'

'No, of course not. I only asked because – well, I'm in the publishing business myself, and I know the kind of sums involved. I know it can't be easy for you.'

'You work in publishing? Who for?'

'Oh, you wouldn't have heard of them. I'm afraid I work at the most disreputable end of the spectrum. Those two deadly words – I can hardly bring myself to utter them.' She leaned forward, and her voice sank to a dramatic whisper: 'Vanity publishing.'

I smiled indulgently. 'Well, most publishing is vanity publishing, when you think about it. I certainly don't earn a living wage, and my writing takes up a lot of time which I suppose I could be spending on other sorts of jobs, so you could say that I was paying for the privilege, in a way.'

'Yes, but we publish the most dreadful kind of rubbish. Terrible novels and boring autobiographies ... Stuff that'll never get within five miles of a halfway decent bookshop.'

'You're an editor for these people, are you?'

'Yes, I have to deal with all these mad authors on the telephone and reassure them that their books are worthwhile, which of course they aren't. And sometimes I have to *find* writers, which is slightly more tricky: you know, somebody wants a book written – a history of their family, or something – and we have to find a writer who'll take it on. That's what I'm trying to do at the moment, as a matter of fact.'

'The arrogance of these people, though: to assume their family histories are worth writing about.'

'Well, they do happen to be quite famous, actually. You've heard of the Winshaws, have you?'

'As in Henry Winshaw, you mean – that maniac who's never off the television?'

She laughed. 'That's right. Well, Henry's . . . aunt, I think it is, wants to have a book written about them all. Only she wants it to be done by – you know, a proper writer. Not just any old hack.'

'God, you'd have to be a glutton for punishment to sign up for that, though, wouldn't you?'

'I suppose you would. All the same, they're absolutely loaded, you know, the lot of them, and it seems she's willing to pay the most absurd amount of money.'

I stroked my chin thoughtfully, beginning to pick up a hint of where this conversation was heading. 'You know, it almost sounds . . . it *almost* sounds as if you're trying to sell this idea to me.'

Alice laughed: she seemed truly shocked by this suggestion. 'To *you*? Goodness, no. I mean, you're a *real* writer, you're *famous*, I'd never in my wildest dreams expect that –'

'But you'd never in your wildest dreams have thought you'd meet me on a train, would you?'

'No, but . . . Oh, I mean, this is ridiculous, it's not even worth talking about. You must have so much to do, so many ideas for new novels . . .'

'As it happens I don't have any ideas for new novels at the moment. I was talking to my editor only a few weeks ago and we reached something of an impasse.'

'But – look, you're not telling me you'd be seriously interested in this, are you?'

'Well, you haven't told me what the deal is yet.'

When she did tell me, I tried to stop my eyes from widening and my jaw from dropping, but it wasn't easy. I tried to look cool and confident in the few seconds it took to work some things out: how I could afford to move out of the flat in Earl's Court, for instance, and buy my own place; how I would be able to live quite comfortably off the sort of sum she was talking about for several years. But there was something else I needed to know, something even more important, before I let myself be taken any further down this dangerous path.

'And this book,' I said: 'this is your project, is it? Your baby.'

'Oh yes, very much so. We'd . . . well, I imagine we'd be working together on it.'

The guard's voice came over the speaker system, announcing that the train was about to arrive in Kettering. Alice stood up.

'Well look, this is where I have to get off. It's been really nice meeting you, and . . . Listen, you don't have to be polite. You wouldn't *really* be interested in taking this on, would you?'

'It's not out of the question, actually. Not by any means.'

She started laughing again. 'I can't believe this is really happening. Honestly, I can't. Look, I've got a card in here somewhere . . .' She fumbled inside her handbag. 'Take this, and give me a call when you've had time to think about it a bit.'

I took the card and glanced at it. The name of the firm, 'The Peacock Press', stood out in red lettering, and beneath it came the legend, 'Hortensia Tonks, Senior Editor'.

'Who's this?' I asked, pointing at the name.

'Oh, that's . . . my boss, I suppose. They haven't given me my own card, yet: I'm a relative newcomer. But who knows,' and here – I can remember this clearly – she touched me lightly on the shoulder, 'you could well turn out to be my passport to promotion. Just wait till I tell them that I've got *Michael Owen* interested in doing the Winshaw book. Just wait.' She crossed out the unfamiliar name and wrote her own, in large, angular handwriting. Then she was taking my hand and pressing it in a formal farewell: 'Well. Bye for now.'

The train was on the point of stopping. Just before she got to the door of the carriage, I said: 'How long did you say you were staying with your sister?'

She turned, still smiling. 'A couple of days. Why?'

'Travelling rather light, aren't you?'

I had suddenly noticed that she had no luggage; just a small black handbag.

'Oh – she keeps a set of things for me. It's lovely – almost like a second home.'

She pushed open the carriage door and left me with a final image of her delighted grin, her waving hand: an image which was to fade slowly into blankness over the eight long years which passed before my next, and final, glimpse of Alice Hastings.

2

. . . necessary *brilliance . . .* necessary *bravado . . .*

Almost. Very close, now. Very close.

*

My spirits continued to rise as the journey progressed. The books I'd brought with me lay unopened on the table, and I abandoned myself instead to dreamy contemplation of the scenery. As we left Derby, the redbricked factories and warehouses backing on to the railway line gave way to rich green countryside: Friesians grazed on hilly pasturelands dotted only with handsome sandstone farmhouses or the occasional village, a few rows of grey slate terraces nestled warmly in a valley. Later, immense heaps of coal began to appear beside the track as Chesterfield announced the beginning of mining country, its skyline dominated at first by cranes and pit shafts and then, incongruously, a crooked church spire which jerked me into nostalgia, taking me back fifteen years or more to the opening credits of a silly comedy series about clergymen which I had enjoyed on television as a teenager. I was sunk deep in the memory of this as we passed through tunnels and long rocky cuttings. The line was planted so thickly with trees that Sheffield itself took me completely by surprise, my first sight of it being a row of terraced houses silhouetted against a sky of Mediterranean blue, and perched on the edge of a ridge, impossibly high: on a clifftop, almost. All at once a spectacular townscape lay before me: the steelworks and factory chimneys beside the railway line were shrunk to insignificance beside the sheerness of the hillsides on which the city had been boldly raised, with phalanxes of tower blocks climbing steeply to their summit. Nothing had prepared me for such sudden, austere beauty.

'Austere beauty': why did I use that phrase, though? Was it

really the city I was describing, or was it the face of Alice which imposed itself on the sombre dignity of these buildings and made them glamorous to my moonstruck eyes? Certainly it was Alice I was thinking of when Joan loomed out of the waiting crowd at the station, her welcoming smile and eager, waving arms striking despondency into my heart in an instant. She had put on weight, and she was not wearing make-up, and she looked very plain and ungainly. (These were not praiseworthy observations, I know: but I might as well be honest about them.) She gave me a bruising hug and a wet kiss on the cheek, and then led me to the car park.

'Let's not go home right away,' she said. 'I'll show you a bit of the city first.'

I'm a Midlander by birth and a Southerner by adoption. Never having lived in the North of England, I've always regarded it from a distance, with a mixture of fear and fascination. It seemed extraordinary, for instance, that I could have been on a train for less than two and a half hours, and disembarked to find myself in a city which felt so palpably and bracingly different from London. I'm not sure whether this difference lay in the architecture, or in the faces of the people surrounding me, or the clothes which they wore, or even in the knowledge that only a few miles away stretched vast and lovely tracts of moorland: but perhaps it went deeper than any of these things, and derived from something fundamental in the very spirit of the place. Joan told me Sheffield's nickname – 'the Socialist Republic of South Yorkshire' – and sang the praises of David Blunkett who at this time led the city's Labour Council. Coming from London, where opposition to Mrs Thatcher was virulent but fatally dispersed and fragmented, I was immediately filled with envy at the thought of a community which could so closely unite itself around a common cause.

'It's nothing like that in the South,' I said. 'Half the socialists I know have defected to the SDP.'

Joan laughed. 'They were routed in the local elections here last month. Even the Liberals only picked up a few seats.' A few minutes later we were driving past the cathedral, and she said, 'I went to a memorial service in there recently, for the people who died on HMS *Sheffield*.'

'They were all from around here, were they?'

'No, not at all. But the local sea cadets were affiliated to the ship, and the crew were always coming to visit children's centres and things like that. We were all devastated when it went down. The "Shiny Sheff", people used to call it. The service was packed: they were turning hundreds away at the door. There was a queue stretching down to York Street.'

'I suppose there must be a lot of anger about the war.'

'Not everybody's angry,' said Joan. 'Not everybody even opposes it. But that wasn't the point. I don't know how to describe it, really, but . . . it was as if we'd all lost relatives on that ship.' She smiled at me. 'This is a very warm city, you see. You can't help but love it, for that very reason.'

Already I felt like a stranger in a foreign land.

*

Joan lived in a small, dark-bricked terraced house not far from the university. There were three bedrooms, two of which she rented out to students in order to help with her mortgage payments. This came as a surprise to me: I'd been expecting that she and I would be alone together for the length of my stay, but it turned out that she was proposing to sleep downstairs while I took over her bedroom. Of course I couldn't allow that to happen, so I found myself facing the prospect of five nights spent on a settee in the living room, to be rudely awoken every morning by the arrival of Joan and her lodgers as they passed through into the kitchen to get their breakfasts.

Both of these lodgers, in fact, were from the polytechnic rather than the university. There was Graham, who was on some sort of film-making course, and a very shy and uncommunicative art student called Phoebe. It soon became obvious that they would not be easy to avoid: Joan presided over a regimented household, and there was a large notice pinned up in the kitchen which set out, in three different coloured inks, the rotas for shopping, washing up and cooking the evening meal. It seemed that I was to be the guest of something closely approximating to a family unit – and, to make matters worse, that there had been much advance discussion of my visit. I had the sense that Joan had been giving me a huge build-up, that by singing the praises of this exotic envoy from literary London she had been trying to stir the others into a state of enthusiasm which they seemed oddly reluctant to share.

These things started to become clear as the four of us sat down to supper together on that first Tuesday evening. It was Joan's turn to cook. We had stuffed avocado with puréed carrot and brown rice, followed by rhubarb crumble. The dining room was small and could almost have been cosy if a little more effort had been made in that direction: instead we ate in the glare of a naked bulb, and beneath the reproachful scrutiny of a number of posters – all of them Graham's, I was to discover – advertising political causes and foreign-language films (of which Godard's *Tout Va Bien* was the only one I recognized). For a while I was more or less excluded from the conversation, which centred on topics of shared interest such as Joan's latest cases and the impending end-of-year assessments at the college. I had to content myself, if that's the word, with munching away at Joan's wholesome food and refilling the wineglasses.

'I'm sorry, Michael,' said Joan finally. 'A lot of this won't mean anything to you. I was thinking perhaps you'd like to come with me on some of my calls tomorrow, and get a sense of what I do. It might be useful to you one day: give you something to write about.'

'Sure,' I said, trying to sound eager and making a poor job of it.

'Then again,' she said, clearly dampened by my response, 'you've probably got some work you want to do. I'd hate to come between you and your Muse.'

'What's this then – another book?' asked Graham, helping himself to more rice.

'Sort of.'

'Graham's been reading your first,' said Joan. 'Haven't you?'

'I started it.' He took an enormous mouthful and swilled it down with some wine. 'Couldn't get beyond the first couple of chapters, though.'

'Fair enough,' I said; but pride wouldn't allow me to leave it at that. 'Do you mind if I ask why?'

'Well, I don't really understand why people write novels any more, to be honest. I mean it's a total irrelevance, the whole thing. Has been ever since the cinema was invented. Oh sure, there are a few people who are still doing interesting things with the form – Robbe-Grillet and the *nouveau roman* crowd – but any serious modern artist who wants to use narrative ought to be working in film. That's my general objection. And more specifically, the problem with the English novel is that there's no tradition of political engagement. I mean, it's all just a lot of pissing about within the limits set down by bourgeois morality, as far as I can see. There's no radicalism. So there's really only one or two novelists in this country that I've got any time for, these days. And I'm afraid you don't seem to be one of them.'

There was a shocked silence. At least, Joan was visibly shocked, and Phoebe was certainly silent. As for myself, I had heard too many speeches like this in my student days to be much put out by it.

'Who would they be, then?' I asked.

'Well, for instance . . .'

Graham mentioned a name, and I smiled: a pleased, private little smile, because it was exactly the name I had been expecting. The ball was very much back in my court now, for this was the same writer whose latest work had fallen into my hands for review. And yes, I had found the word. The word which I had known was out there, all along, just waiting to be matched to its subject.

This was a writer, I should explain, some ten years older than myself, whose three slender novels had been ludicrously overpraised in the national press. Because he made his characters talk in crudely notated dialects and live in conditions of unconvincing squalor, he was hailed as a social realist; because he sometimes played elementary tricks with narrative, in feeble imitation of Sterne and Diderot, he was hailed as an experimental pioneer; and because he made a regular habit of writing letters to the newspapers, criticizing government policy in terms which had always struck me as suggesting a rather timid Leftism, he was hailed as a political radical. More annoying than any of this, however, was his reputation for humour. He had been repeatedly credited with a playful irony, a satiric lightness of touch, which seemed to me to be entirely lacking from his work, characterized as it was by lumbering sarcasm and the occasional abject attempt to jog the reader's elbow with well-signposted jokes. It was this aspect of his style for which I had reserved my final scorn. 'It has become a matter of routine,' I had written, 'to praise Mr —— for his deft combination of wit and political commitment; and even to suggest that here, at last, we have a moral ironist worthy of these ruthless times. We stand badly in need of novels, after all, which show an understanding of the ideological hijack which has taken place so recently in this country, which can see its consequences in human terms and show that the appropriate response lies not merely in sorrow and anger but in mad, incredulous laughter. For many people, it seems, it is only a matter of time before —— writes just such a novel: but this reader remains unconvinced. Whatever his other qualifications for the task, I suspect, finally, that he lacks the necessary –'

And this was where my invention had failed me for so long. What was it that he lacked, exactly? The word that I was looking for had something to do with style, something to do with tone. It wasn't that he lacked compassion, or intelligence, or technique, or ambition: what he lacked was . . . it was an *instinct*, somehow, for putting these things together, but in a nimble, a fleet-footed way. It was a sort of daring, but there also had to be an element of diffidence, because this quality, whatever it was, would only appear truly natural and spontaneous if it was entirely without self-regard. The word was there, and I was only inches away from it. He lacked the necessary *brilliance*, the necessary *bravado*, the necessary . . .

. . . *brio.*

Yes, that was it. Brio. Precisely. It seemed so obvious, already, that I couldn't understand why it had taken me so long to get there. At once an almost mystical sense of its rightness flooded over me: not only was I sure that it put a perfect end to the review, but I also knew, as if by some telepathic process, that it described the single quality which *he*, in his most secret heart of hearts, would yearn to be credited with. I had invaded, penetrated, wormed my way inside him: when the review appeared, on Friday morning, I would wound him; wound him deeply. I had a vision of hallucinogenic intensity, born half from imagination and half from the distant memory of a nameless, black and white, probably American film: a man in a busy, windswept city in the early morning, buying a newspaper from a street-corner vendor, taking it to a coffee bar and thumbing impatiently to a particular page; devouring a sandwich at the counter, and then the movement of his jaws getting slower and slower as he reads, until he screws the newspaper up in disgust, throws it into a bin and storms out of the bar, the anger and disappointment drawn lividly on his face. I knew – as soon as I'd thought of the word, I knew it for a certainty – that this was the scene, in exaggerated form, which would be played out on Friday morning, when he went out to buy the newspaper, or picked it up off his doormat, or as soon as his agent telephoned him with news of my crushing performance. It shames me, now, to think how happy the knowledge made me; or rather, to think how ready I was to mistake for happiness the poisoned stream of satisfaction which welled up inside me.

All I said to Graham was: 'I thought it might be him.'

'Not your cup of tea, I suppose,' he said; and managed to make even this sound like another in my litany of inadequacies.

'He has his moments,' I conceded, and then added casually: 'I've just reviewed his latest, in fact.' I turned to Joan. 'That phone call I had to make just before dinner. I was dictating it to one of the copy-takers.'

Joan blushed with pride, and said to her lodgers: 'Just think – someone makes a phone call from my little sitting room, the words travel all the way down the lines to London, and a few days later, it's in all the papers.'

'The wonders of modern science,' said Graham, and began stacking the plates.

*

The next day, a wet and misty Wednesday, was not a great success. I decided to take Joan up on her invitation and accompany her on some of her visits, but it was a dispiriting experience. The bulk of her work appeared to involve turning up uninvited at family homes in order to conduct furtive interviews with the children while their parents stared on balefully, or beat ungracious retreats to the kitchen to make cups of tea which never got drunk. At first I actually went with her to sit in on these encounters, but my presence was so obviously unwelcome that I gave up on that after the first couple of visits and spent the rest of the day sitting in Joan's car, reading through the pile of old magazines and newspapers which cluttered her back seat and waiting tiredly for her to emerge from the doorway of some council house or tower block.

For lunch we went to a pub in the centre of town. Joan had a vegetable pasty and I had steak and kidney pie, which caused her to tut reprovingly. That evening, it was Graham's turn to cook. The dish he prepared for us may or may not have had a name: it seemed to consist mainly of lentils and walnuts burned down to a black crust, scraped off the bottom of a large saucepan, and served with a dollop of wholemeal pasta ribbons which had the texture of rubber bands. We ate, for the most part, in absorbed silence.

'You ought to show Michael some of your work, tomorrow,' said Joan to Graham at one point. 'He might have some interesting comments to make.'

'I should like that,' I said.

*

Graham sat me down on his bed and switched on the large, unwieldy television which dominated one corner of his bedroom. It took nearly a minute to warm up.

'1970s vintage,' he explained. 'Pretty much on its last legs.'

Yesterday's mist had cleared and the morning was turning out bright but muggy. Not that much of the sunshine would come our way: Graham's room was permanently in shadow, with a tiny, lace-curtained window which looked out over Joan's back yard and the back yards of other houses in the next street. We were alone in the house, it was half past ten and we were both on to our second cups of strong, sugary tea.

'Have you got one of these yourself?' Graham asked, kneeling down to slot a VHS tape into the video machine.

'Can't afford it on what I earn,' I said. 'I'm waiting for the prices to come down. They say they're going to tumble.'

'You don't think I own this, do you? Nobody's buying the things – you do it on the rental. Ten quid a month is all this costs me, down at Rumbelows.'

I sipped my tea and said spitefully: 'When I was a student we used to spend our money on books.'

'Don't give me that.' Graham gestured at the rows of tapes which lined his dresser and window-sill. 'These *are* my books. This is the medium of the future, as far as film-making's concerned. Nearly all our work at college is done on video now. Three hours of tape, there is, on one of these little beauties. Do you know how much three hours' worth of sixteen mill would cost you?'

'I see your point.'

'Not too hot on the practicalities, you literary types, are you? It's all ivory tower with you.'

I ignored this.

'Does it have a freeze frame, your video?'

'Sure. It's a bit shaky, but it does the job. Why, what do you want one of those for?'

'Oh, you know – It's nice to have . . . all the gadgets.'

The screen flickered into action just as Graham finished closing the curtains and seating himself beside me on the bed.

'Here we go, then. This is my end-of-year assignment. See what you think.'

It was a less painful experience than I had anticipated. Graham's film was only about ten minutes long, and proved to be an efficient if unsubtle piece of polemic about the Falklands conflict, called 'Mrs Thatcher's War'. The title was double-edged, because he had somehow managed to find a pensioner called Mrs Thatcher who lived in Sheffield, and shots of warships steaming into battle and extracts from the Prime Minister's speeches were juxtaposed with scenes from the life of her less eminent namesake: making trips to the shops, preparing frugal meals, watching news bulletins on the television and so on. In a disjointed voice-over commentary, the old woman spoke of the difficulties of getting by on her pension and wondered what had become of all the money she had paid in taxes throughout her working life: this was usually the cue for a rapid cut to some brutal and expensive-looking piece of military hardware. The film ended with the Prime Minister's famous speech to the Scottish Conservative Party, in which she described the war as a battle between good and evil and declared that 'It must be finished', followed by a lingering shot of the other Mrs Thatcher carrying a heavy bag of groceries up a steep, forbidding street. Then the screen faded to black and two captions appeared: 'Mrs Emily Thatcher supports herself on a weekly income of £43.37'; 'The cost of the Falklands War has already been estimated at £700,000,000.'

Graham turned off the tape.

'So – what did you think? Come on, your honest opinion.'

'I liked it. It was good.'

'Look, just try to forget that Southern middle-class politeness kick for a minute. Give it to me straight.'

'I told you, it was good. Powerful, and direct, and . . . truthful. It tells the truth about something.'

'Ah, but does it, though? You see, film's such a tightly structured medium, that even in a short piece of work like this, all sorts of decisions have to be made. How long a shot's going to last, how a shot's going to be framed, which shots are going to come before it, which ones are going to come after. Now doesn't that whole process become suspect when you're dealing with something that advertises itself explicitly as a political film? Doesn't it make the role of the film-maker himself intensely problematic, prompting the question – not "Is this the truth?" but "Whose truth is it anyway?"'

'You're absolutely right, of course. Do you think you could show me how this freeze frame business works?'

'Sure.' Graham picked up the remote control, rewound the tape a few minutes and then pressed Play. 'So my point is that the whole thing is deeply manipulative, not just of the audience, but of its subject. Mrs Thatcher invaded the Falklands and I invaded this woman's life – both of us on the same pretext, that we had their best interests at heart.' He pressed Pause and the old woman froze into jittery stillness, in the act of opening a can of soup. 'In a way the only really honest thing for me to do would be to expose the mechanics of my involvement: to have the camera pan round and suddenly rest on me, the director, sitting in the room with her. Perhaps that's what Godard would have done.'

'Can't you get rid of those lines across the screen?' I asked.

'Sometimes you can. You just have to keep pressing the button and eventually they go away.'

He pressed the pause button some more times.

'It's a bit blurred, isn't it?'

'The technology'll improve. Anyway, would it have been anything more than an empty self-referential gesture, that's what I have to ask myself. Because I know exactly what you're going to say next: you're going to say that any attempt to foreground issues of authorship would just be a throwback to formalism, a futile strategy to shift emphasis from the signified to the signifier which can't do anything to alter the basic fact that, at the end of the day, all truth is ideological.'

'Do all the machines have this feature,' I asked, 'or do you have to go to the more expensive end of the market?'

'They've all got them,' he said. 'It's their main selling point. Quite a radical development, when you think about it: for the first time in history, control over cinematic time is being given to the audience and taken out of the film-maker's hands. You could argue that it's the first real move towards the democratization of the viewing process. Though of course' – he switched off the tape and stood up to draw the curtains – 'it'd be naïve to suggest that that's why people were buying them. At college we call it the WP button.'

'WP?'

'Wankers' paradise. All your favourite movie stars in the buff, you see. No more of those tantalizing scenes when some gorgeous actress drops them for a couple of seconds and then disappears out of the frame: now you can stare at her for as long as you like. For an eternity, in theory. Or at least until the tape wears out.'

I looked past him, gazing sightlessly at the window. 'That would certainly . . . have its uses,' I said.

'Anyway, it's been nice having this chat,' said Graham. 'It's always helpful, getting a bit of objective criticism from someone.'

There was a short pause and then I snapped out of my reverie, suddenly hearing him again. 'That's OK,' I said. 'I found it very interesting.'

'Well look, I'm just going into town. Can I get you anything?'

*

I was alone in the house for the first time. There is a sort of quietness I associate with such moments: more than absolute, it insinuates, takes root, and keeps watch. The opposite of a dead silence, it quivers with possibility. It is alive with the sound of nothing happening. You don't get silence like this in London: not silence that you can listen to, savour, swathe yourself in. I found that I was walking around the house on tiptoe, and that the occasional noises of footsteps outside in the street or cars chugging past seemed highly intrusive. I tried to settle down and read the newspaper but could only manage it for a minute or two. With Graham's departure the house had changed its character completely – had taken on a magical aspect, like a forbidden temple which I had somehow managed to infiltrate, and I was seized with the impulse to explore.

I made my way up the staircase, turned right on the landing, and stepped into Joan's bedroom. It was a bright, cheerful room which faced on to the main road. There was a double bed, neatly made, with a pink duvet and several pale blue cushions arranged against the pillows. In the middle of these sat a figure I recognized from one of memory's most distant corners: a battered yellow teddy bear called Barnabas, her bedtime companion since infancy. I noticed that his eyes didn't match any more: one was black and the other was blue. It must have come off quite recently, and a brief, affecting image flickered across my mind – Joan sitting at the end of the bed, a needle and thread in her hand, sewing the button on, patiently restoring eyesight to this worn childhood relic. I didn't touch him. I glanced at the neatly stacked bookshelves, the family photographs, the desk with its gift stationery and Liberty print lamp. In the corner there were more functional-looking ring binders and a cardboard box full of notes and papers. Nothing on her bedside table besides a half-empty glass of water, a box of tissues and a magazine, the cover of which boasted a picture of two green bomber jets in mid-flight, with the caption 'The Mark 1 Hurricane – Britain's wartime triumph'. I smiled and picked it up. This was the Sunday newspaper magazine published a couple of months ago with my juvenile story in it. I wondered whether Joan had simply never got around to putting it away, or if it was there for a reason, to be marvelled at and pored over every night before going to sleep. I wouldn't have been surprised.

If this was the case, anyway, who was I to make fun of her: I had read and re-read the thing often enough myself, and even now I couldn't resist sitting down on the bed, opening the magazine at the familiar page and immersing myself once again in the warm waters of that shallow glory.

Michael Owen [read the introduction] was born in Birmingham in 1952 and has recently received great acclaim for his novels *Accidents Will Happen* and *The Loving Touch*.
Michael was only eight years old when he created his first fictional character, a Victorian detective who went by the exotic name of Jason Rudd. He was the subject of numerous adventures, the longest and most exciting being The Castle of Mystery, *of which we present the opening pages here. Sadly this is not the first in the series – an earlier case, involving a character called Thomas Watson mentioned in this extract, has been lost – but Michael assures us that it provides a good introduction to the world of Rudd and his assistant Richard Marple, which he describes as 'Holmes and Watson revisited, with a healthy dash of surrealism'.*

THE CASTLE OF MYSTERY
Chapter One

Jason Rudd, a distinguished detective of the 19th Century sat at a wooden carved table, opposite his companion Richard Marple, who had accompanied him on many of his adventures.

Jason was middle-sized and had light hair. He was more or less the bravest of the two, but Richard was extremely courageous too. Richard had dark hair and was very tall, but Jason had the brains. He could not do without Richard.

You see, Richard could perform athletic feats, and Jason couldn't. They were about the most formidable combination in Britain.

At this moment however they were engaged in a game of Chess. The board was old and dirty, despite Jason's efforts to polish it. Jason moved his knight and smiled.

'Check', he said.

But Richard moved his bishop and took Jason's knight.

'Bother'!

Jason sat extremely still hardly breathing. He always did this when he was thinking. He moved his queen.

'Checkmate'!

'You've won, well done'.

The two shook hands then sat down.

'I'm getting exceptionally bored', pronounced Jason. 'I want something to think about. I mean, chess is alright but I'd like something like that Thomas Watson business, which reminds me, how is Thomas?'

'Not too good I'm afraid. His arm is yet to heal'.

'Is he in danger of dying, or worse?'

'He is in danger of dying'.

'He is? That is bad. We must see him. What about tomorrow or the next day?'

'Tomorrow would be convenient'.

'Then shall we make a day of it?'

'Certainly, if my wife approves. Er, what is the time please?'

'Five minutes past ten'.

'Then I had better be going'.

'Alright,' said Jason, 'Shall I see you out?'

'No thank you'.

Jason watched Richard get his coat. He heard the door open then close.

Richard walked out. He was half-way home when a man stepped out of the dark and blocked Richard's way.

'I'm Edward Whiter', he said.

He had an American accent, a beard and yellow teeth.

'Are you Richard Marple?'

'I am'.

'I would wish to see you and Mr Jason Rudd together now'.

'For what reason?'

'I want to talk to you. It is about a very frightening business and I wish you would help me'.

'Then when do you want us to start this?'

'Tomorrow'.

'I am sorry but that is impossible'.

'You must do it'.

'Why?'

'Because we don't want our people to believe in it'.

'Believe in what?'

Edward lowered his voice and whispered 'The curse'.

'The curse? What curse?'

'The curse of Hacrio Castle'.

'Alright. I'll take you to see Jason. I'm sure that he'll be very interested'.

'That's good'. He now spoke with an English accent. He sounded much pleasanter. He ripped off a false beard and smiled.

'I'm very pleased to meet you Mr Marple,' he said. Richard, being rather surprised held out his hand. They shook hands.

'I – I'm very pleased to meet you Mr – Mr Whiter'.

'Please, call me Edward. Now come on, where is Mr Rudd's house?'

*   *   *

'I wish to tell you a story Mr Rudd. I imagine that it should interest you greatly. Shall I begin?'

'Most certainly'.

'Then I shall. It was dark. There was a terrible thunderstorm breaking out over Hacrio Castle. Faint cries were coming from inside. The Black Knight was hammering Walter Bimton to death with a spiked mace. Goodbye Mr Rudd'.

He got up and left the room. Jason heard the front door open and then shut.

'A most surprising visitor. I wonder why he left so soon?'

'I don't know', said Richard. 'What do you think of the story?'

'It was most interesting. We must locate Hacrio Castle. It will be most interesting for us to investigate'.

'Yes'.

'However, at present I am more interested in Edward Whiter. Why did he go so quickly? Why, he barely said a few words before he left'.

'It is so, Jason. I wonder also. Perhaps we will get the answer later'.

'It may be. Anyway, Hacrio Castle – have you ever heard of it?'

'No, not at all, and I haven't got any idea of what it might look like, either'.

'Neither have I', admitted Jason. 'Still I don't suppose it would be of any use anyway'.

'You're probably right. Got any ideas as to what mystery may surround it?'

'Oh yes, I think I have'.

'You do?'

'Yes'. He lowered his voice. 'I think it's cursed'.

I closed the magazine, after taking a last look at that silly photograph of me looking precocious and introspective in Mr Nuttall's cowshed, and put it back on Joan's bedside table. It was strange reading that story again; like hearing an unfamiliar voice on a tape recorder and steadfastly refusing to believe that it could be your own. The temptation was to think of it as another potential bridge to the past: a way of retracing my steps until I would be brought face to face with the eight-year-old innocent who had written it, and who now seemed such a perfect stranger. But it was obvious enough, even to me, that it actually said less about the kind of child I had been than about the books I was reading at the time: stories of nice middle-class children spending holidays together in rambling country houses which would turn out to be crammed with trapdoors and secret passages; stories of Gothic adventure unfolding in lurid comic strips, their detail hovering just this side of parental acceptability; stories of remote and enviable American teenagers who formed themselves into detective clubs, and seemed to live in unlikely proximity to any number of haunted castles, ghostly mansions and mysterious islands. It was years since I'd read one of these books. Most of my copies had been given away to church jumble sales by my mother. But it was a safe bet, I thought, that there would be a few such items still to be found on Joan's bookshelf: and I was absolutely right. I plucked at a colourful spine and found myself staring at a cover illustration which instantly gave off the dusty odour of past pleasures. It was tempting to take the book downstairs and start reading it there and then, but some puritanical impulse stopped me, insisting that I had better things to do than to wallow in this sort of nostalgia. So I put it back on the shelf, tiptoed out on to the landing and, resuming my earlier (and certainly no more noble) programme of exploration, pushed open the door to Phoebe's room.

It was the largest of the three bedrooms; also the most cluttered, because it clearly served as both living quarters and studio space. A variety of paint pots, brushes soaking in cleaning fluid, old newspapers scattered over the floor and rags streaked with multicoloured oils all testified to the nature of her work; and in front of the window, catching the best of the sunlight, there was an easel supporting a large canvas, hidden from view by an off-white sheet. I must admit that I hadn't been much prey to curiosity regarding Phoebe up until this point: I had noticed, in a superficial way, that she was very attractive (oddly enough she reminded me of Shirley Eaton, whose image had for so long provided my ideal of feminine beauty), but this would probably have had more effect if I hadn't still been under the spell cast by Alice during our short meeting; and to me, at any rate, she had said scarcely anything of interest – had said scarcely anything at all, if it came to that – since my arrival. And yet there was something irresistible about the idea of spying on her work in progress; something wickedly analogous, I suppose, to the thought of glimpsing her in a state of undress. I took hold of a corner of the sheet and lifted it two or three inches. A tantalizing area of thick, grey-green paint came into view. I raised the sheet some more, until I could just about see a provocative little band of coppery red, placed teasingly on the edge of the canvas. It was more than I could bear, and in one sudden, ruthless movement I whipped the sheet away, so that the entire picture stood exposed to me in all its unfinished glory.

I looked at it for several minutes before it started to make any sense. All I could see at first was this random patchwork of colour, striking enough in itself, but oppressive and disorientating. Then gradually, as I began to make out certain curves and boundaries, it came to seem less like a patchwork and more like a vortex, and I felt myself caught up in a giddying swirl of movement and energy. Finally, some shapes started to emerge, and I began the treacherous business of trying to put a name to them: that globe, which dominated the left-hand side of the painting, and what seemed to be some sort of netted implement . . . Could it be anything as mundane as a clogged and muddled still life? A roughly sketched scrub of waste land – in the corner of Joan's back yard, say – with a football and an old tennis racket in it? It seemed increasingly likely, and I felt my excitement begin to subside, when . . .

'Please don't look at that.'

Phoebe stood in the doorway, clutching a paper bag to her chest.

There was nothing I could say, except, 'I'm sorry, I – I was just curious.'

She carried the paper bag to her desk and took out a drawing pad and some pencils.

'I don't mind you coming in here,' she said. 'But I don't like people looking at my work.'

'I'm sorry, I should have just . . . asked you or something –'

'It isn't that.' She pulled the sheet back over the canvas and started to rearrange the bunch of wilting gyp which stood in a jam jar on her window-sill.

'It's very good,' I said. I could feel her grow suddenly tense, but persisted in blundering on: 'I mean, to fill a picture with so much drama and power, when you're dealing with a couple of everyday objects like that; it's remarkable. I mean, a football and a tennis racket – who would have thought it . . .?'

Phoebe turned to face me, but her eyes remained lowered and her voice muted. 'I don't have much confidence in my abilities as a painter.'

'Well you should.'

'It's the last in a series of six pictures inspired by the Orpheus legend.'

'And if the others are as good as th– ' I stared at her in surprise. 'Pardon?'

'It shows his lyre and his disembodied head being carried along by the waters of the Hebrus.'

I sat down on the bed. 'Ah.'

'Now you see why I don't like to show people my work.'

There was little prospect of an end to the ensuing silence. I looked blankly into the middle distance, too flustered to manage anything in the way of an apology, while Phoebe sat down at her desk and started to sharpen one of the pencils. I had almost come to the conclusion that it would be best if I got up and left without another word, when she said abruptly: 'Has she changed much?'

This threw me at first.

'I'm sorry?'

'Joan. Has she changed much, since you knew her?'

'Oh. No, not really.' Then I thought about it. 'Well to be honest, I can't really say. I mean, I've never really known her as an adult, only as a child. It's been a bit like meeting her for the first time.'

'Yes, I'd noticed. You're almost like strangers.'

I shrugged: but in a rueful rather than a nonchalant way. 'Perhaps it was a bad idea for me to come.'

'No, I don't think so. She's been looking forward to this for weeks. And she loves having you here, I can tell. She's very different with you around. Graham thinks so too.'

'In what way different?'

'Less . . . desperate, I suppose.'

I didn't like the sound of that.

'I think she gets lonely up here, you see. And her work can be very demanding. We both do our best to jolly her along. I know she's dreading the summer, when we're not going to be here to keep her company. Not that we find it a strain, or anything,' she added earnestly. 'We both get on with her all right, and there are really only one or two things which seem – well, beyond the call of duty . . . Like when we have to play games.'

'Games?'

'Quite often, after dinner, she wants us to play board games. Monopoly, Snakes and Ladders, things like that.'

I said nothing; just shuddered, for some reason.

'Anyway, that's one thing you don't have to worry about. She won't be doing it while you're here, that's for sure. Doesn't have to.'

*

'Now – who's for a quick game of Scrabble?'

Joan beamed expectantly around the table, and all three of us did our best to avoid meeting her eye. Graham resorted to his trick of stacking the plates again, Phoebe concentrated on slowly draining what was left in her wineglass, and I developed a sudden interest in translating the Polish Trade Union poster which had been staring me in the face for the last three evenings. But then, after a few seconds, I began to sense that the other two were relying on me to come to the rescue, so I said: 'Actually I could do with an hour or two alone with my notebook, if that's all right. The ideas have been coming thick and fast today.'

Brazen falsehood though it was, it was the only excuse Joan was likely to accept. 'Oh well,' she said, 'I'd hate to come between you and your Muse. But if this is a new book you're working on, you must make me a promise.'

'What's that?'

'That I can be the first person to read it when you've finished, of course.'

I smiled awkwardly. 'Well, this is something of a long-term project: I doubt if it'll see the light of day for years. In the meantime I've got something else to be thinking about. I'm contemplating a move into non-fiction.' It was hard to tell, from her expression, whether Joan was impressed or baffled by this revelation. 'I've been offered the job of writing the history of a certain eminent family. It's quite a distinction, if you must know.'

'Oh – and who might they be?'

I told her, and Graham snorted with incredulous laughter.

'That bunch of vampires? Well, you must be on your uppers,

that's all I can say.' He disappeared into the kitchen, carrying our plates and the remains of Phoebe's excellent *parmigiana*. As he left he could still be heard muttering, 'The Winshaws, eh? That's a good one.'

Joan stared after him, her eyes wide with incomprehension.

'Well I don't understand what he meant by that. What's so special about the Winshaws?' She turned to me for enlightenment, but Graham's reaction had stung me into sulky silence. 'Do you know what he was talking about?' she asked Phoebe. 'Have you heard of the Winshaws?'

Phoebe nodded. 'I've heard of Roderick Winshaw. He's an art dealer. He was meant to come and give a talk to us a few weeks ago, actually, about survival in the marketplace, but he never showed up.'

'Well, Michael,' said Joan, 'you certainly are a dark horse. I want to hear all about it. I insist.'

'Oh, it's all quite –'

'Not now, not now.' She held up a restraining hand. 'You've got work to do, I realize that. No, we'll have plenty of time to hear the whole story tomorrow. We'll have all day, in fact.'

That sounded ominous. 'We will?'

'Did I not tell you? I've managed to get the day off, so we can go out to the dales for a picnic, the two of us.'

'Mm. Sounds lovely.'

'And rather than take the boring old car, I thought we'd cycle.'

'Cycle?'

'Yes. Graham's said that you can borrow his bike. Isn't that nice of him?'

Graham, returning to the table to collect the cutlery, flashed me a malicious grin.

'Very nice,' I said. 'Very nice indeed. Is the weather going to be good enough?'

'Well, it's funny you should mention that,' said Joan, 'because there are storms forecast for the end of the day. But we should be fine if we set off in plenty of time. I thought if we got up at, say . . . six o'clock?'

The will to resist had deserted me. 'Why not?' I said, and handed Graham my fork and empty glass.

*

That night I found it impossible to get to sleep. I don't know what it was: maybe the thick summer heat, or perhaps simply the knowledge that I had to get up early the next morning, but I lay on that sofa for more than an hour, each position more uncomfortable than the last, until there was nothing for it but to try and find something to read; something to clear my mind of the tired spiral of thoughts which seemed to be clogging it up. But there were no books downstairs: only the ones I had brought with me, and three or four vegetarian cookbooks in the kitchen. That wasn't what I needed at all. I needed something undemanding but compulsive, and immediately I found myself thinking of the children's mystery story I'd rediscovered in Joan's room today. If only I'd brought it down with me while I had the chance.

Ten minutes later, I knew that the only solution was to steal up to her room and fetch it.

I was in luck. Her door had been left a couple of inches ajar, and I could tell that her curtains were open, letting in a good deal of light from the street lamps. Since the bookshelf was right next to the door, there should be no problem slipping in there without waking her up. I paused on the landing for just a second or two, listening, then eased the door gently open and stepped inside. It was about half past one in the morning.

Joan was lying on her back, her skin grey and luminescent in the silver lamplight. She was not wearing any nightclothes, and had thrown off most of the duvet in her sleep. It was eight years since I'd seen a naked female body, in the flesh, as it were; and I think it's true to say that I had never seen one as beautiful as this. Verity had been slender, strong-boned and small-breasted; by comparison Joan, basking without shame in the fullness of my hot gaze, seemed almost immorally ample and voluptuous. The word 'generous' came to mind: it was a generous body, both in the heavy grace of its proportions and in the uncomplicated readiness with which it submitted to my scrutiny. I stood there, transfixed, and it seems to me now that those few guilty moments were among the most glorious, the most unlooked-for, the most thrilling of my life. And yet it was all over so quickly. In no time at all, Joan had stirred, turned towards me, and I backed out of the door without making a sound.

3

'Look at these arms,' she said, squinting at them irritably and pinching the pale flesh until it blushed pink. 'Like an Italian peasant woman. I just tell myself it's in the genes and there's no point in fretting.' She spread raspberry jam thickly on to a slice of granary loaf and bit into it, then wiped her mouth with a paper napkin. 'Do you think I'm overweight?'

'Of course you aren't. You know, your body is something you should feel comfortable about. It doesn't have to be a particular shape.'

The shape of Joan's body was very much on my mind that day, I have to admit. It was another hot summer morning and it had taken us nearly two hours to cycle out into open country. As soon as we reached what Joan deemed to be a suitable location we threw ourselves down upon the ground, and for the next few minutes, in spite of my fatigue, I was acutely conscious of the lazy pleasure with which she was stretching her limbs, the movement of her breasts as her breathing rose and fell, the thinness of the pink and blue blouse which she had untucked from her jeans and rolled up at the sleeve. For my part, I was bathed in sweat and panting noisily. For the first part of the ride I hadn't been sure that I was going to make it. Joan had led me on a steady climb, choosing the steeper road every time we came to a junction: sometimes the incline had been so fierce that I nearly keeled over, it was so hard to keep moving. (Graham's bicycle, I need hardly mention, was not equipped with gears.) But then I found myself getting more confident and the going became easier. Soon the terrain had levelled out, and at one point we hit upon a fabulous stretch of road – downhill but not too steep, just enough to get a bit of speed up, take your feet off the pedals and coast forward with the wind skimming your face and rushing through your ears, sweet tears of excitement welling at the corner of each eye. For a brief instant I felt the years slipping away, like a heavy burden which had been breaking my back, and we were children again, Joan and I, riding down the lane towards Mr Nuttall's farm. She told me afterwards that I had let out a whoop of joy. I wasn't aware of it at the time.

'So,' she said, 'are you going to tell me about this mysterious new project of yours?'

'It's not definite yet,' I insisted, and then gave her a full account of my extraordinary meeting on the train.

Joan gasped when I got to the part about sharing a carriage with somebody who was reading one of my books. 'How *amazing!*' she said. As soon as I had finished, she wanted to know, 'I suppose she was pretty, was she, this Alice woman?'

'No, not especially.' It was surprisingly difficult to say this. The mere act of telling the story had brought Alice's beauty vividly back to mind, and Joan at once seemed as plain and ungainly as when I had first caught sight of her on the station platform. I fought hard against this realization but there was no stopping it: I felt a shiver of desire pass through me as soon as I remembered the laughter and the teasing invitation I had glimpsed in Alice's eyes.

'Cold?' said Joan. 'Surely not.'

We talked a little more about the Winshaws and my writing and this somehow got us on to the subject of the stories we used to make up when we were children.

'I suppose it's rather exciting,' Joan said, 'to think that I once collaborated with a famous author.'

I laughed. '*Jason Rudd and the Hampton Court Murders.* I wonder what happened to that little masterpiece. I don't suppose you kept it, did you?'

'You know very well that you had the only copy. And you probably threw it away. You were always ruthless about things like that. I mean, fancy having to come to me for that photograph.'

'I didn't throw that picture away, I lost it. I told you that.'

'I don't see how it could have just got lost, I really don't.

Anyway, I remember you throwing all your Jason Rudd stories away when you started on your science fiction phase.'

'Science fiction? Me?'

'You know, when you wouldn't write or talk about anything except Yuri Gagarin, and you tried to make me read that long story about him flying to Venus or something and I wasn't interested.'

The shapeless memory of some ancient but wounding disagreement arose before me and prompted a smile. For the first time I realized how nice it was to be with Joan again; to be able to feel that life did in fact have a sort of continuity, that the past was not an ignoble secret to be locked away but something to be shared and wondered at. It was a warm, uncomplicated feeling. But then Joan, having finished her meal, turned over and lay at my feet, resting on her elbows, cupping her chin in her hands and affording me a panoramic view of her cleavage; and suddenly I was caught again in a tangle of different impulses, urging me to look and not to look. Of course I turned away, and pretended to be admiring the scenery, so that a difficult silence descended until Joan gave up and asked the inevitable question: 'What are you thinking?'

'I was thinking about my review. He'll have read it by now. I wonder how he's taking it.'

Joan rolled on to her back, plucked a long blade of grass and began chewing it. 'Do you really suppose people care what you say about them?'

'In this case,' I said, my eyes still fixed on the horizon: 'Yes, I do.'

*

Storm clouds gathered. There was a black bank of them, ranged so threateningly in the western sky that by four o'clock in the afternoon we both decided it would be sensible to head for home. Besides, it was Joan's turn on the cooking rota again. 'It wouldn't do to let them down,' she said. 'They'll be counting on me.'

When we got back to the house she went straight into the kitchen and started chopping vegetables. I was so tired by this stage that my legs would barely support me. I asked if she would mind me lying down on her bed for a little while and she said no, of course not, fixing me at the same time with a look of such concern that I felt obliged to say: 'It's been a great day, though. I really enjoyed it.'

'It has, hasn't it?' She went back to her chopping board and added, half to herself, 'I'm so glad I've got you till Sunday. Two more lovely days.'

On my way through the sitting room I passed Graham, who was busy reading the film reviews in the paper.

'Have a good trip, did you?' he asked, without looking up.

'Very nice, thank you.'

'You got back just in time, I reckon. It's going to piss down in a minute.'

'Looks like it.'

'I've just been reading your piece.'

'Oh yes?'

'Very enigmatic.'

I lay on Joan's bed for about twenty minutes wondering what on earth he could have meant by that remark. Enigmatic? There was nothing enigmatic about what I'd written. I'd gone out of my way to make my feelings plain, in fact. If anything it was Graham who was being enigmatic. I knew the piece off by heart and went through it, sentence by sentence, to see if there was anything that might have thrown him. This drew a blank, and for a while I tried to put the whole thing out of my mind, but still his peculiar phrase nagged away at me. Finally I knew that it wouldn't give me any more rest, so I went back downstairs to see if there was an explanation.

Graham was watching a local news programme on Joan's television. I picked up his discarded paper and glanced at my review, pleased to see that it had been laid out prominently at the top of the page.

'I don't see what's so enigmatic about this,' I said, reading the first paragraph to myself and admiring the quietly sarcastic note I had managed to inject into a simple plot summary.

'Look, it's no big deal,' said Graham. 'It's only a bloody review, after all. I just couldn't see what you were getting at.'

'Seems fairly clear to me.' I was on to the second paragraph, where the tone began to get more explicitly frosty. I could imagine my subject starting to bristle with apprehension at this point.

'Look, there's obviously some clever metaphor or figure of speech that I've missed out on,' said Graham. 'I'm sure your metropolitan friends will understand it.'

'I really don't know what you're talking about,' I said. I couldn't help smiling at some of the digs in the third paragraph; they looked even more pitiless in print.

'I mean, what are you trying to say, exactly?' said Graham. 'That this bloke is never going to write a really good novel, because he doesn't own a pen?'

I looked up sharply. 'What?'

'The last sentence. What does it mean?'

'Look, it's simple. He obviously wants to write this fantastic, funny, angry, satirical book, but he's never going to do it, because he hasn't got the necessary –' I was about to read the word aloud for confirmation, when suddenly I saw what they had printed. I froze in amazement: it was one of those moments when the reality is, literally, so horrific that it staggers belief. Then I screwed up the newspaper and threw it across the room in an involuntary fury. 'The *bastards*!'

Graham stared at me. 'What's the matter?'

I couldn't answer at first; just sat there and chewed my nails. Then I said: '*Brio*, is what I wrote. He doesn't have the necessary brio.'

He retrieved the newspaper and examined the sentence again. A smile began to dawn on his face.

'Oh, *brio* . . .' Then the smile became a chuckle, the chuckle became a laugh, and the laugh became a helpless, deafening, maniacal roar which brought Joan, ever anxious to be in on the joke, running from the kitchen.

'What's the matter?' she said. 'What's so funny?'

'Look at this,' said Graham, handing her the paper and struggling to speak through his choking laughter. 'Take a look at Michael's review.'

'What about it?' she said, scanning it with a frown which struggled for precedence with her anticipatory smile.

'The last word,' said Graham, by now gasping for breath. 'Look at the last word.'

Joan looked at the last word, but still she couldn't fathom the mystery. She looked from me to Graham, from Graham to me, more puzzled than ever by our different reactions. 'I don't get it,' she said at last, after reading the sentence one more time. 'I mean, what's so funny about a biro?'

*

It was another subdued meal. We had red kidney bean stew followed by pineapple jelly; the noise of us all eating seemed louder than usual, interrupted as it was only by Joan's occasional abortive attempts to get a conversation started, and Graham's sporadic fits of laughter, which he seemed to be containing only with the greatest difficulty.

'Well I still don't think it's very funny,' said Joan, after his fourth or fifth eruption. 'You'd think they'd have proper proof readers or something, on a national newspaper like that. If I were you, Michael, I'd have a jolly good go at them on Monday.'

'Oh, what's the use,' I said, pushing a bean idly around my plate.

The lashing of rain against the windowpane intensified, and as Joan served us a second helping of jelly there was a flash of lightning, followed by a terrific thunderclap.

'I love storms,' she said. 'They're so atmospheric.' When it became clear that nobody had anything to add to this observation, she asked brightly: 'Do you know what I always feel like doing when there's a storm?'

I tried not to speculate; but the answer turned out, in any case, to be fairly innocuous.

'I like a good game of Cluedo. There's nothing to beat it.'

And this time, for some reason, our opposition was ineffectual, so that after the plates had been cleared away we found ourselves setting out the board on the dining-room table and squabbling over who should be assigned which character. In the end Phoebe was Miss Scarlet, Joan Mrs Peacock, Graham the Reverend Green, and I was Professor Plum.

'Now, you've got to imagine that we're all stuck in this big old house in the country,' said Joan. 'Just like in that film, Michael, that you were always telling me about.' She turned to the others and explained: 'When Michael was little, he saw this film about a family who all got killed one stormy night in this rambling old mansion. It made a big impression on him.'

'Really?' said Graham, pricking up his *cinéaste*'s ears. 'What was it called?'

'You wouldn't have heard of it,' I said. 'It was in English, and it wasn't made by Marxist intellectuals.'

'Ooh, touchy.'

Joan fetched a couple of candlesticks, placing one on the table and another on the mantelpiece, and then turned out all the lights. We could hardly see what we were doing, but the effect, it had to be said, was suitably eerie.

'Now, are we all set?'

We were ready to start, except that Joan, Graham and Phoebe were each provided with pens or pencils to tick off the suspects on their murder cards, and I wasn't. Typically, it was Graham who noticed.

'Hang on a minute,' he said. 'I think Michael lacks the necessary biro.'

Even Joan collapsed into giggles at that, and Phoebe permitted herself an apologetic smirk which soon, in the face of the others' hilarity, turned into laughter too. I fetched myself one of the coloured pens from beneath the rota board in the kitchen, then sat down and waited composedly for the hysteria to subside. It took quite a while, and in the meantime I made a firm, silent resolve: from that day on, I would write no more reviews for the newspapers.

We played three games, each of them fairly long because there were some quite sophisticated bluffs and counter-bluffs going on, usually between Graham and Joan. As for Phoebe, I had the impression that her heart wasn't really in it. Neither was mine, at first: I tried to treat it as no more than a mathematical puzzle, an exercise in probability and deduction, but then after a while –

and I suppose this will seem childish – my imagination began to assert itself and I became thoroughly absorbed. Helped along by the cracks of thunder and flashes of lightning which would momentarily flood the room with garish contrasts of light and shadow, I had no difficulty in believing that this was a night on which terrible things might happen. In my mind, Professor Plum began to take on the characteristics of Kenneth Connor, and once again I had the sense (the sense which had never been far away, ever since my birthday visit to the cinema in Weston-super-Mare) that it was my destiny to act the part of a shy, awkward, vulnerable little man caught up in a sequence of nightmarish events over which he had absolutely no control. The posters on the wall came to resemble ancient family portraits, behind which a pair of watchful eyes was likely to appear at any moment, and Joan's tiny house began to feel as vast and sinister as Blackshaw Towers itself.

Joan won the first game: it was Mrs White, in the study, with the lead piping. Then Graham decided to take a more rigorous approach and fetched himself a clipboard and a large sheet of blank paper, on which he carefully recorded the transactions which took place between every player. He won the second game this way (it was Colonel Mustard, in the billiard room, with the revolver) but was then unanimously disqualified from using similar tactics again. The third game was closely fought. It soon became obvious that the crime had taken place either in the lounge or the conservatory, and either with the dagger or the candlestick; but I was at a significant advantage when it came to naming the murderer, because I held three of the relevant cards in my hand. While the others were still floundering and firing off wildcat suggestions at each other, the solution slowly revealed itself to me: the culprit, of course, was none other than myself, Professor Plum.

As soon as I realized this, it struck me that the game was intrinsically flawed. It seemed wrong that by a simple process of elimination you could find yourself guilty of a crime, and yet still not know how or where you were supposed to have committed it. Surely there was no precedent for this situation in real life? I wondered what it would actually feel like, to be present at the unravelling of some terrible mystery and then to be suddenly confronted with the falseness of your own, complacent self-image as disinterested observer: to find, all at once, that you were thoroughly and messily bound up in the web of motives and suspicions which you had presumed to untangle with an outsider's icy detachment. Needless to say, I could not imagine the circumstances in which such a thing might ever happen to me.

As it turned out, in any case, Graham was ahead of us all. On his next move he crossed over to the conservatory via the secret passage and pointed an accusing finger in my direction.

'I suggest,' he said, 'that it was Professor Plum, in the conservatory, with the candlestick.'

He was right; and at this point we conceded defeat. Joan turned the lights on and made us all a mug of cocoa, and the mood would perhaps have been shattered if the storm had not continued outside, gathering in ferocity, if anything, as midnight approached.

*

This time I didn't have the excuse of a book to fetch; nor was I feeling hot or uncomfortable. I could probably just have lain there, listening to the rain against the window, the occasional crash of thunder, and sooner or later I would have nodded off to sleep. But only half an hour after I was sure that everyone had gone to bed, I climbed out from beneath the blankets and padded up the stairs in my T-shirt and underpants. The door to Joan's room, as before, was standing ajar. As before, her curtains were open, letting in a good deal of light from the street lamps. And as before, she was lying on her back, her skin grey and luminescent in the silver lamplight, flickering sometimes into blueness as gashes of lightning streaked across the night sky. Although she was more than half covered, tonight, by the pale duvet, it was still enough to root me to the spot, my beady, impotent eyes consuming her hungrily from the safety of the shadowed doorway.

I stood, and I watched; but soon, strangely enough, it was her face that I found myself watching – the face I had seen every day for the last four days, and not the body which had been magically offered up to me in these precious, illicit glimpses. Perhaps there is something more private, more secret to be found in a sleeping face than there is even in a naked body. At rest, her lips slightly parted, her closed eyelids seeming to suggest an act of intense concentration on some distant, inward object, Joan was shockingly beautiful. It was now impossible, shameful even, that I could ever have thought her plain.

I watched.

And then suddenly her eyes were open; she was looking back at me and smiling.

'Are you just going to stand there,' she said, 'or are you coming in?'

How different my life might have been, how very different, if I had stepped into her room instead of slipping back into the darkness as quickly and as silently as a dream slips from the waking mind.

*

On Saturday morning I left the house before any of the others were awake, and returned to London. It was the last I saw of Joan for many years. Her parents retired to a village on the South coast, so we never met up again while visiting our families at Christmas. The only news I ever heard was when my mother told me (shortly before we stopped speaking) that she had moved back to Birmingham and married a local businessman.

On Monday morning, I telephoned the Peacock Press and accepted their commission to write a book about the Winshaws.

The same afternoon, I went out and bought my first video recorder.

Thomas

Few people remember anything about the first domestic VCR, launched by Philips as long ago as 1972. The price was high, the recording time was limited to one hour, and it ended up selling mainly to commercial and institutional buyers. Thomas Winshaw bought one, all the same, and had it built into a cupboard behind one of the oak-panelled walls of his office at Stewards. But he decided not to invest at this stage. Although he was both privately excited by the invention and keenly aware of its commercial possibilities, he sensed that its time had not yet come. Almost, but not quite.

1978 saw the first real flurry of activity. In April JVC introduced its Video Home System, retailing at £750, and only three months later Sony launched the rival Betamax machine. Over the next few years these two systems were to slug it out in the marketplace, with VHS finally proving itself the clear winner. In the autumn of 1978, when Thomas Winshaw announced that the bank would be involving itself heavily in the burgeoning industry, his fellow board members' initial reaction was one of dismay. They reminded him that Stewards' flirtation with the film industry in the early 1960s had not been successful, and even invoked the crisis at Morgan Grenfell ten years ago, when a major commitment to film financing had ended in a potential disaster only warded off at the last minute by intervention from the Bank of England. Thomas dismissed these precedents. He was not suggesting anything as risky as investment in film production. He simply proposed taking a modest stake in one of the leading hardware manufacturers; the software market being, as he would be the first to admit, at this stage too new, too unstable and, frankly, too sleazy. As usual, his instincts were right. Over the next five years, imports of video recorders multiplied ten times over, and by 1984 there was a machine in 35.74 per cent of British homes, as opposed to 0.8 per cent in 1979. The bank profited handsomely. Then in 1981 they became advisers and fund managers to a firm which was rapidly building up a strong market share in post-production, distribution and film-to-video transfers. With Stewards' help, this company went on to merge with an independent video duplication house and within a few years more than three quarters of its income was coming from duplication services. Once again, the bank reaped substantial dividends. Thomas slipped up on one occasion, however: he was an enthusiastic proponent of Philips's videodisc system, LaserVision, which was put on the market in May 1982 but after more than a year had only collected sales figures of around 8,000. The obvious explanation was that it did not offer a recording facility, and when, a few months later, JVC abruptly cancelled their own disc system, and RCA decided to halt all player production in 1984, it was clear even to the least sophisticated industry analyst that the new technology had failed to catch on. Yet Thomas maintained his commitment to a £10-million disc-pressing plant in Essex, which was running at a huge loss.

Among themselves, his colleagues would puzzle over this curious blind spot. The amount of money involved was negligible, in Stewards' terms: but it was still the only time in Thomas's fifteen-odd years of chairmanship that he had persisted in offering uncritical support to a palpably loss-making enterprise. And they never did guess the real reason, which was that he was enraptured with the sharp picture quality and perfect still frames offered by the video disc, which suited his own needs so admirably and took him back to the heady, exhilarating days when he used to hang around the film studios and collect discarded footage of beautiful young actresses in various stages of *déshabillé*. The freeze frame, for Thomas, was the very *raison d'être* of video: he was convinced that it would turn Britain into a nation of voyeurs, and sometimes, as he sat spellbound in the dark with the television on, his fly buttons undone and the door to his office securely locked, he would imagine identical scenes being played out in curtained rooms up and down the country, and would feel a strange solidarity with the great mass of ordinary men from whose pitiful lives he normally took such care to insulate himself.

Only once, incidentally, did he forget to lock the office door. It was about seven o'clock in the evening and as luck would have it his secretary, who was also working late, made the mistake of entering without knocking. She was sacked on the spot; but the story still managed to make its way into a few of the City wine bars, and some people maintain that the phrase 'merchant banker' was introduced into the currency of rhyming slang at precisely this time.

*

Thomas loved screens of every description. He loved the lie they sustained: that the world could be given shape by the four sides of a rectangle, and that he, the spectator, was in a position to sit back and watch, untouched and unobserved. In his professional life (not that he had any personal life to speak of) he was at constant pains to screen himself off from the world, which he watched as if it were a silent film from behind the protecting glass of many different screens: the window of a first-class railway carriage, for instance, or of Bob Maxwell's helicopter (which he was occasionally allowed to borrow), or the smoke-tinted, one-way glass of his private limousine. The computerization of the foreign exchange markets, which alarmed some of the older bankers, seemed to him an entirely logical development. So did the abandonment of the stock exchange floor in 1986. At last, to his delight, there was no longer any need for dealers ever to come into contact with one another, and every transaction was reduced to the flicker of electric pulses on a video screen. He had a camera installed in Stewards' own foreign trading room, connected to a monitor in his office, and here, staring at a screen which all day showed nothing but row upon row of his traders, themselves staring at screens, he would swell with quasi-sexual sensations of pride and power. It seemed, at such moments, that there was no end to the glassy barriers which he could put up between himself and the people (did they really exist?) whose money formed the basis of each day's intoxicating speculations.

Banking, as he once told a television interviewer, had become the most spiritual of all professions. He would quote his favourite statistic: one thousand billion dollars of trading took place on the world's financial markets every day. Since every transaction involved a two-way deal, this meant that five hundred billion dollars would be changing hands. Did the interviewer know how much of that money derived from real, tangible trade in goods and services? A fraction: 10 per cent, maybe less. The rest was all commissions, interest, fees, swaps, futures, options: it was no longer even paper money. It could scarcely be said to exist. In that case (countered the interviewer) surely the whole system was nothing but a castle built on sand. Perhaps, agreed Thomas, smiling: but what a glorious castle it was . . .

Watching his foreign exchange dealers as they stared feverishly at their flickering screens, Thomas came as close as he would ever come to feeling paternal love. They were the sons he had never had. This was during the happiest time of his life, the early to mid 1980s, when Mrs Thatcher had transformed the image of the City and turned the currency speculators into national heroes by describing them as 'wealth creators', alchemists who could conjure unimaginable fortunes out of thin air. The fact that these fortunes went straight into their own pockets, or those of their employers, was quietly overlooked. The nation, for a brief, heady period, was in awe of them.

Things were very different when Thomas had first come to work for Stewards: the City was still recovering from the ordeal of the Bank Rate Tribunal which, for two weeks in December 1957, had exposed some of its dealings for the first time to public view. Labour MPs and the popular newspapers had been raising scandalized eyebrows over revelations of multi-million-pound deals being passed through on a nod and a wink in the comfort of gentlemen's clubs, on Saturday morning golf courses and weekend grouse-shooting parties. Although all of the merchant banks involved had been cleared of the charge of acting upon 'improperly disclosed' information about the raising of the Bank Rate, a distinct whiff of scandal lingered in the air, and it remained true that hefty amounts of gilt-edged stock had been unloaded on to the market in the days (and hours) before the Chancellor's announcement. For Thomas, who had become a director of Stewards in the spring of that year, it had been a bruising initiation: Macmillan may have been proclaiming in Bedford that the economy was strong and the country had 'never had it so good', but the foreign speculators thought differently, and embarked upon a fierce campaign of selling sterling short, wiping millions of dollars off the gold reserves and forcing an eventual 2 per cent rise in the Bank Rate (up to 7 per cent, its highest for more than a century).

'It was what you might call a baptism by fire,' Thomas had explained to his young cousin Mark, who was employed in a junior capacity at the bank in the summer of 1961. 'We cleaned up, of course, but to be frank I don't expect to see another sterling crisis like it during my time at Stewards.'

And yet something similar did take place, on September 16th 1992 (Black Wednesday, as it came to be called), when the currency dealers once again managed to raid the country's gold reserves to the tune of billions of dollars, and this time force a devaluation of sterling into the bargain. Thomas was right in one respect, however: he never did see it happen. He had lost the use of his eyes by then.

*

Thomas's world had always been apprehended entirely through the eyes: this was why (among other things) he never felt any desire to touch or to be touched by women. All great men have their idiosyncracies, and his, unsurprisingly, was a neurotic preoccupation with the quality of his eyesight. A private medicine cabinet in his office contained a vast array of eyewashes, moisturizers, baths and drops, and for thirty years the only fixed item in his timetable was a weekly visit to his ophthalmologist, at ninethirty every Monday morning. The doctor in question might have found this arrangement trying had not Thomas's obsession been earning him a ludicrous amount in consultation fees. There wasn't a single ailment in the textbook which he did not believe to have contracted at some time or another. He fancied that he had arc eye, cat's eye, pink eye and cystic eye; gas eye, hare eye, hot eye and lazy eye; ox eye, Klieg eye, reduced eye, schematic eye, scotopic eye, aphacic eye, squinting eye and cross eye. Once, after a fact-finding visit to some hop fields, he became convinced that he had hop eye (acute conjunctivitis found in hop-pickers, caused by irritation from the spinal hairs of the hop plant); after a visit to a shipyard, that he had shipyard eye (epidemic keratoconjuncti-vitis, an infection spread by contaminated fluids in the busy eye casualty stations found at shipyards); and after a visit to Nairobi, that he had Nairobi eye (a severe ocular lesion caused by the secretions of certain vesicating beetles common in Nairobi). On another occasion, when his mother made the mistake of telling him that his grandfather Matthew Winshaw had suffered from a congenital form of glaucoma, he had cancelled all his banking engagements for three days and booked himself a succession of round-the-clock specialist appointments. In turn he was tested for absolute glaucoma, capsular glaucoma, compensated glaucoma, congestive glaucoma, haemorrhagic glaucoma, inflammatory glau-coma, inverse glaucoma, obverse glaucoma, malignant glaucoma, benign glaucoma, open-angle glaucoma, closed-angle glaucoma, postinflammatory glaucoma, preinflammatory glaucoma, infantile glaucoma and myxomatosis. Thomas Winshaw's eyes were insured (with Stewards' own insurance company) for a sum variously rumoured to be between £100,000 and £1 million. There was no organ, in other words, which he valued more highly; and that includes the one towards which his right hand could sometimes scarcely stop itself from wandering – most memorably, perhaps, on the day he entertained a surprised but politely speechless Queen and Prince Charles to sherry in his freshly red-carpeted office.

*

When the Conservative government announced that they were abolishing free eye tests on the NHS in April 1988, Thomas phoned his brother Henry to tell him that they were making a big mistake: there would be a public outcry. Henry told him that he was over-reacting. There would be a whimper of protest from the usual quarters, he said, and then it would all quietly die down.

'And I was right, wasn't I?'

'I should have bowed to your political judgment, as always.'

'Well, it's quite simple, really.' Henry leaned forward and threw another log on the fire. It was a cold, dark afternoon in early October 1989, and they were enjoying tea and muffins in one of the Heartland Club's private rooms. 'The trick is to *keep* doing outrageous things. There's no point in passing some scandalous piece of legislation and then giving everyone time to get worked up about it. You have to get right in there and top it with something even worse, before the public have had a chance to work out what's hit them. The thing about the British conscience, you see, is that it really has no more capacity than . . . a primitive home computer, if you like. It can only hold two or three things in its memory at a time.'

Thomas nodded and bit eagerly into his muffin.

'Unemployment, for instance,' Henry continued. 'When was the last time you saw a newspaper headline about unemployment? Nobody gives a hoot any more.'

'I know: and all this is very reassuring, old boy,' said Thomas, 'but what I really want is some concrete guarantee . . .'

'Of course you do. Of course.' Henry frowned and focused his mind upon the matter in hand, which was the case of Farzad Bazoft, a British journalist recently imprisoned in Baghdad on charges of espionage. 'I understand your point entirely. You and Mark want to protect your investments: I can quite sympathize with that.'

'Well, it isn't even just Mark. We've got plenty of other clients besides Vanguard who are doing very nicely servicing Saddam and his shopping list. We're all committed up to our necks, frankly.'

'You don't have to remind me.'

'Yes, but look: this sounds to me like a very delicate situation. This man's a British subject. Surely this new chap at the Foreign Office – Major, or whatever his name is – is going to come under a bit of pressure to get him released.'

Henry raised his eyebrows in mock innocence. 'How could he possibly do that?'

'Well, sanctions, of course.'

'Really,' said Henry, laughing out loud, 'I'm amazed that you think we'd even contemplate such a thing. We've got a $700 million surplus with Iraq. Confidentially, there's going to be another four or five hundred where that came from in a month or two. If you think we're going to jeopardize all of that . . .'

He tailed off: the sentence didn't need finishing.

'Yes, but what about Mark's little . . . line of business?'

This time Henry's laughter was shorter, more private. 'Put it this way: how on earth can we impose sanctions on something, when we're not even selling it in the first place. Mm?'

Thomas smiled. 'Well, I can see you have a point there.'

'I know Major hasn't been in the job for long and we're all a bit worried that he doesn't know what the hell he's playing at. But take it from me – he's a good boy. He does what he's told.' He took a sip of tea. 'And besides, he might be moving again soon.'

'What, already?'

'It looks that way. Margaret and Nigel seem to be heading for a final bust-up. We suspect there'll be a vacancy at Number Eleven pretty soon.'

Thomas tucked this information away at the back of his mind for future reference. It had considerable implications, which he would need to contemplate and examine at his leisure.

'Do you think they'll hang him?' he asked suddenly.

Henry shrugged. 'Well, he was a rotten chancellor, it has to be said, but that would be a bit drastic.'

'No, no, not Lawson. I mean this journo character. Bazoft.'

'Oh, him. I dare say they will, yes. That's what happens if you're silly enough to get caught snooping around Saddam's arms factories, I suppose.'

'Making trouble.'

'Exactly.' Henry stared into space for a moment. 'I must say, there are one or two snoopers over here that I wouldn't mind seeing strung up on Ludgate Hill, if it came to that.'

'Nosey parkers.'

'Precisely.' Briefly a frown crossed his face, comprised half of malevolence and half recollection. 'I wonder whatever happened to that scruffy little writer that Mad Tabs set on us a few years back?'

'Him! Good God, that fellow got up my nose. What on *earth* she was thinking of . . .' He shook his head. 'Well, anyway: she's just a poor witless old fool . . .'

'You spoke to that chap, then, did you?'

'Invited him up to the office. Gave him lunch. The works. All I got in return was a lot of impertinent questions.'

'Such as?'

'He had a bee in his bonnet about Westland,' said Thomas. 'Wanted to know why Stewards had been so keen to support the American bid when there was a European one on the table.'

'What, and he supposed you were snuggling up to Margaret in the hope of a knighthood or something, did he?'

'Even more devious than that, I'm afraid. Although, now you come to mention it, I seem to remember there *was* something promised . . .'

Henry shuffled uncomfortably in his seat. 'I haven't forgotten, Thomas, really. I'm seeing her tomorrow. I'll bring it up again.'

'Anyway, *he'd* got this absurd theory that Sikorsky had tied up some huge arms deal with the Saudis, and the only reason we all wanted to climb into bed with them was to get ourselves a slice of the cake.'

'Preposterous.'

'Outrageous.'

'And so what did you say to that?'

'I sent him packing,' said Thomas, 'with a few choice words once directed at myself, on one very memorable occasion, by the late, great and much lamented Sid James.'

'Oh?'

'I said – and here I quote from memory – "Do us all a favour, laughing boy: piss off out of it and don't come back." '

And then the room echoed as Thomas attempted his own version of the comedian's smoky, inimitable laugh.

*

It had happened in the late spring of 1961. Thomas arrived at Twickenham Studios at about lunchtime and made his way to the restaurant, where he spied three vaguely familiar faces at a corner table. One of them was Dennis Price, still best known for his leading role in *Kind Hearts and Coronets* twelve years earlier; another was the wizened, eccentric Esma Cannon, who reminded Thomas irresistibly of his mad Aunt Tabitha, still confined to a high-security asylum somewhere on the edge of the Yorkshire moors; and the third, unmistakably, was Sid James, one of the stars of the film currently in production – a loose comic remake of an old Boris Karloff feature, *The Ghoul*, under the new title *What a Carve Up!*

Thomas fetched himself a tray of corned beef hash and jam pudding, and went over to join them.

'Mind if I sit here?' he said.

'It's a free country, mate,' said Sid James, indifferently.

Thomas had been introduced to all three actors a few weeks ago, but he could see that they didn't recognize him, and their conversation, which had been lively, dried up when he sat beside them.

'We have met, I believe,' he said, after taking his first mouthful.

Sid grunted. Dennis Price said, 'Of course,' and then asked, 'Are you working at the moment?'

'Well, erm – yes,' said Thomas, surprised.

'What are you in?'

'Well, I don't know how you'd describe it really: I suppose I'm in stocks and shares.'

'*Stocks and Shares*, eh?' said Sid. 'That's a new one on me. Something the Boultings are cooking up, is it? Taking the lid off the City: Ian Carmichael as the innocent young bank clerk, Terry-Thomas as his conniving boss. Sounds good. Should be very droll.'

'Not exactly: I think there might be a small misunder–'

'Hang about, I knew I'd seen you somewhere before.' Sid had now been studying his face for a few moments. 'Didn't you play the vicar in *Two-Way Stretch*?'

'No, silly, that was Walter Hudd,' said Dennis, before Thomas had had the chance to deny it. 'Surely, though, you were the policeman in *Dentist in the Chair*?'

'No, no, no,' said Esma. 'That was Stuart Saunders. Darling Stuart. But didn't I see you in *Watch Your Stern*?'

'Come off it – I was in that one,' said Sid. 'You think I wouldn't remember? No, I've got it: *Follow That Horse*. You were one of the spies.'

'Or was it *Inn for Trouble*?'

'Or *Life is a Circus*?'

'Or *School for Scoundrels*?'

'I'm sorry to disappoint you,' said Thomas, raising his hand. 'But you're all quite wide of the mark. I'm no thespian, I'm afraid. When I said I was in stocks and shares, I meant it literally. I work in the City. I'm a banker.'

'Oh.'

There was a longish silence, broken at last by Esma, who said cheerfully: 'How fascinating.'

'What then brings you,' said Dennis, 'to these foreign shores? If you don't mind my asking.'

'The bank I represent has invested heavily in these studios,' said Thomas. 'They like to send me down occasionally, to see how things are coming along. I thought that, if it wouldn't be too intrusive, I might watch some of the filming this afternoon.'

Dennis and Sid exchanged glances.

'Well, I hate to say this,' Sid ventured, 'but I think you've cooked your goose there, mate. You see, it's a closed set today.'

'Closed set?'

'Just Ken and Shirl and the technicians. They're filming what you might call a rather intimate scene.'

Thomas smiled to himself: his information had been correct.

'Well, I'm sure that nobody would mind – just for a few minutes . . .'

But this time, it looked as though he'd finally found himself out of luck. When he strolled over to the set a few minutes later, he learned that the scene to be shot that afternoon involved Kenneth Connor wandering into Shirley Eaton's bedroom just as she was getting undressed. Onlookers, the assistant director was at pains to make clear, would not be welcome.

Inwardly seething, Thomas withdrew into the shadows beyond the arc lights and contemplated his next move. He could hear the director and the two performers going over their lines, discussing floor-markings and camera angles; and soon after that, there was a call for quiet, a cry of 'Action!', and the cameras had presumably started rolling.

It was intolerable. Thomas had caught a glimpse of the beautiful Shirley Eaton in her dressing-gown as he came from the restaurant, and he could not bear the thought of such loveliness now being unveiled away from his greedy gaze. Hard-hearted, cool-headed businessman that he was, so used to presiding impassively over the building and wrecking of huge financial fortunes, it made him want to cry. The situation was desperate. Something had to be done.

As he prowled around the outskirts of the studio floor in semi-darkness, salvation presented itself in the form of a stepladder propped up against the back of some scenery. Cocking his ear against the plasterboard, Thomas could hear the actors' voices on the other side as they attempted take two of the bedroom scene. He glanced up and noticed two small pinpoints of light drilled into the wood, just where the ladder was resting. Could it possibly be that they would look out on to the set? (As he later discovered, they were cut out of an oil painting, a gruesome family portrait hanging on the bedroom wall, behind which the watchful eyes of the murderer would sometimes make a chilling appearance.) Silently he climbed the ladder and found that the drillholes were exactly positioned to accommodate a pair of human eyes. They might almost have been designed for that purpose. After taking a few seconds to accustom himself to the glare of the lights, Thomas looked down and found that he now had an uninterrupted view of the forbidden bedroom.

It wasn't immediately clear what was going on, although the scene appeared to revolve around Kenneth, Shirley and a mirror. Kenneth had his back to Shirley while she took most of her clothes off, but he could still see her reflection in the mirror, which was on a hinge and which he was doing his best to keep tilted, for the sake of her modesty. Shirley stood by the side of the bed, facing the portrait through which Thomas's widened eyes were now staring out, unnoticed. He seemed to have arrived during a lull in the proceedings. Kenneth was in conversation with the director while two young assistants made small adjustments to the angle of the mirror in response to shouted instructions from the cameraman. Finally the director called out, 'OK, positions, everyone!', and Kenneth went over to the door to make his entrance. The set went quiet.

Kenneth opened the door, walked in, and looked startled to see Shirley, wearing only her slip and about to put on a nightgown.

He said: 'I say, what are you doing in my room?'

Shirley said: 'This isn't your room. I mean, that isn't your luggage, is it?'

She clutched the nightgown modestly to her bosom.

Kenneth said: 'Oh, blimey. No. Wait a minute, that's not my bed, either. I must have got lost. I'm sorry. I'll – I'll push off.'

He started to leave, but paused after only a few steps. He turned and saw that Shirley was still holding on to her nightgown, unsure of his intentions.

Thomas stirred excitedly on the ladder.

Kenneth said: 'Miss, you don't happen to know where my bedroom is, do you?'

Shirley shook her head sadly and said: 'No, I'm afraid I don't.'

Kenneth said: 'Oh,' and paused. 'I'm sorry. I'll go now.'

Shirley hesitated, a resolve forming within her: 'No. Hang on.' She gestured with her hand, urgently. 'Turn your back a minute.'

Kenneth turned and found himself staring into the mirror, in which he could see his own reflection, and beyond that, Shirley's. Her back was to him, and she was wriggling out of her slip, pulling it over her head.

He said: 'J– just a minute, miss.'

Thomas heard a movement behind him.

Kenneth hastily lowered the mirror.

Shirley turned to him and said: 'You're sweet.' She finished pulling her slip over her head, and started to unfasten her bra.

Thomas felt his ankles suddenly gripped by a strong pair of hands. He gasped and nearly fell off the ladder, and then looked down. He was confronted by the grizzled features of Sid James, who flashed him a menacing smile, and whispered: 'Come on, laughing boy. I think it's time you and I went for a walk.'

Pinning Thomas's arm firmly behind his back, Sid frogmarched him out into a corridor, ignoring the illustrious banker's garbled protestations.

'Now I know this looks bad,' he was saying, 'but I was really just checking on the soundness of the construction materials. It's absolutely essential that we know our investment is being –'

'Look, mate, I've read about people like you in the papers. There are words for people like you: not very nice words, most of them.'

'Perhaps this isn't the best moment,' said Thomas, 'but I really am a huge fan of yours. I don't suppose you could manage an autograph at all . . .?'

'You've really slipped up this time, matey. The thing about Shirley, you see, she's a lovely girl. Very popular round here. Young, too. So you're in big trouble if you ever get caught doing this sort of thing again.'

'I do hope we'll be seeing you back on the television soon,' said Thomas desperately, wincing from the pressure on his arm. 'Another series of *Hancock's Half Hour*, perhaps?'

They had reached a door to the outside world. Sid pushed it open and let go of Thomas, who breathed a heavy sigh of relief and started brushing down his trousers. When he turned to look at Sid, he was surprised to see his face now contorted with fury.

'Don't you read the papers, you ignorant pillock? Me and Tony are history. Finished. Kaput.'

'I'm sorry, I hadn't heard.'

And it was at this point that Sid James took a deep breath, pointed a wagging finger at Thomas, and sent him on his way with the parting words which were still fresh in the old man's mind nearly thirty years later, as he sat chuckling over the incident with his brother Henry by the warm, homely fireside of the Heartland Club.

Perhaps inspired by his visit to Twickenham Studios, Thomas had a number of peepholes installed in various key locations at the Stewards offices when he became chairman of the bank. He liked to know that he could spy on his juniors' meetings whenever he wanted, and to feel that he had an advantage over everyone else who visited or worked in the building. It was for this same reason that he considered the chairman's office itself to be such a masterpiece of design: for the oak panelling on the walls was, to all appearances, unbroken, and any visitor trying to leave at the end of an unsuccessful interview might spend several fumbling minutes looking for the door before Thomas would rise to his assistance with an air of tired expertise.

This feature was itself symptomatic of the secrecy in which all of Stewards' business was habitually cloaked. It was not until the 1980s that merchant banking began to lose its gentlemanly, recreational image and take on a sort of glamour which threatened to encourage a tiny (though still, in Thomas's view, profoundly unhealthy) flicker of public interest. To some extent he brought it upon himself. Recognizing the huge profits which were to be made from advising the government on its privatization programme, he took aggressive steps to ensure that Stewards secured itself a substantial share of this well-publicized business. He thoroughly enjoyed snatching these huge state-owned companies from the taxpayers' hands and carving them up among a minority of profit-hungry shareholders: the knowledge that he was helping to deny ownership to many and concentrate it in the hands of a few filled him with a deep and calming sense of rightness. It satisfied something primeval in him. The only place Thomas could find even greater, more lasting fulfilment, perhaps, was in the area of mergers and takeovers.

For a while Stewards led the way in the upsurge of takeover business which swept through the City during the first half of Mrs Thatcher's reign. It rapidly became clear that if a bank could prove itself capable, against the odds, of helping its clients to swallow up other, more profitable companies (not necessarily smaller ones), then there was no limit to the kind of services it would be able to sell them in the future. Competition between the banks intensified. New terms such as 'bid fees' and 'success fees' were introduced into City parlance, and it became an increasingly important part of Thomas's job to mobilize 'bid teams' made up of banks, brokers, accountants, lawyers and PR advisers. New methods of financing the bids were devised – using the bank's own money, for instance, to buy shares in the target companies, or underwriting generous cash alternatives to share offers – which were benignly waved through by the City's self-regulating watch-dogs. By comparison, the series of largely uncontested mergers which Thomas had negotiated on behalf of his cousin Dorothy and her Brunwin group during the 1960s and 1970s now seemed very modest.

The Guinness trial, carefully timed during the run-up to a general election to prove that the government was taking a strong line on financial malpractice, put a temporary check on the more ruthless procedures. To find a classic instance of Thomas's methods, then, you would have to look back to the halcyon years at the beginning of the decade, when Stewards' profits from corporate finance were running at about £25 million and they were advising on thirty to forty takeovers a year. Of these, the case of Phocas Motor Services is about as representative as any.

Phocas was a profitable and highly regarded engineering firm based in the Midlands, supplying a wide range of parts, designs and accessories to the motor industry. They made batteries, central locking devices, in-car stereos, heaters, ventilators, fans and most small electrical components, and had a permanent research and development team working on safer, more responsive versions of existing steering and braking systems. At the beginning of 1982 it became known that a multi-national company working in a similar field was interested in buying them up. There was every reason to believe that the takeover would have been a friendly and beneficial one: the company in question had a track record of realistic expansion and good industrial relations.

Their bid, however, was contested by a flamboyant tycoon who happened to be one of Stewards' most prestigious clients. He knew very little about the motor industry – most of his holdings were in publishing, retail and sport – and many City observers found it hard to see why he had decided to involve himself at all; but his entry now ensured that this would become one of the most closely fought takeover battles of the year. Both companies were intending to bid for Phocas with their own shares, and so it became the task of their respective bankers to quietly set about the business of mounting share support operations.

It was never going to be a fair contest. At Stewards, Thomas had a limitless range of contacts to whom he could turn for help, both in industry and the City; he was also unhampered by scruple, and had the not inconsiderable advantage of being on terms of close personal friendship with some of the most important members of the Takeover Panel. It was unlikely that any of his more belligerent tactics would earn anything worse than a gentle rap on the knuckles. Precise details are hard to come by, but it's believed that he clinched the deal by going to another, smaller merchant bank and persuading them to buy several million pounds' worth of his client's shares; when their price soared in the closing days of the bid, the bank came back to him and told him they were thinking of selling; and to forestall this disaster, he persuaded his client to mollify them with a deposit, interest free, of the exact sterling equivalent of the current price of the shares in an unnumbered Swiss bank account. Even though this practice – the use of a company's own money (or, if we're going to be finicky about this, the money of its employees and shareholders) to support its own share price – was to become the subject of a criminal prosecution in the wake of the Guinness scandal, Thomas was never able to see anything wrong with it. He liked to refer to it as a 'victimless crime'. It was something of a gamble, admittedly, but one which in his experience almost invariably paid off, and if there was anything at risk, how could he be expected to see it? Blinded by the many screens which had been put up between himself and the rest of the world, he was no longer in a position to catch even the most fleeting glimpse of the people whose money he was gambling with.

Thomas's client won the battle, in any case, and shortly afterwards the reasons for his interest in Phocas Motor Services became very clear. In addition to its long-term profitability, the company had another valuable asset – namely, a pension fund which had been so well managed and so shrewdly invested that it was, at this time, substantially overfunded. Before the takeover, the Phocas employees were about to have been offered – did they but know it – a year's holiday from pension contributions, but one of the tycoon's first decisions upon assuming control was to sack the present fund manager and appoint one of his own men in his place; and when his publishing, retailing and sporting empire collapsed around him like a house of cards less than a year later, the independent auditors brought in to clear up the mess were astonished at the speed and efficiency with which this pension fund had been emptied – not just depleted, but literally emptied – and the money siphoned off to be squandered in a futile attempt to postpone the collapse of various failed imprints, failed chainstores, failed football teams and a dozen other worthless adventures.

Even now, years later, legal manoeuvres to help the pensioners recover their money are still in progress. There is no solution in sight. Thomas Winshaw, whose bank handled every aspect of the flamboyant tycoon's finances, continues to profess his amazement at the scale of the fraud, and to plead his own baffled ignorance.

*

Needless to say, I don't believe him. And I should mention, perhaps, that I have a small personal interest in this case. Phocas Motor Services was the firm my father worked for. He was there for nearly thirty years, and retired just a few months after the pension scandal came to light. The money he had been saving all that time had vanished, and he was left to survive on a state pension, supplemented by a few extra pounds brought in by my mother, who had to return to part-time teaching. It wasn't the retirement they'd been planning for.

There is no doubt, in my mind, that the stress brought on by this situation would have contributed to his heart attack.

Does this mean that Thomas was an accessory to my father's murder?

December 1990

I lose count of the number of times Fiona and I contrived to go to bed together over the next few weeks: although a purist, I suppose, might take issue with my precise interpretation of the phrase 'go to bed'. The procedure was something like this. She would come home from work – exhausted, like as not – and get into bed almost at once. Meanwhile I, in my kitchen, would be preparing some tasty morsel: nothing too substantial, because she didn't have much of an appetite; some scrambled eggs or fish fingers would usually be enough, or sometimes I would just warm up a can of soup and serve it with bread rolls. Then I would take the tray of food across the hallway into her flat, and place it across her legs as she sat propped up against a bank of pillows. I would sit down beside her – technically *on* the bed, you see, rather than in it – and we would eat our little supper together, side by side, for all the world like a couple who'd been married for thirty years or more. And to cap it all, just to make the illusion complete, we would always turn the television on, and sit watching it for hours at a time, barely speaking a word.

I have always associated television with sickness. Not sickness of the soul, as some commentators would have it, but sickness of the body. It probably goes back to the time my father was lying in hospital, following the heart attack which was to finish him off in a matter of two or three weeks at the age of only sixty-one. I'd come up from London as soon as I heard the news and for the first time in many years I was staying under my parents' roof. It was a peculiar experience, to be back in that newly unfamiliar house, in that suburb which was half-town and half-country, and many mornings were spent sitting at the desk in my old bedroom, looking out at the view which had once marked the full extent of my experience and aspiration, while my mother remained downstairs, trying to find housework to occupy herself or solemnly filling in one of the numerous magazine or newspaper crosswords to which she was by then addicted. But for the afternoons we had developed a little ritual, a ritual designed, I suppose, to keep the dread and the grief at a tolerable distance: and this was where the television set came into its own.

Although my parents lived on the outskirts of Birmingham, their lives tended to revolve around a quiescent, reasonably pretty market town which lay some six or seven miles from their home. It boasted one small hospital, to which my father had been admitted on the day of his attack: visiting hours were from two-thirty to three-thirty in the afternoon, and from six-thirty to eight o'clock in the evening. This meant that the hours between our visits were the most tense and problematic of the day. We would emerge from the hospital into the visitors' car park and the bright afternoon sunshine, and my mother, who had completely lost the capacity (although it had never before deserted her in the last twenty-five years) to plan her shopping more than a few hours in advance, would drive us both to the local supermarket to buy some packets of frozen food for our evening meal. While she was making this purchase I would get out of the car and wander down the almost deserted High Street – indeed, the only real shopping street – puzzled to think that I had once been unable to conceive of a metropolis more teeming or animated. I looked into the branch of Woolworth's where I used to spend my long-saved pocket money on budget-priced records; into the newsagent's where it was possible to buy – although I'd had no inkling of it at the time – only a fraction of the titles available in London; and into the town's only bookshop, laid out on one thinly stocked floor about thirty feet square, which for years had seemed to me to resemble nothing less than a modern library of Alexandria. It was here, towards the end of my teens, that I used to linger for hours, staring at the covers of the latest paperbacks while Verity fumed and stamped her feet outside. The very sight of these books had never failed to fill me with wonder: they seemed to imply the existence of a distant world populated by beautiful, talented people and devoted to the most high-minded literary ideals (the same world, of course, into which chance would one day allow me to dip my own uncertain feet, only to find it as cold and unwelcoming as the pool which had numbed me into unassuageable tears on that fateful birthday).

After this, anyway, came the most important part of the ritual. We would get back to the house, make two cups of instant coffee, lay out a plate of digestive or Rich Tea biscuits and then, for half an hour, settle down in front of the television to watch a quiz show: a show of awesome frivolity and tameness which we none the less followed with idolatrous concentration, as though to miss even a few seconds of it were to render the whole experience meaningless.

There were two simple elements to this programme: a game involving numbers, where the contestants had to perform some basic mental arithmetic (I was quite good at this one, whereas my mother invariably got into a muddle and found herself beaten by the clock); and a lexical game, in which they vied with each other to see who could make the longer word out of nine randomly selected letters of the alphabet. My mother took it more seriously than I did, always making sure that she had pencil and paper to hand before sitting down to watch, and every so often she would actually beat the contestants: I can well remember her flush of triumph at making an eight-letter word, 'wardrobe', out of the letters R,E,B,G,A,R,W,O,D, when the best that the winner could manage was 'badger', for six points. She was euphoric for hours afterwards: it was the only time during those weeks that I saw the lines of care wiped smooth from her face. And I can only think it was for this reason that we used to make such strenuous efforts to get back to the television every day at four-thirty, even sometimes, when our shopping expedition had taken longer than expected, driving at fifty or sixty miles an hour through the suburban streets, fearful of missing the early stages of the game. or the host's foolish introduction, peppered with terrible puns and delivered with the beseeching smiles of an overgrown puppy. There was another reason, though, why my mother watched every afternoon, her eyes aglow with the faith of the true believer, and this was that she clung to the possibility that one day she might be granted a vision, a revelation of the Holy Grail after which all of the programme's followers quested: a perfect nine-letter word to be formed out of those randomly selected letters. It would have made her the happiest woman in the world, I think, if only for a few instants; and the ironic thing is that it did happen once and she never knew it. The letters were O,Y,R,L,T,T,I,M and A, and I could see it straight away, but neither of the contestants got it and my mother was struggling, too – all that she found, in the end, was a feeble five-letter word, 'trail'. At least, that's what she said at the time, and it's only now that I wonder if she saw it as well, the word 'mortality' spelled out by those nine random letters, but couldn't bring herself to write down the truth of it on the back of her scribbled afternoon shopping list.

In any case, Fiona and I had more serious matters to occupy us, because the dramatic change which her illness wrought on our viewing habits happened to coincide with a period of political upheaval in both the domestic and the international spheres. Late in November, just a few days after she had been to see her doctor for the second time, the Tory party leadership crisis came to a head and Mrs Thatcher was forced to resign. It was a week of intense, if transient, media excitement, and we were able to gorge ourselves on a diet of end-to-end news programmes, special late-night panel discussions and extended bulletins. And then on the day she went for her outpatients' appointment, we heard that Saddam Hussein had rejected Security Council Resolution 678, an ultimatum authorizing the use of 'all necessary means' if Iraq had failed to withdraw from Kuwait by January 15th, and soon he was on French television saying that he thought there was a 50–50 chance of armed conflict; and even though he now started releasing the hostages, so that they were all home a week or so before Christmas, it still felt as if the politicians and the army leaders were hell bent on dragging us into war. But the strange thing is that Fiona, who was a peace-loving person and not very interested in politics, took a kind of comfort from all of this, and

I began to suspect that, like my mother with her quiz show, she had chosen to use it as a way of shielding herself from the fear which was otherwise liable to swamp her.

This time the doctor had listened more carefully. He examined her neck when she told him about the growth, which was bigger than it used to be, she said, almost two inches across, and he wrote down everything she told him about it but still said there was probably nothing to worry about, that the fevers and night sweats might well derive from something else entirely, some aggressive but treatable infection. But there was no point in taking unnecessary risks, and she was booked in for this out-patients' appointment in the last week of November. They took some blood tests and X-rays, apparently, and she was supposed to go back in three weeks' time to get the results. Meanwhile she had a temperature chart to fill in, and so our evenings together would always conclude with me fetching the thermometer, and faithfully entering the relevant figure before putting out the light and returning to my flat with the tray and the dirty plates or soup bowls.

As I mentioned, there was a good deal of silence between us: on Fiona's part because talking made her throat burn, on mine because I could never think of anything to say. But I do remember one conversation which took place in the dead half hour between the *Nine O'Clock News* and the *News at Ten*, and which began with her making an unexpected remark.

She said: 'You don't have to do this every evening, you know.'

'I know.'

'I mean, if there are other places you want to be, other people you want to be seeing . . .'

'Yes, I know.'

'It can't be much fun for you, being stuck here with me all the time. It's not as if –'

'You're good company. Really. I've told you that before.' (And it was true.)

'I know, but – When I'm better, when I've got this thing licked, I'll be . . . a lot more fun. And then – you know, then we'll really start something, will we? Really try to make a go of it.'

I nodded. 'Yes. Of course.'

'I'm impressed, in a way,' she continued hesitantly. 'I mean, it's not every man – There aren't many men I'd feel comfortable with, having them around here all the time and seeing me in bed and everything. I suppose I'm impressed that . . . you haven't tried anything on.'

'Well I'm not going to take advantage of you, am I? Not while you're feeling like this.'

'No, but we've known each other a couple of months now, and most people, in that time, would have . . . I mean circumstances don't permit, in our case, but – you know. You must have given it some thought.'

And of course I had given it thought, sitting night after night on Fiona's bed, sometimes with her wearing a jumper, sometimes just her nightgown; touching her bare arms, brushing crumbs from her body, feeling her neck for signs of swelling, taking the thermometer in and out of her mouth, giving her consoling hugs and good-night kisses on the cheek. How could all of that attention be innocent, how could it not contain its quota of furtive glances and suppressed excitement? Of course I had given it thought. There was, and we both knew this, a strong undercurrent of feeling between us which it was both difficult to ignore and folly not to acknowledge.

But I merely smiled. 'Don't worry,' I said, making for the kitchen to get two cups of cocoa. 'Sex has never been further from my mind.'

*

suspenders	*black*	*bullwhip*
stockings	*bra*	*unhook*
orgy	*grope*	*panties*
erect	*handcuffs*	*stretch*
unzip	*fishnet*	*tights*
protruding	*take off*	*suck*
cleavage	*juices*	*rubber*
striptease	*Mazola*	*smooth*
nipple	*stroking*	*pink*

mount	*lick*	*moist*
leather	*thighs*	*parted*
probing	*tongue*	*tender*
back	*arching*	*moaning*
softly	*Oh God*	*Yes*
please	*don't stop*	*Yes*

*

I left the contents of the tray unwashed in the kitchen, then went back to my desk and read through this list again. It filled me with apprehension. Ever since my conversation with Patrick, I had been determined to show him that I could write about sex as well as anybody, that it wasn't a subject I would shy away from in my book about the Winshaws. And the situation I'd chosen to describe had presented itself without much difficulty. When meeting Findlay at the Narcissus Gallery, I'd happened to overhear some gossip about how Roddy Winshaw had once seduced a young painter he'd invited up to Yorkshire for the weekend, and since I knew nothing of the circumstances, and had decided that, for the purposes of this book, the boundary between fiction and reality was no longer one which I was interested in observing, the incident seemed to form an ideal starting point. But I'd been working on it, now, for more than four nights, and it was perfectly obvious that I was getting nowhere.

To be honest, I had little experience in this area. My knowledge of sexually explicit books and films was small. Despite all those years of relying on the television for sexual stimuli, I retained, amazingly enough, a fundamental aversion to pornography (an aversion probably based on principle, if you cared to look back into the distant past). In even the tackiest of the films which I bought, rented or taped from the television, there was usually a vestige of artistic justification for the couplings and disrobings which would rapidly become my main focus of interest. And in fact I had only once been to the cinema to see a pornographic film. It was in the mid 1970s, during the final grisly stages of my marriage to Verity. For several months our sex life had been dying a slow, lingering death, and in our mutual panic we decided that a visit to a nearby cinema specializing in blue movies might provide something in the way of resuscitation. Sadly, we were out of luck. The film we'd chosen had attracted a certain amount of attention in our evening newspaper because, although made by a London production company, it had been shot entirely on location in Birmingham itself. As a result it was enormously popular with the locals, and the rest of the audience consisted mainly of middle-aged couples – some of whom had obviously seen it several times before – who would have an annoying tendency to interrupt, for example, a scene of back-seat oral sex with remarks like, 'This is the bit where you can see our Tracy's Morris Minor going past outside', or 'Doesn't the chiropodist's look better now they've given it a lick of paint?' Verity and I left the cinema without feeling noticeably aroused and spent the rest of the evening, I seem to remember, rearranging the holiday snaps from our recent trip to the Scilly Isles.

Shaking this memory off, I returned to the blank sheets of paper in front of me and tried to bring my mind into focus. It was no easy task, for we were only five days away from Christmas, and tomorrow Fiona was supposed to be going back to the hospital for the results of her tests. I'd agreed to keep her company, and we were both apprehensive about it. On top of that, I'd had an alarming phone call earlier that day – from Mrs Tonks, of all people. It seemed there had been another break-in: not at the office, this time, but at Mr McGanny's house in St John's Wood. The burglar had managed to force entry into his safe and several private documents had been stolen. They included letters from Tabitha Winshaw and, for some reason, statements of the firm's accounts for the tax year 1981/82. Even more bizarrely, a number of photographs had been removed from one of Mr McGanny's family albums. She asked me if I could throw any light on this. Naturally I couldn't, and so the only effects of our conversation were to leave the mystery more clouded than ever and to make it even harder for me to concentrate on my work.

After a few minutes I put my list of key words to one side: it had proved inhibiting rather than helpful, and the only way to break the deadlock, I decided, was to go for complete spontaneity.

I should write down whatever came into my head, and worry about the details later. So I fetched a bottle of white wine from the kitchen, poured myself a tumbler-full and wrote my first sentence.

She followed him into the bedroom

That was a good start. Nothing too complicated there. I took a sip of wine and rubbed my hands. Perhaps this wasn't going to be as difficult as I'd thought. Now maybe just a couple of sentences to describe the bedroom, and then we would be getting somewhere.

It was a

It was a what, though? I didn't want to go for anything elaborate at this stage, bogging the reader down in prolix descriptions. A single carefully chosen epithet ought to do the trick. How about –

It was a large room

No: much too boring. It was a sumptuous room? Too clichéd. A charming room? Too twee. It was a large, charming, sumptuous room. It was charmingly sumptuous. It was largely charming. To be honest, I didn't give a shit what kind of room it was. Neither would my readers, in all probability. Best to skip all that stuff and keep things moving.

He pulled her roughly towards the bed

That wouldn't do. I didn't want to make it sound like rape.

He pulled her gently towards the bed

Too wimpish.

He drew her towards the bed

He sat down on the bed and drew her roughly towards him

'Won't you sit down?' he said, and pointed in the rough direction of the bed

He looked in the rough direction of the bed, and raised a provocative eyebrow

A suggestive eyebrow

He raised one of his eyebrows

He raised both of his eyebrows

He raised his right eyebrow provocatively

He raised his left eyebrow suggestively

Raising both of his eyebrows, one provocatively, the other suggestively, he pulled her gently in the rough direction of the bed

Perhaps this section was also best dispensed with. I could imagine exactly what Patrick's criticism would be: I was dithering over these preliminary niceties so as to avoid getting down to the action.

She was wearing a

What was she wearing?

She was wearing a blouse

Yes?

She was wearing a thin muslin blouse
She was wearing a thin muslin blouse, through which her

Go on, write it.

through which her nipples stood out like

Like?

like two cherries
like two maraschino cherries
like two glacé cherries
like two Fox's Glacier Mints
like two peas in a pod
like three coins in a fountain
like Victoria plums
like Victoria Falls
like a sore thumb

Anyway, she had these nipples. That was fairly obvious. What about him, though? I didn't want to be accused of sexism: I was obliged, as far as I could see, to present the male as a sexual object too. And so, for instance:

His tight black trousers could barely conceal

Or better still –

The bulge in his tight black trousers left her in no doubt
as to
    his excitement
    his intentions
    his endowment
    his policy
    the nature of his endowment

the extent of his manhood
the length of his extension
the extent of his full, throbbing manhood
the full extent of his hot, throbbing member

I had to admit it, this wasn't getting me anywhere. Besides, I could always come back later if I wanted to fine-tune these points of descriptive detail. If I didn't get to the heart of the matter soon, the momentum would be gone.

He tore off her blouse

No, too aggressive.

He unbuttoned her blouse and peeled it off like a
like
like the skin on an overripe banana

I threw down my pen and sat back in disgust. What was the matter with me tonight? Maybe it was the wine, or just the fact that I was thoroughly out of practice at this sort of thing, but nothing seemed to be working. I was making all the wrong moves, falling at every fence, fumbling and groping and communicating nothing but my own inexperience.

He laid a tentative, questioning hand on her
soft, milky
warm, silky
yielding, heaving
rising, falling
swelling, bulging
big, bouncy
fleshy, bumpy, heavy, chunky, strapping, whopping,
vast, enormous, massive, monstrous, prodigious, colossal,
gigantic, mountainous, Gargantuan, Titanic, Herculean
her small, pert breasts
her perfectly proportioned breasts
her averagely proportioned yet somehow surprising
breasts
her deformed breasts

All right. Forget that. More wine. Now think carefully. Imagine these two young, attractive people, alone in a room with only their own bodies for amusement. Picture them in your mind.

Now choose your words with confidence, and precision. Be fearless.

> *as he buried his face in her bountiful breasts, she pulled the shirt from his shapely shoulders*
>> *he sank to his knees and nuzzled her navel with his nose*
>> *they fell on to the bed and he lay on top of her, their lips boring greedily into each other in a long, moist kiss*
>> *they fell on to the bed and she lay on top of him, their moist lips meeting hungrily in a long, boring kiss*

Oh, to hell with it.

>> *she was panting with desire*
>> *he was bursting from his pants*
>> *she was wet between the thighs*
>> *he was wet behind the ears*
>> *she was just about to come*
>> *he didn't know whether he was coming or going*

And it was at this climactic juncture, just as I had managed to work myself into a state of rather desperate excitement, that the telephone rang. I sat up in surprise and looked at the clock. It was two-thirty in the morning. Irrationally, I felt obliged to tidy up my desk and make sure that the sheets of paper were positioned face down before I went to answer. Then, when I picked up the receiver, I heard an unfamiliar voice.

'Mr Owen?' it said.

'Speaking.'

'I'm sorry to be disturbing you at this time of night. I hope I didn't get you out of bed. Hanrahan's the name. I'm ringing on behalf of one of my clients, a Mr Findlay Onyx, who claims to be an acquaintance of yours.'

'That's correct.'

'I'm his lawyer, you see. Findlay sends his apologies for not being able to speak to you directly, but he's being held at Hornsey police station, and isn't allowed to make any more phone calls. He is, however, very anxious to meet with you personally at the earliest opportunity. He asked me to say that you should come round to the station first thing tomorrow morning, if it's at all possible.'

'Well, it's ... difficult,' I said, thinking of Fiona and her

outpatients' appointment. 'I suppose if it's absolutely necessary
... I mean, what's going on? Is he in trouble?'

'I'm afraid so. I really think it would be best if you could make
the effort.'

I gave him a tentative assurance and he said, 'Good. Findlay
can count on you, then,' and hung up. The whole conversation
had taken place so quickly that I scarcely knew what had happened. For a start I hadn't even managed to ask him why Findlay
was being held by the police – unless, of course (and suddenly
this seemed the obvious, the only solution), he was the one who
had broken into Mr McGanny's house and stolen the documents
relating to my book. I went into the bedroom, lay down on the
bed and pondered the likelihood of this. Could they have caught
up with him already, if the burglary had only taken place last
night? It was possible. He was old and infirm, and might well
have left a trail of careless evidence. But if that was the case, why
the sudden urgency? Surely he would be let out on bail, and our
meeting could have been deferred until he was back in the privacy
of his flat. There was no way of knowing, anyway, and I spent
the rest of the night mulling over this new development in an
uneasy half-sleep which was broken after only a few hours by the
first shafts of wintry sunlight.

2

It seemed to take most of the morning to get to the police station by bus. Fiona wouldn't have that problem, at any rate: I'd booked a minicab for her before setting out. I'd done this to salve my conscience as much as anything else, because she'd looked so suddenly vulnerable when I left her: she'd put on her smartest work clothes, the way people do when gripped by that strange sense of propriety which insists that, if they are to meet their doom, they should at least be properly dressed. (But then again, I suppose, it gives them a kind of strength.) Having me with her wouldn't have made a lot of difference, anyway. That's what I tried to believe as the bus stopped and started on its throttled course across London, carrying me ever closer towards the next stage in a mystery from which I was, to tell the truth, beginning to feel more and more detached. It was a good feeling, too, this detachment: quite a relief, after all those years of puzzlement and struggle. It never occurred to me that I would have lost it by the time the morning was out.

I was kept waiting for only a few minutes by the desk sergeant, and then taken to a bright but grubby cell on the ground floor. Findlay was sitting rigidly on a bench, his raincoat again draped over his shoulders, his white hair turned to a halo by beams of light from one small window high up in the wall.

'Michael,' he said, taking my outstretched hand. 'You do me an honour. I could only wish our second meeting had not been fated to take place amid such squalor and uncleanness. The fault, I'm afraid, is entirely my own.'

'Entirely?'

'Well, you can probably guess what has brought me here.'

'I have – let's say an inkling.'

'Of course you have, Michael. A man of your discernment,

your intuition. You know the frailties an old man is subject to, when his resolve is weak but his desires – alas – remain strong. Strong as they ever were.' He sighed. 'I think that I mentioned, the last time we met . . . the bender?'

I nodded uncertainly. To be honest, I had lost his drift.

'Well, I'm in breach of it. That's the sad fact of the matter, and I have only myself to blame.'

Light began to dawn. 'You mean your suspended sentence?'

'Quite. Once again I find myself flattened by the demands of a reckless libido. Once again the power of flesh over the spirit –'

'So it wasn't you who broke into McGanny's house the other night?'

He looked up sharply, hissed me into silence and shot a warning glance towards the door. 'For Heaven's sake, Michael. Do you want to make things even worse for me?' And then, in a whisper: 'Why do you think I brought you here, if not to discuss that very matter?'

I sat down on the bench beside him and waited for enlightenment. After a while I realized that he was sulking.

'I'm sorry,' I prompted.

'Apart from anything else,' he said, 'you impugn my professional competence, if you think that I'm incapable of carrying out such a routine little assignment without getting caught. I slipped in and out of that house, Michael, with the grace and the lithe energy of a jungle cat. The great Raffles himself might have stood back and gasped in envy.'

'So what went wrong?'

'Sheer loss of control, Michael. Lack of will-power, and nothing else. I spent the whole of yesterday sifting through the documents which I had borrowed – borrowed, I repeat, for I have a scrupulous regard for property – and by the evening, I was quite satisfied that they provided everything I might have required to forge the missing links in the chain of this most perplexing investigation. Imagine my exhilaration, Michael. Imagine the surge of adrenalin and the rush of blood, coursing through my ancient veins in a torrent of pride and excitement. Suddenly I felt like a young man of thirty.'

'And so?'

'Naturally I went out to look for one. The pubs were shut, by now, but just a few streets away from my flat there is a public convenience which, thanks to an uncharacteristically enlightened decision on the part of our council leaders, provides a haven at all hours of the day and night for anyone seeking relief, in its various forms. I'd been trying to stay away from the place for weeks, ever since I was last hauled up in front of a judge and told that one more slip would land me behind bars – only for a couple of months, he said, but who knows what effect even a brief confinement might have on the constitution of a frail and feeble-hearted relic such as myself. Last night, however, the majesty of the law seemed to hold no terrors, and I found myself unable to resist an approach to this sink of delicious iniquity. I had been there for only a few seconds when a man (man! what am I saying! – an apparition, Michael, a perfectionist's fantasy sprung to life: Adonis himself, in bomber jacket and sky-blue jeans) emerged from one of the cubicles.' Findlay shook his head, rapture and regret seeming to vie for precedence in his thoughts. 'Needless to say, he was to be my undoing. And vice versa.'

'Vice versa?'

'Precisely: I undid his shirt, I undid his trousers, I undid the buttons on his fly. I won't offend your breeder's sensibilities, Michael, with a detailed account – a blow-by-blow account, one might almost say – of the pleasantries which ensued. I ask you only to imagine my shock, my outrage, my sense of betrayal, when he suddenly introduced himself as a detective superintendent, no less, of the Metropolitan Police, clapped a pair of handcuffs on me, and whistled for the accomplice who had been waiting out by the doorway. It all happened so very quickly.' He bowed his head and we both fell silent. I struggled for words of consolation but couldn't find any; and when Findlay spoke at last, there was a new note of bitterness in his voice. 'It's the hypocrisy of these people I can't stand, you know. The lies they tell themselves and the rest of the world. The little shit was enjoying himself every bit as much as I was.'

'How do you know?'

'Please, Michael,' he said, with an indulgent glance. 'Either that, or it was his truncheon I'd had between my teeth for the last ten minutes. Allow me some credit for my reading of the situation.'

Chastened, I waited a moment or two before asking: 'So then what happened?'

'I was brought back here, and now it appears they can have me banged up in a day or two. Which is why I wanted to see you as soon as possible.'

There were footsteps in the corridor outside. Findlay waited until they had gone by, then leaned towards me conspiratorially. 'I have made,' he said, in a low voice, 'some startling discoveries. You will be pleased to hear – though not especially surprised, if you are at all acquainted with my rate of success in these matters – that my hunch has proved to be accurate.'

'Which hunch is that?'

'Cast your mind back, Michael, to that discussion we had the last time we met. At one point, I seem to recall, you made an assertion to the effect that you had merely "drifted in" to this business, and I ventured to suggest that it may have been a little more complicated than that. I was right.' He left an impressive pause. 'You were chosen.'

'Chosen? Who by?'

'By Tabitha Winshaw, of course. Now listen carefully. Hanrahan will give you a spare set of keys to my flat, and you will find all the relevant papers in the top drawer of my desk. You should go up there as soon as you can and take a good look at them. The first thing you'll find is Tabitha's letter to the Peacock Press, dated the twenty-first of May, 1982, putting forward the idea of a book about her family. Immediately, then, a question comes to mind: how had she found out about these particular publishers?'

'Answering this question turned out to be simple enough, and involved nothing more devious than some research into the chequered history of McGanny's entrepreneurial career. I found documents suggesting that he had, over the last thirty years, been involved in the formation of no less than seventeen different companies, most of them having gone into receivership and several having been the subject of criminal proceedings under the tax laws. He had run night clubs, drug companies, dating agencies, insurance firms, correspondence courses and had set himself up, finally, as a literary agent: no doubt it was this which gave him the idea of establishing the Peacock Press – having learned that if there is one class of person, out of all of society's most naïve and defenceless members, who is simply crying out to be conned, it's the aspiring but untalented writer. Now it seems that one of McGanny's enterprises, in the mid 1970s, was a chain of bingo halls which ran foul of the authorities in Yorkshire, among other places: and who should have taken charge of his defence on that occasion but our old friend Proudfoot – solicitor to none other than Tabitha Winshaw herself – who continued to provide him with legal representation until meeting with an untimely end, so I gathered, in 1984. So there we have our connection. Tabitha approaches Proudfoot, asking him to locate a suitable publisher, and Proudfoot, miraculously, is able to produce just the man.

'He would also have known that Tabitha's proposal had a good chance of being accepted, because the state of the company finances at that time was fairly desperate. You will be able to see that yourself from the year's accounts, which I took the precaution of including in my haul. Add financial insecurity, then, to Mc-Ganny's proven willingness to engage in unscrupulous transactions, and you will see that he could hardly be expected to refuse Tabitha's generous terms. And he would not even have baulked, as most men would have done, at her one extraordinary precondition.' He looked up at me sharply. 'You can guess what it was, of course?'

I shrugged. 'I've no idea.'

Findlay permitted himself a dry laugh. 'Well, from her letter, it seems that she insisted – insisted, mind – that the book could only be written by you.'

This made no sense at all.

'But that's ridiculous. I haven't even met Tabitha Winshaw. Back in 1982 we didn't even . . . know of each other's existence.'

'Well, she obviously knew of yours.'

Findlay sat back against the wall, examining his fingernails and clearly relishing the confusion into which his information had thrown me. After a while – and, I suspect, more out of mischief than anything else – he speculated coolly: 'Perhaps news of your literary reputation had reached her, Michael. She may have read a review of one of those widely admired novels of yours, and decided that here was a man whose services she could not afford to do without.'

But I scarcely heard this remark, because a number of new questions, distinctly uncomfortable ones, had just occurred to me.

'Yes, but look, I told you how I came to be offered that job. There was this woman called Alice Hastings, and I met her on the train, quite by chance.'

'Quite by arrangement, I think you'll find.' Findlay had produced a toothpick from somewhere and was now scraping out the dirt from beneath his thumbnail.

'But I'd never seen her before in my life.'

'And have you seen her since?'

'Well no, I haven't – not to speak to, anyway.'

'That's rather curious, isn't it, in – what? – eight years of dealing with the firm.'

'Actually,' I said, on the defensive, 'I caught a glimpse of her outside the office only a few months ago, getting out of a taxi.'

'I seem to remember,' said Findlay, now pointing at me with the toothpick, 'that when you first told me this story, you furnished me with a brief description.'

'That's right: long dark hair, long thin neck –'

'– and a face like a horse.'

'I can't believe those were my exact words.'

'Equine, then. That was the detail that stuck in my mind. Or rather, that was the detail which came back to me when I broke into the house the other night and first saw a photograph of' (bringing the toothpick even closer to my face) '*McGanny himself.*'

'What are you saying?'

'Did you know that Hastings is the maiden name of McGanny's wife?'

'No, of course not.'

'And that he has a daughter called Alice – an actress?'

'Yes, I did, as a matter of fact.'

'You knew her name was Alice?'

'I knew she was an actress. She phoned him up the last time I was in there, a few months –'

I stopped short.

'The same day,' Findlay suggested, 'that you thought you'd seen Miss Hastings getting out of a taxi?'

I didn't reply to this; just got up and walked to the window.

'If the name Alice McGanny,' Findlay continued, 'is not one which is widely known in theatrical circles, this is because the young lady's career has, from what I was able to piece together of her CV, obstinately refused to take off. She's understudied, she's dressed, she's ASM-ed, she's had walk-on parts, one-line parts and no-line parts, and in between these triumphs she's been in and out of a drug rehabilitation centre and posed naked for one of the sleaziest magazines in the business. (There was a copy in McGanny's safe, which I was considerate enough to retrieve on your behalf: it did nothing for me, I'm afraid, but they tell me that this sort of thing can sometimes provide a small *frisson* to those who share your rather sad and routine inclinations.) And so it's hardly surprising, given all of this, that she's repeatedly been obliged to borrow large sums of money from her father; and I dare say that on this occasion she was willing enough to undertake a little role-playing on his behalf, if the price was right.'

I stayed over by the window. It was too high up in the wall for me to be able to see anything, but that didn't matter: my mind's eye was focused on our meeting in the railway carriage all those years ago. I replayed it again and again, fast-forwarding, rewinding. They must have found out my address somehow – from Patrick, maybe, or from my literary editor at the newspaper – and then she must have kept watch on the flat for hours, perhaps even a day or two, while I sat inside writing my precious review . . . Followed me to the tube station, followed me to King's Cross, and then that stupid story about going to visit her sister in Kettering, and not needing her own suitcase. How could I have fallen for it: what, precisely, had been blinding me?

'Well, you're not the only man who would have walked into that trap, I'm sure,' said Findlay, appearing to read my thoughts. 'She is rather attractive, after all; even I can see that. Still, they were taking a bit of a gamble, when you think about it, if her looks were all they had to rely upon. I'm surprised they didn't try to bait the hook with something else while they were about it.'

'They did.' I turned, but was still unable to look Findlay full in his questioning face. 'She was reading one of my novels. It had never happened to me before. She didn't have to approach me. I introduced myself.'

'Ah.' Findlay nodded wisely, but there was no mistaking the amusement in his eye. 'Of course. The age-old appeal. And McGanny would know more about authorial vanity than most. After all, he had built a whole business on it.'

'Quite.' I paced the cell briskly now, anxious for the conversation to be over as quickly as possible. I waited for what seemed like an age for Findlay to break his silence, and then could contain my impatience no longer. 'Well?'

'Well what?'

'So what's the missing link?'

'Missing link?'

'Between me and Tabitha. How had she found out about me, why did she choose me?'

'I've already told you, Michael: unless your name had become a watchword, in those days, among Yorkshire's many discerning readers of contemporary fiction, I haven't the vaguest notion.'

'But you're a detective: I thought that's what you were trying to find out.'

'I have found out a great deal,' said Findlay sharply, 'much of it on your behalf and all of it at considerable personal risk. If some of my discoveries have upset you then perhaps there are lessons to be learned from your own conduct in this affair. Don't blame the messenger.'

I sat down beside him and was about to apologize when the cell door opened. A constable popped his head round and said, 'One more minute,' and there was something about his manner as he did this – the sense of a token civility pared down to its

absolute minimum – which, combined with the fearsome clang of
the cell door when it slammed behind him, suddenly brought
home all the injustice of Findlay's predicament.

'How can they do this to you?' I stammered. 'I mean, it's crazy,
putting you away like this. You're an old man: what do they hope
to achieve?'

Findlay shrugged. 'I've had a lifetime of this sort of treatment,
Michael. You stop asking questions. Thankfully I remain sound
in mind and body, so I shall survive the ordeal, you can be sure of
that. But talking of survival' (and here his voice sank to a whisper
again) 'I hear on the grapevine that the members of a certain
eminent family are steeling themselves for a tragic loss. Mortimer
Winshaw is fading fast.'

'That's sad. He's the only one who was ever nice to me.'

'Well, I smell ructions, Michael. I smell upheaval. You know as
well as I do the nature of Mortimer's feelings towards his family.
If he leaves a will there may be some nasty surprises for them in
it; and of course, if there's a funeral, Tabitha will be expected to
attend, and it will be the first time *she's* seen any of them for a
very long time. You should keep your ear to the ground. It might
make for an interesting chapter in your little chronicle.'

'Thank you,' I said. 'I mean, thank you for all your help.'
There was a valedictory feeling in the air, suddenly, and I found
myself trying to make a speech. 'You've been to a lot of trouble. I
– well, I hope you got something out of it, that's all: you know,
whatever it was you wanted . . .'

'Professional satisfaction, Michael. This is all that the serious
detective ever asks from his work. This business has been nagging
away at me for more than thirty years: but all my instincts tell me
that it will be unravelled soon, very soon. I'm just sorry that the
forces of law have intervened to stop me from playing an active
part.' He took my hand and held it in a fragile but determined
grip. 'For the next two months, Michael, you're my ears and eyes.
Remember that. I'm relying on you now.'

He smiled bravely, and I did my best to smile back.

3

Christmas Day dawned cloudy, dry and without character. As I stood at the window of my flat overlooking the park, I could not help thinking back, as I thought back on this day every year, to the white Christmases of my childhood, when the house would be swathed in my mother's home-made decorations, my father would spend hours on his hands and knees trying to locate the one faulty bulb which was preventing our tree from lighting up, and on Christmas Eve I would sit by the window all afternoon, awaiting the arrival of my grandparents who invariably drove over from their neighbouring suburb to stay with us until the New Year. (I mean my mother's parents, for we had nothing to do with my father's; had not even heard from them, in fact, for as long as I could remember.) For a few days the atmosphere in our house, usually so quiet and contemplative, would be lively, boisterous even, and it's perhaps because of this memory – and the memory of the fabulous whiteness which could always be relied upon, in those days, to blanket our front lawn – that there was still an air of unreality about the grey, silent Christmases to which in recent years I had become numbly resigned.

But today would be different. Neither of us could stomach the thought of eight hours' Christmas television, and by mid-morning we were in a hired car heading down towards the South Coast. I hadn't driven for ages. Luckily South London was more or less empty of traffic, and apart from a close shave with a red Sierra and a bruising encounter with the edge of a roundabout just outside Surbiton, we managed to get out into the countryside without serious incident. Fiona had offered to drive, but I wouldn't hear of it. Maybe this was silly of me, because she was feeling (and looking) better than she'd done for weeks, and if anything I think I'd been more upset than she had by the absurd mix-up over the results of her tests at the hospital, when she'd turned up for her appointment only to be told that it had been cancelled, and somebody was supposed to have telephoned her about it, and the specialist who was supposed to be dealing with her case was at a protest meeting to complain about the administrator's decision to close down four surgical wards immediately after Christmas, and could she please come back in a week's time when everything would be sorted out. I couldn't contain my frustration when she told me this story, and no doubt my frenzy of shouting and foot-stamping had shaken her far more badly than her nervous taxi ride and wasted three-quarters of an hour in the clammy hubbub of the outpatients' waiting room. I suppose I was out of practice when it came to dealing with a crisis. Anyway, she'd recovered – we'd both recovered – and here we were, gazing in rapture at the barren hedgerows, the converted farmhouses, the diffident rise and fall of dun-coloured fields, like two children from an inner-city ghetto who had never been let out into the countryside before.

We arrived in Eastbourne at about twelve o'clock. Ours was the only car parked by the front, and for a few minutes we sat in silence, listening to the wash of sea against grey shingle.

'It's so quiet,' said Fiona; and when we got out, the opening and shutting of the car doors seemed both to shatter and to be absorbed by the surrounding hush: making me think – I can't imagine why – of lonely punctuation marks on a blank sheet of paper.

As we walked down to the ocean our footsteps made a pebbly crunch; you could also, if you listened closely, hear a whispered breeze, sibilant and fitful. Fiona unfolded a rug and we sat at the water's edge, leaning into one another. It was extremely cold.

After a while she said: 'Where are we going to eat?'

I said: 'There's bound to be a hotel or a pub or something.'

She said: 'It's Christmas Day. They might all be booked out.'

A few minutes later, the near-silence was broken by the click and whirr of an approaching bicycle. We looked round and saw an old and very corpulent man parking his bike against the wall, then descending the steps and crunching his way towards the sea, a knapsack across his shoulder and a resolute look on his face. When he was about ten yards away from us he put down his knapsack and started taking his clothes off. We tried not to watch as more and more of his huge, pink, astonishing body came into view. He was wearing bathing trunks instead of underpants and, much to our relief, he stopped at these, then folded his clothes in a neat pile, took a towel from his knapsack and shook it out. After that he started picking his way towards the water, pausing only to glance at us and say, 'Morning.' He was still wearing his wrist-watch, and a few steps later he stopped to look at it, turned back towards us and qualified his greeting with: 'Afternoon, I should say.' Then another afterthought: 'You wouldn't mind keeping an eye on my things, would you? If you're going to be here a minute or two.' His accent was Northern: Mancunian, at a guess.

Fiona said: 'Not at all.'

'How old do you reckon he is,' I asked under my breath, as we saw him wade, without flinching, into the icy shallows: 'Seventy? eighty?'

In another moment he had submerged himself and all we could see was his reddened pate bobbing up and down. He wasn't in for long, only about five minutes or so, starting off with some easy-going breast-stroke, then switching to a vigorous crawl as he charged up and down the same stretch of water ten or twelve times, and ending up on his back for a leisurely return to the shore. When he hit the pebbles he rolled over and clambered out, rubbing his hands together and slapping his flabby upper arms to restore the circulation.

'Bit nippy in there today,' he said, as he walked past us. 'Still, it wouldn't do to miss. Couldn't do without my constitutional.'

'You mean you do this every day?' asked Fiona.

'Every day for the last thirty years,' he said, returning to his pile of clothes and beginning to towel himself dry. 'First thing in the morning, as a rule. Of course, today's a bit different: it being Christmas, and so forth. We've a house full of grandkids and this was the earliest I could escape, what with all the presents having to be opened.' Fiona averted her eyes as he began the tortuous business of getting his trunks off while holding the towel in place. 'Are you from round here?' he asked. 'Or just down for the day?'

'We've come down from London,' said Fiona.

'I see. Getting away from it all. And why not. Couldn't face a day of screaming children and Granny hurting her teeth on the walnuts.'

'Something like that.'

'Can't say I blame you. Madness it is, round at our place this morning.' He pulled his ample stomach in a few inches and fastened his belt. 'Mind you, it's the wife I feel sorry for. Turkey, roast potatoes, stuffing and two veg for fourteen people. That's a lot to expect of any woman, isn't it?'

Fiona asked if he could recommend somewhere for us to have lunch, and he mentioned the name of a pub. 'It'll be full up, mind, but the landlord's a friend of mine, so if you just mention my name they might find you a corner. Tell them Norman sent you. I shouldn't waste much time about it, either, if I was you. Come on and I'll point you in the right direction.'

We thanked him and, once he had finished dressing and had re-packed the towel carefully in his knapsack, followed him up to the road.

'Crikey, what a lovely bike,' said Fiona, as soon as she saw it at close quarters. 'Cannondale, isn't it?'

'D'you like it? This is its maiden voyage. It was a present from my eldest: they sprang it on me this morning. I do know a thing or two about bikes – been riding them all my life, you see – and I reckon this one ought to be a beauty. Only weighs about half as much as my old Raleigh: here, look at this, I can lift it up with one hand.'

'How does it feel on the road?'

'Well, not as nifty as I was expecting, funnily enough. I've come from a little way out of town and it's a bit of a climb. I was finding it quite hard going.'

'That's odd.' Fiona knelt down and started to examine the back wheel. I looked on, bemused.

'You'd think with seven gears I wouldn't have any problem at all, wouldn't you?'

She peered even more intently at a cluster of very intimidating-looking cogs and ratchets at the centre of the wheel. 'You know, you might have the wrong sort of cassette on here,' she said. 'If this is designed for racing then the ratios may be too high for you. It's all to do with the cadence. This'll be designed for about ninety r.p.m. and you're probably doing nearer seventy-five.'

Norman looked worried. 'Is that serious, then?'

'Not really. You're in luck, because you've got individually replaceable sprockets. You'll need a chain whip and a lockring remover, and then you can do it yourself.' She stood up. 'Well, it's just a hunch.'

'You can have a ride if you like,' said Norman. 'See what you think.'

'Can I? Gosh, that would be a treat.' She turned the bike round and swung herself into the saddle. 'I'll just go up to the roundabout and back, shall I?'

'Whatever you like.'

We both watched as she pedalled off down the road, uncertainly at first, then gathering speed and confidence. She receded from view until the only distinct feature was her windswept trail of copper hair.

'Getting a good bit of speed up, there,' said Norman.

'She's an old hand,' I said, surprised at the pride I took in being able to tell him this. 'Did a forty-mile sponsored ride a couple of months ago.'

'Well' – he winked at me in a manly, confidential sort of way – 'you're a lucky bugger, that's all I can say. No wonder you don't want to share her with anybody else on a day like this. She's a cracker.'

'That's not really why we're here.'

'Oh?'

'No. We came down for ... well, for health reasons, I suppose you'd call it.' The urge to confide in someone was suddenly strong. 'I'm so worried, I couldn't begin to tell you. We've been trying to get some sense out of the doctors, but it's been going on for months: fevers, night sweats, dreadful sore throats. I just thought a change of scene might do some good – you know, sea air, and all that sort of thing. She'd never say anything about it, but it's been tearing us both apart; and if it turns out to be something serious, I don't know how I'd cope, I really don't.'

'Aye, well.' Norman sighed, looking away, and shuffled his feet in embarrassment. 'I didn't like to say anything, but now you've mentioned it, you do look bloody terrible.' And just before Fiona cruised back into earshot, he added: 'Let's hope she doesn't wear you out, eh?'

*

We tried our luck at the pub he'd recommended. The dining area was very hot, very full, and very stuffy, but when we mentioned Norman's name the landlord did indeed manage to find us a table in the corner, boxed in by a family party of eight, all of them highly boisterous except for a lanky teenager with a streaming cold. He could never quite get to his handkerchief in time, and whenever he sneezed I could see the fine droplets of saliva flying in our direction. We passed on the first course and went straight on to the turkey, which was dry, thinly sliced to the point of transparency, and served with a small mountain of waterlogged vegetables.

'How come you know all that stuff about bicycles, then?' I asked Fiona, as she made her first brave inroads into this daunting confection. 'You were coming across like a real expert.'

She had her mouth full of sprout and turkey, and was unable to answer at first.

'I did an abstract of some articles about new gear systems just a couple of weeks ago,' she said, and then embarked upon some serious chewing. 'I've got a good memory for that sort of thing: don't ask me why.'

'I wouldn't have thought it fell within your brief.'

'We have a very wide brief. It's not just specialist journals: we cover lots of different subjects. Cycling, cybernetics, sexually transmitted diseases, space travel . . .'

'Space travel?'

She noticed my sudden interest.

'Why, is this another little obsession that you've been keeping quiet about?'

'Well, it used to be, I suppose. When I was little I wanted to be an astronaut when I grew up. I know probably every other boy of my age felt the same way but those enthusiasms never really leave you, do they?'

'Strange,' she said. 'I never really thought of you as the macho type.'

'Macho?'

'Well, the symbolism of all those rockets isn't exactly hard to fathom, is it? I'm sure that's the appeal for the average male: thrusting your way into the unknown regions . . .'

'No, that wasn't how I felt at all. Perhaps this sounds strange, but it was the' – I cast around for the word, failed to find it, and had to settle for – 'the lyricism of it, I suppose, that attracted me.' Fiona seemed unconvinced. 'Yuri Gagarin was my real hero. Did you ever read his description of what he could see from the rocket while it was in orbit? It's almost like a poem.'

She laughed incredulously. 'You're going to recite it to me now, aren't you?'

'Hang on.' I closed my eyes. It was years since I'd last tried to remember these words. ' "The day side of the earth was clearly visible," ' I began, and then repeated slowly: ' "The coasts of continents, islands, big rivers, big surfaces of water . . . During the flight I saw for the first time with my own eyes the earth's spherical shape. You can see its curvature when looking to the horizon. The view of the horizon is unique and very beautiful. You can see the remarkable change in colour from the light surface of the earth to the completely black sky in which you can see the stars. This dividing line is very thin, just like a belt of film surrounding the earth's sphere. It's a delicate blue, and this transition from the blue to the black is very gradual and lovely." '

Fiona laid down her knife and fork while I was saying this, and listened with her chin cradled in her hands.

'I had pictures of him plastered all over my bedroom. I even used to write stories about him. And then the night he died in that plane crash' – I laughed nervously – 'and you don't have to believe this if you don't want to – but the night he died, I had a dream about him. I dreamed that I *was* him, plummeting down to earth in this burning plane. And at that stage I hadn't really given him a thought for years.' From the blankness of Fiona's expression, I gathered that she was sceptical about this revelation. So I concluded with an apology: 'Well, it made an impression on me at the time.'

'No, I believe you,' she said. 'I was just trying to remember something.' She sat back and gazed at the window, now dotted with spluttering rain. 'Some time last year, I had to do an abstract of a piece in one of the newspapers. It was about that crash – somebody's theory about what might have happened, based on new information. You know, post-glasnost, and all that.'

'What did it say?'

'I've forgotten a lot of it; but the whole thing was pretty indecisive, anyway, I think. Something about another plane, a much larger one, crossing his flight path and creating a lot of turbulence just as he was coming out of the cloud. Throwing him off course.'

I shook my head. 'My theory's better than that. Well, it's the same theory that a lot of people have, actually. The idea is that the Soviet authorities bumped him off, because he'd seen a bit too much of the West and he liked it and he was probably going to defect.'

Fiona smiled: an affectionate but challenging smile.

'You think you can reduce everything to politics, don't you, Michael? It makes life so simple for you.'

'I don't see what's simple about it.'

'Well of course politics can be complicated, I realize that. But I always think there's something treacherous about that sort of approach. The way it tempts us to believe there's an explanation for everything, somewhere or other, if only we're prepared to look hard enough. That's what you're really interested in, isn't it? Explaining things away.'

'What's the alternative?'

'No, that's not the point. I'm just saying there are other possibilities to be taken into account. Larger ones, even.'

'Such as?'

'Such as ... well, supposing he really did die by accident? Suppose it was circumstance that killed him: nothing more, nothing less. Wouldn't that be more frightening to face up to than your little conspiracy theory? Or supposing it was suicide. He'd seen things that nobody else had seen, after all – incredibly beautiful things, by the sound of it. Perhaps he never really came back to reality, and this was the culmination of something irrational, some madness which had been burning away *inside him* – well out of the reach of you and your politics. I don't suppose you'd like the sound of that much, either.'

'Well, if you're determined to get sentimental about it . . .'

Fiona shrugged. 'Maybe I am sentimental. But there are dangers in being too dogmatic, you know. Seeing everything in black and white.' I couldn't think of an answer to this, and concentrated instead on impaling a trio of spongy peas on the end of my fork. Her next question took me by surprise. 'When are you going to tell me why you fell out with your mother in that Chinese restaurant?'

I looked up and said: 'That's a rather abrupt change of subject.'

'It's not a change of subject at all.'

'I'm not with you,' I muttered, returning to my food.

'You've been promising to tell me for months. You even *want* to tell me: it's obvious.' Since no response was forthcoming, she continued to think aloud. 'What could she have said, to hurt you so badly? So badly that it split you in two. The half that refuses to forgive her because it insists on seeing things in black and white, and the other half – the one you've been trying to smother ever since it happened.' I said nothing; just pushed a piece of turkey around my plate, soaking it in thick, oily gravy. 'Do you even know where she is this afternoon? What she'll be doing?'

'She'll be sitting at home, I expect.'

'By herself?'

'Probably.' I gave up and pushed the plate aside. 'Look, there can't be any going back. It was my father who held us together, anyway. Once he died, then . . . that was that.'

'But you still saw each other after he died. That's not why it happened.'

I did want to tell her, that's the strange thing. I desperately wanted to tell her. But it was going to have to be torn out of me, one piece at a time, and the process was only just beginning. I didn't mean to be unhelpful: I didn't mean to sound wilfully enigmatic. That was just how it came out.

I said: 'People can die more than once.'

Fiona stared at me. She said: 'Why don't we just skip the pudding and leave?'

*

It was an argument, of sorts, even if neither of us could be quite sure how it had happened. We left the pub in silence and spoke only a few words on the way back to the car. Driving home, not wanting to waste the last half hour of daylight, I suggested a quick walk on the South Downs. We walked arm in arm, having silently buried our differences, whatever they were, through a landscape which might have been attractive on a sunny day but now, what with the cold and the encroaching dusk, felt bare and forbidding. Fiona seemed very tired.

I was amazed, in fact, that she'd managed to last this long, and it was no surprise to see her nodding off as we resumed our journey. I looked at her reposeful face and was reminded of the intimacy I'd felt, the sense of privilege, the night that I'd sneaked up to Joan's room and watched her for a few minutes as she slept. But this was deceptive, because looking at Fiona was not like looking into the past: quite the opposite. For with every snatched glance (I was trying to keep my eyes on the road) I felt that I was being offered a glimpse of something new and unthinkable, something that I had been needlessly denying myself, now, for many years: a future.

We stopped off only once more, at a service station where I went to buy myself some Smarties and a Yorkie bar. By the time I got back to the car she was fast asleep.

*

And yet, only six days later –
  Can this be true?
  And yet, only six days later

*

I'm not sure I can go through with this.

4

The day after Boxing Day, my Christmas parcel of books arrived from the Peacock Press. There was a note from Mrs Tonks, apologizing for having sent them later than usual. I couldn't motivate myself to look at them or even take the wrapping off. In the afternoon I went over to Findlay's flat to see the papers he had stolen. They didn't really tell me anything new. Instead of feeling intrigued, or baffled, or worried by Tabitha's letter and the concrete evidence it provided that she had once written to the publishers and implored them to procure my services when I didn't even know of her existence, I was able to register barely a flicker of interest. The Winshaws and their ruthless, fantastic, power-hungry lives had never seemed so distant. As for the envelope which presumably contained the incriminating photographs of Alice, I didn't even open it.

Fiona was everything now.

The next day she had her rescheduled appointment at the clinic, and this time I was determined to accompany her. For some reason, she'd been feeling quite a lot worse since her day out by the seaside. I thought it would have done her some good. But her cough had returned, more insistent than before, and she complained of feeling short of breath: climbing the stairs to her flat the previous evening, she had had to rest on three of the four landings.

The appointment was at eleven-thirty. We waited ages for a bus and were a few minutes late arriving at the hospital, a black-bricked Victorian monstrosity more conducive, I would have thought, to the punishment of long-term offenders than the treatment of the sick. It didn't matter, anyway: it was well past twelve when Fiona got called into the consulting room. I waited outside, struggling to sustain a vestige of optimism in the face of these relentlessly dispiriting surroundings: the queasy, pale yellow décor, the malfunctioning coffee machine, which had already robbed us of 60p, the erratic heating system (one enormous cast iron radiator was on full-blast, the other not at all; and every so often the pipes would gurgle and splutter and shake visibly against the walls, dislodging crumbs of plaster). I could only stand it for about five minutes, and was about to go out for a walk when Fiona returned, looking flushed and agitated.

'Out already?' I said. 'That was quick.'

'They can't find my notes,' she said, walking straight past me and heading for the exit.

I hurried after her.

'What?'

We were outside again. It was bitterly cold.

'What do you mean, exactly?'

'I mean that they can't find the notes to my case. They looked for them this morning and they weren't there. Some secretary's probably got them. Lost in the system, basically. They blamed it on the holiday.'

'So where does that leave you?'

'I've got another appointment for next week.'

Tides of righteous frustration welled up inside me.

'Fiona, they can't keep doing this to you. You're ill, for God's sake. You can't let your health be tampered with by a bunch of idiots. We're not going to stand for it.'

This was just empty bravado, and we both knew it.

'Shut up, Michael.' She coughed furiously for about thirty seconds, doubled up against the hospital wall, and then straightened herself. 'Come on. We're going home.'

*

It was New Year's Eve.

The original plan had been to go back to the Mandarin. I'd phoned them at lunchtime and with a little persuasion had managed to secure a table for two; but by early in the evening it was obvious that Fiona wasn't well enough to go out, so I promised to cook her dinner instead. There was a large continental grocer's open on the King's Road: I bought some fish and cheese and pasta and tinned prawns, in the hope of improvising a seafood lasagne. I got some wine and some candles. I was determined to make an occasion of it. I looked in on Fiona at about seven o'clock and she was sitting up in bed, a bit pale and breathless. Her temperature was high. She wasn't very hungry, but she liked the sound of this meal. The idea seemed to amuse her.

'Do you want me to get dressed up?' she said.

'Of course. I may even get out my old dinner suit, if I can find it.'

She smiled. 'I can hardly wait.'

'I'll come and get you at nine. How does that sound?'

The dinner suit had a stale and musty smell, and the collar on my dress shirt was much too tight, but I put them on anyway. At nine o'clock the lasagne was bubbling away quite satisfactorily, the table was laid, the wine was nicely chilled. I let myself into Fiona's flat. She wasn't in the sitting room and there was no answer when I called out her name. A sudden premonition drew me into the bedroom.

Fiona was kneeling on the floor in front of the open wardrobe. She was wearing a long blue cotton dress which was not yet zipped up at the back. She was rocking slowly backwards and forwards and struggling for breath. I knelt down beside her and asked what was wrong. She said that she'd felt more and more exhausted as she was trying to get dressed, and then she'd been looking for a pair of tights in the bottom drawer of the wardrobe when she found that she couldn't get her breath. I put my hand to her forehead, which was very hot, and beaded with sweat. Could she breathe now, I asked. She said yes, but she didn't think she could get up just yet. I said that I was going to phone for the doctor. She nodded. I asked her where the number was. Between short, high breaths, she managed to say: 'Phone.'

There was an address book by the telephone in the hallway. It took me a minute or two to remember the doctor's name.

'Dr Campion?' I said, when the call was answered, and then realized that I was talking to a machine. There was a recorded message which told me to try another number. This time I got put through to an answering service. The man at the other end of the line asked me which doctor I was trying to contact, and whether it was an emergency. When I'd given him the details he told me that the deputizing doctor would call back as soon as possible.

The phone rang after about three or four minutes. I started to tell the doctor what was wrong. I wanted to be as quick and as clear as possible, so I could get back to Fiona, but it wasn't that easy. Because he'd never heard of her before, never examined her, never seen any notes, never been told about the case, I had to explain everything from the beginning. Then he asked me if I thought it was serious. I told him I thought it was very serious, but I could tell that he didn't really believe me. He thought I was talking about someone with a bad cold. I wasn't going to be put off. I told him he had to come out and see her. He said that he had two other patients to see first – urgent cases, was how he described them – but that he'd come out as soon as he could.

I helped Fiona back into bed. Her breathing was marginally better by now. I went back to my flat and turned off the oven and blew out the candles. Then I changed out of my dinner suit and came back to sit with her.

She looked so beautiful, so

*

The doctor arrived at about ten-fifteen. I tried to be angry with him for taking such a long time but he made this difficult by being so kind and efficient. He didn't do much, just listened to her chest and took her pulse and asked me a few questions. He could see that she was ill.

He said: 'I think she'd better go into casualty.'

This was the last thing I'd been expecting.

'Casualty? But I thought that was for accidents.'

'It's for emergency cases,' he said. He tore a page out of his notebook, scribbled four words on it, and then sealed it in an envelope from his briefcase. His own breathing while he did this seemed wheezy and over-emphatic. 'Take this letter with you. It's for the casualty doctor. Do you have a car?'

I shook my head.

'You'd probably have a long wait for a taxi tonight. I'd better drive you both in. It's on my way home.'

We prepared Fiona for the journey by helping her to put on two thick jumpers over her dress, and some thick woollen socks and a pair of boots. By the time we'd finished with her, she looked slightly ridiculous. I half-carried, half-walked her down the stairs and within a few minutes we were in the doctor's shiny blue Renault. I was trying to stay calm but found that without realizing it I had screwed his envelope up into a tight ball in the palm of my hand. I did my best to smooth it out as we arrived.

*

The casualty unit, while not quite as run-down as the outpatients' clinic, none the less managed to feel both crowded and desolate. Business was brisk. There was frost on the pavements and several people had showed up with minor injuries from slips and falls; and because it was New Year's Eve, there were already one or two victims of pub fights nursing swollen eyes and head wounds. They were expecting more of those later. At the same time there was an atmosphere of rather desperate levity and celebration in the air. Threadbare decorations adorned the walls and I got the impression that there was some sort of low-key staff party going on in a distant room. Some of the nurses running backwards and forwards were wearing silly brightly coloured hats, and the woman at reception had a radio on her desk, tuned to Radio 2. I gave her the doctor's note and pointed to Fiona sitting over on a bench, but she didn't seem to think it was any big deal. That was when I realized that the doctor hadn't actually been as efficient as I'd thought, because he'd forgotten to phone up and let them know that we were coming in. She told us to wait and that a nurse would be along soon to take down all the details. We waited twenty minutes and there was no nurse. Fiona was shivering in my arms. Neither of us said anything. Then I went over to the desk again and asked what was going on. She apologized and told us we wouldn't have to wait much longer.

Ten minutes later a nurse turned up and started asking questions. I answered most of them: Fiona wasn't up to it. The nurse marked the answers off on a clipboard. Quite soon she seemed to reach a decision and said, 'Follow me, please.' As she led us off down a corridor I ventured a meek complaint: 'There don't seem to be many doctors about.'

It was already after eleven o'clock.

'There's only one casualty officer tonight. He's seeing the majors and the minors, so he's got a lot on his plate. There was one very sick patient in earlier. Rotten luck, isn't it, on New Year's Eve?'

I didn't know whether she meant it was rotten luck for the patient or for the medical staff, so I didn't answer.

She took us into a tiny windowless cubicle, equipped with a trolley and not much else, and fetched Fiona a gown.

'There you are, dear. Can you put that on?'

'Perhaps I'd better step outside,' I said.

'It's all right, he can stay,' said Fiona, to the nurse.

I turned to the wall and didn't look while she took off her clothes and put the gown on. I'd never seen her naked.

The nurse took her temperature and her pulse and blood pressure. Then she disappeared. About a quarter of an hour later we were seen by the casualty officer, a harassed-looking man who went through only the most cursory introductions before putting his stethoscope to Fiona's chest.

'Nothing very startling there,' he said. After that he took her pulse, and glanced at some figures from the chart which had been left by the bedside. 'Hmm. Bit of a chest infection, by the looks of things. You may have to come in for a few days. I'll get on to the admitting team, and in the meantime we'll see if we can get you X-rayed tonight: assuming there isn't too much of a queue.'

'She's been X-rayed already,' I said. He looked at me questioningly. 'I don't mean today. I mean a few weeks ago. Her GP – Dr Campion – sent her up here and they took X-rays then.'

'Who was the consultant?'

I couldn't remember.

'Dr Searle,' said Fiona.

'What did they show?'

'We don't know. The first time she came for the results he

didn't turn up, and the next time – a couple of days ago – they couldn't find the notes. Said they were lost in the system.'

'Well, they're probably back in medical records by now. We can't get at them tonight.' He put the chart back on the bed. 'I'll bleep the registrar right away, and she can get hold of Dr Bishop for you. Our houseman,' he explained to Fiona. 'He'll be down to see you in a few minutes.'

With that he left, pulling the curtain behind him. Fiona and I exchanged glances. She smiled bravely.

'Oh well,' she said. 'At least he didn't seem to think there was anything wrong with my chest.'

'I've never thought there was anything wrong with your chest,' I said. Don't ask me why: I know people are supposed to make stupid jokes at moments of crisis, but surely not *that* stupid. But she did her best to laugh, and perhaps it was, in a way, a kind of turning point: a final acknowledgement of the physical attraction I'd been running away from these last few weeks.

The moment soon passed.

Dr Bishop wasn't long coming. He was young and gangly, with heavy bags under his eyes and an alarming shell-shocked, punch-drunk expression. It looked to me as if he'd had no sleep for thirty hours or more.

'OK, I've been talking things over with the sister,' he said, 'and we've decided the best thing would be to find you a bed as soon as we can. It's a busy night tonight and we need all the casualty bays we can get, so it'll be better for us and better for you. They're snowed under in radiology at the moment so we'll have to get the X-rays done in the morning. We'll get them done first thing. Anyway, as soon as you're on the ward, you can have your first lot of antibiotics.'

'The thing is, though,' I said, 'she's got this lump on her neck. We wondered if that might have anything –'

'The important thing is to find a bed,' said Dr Bishop. 'That's the difficult part. If we can find you a bed, then we're laughing.'

'Well will that take long? We've been waiting –'

'It's pot luck in this place at the moment.'

And with that unsettling remark, he disappeared. A couple of minutes later the nurse popped her head around the curtain.

'Everything all right in here?'

Fiona nodded.

'Some of the staff are having a few drinks upstairs. Soft drinks, that is. Just to see in the New Year. I wondered if you might like anything.'

She considered. 'Some fruit juice would be lovely. Orange juice, or something.'

'They were looking a bit low on orange juice,' the nurse said doubtfully. 'I'll see what I can do. Would Fanta be all right?'

We gave her to understand that Fanta would be fine, and then we were left alone again, for what seemed like a very long time. I could think of nothing to say except to keep asking Fiona how she was feeling. She said she was tired. That was all she ever complained about, feeling tired. She didn't want to move, or sit up: she just lay on the trolley, holding my hand. She clutched it tightly. She looked terrified.

'What's taking them so long?' That was my other heavily overworked piece of small talk. Just before midnight I went out into the corridor to see if anything was happening. Looking around for a familiar figure, I caught a glimpse of the casualty officer. He was rushing towards reception. I chased after him, shouting out, 'Excuse me,' but then he was met by a team of nurses pushing an unconscious patient along on a trolley. I stood at a short distance while he started asking questions. The patient had only just been brought in, apparently, after being found almost dead in a car. There was talk of carbon monoxide poisoning, and some earnest, low-voiced remarks were exchanged about his chances of survival. I wouldn't have taken much notice of this, but as the trolley passed by I caught a glimpse of the patient's face and for some reason it seemed distantly familiar. For a moment I was almost certain that I had seen this man somewhere before. But the feeling could have come from anywhere – it might just have been someone I'd passed in the street a few times – and I soon forgot about it when I felt a tap on my shoulder and found myself looking into the nurse's beaming face as she said: 'Mr Owen? I've some good news for you.'

I didn't understand at first, but as my mind came gradually

into focus, thinking only of Fiona and the urgent search to find her a bed, I too broke into a relieved, helpless smile. It froze when I realized that the nurse was trying to place two plastic beakers into my outstretched hands.

'There *was* some orange juice left after all,' she said. 'And listen.' From the radio on the receptionist's desk, we could hear the chimes of Big Ben as it sounded the hour. 'It's twelve o'clock. A very happy New Year to you, Mr Owen. Ring out the old, ring in the new.'

Mark

December 31st 1990

When it became clear that a war against Saddam Hussein was inevitable, Mark Winshaw decided to celebrate by throwing an especially elaborate party on New Year's Eve. He had no friends as such, but still managed to attract more than a hundred and fifty guests, drawn partly by the promise of each other's glittering company and partly by stories of the extravagant hospitality for which Mark's house in Mayfair was famous. There was a smattering of politicians and media people (including his cousins Henry and Hilary), and a few celebrities, but the bulk of the guest list was made up of middle-aged men whose dull grey paunchiness gave little indication that they were among the richest and most powerful captains of commerce and industry. Mark wandered between the groups of people, occasionally stopping to say hello, even more occasionally stopping to say a few words, but otherwise as aloof and inscrutable as ever. Meanwhile his young and beautiful German wife (he had remarried quite recently) seemed to be so busy attending to the guests that nobody saw her speak to her husband once all evening. The atmosphere was high-spirited, but Mark did not join in the hilarity. He drank hardly anything; he danced only once; even when he came upon a group of models taking turns to throw each other into the basement swimming-pool, he watched from a distance, without a tremor of feeling.

Nobody saw anything unusual in this: those who knew Mark were accustomed to his reserve. He was clearly not enjoying himself, but then he had probably never learned how to enjoy himself, and he certainly never allowed himself to relax. Eternal vigilance was one of the preconditions of his wealth. At ten thirty-five, purely as a matter of routine, he went upstairs to check on security. Next to the one (single) bed in the master bedroom, a panelled door gave on to a small windowless room containing a wall of television screens and a control panel. Patiently he flicked the monitors on, one at a time, and looked for irregularities. The dining hall, the kitchens, the conservatory; the pool, the bedrooms, the lifts. The study.

If Mark felt any shock or alarm at what he saw in the study, there was again no trace of it in his eyes. He watched closely, making sure that he had not misread the image. But it was plain enough. A man in a tuxedo was crouched over his desk. Somehow he had managed to pick the lock, and a set of papers had been laid out on the desk top. The man had a small camcorder and was slowly tracking along the desk, recording the contents of each document.

When the man had finished, he put the papers back in the desk and slipped the miniature camera down the leg of his trousers. He looked around furtively, and looked up, although he failed to see the camera hidden behind a wall-lamp which was following his every movement. It was at this point that Mark recognized him. It was Packard.

Mark left the monitoring room and took a lift down to the ground floor, calmly sifting this new information in his mind. He was angry, but not surprised. He'd been expecting something like this to happen: you always expected something like this to happen. And it made sense, in a way, because Mark now remembered a small detail: Packard had been carrying a video camera the very first time they met.

*

1983–1990

Graham had left college with his ideals intact, but seven years later his student radicalism was, to all appearances, a thing of the past: he now occupied a managerial position with Midland Iron-masters, who supplied precision machine tools for the inter-national market and were based just outside Birmingham. He had a house, a wife and a company car, spent a good part of the year travelling abroad at his employers' expense and was on first-name terms with a handful of Britain's most influential businessmen and entrepreneurs. His career gave every sign of being well thought out and perfectly on course; but his fellow board members would have been shocked if they had known its secret goal.

He had come to Birmingham soon after graduating, to take up a job programming films for a small arts cinema which went bankrupt within weeks of his arrival, halfway through a John Cassavetes season. Graham signed on the dole and didn't work again for several months, when one of his new flatmates got married and asked if he would make a video of the wedding. The result was considered so professional that Graham decided to set himself up in business on one of Mrs Thatcher's Enterprise Allowance schemes, confining himself to weddings at first and then branching out into promotional videos for local businesses. It was a far cry from his own self-image as subversive visionary, but the money was good and in the meantime he salved his conscience by doing unpaid work for the Labour Party and for various co-ops, unions and women's groups in the area. In the evenings he pored over copies of *Screen*, *Tribune*, *Sight and Sound* and the *Morning Star*, and dreamed of the documentary he would one day make: a feature-length masterpiece using all of the cinema's most dazzling resources, which would hold the world-wide capitalist conspiracy up to merciless, irresistible scrutiny. He dreamed, in particular, of making a film about the arms market, a subject which called for the politics of a Ken Loach or a Frederick Wiseman, combined with the outrageous plot and seductive glamour of a James Bond movie.

It seemed a long way off: but Graham was to find his opening sooner than he imagined, and through an unexpected quarter. Packard Promos – as the one-man company now styled itself – was approached by Midland Ironmasters in the spring of 1986. It was the most important contract Graham had yet been offered: they wanted a thirty-minute video which would showcase every stage of their production process. The budget was comparatively big and he was shooting on to high resolution tape with stereo sound. Graham followed his brief carefully, and when he presented a rough cut of the film to the firm's directors it was received with great excitement. There followed an animated discussion during which he was quizzed relentlessly for ideas about packaging and distributing the finished product: it quickly became obvious that he was dealing with novices, who seemed inordinately impressed by his routine proposals. The next day the managing director, a Mr Riley, invited him into his office and offered him a job as Head of Marketing. Graham had no intention of moving into this area and politely turned the offer down.

Two days later something happened to change his mind. In preparation for the final edit he was making some establishing shots of the factory floor, when Mr Riley appeared, accompanied by a neat, ratty-looking man who seemed to be taking a guided tour of some of the latest machinery. When they spotted Graham and his camera, they approached and Mr Riley asked him if he would stop filming for a few minutes: clearly at the personal instigation of his guest. Now, at close quarters, Graham recognized him, even though it was some years since he had seen his picture, in a magazine article about illegal arms sales to South Africa.

'No problem,' he said, clipping the lens cap on to his camera. Then he held out his hand. 'Graham Packard, Packard Promos.'

The stranger took his hand and shook it reluctantly. 'Mark Winshaw. Vanguard Import and Export.'

'Pleased to meet you.' He turned to Mr Riley. 'A new contract in the offing?' he asked, blandly.

Mr Riley puffed out his chest and said, with a mixture of pride and obsequiousness: 'The start of a long and fruitful relationship, I hope.'

At that moment Graham took several decisions very quickly. If Ironmasters were doing business with Mark Winshaw this could only mean that they were going to let their machines, whether knowingly or not, be used for munitions production, probably in Iraq which was militarizing itself more rapidly than any other Middle Eastern country. From Mr Riley's remark it sounded like a big, long-term contract. If he took a job with this company, he might be in a position to follow the progress of the deal, perhaps even to start building up contacts: in short, to worm his way inside the very network which he wanted to make the subject of his film, and which until now had seemed so hopelessly inaccessible.

And so before going home that evening he asked to see Mr Riley, and much to his surprise and delight told him that he had reconsidered his offer and wanted to accept the marketing position. And over the next two years he would prove himself such an enthusiastic member of the team that promotion and extra responsibilities came swiftly, until he had moved from Marketing into Planning, and moved from Planning into Expansion, and in 1989 (not long after his wedding) reached the apogee of his career with Ironmasters when he was invited to represent the firm at the First Baghdad International Exhibition for Military Production which opened on Saddam Hussein's birthday in April of that year.

Meanwhile, as soon as Mr Riley and Mark Winshaw had left the shop floor, he took his camera and hurried upstairs to the boardroom, which commanded a good view of the car park and forecourt. Luckily it was empty. He knelt out of sight and, with only his lens peering over the window-sill, zoomed in on the two men, getting a good shot of them chatting and shaking hands next to Mark's red BMW.

Work on the masterpiece had already begun.

*

1990

'*The base at Qalat Saleh,*' said Graham, '*contained twelve reinforced concrete underground aircraft hangars large enough to house two dozen planes, which would take off from an underground ramp, with their brakes on and afterburners lit.*'

Listening to his own voice on the headphones, he found it flat and less than compelling. But this was only a test commentary, to help him synchronize the words and the images. When the film was finished, he would hire an actor, someone known for his left-wing sympathies, and whose voice would carry immediate authority. Alan Rickman, perhaps, or Antony Sher. Of course, this would only happen if he managed to get some real money put behind the project, but he was starting to feel quite optimistic on that front. Preliminary discussions with Alan Beamish, head of current affairs at one of the largest ITV companies, had been very encouraging: as long as he still had a job, Beamish had said, he would do everything in his power to see that the film was supported.

It was getting dark. Graham switched the light on and drew the curtains. The editing suite – actually the back bedroom of their house in Edgbaston – was directly above the kitchen, and he could hear Joan moving about downstairs, putting the finishing touches to dinner.

'*The 3,000 metre runways,*' said his voice on the tape, '*were built behind mounds of desert clay, making them invisible to all but the closest observers.*'

*

April 1987

In the jeep taking them from Qalat Saleh to the test site, the Iraqi general had asked Mark for his opinion.

'Not bad,' said Mark. 'Although the crew quarters seemed rather vulnerable.'

The general shrugged. 'You can't have everything. Men are easier to replace than machines.'

'You think those blast doors are safe?'

'We think so,' said the general. He laughed and put his arm around Mark. 'I know, you only wanted us to buy them from the British because they were more expensive.'

'Far from it. I'm a patriot, that's all.'

The general laughed again, louder than ever. Over the years he had come to appreciate Mark's sense of humour. 'You're so old-fashioned,' he teased. 'We are living in an age of internationalism. These bases are a testament to that. Swiss airlocks, German generators, Italian doors, British communication systems, French hangars. What could be more cosmopolitan?'

Mark didn't answer. His eyes were hidden behind mirror sunglasses which reflected nothing but desert.

'A patriot!' said the general, still chuckling over the joke.

The test was noisy but gratifying. They watched from a bunker dug deep into the sand as the target area, set up to resemble convoys of Iranian tanks, exploded with deafening blasts of fire from the 155mm GCTs positioned more than twenty kilometres away. The guns were performing more accurately than even Mark would have thought possible, and as he saw the general's eyes light up with excitement, he knew that he was going to make an easy sale. They were both in excellent humour as the driver took them back to Baghdad.

'You know, it's not that our leader doesn't admire your country,' said the general, returning to the subject of Mark's patriotism. 'It's just that you make it difficult for him to trust you. So it's a sort of love-hate thing with him. Our armies are still using manuals prepared by your War College. We still send our men to be trained at your air bases, and draw upon the expertise of your SAS. There is nothing better than a British military education. I should know: I was at Sandhurst myself. If only your military genius were backed up by honourable intentions in the diplomatic field.'

Before returning to central Baghdad, they detoured to the Diyala Chemical Laboratory in Salman Pak, where a plant for the manufacture of nerve gas had been established under the guise of a university research facility. It was Mark's third or fourth visit, but as they were waved through the heavily guarded entrance gates and escorted to one of the labs, he could not help being impressed, as before, by the scale and efficiency of the operation.

'German engineering is the best in the world, there is no doubt about it,' said the general. 'And you know why? Because they are not just a nation of opportunists. There are people in Germany who really believe in what we are trying to achieve in Iraq. There's something there that the British could learn from. You and I are not old enough to remember the days before '58, when nearly all of our equipment used to come from Great Britain, but it's possible to be nostalgic for such an arrangement. There can be no dignity when business has to be done clandestinely, behind closed doors. We want allies, you see. We want relationships. But all you are interested in is doing deals.'

As they continued their tour, the general explained why he had brought Mark back to the laboratory. Nervous of the side-effects of the highly volatile chemicals, they wanted to find a contractor who could install a new air cleaning plant.

'I'm pleased to hear you're so concerned about environmental protection,' said Mark.

His friend seemed to like this joke even more than the one about patriotism.

'Well, we must give our technicians the best possible working conditions,' he said. 'After all, they are making important researches in the field of veterinary science.'

As if to illustrate his point, he took Mark past the animal house on their way back to the vehicle. For a while their conversation was drowned out by the howling of the beagles which would be used to test the effectiveness of the nerve gas agents. A nearby garbage dump was piled high with the corpses of their predecessors.

*

May 1987

Mark did not have to look far to find his air cleaning plant. He went to a senior German industrialist who had already sent equipment over to the Salman Pak laboratory and had proved himself a reliable, prompt supplier. Mark always enjoyed visiting his country house in the Rhine valley, where the contracts would be signed in a magnificent study beneath a large, gold-framed portrait of Hitler, and tea would be served by his beautiful young daughter. And today, as a sign of special favour, he was offered some extra entertainment, when the industrialist unlocked a cabinet containing a reel-to-reel tape recorder, wired up to a speaker which had been mounted inside a radio console of 1930s vintage. When he started the tape a familiar voice could be heard, and for the next ten minutes the Führer himself, in full oratorical flight, roared out through the bay windows, across the summer lawns and down to the sparkling river's very edge.

'I can still remember where I was when I heard that speech,' said the industrialist, when the tape was over. 'Sitting in my mother's kitchen. The windows open. The play of light on the table. The air filled with hope and energy. A fabulous time. Well – why shouldn't an old man be allowed to get a little wistful about his youth now and again? Some people do it with a trite, romantic poem or sentimental song. For me it will always be that wonderful voice.' He closed the cabinet door and locked it carefully. 'Saddam Hussein is a good man,' he said. 'He makes me feel young again. It's an honour to help him. But I don't suppose you'd understand that: you were born into an age when principles have ceased to mean anything.'

'If that concludes our business, Herr —'

'You're a puzzle to me, Mr Winshaw. To me, and to many others who are old enough to have served the Reich, and who were well acquainted with your family name long before you appeared on our doorsteps.'

Mark rose to his feet and picked up his briefcase. He appeared not to be interested.

'I know exactly what Saddam Hussein is making at his so-called research facility. I also know that Israel will be his first target. This is why I support him, of course. He will resume a process of cleansing which we were never allowed to complete. Do you take my meaning, Mr Winshaw?'

'I make a habit,' said Mark, 'of not inquiring into the uses –'

'Come now, there's no need to be modest. You're a qualified engineer: a chemical engineer. I'm well aware that you've been instrumental in helping one of our largest firms to supply Iraq with quantities of Zyklon B, for instance. The cleansing process of which I spoke depends upon the free circulation of such commodities, and yet our own laws, placed under absurd international constraints, prohibit us from exporting them. And so, ironically, it's left to men like you – bounty hunters – to keep our ideals alive.' He watched for Mark's response, but saw none. 'You do know where Zyklon B is manufactured, don't you?'

'Of course,' said Mark, who had visited the plant many times.

'I wonder if you are familiar with the history of that factory. It narrowly escaped being destroyed by allied bombers in 1942. A British plane was sent out on a secret mission to reconnoitre the area, but the Luftwaffe were alerted and the unfortunate pilot and his crew were shot down. Does any of this mean anything to you?'

'I'm afraid not. You forget that it happened a long time ago. Before I was even born.'

The old man held his gaze for a moment and then pulled on the bell-rope beside the door.

'Quite true, Mr Winshaw. But as I say, you remain a puzzle.' As Mark left, he added: 'My daughter, if you wish to see her, is in the library.'

*

December 1961

To his mother, Mark had long ago become a puzzle which there was nothing to be gained from solving, and so she had offered no protest when he told her – several weeks after the event – that he had decided to give up his law degree and enrol as a student of chemical engineering. The letter in which he communicated this news was one of the last he ever sent her. It had become pointless to maintain the pretence that mother and son still had anything to say to each other: and in another couple of years there would be physical distance between them to compound the gulf of incomprehension and indifference.

Her invitation to Mortimer's fiftieth birthday party had provided Mildred with a rare glimpse into the Winshaws' prosperous lives. For most of her long years of widowhood the family seemed to have forgotten her, and offered little in the way of financial help beyond the paying of Mark's school and university fees. As she neared the age of fifty, she was still struggling to subsist on her modest income as secretary to an American wine merchant based in London. One day he announced his intention of winding up the business and moving back to Florida, and she was about to resign herself to the prospect of several gloomy weeks haunting the employment agencies, when he astonished her by asking if she would come to America with him, in the capacity not of his secretary, but his wife. It took her three days to recover from the shock; at which point she accepted.

They lived comfortably in a beach house outside Sarasota until their peaceful deaths, within two months of one another, in the winter of 1986. Mildred never spoke to her son again after leaving England. Their last conversation was over lunch one afternoon in Oxford, and they had both found it difficult to remain civil even then. She had ended up accusing Mark of despising her.

'"Despise" is putting it rather strongly,' he said. 'I just can't really see the point of the sort of life you're leading.'

It was a remark which came back to her every so often: perhaps as she sat with her husband on the verandah after dinner, looking out over the ocean and trying hard to think of any place she would rather be.

*

1976

Although Mark never spoke to his mother after she had left for America, he did see her once. This was during the early days of his dealings with Iraq, when he was first introduced to a curt, bearlike man called Hussein who represented the 'Ministry of Industry' and seemed in a hurry to procure specialized equipment for the building of a large pesticides factory. Mark discussed his requirements and recognized at once that several of the compounds he intended to manufacture – including Demeton, Paraoxon and Parathion – could easily be transformed into nerve gas. None the less he saw no reason why the project shouldn't be represented to potential clients as part of an agricultural programme, and he promised to put Hussein in touch with an American firm which would be able to supply him with the huge corrosion-resistant vats necessary for the mixing of the chemicals.

Representatives of the company were flown to Baghdad and fed a convincing story about the plight of Iraqi farmers who could not protect their crops from desert locusts. They returned to Miami and set about preparing blueprints for a pilot plant which would enable the local workforce – which had no experience of work in this dangerous field – to be trained in the handling of toxic chemicals. But before they had time to complete the designs they were informed, via Mark, that Hussein had no interest in building a pilot plant. He wished to embark upon full-scale production immediately. This was not acceptable to the safety-conscious Americans, and Mark, who expected to make some six million dollars in commission on the deal, was forced to intervene and set up a meeting between the two sides in a conference room at the Miami Hilton.

It was not a success. Mark stood at a window overlooking the beach and listened in silence as the negotiations broke down amid accusations of hidden agendas on the one hand and over-regulation on the other. Never once taking his eyes from the strip of silver sand, he heard the Americans snap their cases shut and walk out. He heard Hussein grunt and complain that 'Those guys need their brains examining. They just threw away the chance to become rich.' Mark didn't answer. He was the only person in the room not to have lost his temper. The money would have been useful, but he would make it up. He'd try the Germans next.

The day before, he had driven out through the Everglades to the Gulf Coast. A morning's drive took him to Naples, along the Tamiami Trail with its Indian villages reconstituted as tourist attractions, its airboat rides and roadside cafés offering frogs' legs and gator-burgers. From there he took the freeway north through Bonita Springs and Fort Myers, and arrived outside Sarasota late in the afternoon. His mother's address, although he had never used it on any letter, was committed to memory. But Mark did not want to speak to her even now. He didn't even ask himself why he had come. Once he had found the house, he drove another half a mile down the ocean road and turned off down a dirt track which led to the beach. When he parked at the end of this track, he had a good view of the house.

Her husband was shopping in town that afternoon, but as chance would have it Mildred herself was in the garden. She'd meant just to sit out and read a magazine, maybe start a letter to her stepdaughter in Vancouver, but she could see that the gardener had made a poor job of weeding the lawn, as usual, and was soon down on her knees pulling the more obstinate specimens up by the root. Almost at once she noticed the man leaning against the bonnet of his car and staring at her. She stood up and looked at him, shielding her eyes against the sun. She recognized him now, but didn't move, didn't wave, didn't call out his name; just returned his impassive gaze. There were hollow spaces where his eyes should have been. At closer quarters, she would have realized that he was wearing mirror sunglasses which reflected nothing but the sky's deep blue. But Mildred stayed where she was, and after a minute or two she knelt down again and resumed her weeding. The next time she looked up, the man was gone.

*

September 1988

As Graham's researches progressed, he began to feel that it would be useful to know something about Mark's family background, and he remembered that there was someone who could probably help him. Michael Owen's name had disappeared from the arts pages of the newspapers over the last few years, his novels were no longer to be found anywhere in the shops, and his book about the Winshaws was yet to be published. Perhaps the whole project had never come to anything; but it was just possible, Graham reasoned, that he would still be working on it, and if this was the case, he might have gained access to any amount of valuable inside information (not that he would know what to do with it, since the depth of his political naïvety had been made fairly clear even from their few conversations). It was, at the very least, worth making a few phone calls.

The first of these calls was to Joan. It was two or three years since they had been in touch, and he wasn't even sure that she would still be living in Sheffield, but she answered on the third ring and there was no mistaking the delight in her voice. Yes, she was still in the same job. No, she didn't let out rooms to students any more. No, she hadn't got married or started a family or anything like that. Yes, she could certainly try to contact Michael for him, although she didn't have a current address. Funnily enough she'd been thinking of phoning Graham in the next couple of weeks, because there was a conference in Birmingham at the end of the month, and she'd wondered if he might be interested in meeting up for a drink or something. For old times' sake. Graham said yes, of course, why not. For old times' sake.

The strange thing was, as they both reflected afterwards, that in all of the 'old times' for the sake of which they had agreed to meet up, they could not remember a single evening which had ended with them leaning across the table to kiss each other, or lying down on the sofa with their arms around each other and their tongues in each other's mouths, or falling into bed together and making love as if their lives depended on it. And yet all of these things happened, in sequence, when Joan came down for her visit to Birmingham. And once they had happened, she found herself curiously reluctant to leave and return to her house, and her job, and her solitary life back in Sheffield. And although she did return, after taking a few days' unpaid leave (quite a bit of it being spent in bed with Graham), one of the first things she did was to put the house up for sale. At the same time she started looking for jobs in the Midlands. It took a while, because jobs were not easy to come by, not even for someone as experienced and well-qualified as Joan, but in the new year she managed to get a position running a women's refuge in Harborne, and she moved in with Graham, and one day in February they both took time off to visit the local register office, and then suddenly they were married: he who had always believed that he wasn't the marrying type, and she who had begun to think she had left it too late to find anyone to marry her.

And so Graham's initial phone call had by no means been wasted, even though he never did manage to get in contact with Michael. He seemed to have gone away for a long holiday: or perhaps he just wasn't answering the telephone any more.

*

1981

The wedding of Mark Winshaw to Lady Frances Carfax in the chapel of St John's College, Oxford, had been an altogether grander affair. Britain may have been in the grip of recession, but it seemed to have had little impact on those select members of the aristocracy and business community who attended the ceremony and afterwards convened at the country seat of the Carfax family for a lavish party which was still going strong (according to at least one of the newspaper reports) at four o'clock the next afternoon.

The party, in fact, lasted longer than the marriage.

Mark and Lady Frances had departed the revels early in the evening and joined a flight to Nice: from there, a taxi took them to Mark's villa on the Riviera, where they were to begin their honeymoon. They arrived shortly after midnight, and slept in until lunchtime the next day, when Lady Frances borrowed one of Mark's cars to drive into the nearest village and buy some cigarettes. She had only driven a few hundred yards when there was a huge explosion and the car burst into flames, careering off the road and into the stony mountainside. She was killed instantly.

Mark was devastated by the loss. The car was a 1962 Morgan Plus 8 Drop Head Coupé in midnight blue, one of about three or four left in the world, and it would be impossible to replace. He contacted his cousin Henry, who instructed the intelligence services to find out who was responsible, but didn't have to wait for the results of their inquiry. Three weeks later an Iraqi diplomat contacted him and arranged a rendezvous in Cavendish Square. From there they drove to a secluded house in the Kent countryside. A pristine, off-white 1938 La Salle convertible sedan was parked in the forecourt.

'It's yours,' said the diplomat.

He explained that a comical misunderstanding had arisen. They were well aware, of course, that Mark did business with the Iranians as well as with themselves: they would have expected nothing less from any serious entrepreneur. However, it had been wrongly suggested by an informer that Mark had also been using his position to trade military secrets. Saddam had been most upset to hear this, and had ordered swift retribution. Now the information was found to have been false: the real culprit had been identified and promptly disposed of. They could only be grateful, he said, that chance had intervened to save the life of an innocent man and a most valued friend of the Iraqi people. They were acutely conscious of the damage done to his property, and hoped that he would accept the gift of this car as a token of their continued affection and esteem.

Mark's formal expressions of gratitude concealed his genuine annoyance at this incident. Marriage to Lady Frances would have been useful. He had been rather looking forward to the sexual aspect – although, to be honest, in terms of imagination and athleticism she could not really compare with the prostitutes whose services he was usually offered on his trips to Baghdad – but, more importantly, her father had a number of influential contacts in the South American market, which he was anxious to infiltrate. In all probability he would still be able to use them, but it would have been easier if his young and glamorous wife had been there to help.

Above all, Mark found it unacceptable that someone should have been telling lies about him, and he was determined to have his revenge. After several months' sporadic investigation it emerged that the informer had been a leading Egyptian physicist recently recruited to Iraq's nuclear programme. Anxious to ingratiate himself with his new employers, he had repeated this piece of idle gossip after overhearing it from a conversation between two colleagues; but he had not bothered to find out whether it was accurate or not. Although the Iraqis were furious to discover that they had been misled, the physicist himself was too valuable to be eliminated, and nothing was ever done about it. Mark, however, had other ideas. He knew that the Israelis would be only too pleased to be presented with an opportunity for thwarting Saddam's military ambitions, and some discreet words in the ear of a contact at Mossad were enough to seal the luckless Egyptian's fate. It happened when he was staying in Paris, *en route* from the experimental research centre at Saclay where Iraqi technicians were routinely trained under a nuclear cooperation programme with France. He retired to his hotel bedroom early and the next morning his crushed and battered body was found at the foot of his bed by a chambermaid. Beating a man to death is a long, noisy and difficult business, and Mark was surprised that they had chosen this method. Even so, he permitted himself a private smile when the news was announced on Israel radio the next evening; and when he heard the reporter add that 'Iraqi projects to acquire an atomic bomb have been set back by two years', he smiled again, because his own fortunes, after all, were hardly likely to suffer as a result.

*

October 1986

'So tell me about this Hussein character,' said Henry, as he and Mark sat in a state of post-prandial near-collapse on opposite sides of a blazing log fire in the withdrawing room of the Heartland Club. The family small talk had been disposed of (never a lengthy process with the Winshaws) and they had just lit up two enormous Havana cigars.

'What do you want to know?' said Mark.

'Well, I mean, you've met him personally, haven't you? Done business with him, and so on. What sort of cove is he?'

Mark puffed thoughtfully. 'Difficult to say, really. He doesn't tend to give much away about himself.'

'Yes, but look,' said Henry, leaning forward. 'We're treading on very delicate ground here. The man's offering to write a blank cheque for us, as far as I can see. Guns, planes, missiles, bombs, bullets – you name it, he wants it, and if we aren't prepared to sell then he's just going to go to the French or the Germans or the Yanks or the Chinese. We can't afford to let this opportunity slip. The export figures are terrible enough as it is – even after we've finished tinkering with them. But, you know, there may be a few eyebrows raised if we start getting too friendly with a chap whose idea of fun is shooting a couple of thousand volts through the odd political prisoner. Which I gather he's not averse to doing.'

'Malicious rumour,' said Mark, waving his cigar smoke away airily. 'I've seen nothing to substantiate it.'

'Take a look at this, for instance,' said Henry, producing a crumpled pamphlet from the pocket of his waistcoat. 'We were sent this thing from' (he looked at the name on the first page)

'SODI, they seem to call themselves. The Supporters of Democracy in Iraq. I tell you, it makes pretty nasty reading. What do you make of it?'

Mark glanced over the pamphlet, his eyelids half-closed. Most of the details were already familiar to him. He knew all about the arbitrary arrests, the midnight raids, the trumped-up charges of dissidence or subversion, of belonging to the wrong sort of organization or attending the wrong sort of meeting, of refusing to join the Ba'ath party or agreeing to join the wrong wing of the Ba'ath party. He knew all about the unimaginable conditions in Baghdad's 'Department of Public Security', where detainees would be held in solitary confinement for months at a time, or made to lie on the floor of a cell with fifty or sixty other prisoners, listening to the recorded screams of torture victims by night and the real screams by day. And he knew all about this torture, too: how men and women were flayed, burned, beaten and sodomized with truncheons and bottles; scalded with domestic irons, their eyes, ears, noses and breasts cut off, electric shocks applied to their fingers, genitals and nostrils; how the torturers would wear animal masks and play tape recordings of wild animals as they went about their business; how children were tortured in front of their mothers, and placed blindfold in sacks filled with insects or starved cats; how men and women would be made to lie on their backs on the floor, their feet supported by wooden stocks, then beaten on the soles of their feet with truncheons and forced to walk or run over floors soaked with hot salty water. Mark had heard it all before, which was why he barely glanced at the pamphlet through half-closed lids before handing it back to his cousin.

'Wildly exaggerated, if you ask me,' he said. 'These fringe groups do tend to attract fanatics: you can't take anything they say at face value.'

'So you don't think Hussein is involved with any of this?'

'Well, he's firm, there's no denying that,' said Mark, pursing his lips. 'Firm but fair: that's how I'd describe him.'

'A bit of a rough diamond, you mean?'

'A rough diamond. Exactly.'

'And what does he intend to do with all these weapons,

anyway?' said Henry. 'Once he's put Iran in its place, that is.'

Mark laughed in exasperation. 'Henry, what does it *matter* what he intends to do with them? If it starts to look as though he's in a position to do any harm, then we find an excuse to attack him and wipe out the whole arsenal. And then we start selling again.'

Henry considered the logic of this argument and could find no flaw in it.

'If I may say so,' Mark continued, 'it's not like you to give way to fashionable squeamishness on these matters.'

'Oh, it isn't me,' said Henry. 'It's the Foreign Office we're worried about, and that soppy little wet blanket Howe. He's the one who's coming over all coy about selling any of this stuff.'

'So what's going to happen?'

'Well, on the basis of what you've told me,' said Henry, settling deeper into his chair, 'I'd say that the DTI had won the battle for the time being. I'm going to suggest they send someone over to Baghdad in the next couple of months and offer the Iraqis a nice fat credit agreement. How much have the Americans given them?'

'Several billion, I think: but that's only for grain and so on. Officially, anyway.'

'Hm. Well I would have thought we could run to seven or eight hundred million quid. How does that sound?'

'Sounds good. Should come in very handy.'

'I *assume*,' said Henry, leaning forward and looking Mark in the eye, 'that Hussein can actually lay his hands on this money, at the end of the day. I mean, credit's one thing but we want to know that he's going to pay up eventually.'

Mark thought carefully before saying: 'Iraq has good natural resources. Obviously the money is going to run out if he keeps on spending at this rate: but don't forget that he has a very wealthy neighbour. A wealthy and vulnerable neighbour.'

'Kuwait?'

Mark nodded.

'You think he'd invade?'

'Wouldn't hesitate for a moment.' He smiled as Henry digested this information. 'But that's a long way off,' he said. 'Which lucky boy gets the job of taking the good news to Baghdad?'

'Clark, probably. D'you know him?'

'Vaguely. Seems a decent sort of chap.'

'Bit of a live wire, to be honest,' said Henry. 'We're not quite sure what to make of him. But he's definitely with us on this one.' He crumpled the pamphlet slowly. 'Well, into the fire with this, I suppose,' he said, and leaned towards the hearth.

'Or alternatively,' said Mark, stopping him just in time, 'you could pass it on to Hilary. Get her to do one of her famous hatchet jobs.'

Henry thought about this for a moment.

'Good thinking,' he said, and replaced it in his pocket.

*

January 20th 1988

It was getting on for six in the evening, and everybody else had gone home, but Graham was still sitting in his grey, sparsely furnished office at Midland Ironmasters, waiting for the phone to ring. A recording device was attached to the receiver. Over the last couple of years he had recorded about fifty hours' worth of telephone conversations, but he knew there were only a few minutes that would ever be usable, and he had not yet been able to face the task of editing it all down. It would have to be done soon. He was already aware of an alarming imbalance in the material he had assembled for his film: too much sound, too many still photographs, not nearly enough video. Perhaps it was about time he started taking a few serious risks.

He was waiting for a call from a senior colleague in the machine tools industry, who had been to a meeting in London that day and had promised to phone Graham with news of the outcome. The meeting was with a minister from the Department of Trade and Industry, and concerned the granting of export licences.

Manufacturers of machine tools who wished to export to Iraq were still facing trouble from the Foreign Office. Only recently Geoffrey Howe had suggested to the cabinet that further restrictions should be imposed, and this alone was enough to send shockwaves through the membership of the Machine Tool Technologies Association, now a powerful voice in the British pro-Iraq lobby (one of whose most influential members, Matrix Churchill, had been bought by the Iraqis in order to secure a manufacturing foothold in Britain). Formal requests had been made to the DTI for clarification, and this meeting was the reward. It promised to offer a clear indication of the direction government policy was taking.

The call could have come at any time. Graham had been sitting by the telephone all day. By now he was ravenously hungry, and he had watched a crisp blue wintry sky turn to black.

The phone rang at ten past six.

Playing the tape back on his car stereo as he drove home later that evening, he would hear:

– *Graham. Sorry to keep you so long waiting.*

– *That's OK, that's OK.*

– *Some of us went out to lunch, and it went on a bit, I'm afraid.*

– *That's OK, really. You had something to celebrate, then, did you?*

– *It was a good meeting. Very positive.*

– *What, did they –*

– *A green light. They gave us a green light.*

– *You mean they –*

– *The all-clear. No problem at all. We're a credit to our country, as far as they're concerned. Leading the export drive, and all that.*

– *But I mean, what about the restrictions –*

– *Well, you know, we've just got to be a bit careful, that's all.*

– *Careful? How do you –*

– *Well, we've been advised to, you know, play down the military . . . the military application of the machines. We've got to be a bit careful saying what they're for, and so on.*

– *What, like general –*

– *Like 'general engineering', or, you know, emphasize that these machines can have peaceful –*

– uses –

– peaceful applications, and you know, stress that whole aspect of why we're applying.

– But I mean, they do know, obviously . . .

– Oh I mean, they all know, yes.

– I mean it is obvious, that that's what we're . . . selling.

– Well as we said, they're not going to be making many cars in the middle of a war, are they?

– To them, you said it?

– No, I mean, afterwards, that's what someone said.

– But they don't mind?

– Oh, nobody bloody minds. They all don't mind.

– So it's OK to –

– They don't give a flying fuck what we're selling, basically.

– I can tell the boss that, then. He'll be –

– Pretty chuffed, I should –

– I mean I bet everybody is.

– Well, we've been making the most of it here. You should crack a few open at your end.

– I think I will. I mean why not.

– Look, I've got to go then.

– Well thanks for taking the time to – to ring. It's a weight off my mind. You know, there's some things I can – press ahead with, which had been looking a bit –

– I've got to go now, OK? We'll have another talk.

– OK. We'll talk in the next few days.

– Next few days. OK then.

– Righto. Thanks for taking the time.

– OK. All the best then.

– All the best. Bye now.

Graham ejected the tape, and the radio came back on. It was BRMB, playing an old Huey Lewis song. Not one of his favourites.

*

April 28th 1989

'I see you are taking plenty of photographs. Holiday snaps for the wife and kids back at home?'

Graham whirled around, expecting to be confronted by a uniformed guard, but instead found himself being addressed by a short, stocky, dark-haired man with a rubbery smile which gave him the appearance of a benevolent goblin. He introduced himself as Louis and explained that he was a salesman from Belgium. He handed Graham a card.

'There's so much to see,' said Graham. 'I wanted to remember it all.'

'You're right: this is quite something, isn't it? You know, Saddam Hussein's birthday is always a big day in Baghdad. All the buses are covered in flowers, and in the schools the children sing special birthday songs. But this year, he's really done something special.'

The First Baghdad International Exhibition for Military Production had indeed lived up to the grandeur of its name. Twenty-eight countries were represented, and almost a hundred and fifty different companies had set up tents and pavilions: from smallish firms like Ironmasters and Matrix Churchill to the international giants – Thomson-CSF, Construcciónes Aeronauticas and British Aerospace. All of the star names were there: maverick designer Gerald Bull was showing a scale model of his supergun at the Astra Holdings stand, French dealer Hugues de l'Estoile was engaged in friendly rivalry with Alan Clark's top aide, David Hastie, over who would win the contract for the Fao Project – a long-term aerospace programme to help Iraq establish its own aircraft manufacturing base – while Serge Dessault, son of the great Marcel Dessault who had single-handedly built up France's military aircraft industry, was given an ovation by the Iraqis like a visiting pop star when he approached the reviewing stand.

'I thought there might have been more restrictions,' said Graham, who had been worried enough about taking his camera into Iraq and was now cursing himself for not bringing a camcorder.

Louis seemed surprised. 'But why? This is not a secret assembly. The whole point is for everyone to be open, to show our achievements with pride. There are journalists here from all over the world. We have nothing to hide. Nobody is doing anything illegal. We all believe in deterrence, and the right of every country to defend itself. Don't you agree?'

'Well, yes —'

'Of course you do. Otherwise, why else would your company have sent you out here to show off such splendid examples of modern technology. Would you care to show me, please?'

Louis was clearly impressed by what he saw at the Ironmasters pavilion: it certainly compared well with the rather sorry-looking 1960s machine tools on offer from the Polish, Hungarian and Romanian exhibitors. He dropped a few hints to the effect that he might be able to fix up a deal with some Iranian buyers: but this was left vague. In the meantime he seemed to have taken a liking to Graham, and performed the function of his unofficial guide over the next few days. He took him on to the VIP reviewing stand to watch the Iraqi pilots perform hair-raising stunts in their MiG-29s, sometimes flying so low that the spectators had to throw themselves to the ground. (Only one of the displays went seriously wrong, when an Egyptian pilot mistakenly flew over the presidential palace and was at once gunned down by the Republican Guard, his Alphajet crash-landing in a residential area of Baghdad and killing some twenty civilians.) He took Graham to meet Colonel Hussein Kamil Hasan al-Majid, one of the Ba'ath party's rising stars and the host of this event, who greeted his guests in a huge pavilion set up to resemble a desert encampment. And he was always on hand to introduce him to the more influential figures, such as Christopher Drogoul and Paul Van Wedel, the American bankers from BNL Atlanta who had supplied Iraq with some four billion dollars in long-term loans.

'Did you notice their watches?' Louis asked.

'Their watches?'

'Take a look at their watches next time you see them. They are specially made: Swiss manufacture. And they have Saddam Hussein's face on them. They were personal gifts: a very great honour, I think. I think very few people here, maybe three or four, have been shown such honour. Monsieur de l'Estoile, conceivably. And, of course it goes without saying, your own Mr Winshaw.'

Graham tried to hide his sudden surge of interest. 'Mark Winshaw of Vanguard?'

'You are known to Mr Winshaw, I think. You have been doing business with him on some occasions.'

'Once or twice, yes. Is he here at the moment, by any chance?'

'Oh yes, he's here, you can be sure of it. But he likes to keep a low profile, as you know. As a matter of fact I'm dining with him myself tonight. Shall I give him your regards?'

'Please do,' said Graham; then hesitated before asking boldly, 'A business meeting, I take it?'

'In a manner of speaking,' said Louis. 'We both belong to a certain organization: a sort of rather exclusive club. It's to do with technical matters, really. We meet regularly to discuss problems of safety in the manufacture and distribution of our weapons systems.'

Graham knew which organization he was talking about: AESOP, the Association of Europeans for Safety in Ordnance and Propellants. But he was surprised to hear that Mark was a member. He wouldn't have thought he'd have time for such concerns.

'Anyway,' said Louis, 'I don't think there will be much business to discuss tonight. I expect it to be more of a social occasion. You should come along, Mr Packard. You would really be most welcome.'

Graham accepted.

A small private room had been booked towards the back of a very quiet and expensive restaurant in central Baghdad. There were only five guests: Mark, Louis, Graham, a severe Dutchman and a boisterous German. The food was French (they were all highly vocal in their condemnation of Middle Eastern cuisine); the champagne vintage (Roederer Cristal 77) and plentiful. Each guest enjoyed the attentions of his own pretty, petite Filipino waitress, who would giggle and affect to be pleased when a hand was thrust up her miniskirt or her breasts were roughly fondled as she attempted to serve the food. Graham's waitress was called Lucila: so far as he could tell, none of the others were ever asked to say what their names were. He was seated between Louis and Mark, who seemed noticeably less self-contained and guarded than on previous occasions. He chatted freely about his work and the Baghdad Fair and what it revealed about Saddam's military ambitions to anyone who had eyes to see. Graham was recording this conversation on to a slimline tape machine in the inside pocket of his jacket: it meant that he had to keep a careful track of the time, so that he could slip away to the toilet whenever the tape needed turning over (he'd brought two C90s with him) before the machine switched itself off with a giveaway click.

For personal reasons, in any case, he would erase these tapes after he got home.

Louis was the first to disappear upstairs with his waitress, between the first and second courses. They were away for nearly half an hour. As soon as they came back, it was the Dutchman's turn. While this was going on the party had still managed to consume, by Graham's reckoning, eight bottles of champagne. He could sense Lucila's puzzlement that he was not behaving towards her as his companions would have done. She was not as conventionally attractive as the others: her skin was slightly blemished and pock-marked, and she wasn't as good at hiding her sadness behind a façade of blank-eyed gaiety. She was nervous and sometimes spilled things while serving the food. Graham knew that if he could have relaxed more himself, it would have helped to put her at ease, but this was difficult because he was trying hard to remain sober.

Just as the main course – a shoulder of beef – was about to be served, Mark turned to him and said: 'I hope you won't think us rude, Mr Packard, but there are a few private business matters we have to attend to at this point. I think this might be a good moment for you to withdraw.'

'Withdraw?'

Mark pointed towards Lucila and made a gesture with his eyes. Graham nodded and left the table.

They went upstairs to a small uncomfortable bedroom where the bed was unmade and dishevelled from recent use. The room was clean but dimly lit and inelegant. There were bloodstains on the carpet which seemed to have been there for some time. As soon as the door was closed Lucila began to undress. She looked bewildered when Graham asked her to stop. He explained that he did not want to make love to her because he was married and did not think it was right that women should be expected to go to bed with men they hardly knew. She nodded and sat down on the bed. Graham sat beside her and they smiled at each other. He could tell that she was both relieved and offended. He tried asking her a few questions about where she came from and what she was doing in Iraq, but her English wasn't good and she seemed, besides, a little resentful of these inquiries. They both knew that a decent interval would have to pass before they went back downstairs. Then Lucila remembered something and, opening one of the drawers in the cupboard, she took out a pack of cards. Neither of them knew any proper card games, so they played a few hands of Snap. There was some more champagne in a bottle on the bedside table, and before long they both became hopelessly giggly. After all the subterfuge, the watchfulness, the perpetual tension of the last few days, Graham felt suddenly liberated: there was nothing on earth he would rather be doing than playing this mindless card game with a tipsy and lovely young woman in a strange room, and all at once he felt a wave of desire, which Lucila recognized as soon as she saw it in his eyes. She looked away. They finished the game on a quieter note and then it was time to go back to the restaurant.

He found Mark and his friends arguing with each other noisily but in a teasing vein while drawing a number of pencilled circles on their napkins and on the tablecloth. Each of these circles was divided up into four unequal segments, with the letters GB, D, NL and B written inside. With a bit of effort, Graham was able to coax a drunken explanation out of Louis: later on, the details would be confirmed by his own researches. AESOP, it turned out, had nothing at all to do with research into safety measures. It was an informal cartel of European arms dealers set up to tackle one of the biggest problems posed by Iraq's military requirements: how – given that the demand was so enormous – could the munitions companies meet it without raising their production quotas to the point where government suspicions were aroused? AESOP was the answer: a forum in which leading dealers from each of the member countries could get together and share the work out equitably among their own manufacturers.

'We have decided that these are the figures,' said Louis, handing him a napkin and pointing at the segmented circle, 'which will represent our commissions. Our commissions for the next year.'

'But they don't add up to a hundred,' said Graham.

Louis laughed wildly.

'These are not percentages,' he said, his eyes shining. 'These are millions of dollars!' He laughed even louder when he saw Graham's undisguised astonishment, and his whole body shook as he extended his arm in an expansive gesture which took in the room, the waitresses, his three friends and the gutted carcass of beef on its silver platter. 'What a carve up, eh, Mr Packard? What a carve up!'

Over the next half hour, the atmosphere around the table grew more and more hilarious, and Graham knew that he had begun to seem increasingly out of place.

'Your lips have a look of pursed disapproval,' Mark Winshaw remarked, at one point. 'I don't see why. I've just secured your company the lion's share of the Iraqi market for the foreseeable future.'

'I'm a little tired, that's all,' said Graham. 'It's all been a bit much.'

'Or perhaps, like me, you find this orgy of celebration all rather loud and vulgar.'

'Perhaps.'

'And yet I understand you were quite the young firebrand at college, Mr Packard.'

Graham paused in the act of sipping his coffee.

'Who told you that?'

'Oh, I've made a few little routine inquiries, just as any sensible businessman would. You've grown up quite a lot in the last few years, it would seem.'

'In what way?'

'Politically, I mean. Let me see: now was it the Socialist Workers, or the Revolutionary Communists who enjoyed your services as treasurer?'

Graham smiled bravely even as his spirits started to plunge. 'It was the Socialist Workers.'

'Quite a long journey, then, isn't it, from that hotbed of revolution to this restaurant in Baghdad?'

'As you say,' Graham answered, 'I've grown up a lot.'

'I hope so, Mr Packard. We are playing for high stakes here, after all. I'd like to think you were a man I could trust: a man, for instance, who can keep a cool head in a difficult situation.'

'I think I can do that,' said Graham. 'I think I've shown that already.'

Mark grabbed one of the waitresses by the edge of her miniskirt and pulled her towards him.

'Apples,' he said. 'We need some apples.'

'Yes, sir. You want them baked, or perhaps glazed in some way?'

'Just bring five apples.'

'And turn up that music!' Louis shouted after her. 'Make it loud, make it really loud!'

When she returned, Mark got all the waitresses to stand up against the wall.

'Oh, it's the game!' said Louis, clapping his hands delightedly. 'I *love* this game.'

Mark rested an apple on top of each of the waitresses' heads, then reached inside his jacket and took out a revolver.

'Who's going to be first?' he said.

Although drunk, the others turned out to be excellent shots – with the exception of Louis, whose bullet went some three feet wide of the mark and shattered one of the light fittings. The women screamed and whimpered, but they did not move, not even after their own apples had been targeted.

Finally it was Graham's turn. He had never even known the feel of a gun in his hand before; but he knew that Mark Winshaw was putting him to some sort of monstrous test, and that if he were to back down, if his nerve were to fail, then his cover would be blown and before long, in a matter of weeks if not days, his own life would be taken. He raised the gun and pointed it at Lucila. Tears were streaming down her face and in her terrified eyes he could also read incomprehension: an imploring echo of the laughter and intimacy they had shared in the upstairs room. His hand was shaking. He must have stood like that for some time because he heard Mark say, 'In your own time, Mr Packard,' and then he heard the others clapping their hands and starting to sing the William Tell Overture, buzzing it through their lips as if they were playing on a kazoo. And then just as Lucila let out her first compulsive sob, he did it: the thing for which he would always hate himself, whenever he woke up in the middle of the night, chilled and sweating with the recollection of it; whenever he had to leave the room in the middle of a conversation, or pull over abruptly to the hard shoulder of the motorway, the gorge rising in his throat at the sudden clarity of the memory. He pulled the trigger.

Graham blacked out almost immediately, so he didn't see his bullet split the stalk of the apple and lodge in the wall behind Lucila, or see her sink to her knees and vomit over the polished floorboards. He was dimly conscious of loud music and voices, of people slapping him on the back and making him drink more coffee, but he didn't fully come back to his senses until he found himself sitting on the toilet, his head in his hands and his trousers around his ankles, the air thick with the stench of his diarrhoea, the tiny windowless room silent but for his robotic intonation of one word, toneless and mechanical.

Joan. Joan. Joan.

*

Graham had earned Mark Winshaw's respect. It came in the form of twenty months' silence, followed by an invitation to a New Year's party at his house in Mayfair.

*

December 31st 1990

Eleven o'clock was about the earliest Graham thought he could politely make his excuses and leave. He told Mark that he was driving home to Birmingham that night, to be back with his wife and their eight-month-old daughter.

'But I haven't introduced you to Helke yet,' Mark protested. 'You really must say a few words to her before you go. Is your car parked near here?'

It was. Mark took the keys and gave them to one of his drivers, who was told to bring the car round to the front door immediately. In the meantime, Graham was obliged to swap a few pleasantries with the new Mrs Winshaw, whom he was surprised to find dauntingly attractive. He had wanted to dislike her – knowing that she was the daughter of a wealthy industrialist and notorious Nazi sympathizer – but her pale beauty and oddly coquettish manner made this difficult, even during such a brief meeting.

A few minutes later, as he slumped into the driver's seat, Graham breathed a sigh of relief. He was damp with sweat. Then he was knocked unconscious with a blow to the back of the head.

He was driven to a lock-up garage in Clapham. The driver pulled him out of the car while the engine was still running, and laid him on the ground near to the exhaust pipe. He kicked him four or five times in the face, and once in the stomach. He stripped him of his trousers, took the camcorder, and jumped up and down on Graham's legs. Then he left the garage and locked the doors behind him.

That kick in the stomach had been a mistake, for it had the effect of shocking Graham into semi-consciousness. But he was unable to move for several minutes, during which time even as his body got stronger, his brain was fast running out of oxygen. Eventually, with tremendous effort, he dragged himself back to the driver's seat. He put the engine into gear, and reversed back into the garage doors. It wasn't enough to smash them open, so he tried again. It still wasn't enough: and that was as much as he could manage.

But the noise had caught the attention of a group of drunken passers-by, who succeeded in forcing the doors open and getting the car out into the street. One of them ran off to find a phone box.

Graham was on the pavement, surrounded by strangers.

He was in an ambulance. Lights were flashing and there was a mask on his face.

He was in a hospital. It was very cold.

Big Ben was chiming midnight.

January 1991

I took the beakers of orange juice and carried them back to the cubicle. Fiona drank hers slowly and gratefully: then she drank half of mine. She said that I looked a bit distracted and asked me what had happened.

'This guy's just been brought in. He's unconscious, and he's in a pretty bad way. It just gave me a bit of a shock.'

Fiona said: 'I'm sorry. This is a terrible way to start the New Year.'

I said: 'Don't be silly.'

She was getting weaker, I could see. After her drink she lay back on the trolley and didn't try to speak again until the nurse reappeared.

'Progress report,' she said brightly. 'The sister's trying to find you a bed, and as soon as we've got one, you can go on to the ward and Dr Bishop will give you your antibiotics. Dr Gillam, our registrar, is very busy at the moment, so she'll have to come and see you in the morning.'

This didn't sound very much like progress to me.

'But they've been looking for a bed for more than half an hour, now. What's the problem?'

'Things are very tight,' she said. 'There were some surgical wards closed just before Christmas and that has a knock-on effect. It means that a lot of the surgical patients are now on the medical wards. We keep a chart of all the beds available but it has to be updated all the time. We did think we'd found one for you just now, and we sent the sister along to check but she found there was already someone in it. Anyway, it really shouldn't be much longer.'

'Fine,' I said, with a touch of grimness.

'There is one problem, though.'

'Oh?'

There was a pause. I could tell it was something she felt bad about.

'Well, the thing is, we need this cubicle. I'm afraid we're going to have to move you.'

'Move us? But I thought you didn't have anywhere to move us *to.*'

It turned out that they did. They wheeled Fiona's trolley out into the corridor, pulled up a chair for me to sit beside her, and left us there. It took another ninety minutes to find the bed. We didn't get to see any more doctors in that time: both the houseman and the elusive Dr Gillam were fully occupied, so I gathered, dealing with the new arrival – the man I'd half-recognized – who it seemed they had somehow managed to revive. It was almost two o'clock when the nurses came to take Fiona away, and by then she looked helpless and frightened. I clasped her hand tightly and kissed her on the lips. They were very cold. Then I watched as they wheeled her off down the corridor.

*

The staff had insisted that I went home and got some rest, but I was only able to carry out the first half of this instruction. Physically I was exhausted, not least because I walked all the way back from the hospital, reaching the flat some time after four o'clock. But I'd never felt less like sleep, knowing as I did that in a darkened ward three or four miles away Fiona too was lying awake, her gaze fixed blankly on the ceiling. How could it have taken them so long to get her there? After I'd found her kneeling in front of the wardrobe, it had been more than five hours before she was put safely in that bed – hours in which her condition had clearly worsened. And yet nobody had been negligent, as far as I could see: the atmosphere had been one of frantic, resolute efficiency under pressure. So how could it have taken them so long?

I lay fully clothed on my bed, with the curtains open. A bed was a simple thing, or so I'd always thought. As far as I could remember there could hardly have been more than a dozen nights in my whole life when I hadn't slept in a bed somewhere or other. And hospitals were full of beds. That was the whole point about hospitals: they were just rooms full of beds. It was true that my faith in medical science had always been limited. I knew there were many ailments which it was powerless to treat, but it would never have occurred to me that a bunch of highly qualified doctors and nurses could have such difficulty simply transferring a patient from one place to another: from a cubicle to a bed. I wondered who was responsible for this state of affairs (yes, Fiona, I still believed in conspiracies), what vested interest they might have in making these people's lives even harder than they already were.

I'd been told to phone the hospital at about ten o'clock in the morning. Was there anyone else I should contact in the meantime? I got up and went into Fiona's flat to fetch her address book. It was full of names she'd never mentioned to me, and there was a letter folded inside the back cover, dated March 1984. Probably most of the people in this book hadn't heard from her in about six or seven years. One of them, presumably, was her ex-husband, the born-again Christian. As far as I knew they hadn't spoken to each other since the divorce, so there was no point involving him. She always spoke quite fondly of her colleagues at work: perhaps I should give them a call. But of course they wouldn't be in for another day or two.

She was alone: very much alone. We both were.

The table in my sitting room was still laid for our candlelit dinner, so I cleared everything away and then watched the first day of the New Year dawn feebly over Battersea. When it was light I considered taking a shower but settled for two cups of strong coffee instead. The prospect of waiting another three hours appalled me. I thought of my mother, and how she had done her best to fill out the empty days while my father lay in hospital. There were plenty of old newspapers in the flat so I gathered them together and started doing the crossword puzzles. I did half a dozen of the quick crosswords in no time at all and then got stuck into a jumbo-sized cryptic puzzle which required the use of dictionaries and reference books and a thesaurus. It didn't actually take my mind off anything, but it was better than just sitting around. It kept me going until twenty to ten, when I phoned the hospital.

I was put through to a nurse who told me that Fiona was still looking 'pretty poorly', and said that I could come in and see her now if I wanted to. Rudely, I put the receiver down without even thanking her, and almost broke a leg running down the staircase.

*

The ward was full but quiet: most of the patients looked bored rather than seriously ill. Fiona was in a bed near the nurses' room. I didn't recognize her at first, because she had an oxygen mask over her nose and mouth. There was a drip attached to her arm. I had to tap her on the shoulder before she realized I was there.

'Hello,' I said. 'I didn't know what to get you, so I brought some grapes. Not very original.'

She took the mask off and smiled. Her lips were turning slightly blue.

'They're seedless,' I added.

'I'll have some later.'

I held her hand, which was icy, and waited while she took some more breaths from the mask.

Fiona said: 'They're going to move me. To another ward.'

I said: 'How come?'

She said: 'Intensive care.'

I tried not to let the panic show in my face.

She said: 'They did all these things to me this morning. It took about an hour. It was awful.'

I said: 'What sort of things?'

She said: 'First of all, I saw Dr Gillam. The registrar. She was very nice, but she seemed a bit angry about something. She made them do an X-ray here. Right away. I had to sit up in bed and they put this plate behind my back. Then I had to keep breathing in. That was quite bad. Then they wanted to do a blood gases test, so they got this needle and had to find an artery. Here.' She showed me her wrist, which had several puncture marks. 'I think it must be difficult to get it right first time.'

I said: 'When are they moving you?'

She said: 'Soon, I think. I don't know what the delay is.'

I said: 'Have they told you what's wrong?'

She shook her head.

Dr Gillam took me aside into a private room. First of all she asked me if I was next of kin, and I said no, I was just a friend. She asked me how long I'd known Fiona and I said about four months, and she asked me if Fiona had any family and I said no, not unless there were uncles or cousins that I didn't know about. Then I asked her why Fiona was suddenly so ill and she told me everything, starting with the pneumonia. She'd picked up a severe pneumonia from somewhere and her body wasn't fighting it properly. The explanation for that lay in the X-rays (and, of course, in the consultant's notes, locked up somewhere in a filing cabinet), which revealed large growths in the centre of her chest: a lymphoma, in fact. The word meant nothing to me so Dr Gillam explained that it was a form of cancer, and seemed, in this case, to be quite advanced.

'How advanced?' I said. 'I mean, it's not too late to do anything about this, is it?'

Dr Gillam was a tall woman whose jet-black hair was cut in a bob and whose small, gold-rimmed glasses framed a pair of striking and combative brown eyes. She thought carefully before answering.

'If we could have got at this a bit earlier, we may have had a better chance.' She gave the impression of holding something back, at this point. Like Fiona, I could sense a closely guarded anger. 'As it is,' she continued, 'her blood oxygen level's been allowed to get very low. The only thing we can do is move her to intensive care and keep a close eye on her.'

'So what are you waiting for?'

'Well, it's not quite that simple. You see, first of all –'

I knew what was coming.

'– we've got to find her a bed.'

*

I stayed at the hospital until the bed was found. This time it only took about another half hour. It involved several telephone calls and appeared to depend, finally, on finding a patient two or three beds down the chain, throwing him off his ward and making him wait in the day room until he could be officially discharged. Then Fiona was taken away from me again and there was nothing I could do. I went home.

I didn't have any medical books but the dictionaries I'd used for the crossword were still lying on the table, so I looked up 'lymphoma'. All it said was 'a tumour having the structure of a lymphatic gland'. Put like that it didn't sound very frightening but apparently this was the cause of all those months of sore throats and fevers, and this was the reason her immune system had all but closed down and surrendered to the first infection that came its way. I stared at the word again, stared at it for so long that it stopped making any kind of sense and began to look like nothing but a meaningless jumble of letters. How could anything so small, so random as this silly little word possibly do so much damage? How could it (but this wasn't going to happen) *destroy* a person?

It wasn't going to happen.

Suddenly revolted by the sight of the half-finished crossword, which seemed trivial and offensive, I screwed the newspaper up into a ball and in the process knocked over the cold remains of my second cup of coffee. Then, after fetching a cloth and wiping away the stain, I fell into a frenzy of cleaning. I polished the table, dusted the shelves and attacked the skirting-board. I marshalled scourers and J-cloths, Pledge, Jif and Windolene. I went at it so ferociously that I started to take the paint off the window frames and the veneer off the coffee table. But even this wasn't enough. I piled all the furniture from my sitting room into the hallway and vacuumed the carpet. I took a mop to the bathroom floor and polished the taps and the shower fittings and the mirrors. I cleaned out the lavatory bowl. Then I went round the flat with two big black dustbin liners, throwing in every out-of-date magazine, every wad of yellowing newsprint, every discarded note and scrap of paper. I didn't stop until I came upon an unopened Jiffy bag, containing my parcel of books from the Peacock Press: then, seized by an absurd, almost hysterical curiosity, I tore it open and looked at the three volumes. I wanted to see something that would make me laugh.

There was a slender pamphlet entitled *Architectural Beauties of Croydon*, which boasted, according to the flyleaf, 'three black and white illustrations'. *Plinths! Plinths! Plinths!*, by the Reverend J.W. Pottage, promised to be 'the most accessible and humorous offering yet to fall from the pen of an author now internationally recognized as an authority in his field'. And the third book seemed to be yet another volume of war memoirs, bearing the somewhat enigmatic title, *I Was 'Celery'*.

Before I'd had time to attach any significance to this, the telephone rang. I threw the book down at once and went to answer it. It was the hospital. They were putting Fiona on to a ventilator and if I wanted to talk to her I should come right away.

*

'There's been a circulatory collapse,' Dr Gillam explained. 'We've been treating her with high concentrations of oxygen, but the level in her blood's still very low. So we'll have to try the ventilator. Once she's on it, though, she won't be able to talk. I thought you'd better see her first.'

She could barely talk even now.

She said: 'I can't understand it.'

And: 'Thanks for being here.'

And: 'You look tired.'

And: 'What happened to the lasagne?'

I said: 'You'll be all right.'

And: 'Are you comfortable?'

And: 'The doctors here are very good.'

And: 'You'll be all right.'

It was nothing special, as conversations go. I suppose none of our conversations had ever been all that special. Especially special, I nearly wrote. I think I must be going to pieces.

*

They said it would take about ninety minutes to set the ventilator up and fit all the necessary drips, and after that I could go back to see her. I lingered for a few minutes in the Relatives' Room, a functional-enough waiting area with a few unyielding black vinyl chairs and a selection of newspapers and magazines which seemed slightly more upmarket than usual. Then I went to get a cup of coffee, and managed to find a canteen which I think was intended for the use of staff rather than visitors, although nobody seemed to object when I took my seat. I'd been there for a while, drinking black coffee and getting through two and a half bars of Fruit and Nut, when someone stopped by my table and said hello.

I glanced up. It was the nurse who had been looking after Fiona that morning.

'How is she now?' she asked.

'Well, they're putting her on a ventilator at the moment,' I said. 'I assume that means things are fairly serious.'

Her response was noncommittal. 'She'll be very well looked after.'

I nodded glumly, and she sat down in the chair opposite me.

'How are *you* feeling, though?'

I hadn't really thought about this. After a second or two I said, rather to my own surprise: 'I'm not sure. Angry, if anything.'

'Not with Dr Bishop, I hope.'

'No, not with anyone specific. I'd say it was with fate, except that I don't actually believe in fate. With the particular chain of circumstances, I suppose, which has brought –' Suddenly it struck me that I hadn't understood her remark. 'Why should I be angry with Dr Bishop?'

'Well, it probably *would* have been better if she'd been given the antibiotics last night,' she said doubtfully. 'She might at least have been more comfortable that way. Not that it ought to make that much difference, in the long run . . .'

'Hang on,' I said. 'I thought she did have them last night. I mean, that's what they told me was going to happen.'

I could see it dawning on her that she shouldn't have told me. She must have assumed that I already knew.

'Look,' she said, 'I ought to be getting back to the ward . . .'

I followed her into the corridor but she wouldn't answer any more of my questions, and I gave up when I caught sight of Dr Gillam out in the car park, wrapped up against the winter cold in her gloves and trench coat. I hurried to the main entrance and ran after her, catching up just as she was fumbling in her pocket for the car keys.

'Can I have a word with you?' I said.

'Of course.'

'I don't want to keep you, if you've finished for the day . . .'

'Never mind that. Was there something you wanted to know?'

'Yes, there was.' I hesitated. There seemed to be no tactful way of approaching this. 'Is it true that Dr Bishop forgot to give Fiona her antibiotics last night?'

She said: 'Where did you hear that?'

I said: 'Is that what you were so angry about this morning?'

She said: 'It might be a good idea if we went for a drink.'

As it was a Bank Holiday and the middle of the afternoon, all the pubs were shut. We were in a gloomy backwater of South West London. The best we could manage, in the end, was a bleak and characterless little café, rendered all the more tacky by the fact that it had obviously been designed to fool unwary customers into thinking that it was part of a well-known fast food chain. It called itself 'Nantucket Fried Chicken'.

'I think I've got the coffee,' said Dr Gillam, after sipping from her paper cup. We swapped drinks.

'No, this could be the tea,' I said, testing it doubtfully. But we didn't swap again. There didn't seem much point.

'You went through quite an ordeal last night,' she began, after a few moments' thought. 'To tell the truth, what you went through was unacceptable. But I'm afraid I can't apologize, because it happens all the time, and it would have happened anywhere else.'

'It wasn't quite what I . . . would have expected,' I said, not sure where any of this was leading.

'This is my last month as a doctor,' she now announced, abruptly.

I nodded, more confused than ever.

'I'm going to have a baby.'

'Congratulations.'

'I don't mean that I'm pregnant. I mean that I might as well have a baby now, while I'm trying to decide what to do next. The fact is that I can't really put up with this job any more. It depresses me too much.'

'Why become a doctor in the first place,' I asked, 'if illness depresses you?'

'Illness is only one of the things we're fighting against.'

'What are the others?'

She considered. '"Interference" would be the best word, I suppose.' She brushed this line of argument aside angrily. 'I'm sorry, I don't want this to turn into a political lecture. We should be talking about Fiona.'

'Or Dr Bishop,' I said. Then asked: 'Is it true?'

'The point is,' she said, leaning forward, 'that it's no use trying to find scapegoats. He'd been on call for twenty-six hours. And they found the bed as quickly as they could. I was horrified when I heard about it this morning, but I don't know why. As I said, it happens all the time.'

I tried to take this in. 'So . . . I mean, what kind of effect are we talking about here?'

'It's hard to say. I don't think the pneumonia would necessarily have taken hold the way it did. Not if she'd been put on to a ward straight away, and given her antibiotics last night.'

'Look, if you're telling me that her life' – I didn't want to say this; just by saying it, there was a danger of making it real – 'that her life has been put in danger through somebody's *negligence* –'

'I'm not talking about negligence. I'm talking about people trying to work under conditions which are becoming impossible.'

'Somebody must create those conditions!'

'The decision to close wards is taken by managers.'

'Yes, but on what basis?'

She sighed. 'These are not people who feel a personal involvement with the hospital. They're brought in from outside on short-term contracts to balance the books. If they balance the books by the end of the financial year then they get their bonus. Simple.'

'And whose bright idea was that?'

'Who knows? Some cabinet minister, some civil servant, some academic guru sitting on a policy-making committee.'

A name immediately flashed through my mind: Henry.

I said: 'But that's the only consideration, is it – finance?'

'Not always.' Dr Gillam smiled bitterly. 'Another ward was closed a few days ago. Do you know why?'

'Go on, I'll buy it.'

'War casualties.'

'But we're not at war,' I said, not even certain that I'd heard her properly.

'Well, somebody obviously thinks we will be soon, unless Saddam pulls his finger out. And this is one of the hospitals which has been told to clear some room for our gallant lads out at the front.'

There was no option but to believe her, however incredible it might seem. But I hated the way we were now expected to take this war for granted: where had it come from, this breezy assumption of inevitability? In any case, it was supposed to be nothing to do with me – something that was happening thousands of miles away, on the other side of the world: on the other side (which was further still) of a television screen. So how could I suddenly accept that it was now one of the forces conspiring against Fiona – that it had already crept into her blameless life? It was as if cracks had started to appear in the screen and this awful reality was leaking out: or as if the glass barrier itself had magically turned to liquid and without knowing it I had slipped across the divide, like a dreaming Orpheus.

All my life I'd been trying to find my way to the other side of the screen: ever since my visit to the cinema in Weston-super-Mare. Did this mean that I'd made it at last?

*

Dr Gillam warned me about the ventilator. She told me not to be alarmed by what I saw. A chatty and efficient nurse led me on to the ward and, as before, I was struck by the contrast with the rest of the hospital. Everything here seemed quiet, modern and clinical. There were expensive-looking machines next to every bed. Lights flashed and pulsed, and I was subliminally conscious of a discreet electric hum which had a strangely calming effect. I walked straight past the other beds, not glancing to either side. I felt that to look at any of the other patients would be invasive.

Was the woman I saw that evening really Fiona? She bore no relation to the woman who had come with me to Eastbourne seven days earlier, or even to the woman who had sat up in bed and smiled at the prospect of our formal dinner for two on New Year's Eve. She looked like a victim on a sacrificial altar. She looked like she was being attacked by snakes.

There was:

a tube for oxygen coming out of her mouth, its corrugated
    pipes forming a T-junction
a tube attached to a vein in her neck
a tube thrust into an artery in her wrist
a tube coming out of her bladder
a temperature probe on her finger
a drip for liquids
a drip for antibiotics
a mass of wires and tubing and pumps and brackets and
    supports and tape and cords, all connected up to a box-like
    machine which was covered with knobs and dials.

Fiona herself had been heavily sedated, and paralysed. Her eyes were open but she was barely conscious.

I asked her if she could hear me. There was a tiny movement behind her eyes, unless I was imagining it.

I said: 'You don't need to worry about a thing, Fiona. Dr Gillam's been explaining everything, and I understand it all now. It turns out that I was right all along. I was right, and you were wrong. I don't believe in accidents any more. There's an explanation for everything: and there's always someone to blame. I've found out why you're here, you see. You're here because of

Henry Winshaw. Ironic, isn't it? He wants you to be here because he can't bear to think that his money or the money of people like him might be used to stop things like this from happening. It's obvious, really. Not very difficult, as whodunits go. An open and shut case. All we need now is to get hold of the murderer and bring him to justice. And bring in the rest of the family, while we're at it. They've all got blood on their hands. It's written all over their faces. There's no end to the people who've died because of Mark and his obscene trade. Dorothy was the one who killed off my father, feeding him all that junk; and Thomas added a twist of the knife, making his money vanish into thin air just when he needed it. Roddy and Hilary have certainly done their bit. If imagination's the lifeblood of the people and thought is our oxygen, then his job's to cut off our circulation and hers is to make sure that we all stay dead from the neck up. And so they sit at home getting fat on the proceeds and here we all are. Our businesses failing, our jobs disappearing, our countryside choking, our hospitals crumbling, our homes being repossessed, our bodies being poisoned, our minds shutting down, the whole bloody spirit of the country crushed and fighting for breath. I hate the Winshaws, Fiona. Just look what they've done to us. Look what they've done to you.'

Perhaps I didn't say any of this. It becomes so hard to remember.

*

I sat on a black vinyl chair in the Relatives' Room and tried to read a newspaper, but must have been so tired that I dozed off. I had a strange dream in which the hospital became a film set and I was sitting in the darkened auditorium of a cinema, watching myself on the screen as I held Fiona's hand and spoke to her. Such scenes, I find, are rarely very involving, and after a while I got up from my seat in the stalls and went to find the bar, where I was served a drink by Dr Gillam. I swallowed it in one draught, then sat down on a black vinyl chair in a corner of the bar and started to doze. Some time later I awoke and looked up to find Joan standing over me and smiling in recognition. It took me several seconds to realize that this was not part of my dream. It really was Joan: here, in the Relatives' Room, before my very eyes.

'What are you doing here?' I said.

'Oh, Michael.' She knelt down and hugged me. 'It's so nice to see you. It's been ages. It's been years.'

'What are you doing here?'

She told me that she was now married to Graham, and that Graham was the patient who had been brought into the hospital unconscious last night. Thanks to the attention he had received from Dr Gillam and Dr Bishop in the early hours of the morning he was now out of danger and they expected to be able to discharge him soon. Possibly I should have been astonished by these revelations but I found myself wearily incapable of rising to the occasion: even when she told me that Graham had almost been killed while trying to make a documentary about Mark Winshaw, it didn't provoke either laughter or outrage. I simply chalked it up mentally as another point against the family, to add to my already substantial tally. I told her about Fiona, and tears came into her eyes. She wanted to start hugging me again and saying how sorry she was, but I wasn't having any of that. I had to keep holding things in for a little longer. So I started asking her questions instead about how she'd been and what she'd been up to. She was still in the same line of work, it seemed, but she'd moved back to Birmingham now. They lived no distance at all from where the two of us had grown up together. None of this information was really sinking in, and I can't have been thinking straight, because I now asked her a very stupid question: I asked why she'd never tried to get in touch.

'Michael,' she said, 'we did our best, but it was as if you'd gone into hiding. First I tried to get hold of you, then Graham tried to get hold of you. You never answered letters, you never picked up the phone. What could we do? And whenever I spoke to your mother, she just said that you'd gone a bit strange, and I got the impression that you didn't see each other much any more.'

I said: 'You've been seeing my mother?'

'Now and again. Not as often as I'd like.'

'Well, how often is that?'

'I hardly see her at all at home,' said Joan, sighing. 'It's silly really, with us living so close. But of course, I was with her a couple of days ago. We both were.'

'Both of you? How come?'

'She was down at my parents' house for Christmas. You know that perfectly well, Michael, and don't try to pretend otherwise. You were invited, as usual, but of course you wouldn't come.'

Needless to say, I'd heard nothing of this. 'What reason did she give?'

'She didn't.' Joan turned to me, her gaze a gentle accusation. 'Look, *I* know why you haven't wanted to see me. It's to do with what happened in Sheffield, isn't it? But that was ages ago, Michael. We can both forget about that now.'

I could see that Joan wanted only to console and reassure me, and it wasn't her fault if her presence in the hospital was having the opposite effect: confronted by this impossible, freakish development, I felt more disorientated than ever. She hadn't aged at all in the last eight years: the same round, trusting, open face; the slight plumpness which she none the less carried so lightly; the hidden, toothy innocence which was liable to reveal itself in a sudden smile. I had missed all of these things.

'Did something go wrong between you, Michael?' she said. 'You've changed, you know. You look so much older. I hope you don't mind me saying that, but it's true. I hardly recognized you. I wasn't even going to say hello at first: I wasn't sure it was you. Did something go wrong between you? I was so sorry to hear about your father. I know how close you were to him. I was going to write you a letter or something. It must have been awful for you. It wasn't anything to do with him, was it, Michael? Is that what went wrong?'

*

Joan had hit upon the truth, and there was no getting away from it: I did look older. Patrick had noticed it too. Perhaps I had been flattering myself the night Fiona first came to visit me, when I had stared at my own reflection in the kitchen window and tried to imagine how it would have appeared to her. Or maybe the events of the last twenty-four hours had taken a dreadful toll. Whatever the reason, when I looked at myself in the mirror of the men's washroom later that night, I could scarcely believe what I saw. It was the face which had once been revealed to me in a nightmare more than thirty years ago: the face of an old man, ravaged with age and grooved like an ancient carving with the traces of pain.

*

It was about two o'clock in the morning when the nurse came into the Relatives' Room to wake me up. I was in the middle of a deep sleep. She didn't say anything, and I didn't ask why she had come. I just followed her down the corridor. As we approached the ward she did make some remark, but I can't remember what it was. She hesitated before opening the door and said: 'You were fast asleep, weren't you?'

And, when I didn't answer: 'Shall I get you a cup of coffee?'

And, when I didn't answer: 'Strong and black?'

Then she pushed open the door and led me into the cinema. It was very quiet in there. The rest of the audience seemed to be asleep. I followed the bobbing light of her torch and took a seat towards the front of the stalls. Then she left.

The image on the screen hadn't changed. There was still this woman, Fiona, lying there surrounded by tubes and gadgets and drips. She was staring straight ahead, motionless. And sitting next to her was Michael, her lover or friend or whatever he liked to call himself. He was holding her hand. Neither of them said anything for a long time.

Then he said: 'I suppose now you're going to die on me.'

He said this very quietly. In fact I'm not sure that he said it at all. It seems a strange thing to say, in any case.

There was another long silence. I began to get a bit fidgety in my seat. I hoped this wasn't going to be too boring. I don't like death-bed scenes, as a rule.

Then he said: 'Can you hear me?'

Another pause.

Then he said: 'I suppose thank you is the most important thing I've got to say. You were so kind to me.' There was some fairly sentimental stuff after this. His voice was shaking and he started to get incoherent. There was a lot I couldn't understand, and then he started alluding to some secret he'd been keeping from her, some story to do with a Chinese restaurant he'd never explained to her properly.

He said: 'It isn't too late to tell you now, is it? You're still interested?'

Personally, I don't think she could hear him by this stage. That's my theory. But he carried on anyway. He was the persistent sort.

He said: 'It was a Friday night. We'd booked a table for two, for eight o'clock. Mum had come down about five. I thought she seemed a bit edgy, for some reason. I mean, she'd just had a long drive and everything, but it was more than that. So I asked her if there was anything the matter, and she said yes, she'd got something to tell me, some news, and she wasn't sure how I was going to take it. I asked her what it was and she said it was probably best to wait till we got to the restaurant. So that's what we did.

'Well, you know how busy the Mandarin gets, especially on a Friday night. It was pretty full. The food was a long time coming but she insisted on waiting for the main courses before saying whatever it was she had to say. She was getting very nervous. I was getting nervous, too. Finally she took a breath and told me that there was something I had to know about my father. Something she'd been meaning to tell me ever since he died, but had never had the nerve because she knew how much I worshipped him – how he'd always been my favourite, out of the two of them. Of course I denied this at the time, but it was true. He used to write me these letters when I was little. Made-up letters, full of all these silly jokes. They were the first letters I ever got. My mother would never have done anything like that. So, yes, it was true: he was my favourite. Always had been.

'And then she started telling me about how they'd met, how they'd both belonged to the same badminton club, and how he'd courted her for months and kept asking her to marry him and she'd kept refusing. I knew most of this already. But what I didn't know was the reason she finally accepted, which was that she was pregnant. Pregnant by another man. She was three or four months pregnant by then and she asked him if he would marry her and help her to bring the baby up and he said yes he would.

'So I said: Are you telling me that the person I called my father all those years wasn't my father at all? That he had nothing to do with me?

'And she said: Yes.

'So I said: Who knew about this? Did everybody know? Did his parents know? Is that why they never wanted to speak to us?

'And she said: Yes, everybody knew, and yes, that was why his parents had never wanted to speak to us.

'We'd both stopped eating by now, as you might have guessed. My mother was crying. I was beginning to raise my voice. I don't know why I was starting to feel angry: maybe it was just because anger was so much easier to deal with than the emotions I should have been feeling. Anyway, I asked her, in that case, could she possibly see her way clear to telling me who my real father was, if it wasn't too much to ask. And she said his name was Jim Fenchurch, and she'd met him twice, once at her mother's house in Northfield and once again about ten years later. He was a salesman. She'd been on her own in her mother's house and he'd come round to sell her a vacuum cleaner and after a while they'd gone upstairs and that was when it had happened.'

The nurse came back at this point. She tapped Michael on the shoulder and put a cup of coffee on the table next to the bed, but he didn't seem to notice, and carried on talking in this low, murmurous monotone. He was gripping Fiona's hand quite hard by now. The nurse didn't leave, she just stepped back a few paces and stood in the shadows, watching.

'So then I started losing my temper. Then I started thumping the table and sent a couple of chopsticks flying, and I said: You went to bed with a *salesman*? You went to bed with a man who came to sell you a *vacuum* cleaner? Why did you do it? Why? And she said she didn't know, he was so charming, and so nice to her, and he was handsome, too. He had lovely eyes. Like your eyes, she said. And I just couldn't stand it when she said that. I shouted: I do not! I don't have his eyes! I've got my father's eyes! And she said: Yes, that's exactly it, you've got your father's eyes. And that was when I got up and walked out, only you know how close together the tables are in the Mandarin, I was so angry and I was in such a hurry, I bumped into this couple's table and knocked their teapot over and I didn't even stop or anything. I just walked straight out into the street and didn't look to see if my mother was following. I walked straight out into the street and didn't go back to the flat for hours, not till some time after midnight. And my mother was gone by then. Her car was gone and she left a note for me which I never read and a few weeks later she sent me a letter which I never opened and I've never heard from her since. After that night I just stayed in my flat and didn't really go out or speak to anyone for two, maybe three years.'

He paused. Then his voice was even quieter: 'Till you came along.'

And then, quieter still: 'So now you know.'

Then the nurse stepped forward and put her hand on his shoulder. She whispered, 'She's gone, I'm afraid,' and Michael nodded, and bowed his head, curling in upon himself. He might have been crying, but I think he was just very very tired.

He was like that for about five minutes. Then the nurse made him let go of Fiona's hand, and said: 'I think you'd better come with me.' He stood up slowly and took her arm, and they walked off the screen together, to the left of the frame. And that was the last I ever saw of him.

As for me, I stayed right there in my seat. I wasn't going to move until Fiona did. There seemed no point in leaving the cinema, this time.

PART TWO

＊

'AN ORGANIZATION
OF DEATHS'

CHAPTER ONE

Where There's a Will

THE short January afternoon was fading into premature dusk. Thin, silent rain fell drearily. A dank, clinging fog had risen from the river, and was creeping furtively over the city. Through this grey pall the familiar roar of London's traffic penetrated, persistent, yet with an eerie, muffled effect.

Michael turned away from the window and sat down in front of the silently flickering television screen. The room was dark, but he didn't bother to turn on the lights. He picked up the remote control and switched idly from one channel to another, settling finally for a news bulletin which he watched for a few minutes with bored incomprehension, dimly aware that his eyelids were beginning to droop. The radiators were on full, the air was thick and heavy, and before long he had slipped into a light, uneasy doze.

It had already become his habit, in the two weeks since Fiona's death, to leave the front door of his flat unlocked and slightly ajar. He had taken a resolve to stay on closer terms with the other residents, and this gesture was intended to express the character of a friendly, approachable neighbour. Today, however, it had another effect, for when an elderly stranger, clad from head to foot entirely in black, arrived at Michael's threshold and received no answer to his inquiring knock, he was able to push the door noiselessly open and make his own way, unseen, into the darkened hallway. Proceeding into the sitting room, the stranger positioned himself next to the television set and stood a little while in impassive contemplation of Michael's slumped, recumbent figure. When he had seen all that he wanted to see, he coughed, loudly, twice in succession.

Michael awoke with a start and brought his sleepy eyes into focus, whereupon he found himself staring at a face which would have struck terror into the heart of many a stronger man. Gaunt, misshapen and unhealthy, it expressed at once a meanness of spirit, a slowness of intelligence and, perhaps most chillingly of all, an absolute untrustworthiness. It was a face from which all marks of love, compassion, or any of those softer feelings without which no man's character can be called complete, had been viciously erased. It had, one might have thought, a touch of madness in it. It was a face which gave out a simple, dreadful message: abandon hope, all you who look upon this face. Give up every thought of redemption, every prospect of escape. Expect nothing from me.

Shivering with disgust, Michael turned off the television, and President Bush disappeared from the screen. Then he switched on a nearby table lamp, and looked for the first time at his visitor.

He was not a man of forbidding aspect: the austerity of his clothing and steadiness of his gaze made him more severe than sinister. He was, Michael surmised, very much on the wrong side of sixty; and he spoke flatly, with a Yorkshire accent, his voice deep, cold and expressionless.

'You'll forgive me for intruding, unannounced, upon your personal domesticity,' he said. 'But as your door had been left ajar . . .'

'That's quite all right,' said Michael. 'How can I help you?'

'You are Mr Owen, I take it?'

'Yes, I am.'

'My name is Sloane. Everett Sloane, solicitor, of the firm of Sloane, Sloane, Quigley and Sloane. My card.'

Michael struggled into an upright position and took the proffered instrument, which he examined blinkingly.

'I'm here under instructions from my client,' the solicitor continued, 'the late Mr Mortimer Winshaw, of Winshaw Towers.'

'Late?' said Michael. 'You mean that he's dead?'

'That,' said Mr Sloane, 'is precisely my meaning. Mr Winshaw passed away yesterday. Quite peacefully, if reports are to be believed.'

Michael received this news in silence.

'Won't you sit down?' he said at last, remembering his visitor.

'Thank you, but my business can be kept very brief. I have

only to inform you that your presence is requested at Winshaw Towers tomorrow evening, for the reading of the will.'

'My presence . . .?' Michael echoed. 'But why? I only met him once. Surely he wouldn't have left me anything?'

'Naturally,' said Mr Sloane, 'I am not at liberty to discuss the contents of this document until all the concerned parties are gathered, at the appointed time and place.'

'Yes,' said Michael, 'I can see that.'

'I can count on your attendance, then?'

'You can.'

'Thank you.' Mr Sloane turned and was about to leave, when he added: 'You will, of course, be staying the night at Winshaw Towers. I would advise you to bring plenty of warm clothing. It is a cold and desolate spot; and the weather, at this time of year, can be uncommonly fierce.'

'Thank you. I'll bear that in mind.'

'Until tomorrow, then, Mr Owen. And don't worry: I can see myself out.'

*

There was a strange sense of expectancy in the air the following day, which had nothing to do with Michael's impending journey to Yorkshire. It was January 16th, and at five o'clock that morning, the United Nations' final deadline for Iraq's withdrawal from Kuwait had expired. The allied attack on Saddam Hussein might be launched at any moment, and every time he turned on the radio or the television, Michael was half-expecting to hear that the war had begun.

Boarding a train at King's Cross station late in the afternoon, he glimpsed some familiar faces among the other passengers: Henry Winshaw and his brother Thomas were both taking their seats in a first-class carriage, along with their young cousin Roderick Winshaw, the art dealer, and Mr Sloane himself. Michael, needless to say, was travelling second class. But the train was not busy, and he was able to spread his coat and suitcase over a pair of seats with a clear conscience, while he took out an exercise book and attempted to make notes on the most important passages from what was obviously a well-thumbed volume.

I Was 'Celery', published by the Peacock Press in late 1990, had turned out to be the memoir of a retired Air Intelligence Officer who had worked as a double agent for MI5 during the Second World War. Although it offered no direct information about Godfrey Winshaw's disastrous mission, it did at least explain the meaning of Lawrence's note: BISCUIT, CHEESE and CELERY, it appeared, had all been the codenames of double agents controlled and supervised by something called the Twenty Committee, established as a collaborative venture by the War Office, GHQ Home Forces, MI5, MI6 and others in January 1941. Might Lawrence have been a member of this committee? Very likely. Might he also have been in secret radio communication with the Germans, supplying them not only with the names and identities of these double agents, but with information about British military plans – such as the proposed bombing of munitions factories? This would be difficult to establish, fifty years after the event, but the evidence was beginning to suggest that Tabitha's worst accusations about her brother and his wartime treachery were very close to the truth.

As the train sped on through the grey, mist-shrouded landscape, Michael found it harder and harder to concentrate on this puzzle. He laid the book down and stared vacantly out of the window. The weather had hardly changed in the last two weeks. It was on just such an afternoon, some ten days ago, that Fiona's body had been cremated in the drab, cheerless setting of a suburban funeral parlour. The ceremony had been sparsely attended. There had been only Michael, a forgotten aunt and uncle from the South West of England, and a handful of her colleagues from work. The hymn singing was unbearably thin, and the attempt to convene at a pub afterwards had been miscalculated. Michael had only stayed a few minutes. He had gone back to his flat to pick up an overnight bag, then taken a train up to Birmingham.

His reconciliation with his mother, too, was less than he had expected it to be. They spent an awkward evening together at a local restaurant. Michael had presumed, rather naïvely, that his very reappearance would fill her with such delight as to compensate fully for all the pain he had inflicted by breaking off communications for so long. Instead, he found himself called upon to justify his conduct, which he attempted to do in a succession of halting and poorly argued speeches. In effect, he maintained, his father had died twice: the second, and more devastating death being when Michael learned the truth about his parentage. He now believed that his two or three years' subsequent withdrawal from the world could be seen as a period of sustained mourning – a theory supported, if support were needed, by Freud's essay on the subject, 'Mourning and Melancholia'. His mother seemed less than convinced by this appeal to scientific authority, but as the evening wore on, and she saw the sincerity of her son's contrition, the atmosphere nevertheless began to thaw. After they had arrived home and made two cups of Horlicks, Michael felt emboldened to ask a few questions about his lost parent.

'And did you never see him again, after that one time – the day it happened?'

'Michael, I told you. I saw him once again, about ten years later. And so did you. I told you that already.'

'What do you mean, *I* saw him? I never saw him.'

His mother took another sip of her drink and embarked upon the story.

'It was a weekday morning, and I was in town doing some shopping. I felt like a bit of a break, so I went to Rackham's, to get a cup of tea in the café. It was quite full, I remember, and I stood there for a while with my tray, wondering where I was going to sit. There was this gentleman sitting by himself at a table, looking very gloomy, and I was wondering whether it would be all right to join him. And then suddenly I realized that it was him. He'd grown old, he'd grown dreadfully old, but I was sure that it was him. I would have known him anywhere. So I thought about it for a minute, and then I went over to the table, and I said, "Jim?", and he looked up, but he didn't recognize me; and so I said, "It's Jim, isn't it?", but all he said was, "I'm sorry, I think you must be mistaken." And then I said, "It's me, Helen," and I could see it beginning to dawn on him who I was. I said, "You do remember, don't you?", and he said yes, he did, and then I sat down and we got talking.

'He wasn't much fun to talk to: just a shadow of the man I'd met before. He seemed very angry with himself for never having settled, for not finding someone he could build a home with and start a family. He seemed to think it was too late to do any of that now. So then when I began talking about myself, I just couldn't help it. I had to tell him about you. I thought perhaps it might mean something to him. And of course he'd no idea. He was completely flabbergasted. He wanted to know all about you, when you were born, what you looked like, how you were doing at school, all that sort of thing. And the more I told him, the more he wanted to know; until in the end, he asked me if he could come and see you. Just the once. So I thought about it and to be honest I didn't really like the idea, but finally I said all right, but I'll have to ask my husband, thinking of course that he'd say no, and that would be an end to it. But you know what Ted was like, he could never deny anybody anything, and when he got home that evening I *did* ask him, and he said yes, he didn't mind, he thought it was the least the poor man deserved. And so later that night, after you'd gone to bed, he came round to the house and I took him up to your bedroom and he stood and looked at you for about five minutes, until you woke up and caught sight of him and started screaming fit to bring the roof down.'

'But that was my dream,' said Michael. 'That was my nightmare. I dreamed that I was staring into my own face.'

'Well you weren't,' she said. 'It was your father's.'

For some time Michael said nothing. He was too astonished to speak – until, brokenly, he managed to ask: 'Then what?'

'Then nothing,' said his mother. 'He left and none of us ever saw him again. Or heard from him.' About to take another sip, she hesitated. 'Except that . . .'

'Yes?'

'He asked if he could have a photograph. I can still remember how he described you – "the only trace of myself I've managed to leave behind these last twenty years" – and when I heard that, I didn't feel I could refuse him, very well. So I gave him the first one I could find. It was the one you always kept out, the one of you and Joan, writing your books together.'

Michael looked up slowly. 'You gave him that picture? So I never lost it?'

She nodded. 'I meant to tell you, but I just couldn't. I couldn't think of any way to tell you.'

His capacity to absorb these revelations almost, but not quite, exhausted, Michael said: 'When was all this? When did it happen?'

'Well,' said his mother, 'it was in the spring. That I do know. And it was before your birthday, the day we took you down to Weston. You were never the same after that day. So I suppose it must have been . . . 1961. It must have been spring, 1961.'

*

It was already dark when Michael disembarked from the train at York. The three Winshaws and Mr Sloane, without noticing him, immediately hailed a taxi and drove off into the city traffic. Having established that the fare would leave him little in the way of change out of seventy pounds, Michael decided that he would have to forego that means of transport, and waited instead for a bus, which was due to depart in forty-five minutes. He passed the time consuming two packets of Revels and a Curly-Wurly in the station waiting-room.

The bus journey lasted for more than an hour, and for almost half of that time, as the tired, spluttering vehicle carried him along ever darker, narrower, wilder and more tortuous roads, Michael was the only passenger. When he left the bus he was still, by his own calculations, some seven or eight miles from his destination. The only sounds, at first, were the forlorn bleating of sheep, the soft moan of a gathering wind, and the falling of a thick rain which looked ready to settle, before too long, into a steady downpour. The only lights came from the windows of a few isolated houses, scattered and remote. Michael buttoned his coat up against the rain and began walking; but after only a few minutes he heard the distant rumble of an engine, and turned to see the twin beams of a car's headlights, no more than a mile away and advancing in his direction. He put down his suitcase and, as the vehicle approached, stuck out a plaintive thumb. The car braked to a halt.

'Going anywhere near Winshaw Towers?' he asked, as the driver's window was wound down to reveal a dark, clean-shaven man wearing a flat cap and green Barbour.

'I go within a mile of it: and I'll go no closer,' said the man. 'Get in.'

They drove for several minutes in silence.

'It's a poor night,' said the driver at last, 'for a stranger to be lost on the moors.'

'I thought the bus might get me a bit further,' said Michael. 'The service up here seems rather erratic.'

'Deregulation,' said the driver. 'It's a crime.' He sniffed. 'Mind you, I wouldn't vote for the other lot.'

He dropped Michael at a crossroads and drove off, leaving him once again at the mercy of the wind and the rain, which already seemed to have doubled in intensity. Nothing was visible in the surrounding darkness but the rough, stony road ahead, fringed on either side by a narrow strip of moorland, ever alternating between black, naked peat, straggling heather, and piled, weirdly shaped rocks; not, at least, until Michael had been walking ten minutes or more, when he became aware that the road had begun to run alongside some sort of man-made lake, illuminated at one end by parallel rows of lights which called to mind an airport runway. He could even distinguish the outline of a small seaplane parked at the water's edge. Shortly after that, he came upon a patch of thick woodland, cordoned off by a long brick wall which was interrupted, at last, by a pair of wrought-iron gates. They creaked open at his touch, and Michael guessed that his journey must nearly be at an end.

By the time he emerged from the seemingly endless, mudcaked and densely overgrown tunnel of blackness which constituted the driveway, the golden squares of lamplight shining out from the windows of Winshaw Towers might have seemed almost welcoming. This impression, however, could not survive even a cursory glance over the bulk of the squat, forbidding mansion. A shudder passed through Michael's body as he approached the front porch and heard the ghastly howling of dogs, protesting at their confinement in some hidden outhouse. To his own surprise he found that he was muttering the words: 'Not exactly a holiday camp, is it?'

The line should have been Sid's, of course: but there was no Sid to keep him company now. For the moment, he would have to keep the dialogue going by himself.

CHAPTER TWO

Nearly a Nasty Accident

As soon as Michael attempted to lift the immense, rusty knocker, he found that the door promptly swung open of its own accord. He stepped inside and looked around him. He was in a huge, dingy, stone-flagged hall, lit only by four or five lamps set high in the wood-panelled walls, with badly weathered tapestries and oil paintings adding to the crepuscular impression. There were doors leading off on either side, and, directly in front of him, a broad oak staircase. He could see light coming from beneath one of the doors to his left, and from the same direction occasional voices could be heard, raised in desultory conversation. After hesitating briefly, he put his suitcase down near the foot of the stairs, brushed the wet and tangled hair away from his eyes, and advanced boldly forward.

The door led into a large and cheery sitting room, where a log fire burned merrily, throwing antic, dancing shadows over the walls. In an armchair beside the fire sat a tiny, crook-backed woman, wrapped up in a shawl and squinting with intent bird-like eyes at her knitting needles as she worked them dexterously with busy fingers. This, Michael guessed, was Tabitha Winshaw: her resemblance to Aunt Emily, the deranged old spinster played by Esma Cannon in the film *What a Carve Up!*, was unmistakable. Opposite her, on a sofa, staring phlegmatically into space with a whisky glass in his hand, was Thomas Winshaw, the merchant banker, while at a table on the far side of the room, nearest the rain-spattered window, Hilary Winshaw was quietly tapping away at a laptop computer. Reaching the end of a paragraph, and looking around the room in search of further inspiration, she was the first to notice Michael's appearance.

'Hello, who's this?' she said. 'A stranger in the night, if ever I saw one.'

'Not quite a stranger,' said Michael, and was about to introduce himself when Thomas broke in with, 'For God's sake, man, you're dripping all over the carpet. Call for the butler, someone, and get him to put that coat away.'

Hilary stood up and pulled on a bell-rope, then came to take a closer look at the new arrival.

'You know, I *have* seen him somewhere before,' she said. And then, addressing Michael directly: 'You don't ski at Aspen, do you?'

'My name's Michael. Michael Owen,' he answered, 'and I'm a writer. Among my unfinished works is a history of your family: parts of which you might even have read yourself.'

'Why, Mr Owen!' cried Tabitha, putting down her needles and clapping her hands in delight when she heard this news. 'I was wondering if you'd be able to come. I've been so looking forward to meeting you. Of course, I've read your book – your publishers have been sending it to me, as you know – and read it, I must say, with the greatest interest. We must sit down together and have a long talk about it. We really must.'

Thomas now rose to his feet and pointed at Michael accusingly.

'I remember you. You're that damned impudent writer fellow. Turned up at the bank one day and started asking a lot of fishy questions. I was obliged to throw you out, if I'm not mistaken.'

'Not mistaken at all,' said Michael, extending his hand, which Thomas declined to take.

'Well what the deuce do you think you're doing here, turning up at a private family get-together? This is tantamount to breaking and entering. You could find yourself in very serious trouble.'

'I'm here for the same reason as yourself,' said Michael, unruffled. 'I'm here for the reading of the will: at your late uncle's invitation.'

'Poppycock, man, pure poppycock! If you expect us to swallow a story like –'

'I think you'll find that Mr Owen is telling the truth,' said a voice from the doorway.

They all turned to see that Mr Sloane had entered the room.

He was still wearing his black, three-piece suit, and he had with him a slim briefcase, gripped firmly in his right hand.

'It was Mortimer Winshaw's specific request that he should be present this evening,' he continued, coming to warm himself at the fire. 'We shall not know why, until the will itself has been read. Perhaps if Mr Owen were now to go upstairs and refresh himself, that happy event might be expedited.'

'Fair enough,' said Michael.

'And here's your taxi,' said Hilary, as the ancient, shambling figure of Pyles, the butler, came unsteadily into view.

He and Michael proceeded slowly up the staircase together. Not having much experience of making small talk with servants, Michael waited some time before venturing his first sally.

'Well, I can't say I think much of the climate up here,' he said, with a nervous chuckle. 'Next time, I think I'll bring a sou'wester and wellington boots.'

'The worst is yet to come,' said Pyles curtly.

Michael thought about this.

'You mean the weather, I take it.'

'There'll be storms tonight,' he muttered. 'Thunder, lightning, and blinding rain enough to soak the dead in their very graves.' He paused briefly, before adding: 'But to answer your question, I did not mean the weather, no.'

'You didn't?'

Pyles put the suitcase down in the middle of the corridor, and tapped Michael on the chest.

'It's nearly thirty years since the family were last met together in this house,' he said. 'Tragedy and murder visited us then, and so they will tonight!'

Michael stepped back, reeling slightly from his close contact with the butler's alcoholic aura.

'What, erm . . . what did you have in mind, exactly?' he asked, picking the suitcase up himself, and continuing down the corridor.

'All I know,' said Pyles, limping after him, 'is that dreadful things will happen here tonight. Terrible things will happen. Let us all count ourselves lucky if we wake tomorrow morning, safe in our beds.'

They stopped outside a door.

'This is your room,' he said, pushing it open. 'I'm afraid the lock has been broken for some time.'

*

The walls and ceiling of Michael's bedroom were panelled in dark oak, and there was a small electric fire which had not yet had time to warm the dank air. Despite the light from this and a couple of candles which stood on the dressing table, a sombre gloom shrouded every corner. The air of the room, too, had a strange quality: a suggestion of mouldering decay, a cold damp mustiness such as is found in underground chambers. The one tall, narrow window rattled unceasingly in its frame, shaken by the storm until it seemed that the glass would splinter. As Michael unpacked his suitcase and arranged his comb, razor and sponge-bag on the dressing table, a mounting sense of unease began to steal over him. Preposterous though the butler's words had been, they had planted in him the seeds of a shapeless, irrational fear, and he started to think wistfully of the downstairs sitting room, with its blazing hearth and promise of human company (if a roomful of Winshaws could be said to offer any such thing). He changed out of his damp clothes as quickly as he could, then closed the door of the bedroom behind him with a quiet sigh of relief, and lost no time in attempting to retrace his steps.

This, however, was easier said than done. The upper floor of the house presented a maze of corridors, and Michael had, he now realized, been so distracted by the butler's prophecies that he had not taken proper notice of their various twists and turns. After several minutes' walking up and down the shadowy, thinly carpeted passages, his unease had begun to grow into something approaching panic. He also had the feeling – a ridiculous feeling, he knew – that he was not alone in this part of the house. He could have sworn that he had heard doors being stealthily opened and closed, and even that, once or twice, he had caught a fleeting glimpse of something moving in the darkest corner of one of the landings. This feeling was not completely shaken off even when he arrived (just when he was least expecting it) at the top of the Great Staircase. Here he paused, standing for a moment between two rusting suits of armour, one of them wielding an axe, the other a mace.

Now: was he ready to face the family? He patted his hair into shape, straightened his jacket, and checked that he hadn't left his flies undone. Finally, noticing that one of his shoelaces had come loose, he knelt down to tie it up.

He had been in this position for only a few seconds when he heard the scream of a woman's voice behind him.

'Look out! For God's sake look out!'

He wheeled around, and saw that the axe-wielding suit of armour was toppling slowly towards him. With a cry of alarm he flung himself forward, just half an instant before the blade of the venerable weapon embedded itself with a thud on the very spot where he had been kneeling.

'Are you all right?' said the woman, running to his side.

'I think so,' said Michael, who had in fact knocked his head on the banister. He tried to get up and failed. Noticing his difficulty, the woman sat down on the topmost step, and allowed him to lie across her lap.

'Did you see anyone?' asked Michael. 'Somebody must have pushed it.'

Just then, as if on cue, a large black cat crept out from the alcove where the suit of armour had been standing, and ran off down the stairs with a guilty miaow.

'Torquil!' said the woman, scoldingly. 'What were you doing out of the kitchen?' She smiled. 'Well, there's your assassin, I suppose.'

A door had opened downstairs, and several members of the family rushed out from the sitting room to investigate the disturbance.

'What was that noise?'

'What's going on here?'

Two men, whom Michael recognized as Roderick and Mark Winshaw, were heaving the suit of armour back into place, while Tabitha herself bent over him and asked: 'He isn't dead, is he?'

'Oh, I don't think so. He's had a knock on the head, that's all.'

Michael was slowly coming back to his senses, and now found himself gazing up at his rescuer, a very attractive and intelligent-looking woman in her early thirties, with long blonde hair and a kind smile; and as soon as he did so, his eyes widened in amazement. He blinked, three or four times. He knew this woman. He had seen her before. At first he thought it was Shirley Eaton. Then he blinked again, and a distant, more elusive memory rose to the surface. Something to do with Joan . . . With Sheffield. With . . . yes! It was the painter. The painter from Joan's house. But it couldn't be! What on earth would she be doing here?

'Are you sure you're OK?' asked Phoebe, seeing the change in his expression. 'You look a bit odd.'

'I think I must have gone mad,' said Michael.

Tabitha laughed hysterically at these words.

'How amusing!' she cried. 'That makes two of us.'

And with this enlightening remark, she led everyone back downstairs.

CHAPTER THREE

Don't Panic, Chaps!

'Mr Mortimer Winshaw's will,' said Everett Sloane, looking gravely around the table, 'takes the form of a short statement, which he composed only a few days ago. If nobody objects, I shall now read it in full.'

Before he was able to proceed, the first crack of thunder sounded outside, causing the windows to vibrate and the candlesticks on the mantelpiece to rattle loudly. It was followed almost at once by a streak of lightning, which for a brief, hallucinatory moment made the intent and hawkish faces of the expectant family look suddenly pale and wraithlike.

'"I, Mortimer Winshaw,"' the solicitor began, '"pen these last words to the surviving members of my family, in the sure and certain knowledge that they will be present to hear them. I must therefore begin by extending the warmest of welcomes to my nephews, Thomas and Henry, to my niece, Dorothy, to my younger nephew, Mark (son of dear, departed Godfrey), and last, but by no means least, to Hilary and Roderick, the offspring – though it almost shames me to acknowledge it – of my own loins.

'"To the three other guests, of whose attendance I am perhaps not quite so confident, I offer more tentative greetings. I hope and pray that, for one night at least, my dear sister Tabitha will be released from her outrageous confinement in order to be present at what promises to be a unique and, dare I say it, never-to-be-repeated family gathering. I hope, too, that she will be joined by my most loyal and selfless nurse, Miss Phoebe Barton, whose grace, charm and gentleness have been a source of great comfort to me in the last year of my life. And finally, I trust that the family's luckless biographer, Mr Michael Owen, will be on hand to make a complete record of an evening which will, I believe, provide a most fitting conclusion to his eagerly awaited history.

' "The following remarks, however, are addressed not to this trio of interested bystanders, but to the six relatives previously mentioned, whose presence around this table tonight is already a foregone conclusion. And yet how, you might ask, can I possibly make this prediction with such assurance? What force could possibly motivate six people, whose lives keep them so busily and gloriously occupied on the world's stage, to abandon their commitments at a moment's notice and to travel to this lonely, godforsaken spot – a spot, I might add, which they found no difficulty in avoiding while its owner was still alive? The answer is simple: they will be propelled by the very same force which has always – and solely – driven them throughout the entire conduct of their professional careers. I refer, of course, to greed: naked, clawing, brutish greed. Never mind that we have, gathered around this table tonight, six of the wealthiest people in the country. Never mind that they all know, for a certain fact, that my personal fortune can only amount to a tiny fraction of their own. Greed is so ingrained in these people, has become such a fixed habit of mind, that I know they will not be able to resist making the journey, merely in order to scrape whatever leavings they can from the rotten barrel which is all that remains of my estate." ' '

'Poetic old thing, wasn't he?' said Dorothy, seemingly not at all discomfited by the tone of the document.

'If rather prone to mixing his metaphors,' said Hilary. 'You scrape the *bottom* of barrels, don't you? And aren't they only meant to be rotten if there's a rotten apple in them?'

'If I may continue,' said Mr Sloane. 'There is only one more paragraph.'

Silence fell.

' "And so it gives me no small pleasure to announce to these parasites – these leeches in human form – that all their hopes are in vain. I die in a condition of poverty such as will be beyond their imaginations to grasp. Throughout the long, happy years of our marriage, Rebecca and I did not live wisely. What money we had, we spent. Doubtless we should have been busy hoarding it, investing it, putting it to work, or devoting all our energies to sniffing it out and laying our hands on even more of it. But that, I'm afraid, was not our philosophy. We chose to enjoy ourselves,

438

and the consequence was that we ran up debts: debts which remain unpaid to this day. Debts so large that even the sale of this accursed residence – always assuming that we could find someone foolish enough to buy it – would not be sufficient to cover them. I therefore bequeath these debts to the six aforementioned members of my family, and instruct that they be shared out among them equally. A full schedule is attached as an appendix to this statement. It only remains for me to wish that you all pass a safe and pleasant evening together under this roof.

'"Dated this eleventh day of January, in the year nineteen hundred and ninety-one. Signed, Mortimer Winshaw."'

There was another crack of thunder. It was closer, now, and it rumbled on for some time. When it had finally died down, Mark said: 'Of course, you all realize that legally he can't get away with that. We're under no obligation to bail him out with his creditors.'

'Doubtless you're right,' said Thomas, rising to his feet and making for the whisky decanter. 'But that's hardly the point. The point, I suppose, was to have a damned good joke at our expense: and in that respect, I'd say he succeeded rather well.'

'Well, at least it shows the old boy still had a bit of spirit in him,' said Hilary.

'How much was he paying you?' barked Henry, suddenly turning in Phoebe's direction.

'I beg your pardon?'

'The fellow claims he didn't have any money – so how come he was employing a private nurse?'

'Your uncle paid Miss Barton,' said the solicitor, pouring suave oil on troubled waters, 'out of a capital sum raised on a mortgage against this property.' He smiled at the angry faces ranged against him. 'He really was a very poor man.'

'Well, I don't know about anybody else,' said Hilary, getting up and pulling on the bell-rope, 'but I could do with some supper after sitting through all that lot. It's after ten and I've had nothing to eat all evening. Let's see what Pyles can come up with.'

'Not a bad idea,' said Roddy, as he too gravitated towards the drinks cabinet. 'And make sure he goes down to the wine cellar while he's at it.'

'Damn this weather,' said Dorothy. 'I could normally have

439

driven back to the farm before midnight: but there's no point in risking the roads tonight.'

'Yes: looks like we're here for the duration,' Thomas agreed.

Tabitha rose stiffly from her chair.

'I hope no one will mind,' she said, 'if I resume my former station. Only, this armchair is so comfortable, and you've no idea what a treat it is to sit beside a real fire. My room at the Institute is quite chilly, you know: even in the summer. Won't you come and join me, Mr Owen? It's so long since I've enjoyed the company of a real man of letters.'

Michael had not yet had a chance to talk to Phoebe, and had been about to reintroduce himself with a view to finding out if she remembered their earlier acquaintance; but he did not see that he could very well refuse his patron's summons, and now went to join her by the hearth. As he took his seat, he glanced up at the portrait which hung above the fireplace, wondering if there was a pair of watchful eyes looking out from behind it. But this, he had to admit, was unlikely: it was a Picasso, and both eyes had been painted on the same side of the face.

'Now tell me,' Tabitha began, laying a thin hand on his knee. 'Have you published any more of those fascinating novels?'

'I'm afraid not,' he answered. 'Inspiration seems to have deserted me recently.'

'Oh, what a shame. But never mind: I'm sure it will return. At least you are well established in the literary world, I hope?'

'Well, it's been a number of years, you see, since –'

'You're well known to the Bloomsbury group, for instance?'

Michael frowned. 'The . . . Bloomsbury –?'

'We haven't corresponded for some years, to my regret, but Virginia and I were very close, at one time. And dear Winifred, of course. Winifred Holtby. You're familiar with her work?'

'Yes, I –'

'You know, if it would help you at all in your career, I could quite easily supply you with a number of introductions. I have a certain amount of influence with Mr Eliot. In fact the truth of it is, if you can keep a secret' (and here she lowered her voice to a whisper) 'I'm told that he has quite a crush on me.'

440

'You mean – T.S. Eliot?' Michael faltered. 'Author of *The Waste Land*?'

Tabitha let out a bright, musical laugh.

'Why, you silly boy!' she said. 'Hadn't you heard: he's been dead for years!'

He joined in her laughter uncertainly. 'Yes, of course.'

'I hope you're not trying to tease an old lady,' she said, poking him playfully in the ribs with a knitting needle.

'Who, me? Of course not.'

'My reference,' she explained, her eyes still twinkling at the joke, 'was to Mr George Eliot. Author of *Middlemarch* and *Mill on the Floss*.'

Tabitha took up her ball of wool and began knitting again, smiling benignly all the while. She was only able to bring an end to Michael's dumbfounded silence by introducing an abrupt change of subject.

'Ever flown a Tornado?'

*

Supper at Winshaw Towers that night was not a cheerful meal, consisting as it did of cold meat, pickles, cheese and an indifferent Chablis. They were only eight at table: Henry and Mark chose to remain in an upstairs room, watching the news on television. They both seemed to think that an announcement of American air strikes against Saddam Hussein might be imminent. The others all sat together at one end of the long table in the dining room, which was draughty and inhospitable. The radiators were not working, for some reason, and the electric chandelier was lacking several bulbs. They ate for some minutes in near-silence. Michael did not feel that he could initiate a private conversation with Phoebe in these circumstances, and the Winshaws them-selves appeared to have little enough to say to one another. Meanwhile the constant howling of the wind, and the hammering of rain against the windowpanes, did nothing to raise anybody's spirits.

The monotony was broken, at last, by the sound of heavy knocking upon the front door. Shortly afterwards they could hear the door being opened, and there were voices in the hall. Then Pyles shuffled into the dining room, where he informed the assembly as a whole: 'There's a gentleman outside, says he's a policeman.'

Michael thought this a most dramatic announcement, but the others evinced no particular interest. It was finally Dorothy, seated nearest to the door, who got up and said: 'Better have a word with him, I suppose.'

Michael followed her into the hall, where they were met by Mark, coming down the Great Staircase.

'What's all this about, then?' he said.

A thickly bearded, beetle-browed figure of indeterminate age, his policeman's uniform soaked through with the rain, introduced himself as Sergeant Kendall of the village constabulary.

'By crimes!' he exclaimed, his local accent almost impenetrable to Michael's ear. 'It's a night when we'd all want to be tucked up safely at home, and no business to take us out of doors.'

'What can we do for you, Sergeant?' Dorothy asked.

'Well, I've no wish to alarm you, Madam,' the policeman said, 'but I thought it best you were warned.'

'Warned? About what?'

'You have a Miss Tabitha Winshaw staying with you tonight, I believe.'

'We do, yes. Is there any harm in that?'

'Well you know, I suppose, that at the . . . hospital where Miss Winshaw usually resides, a number of highly dangerous cases – mental patients, you understand – are also held, under conditions of absolute security.'

'What of it?'

'It seems there was a break-out this afternoon, and one of these patients escaped – a murderous cut-throat, no less: a killer without mercy or remorse. By crimes! The life of the man unlucky enough to cross his path on a night like this would not be worth an hour's purchase!'

'But surely, Sergeant, the Institute lies more than twenty miles away. This incident, distressing though it may be, can hardly concern us.'

'I'm very much afraid that it does. You see, the vehicle of his escape, we believe, was the very same car which brought Miss Winshaw here tonight. The cunning fellow must have concealed himself in the boot. Which means, in all probability, that he's still somewhere hereabouts. He can't have got far, in this weather.'

'Let me get this straight, Sergeant,' said Mark Winshaw. 'Are you telling us, in effect, that there's a homicidal maniac at loose in the grounds?'

'That's about the size of it, sir.'

'And how would you advise that we adapt ourselves to this regrettable state of affairs?'

'Well, there's no need to panic, sir. That would be my first advice. Don't panic, whatever you do. Simply take the precaution of locking all the doors to the house – bolt them, too, if you can – set a few dogs out to roam the gardens, fortify yourselves with whatever guns and firearms you happen to have about the place, and make sure there's a light burning in every room. But whatever you do, don't panic. These creatures can sense fear, you know. They can smell it.' Having thus reassured them, he set his cap firmly on his head and made for the door. 'I'd better be getting along, now, if you don't mind. My colleague's waiting for me out in the car; and we've several more houses to visit tonight.'

After seeing him out – and letting in a torrent of rain and swirling leaves in the process – Mark, Dorothy and Michael returned to the dining room to inform the others of this extraordinary news.

'Well, that just about puts the tin lid on a delightful evening,' said Hilary. 'Now we get to spend the night here with Norman Bates for company, do we?'

'There might, even now, be time to leave,' Mr Sloane murmured, 'if anyone cares to try it.'

'I may well take you up on that,' said Dorothy.

'I can't believe that one of my neighbours would ever do such nasty things,' said Tabitha, half to herself. 'They all seem such quiet and pleasant people.'

Several of her relatives snorted at this point.

'Incidentally, you know, you mightn't be far wrong,' Michael remarked, turning towards Hilary. 'I don't know about Norman Bates, but of course there *are* films where this sort of thing happens.'

'Such as?'

'Well, like *The Cat and the Canary*, for instance. Did anybody see that?'

'I know it,' said Thomas. 'Bob Hope and Paulette Goddard.'

'That's right. All the members of a family are summoned to an isolated old house for the reading of a will. There's a terrible storm. And a police officer turns up to warn them that there's a killer in the area.'

'And what happens to the members of this family?' asked Phoebe, looking directly at Michael for the first time.

'They're murdered,' he said calmly. 'One by one.'

The crash of thunder which followed this statement was louder than ever. It was succeeded by a long pause. Michael's words seemed to have had a powerful effect: only Hilary remained determinedly unimpressed.

'Well, to be honest, I don't see what we've got to be worried about,' she said. 'After all, you're the only one who's been attacked so far.'

'Oh, come on,' said Michael. 'We all know that that was an accident. Surely you're not suggesting –'

'Do you mind?' Roddy now broke in abruptly. 'I'm beginning to find the tenor of this conversation almost as tasteless as this confounded Stilton.'

He pushed his plate away in disgust.

'And you know all there is to know about *taste*, of course,' said Phoebe.

This remark was accompanied by a very meaningful look, which provoked him to point a finger at her and stammer furiously: 'You've got a damned nerve, you know, being here at all. One weekend, you spent up here, but it was still long enough for you to get your claws into my father. How much money did you squeeze out of him, that's what I want to know? And more to the point, what's he supposed to have died of, anyway? Nobody seems to be talking about that.'

'I don't know, exactly,' said Phoebe, on the defensive. 'I was away when it happened.'

'Look, we're wasting time here,' said Dorothy. 'Somebody should fetch Henry and let him know what's going on.'

444

This struck everyone as a very sensible idea.

'Where is he, though?'

'Up in Nurse Gannet's old room, watching television.'

'Well where on earth's that? Does anyone know their way around this blasted house?'

'I do,' said Phoebe. 'I'll go and get him myself.'

Michael was slow to oppose this course of action, because he had been confused and intrigued by the sudden display of animosity between Roddy and Phoebe, and was beginning to wonder if it had any sort of history behind it. But as soon as he realized that she had departed on what might well be a dangerous errand, he turned to reproach the others.

'She shouldn't be wandering around by herself,' he protested. 'You heard what the sergeant said. There might be a killer in the house.'

'What nonsense,' scoffed Dorothy. 'We're not in a film now, you know.'

'That's what you think,' said Michael, and ran off in pursuit.

But once again he had occasion to curse the fiendishly convoluted architecture of the building. Reaching the top of the Great Staircase, he found that he had no idea which direction to take, and wasted several breathless minutes tearing up and down the winding, intersecting corridors until all at once he turned a corner and ran straight into Phoebe herself.

'What are *you* doing up here?' she said.

'Looking for you, of course. Did you find him?'

'Henry? No, he's not there any more. Perhaps he went back downstairs.'

'Probably. Still, let's have another look, just in case.'

Phoebe led him around the corner, up a small flight of steps, and then along three or four short, gloomy passages.

'Ssh! Listen!' said Michael, laying a hand on her arm. 'I can hear voices.'

'Don't worry, it's only the television.'

She flung open a door upon an empty room, containing only a sofa, a table, and a portable black and white television which was tuned to *Newsnight*. Unwatched, Jeremy Paxman was interviewing a harassed-looking junior defence minister.

445

'See?' said Phoebe. 'Nobody here.'

'It would be wrong to regard the UN deadline simply as a trigger point,' the minister was saying. 'Saddam knows that we now have the *right* to take military action. When – and indeed whether – we choose to *exercise* that right, is another thing altogether.'

'But nearly nineteen hours have elapsed since the deadline expired,' Paxman insisted. 'Are you saying that you still have *no* information as to when –'

'Oh my God.'

Michael had noticed something: a stream of blood was running down the side of the sofa and dripping on to the floor. He peered gingerly over the back and saw that Henry was lying face down on the sofa, a carving knife sticking out from between his shoulder blades. Phoebe followed him and gasped. They stared speechlessly at the corpse for some time; until they became aware that a third person had entered the room and was standing between them, looking down with blank indifference at the dead man.

'Stabbed in the back,' said Hilary drily. 'How appropriate. Does this mean that Mrs Thatcher is somewhere in the house?'

CHAPTER FOUR

Carry On Screaming

MICHAEL, Phoebe, Thomas, Hilary, Roddy, Mark and Dorothy stood in a solemn circle and contemplated the body. They had raised Henry into a sitting position, and he now stared back at them with the same outraged, incredulous expression which had been the hallmark of all his public appearances.

'When do you think it happened?' asked Roddy.

Nobody answered.

'We'd better get back downstairs,' said Hilary. 'I suggest we find Tabitha and Mr Sloane and all have a good talk about this.'

'Are we just going to leave him like that?' asked Thomas, as the others started to leave.

'I'll . . . clean him up a bit, if you like,' said Phoebe. 'I've got some things in my bag.'

'I'll stay and help you,' Dorothy volunteered. 'I've had a bit of experience with carcasses.'

The rest of the party proceeded downstairs in a silent cortège, and convened in the dining room, where Tabitha was once again placidly employed with her knitting, and Mr Sloane sat beside her, a look of the utmost horror drawn on his face.

'Well,' said Hilary, when nobody else showed signs of beginning the conversation, 'Norman seems to have claimed his first victim.'

'So it would appear.'

'But then, appearances can be deceptive,' said Michael.

Thomas rounded on him.

'What on earth are you blathering on about, man? We know there's a lunatic on the loose. Are you telling me you don't think he's responsible for this?'

'It's one of the theories available: that's all.'

'I see. Well perhaps you'd be so good as to tell us what the others are, in that case.'

447

'Yes, come on, out with it,' said Mark. 'Who else could have killed him?'

'Why, any one of us, of course.'

'Stuff and nonsense!' said Thomas. 'How could any of *us* have done it, when we were all down here having supper?'

'Nobody had seen Henry since the will was read,' Michael pointed out. 'Between then and supper, we were all of us alone, at one time or another. I don't rule anybody out.'

'You're talking rubbish,' said Mark. 'He can only have been killed a few minutes ago. You forget that I was watching the television with him, for a while, when you were all down here eating.'

'Well, that's *your* story,' said Michael coolly.

'Are you calling me a liar? What else do you suppose I was doing?'

'You could have been doing anything, for all I know. Perhaps you were on the telephone to your friend Saddam, helping him out with a last-minute order.'

'You impudent swine! Take that back.'

'I'm afraid that intriguing hypothesis will have to be discounted,' said Roddy, who had slipped out into the hall, and now returned carrying a telephone. The cord had been roughly snapped in two. 'As you can see, the service seems to have been temporarily suspended. I found this out because, unlike the rest of you, I had the sense to think of phoning for the police.'

'Well, it isn't too late,' said Hilary. 'There's a telephone in my room as well. Come on – if we hurry, we might still get to it before he does.'

Mark smiled a superior smile after them as they hurried out of the room.

'I'm amazed that people still rely on these primitive methods of communication,' he said. 'You brought your cell-phone up here, didn't you, Thomas?'

The elderly banker blinked in surprise. 'That's right: of course I did. Never without it. Can't imagine why I didn't think of it before.'

'Where did you leave it, can you remember?'

'Billiard room, I think. Had a few frames with Roddy before you arrived.'

'I'll just go and get it. We should have this business wrapped up in no time at all.'

He sauntered out, leaving Michael and Thomas to glower silently at one another. Meanwhile Mr Sloane began to pace the room, and Tabitha carried on with her knitting as if nothing had happened. Before long she was quietly humming a tune to herself – dimly identifiable, after a few bars, as 'Those Magnificent Men in Their Flying Machines'.

'Has anyone seen Pyles lately?' Thomas asked, when he could stand no more of this.

Mr Sloane shook his head.

'Well, hadn't someone better find him? He certainly wasn't with us in the dining room all the time. What do you say, Owen – shall we try to track him down?'

Michael was lost in thought, and didn't appear to have heard this question.

'All right then – I'll go and find the fellow myself.'

'And now we are three,' said Tabitha happily, once Thomas had gone. 'I've never known so much running about. What a to-do! Have we started to play sardines?'

Mr Sloane shot her a withering glance.

'What a long face you're wearing, Michael!' she exclaimed, after a little more humming. 'Not entering into the party spirit? Or perhaps you're beginning to get a few thoughts about how your book might end?'

'There was something strange about those suits of armour at the top of the stairs,' said Michael, taking no notice, and continuing with his own line of thought. 'Something about them had changed, when we came past them just now. I can't put my finger on it.'

Without another word, he got up and made his way to the hall. He was about to climb the staircase when he saw Pyles coming from the kitchen, a silver tray balanced precariously on his arm.

'Enjoying your visit, Mr Owen?' he asked.

'Thomas has been looking for you. Did you see him?'

'No, I didn't.'

'Did they tell you what had happened?'

449

'Yes. And it's only the start. I've known it all along, you see: this whole house is doomed, and everyone in it!'

Michael patted him on the back. 'Keep up the good work.'

When he reached the top of the staircase, he examined both suits of armour in detail. They were still in the same positions, and nothing seemed obviously awry. And yet surely, some subtle alteration had been made . . . Michael had the sense that he was being very obtuse, that he was missing something important which was staring him in the face. He looked again.

And then he saw it. At once a dreadful suspicion stole over him.

There was a loud crash from the direction of the billiard room. Michael ran down the stairs and almost collided with Mr Sloane in the hall. Together they ran towards the noise and burst in to discover Pyles collapsed in a chair, having dropped his tray to the floor.

'I came in to collect the empty glasses,' he said. 'And then I saw –'

Their eyes followed his trembling finger. Mark Winshaw was slumped against the wall. At first Michael thought that his hands had been tied behind his back: then he realized that the body had been horribly mutilated. The missing axe from the suit of armour, its blade red and sticky, had been left on top of the billiard table; and protruding hideously from the two pockets at the baulk end were Mark's severed limbs. To complete the macabre joke, a message had been scrawled in blood on the wall.

It said: A FAREWELL TO ARMS!

CHAPTER FIVE

A Lady Mislaid

'Now the important thing,' said Thomas, 'is that we all remain calm, and civilized.'

They were gathered in the dining room again, sitting amid the debris of their supper. Their faces, for the most part, were chalky and haggard. Tabitha alone was blissfully unmindful of the latest shocking turn of events, while Pyles, who had now joined them at the table, wore a crooked, fatalistic smile, having already delivered himself of the helpful opinion that 'There'll be more to come, before the night is out! Many more!' The only (living) member of the family not in attendance was Dorothy, who for the time being was nowhere to be found. Out of doors, there seemed little promise of an end to the storm.

'I suggest that we proceed on the assumption,' Thomas continued, 'that a madman is loose in the house, bent on the random slaughter of anyone with whom he comes into contact.'

Michael sighed. 'You don't get it, do you?'

The others looked to him for explication.

'There's been nothing random about these killings so far,' he said.

'Would you care to explain yourself?'

He turned towards Hilary. 'All right then: what were your first words when you saw that Henry had been stabbed in the back?'

'I can't remember,' said Hilary, shrugging carelessly.

'They were "How appropriate". They struck me as rather curious, even at the time. What did you mean by them, exactly?'

'Well . . .' Hilary gave a guilty laugh. 'We all know that personal loyalty wasn't the most obvious distinguishing feature of Henry's political career. And certainly not towards the end.'

'Quite. He was a turncoat, and, indeed, a backstabber. Can we all agree on that?'

From the ensuing silence, it appeared that they could.

'And as for Mark, I don't think we need have any illusions about what he was up to in the Middle East. Hence, I suppose, the message written on the wall above his body.'

'Your theory, insofar as I understand it,' said Roddy, 'seems to be that each of us is on the point not only of being killed, but of being killed in a manner ... appropriate, as it were, to our professional activities.'

'That's correct.'

'Well, it's a ridiculous theory, if you don't mind my saying so. It smacks of the scenario to a third-rate horror film.'

'Interesting that you should say that,' said Michael. 'Perhaps some of you saw a film called *Theatre of Blood*, made in 1973?'

Mr Sloane tutted reprovingly. 'Really, I think we're getting a long way from the point here.'

'Not at all. Vincent Price plays a veteran actor who decides to revenge himself on his critics, and murders each of them using methods inspired by some of the grisliest scenes from Shakespearian tragedies.'

Roddy stood up. 'Boredom, if nothing else, compels me to suggest that we abandon this wearisome line of inquiry and take some practical course of action. I'm worried about Dorothy. I think we should split up and go looking for her.'

'Just one moment,' said Thomas. 'I'd like to play our film expert at his own game, if I may.' He settled back in his chair and looked at Michael with the light of challenge in his eye. 'Isn't there a film where some crackpot – he turns out to be a judge – invites a lot of people to a remote house and does 'em all in: the point being that they all have guilty secrets to hide, and he sees himself as their executioner – a sort of angel of justice?'

'The plot is from Agatha Christie's *Ten Little Niggers*. There are three different film versions. Which did you have in mind?'

'The one I saw was set in the Austrian Alps. Wilfrid Hyde-White was in it, and Dennis Price.'

'That's right. And Shirley Eaton, I seem to remember.'

Michael glanced at Phoebe as he said this; and noticed, in passing, that Roddy was now looking at her too.

452

'Well,' said Thomas, 'doesn't that little set-up seem remarkably close to what appears to be going on here tonight?'

'I suppose that it does, yes.'

'Fine. Now listen to this: what was the name of the fellow who did the killing? The one who organized the whole shindig? Can't remember? Well I'll tell you.'

He leaned forward across the table.

'He called himself Owen. Mr U. N. Owen.' Thomas paused triumphantly. 'Now: what do you say to that?'

Michael was taken aback. 'Are you accusing me?'

'Damn right I am. We've all seen parts of that nasty little book of yours. We all know exactly what you think of us. It wouldn't surprise me if you've lured us all here as part of some insane scheme of your own.'

'Lured you here? How would I have done that? You're not accusing me of organizing Mortimer's death as well, surely?'

Thomas narrowed his eyes and turned towards Phoebe. 'Well, perhaps that's where Miss Barton comes in.'

Phoebe laughed angrily and said: 'You've got to be joking.'

'It makes sense to me,' said Roddy. 'I know for a fact she has a grudge against the family. And look at it this way: she and Owen go upstairs to look for Henry together – five minutes later, he's dead. That makes them the prime suspects, in my book. What do you think, Hilary?'

'I agree entirely. Apart from anything else, have you noticed the way they've been looking at each other all evening? Lots of little meaningful glances have been passing back and forth. I don't think this is the first time they've met at all. I think they've known each other all along.'

'Well, is this true?' said Thomas. 'Have you two met before?'

Phoebe gazed at Michael helplessly, before admitting: 'Well, yes . . . We did meet once. Years and years ago. But that doesn't mean –'

'Ha! So now it's all coming out!'

'I'll tell you another thing,' said Roddy. 'Owen's already condemned himself out of his own mouth. Hilary and I were both upstairs when Mark was found: so was Dorothy, and so were you, Thomas – looking for Pyles. Now, Owen says that he

453

was standing at the top of the staircase looking at the suits of armour all this time. So if any of *us* had tried to leave the billiard room and get past him, he would have seen us, wouldn't he? But he says that nobody came by!'

Thomas rubbed his hands. 'All right,' he said to Michael. 'Talk your way out of *that*!'

'There's a perfectly simple explanation,' he answered. 'The murderer didn't enter *or* leave the billiard room by the door. There's a passage from that room. It leads to one of the bedrooms upstairs.'

'What the *devil* are you talking about, man?' Thomas thundered.

'It's true. Ask Tabitha: she knows. She knows because Lawrence used to use it, during the war.'

'What tommyrot.' He turned to his aunt, who had been listening to this conversation with every appearance of enjoyment. 'Did you hear that, Aunt Tabitha?'

'Oh yes. Yes, I heard it all.'

'And what do you think?'

'I think it was Colonel Mustard, in the kitchen, with the candlestick.'

'Oh, for God's sake,' said Hilary. 'We're wasting valuable time. Dorothy hasn't been down for half an hour or more: we must try to find her.'

'All right,' said Thomas, getting up. 'But these two aren't coming with us.'

The curtains in the dining room could only be opened and closed by means of a thick cotton rope. Thomas cut off two lengths from this and lashed Michael and Phoebe securely to their chairs. Care of the prisoners was left to Mr Sloane (and Tabitha, for what she was worth), while Roddy, Hilary, Thomas and Pyles set off to search the house, agreeing to meet back in the dining room in twenty minutes' time.

Hilary was the first to return, followed shortly by the butler.

'Any luck?' she asked him.

Pyles shook his head. 'You won't be seeing her again,' he said, in his most lugubrious tone. 'Not on this side of the grave.'

Roddy arrived with more bad news.

'I went out to look in the garages. I thought she might have driven off without telling us.'

'And?'

'Well, her car's still there, but it wouldn't be any use to her in any case. One of those huge beech trees has blown right over, and the driveway's completely blocked. So now we're all well and truly stuck.'

Michael laughed. 'What did you expect?' he said. He was still tied to his chair, and not in the best of tempers. 'We psychopaths think of everything, you know.'

Roddy ignored him. 'I've had a thought, though, sis: what about your plane? Could we get away in that?'

'Well, *I* can't fly the thing,' said Hilary. 'And my pilot's staying in the village tonight. He won't be round till the morning.'

'Do you mean Conrad?' asked Phoebe mischievously. 'I should like to meet him again.'

Hilary gave her a furious look, and Roddy couldn't resist explaining, with a smirk: 'Conrad got the push a few months ago – on Sir Peter's orders. His replacement isn't quite in the same league.'

'Do you think he could *possibly* take me for a ride, when he comes round tomorrow?' cried Tabitha, her eyes alight with anticipation. 'I love aeroplanes, you know. What sort is it?'

'A Buccaneer,' said Hilary.

'The Lake LA-4-200, I suppose? With the four-cylinder Avco Lycoming engine?'

'Oh, shut up, you old fool.'

Hilary picked a grape from the fruit bowl and began tossing it nervously between her hands.

'Now there's no need to get bad tempered, you naughty girl,' said Tabitha. 'A kind word and a happy smile don't cost much, do they? Always look on the bright side, I say. Things could easily be so much worse.'

'Aunty,' said Hilary slowly. 'We're trapped in an isolated house, with a homicidal maniac, in the middle of a thunderstorm. All the phone lines have been cut off, we have no means of escape, two of us have been killed and another has gone missing. How could things possibly be worse?'

At that moment, the lights went out and the house was plunged into darkness.

'Oh God,' said Roddy. 'What's happened?'

The blackness to which they had been consigned was absolute. The heavy dining-room curtains were closed, and it was impossible to see even an inch or two ahead in such thick, impenetrable gloom. To add to the eeriness of the situation, it seemed to all of the company that the sounds of the raging weather outside had increased tenfold as soon as their powers of vision were taken away.

'It must be a fuse,' said Pyles. 'The fuse box is in the cellar. I'll see to it at once.'

'Good man,' said Roddy.

Whether he would succeed on this mission seemed open to doubt, for his progress towards the door was marked by any number of thuds, crashes, smashes and tinkles as he collided heavily with various objects of furniture scattered around the room. But finally he made it: the door creaked open and shut, and they could hear his receding footsteps echoing faintly as he made his halting way across the stone-flagged hall.

Then the clicking of Tabitha's needles resumed, and she started humming another tune. This time it was 'The Dambusters' March'.

'For God's sake, Aunty,' said Roddy. 'How on earth can you do any knitting in this dark? And would you kindly desist from singing those infuriating songs?'

'I must say, Mr Owen, your ingenuity compels admiration,' said Hilary; and her brother could recognize in her voice a forced, brittle cheerfulness – a sure sign that her spirits were violently agitated. 'I can't help wondering what sort of fate you had in mind for the rest of us.'

'I hadn't really thought, to be honest,' said Michael. 'I was more or less improvising the whole thing, you see.'

'Yes, but surely you must have had a few ideas. Henry's back; Mark's arms. What about Thomas? What part of *his* anatomy were you intending to go for?'

'Where is Thomas, anyway?' said Roddy. 'He should have been here ages ago. The last I saw of him he –'

'Ssh!' It was Hilary who cut him short. The atmosphere in the room grew suddenly tense. 'Who's that moving about?'

They all strained to listen. Was that a footstep they had just heard? Was there someone (or something) in the room with them, a furtive, watchful presence, creeping through the inky shadows – and now very close at hand? Was that the sound of something on the table itself – where they were all sitting, rigid with expectation – being very quietly, very stealthily moved?

'Who's there?' said Hilary. 'Come on, speak up.'

Nobody breathed.

'You were imagining it,' said Roddy, after about a minute.

'I don't *imagine* things,' Hilary answered, indignantly. But the tension had gone.

'Well, fear can play strange tricks,' said her brother.

'Look: I am *not* afraid.'

He laughed scornfully. 'Afraid? You're scared witless, old girl.'

'I don't know what gives you that idea.'

'After all these years, darling, I can read you like a book. Anyone can tell when you're upset. You start messing around with the grapes.'

'The grapes? What are you on about?'

'You start playing around with them. Peeling them. Taking the skins off. You've done it since you were a kid.'

'I may have done it since I was a kid but I'm not doing it tonight, I can assure you.'

'Oh, come off it. I've got one of them in my hands right now.'

Roddy stroked the fruit between finger and thumb – it felt smooth and oily without its skin – and then popped it into his mouth. He closed his teeth upon it, but instead of the expected release of fresh, tangy syrup upon his tongue, he felt only a rubbery squelch, and his mouth was filled with an appalling taste, the nameless virulence of which he had never known before.

'Jesus Christ!' he shouted, and spat it out. He began to retch violently.

Just then, the lights came back on. Squinting in the sudden brightness, it took him a few seconds to identify the object he had just coughed up, which was now lying on the table in front of him. It was a half-chewed eyeball. Its fellow stared balefully at him from the fruit bowl: the bloodshot eye of Thomas Winshaw, fixed for ever in its last, unblinking, lifeless gaze.

CHAPTER SIX

The Crowning Touch

'He should sleep now,' said Phoebe, as Roddy lay back on the pillow, his breathing gradually taking on a slower, more regular rhythm. She gently took the glass from his hand, set it down on the bedside table, and put the bottle of pills away in her bag.

Hilary regarded her brother dispassionately. 'He always was a squeamish little thing,' she said. 'Still, I've never seen him perform in quite that way before. Will he be all right, do you think?'

'I expect he's just in shock. A few hours' rest ought to take care of it.'

'Well, we could all do with that.' Hilary glanced around the room, and went to check that the window was securely fastened. 'I suppose he'll be safe in here, will he? There's not much point leaving him sleeping like a baby if our resident maniac is just going to sneak in and bump him off the minute our backs are turned.'

They decided that the best thing would be to lock him in. Phoebe didn't think that he would wake before morning, and even if he did, the temporary inconvenience of being held captive was surely of little importance when set beside his personal safety.

'I think I'd better keep the key,' said Phoebe, slipping it into the pocket of her jeans as they set off down the corridor together.

'Why's that?'

'I would have thought it was obvious. Michael and I were tied up when Thomas was killed. That puts us in the clear, doesn't it?'

'I suppose so,' said Hilary curtly, after a moment's thought. 'In any case, my congratulations go to whoever's behind this whole set-up. They haven't missed a trick. Disconnecting all the phones, for instance. I think I could forgive just about everything apart from that.'

'Preventing us from calling the police, you mean?'

'Worse than that – I can't even use my modem. First time in six years I've missed a copy deadline. I'd got an absolute corker for them, too. All about the Labour Party peaceniks and how the Iraqis would have run rings around them. Ah well.' She sighed. 'It'll just have to wait.'

They made their way back to the sitting room, where Tabitha was once again installed by the fire, now preoccupied not with her knitting but with the perusal of a bulky paperback which on closer inspection turned out to be Volume Four of *The Air Pilot's Manual*. She looked up when Hilary and Phoebe came in, and said: 'Why, there you are! I was beginning to think you were never coming back.'

'What about Michael and Mr Sloane?' Phoebe asked. 'Are they still outside?'

'I suppose they must be,' said Tabitha. 'Really, you know, I find it hard to keep track of all your comings and goings.'

'And there's been no sign of Dorothy, I suppose?' Hilary ventured.

'The only person I've seen,' said the old woman, 'was your father. He stopped by a few minutes ago. We had a lovely little chat.'

Phoebe and Hilary exchanged worried looks. Hilary knelt down beside her aunt and began to speak very slowly and distinctly.

'Aunty, Mortimer isn't with us any more. He died, the day before yesterday. That's why we're all here, remember? We came for the reading of his will.'

Tabitha frowned. 'No, I think you must be quite mistaken, dear. I'm certain it was Morty. I must say, I didn't think he was looking his best – he was very tired and out of breath, and he did have blood all over his clothes, now I come to think of it – but he wasn't dead. Not a bit of it. Not at all like Henry, or Mark, or Thomas.' She smiled at the last name, and shook her head fondly. 'Now *that's* what I call dead.'

There were footsteps outside the room, and Michael returned, with Pyles and Mr Sloane in tow. Hilary rose from her kneeling position and took Michael aside to acquaint him with the latest turn of events.

'Loony alert,' she said, in a loud whisper. 'The old biddy's completely lost it this time.'

'Why, what's happened?'

'Says she's just been talking to my father.'

'I see.' Michael paced the room for a few moments, sunk in thought. Then he looked up. 'Well – who's to say she's not telling the truth? I mean, did anyone actually *see* Mortimer die?'

'I didn't,' said Phoebe. 'As I said, I wasn't here when it happened. I'd gone back to Leeds for a couple of days.'

'And was that your idea?'

'Not really. He more or less forced it upon me. Told me I was looking under the weather and insisted that I took a break.'

'And what about you, Pyles – did you ever see Mortimer's body?'

'No,' said the butler, scratching his head. 'Dr Quince – Dr Quince the younger, that is – simply came down that morning and informed me that the master had passed away. And then he very kindly offered to make all the arrangements with the funeral director himself. I wasn't involved at all.'

'But my father couldn't be running around here killing people,' Hilary protested. 'He was confined to a wheelchair, for God's sake.'

'That was the impression he liked to give,' said Phoebe. 'But I saw him get up and walk once or twice, when he thought nobody was looking. He wasn't nearly as ill as he liked to make out.'

'I cannot find it in me to believe,' the solicitor maintained, 'that Mr Winshaw himself is still alive, somewhere in this house, and is responsible for all these dreadful murders.'

'But it's the only possible solution,' said Michael. 'I've known it all along.'

Hilary raised her eyebrows.

'That's a rather extraordinary statement,' she said. 'Since when have you known it, exactly?'

'Well . . . since Henry was killed,' said Michael; and then thought again. 'No, before then: since I arrived here. No, before that, even: since Mr Sloane turned up at my flat yesterday. Or – oh, I don't know: since I was first approached by Tabitha and started writing this wretched book about you all. I can't say. I really can't say. Perhaps it's even longer than that. Perhaps it goes all the way back to my birthday.'

'Your birthday?' said Hilary. 'What on earth are you talking about?'

Michael sat down and put his head in his hands. He spoke wearily, without emotion.

'Years ago, on my ninth birthday, I was taken to see a film. It was set in a house rather like this one, and it was about a family, rather like yours. I was an over-sensitive little boy and I should never have been allowed to see it, but because it was supposed to be a comedy my parents thought it would be all right. It wasn't their fault. They could never have known the effect it was going to have. I know it sounds hard to believe, but it was . . . well, easily the most exciting thing that had ever happened to me. I'd never seen anything like it before. And then half-way through – less than half-way through, probably – my mother made us get up and leave. She said we had to go home. And so we left: we left and I never found out what happened in the end. All I could do was wonder about it, for years afterwards.'

'Enchanting though I find these childhood reminiscences,' Hilary interrupted, 'I can't help thinking you've chosen an odd time to share them with us.'

'I've seen the film since then, you understand,' said Michael, apparently not having heard her. 'I've got it on video. I know how the story works out: that's how I know that Mortimer's still alive. But that isn't the point. It was never enough, being able to see it whenever I wanted: because I wasn't just *watching* it, that day. I was *living* it: that's the feeling I thought would never come back, the one I've been waiting to recapture. And now it's happening. It's started. All you people' – he gestured at the circle of attentive faces – 'you're all characters in my film, you see. Whether you realize it or not, that's what you are.'

'Just like Alice, and the Red King's dream,' Tabitha chipped in.

'Exactly.'

'If I may make a suggestion, Michael,' said Hilary, in a sweet tone of voice which rapidly turned sour, 'why don't you and Aunt Tabitha retire to a quiet corner together, for a private meeting of Nutters Anonymous, while the rest of us apply our minds to the trifling little question of how we're going to get through the rest of the night without being slashed to ribbons?'

'Hear hear,' said Mr Sloane.

'We all seem to be forgetting, apart from anything else, that according to the local police there's an escaped killer in the area. Forgive me for being so prosaic, but I can't help thinking that this has slightly more bearing on our predicament than Mr Owen's admittedly diverting fairy stories.'

'That business with the policeman was all a red herring,' said Michael.

'What's this? Another theory? Why, the man's a perfect magician! What's it to be this time, Michael – Plan Nine from Outer Space? Abbott and Costello Meet the Wolf Man?'

'Mr Sloane and I have been out to check the driveway,' Michael said. 'It's covered with mud, so any tyre tracks would show up quite clearly. But you can still see my footprints: they're the most recent marks on the drive. There's been no police car here since I arrived.'

Hilary seemed momentarily chastened. 'Well you saw this policeman, and so did Mark and Dorothy. Are you saying he was an impostor?'

'I think it was Mortimer himself. I only ever met your father once, so I can't be sure. *They*, of course, hadn't seen him for years. But it's what happens in the film. The man who's supposed to be dead turns up and pretends to be a policeman, to throw them off the scent.'

'I don't know about anybody else, but my head's beginning to spin with all this theorizing,' said Mr Sloane, breaking the uneasy silence which followed this exchange. 'I propose that we all go to our rooms, lock the doors, and stay put until the storm blows over. Explanations can wait until the morning.'

'What a splendid idea,' said Tabitha. 'I'm quite worn out, I must say. I wonder if someone would be so good as to fill me a hot-water bottle, before they retire? This house seems so frightfully chilly tonight.'

Phoebe said that she would take care of it, while Michael, Pyles and Mr Sloane decided to make one final search of the house, to see if there was any sign of Dorothy.

'We still haven't talked about your book, Michael,' Tabitha reminded him, just as he was about to leave. 'Now you won't disappoint me tomorrow, will you? I've been looking forward to it for so long. So very, very long. It will be just like talking to your father again.'

Michael stopped in his tracks when she said this. He wasn't sure that he had heard correctly.

'You're very like him, you know. Just as I expected. The same eyes. Exactly the same eyes.'

'Come on,' said Mr Sloane, pulling at Michael's sleeve. He added in a whisper: 'She's not all there, poor soul. Take no notice. We don't want to confuse her even further.'

Hilary was left alone with her aunt. She stood for a while in front of the fire, biting her nail and doing her best to make sense of Michael's latest baffling suggestion.

'Aunty,' she said, after a minute or two. 'Are you quite *sure* it was my father you were talking to in here?'

'Quite sure,' said Tabitha. She closed her book and put it away in her knitting bag. 'You know, it's very confusing, with everyone saying that he's dead one minute and alive the next. But there is a way you could prove it beyond question, isn't there?'

'Really? How would I do that?'

'Why, you could go down to the crypt, of course, and see if his body's in the coffin or not.'

Hilary had never wanted for courage, and she thought that this plan was well worth putting into action; but the journey involved was not one to relish. She was determined to complete it as quickly as possible, and so didn't stop to fetch her raincoat before unbolting the front door and throwing herself into the heart of the howling storm, which had been continuing now for two hours or more. Barely able to see through the thick sheets of rain, almost thrown off her feet by the buffeting wind, she struggled across the forecourt and made for the bulky outline of the family chapel, which stood in a small glade near the head of the densely wooded driveway. All around her the trees groaned, creaked and rustled as the gale came and went in a series of wild and unpredictable gusts. Very much to her surprise, the door to

464

the chapel was open, and there was a light flickering inside. Two candles burned on the altar. They had been recently lit, even though the chapel itself appeared to be deserted. Shivering violently – half with the cold, half with apprehension – she hurried across the aisle and pushed open a small, oak-framed door which gave upon a steep flight of stone steps. These were the steps which led down to the family vaults, where generation after generation of Winshaws had been interred, and where one vacant but elaborately inscribed tomb bore witness to the memory of Godfrey, the wartime hero, whose body they had never been able to recover from enemy soil.

Hilary descended the steps in complete darkness, but on reaching the entrance to the vault itself, she could see a thin band of light coming from beneath the door. Fearfully, hesitantly, she eased it open: and saw –

– and saw an empty coffin raised on a dais in the middle of the chamber, its lid removed, and beside it her father, Mortimer Winshaw, standing at a rakish angle and smiling warmly in her direction.

'Come in, daughter dearest,' he said. 'Come in, and all will be explained.'

As Hilary stepped forward and opened the door to its fullest extent, she heard a sudden whirr above her head. Glancing upwards with a short scream, she had the briefest impression of a bulky parcel falling towards her on the end of a rope: a parcel compounded – although she was never to know it – of all the newspapers for which she had written a column over the last six years. But before she could guess what had hit her, Hilary was dead: crushed by the weight of her own opinion, and knocked to the ground, as senseless as any reader who had ever been numbed into submission by her raging torrent of overpaid words.

CHAPTER SEVEN

Five Golden Hours

ALL was quiet at Winshaw Towers. Outside, the wind was beginning to die down, and the rain had dwindled to a soft patter against the windowpanes. Within, there was no sound save the reproachful creaking of the stairs as Michael made his way back to the upper floor, his final inspection of the house completed.

Whether from simple fatigue, or confusion at the dizzying events of the last few hours, Michael once again let the labyrinthine corridors get the better of him, and as he walked into what he had assumed was his bedroom, the first thing he saw was a large and unfamiliar item of furniture: a mahogany wardrobe, with a full-length mirror fixed to its open door. Phoebe had her back to the mirror and was reflected in it, bending over and about to step out of her jeans.

'What are you doing in my room?' said Michael, blinking in confusion.

She turned round with a start, and said: 'This isn't your room.' She gestured at the hairbrushes and make-up laid out on the dressing table. 'I mean, those aren't your things, are they?'

'No, of course not,' said Michael. 'I'm sorry, I can't seem to get the hang of this place at all. I didn't mean to disturb you.'

'That's all right.' Phoebe pulled her trousers back up and sat on the bed. 'Perhaps it's about time we had a talk anyway.'

He needed no further invitation to come inside.

'I've been wanting to speak to you properly all evening,' he said. 'But the opportunity just never seemed to arise.'

Phoebe appeared to regard this as an understatement.

'I know,' she said, with a slightly cutting edge to her voice. 'There's something terribly distracting about mass murder, isn't there?'

There was an awkward pause, before Michael blurted out:

'Well what are you *doing* here, for Heaven's sake? How did you come to be involved in all this?'

'Through Roddy, of course. I met him just over a year ago: he offered to show some of my work at the gallery, and like a fool I believed him, and then like an even bigger fool I went to bed with him, and then as soon as he'd got what he wanted he dropped me like a stone. But while I was up here I met Mortimer. Don't ask me why, but he took a liking to me and offered me this job.'

'And you accepted? Why?'

'Why do you think? Because I needed the money. And don't look so disapproving about it: why did *you* agree to take on this book, for that matter? Artistic integrity?'

It was a fair point.

'Mind if I sit here?' said Michael, indicating the space beside her on the bed.

Phoebe shook her head. She looked tired, and ran a hand through her hair.

'How've you been, anyway?' she asked. 'I've been looking out for your novels.'

'I never wrote any more. I dried up.'

'That's a shame.'

'Still painting?'

'On and off. I can't really see much future in it at the moment. Not while the Roddy Winshaws of this world continue to rule the roost.'

'Well, there'll be one less of them by tomorrow morning, at this rate.' Not wanting to dwell on this macabre prospect, Michael added: 'You mustn't give up, though. You were good. Anyone could see that.'

'Anyone?' Phoebe echoed.

'Do you remember that time,' said Michael, not noticing her question, 'when I came into your room and saw the painting you were working on?' He began to chuckle. 'And I thought it was a still life, when it was really a picture of Orpheus in the underworld or something?'

'Yes,' said Phoebe, quietly. 'I remember.'

Michael had a flash of inspiration. 'Could I buy that painting? It would be so nice to have – just as a sort of . . . keepsake.'

'I'm afraid I destroyed it. Soon afterwards.'

Phoebe got up and sat at the dressing table, where she began brushing her hair.

'You don't mean – not because of what I said, surely?'

She didn't answer.

'I mean, it was just a silly mistake.'

'Some people bruise easily, Michael.' She turned around. Her face was flushed. 'I don't, any more. But I was young at the time. And not very sure of myself. Anyway, it's all forgotten now. It was a long time ago.'

'Yes, but I had no idea. Really I didn't.'

'You're forgiven,' said Phoebe, and then tried to rescue the mood by asking: 'Have I changed much since then?'

'Hardly at all. I would have recognized you anywhere.'

She decided not to point out that he had noticeably failed to recognize her at the Narcissus Gallery's private view a couple of months ago. 'Do you ever hear from Joan?'

'Yes, I saw her. Saw her just recently, as it happens. She married Graham.'

'That figures.' Phoebe rejoined him on the bed. 'And they're both well, are they?'

'Fine, yes, fine. I mean, Graham was almost dead when I last saw him, but I should think he's recovered by now.'

This required a certain amount of explanation, so Michael told her all that he knew about Graham's documentary and Mark's abortive assassination attempt.

'So now *he's* fallen foul of the Winshaws, too,' said Phoebe. 'They seem to get everywhere, this family, don't they?'

'Of course they do. That's the whole point about them.'

She thought a little more about his story, and asked: 'What were you doing in this hospital over New Year?'

'I was visiting someone. A friend. She got taken ill unexpectedly.'

Phoebe detected an abrupt change of tone. 'You mean – like a girlfriend?'

'Something like a girlfriend, I suppose.'

He lapsed into silence, and she suddenly felt that her questions had been intrusive and unnecessary.

'I'm sorry, I – didn't mean to pry . . . I mean, it's none of my business –'

'No, that's all right. Really.'

He forced a brief smile.

'She died, didn't she?' said Phoebe.

Michael nodded.

'I'm so sorry.' She put her hand on his knee for a few, embarrassed moments; then withdrew it. 'Do you want – I mean, would it help to talk about it?'

'No, I don't think so. Not really.' He squeezed her hand, to show that her gesture had not gone unnoticed. 'It's silly, really, I'd only known her for a few months. We never even slept together. But somehow or other, I managed to . . . invest in her, quite heavily.' He rubbed his eyes, adding: 'Makes her sound like a public company, doesn't it? I'm starting to talk like Thomas.'

'What did she die of?'

'The same thing that gets everybody, in the end: a combination of circumstances. She had a lymphoma, which could have been treated, but certain people chose to arrange things so that it didn't happen. I'd been meaning to have a word with Henry about it, while I was up here, but . . . there's no point, now, is there. Nothing . . . more to be . . .' His words dried up and he stared into space for what seemed a very long time. Finally he said one more word, very softly, but with emphasis: 'Shit.' Then he keeled over and lay curled up on the bed in a foetal position, with his back towards Phoebe.

After a while she touched him on the shoulder, and said: 'Michael, why don't you stay here tonight? I don't fancy spending the night alone, and we'd be company for each other.'

Michael said: 'OK. Thank you.' He didn't move.

'You'd better get undressed.'

Michael undressed down to his underwear, slipped between the sheets of the double bed and fell asleep almost instantly; just finding the time to murmur: 'Joan asked me to stay in her bedroom once. I ran away. I don't know why.'

'She was very fond of you, I think,' said Phoebe.

'I've been so stupid.'

Phoebe put on her nightshirt and got into bed beside him. She turned off the lamp. They lay back to back, with an inch or two of space between them.

Michael dreamed about Fiona, as he had done every night for the last two weeks. He dreamed that he was still sitting beside her hospital bed, holding her hand and talking. She was listening to him and smiling back. Then he dreamed that he had woken up to the realization that she was dead, and started to dream that he was crying. He dreamed that he was reaching out in the bed and touching a warm female body. He dreamed that Phoebe had turned towards him and put her arms around him and was stroking his hair. He dreamed that he was kissing her on the lips and that she was returning his kiss, her mouth open, her lips soft and warm. He dreamed the warm smell of her hair and the warm smoothness of her skin as his fingers touched the small of her back beneath her nightshirt. He tried to remember when he had last had this dream, this dream of waking up and finding that he was in bed with a beautiful woman, waking up in the joyful awareness that she was touching him, that he was touching her, that they were dovetailed, entangled, coiled like dreamy snakes. This dream where it seemed that every part of his body was being touched by every part of her body, that from now on the entire world was to be apprehended only through touch, so that in the musty warmth of the bed, the curtained darkness of the bedroom, they could not but find themselves starting to writhe gently, every movement, every tiny adjustment creating new waves of pleasure. Michael was dreading the moment when the dream would end: when he would wake up for the last time and find himself alone in bed, or when he would be overtaken by a still deeper sleep and fall into another dream of emptiness and loss. But it didn't happen. Their love was long, slow and sleepy, and although there were times when they did nothing but lie together, drowsily entwined, these intervals of huddled stillness were all part of a single movement, perpetual and effortless, during which they slid rhythmically in and out of sleep, rocked back and forth between dreaming and waking, and had no knowledge of the passing of time until Michael heard the grandfather clock in the hallway strike five, and turned his head to see Phoebe's eyes smiling at him in the dark.

'Kenneth,' he said, 'you'll never know what you missed.'

'My name isn't Kenneth,' said Phoebe. She laughed as she rummaged around in the tousled sheets for her nightshirt, then struggled into it. 'Don't tell me you were thinking about someone called Kenneth all that time. Although I suppose it would at least explain why you and Joan never got it together.'

She climbed out of bed and made for the door. Michael sat up, his mind still foggy with sleep, and said in an abstracted way: 'Where are you going to go now?'

'To the lavatory, I thought, if I have your permission.'

'No, I meant – whenever. You know, as soon as all this is over.'

Phoebe shrugged. 'I don't know: back to Leeds, maybe. I can hardly stay here, at any rate.'

'Come and live with me in London.'

She didn't say anything to this at first, and Michael couldn't see how she had reacted.

'I'm serious,' he added.

'I know you are.'

'I mean, I know you must like me. Otherwise –'

'I don't really think this is the time. And it certainly isn't the place.' She opened the door. He could hear her pause before leaving. 'Slow down, Michael,' she said: not unkindly. 'We're neither of us ready to make plans.'

A few minutes later she returned and climbed back into bed. They held hands beneath the sheets.

'I knew you'd ask me to stay the night in here,' Michael said, surfacing from some private train of thought.

'Women usually find you irresistible, do they?'

'No, but it happens in the film, you see. Almost exactly this situation. That was when I had to leave the cinema. And now that it's actually happened, it's almost as if . . . a spell's been broken.'

'All sounds very fatalistic to me. I suppose I had no choice in the matter, then?'

'There *is* a film, you know,' Michael insisted. 'I wasn't making it up, whatever Hilary may have thought.'

'I believe you,' said Phoebe. 'Anyway, I'd heard about it before.'

'You had? When?'

'Joan mentioned it once: don't you remember? That night when she made us all play Cluedo, and there was a terrible storm.'

All at once the memory came back to Michael in vivid detail. The four of them clustered around the table in Joan's sitting room . . . Graham laughing at him because of the misprint in his review . . . And the feeling he'd had – a premonition, you might call it – when he'd found out that his character, Professor Plum, was the murderer, and it had no longer been possible to think of himself as detached, disinterested . . . To find yourself suddenly at the centre of things . . .

Then he remembered Tabitha's last, enigmatic words, and light dawned.

'I thought I was supposed to be writing this story,' he said, 'but I'm not. At least not any more. I'm part of it.'

Phoebe stared at him. 'What?'

Michael sprang to his feet, saying: 'God, I've been slow. Of course I'm part of it – *that's* why Tabitha chose me.'

'I haven't the faintest idea what you mean.'

'She said I had his eyes: my father's eyes. There's only one person she could have been talking about. My mother said the same thing. That was what made me so angry in the restaurant. Even Findlay noticed it. He said they were like . . . blue velvet, or something. And I thought he was just trying to get me into bed.'

'You've lost me, Michael. Completely lost me. Who on earth's Findlay?'

'He's a detective. Tabitha hired him, years ago. Listen.' He made Phoebe sit up, and explained: 'Tabitha had a brother called Godfrey, who was killed in the war. Shot down by the Germans.'

'I know all that. And she also had a brother called Lawrence, who she hated, and when she went mad she started accusing him of murder, or something.'

'That's it. Only she was right: he did tip the Germans off about Godfrey's mission, and that was why he got shot down. I'm almost certain of it. But there was also a co-pilot, who *didn't* get killed. He was put in a POW camp and after the war he came back to this country. He drifted around and went to seed a bit, and did all sorts of jobs under different names. John Farringdon was one of them, and Jim Fenchurch was another.'

'Yes, and what about him?'

'Well I'm his son.'

Phoebe's eyes widened in disbelief.

'You're what?'

Michael said it again, and she let out a cry of exasperation. 'Well, don't you think it might have been a good idea to share this with us earlier?'

'But I've only just realized. In fact, I'm going to have to ask Tabitha about it right now.' He got up, turned the light on, and began dressing as quickly as he could.

'Michael, it's five o'clock in the morning. She'll be fast asleep.'

'I don't care. This is urgent.' He squeezed himself clumsily into his shoes. 'You know, I don't think Tabitha's mad at all. I think she's been playing a very clever game.' Opening the door, he concluded dramatically: 'Unless I'm very much mistaken, she's as sane as I am.'

'Saner, perhaps,' said Phoebe. But not loud enough to hear.

CHAPTER EIGHT

Back Room Boy

MICHAEL needn't have worried about interrupting Tabitha's sleep. There was a light coming from her room, the door was unlocked, and she was sitting up in bed, knitting and listening to a transistor radio placed on the bedside table.

'Why, Michael,' she cried. 'You've come even sooner than I expected! Is it time for our little chat already?'

'John Farringdon,' he said, coming straight to the point. 'He was my father, wasn't he?'

'So, you're there at last, are you? Well done, Michael. Very well done! Although, to be perfectly frank with you, I *was* expecting you to get there a little earlier. How long has it taken you now? Nearly nine years, I think. And yet, from reading your books, I'd formed the impression that you were quite an intelligent man.'

Michael drew up a chair next to the bed. 'All right,' he said. 'I know you're playing with me now. Have you been playing with me all along?'

'Playing with you, Michael? That's not a very nice accusation to make. I've been helping you. I've always wanted to help you. It's been my only thought.'

'Look – I've had no help from you: none at all. You never even contacted me in all that time.'

'I've given you rather a lot of money, none the less. Hasn't that been of any use?'

'Yes, of course.' Michael blushed, ashamed to be reminded that he hadn't even thanked her for her generosity in this area. 'Of course it has. But how was I to – I mean, if it hadn't been for Findlay, I would never even have got *near* the truth of this whole business.'

'Findlay? Surely you don't mean Mr Onyx? Mr Findlay Onyx, the detective? Is he still alive, Michael?'

'Certainly he is. Alive and in prison even as we speak.'

'And I can guess what for!' said Tabitha, laughing merrily. 'Oh, he was a naughty little man. Very naughty indeed. But most professional, I have to admit. It was Mr Onyx who managed to locate your father for me, of course. He told you all about that, I take it?'

'Yes, he did.'

'So you know that your father was killed by Lawrence, in this very house? The night of Morty's birthday party?'

Michael nodded.

'I was very disappointed, I must say,' said Tabitha. 'I really thought that Mr Farringdon would have had no difficulty finishing my brother off. But clearly one should never take these things for granted. I was in extremely low spirits when Mr Onyx came to see me the next morning.' She shook her head, smiling. 'He was a most conscientious man. Most reliable. He came – at some risk to himself, I must say – to deliver an envelope, containing some of Mr Farringdon's effects. Among which, I found –'

'– a photograph?'

'Exactly, Michael! A photograph. Perhaps you're not quite as slow as I thought. A photograph of you, sitting at your desk and writing. You can only have been about ... eight years old, would you say? There was a little girl in the picture as well. Not very pretty, I'm afraid. Rather prominent teeth. Mr Farringdon was very attached to this photograph, anyway. He'd told me all about it, in one of our long conversations at the Institute, where he had been kind enough to come and visit me on a number of occasions. Oh, yes, those were pleasant afternoons. We talked about all sorts of things. One day, I remember, we had a long and most stimulating discussion about the Lockheed Hudson. I'd always been concerned, you see, about the high amount of magnesium alloy used in construction. It seemed to me that it made the aircraft very vulnerable to fire, particularly if the integral fuel tanks were to rupture. Now, of course, Mr Farringdon had never flown one himself, but ...' Her eyes had glazed over, and she now turned to Michael with a look of bewilderment. 'I'm sorry, dear, what was I saying?'

'The photograph.'

'Ah, yes, the photograph. Well, I held on to it, of course, just as he'd asked me to, although I'm afraid it gave me no means of finding you, because he'd neglected to tell me your name. Perhaps he never even knew it himself. And then one day – it would have been, oh, almost twenty years later – a most extraordinary thing happened. One of the doctors came up to my room and brought me a magazine. Wasn't that thoughtful of him? All of the staff are familiar with my little hobby, you see, and this was a colour magazine with a lovely long article in it, all about the Mark I Hurricane. Well, I have to say that it *wasn't* very well researched: I was most disappointed. The author missed several important points – never even mentioned, would you believe, its one real advantage over the Spitfire, which, as you know, was the thickness of the section wings. I actually wrote a letter of complaint to the editor, but it was never published. I wonder why . . .'

There was a dangerously long silence, and Michael realized that she had drifted off again.

'Anyway, about this magazine.'

'I'm sorry: I do tend to get distracted sometimes. The magazine. Precisely. Well, after I'd read this article, I started to look at some of the other items, and imagine my surprise, Michael – imagine my delight, and astonishment – when I found, tucked away at the very back, a charming little short story about a castle and a detective, and at the top of it, the very same picture which Mr Farringdon had given me all those years ago. A picture of you, Michael! You as a little boy! Fate had delivered you into my hands, at last, and not only that, but it turned out that you'd become a *writer*. It was all too, too perfect! I began to think of a little plan, which would enable me to make financial reparation for what my family had done to you – I knew that you would be short of money, it went without saying: *all* writers are short of money – and which, at the same time, would inevitably lead you to find out the truth about your father and how he died. You would discover the truth about my family, Michael, and reveal it to the world, in the form of a book. And what a book it would be! I envisaged . . . a tremendous book, an *unprecedented* book – part personal memoir, part social commentary, all stirred together into one lethal and devastating brew.'

'Sounds wonderful,' said Michael. 'I should have hired you to write the blurb.'

'I think, in retrospect, that I overestimated you,' said Tabitha. 'Much as I enjoyed the extracts which you sent to me, my expectations had been too high. I see now that you weren't quite equal to the task. You lacked the necessary . . . dash, the necessary . . . daring, the necessary . . . what *is* the word?'

'Brio?'

'Perhaps, Michael. Perhaps that's what you lacked, in the end.' She sighed. 'But then, who could really do justice to my family? Liars, cheats, swindlers and hypocrites, the lot of them. And Lawrence was the worst. By far the worst. To betray your country for money is bad enough, but to send your own brother to his death . . . Only my family could do such a thing. When it happened, I realized for the first time what they were really like: and after that, what did it matter if they locked me away? I didn't care what became of me.' She sighed again, even more heavily. 'It quite spoiled my war.'

'You say that almost as if you'd been enjoying it,' said Michael.

'But of course I was enjoying it,' said Tabitha, smiling. 'We all were. It's so hard for you young people to understand, I know, but there's nothing like a good war for pulling a country together. Everyone was so *nice* to each other, for a while. Everything that had divided us suddenly seemed so petty and inconsequential. Things have changed, since then. Changed terribly. Changed for the worse. We were all so *polite*, you see. We observed the niceties. Mortimer, for instance . . . He would never have behaved like this, running around the house and chopping his family up with axes and knives and what have you. It would never have entered his head, in those days.'

'I imagine not,' said Michael. 'Still, it won't happen again, I don't suppose.'

'What won't happen again, dear?'

'A war like that.'

'But we're at war now,' said Tabitha. 'Hadn't you heard?'

Michael looked up. 'We are?'

'Of course. The first bombers were sent out shortly after midnight. I've been listening to it on the wireless.'

Michael was stunned. Even after the expiry of the UN deadline, he had somehow never believed that it would happen. 'But that's terrible,' he stammered. 'It's a disaster.'

'Not at all, not at all,' said Tabitha cheerfully. 'The allies will have no difficulty establishing air superiority. The F-117A Nighthawk is a most sophisticated craft. The navigation system, you know, features an INAS with both Forward-Looking and Downward-Looking Infra-Red sensors, and it can carry up to four thousand pounds of explosives at speeds of five hundred and fifty miles an hour. The Iraqis have got nothing like it. And then there are the F-111s: well, Colonel Gadaffi already knows what *they* can do. With EF-111A Ravens blinding the enemy's acquisition radars, they can fly through an attack corridor at more than fifteen hundred miles an hour. Their weapons bay accommodates up to fourteen tons of ordnance –'

Michael had already lost interest. There were more urgent matters to consider. 'So you think it *is* Mortimer?' he asked.

'Of course it is,' said Tabitha. 'Who else would it be?'

'It's just that these killings – they've obviously been carried out by someone who knows all about the family. What they've been up to, over the years. But Mortimer hasn't really seen any of them for a long time, has he? How would he know those things?'

'Why, that's simple,' said Tabitha. 'Mortimer's read your book, you see. Whenever you sent me part of your manuscript, I would always forward a copy on to him. He found it most interesting. So in a way, Michael, you *are* responsible for all of this. You should feel very proud of yourself.'

She went back to her knitting, while Michael brooded over the role he could now be seen to have played in this bizarre story. He felt anything but proud.

'Where is he now?' he asked.

'Morty? Well, I'm afraid that's very difficult to say. He's hiding somewhere, that's for sure, but this house is full of secret passages. It's a veritable warren. I found that out the night I locked Lawrence in his bedroom. A few minutes later, you know, he was downstairs playing billiards, so there *must* be some hidden link between the two rooms.'

'That's right – you'd heard him in his room, hadn't you,

speaking in German?' It was all starting to become clear. 'Could he have been talking into a radio set, do you think?'

'Certainly he could.'

Michael leapt up. 'Which room was it?'

'It's at the far end of the corridor. The one where young Roderick has been staying.'

He ran out into the corridor and went to find Phoebe, knowing that she had the only key. But she was no longer in bed. Gripped by a sickening anxiety, Michael swung around only to find that she was now standing in the doorway behind him, a grim expression on her face.

'Quick,' he said. 'We've got to get into Roddy's room.'

'Too late. I've just come from there.' Her voice was shaking. 'Come and have a look.'

It was not a pleasant sight. Roddy was lying on top of the bed, naked and motionless. He had been covered from head to foot in gold paint, and must have been dead for two or three hours.

'Suffocation, I assume,' said Phoebe. 'Painted to death: I suppose we should have guessed it.' She frowned. 'Isn't that from a film as well?'

'Shirley Eaton in *Goldfinger*,' said Michael. 'Mortimer's certainly been doing his homework.'

'I still don't see how he could have got in. The key's been in my trouser pocket all night. Unless he's got another copy, of course.'

'This used to be Lawrence's bedroom,' said Michael. 'Which means there's a secret door somewhere, and a passage which leads downstairs. Come on, let's see if we can find it.'

They circled the room, knocking on each of the panels to see if any of them gave off a hollow sound. When this produced no result, Michael unlocked the double-doored wardrobe which had been built into one of the walls, and peered inside.

'Hello, what's this?' he shouted.

Phoebe ran over. 'Have you found it?'

'Well, I've found something.'

He reached into the wardrobe and pulled out a pair of garments – a jacket and trousers, in navy blue. On closer inspection they turned out to comprise the uniform of a police sergeant.

479

'What did I tell you? That wasn't a policeman at all. And look, here's the rest.'

He handed Phoebe a peaked cap, and as he did so, a small glass vial was disclosed on the shelf behind it.

'Potassium chloride,' he read slowly, examining the label. 'Have you ever heard of this?'

'It's a poison,' said Phoebe. 'Mortimer used to keep it in his medicine chest. Only the last time I saw it, it was full.'

She pointed at the level of the liquid, which now filled only about a quarter of the bottle.

'Is it deadly?'

Phoebe nodded. 'I remember now – the day he sent me away, just before I left, he was asking me where the syringes were. I didn't think anything of it at the time. Perhaps this might have something to do with it.'

'Could be.'

'Hang on, then – I'll go and check if they're still there.'

She hurried off in the direction of her former employer's sick chamber, where it took very little time to establish that at least one syringe had gone missing from its case. But when she returned to inform Michael of this news, a surprise awaited her. Roddy's naked corpse was still lying on the bed, but otherwise the room was empty. Michael himself had vanished.

*

It had been instinct, more than anything else, which had drawn him to the elaborately gilt-framed mirror on the bedroom wall. A mirror was a doorway to the underworld: Michael had learned this by now, and so it was the work of only a few moments to slide his fingers behind the frame and ease it away from the wall. The mirror swung open on a stiff hinge, revealing a black, rectangular cavity; and as soon as he stepped through into the darkness, it closed behind him without a sound. When Michael tried to push it open again he could obtain no purchase, and he knew that, for the time being, the only way to go was forward. He could see and hear nothing; but there was a stale, musty smell in the air, and the bare-bricked walls to either side of him were dry and flaking. Very tentatively, he put one foot in front of the other, and immediately realized that he was standing at the top of a staircase; but he had descended only three steps when the floor beneath him levelled out, and he could sense that he had now entered upon a wider space. He took six paces to his right, and found himself touching a wall: this time it was smooth and plastered. He started edging around this wall, and after taking two changes of direction and bumping into something heavy – a table, perhaps – his hands touched upon the very thing that he had been praying for: a light switch. And, miraculously, it worked.

Michael was standing in a very narrow but high-ceilinged chamber, apparently built into the thickness of the wall. Besides the short staircase he had just descended, there was also a tiny doorway leading off to the left. Standing against one of the walls, but large enough to take up most of the available space, was a desk; and placed on top of it, a heavy, unwieldy set of radio apparatus. The desk and the radio were thick with dust, and in the four or five decades (so Michael hazarded) since they had last been touched, whole dynasties of spiders had been busy weaving blanket upon blanket of fine, powdery webs. The room was windowless; but a thin trail of aerial wire could be seen running up the wall and through a hole in the ceiling, presumably to emerge on the roof of the house itself.

'So this is where you did it, you cunning devil,' Michael muttered. 'A regular little back room boy!'

Impatiently he swept aside most of the dust and the cobwebs. The radio seemed to have been battery operated and, unsurprisingly, it did not respond when he tried flicking the various switches; but a quick search of the desk drawers proved more rewarding. There were maps, almanacs and railway timetables from the 1940s, along with a German–English dictionary and what appeared to be some sort of address book. Leafing through it, Michael came across not only BISCUIT, CHEESE and CELERY but also the codenames of other double agents – CARROT, SWEETIE, PEPPERMINT, SNOW, DRAGONFLY – all with addresses and telephone numbers written alongside them. Personal details of many high-ranking figures from the military, the War Cabinet and the coalition government had also been noted down. A leather-bound accounting book was filled with parallel rows of figures in pounds and Deutschmarks, while a page at the back listed the names and addresses of several British and German bank accounts. And there were, in addition, some loose sheets of paper, one of which in particular caught his eye. It was headed:

$$L\,92\,65 - 53\;Sqn.$$

This, Michael knew, had been the number of Godfrey's plane and squadron. Most of the figures which followed were incomprehensible to him, although '30/11' was clearly an indication of the date, and some of the other numbers looked as though they might refer to positions of latitude and longitude. It was certain, in any case, that he had at last stumbled upon the proof of Lawrence's treachery: his calculated betrayal of Godfrey for financial gain.

Michael was now torn between two conflicting impulses: to return to Phoebe (if he could) and explain his discovery, or to try his luck with the other doorway and continue exploring. For once, his spirit of adventure won the day.

The second exit led directly on to another staircase, this one steeper and more uneven than the last. By leaving the door to the little room wedged open, Michael found that he had just enough light to illuminate his progress, and before long he calculated that he had descended to the level of the ground floor, at which point the steps ended. He was now standing at the entrance to a narrow passage. Darkness began to encroach.

In the wall of the passage, after only a few paces, he came upon a wooden door. It was bolted at the top, but the mechanism was well oiled and seemed to have been in recent use. He opened it without difficulty, and found himself looking out, as he had expected, into the billiard room. Dawn would not come for an hour or two yet, but a certain amount of moonlight was peeping through gaps in the curtains, and in the shadows he could make out Mark's corpse, which had now been covered with a blood-stained sheet. His severed arms still rose grotesquely, like savage totems, from the pockets of the billiard table. Michael shuddered, and was about to withdraw when he noticed a metallic glint at the table's edge. It was Mark's cigarette lighter. This was too useful to pass up, so he stole across the room and grabbed it before beating a grateful retreat into the tunnel, the entrance to which was seamlessly concealed behind a rack of billiard cues clamped to the oak panelling.

Michael had not gone much further along the passage before the roof and walls began to close in, making movement more difficult. For a while he had to crouch almost on his hands and knees, and he could tell that the floor was beginning to slope steeply downwards. Once or twice, twin pinpoints of light in the distance would betoken the presence of a watchful rat, which would then scurry away at his approach. The tunnel remained dry, however, and the mortar would sometimes crumble as he brushed against it, so he was surprised when he began to hear a distinct dripping noise, irregular but insistent.

Plip. Plip. Plip.

At this point, too, a flickering light began to appear, getting stronger all the time, and the space between the walls began to broaden out. Suddenly the passage opened into what was almost a room. The roof, composed of stone flags, was supported by beams, and the four walls formed a square some sixteen feet across.

Plip. Plip.

The source of the dripping was readily apparent. The first that Michael saw of it was a fantastically enlarged shadow, dancing unsteadily in the light from a burning candle set on the floor. It was the shadow of a human body, trussed up neatly and tied by the ankles to a meat hook screwed into one of the beams. A small incision had been made in the neck, from which blood flowed in a steady trickle, across the face, down through the tangle of clotted hair, and into a heavy steel bucket which was now almost full.

Plip. Plip. Plip.

It was the body of Dorothy Winshaw; and beside it, sitting on a little three-legged stool, was her uncle Mortimer. He looked up at Michael as he emerged from the tunnel, but it was impossible to say whose eyes were more tired and expressionless: the eyes of Mortimer, or those of the frozen, slowly rotating cadaver.

Plip.

'Is she dead?' said Michael at last.

'I think so,' said the old man. 'But it's rather hard to say. It's taken longer than I thought.'

'What a horrible way to kill someone.'

Mortimer thought about this for a moment.

'Yes,' he agreed.

Plip.   Plip.

'Mr Owen,' Mortimer continued, speaking with great effort. 'I do hope you aren't going to expend any pity on members of my family. They don't deserve it. You should know that better than anybody.'

'Yes, but all the same . . .'

'It's too late now, in any case. What's done is done.'

Plip.   Plip.   Plip.

'We're underneath the sitting room, in case you were wondering,' said Mortimer. 'If there was anybody up there now, we could hear them. I stood here some hours ago, and listened to all the fuss they made when Sloane read out the will, and they realized they weren't going to get a penny out of me. A childish contrivance, I suppose.' He grimaced. 'Vain. Foolish. Like everything else.'

Plip.

Mortimer closed his eyes, as if in pain.

'I've led an idle life, Mr Owen. Wasted, for the most part. I was born into money and like the rest of my family I was too selfish to want to do any good with it. Unlike them, at least, I never did anyone much harm. But I thought I might redeem myself, slightly, by doing mankind a small favour before I died. Ridding the world of a handful of vermin.'

Plip.   Plip.

'It was you, Mr Owen, who finally persuaded me. That book of yours. It gave me the idea, and suggested one or two possible . . . approaches. Now that it's done, however, I must confess to a certain sense of anti-climax.'

As he spoke these words, Mortimer was toying in his right hand with a large syringe filled with clear liquid. He noticed that Michael was watching him apprehensively.

'Oh, you needn't worry,' he said. 'I don't intend to kill you. Or Miss Barton.' His expression seemed to soften for a moment at the mention of this name. 'You will look after her, won't you, Michael? She's been good to me. And I can see that she likes you. It would make me happy, to think . . .'

'Of course I will. And Tabitha, too.'

'Tabitha?'

'I'll make sure that she's not taken back to that place. I don't know how, but – I won't let it happen.'

Plip.

'But you do know, of course,' said Mortimer, 'that she's mad?'

Michael stared at him.

'Oh, yes.' He smiled distractedly. 'Quite, quite mad.'

'But I've just been talking to her. She seemed perfectly –'

'It runs in the family, you see. Mad as hatters, queer as coots, and nutty as fruitcakes, every one of us. Because there comes a point, you know, Michael' – he leaned forward and pointed at him with the syringe – 'there comes a point, where greed and madness become practically indistinguishable. One and the same thing, you might almost say. And there comes another point, where the willingness to tolerate greed, and to live alongside it, and even to assist it, becomes a sort of madness too. Which means that we're all stuck with it, in other words. The madness is never going to end. At least not . . .' (his voice faded to a ghostly whisper) '. . . not for the living.'

Plip.   Plip.

'Take Miss Barton, for instance.' Mortimer's speech was starting to slur. 'Such a kind girl. So trusting. And yet I was deceiving her all that time. My legs were in reasonable shape. A few ulcers, here and there, but nothing to stop me walking around. I simply liked to be fussed over, you see.'

Plip.   Plip.   Plip.

'I'm so tired, Michael. That's the irony of it, really. There's only ever been one thing wrong with me, and I haven't even mentioned it to Miss Barton. She has no idea. Can you guess what it is?'

Michael shook his head.

'Insomnia. I can't sleep. Can't sleep at all. An hour or two, every now and again. Three, at the most. Ever since Rebecca died.'

Plip.

485

'And what a night it's been! It's all been far, far too much. The exertion. I thought I'd never make it, to be frank with you.' He slumped forward, his head in his hands. 'I'd so like to sleep, Michael. You will help me, won't you?'

Michael took the syringe from his outstretched hand, and watched as Mortimer rolled up his sleeve.

'I don't think I have the strength left in my fingers any more, that's the pity of it. Just put me to sleep, Michael, that's all that I ask.'

Michael looked at him, undecided.

'Out of the kindness of your heart. Please.'

Michael took hold of Mortimer's hand. The skin was hanging off his arms. He had the eyes of an imploring spaniel.

Plip. Plip.

'They send dogs to sleep, don't they? When they're old, and sick?'

And he supposed, put like that, that it didn't sound so bad.

CHAPTER NINE

With Gagarin to the Stars

'No explanations,' said Michael. 'If you sleep, if you dream, you must accept your dreams. It's the role of the dreamer.'

Phoebe shielded her eyes against the sunlight. 'Sounds plausible. What does it mean?'

'I was just thinking: there are three dreams I had when I was a kid which I can still remember clearly. And now two of them have come true: more or less.'

'Only two? What about the third?'

Michael shrugged. 'You can't have everything.'

They were standing on the terrace at Winshaw Towers, looking out over the lawns, the gardens, the tarn, and the magnificent sweep of the moors beyond. Bright sunshine had succeeded the storm, although there were felled trees, fallen tiles and windswept debris everywhere to testify to its effect.

It was almost midday: the end of a long, gruelling morning, during which they seemed to have done nothing but give statements to the policemen who had been swarming all over the house ever since Phoebe had walked to the village and raised the alarm. Shortly after ten o'clock, the first journalists and press photographers had arrived. So far the police had been successful in holding them at bay, but they were even now spread out on the road like an army waiting in ambush, keeping the house covered with a whole arsenal of telephoto lenses, or sitting sulkily in their cars hoping to pounce on anybody who dared venture down the drive.

'I wonder if things will ever get back to normal,' said Michael. He turned urgently to Phoebe. 'You will come and see me in London soon, won't you?'

'Of course: as soon as I can. Tomorrow, or the day after.'

'I don't know what I'd have done, if you hadn't been here.' He smiled. 'Every Kenneth needs his Sid, after all.'

'What about "Every Orpheus needs his Eurydice"? Just to clear up any gender confusion.'

But Michael seemed dejected by this analogy. 'I'll never forgive myself, you know, for what happened about that painting.'

'Look, Michael, let me just say something. We're never going to get anywhere, you and me, by harping on about the past. The past is a mess, in both our cases. We've got to put it behind us. Agreed?'

'Agreed.'

'All right, so repeat after me: DON'T - LOOK - BACK.'

'Don't look back.'

'Good.'

She was about to reward him with a kiss when they were joined on the terrace by Hilary's pilot, Tadeusz, who had also arrived that morning. He was, it had to be said, a far cry from Conrad, the previous holder of this desirable position: for he was barely five feet tall, well over sixty years old, and, having only recently settled in this country from his native Poland, could not speak a word of English. He nodded brusquely to Michael and Phoebe and then stood at some distance from them, leaning against the balustrade.

'I think Hilary's husband must have put his foot down,' Phoebe whispered. 'Her last pilot was this godlike specimen. They came up here once and romped naked on the croquet lawn for most of a weekend. Somehow I can't see this one entering into quite the same spirit.'

'Oh well, as long as he knows how to fly a plane,' said Michael. 'He's supposed to be taking me home this afternoon.'

*

Little more than an hour later, Michael was packed and ready to leave. Phoebe, who was planning to take an afternoon train to Leeds in the company of Mr Sloane, walked with him down to the edge of the tarn. They had been unable to find Tadeusz anywhere in the house, but the agreed take-off time was one o'clock, and Michael was relieved to see the pilot's diminutive figure already squeezed into the cabin. He was fully dressed for the part, in what seemed to be an authentic World War I flying ace costume, complete with goggles and leather helmet.

'My God, it's the Red Baron,' said Phoebe.

'I hope this guy knows what he's doing.'

'You'll be fine.'

He put his case down and hugged her.

'See you soon, then.'

Phoebe nodded, stretched up on her toes, and kissed him on the mouth. He clung on to her tightly. It was a long kiss, which after a fierce start became more leisurely and tender. Michael enjoyed the feel of her hair blowing in his face, the coldness of her cheek.

Reluctantly, he climbed into the cabin.

'So, this is it, I suppose. I'll phone you tonight. We'll make plans.' He was about to close the door, but hesitated. There seemed to be something on his mind. He looked at her for a moment, and then said, 'You know, I had an idea about that painting. I can remember it quite clearly: so I was thinking that if we sat down and I described it to you, and you found your old sketches, you could maybe – Well, at least do something similar . . .'

'What did I say to you up on the terrace?' said Phoebe sternly.

Michael nodded. 'You're right. Don't look back.'

Phoebe waved as the plane taxied round into the take-off position, and blew a kiss after it as it gathered speed and cleared the surface of the water, rising smoothly into the air. She watched until it was nothing more than a black speck against the blueness of the sky. Then she turned and walked back up to the house.

Her heart was heavy with foreboding. She was worried about Michael: worried that he already expected too much of her, worried that his preoccupation with the past was somehow obsessive; or adolescent, even. It was hard to remember, sometimes, that he was seven or eight years her senior. She was worried that the relationship might proceed too quickly, taking directions over which she had no control. She was worried that she could actually think of no good reason – if she was honest with herself – for having started it in the first place. It had all happened too quickly, and she had been acting out of the wrong motives: because she had felt sorry for him, and because she too had been scared and in need of comfort. Besides, how could they ever hope to forget the horrific circumstances which had brought them together? How could anything good come from such a beginning?

She went up to her bedroom, packed her suitcase, and then looked around to see if she had forgotten anything. Yes – there were some first-aid things, she now remembered, which would still be in the room where Henry's body had been found. It would only take a minute to retrieve them, and yet for some reason the prospect filled her with disquiet. She found that she was shivering as she walked along the corridors, and climbing up to the second floor of the house, she had the sudden, ominous sense that she had begun to relive the events of the night before: an impression reinforced as she turned the last corner and heard the sound of the television set, tuned to the one o'clock news.

She opened the door. President Bush was addressing an empty room. It was a re-run of his broadcast to the American people, made shortly after the first bombers had been sent in to Baghdad.

Just two hours ago, allied air forces began an attack on military targets in Iraq and Kuwait. These attacks continue as I speak.

Phoebe noticed something: a stream of blood was running down the side of the sofa and dripping on to the floor.

The twenty-eight countries with forces in the Gulf area have exhausted all reasonable efforts to reach a peaceful resolution, and have no choice but to drive Saddam from Kuwait by force. We will not fail.

She peered gingerly over the back and saw that a man was lying face down on the sofa, a carving knife sticking out from between his shoulder blades.

Some may ask: Why act now? Why not wait? The answer is clear: the world could wait no longer.

She turned the man over and gasped. It was Tadeusz.

This is an historic moment.

There was a knock on the door, and one of the police officers on duty popped his head round.

'Has anyone seen Miss Tabitha?' he said. 'We can't seem to find her anywhere.'

Our operations are designed to best protect the lives of all the coalition forces by targeting Saddam's vast military arsenal. We have no argument with the people of Iraq. Indeed, for the innocents caught in this conflict, I pray for their safety.

Would the madness never come to an end?

*

Michael sits in the cabin of the seaplane, craning forward and watching the South Yorkshire landscape unroll beneath him.

The pilot, sitting up ahead, starts humming a tune: *Row, row, row the boat, gently down the stream.* The pilot's voice seems unusually high and musical.

The world could wait no longer.

The plane starts to climb sharply. Michael cannot see the reason for this, and stiffens in his seat. He thinks it will surely level out, in a second or two. But the ascent becomes steeper and steeper, until suddenly they are vertical, and then they are upside down, and then before Michael has even had a chance to scream, they have looped a complete loop and regained their original position.

'What the hell do you think you're doing?' he shouts, grabbing the pilot by the shoulder. But the pilot is quivering with laughter – hysterical, unstoppable laughter – and crying out for joy.

Merrily, merrily, merrily, merrily

'I said, what the hell do you think you're doing?' Michael repeats.

We have no argument with the people of Iraq.

'Have you gone raving mad?'

The pilot's laughter grows even more hysterical when Michael says this, and then the goggles and the leather helmet are torn off, and Tabitha Winshaw turns around to say: 'You know, Michael, it's just as I thought – these things are terribly easy, once you get the hang of them.'

Row, row, row the boat, gently down the stream
Merrily, merrily, merrily, merrily
Life is but a dream.

'Where's Tadeusz, for God's sake?' shouts Michael.

Our goal is not the conquest of Iraq. It is the liberation of Kuwait.

'Do you want me to show you how it's done?' says Tabitha.

Michael is shaking her roughly backwards and forwards.

491

'Do you know how to land this thing? Just tell me that.'

'This dial, you see,' says Tabitha, pointing at one of the flight instruments, 'is the Air Speed Indicator. Green for normal, yellow for caution. See here, where it says VNO? That means the normal operating limit speed.'

Indeed, for the innocents caught in this conflict, I pray for their safety.

Michael watches as the arrow on the dial starts pushing its way out of the green arc and into the yellow arc. The speed of the acceleration is making him feel sick. The arrow is now at the upper end of the yellow arc, at a point marked VNE.

'What does that mean?' he says.

'Never exceed,' cries Tabitha. She is almost jumping out of her seat with excitement.

'For God's sake, Tabitha, slow down. This is dangerous.'

She turns around again and says, reprovingly: 'Flying, Michael, is *never* dangerous.'

'It isn't?'

'Not at all. It's *crashing* that's dangerous.'

And then, with a shrill, lunatic howl of laughter, she pushes the joystick forward to its fullest extent, the plane tips forward and now they plunge, hurtling downwards at unthinkable speed, and Michael is hollow, his body is an empty shell, his mouth is open and everything that was inside him has been left way behind, way up in the sky . . .

I'm going down, I'm going down, I'm going down.

Tonight, as our forces fight, they and their families are in our prayers.

Row, row, row the boat, gently down the stream

The noise is deafening, the terrible whine of engine and airstream, and yet above it all he can still hear Tabitha's mad laughter: the endless, hideous laughter of the irredeemably insane . . .

Merrily, merrily, merrily, merrily

No president can easily commit our sons and daughters to war.

I'm going down, I'm going down.

May God bless each and every one of them.

Going down . . .

This is an historic moment.

Until there comes a point . . .

Merrily, merrily
Comes a point where greed . . .
Merrily, merrily
A point where greed and madness . . .

And then there is the final scream of metal, the piercing laceration as sections of the fuselage start to tear themselves apart, until at once the whole plane breaks up and shoots off in a million different directions, and he is in freefall, diving, unshackled, nothing but blue sky between Michael and the earth which he can see clearly now, rising up to meet him, the coasts of continents, islands, big rivers, big surfaces of water . . .

Merrily, merrily, merrily, merrily
I am no longer in pain . . .
Life is but a dream
I am no longer afraid . . .
Life is but a dream

. . . because there comes a point where greed and madness can no longer be told apart. This dividing line is very thin, just like a belt of film surrounding the earth's sphere. It's a delicate blue, and this transition from the blue to the black is very gradual and lovely.

The world could wait no longer.

THE
WINSHAW LEGACY
*
A Family Chronicle

MICHAEL OWEN

PEACOCK PRESS

Preface

by Hortensia Tonks, B.A., M.A.(Cantab.)

Signor Italo Calvino, an Italian writer held in some considerable esteem among the literary *cognoscenti*, once remarked – very beautifully, in my view – that there is nothing more poignant than a book which has been left unfinished by its author. Such fragmentary works, in the opinion of this distinguished gentleman, are like 'the ruins of ambitious projects, that nevertheless retain traces of the splendour and meticulous care with which they were conceived'.

How appropriate, how sweetly ironic, that Sig. Calvino should have delivered himself of this lofty sentiment in the course of a series of essays which were themselves left incomplete at the time of his death! And how fitting the phrase now seems, when applied to the present volume, the truncated work of an author cut down, as it were, in his literary prime, which shows him writing at the height of his powers (and which in time, perhaps, will be recognized as his masterpiece)!

I knew Michael Owen well, and feel towards his book much as a doting parent must feel towards a favourite child, for it blossomed and took shape under my benign aegis. And so when we at the Peacock Press heard the bitter news of his death, our initial sense of shock and bereavement was succeeded by the knowledge that we could do no better justice to his memory than by sending his last work upon its way with all despatch. It is for this reason alone (despite the malicious hints which have been dropped in various quarters of the press) that we publish it so soon after the sensational events which have recently aroused keen public interest in the Winshaw family and all its doings.

One might lament the keenness of this interest; but to ignore it altogether would surely be folly. I have therefore taken the liberty of including, by way of introduction to Michael's history, a full and detailed account of the horrific murders which took place at Winshaw Towers on the night of January 16th this year. The composition of this chapter – compiled on the basis of authentic police records and photographs (more graphic and distressing, I am told, than any previously encountered in the long career of the pathologist who supplied them) – gave me no pleasure at all; but the public has an absolute right of access to even the most disagreeable particulars of such an affair. This is a point of high principle, and one which we, as publishers, have always been proud to uphold.

It also occurred to me, in my capacity as editor, that there were certain passages in Michael's manuscript so laudably academic in tone, so rigorous in their historical perspective, that they might have proved a trifle daunting to those readers who were drawn to the book out of little more than a natural and wholesome curiosity to know more about the January massacre. My advice to such readers, then, would be that they can safely ignore the main body of his narrative, for my intention in the remainder of this Preface is to summarize, in a few concise, vivid pages, the entire early history of the family whose very name – once a by-word for all that was prestigious and influential in British life – has now become synonymous with tragedy.

*

Tragedy had struck the Winshaws twice before, but never on such a terrible scale.

Author's Note

I'd like to thank Monty Berman, co-producer of the film *What a Carve Up!*, for kindly allowing me to quote from the screenplay (written by Ray Cooney and Tony Hilton). Thanks also to Louis Philippe for permission to quote from his song 'Yuri Gagarin' (words and music by Louis Philippe, published by Complete Music, copyright © 1989); to Raymond Durgnat, whose marvellous essay on *Le Sang des Bêtes* (in *Franju*, published by Studio Vista, 1967) furnished me with a quotation in Dorothy's chapter and eventually suggested the title of Part Two; and to International Music Publication Ltd for permission to reproduce 'La Mer' by Charles Louis Augustine Trenet, copyright © 1939 Brenton (Belgique) Editions Raou, administered by T.B. Harms Co., Warner Chappell Music Ltd, London.

My novel owes a shadowy debt to the works of Frank King, author of *The Ghoul* (1928), upon which the film *What a Carve Up!* was distantly based. Paragraph one of my chapter 'Where There's a Will' is copied from the first chapter of *The Ghoul* (with one word changed), and throughout Part Two there are several smaller instances of what Alasdair Gray has called 'Implags' (imbedded plagiarisms) both from *The Ghoul* and from the equally wonderful *Terror at Staups House*. Having been unable to trace any information on Mr King, the only repayment I can offer him is to recommend that readers make every effort to seek out these and other novels (*What Price Doubloons?*, for instance, or *This Doll is Dangerous*) and campaign vigorously for their reissue.

Among the other people who helped me in various ways were Harri Jenkins and Monica Whittle, who gave generously of their time to fill me in on Health Service issues and hospital procedure; Andrew Hodgkiss and Stephanie May, who provided further medical background; Jeremy Gregg, for computer literacy; Michèle O'Leary, for legal expertise; Paul Daintry, for Findlay's signature and general encouragement; Tim Radford, for Yuriology; plus Russell Levinson, Ralph Pite, Salli Randi, Peter Singer, Paul Hodges, Anne Grebby and Steve Hyam. I'm especially grateful to everyone at Viking Penguin who has worked so hard for the book, and to the inestimable Tony Peake, Jon Riley and Koukla MacLehose, whose efforts on its behalf have been tireless.

As for my printed sources, Mark's chapter is based largely on information gleaned from Kenneth Timmerman's *The Death Lobby* (Fourth Estate, 1992) – surely the best book ever written about the arms market – which gave me the dead beagles and the apple-shooting, among other things. Details of Iraqi torture practices were obtained from publications by Amnesty International and CARDRI (the Campaign Against Repression and for Democratic Rights in Iraq); SODI is a fictitious organization. Dorothy's chapter draws on the pioneering work of Ruth Harrison in her book *Animal Machines* (Vincent Stuart, 1964), supplemented by Mark Gold's *Assault and Battery* (Pluto, 1983), Geoffrey Cannon's *The Politics of Food* (Century, 1987) and Richard Body's *Our Food, Our Land* (Rider, 1991). Of the many books consulted for Thomas's chapter, by far the most readable and informative were two by Paul Ferris: *The City* (Gollancz, 1960) and *Gentlemen of Fortune* (Weidenfeld, 1984). NHS data was furnished by Chris Ham's *The New National Health Service: Organization and Management* (Oxford, 1991), and I learned about wartime codenames from Sir John Cecil Masterman's fascinating book, *The Double-Cross System in the War of 1939 to 1945* (Yale, 1972).

This novel owes its existence, finally, to Janine McKeown, not least because she supported me financially while I was writing it. For this and other reasons, I dedicate it to her with love and gratitude.

ANIMAL DREAMS

ANIMAL DREAMS

A NOVEL BY

BARBARA KINGSOLVER

HarperCollins*Publishers*

FIRST EDITION

Designed by Helene Berinsky

Library of Congress Cataloging-in-Publication Data

Kingsolver, Barbara.
  Animal dreams : a novel / by Barbara Kingsolver.—1st ed.
    p.   cm.
  ISBN 0-06-016350-X
  I. Title.
PS3561.I496A86   1990   86-46571
813'.54—dc20

---

90 91 92 93 94 NK/HC 10 9 8 7 6 5 4 3 2

in memory of Ben Linder

CONTENTS

AUTHOR'S NOTE

Grace, Arizona, and its railroad depot are imaginary, as is Santa Rosalia Pueblo, although it resembles the *Keresan* pueblos of northern New Mexico. Other places, and crises, in the book are actual.

I'm grateful for the example provided by many nonfictional volunteers from the United States who went to live and work for a new social order in Nicaragua during the decade following the 1979 revolution. Alongside the Nicaraguan people, they have made indelible contributions to that country, and to history.

For their support and contributions to this book I also owe a warm debt of thanks to my editor at Harper & Row, Janet Goldstein, my literary agent, Frances Goldin, and my remarkable family, especially Jessica Sampson (locomotive engineer extraordinaire), Wendell and Ginny Kingsolver, Joe Hoffmann, and Camille Hoffmann Kingsolver, who has attached me securely to this world.

1

THE NIGHT OF ALL SOULS

His two girls are curled together like animals whose habit is to sleep underground, in the smallest space possible. Cosima knows she's the older, even when she's unconscious: one of her arms lies over Halimeda's shoulder as if she intends to protect them both from their bad dreams. Dr. Homer Noline holds his breath, trying to see movement there in the darkness, the way he's watched pregnant women close their eyes and listen inside themselves trying to feel life.

A slice of white moon from the window divides their bodies deeply into light and shadow, but not one from the other. No light could show where one body ends and the other begins when they're sleeping like this. Maybe a mother's eye could tell, but that is the one possibility that can't be tried.

Halimeda's bed is still made. In the morning she'll rumple it so he'll believe she slept by herself, and then the girls will make it again. Their labors at deceiving him are as careful as surgery. But morning is worlds away now, it's still early night on the Day of All Souls. The two of them spent the whole day playing in the cemetery with neighbor children, Pocha and Juan Teobaldo and Cristobal and the twin babies, helping Viola Domingos build a bower of marigolds over the grave of a great-grandmother who is no part of this family.

3

For a long time he stands gripping the door frame, which is exactly the width of a newborn's skull and curves similarly against his palm. He watches his daughters, though there's nothing to watch, and thinks these words: "A great-grandmother who isn't their business." He decides this will be their last year for the cemetery and the Day of All Souls. There are too many skeletons down there. People count too long on the oblivion of children.

They're deep in the corpselike collapse that takes hold of children when they are exhausted, but still he won't risk going in to stand over the bed the way he once would have. He would see the usual things: unraveled braids and the scraped shins hidden from his punishing antiseptics. Tonight he would also see cheeks and eyelids stained bright yellow from marigold pollen. He's spent a lifetime noticing small details from a distance. From the doorway he smells the bitterness of crushed marigold petals on their skin.

There is a deeper draft of breath and they both move a little. Their long hair falls together across the sheet, the colors blending, the curled strands curving gently around the straight. He feels a constriction around his heart that isn't disease but pure simple pain, and he knows he would weep if he could. Not for the river he can't cross to reach his children, not for distance, but the opposite. For how close together these two are, and how much they have to lose. How much they've already lost in their lives to come.

COSIMA

2

HALLIE'S BONES

I am the sister who didn't go to war. I can only tell you my side of the story. Hallie is the one who went south, with her pickup truck and her crop-disease books and her heart dead set on a new world.

Who knows why people do what they do? I stood on a battleground once too, but it was forty years after the fighting was all over: northern France, in 1982, in a field where the farmers' plow blades kept turning up the skeletons of cows. They were the first casualties of the German occupation. In the sudden quiet after the evacuation the cows had died by the thousands in those pastures, slowly, lowing with pain from unmilked udders. But now the farmers who grew sugar beets in those fields were blessed, they said, by the bones. The soil was rich in calcium.

Three years later when my sister talked about leaving Tucson to work in the cotton fields around Chinandega, where farmers were getting ambushed while they walked home with their minds on dinner, all I could think of was France. Those long, flat fields of bone-fed green. Somehow we protect ourselves; it's the nearest I could come to imagining Nicaragua. Even though I know the bones in that ground aren't animal bones.

7

▼▼▼

She left in August after the last rain of the season. Summer storms in the desert are violent things, and clean, they leave you feeling like you have cried. Hallie had never left me before. It was always the other way around, since I'm three years older and have had to do things first. She would just be catching up when I'd go again, swimming farther out into life because I still hadn't found a rock to stand on. Never because I wanted to leave. Hallie and I were so attached, like keenly mismatched Siamese twins conjoined at the back of the mind. We parted again and again and still each time it felt like a medical risk, as if we were being liberated at some terrible cost: the price of a shared organ. We never stopped feeling that knife.

But she went. And true to the laws of family physics, the equal and opposite reaction, I was soon packed up too and headed northeast on a Greyhound bus. In our divergent ways, I believe we were both headed home. I was bound for Grace, Arizona, where Hallie and I were born and raised, and where our father still lived and was said to be losing his mind. It was a Sunday. I had a window seat, and in a Greyhound you're up high. You pass through the land like some rajah on an elephant looking down on your kingdom, which in this case was a scorched, bristling landscape and the tops of a lot of cars. It wasn't all that different from my usual view of life, because I'm tall, like my father and Hallie. I don't look like who I am. They do, but I don't.

It was midmorning when I stepped down off the bus in Grace, and I didn't recognize it. Even in fourteen years it couldn't have changed much, though, so I knew it was just me. Grace is made of things that erode too slowly to be noticed: red granite canyon walls, orchards of sturdy old fruit trees past their prime, a shamelessly unpolluted sky. The houses were built in no big hurry back when labor was taken for granted, and now were in no big hurry to decay. Arthritic mesquite trees grew out of impossible crevices in the cliffs, looking as if they could adapt to life on Mars if need be.

I was the only passenger getting off. The short, imperious

bus driver opened the baggage door and made a show of dragging out luggage to get to mine, as if I were being difficult. A
more accommodating woman, he implied, would be content
with whatever bags happened to be right in front. Finally he
slapped my two huge suitcases flat out in the dust. He slammed
the doors and reclaimed his throne, causing the bus to bark like
a dog, leaving a cloud of exhaust in the air, getting the last word,
I suppose.

The view from here was orchards: pecan, plum, apple. The
highway ran along the river, dividing the orchards like a long,
crooked part in a leafy scalp. The trees filled the whole valley
floor to the sides of the canyon. Confetti-colored houses perched
on the slopes at its edges with their backs to the canyon wall.
And up at the head of the canyon was the old Black Mountain
copper mine. On the cliff overlooking the valley, the smelter's
one brick smokestack pointed obscenely at heaven.

I dragged my bags to the edge of the street. Carlo, my lover
of ten years, whom I seemed to have just left, would be sending
a trunk from Tucson when he got around to it. I didn't own very
much I cared about. I felt emptied-out and singing with echoes,
unrecognizable to myself: that particular feeling like your own
house on the day you move out. I missed Hallie. Carlo, too—
for the lost possibilities. At the point I left, he and I were still
sleeping together but that was all, just sleeping, with our backs
touching. Sometimes Hallie would cough in the next room and
I'd wake up to find my arm over his shoulder, my fingers touching his chest, but that's only because it takes your sleeping self
years to catch up to where you really are. Pay attention to your
dreams: when you go on a trip, in your dreams you will still be
home. Then after you've come home you'll dream of where you
were. It's a kind of jet lag of the consciousness.

Carlo loved Hallie. When he and I moved back to Tucson the
three of us contrived a little household in a bad neighborhood,
with jade plants on our front steps that kept getting stolen till
Hallie thought to bolt down the pots. We played house to beat
the band. Hallie and I made prickly-pear jelly, boiled and
strained and poured blood-red into clean glass jars. We'd har-
vested the fruits from the physical therapy garden of the hospital

where Carlo worked. A nun saw us out there with our grocery sack while she was walking an old man around the little race track, and Hallie and I just waved. We said we were living off the land.

Our home fell apart when she left. She was our center of gravity, the only one of us who saw life as a controllable project. Carlo was an orphan like me. We forgot about the jade plants, they went crisp as potato chips out on the porch, and Carlo withered as if he needed water also. Every man I'd ever loved had loved Hallie best and settled for me. It didn't bother me as much as you might think; I could understand it. I loved her too.

And now his life with the Noline women had run its course. He could go where he pleased. Carlo was a rolling stone: an emergency-room doctor, which gave him a kind of freedom almost unknown to the profession. You can always find work if you're willing to take up with a human body as soon as possible after one of life's traumas has left off with it. Carlo and I met in medical school, and in our years together he and I probably had more addresses than the Grace, Arizona, phone book. Along the way I'd landed a few presentable jobs, but in between I tended to drift, like a well-meaning visitor to this planet awaiting instructions. My career track had run straight down into the weedy lots on the rough side of town. It's the truth. For the last six months in Tucson I'd worked night shift at a 7-Eleven, selling beer and Alka-Seltzer to people who would have been better off home in bed. There wasn't a whole lot farther I could go. Now I was here.

A high-school friend, Emelina Domingos, had offered to meet my bus but I'd told her, No, don't bother, I'll make my own way. The plan was for me to live in the Domingos' guesthouse. Not with my father. My relationship with Doc Homer had always improved with distance, which is to say that mail was okay and short, badly connected phone calls were best. I thought I should still keep some miles between us, even though he was ill and conceivably dying. It was going to be touchy. He would be an unwilling candidate for rescue, and I was disaster in that department myself. But he had only two living relatives and the other one was behind the wheel of a Toyota pickup headed for

Nicaragua. I stood my suitcases side by side and sat on them for a minute to get my bearings. I think I was hoping Emelina might still show up.

There was no evidence of human life, or life that was *ongoing* in any obvious way. The one vehicle parked in front of the courthouse, a blue station wagon, had four flats and a bumper sticker stating "ONE DAY AT A TIME." I suspected it had been there in 1972, the year I finished high school, when I last climbed on a Greyhound and turned my back on Grace. There wasn't a soul on the street today and I thought of those movies in which a town is wiped clean of its inhabitants, for one reason or another—a nuclear holocaust, say, or a deadly mutant virus—leaving only a shell of consumer goods. The point, I think, is to make some statement about how we get carried away with all our trappings, but this wasn't the place to shoot a movie like that. Grace hadn't yet entered the era of parking meters, for example. There were iron rings mortared into the block wall of the courthouse where a person could tie a horse.

I tried to imagine Doc Homer coming downtown on horseback, looking silly, his tall, stiff spine bouncing up and down against his will. I erased the fantasy from my mind, feeling guilty. It was too late to be taking imaginary revenge on my father.

There wasn't much to Grace's commercial district. The window of the Hollywood Dress Shop leered from across the street, framing a ferocious display of polyester. The headless mannequins were dressed to the nines, with silver vinyl loafers and red nail polish. If I moved a little I could put my reflection there in the window with them: me in my Levi's and Billy Idol haircut. (I was the one with a head.) A friend of mine used to make bizarre collages like that—Nancy Reagan in mink among the slaves on an Egyptian mural; Malibu Barbie driving sled dogs in the Iditarod. She sold those things for good money.

The Hollywood Shop was flanked by Jonny's Breakfast (open all day) and the movie theater. Back behind these buildings ran the railroad tracks. On the other side of Jonny's were the State Line Bar and the Baptist Grocery. I tried to place myself inside these stores; I knew I'd been there. Directing Hallie through the grocery aisles on a Saturday, ticking off items from Doc Homer's list. Sitting in Jonny's afterward, hunched in a booth drinking forbidden Cokes, reverently eying the distant easy grace of the girls who had friends and mothers. But I couldn't see it. Those things didn't seem so much like actual memories as like things I might remember from a book I'd read more than once.

I had lied on the bus. I'd told the woman sitting next to me that I was a Canadian tourist and had never been to Grace. Sometimes I used to do that, tell tales on buses and airplanes—it passes the time. And people love you for it. They'll believe anything if you throw in enough detail. Once I spent a transatlantic flight telling a somber, attentive man about a medical procedure I'd helped develop in Paris, in which human cadavers could be injected with hormones to preserve their organs for transplant. I would be accepting a prestigious medical prize, the name of which I devised on the spot. The man seemed so impressed. He looked like my father.

I didn't do it anymore, I was more or less reformed. What I'd said that morning was the truest kind of lie, I guess, containing fear at its heart: I *was* a stranger to Grace. I'd stayed away fourteen years and in my gut I believe I was hoping that had changed: I would step off the bus and land smack in the middle of a sense of belonging. Ticker tape, apologies, the luxury of forgiveness, home at last. Grace would turn out to be the yardstick I'd been using to measure all other places, like the mysterious wornout photo that storybook orphans carry from place to place, never realizing till the end that it's really their home.

None of this happened. Grace looked like a language I didn't speak. And Emelina wasn't coming. I hefted up my suitcases and started to walk.

Oh Lord, the terror of beginnings. I dreaded having to see all the people who were going to say, "How long are you home for, honey?" Possibly they would know I'd come for the school year. We would all carry on as if this were the issue: the job. Not Doc Homer, who'd lately begun addressing his patients by the names of dead people. Since I really did need to come, I'd gotten myself hired to replace the high-school biology teacher who'd recently married and defected without warning. I had practically no teaching qualifications, I should add, and things like that get around. It's tough to break yourself as news to a town that already knows you. Grace formed its opinions of Hallie and me before we had permanent teeth. People here would remember our unreasonable height in seventh grade, and our unfortunate given names; our father actually named my sister Halimeda, which means "thinking of the sea," however reasonable a thing that might be to do in a desert. And my own name, Cosima, means something to the effect of "order in the cosmos" which is truly droll, given my employment history. I must have sensed the lack of cosmic order in my future, early on. Maneuvering for approval, I'd shortened it to Codi in the third grade, when Buffalo Bill and the Pony Express held favor with my would-be crowd.

Hallie was a more natural abbreviation, from the time she could walk people never called her anything but that, although *Halimeda* actually had some truth in it; she made you look for things beyond what you could see. I could imagine Doc Homer dreaming up these names, confident we'd both take noble courses. Suddenly I felt dragged down by emotions as I walked along, as if I'd swum out into a calm sea and encountered a bad undertow. I carried my suitcases toward the edge of town.

An old, densely planted pecan orchard stretched out from the edge of the courthouse square, and somewhere behind it lay Emelina's place. The reflected sky ran like a vein of silver in the irrigation ditch, but when I left the street and stepped under the canopy of trees it was dark. If you've never walked through an old orchard, you have to imagine this: it presents you with an optical illusion. You move through what looks like a hodgepodge thicket of trees, but then at intervals you find yourself at the center of long, maddeningly straight rows of trees, standing like soldiers at attention. There's a graveyard in northern France where all the dead boys from D-Day are buried. The white crosses reach from one horizon to the other. I remember looking it over and thinking it was a forest of graves. But the rows were like this, dizzying, diagonal, perfectly straight, so after all it wasn't a forest but an orchard of graves. Nothing to do with nature, unless you count human nature.

A bird scream rang out from the leaves and echoed up my spine with a shiver that ended in my scalp. I believe it was the first sound I'd heard since the gear grinding of the bus. I stopped to listen. Quiet. Then another bird answered from behind me, close by. It sounded like the throaty, exotic laughter of a foreigner—like a jungle bird. The peacocks. These orchards were full of peacocks, living more or less wild and at the mercy of coyotes but miraculously surviving in droves. There was a local legend, supposedly true, about how they got here a hundred years ago: the nine blue-eyed Gracela sisters came over from Spain to marry nine lucky miners in the gold camp, sight unseen. Back then these hills were run through with gold veins and drew a crowd of men who had too much money and too little love. The sisters were just children, and only agreed to come if they could bring their birds with them in the hold of the ship. Their legacy in Gracela Canyon was a population of blue-eyed, dark-haired descendants and a thousand wild peacocks. Their father stayed behind and got rich by proxy, for he'd literally sold his girls for a gold mine.

The branches were ringing with bird calls now. And I could hear kids laughing. A whole chorus of them screamed at once. Toward the far end of the orchard I could make out children's silhouettes jumping and dancing under the trees. It was dark in there for midday but I definitely saw kids: little girls in billowy dresses and boys in white shirts. I couldn't make out their game. The tallest boy had a stick and they were chasing something and flailing at it. I walked down the row toward them, towing my bigger suitcase like an anchor. I was traveling light in theory, but I'd dragged with me into Grace a substantial reference library. It had taken me a lot of nervous weeks to narrow down what books to bring. At the very last minute I'd thrown out Gray's *Anatomy* because Doc Homer would have it.

I stepped over the irrigation trenches, mindful of my Italian leather uppers. I'm picky about shoes, and there was no replacing these now. I smiled, thinking of the awful silver loafers in the Hollywood Shop. I envisioned my predecessor at the high school dressed like that, standing in front of a classroom of fifteen-year-olds, twisting her white chiffon scarf as she explained cell division. What would these kids make of me? My shoes were pointed and my, as the magazines say, personal style leaned toward apologetic punk. I'd never had a teacher who looked like me; probably there was a reason.

I stopped to massage my aching shoulder. There was something up there at the edge of the orchard all right, a bunch of kids, and something in the trees over their heads. I thought about skirting around the little gang to avoid spoiling their fun, or maybe, actually, because I was afraid. I tried to move quietly. Whatever it was they were chasing, they were going to get it.

I could see plainly then that it was a heavy-bodied peacock shuffling from side to side on a low branch. Apparently the creature was too dull-witted or terrorized to escape, or possibly already injured. The children pursued it ferociously, jumping up and pulling at its long tail feathers, ready to tear it to pieces. The boy with the stick hit hard against the belly and they all shrieked. He hit it again. I couldn't see the stick but I heard the sickening whack when it made contact.

I looked away. I'd arrived in Grace, arrived at that moment in my life, without knowing how to make the kind of choice that was called for here. I'm not the moral guardian in my family. Nobody, not my father, *no one* had jumped in to help when I was a child getting whacked by life, and on the meanest level of instinct I felt I had no favors to return. Especially to a bird. It was Hallie's end of my conscience that kept pinching me as I walked. I dropped my bags and walked a little faster, trying to think of some commanding thing to say. If they didn't stop soon the thing would be maimed or dead.

"Stop it!" I yelled. My heart was thumping. "You're killing that bird!"

The boy froze like a rabbit in headlights. The other kids, down on their knees, stared too. I'd arrested them in the act of grabbing fistfuls of bright paper and candy that sparkled on the ground. The mute peacock swung over their heads on a wire. Its fractured body hung in clay shards the size of plates, held together by a crepe-paper skin.

When I was ten I'd demolished a piñata exactly like this one, with blue paper wings and a long glossy tail of real feathers. At a birthday party. At some time or other every child in Grace had done the same.

After an impossible few seconds they went back to scrambling for their prize. Two older girls helped the smallest kids scoop candy into piles in their laps. A cluster of boys elbowed and slapped each other behind the girls' backs.

I felt disoriented and disgraced, a trespasser on family rites. I walked away from the little group of kids back toward the place in the center of the orchard where I must have left my suitcases. I wondered in what dim part of Grace I'd left my childhood.

3

THE FLOOD

The leaves shine like knife blades in the beam of his flashlight. The rain has slowed, but the arroyo is still a fierce river of mud and uprooted trees that won't crest until dawn. He is wet and chilled to his spine. The girls are lost. The sound of the flood makes his blood cold.

They wanted to gather prickly-pear fruits for jelly. They knew a storm was coming and they went anyway, while he was in his workroom. He follows the narrow animal path between thickets of thorn scrub along the bank, shining his light along the edge of the rising water. Acacias lean into the river with their branches waving wildly in the current, like mothers reaching in for lost babies. The girls ignore his cautions because they are willful children who believe nothing can harm them. Hallie is bad but Cosima is worse, pretty and stubborn as a wild horse but without an animal's instincts for self-preservation—and she's the older. She should have some sense.

He forces his body through the bank of oleanders near the house and turns back toward the riverbed to search the arroyo to the south. He has no idea which way they would have gone; they roam this desert like pocket mice. And everything in a desert is poisonous or thorned. Good Lord, he has already lost a wife, and did not think his heart would live beyond her. *Wished* it wouldn't. He slashes at the oleanders with the metal flashlight. He'd meant to cut these down when Cosima was born. One well-chewed leaf could bring on cardiac arrest in a child. He'd seen a case years ago, or was it later, after the girls left home? That blue girl?

Doc Homer sits up in his bed and stares at the orange pill bottles on the windowsill. There is light at the window. It's a Sunday morning in August. It is only a month ago he lost that blue girl. His own daughters are grown and living somewhere else, looking after themselves, but his heart is still pumping hard. His circulatory system believes they are still lost.

He turns his pillow and rests his head on it carefully because his brain gets jostled and things move around inside his head like olives in a jar of brine. Think about the flood. He is going south on the near side of the arroyo. He stops to look back upstream and his light finds them, by pure luck, on the opposite bank. Cosima's thin, waving arms shine like the crisscrossing blades of scissors. They are screaming but he only sees their mouths stretched open like the mouths of fledgling birds. Absolute expectation, Papa will save us. The road is washed out, and he has to think how else he will get to them. He realizes, stunned, that they have been huddled there for half a day. The road has been washed out that long.

How does he reach them? A boat? No, that wouldn't have been possible. He sits up again. He has no clear image of reaching them, no memory of their arms on his neck, he only hears them crying over the telephone. And then he understands painfully that he wasn't able to go to them. There is no memory because he wasn't there. He had to call Uda Dell on the other side of the arroyo. Her husband was alive then, and went down the bank on his mule to find them in a washed-open coyote burrow with seven pups the girls wanted to save.

"There were seven," she'd wailed over the telephone. "I could carry four but Hallie could only get one in each hand and we didn't want to leave the other one. He would have gotten drowned." Cosima is sobbing because in the end, after crouching for half a day in the small shelter of that gravel bank, waiting for the mother coyote to come back and save her children, they had to leave them. He hears Hallie shrieking in the background. They're both crying as if they are drowning themselves. Drowning pups.

When he gets them home they sit hugging each other on the davenport, wrapped in the black-and-red crocheted afghan. They won't stop shaking. They want to know if the baby coyotes died. If animals go to heaven. He has no answers. "We tried to put them in the paper bag we used for the prickle pears, but it fell all apart." The tears stream out until the afghan is wet and he thinks there will be no more fluid in them to run the blood cells through their veins. He makes them drink orange juice. God, why does a mortal man have children? It is senseless to love anything this much.

COSIMA
▼▲▼▲▼▲▼▲▼▲▼

4

KILLING CHICKENS

Emelina's was a pleasant, ramshackle place with animals, an old plum orchard and five boys. When I walked up the drive with my suitcases they were preparing to kill roosters. Emelina's eyes and mouth drew wide and she looked briefly like a surprised fish. "Codi, this is *Sunday*, I thought you said *tomorrow*."

"No, it was today, I'm here," I said apologetically. I was glad I hadn't waited any longer at the courthouse.

"Shoot, you look like a fifty-dollar bill. Where'd you get that haircut, Paris, France?" She gave me a hug and waved her hand at the driveway. "I'm sorry about this mess. We've just got the water boiled for the birds. Shoot."

I'd just witnessed what I'd thought was going to be the slaughter of a peacock, so I laughed, but this time it was real murder and mayhem. The drive was lined with pails, paper bags, and a tragically stained wooden block that had been used before. Emelina's twins, who were about ten, each held a fat white rooster by the feet. A younger brother was riding a tricycle precariously over the rocky ground. I put down my suitcases.

"Curty and Glen, look at you," I said. "And Mason. You guys are getting too big."

"Aunt Codi, look. If you hold them upside down they go to sleep," Glen said.

Curty said, "No, they get hypnotized."

"Well, either way it's a handy trick," I said. "You don't want them to see what's coming."

Emelina looked dismayed. "Codi, we don't have to do this now. What a god-awful thing to do in front of company."

"I'm not company. You're all set up, so do it. You can't go out of your way for me if I'm going to live here."

She rolled her eyes. "Go on back to the granny house then. John Tucker was supposed to sweep it out this morning before he went to his baseball practice but I'll fall over dead if he did it right now, instead of feeding the baby. I'll bet you fifteen dollars he's laying in the house watching the MTV."

John Tucker was Emelina's oldest, but I couldn't picture him old enough to feed the baby. I hadn't yet seen the baby, since he'd only arrived six months ago. But over the years Emelina and I had kept up. I'd taped her kids' school pictures to the woodwork of Carlo's and my many ill-furnished apartments. Sometimes repairmen would ask if they were my boys.

I went around to the side yard and pushed open a wire gate that wouldn't have kept out a determined hen. The guesthouse in the back faced the big ranch house across a huge brick court-yard that was wild and overrun with flowering vines. Every inch of space was taken up with fruit trees, painted flowerpots, and lawn chairs that looked like they'd been there since the last war. I could hear chickens clucking softly somewhere out of sight, and at the back of the courtyard a goat stretched its neck to get at a fig tree.

The guesthouse had a pink door flanked by pots of geraniums, whose crimson flowers stood out against the white walls like wine stains blooming on a tablecloth. Inside, the little house was whitewashed and immaculate. There were two brick-floored rooms: a living room and bedroom. The light pouring in the windows was stirred up by the motion of fig branches outside. The bed had a carved headboard, painted with red enamel, and a soft-looking woven spread. It was a fairytale bed. I wished I could fall down and sleep a hundred years in this little house with pale crisscrossing shadows on the walls.

I heard the goat moving around outside, munching loudly and bumping against the wall. I opened cupboards. Everything was spotless. The east window in the living room looked straight out onto the granite wall of the canyon a few yards away, a startling lack of view. Emelina's place was the last and highest on her street, backed up against the canyon. The floorboards of her front porch were on a level with her neighbors' roofs.

I took my time exploring. I savored the first minutes in a new home. Carlo would always go straight to unpacking boxes, looking for the sheets and coffeepot and swearing that we were going to get better organized, while I stepped stealthily over the bare floors, peeking around corners and into alluring doors, which generally turned out to be the broom closet. But there was that thrilling sense that, like a new lover, the place held attributes I had yet to discover. My favorite book as a child was *The Secret Garden*. It's embarrassing to think I'd merrily relocated again and again, accompanying Carlo to the ends of the earth, because of the lure of a possible garret or secret closet. But it might be true.

I tried out the two very old chairs in the living room. They had rose slipcovers and were comfortable. In a corner near the window was a beehive fireplace, and next to it, a clay vase of peacock feathers. Every home in Grace had one of those; it was a local feature. You could pick up half a dozen peacock feathers on any given day, in the orchards, as you went about your business. When the vase was full, you took them to one of the old women who made real-feather piñatas, and then you started your collection over. The practice had not been allowed in our house because Doc Homer said the feathers were crawling with bird mites; he dreaded to think what those old women's houses were harboring in the way of microorganisms. It became Hallie's and my joke. Whenever he unreasonably forbade us to do something, we'd look at each other and mouth the words "bird mites."

The bathroom and kitchen must have been added on about mid-century. The refrigerator looked prehistoric, but worked. It contained a loaf of fresh bread in a paper bag, some tomatoes and figs, a block of goat cheese, and a six-pack of Miller Lite.

Emelina's estimation of the bare essentials. I popped open a beer and went back around the house in time to witness the demise of the second rooster.

"Is it okay that there's a goat loose in the courtyard?" I asked Emelina.

"Shit! I'm going to tan John Tucker's hide. *John Tucker!*" she yelled. "Get your damn goat out of the garden, please, or we'll have him for dinner!"

There was a noise from inside and the back door slammed.

"You don't really want to watch this, Codi," she said. "But I guess you see a lot worse in your line of work."

I sat on the porch rail. I was no longer in the doctoring line of work. It's true I'd been educated to within an inch of my life, and had done well in medical school. My mistake was assuming medicine was a science like any other. If it's carburetors you know, you can fix cars, I reasoned; if it's arteries and tendons you fix people. For reasons that were unclear to me, I'd learned the science but couldn't work the miracle: I'd had a crisis while trying to deliver a baby. My problem turned out to be irreversible. Emelina knew all this. I was *here*, after all, with no more mission in life than I'd been born with years ago. The only real difference between then and now was wardrobe.

"Tell me if I can help," I said.

She ignored me. "Okay, watch your hands, Curty. Keep them way back." Emelina was small, but didn't give that impression. Her jeans had "Little Cowboy" stitched on the label, and undoubtedly belonged to one of her sons. Emelina and I graduated from high school the same year, 1972. Under my picture in the yearbook it said, "Will Go Far," and under Emelina's it said, "Lucky in Love." You could accept this as either prophecy or a bad joke. I'd gone halfway around the world, and now lived three-quarters of a mile from the high school. Emelina had married Juan Teobaldo Domingos the same June we graduated. Now J.T. worked for the railroad and, as I understood it, was out of town most of the time. She said it didn't bother her. Maybe that's as lucky as love gets.

Curty laid his hypnotized rooster on the block and held its

feet, keeping the rest of his body as far away as possible. It never regained consciousness. Emelina swung the axe over her shoulder and brought it down on the mark. The pink, muscular neck slipped out of the collar of feathers as if the two parts had been separately made. The boys hooted and chased after the body as it thrashed across the dirt. But I was fascinated by the head: the mouth opened and closed, silently, because the vocal cords were in the part that had been disconnected.

"That's the way, Curty," Emelina directed. "Don't get blood on your brother. Dip him all the way in. Now pluck him quick or he'll go stiff on you. Start with the wings, see how Glen's doing?" She wiped perspiration out of her eyes.

I was amazed by the muscle definition in her upper arms and her easy command of the axe. Her hands stayed surprisingly clean through the whole operation. She reminded me of Hallie, the way she could do things. Though of course Hallie would never decapitate anything.

"I can't believe you're watching this," she said when both boys were settled down to plucking feathers. She went inside and came out with a beer. She sat down next to me on the wide wooden rail, knocking the heels of her sneakers against the crossbar like a child. I was very conscious of my height. Sometimes I had an acute feeling that small women were better put together somehow, more in control of their bodies.

"You used to have a hissy fit when we'd go over to *Abuelita's* and she'd be killing chickens," Emelina said. "Remember? Even when we were big, twelve or thirteen."

"No, that was Hallie. She's the one that had such a soft heart. We've always been real different that way. She'd cry if she stepped on a bug." I drained my beer. "She's still like that, except now she cries about bag ladies. I swear. She gives them quarters and then she wishes she'd given them a dollar."

I stared out at the treetops and the leaf-green gables of the roof on a house below us. The shingles were an odd, elaborate shape like the spade in a deck of cards. I wondered in what decade they'd stopped making shingles like that, and how this neighbor might repair the roof after a bad storm.

"You really do look great," Emelina said. "That's a terrific haircut, I mean it. You'll stand out in a crowd here till you get your first cut down at Beth's Butcher Shop."

I ran my fingers over my weedy scalp, feeling despair. I'd spent my whole childhood as an outsider to Grace. I was willing to march downtown and submit myself to butchery this minute if that would admit me to the club. I'd led such an adventurous life, geographically speaking, that people mistook me for an adventurer. They had no idea. I'd sell my soul and all my traveling shoes to *belong* some place.

"I always forget you have so much auburn. Doc Homer had the same coloring, didn't he? Sort of reddish before he went gray?" She fingered her own shoulder-length hair. "Speaking of him . . ."

"Speaking of him," I said.

"Have you talked to him?" She looked apprehensive. Emelina was my informant. When he started getting lost on his way home from the drugstore, she was the one person in Grace who thought to call me, rather than just draw him a map.

"I'll go up and see him tomorrow."

"And where's Hallie gone? You told me, but I forgot."

"Nicaragua," I said. "To save the crops. Cross between Johnny Appleseed and a freedom fighter."

Emelina laughed and I felt disloyal. I hadn't meant to sound glib. It was just hard to put Hallie into the context of regular life. "I guess it's really dangerous," I said. "But she's excited about it. She'll be happy." I was sure of this. Hallie didn't have my problem. She belonged wherever she was.

Emelina nodded. She watched the boys, who sat cross-legged on the driveway, transfixed by the importance of their task. They were dappled with blood and looked like they'd been through a strange war themselves—a children's war.

A scarlet bougainvillaea covered the front porch. In fact, it was so overgrown that the wood of the vine seemed to be supporting the structure over our heads. The breeze coming up the valley felt like a warm liquid against my arms and face. I held the sweaty beer can against my temple and watched the bougainvillaea arms swaying around us like seaweed under the ocean.

"No," Emelina said after a while. "I'm sure it was you that had a fit over the chickens. You'd start, and then Hallie would do it too. She always followed whatever you did."

"No. Hallie? We're chalk and cheese. Somebody ought to do a study on us, if they want to know how kids in the same family can turn out totally different. She was born with her own mind."

"Maybe she was, but she copied you like a picture," Emelina said. "She used to get so pissed off at me because I wouldn't go along with your boycott of *Abuelita's* chicken and rice."

I didn't remember organizing boycotts. "Well, you're the witness here. Blood all over the driveway and I didn't faint."

"People change," she said. "Not everything stays with you all your life."

▼▼▼

I sat watching my suitcases for a good fifteen minutes, as if they might become inspired to unpack themselves, and then I went into the bedroom and lay down for just a minute, letting my shoes drop one at a time onto the brick floor. I tried to think how far Hallie might have gotten by now. Guatemala. Maybe farther. It was frightening to speculate on specifics; I'd been rationing my thoughts about her, but now I was exhausted and my mind ran its own course. I thought of Hallie at border crossings. Men in uniforms decorated with the macho jewelry of ammunition. No, not that far. I pulled her back to Tucson, where I'd seen her last and she was still safe.

She'd come by the 7-Eleven, all packed up, at the end of my graveyard shift. She knocked her knuckles on the plate glass to get my attention. I locked the cash drawer and took off. Sparrows were ruffling themselves in the sheets of fresh rain on the asphalt. As I walked her across the parking lot to her truck I could see just how we'd look to somebody, hanging on to each other by the elbows: like two swimmers in trouble, both of us equally likely to drown.

Or maybe only one of us was holding on for dear life. It was hard to believe I'd once been the one to strike out bravely for college, leaving Hallie crying in front of the Baptist Grocery. Now it seemed like I was the baby of the family, the one with no firm plans who's allowed to fiddle around forever keeping everyone young.

Hallie was headed for a war zone. She walked straight through the puddles, dragging me along, and I had to stretch out my legs and drench my shoes to keep up with her. When Hallie was intensely excited she had a wild-animal look to her that could stop people in their tracks. A vibration came from her skin, like a bell that has just been struck. Her hair was long and reckless, curling wildly in the humidity. Every part of my sister could stir rebellion. I was thinking that if anything happened to her I wouldn't survive. I couldn't see that there would be any method, or any point.

As long as I held Hallie's arm she would still be here, she wouldn't be climbing into the truck, turning the key, driving south through Arizona and Mexico and the perilous places farther on, wouldn't be stopped at a roadblock by men who might blandly shoot her in the head for being twenty-nine years old and alone and female, wearing blue jeans, carrying antihistamine pills in her glove compartment. It seemed like a chain of events I could hold back, there in the parking lot, with the bones of her elbow securely gripped in my hand.

Her little beat-up pickup looked impossibly loaded, like the tiny burros you see in postcards carrying elephant-sized burdens without complaint. I wasn't worried about the truck. I asked where she'd put her antihistamines. We knew of a photographer who'd been shot, ostensibly for running drugs, because he had a baby-food jar of aspirin and vitamin tablets in his camera bag.

Hallie said her pills were no place easy to find.

I put my head on her shoulder. "What if our houseplants die?"

"They won't," she said. Hallie knew I wanted easy answers.

I lifted my head again and she stared at me, thoughtfully. The sky had cleared. The early-morning light behind her head was orange, making her hair glow, and she looked like an angel.

She never had any idea how she looked to other people; she thought she was plain.

"If the flea beetles start getting at the ones on the porch," she said slowly, "dust them with Celite." Hallie worked for the Extension Service and answered the Garden Hotline, 626-BUGS. For a period of years ending on that day, garden pests were her life.

I hugged her with all the strength in my arms. "Hallie," I said, "could you please just change your mind now and not go?"

"You really love me, so you want me to stay here and keep the suburbs safe for geraniums."

"I know how I ought to feel," I said. "I just don't."

Her breath expanded her chest against my arms, and I thought of the way a tree will keep on growing after a fence is wired around its trunk. The unbelievable force of that expansion. And I let her go.

She started up her truck and waved from the corner, not a mournful gone-forever wave but a chin-up wave like you see in the World War II movies, where everybody is brave because they all believe in the same thing. I told myself because I had no other choice that Hallie would do all right. That we were both going to live.

I walked the six blocks home under dripping trees and a sun that was already too hot. Across the street I heard a woman say to her companion in an odd accent, "It's the *Desert* Museum. I had understood him to say the 'dessert museum,' and obviously I was expecting something quite different." I thought: this is how life is, ridiculous beyond comprehension. What I felt wasn't pain but a hollowness, like a drum with the skin stretched tight. It took me five minutes to get our front door open, because everything in Tucson with moving parts gets cantankerous in the rainy season. Hallie had meant to put graphite in the lock before she left.

A white balloon left over from her going-away party followed me from the living room into the kitchen. It was the size of a head, and had lost some helium so it hung at eye level, trailing its string along the floor like a tired old ghost. Static electricity drew it along behind me. I swatted it away from my head while I plundered the refrigerator. I found some red bell peppers that had been absurdly expensive at the health-food market, and washed one and ate it standing up in the kitchen. After that I found a paring knife and went to work on a cucumber. I didn't feel like cooking breakfast just for myself. Carlo was at the hospital and I had no idea when he was due back.

The phone rang and I jumped, I suppose because I felt guilty for standing in the kitchen eating costly vegetables. I was afraid it was going to be somebody with garden pests, but they'd already turned off the Garden Hotline. It was Hallie calling from a pay phone this side of the border to tell me she'd forgotten to graphite the lock.

"I knew you'd call about that." I was filled with a strange joy because she felt the same way I did: that we couldn't survive apart. I just stood still for a minute, giving Hallie's and my thoughts their last chance to run quietly over the wires, touching each other in secret signal as they passed, like a column of ants. You couldn't do that kind of thing at international rates.

"There's a library book, too," she said. "Those Baron Münchhausen stories. I found it in with my books when I was cleaning out my room."

"I know. I saw it. I'll take it back today."

"That book's got to be overdue, Codi. You were reading it in the car a month ago when we drove to Bisbee."

I took a bite out of the cucumber and chewed before answering. I wanted this phone call to last forever. I wanted to recall every book we'd ever read aloud together while driving. "You're right. It's overdue."

"Take it back and pay the fine, okay? Libraries are the one American institution you shouldn't rip off."

"Yes, ma'am," I said. "Miss Patty Hearst the Second." I heard her trying not to laugh. Hallie was intellectually subversive and actually owned a copy of Abbie Hoffman's *Steal This Book*, but by nature she was perversely honest. I'd seen her tape dimes to a broken parking meter.

"Apart from moral reasons, they'll cancel your card."

"I don't know why you think I'm such a library outlaw. I'm

all paid up over there." I munched on the cucumber. It wasn't that different from eating an outsize apple, say, or a peeled peach, and yet anyone looking in the window would judge me insane. "Don't worry about me, Hallie," I said finally. "Just worry about yourself."

"I'm not worried about myself. I'm the luckiest person alive."

It was an old joke, or an old truth, grown out of all the close shaves she'd walked away from. Bike wrecks, car wrecks, that kind of thing. I'd always been more or less a tragedy magnet, but Hallie was the opposite. One time she started out the door of the old science library at the university, and then turned around and went back in because she'd left her sunglasses by the microfiche machine, and two seconds later the marble façade fell off the front of the building. Just slid straight down and smashed, it looked like Beirut.

Hallie didn't believe she was invulnerable. She was never one of those daredevil types; she knew she could get hurt. What I think she meant was that she was lucky to be on her way to Nicaragua. It was the slowest thing to sink into my head, how happy she was. Happy to be leaving.

We'd had one time of perfect togetherness in our adult lives, the year when we were both in college in Tucson—her first year, my last—and living together for the first time away from Doc Homer. That winter I'd wanted to fail a subject just so I could hang back, stay there with her, the two of us walking around the drafty house in sweatshirts and wool socks and understanding each other precisely. Bringing each other cups of tea without having to ask. So I stayed on in Tucson for medical school, instead of going to Boston as I'd planned, and met Carlo in Parasitology. Hallie, around the same time, befriended some people who ran a safehouse for Central American refugees. After that we'd have strangers in our kitchen every time of night, kids scared senseless, people with all kinds of damage. Our life was never again idyllic.

I should have seen it coming. Once she and I had gone to see a documentary on the Abraham Lincoln Brigade, which was these Americans who volunteered without our government's blessing to fight against Franco and Hitler in the Spanish Civil

War. At that point in U.S. history fascism was only *maybe* wrong, whereas communism was *definitely*. When we came home from the movie Hallie cried. Not because of the people who gave up life and limb only to lose Spain to Franco, and not for the ones who came back and were harassed for the rest of their lives for being Reds. The tragedy for Hallie was that there might never be a cause worth risking everything for in our lifetime. She was nineteen years old then, and as she lay blowing her nose and sobbing on my bed she told me this. That there were no real causes left.

Now she had one—she was off to Nicaragua, a revolution of co-op farms and literacy crusades—and so I guess she *was* lucky. Few people know so clearly what they want. Most people can't even think what to hope for when they throw a penny in a fountain. Almost no one really gets the chance to alter the course of human events on purpose, in the exact way they wish for it to be altered.

I loved her for feeling so strongly about things. But I'd watched Doc Homer spend a lifetime ministering his solemn charity to the people of Grace and I'm not sure whose course was altered by that, other than Hallie's and mine, in a direction we grew to resent. It's true that I tried myself to go into medicine, which is considered a helping profession, but I did it for the lowest of motives. I did it to win love, and to prove myself capable. Not to move mountains. In my opinion, mountains don't move. They only look changed when you look down on them from a great height.

5

THE *SEMILLA BESADA*

I'd agreed to move into the guesthouse on the condition that I wasn't going to impose on Emelina's family life, but apparently her life was beyond imposition. She sent John Tucker over in the morning to fetch me for breakfast.

He stood tentatively outside my screen door, unsure of what to do with all his limbs. "Mom says she'll break your face if you don't come over for breakfast."

"Okay, sure," I said, following him back to the house. John Tucker was the most appealing kind of adolescent. I couldn't begin to picture the man he would soon become—armpits and arrogance, scratching the back of his neck, throwing a baseball. Out of the question. He was wearing a cap to cover what looked like an overly enthusiastic summer haircut.

"I know you don't have anything to eat over there yet," Emelina said. "Everything was closed, yesterday was Sunday. Today you can get on your feet. J.T. called from El Paso and said to be sure and give you a kiss." Emelina buttered a piece of toast and handed it to Mason, who was four going on five. "Glen, don't put jam on your brother. If you want to wear plum preserves today that's your nickel, but not Curtis's. Curty, honey, don't hit. John Tucker, help him with that, will you?"

"He called from El Paso?" I prompted. Conversations with a mother of five are an education in patience.

"Yeah, he's in Texas. He's got to stay for an investigation. So are you going to be able to stand living in that shack?"

"It's not a shack, Em. It's nice out there. I like it."

"Codi, honey, there was goats living in there at one time. And Grammy lived there too, before the goats. But she said she got the ague in her bones and she decided she had to move in upstairs." Grammy was J.T.'s mother, Viola Domingos.

"Mom, make Glen stop," Curtis said.

"Glen, for heaven's sakes, just eat that toast and put it out of its misery. The bus is going to be here in a minute and you don't even have your shoes on."

"No, but I know where they are," Glen declared.

"Well, go get them."

"School doesn't start till next week," I said, alarmed that I might be wrong. I was always having dreams like that.

"No, but they've got this summer thing for kids. They go up there to the river park and shoot each other with bows and arrows or something. Tomorrow's the last day. So you think you'll like it out there? We make enough noise over here to raise up the quick and the dead."

"It's fine. I used to live three blocks from a hospital ambulance entrance." I didn't add: with a man who reattached severed body parts for a living. I buttered my toast, holding my elbows in close and keeping an eye out for wayward jam knives. "So what kind of an investigation?"

"Oh, J.T.? He put sixteen cars on the ground outside El Paso. A derailment. Nobody got hurt. Oh shoot—John Tucker, honey, will you take the baby in the living room and watch him a minute? I can't hear myself think."

John Tucker took the baby from Emelina's lap and carried him under one arm into the next room. The baby waggled his arms and legs like a swimmer in green stretch pajamas.

"Okay. Mason, sweetie, put your feet up here on my lap and I'll tie your sneakers for you." Emelina took a gulp of coffee. "So they all had to give a urine sample—J.T., the fireman, the brakeman, and some other person, I can't remember who.

Maybe another engineer. It all had to happen within a half hour of the accident; the company made a very big deal out of that. J.T. says, here they were out in some cow pasture with sixteen boxcars of frozen mixed vegetables scattered from hell to break-fast, and all the damn supervisor cared about was making sure which person pissed in what jar."

The boys seemed unmoved by this off-color narrative. Having Emelina for a mother would neutralize the thrill of swear words.

"You know what, though," she said, looking startled. "Damn. We were just joking about drug tests, the day before yesterday. Grammy made a poppyseed cake for Curty's and Glen's birthday and J.T. said . . ."

"Mo-om."

"I'm sorry, Curtis, I forgot. He doesn't want us to call him Curty. Their actual birthday was yesterday."

I wanted to hear the rest of the derailment story, but this conversational flow was akin to freeway driving in L.A.; you don't back up. "Well, happy birthday," I said. "You boys get handsomer every time I see you, you know that?"

Curtis's ears turned red.

"You can say 'Thank you, ma'am,' can't you? Codi, they've all been asking me when you were going to get here till I thought they'd turn blue in the face, and now they're acting like they were raised outside in a pen with the dogs."

"That's okay." I felt a little intimidated myself. Even though I'd kept up with the family, it was inconceivable that in my absence from Grace Emelina could have produced this whole blue-eyed tribe of human beings.

"Mom, can I sleep out in the pen with Buster tonight?" Mason asked.

"No sir, you can't. So when we were eating that cake, J.T. was saying how he'd better not have an accident on the railroad, because poppyseeds show up some way on the drug test."

"That's true, they would." I reconsidered this. "He'd register positive for opiates. Poppyseeds are related to heroin. Is he going to be in trouble?"

"No, they know it wasn't his fault. It was a sun-kink or some darn thing with the rails. The drug test is just to cover their ass.

You know who else was on the train? The other engineer and the brakeman were both guys we went to school with, you might remember them. Roger Bristol and Loyd Peregrina. Loyd lived up at Whiteriver for a while but he's moved back."

I paid attention to my heart rate, to see if it would react in any way to this information. It didn't seem to.

"Aunt Codi, say something in Greece," Glen said.

"In Greek," Emelina corrected, giving me an apologetic look. "I already told them you looked like a fashion model and had lived overseas. They think you know David Bowie."

"Your mother exaggerates," I said.

Glen didn't seem too disappointed.

"So, Em, if I'm going to live here do I have to buy a pair of those silver loafers from the Hollywood Shop?"

She nodded seriously. "I'm pretty sure they won't let you teach down at the high school without them."

The school bus honked outside. "Okay, scoot," Emelina said. "Mason, give me a kiss."

The boys stampeded out the kitchen door, all legs, leaving the baby beached on Emelina's lap. His eyes roamed anxiously around the quiet kitchen, taking in the emptiness.

Emelina and I took each other in. All morning I'd felt the strange disjuncture that comes from reconnecting with your past. There's such a gulf between yourself and who you were then, but people speak to that other person and it answers; it's like having a stranger as a house guest in your skin.

"So what's new?" she asked.

"I don't know, everything. I don't think Grace has changed, but it feels different. There's a lot I don't remember."

Emelina smiled. "I know what you mean. Senility strikes." It was an odd thing to say; Doc Homer's exact problem was that his mind had begun to roam in alarming new pastures.

"I guess so," I said.

"Well, some things never change." She leaned forward and said in a low voice, "Grammy still collects figurines of Elvis."

I had to laugh. We'd known J.T.'s mother as children, of course—people here spent their childhoods tearing through the homes of their future in-laws—and I remembered her living

room, which we used to call the Elvis Museum. She denied that
the ones that were whiskey bottles were whiskey bottles. She'd
always told us aftershave.

"So it's all over with Carlo? Or just a vacation?"

"I don't know. Over, I think. It's taken me all this time to
figure out he's not going to tell me the secret to a meaningful
life." I was serious. I'd loved Carlo best when he provided me
with guidance.

"I used to think the ideal husband would be Doctor Kildare."

"Carlo's an emergency-room surgeon. A man that decides
which way to sew a thumb back on would have a good hold on
life, wouldn't you think? I just assumed it would rub off."

"Gross," Emelina remarked.

"I think it was his eyebrows. You know how he has those
kind of arched, Italian eyebrows?"

"No, I never got to meet him. He was always at the hospital."

That was true. He was shy. He could face new flesh wounds
each day at work, but he avoided actual people. "Well, he had
this look," I said. "He always seemed right on the verge of saying
something that would change your life. Even when he was asleep
he looked like that."

"But he never did?"

"Nope. It was just his eyebrows."

I did miss him, or at least I missed being attached to someone
in theory. Carlo had beautiful hands and a legendary sense of
direction. Even when we were in Venice, where the tourist books
advise you that "part of the Venice experience is wandering the
narrow *strade* until you find yourself lost," we wandered but
never got lost. The man had a compass needle in his cerebral
cortex. And for all that, he'd still in the long run declined to be
the guiding star I needed. Just as my father did. My father was
dying on me.

Emelina collected the plates and cups. She stood up and tied
on an apron over her bathrobe, miraculously keeping the baby
situated on her hip throughout the operation.

"Well, you're no worse for the wear of five children in fourteen years," I said, and she laughed, probably not believing it.
Emelina was noticeably pretty. That combination particular to

Grace, the pale blue eyes and black hair, never failed to be arresting, no matter how many versions of it you saw. The eyes were a genetic anomaly—in the first hours after birth, the really pure specimens of Grace's gene pool were supposed to have whitish, marblelike irises. I'd seen pictures. Doc Homer had written it up for the *American Journal of Genetics*, years ago.

"And John Tucker's a teenager," I said. "Are we that old?"

"I am. You're not." She started to clear the table with one hand. "Every minute in the presence of a child takes seven minutes off your life." I took the baby from her and she said, "Don't say I didn't warn you."

"They're your treasures, Em. You've got something to show for yourself."

"Oh, yeah. I know," she said.

The baby's name was Nicholas, but nobody called him anything but "the baby." I'd read somewhere that the brain organizes information in sets no larger than four—that's why Social Security and phone numbers are subdivided; possibly four children's names were the limit on parental memory. I sat in the rocker and settled nameless Nicholas on my lap, his head at my knees. My long thigh bones exactly accommodated his length.

Emelina scraped toast corners into a blue enamel pail and ran a sinkful of hot water. "I don't think I could stand to let Mason go off to kindergarten next year if it wasn't for the baby. It kills you to see them grow up. But I guess it would kill you quicker if they didn't."

"I remember you saying you were calling it quits after four."

"Famous last words."

While I watched her move around the kitchen, my fingers tingled with the pleasure of stroking the baby's fine black hair. It was longer by several inches than his big brother John Tucker's; someone had taken shears to that boy with a vengeance. Probably Emelina. A woman who beheaded her own chickens would cut her kids' hair herself.

Emelina washed and rinsed the plates and set them into the wire rack to drain. I sat feeling useless, though Nicholas seemed comfortable and was falling asleep on my lap. When that happens you feel them grow heavier, as if relaxation allowed them to be flooded with extra substance. A constriction ran across my lungs. I'd come close to having a baby of my own once, but I thought of it now so rarely that the notion of myself as a mother always caught me off guard.

In spite of the heat outside, Emelina's dishwater was fogging the window. A little collection of potted plants stood in a row on the windowsill. Prayer plants. I was struck with a sudden, forceful memory of Emelina's grandmother's house. Hallie and I called her *Abuelita* too, though of course she was no relation, and the old woman called us "the orphan girls," *huérfanas*. Nobody ever thought we could understand Spanish. The house had a stale, old-lady smell, but we loved her boxes of "pretties": cast-metal carts with broken wheels, lead soldiers, huge washers and carriage bolts, every species of unidentifiable metal part. Her dead husband was a blacksmith. There were also boxes of ancient dress-up clothes in satiny fabrics as brittle as paper. Our best playroom was the sunny alcove crammed with plants where we stalked lions through the parlor palms, dressed in our finery, more glamorous than Beryl Markham and the Baroness von Blixen could have managed to be in their dreams. We confronted real dangers in the form of rickety iron stands holding heavy, breakable pots and fragile plants. The African violets were furred like pets, and the prayer plants had leaves like an old woman's hands, red-veined on the back, that opened wide in the sun and folded primly together in the shade. *Abuelita* instructed us to sit and watch them, to try and catch them in the act of closing their leaves. Hallie always waited the longest, patient for enlightenment long after Emelina and I had returned to our rowdy diversions.

"You know, I'm so used to J.T. being gone," Emelina said, bringing me back. "I think he'd be underfoot if he were here. I'd give us about ten days, then I'd probably shoot him. Husband murder in Grace, oh boy." She seemed to be answering a question, however circumspectly, that I wasn't sure I'd asked.

"How long has he been on the railroad?"

"Just since the mine shut down, which was . . ." She frowned at the glass she was drying, decorated with white pigs in red bow ties. "Ten years, about."

"They used to always say they'd hire again up there when the price of copper went up."

"Well, you know, that's talk. Nobody's waiting around anymore. Now it's pecans and plums. And the railroad, thank God for that. I think we could live off the orchards if the boys didn't eat like horses and outgrow their shoes every ten days. Get this, now they're too fashion conscious to wear each other's hand-me-downs. Remember when boys didn't give a shit what they wore? We never should have got satellite TV." She turned around, drying her hands on her apron. "Is that rascal gone to sleep? Thanks, Codi. I'll take him upstairs and put him down for his nap." She lifted the baby onto her shoulder like a sack of valuable flour. "You got big plans for today?"

"I thought I'd make an excursion into the city," I said. "Check out the dry goods at the Baptist Grocery."

She laughed. "If you can wait awhile I'll go with you. Grammy can listen for the baby. She ought to be home pretty soon from her meeting." Emelina rolled her eyes as she left the kitchen. "Stitch and Bitch Club on Mondays, bright and early."

I stood at the window looking out at the grove of trees that ran the length of the canyon. Plum, pear, apple. And quince, I believe, though I couldn't identify a quince tree to save my life. I only remembered the word because of the way people here pronounced it—"queens"—with their Spanish-influenced vowels. In the distance I could make out white satellite dishes perched among the cacti on the red cliff—one to each house, like dogs. Well, that was something new. The sky was overcast. In the orchards on the other side of the river I could see men working among the trees. I remembered them beating the branches with long poles, bringing down scattered showers of pecans. Frailing, that was called. In the older orchards sometimes they had to climb up into the tallest trees to reach the upper branches with their poles. But it was too early in the year for that. Pecans didn't ripen till late fall.

Hallie and I had played in this house once or twice as children, when a pair of pigeon-toed girl cousins of J.T.'s had lived here. Now it belonged so securely to Emelina. It was hard to realize how fully life had gone on. Of course, it would. I could have stayed here, or gone away as I did, it made no difference to Grace.

I washed the baby's cup, running my finger around the inside rim. While the sun left the windowsill and moved on to other things, I noticed, the prayer plants had closed up when I wasn't watching. They stood in a self-satisfied row, keeping their thoughts to themselves.

▼▼▼

"You keep some of the dirt on them, and you just stuff them down in paper bags and keep them somewhere dark," said Lydia Galvez. "Do you have a root cellar?"

"No, uh-uh. We did, but the boys got into it and figured out how to cave it in some way," Emelina said.

"Well, you could put them anyplace dark. The bottom of a closet would do."

Lydia Galvez was the wife of John Tucker's little league coach. I'd been introduced. We'd discussed John Tucker, baseball, and Emelina's talent for producing boys. The whole town had been betting this last one would be a girl, Lydia Galvez told me. Now they were talking about dividing gladiolus bulbs.

"I've got some black," Lydia was saying. "Do you have any black? I could spare you some. They're not a *true* black, I'd really call it purple, but they're supposed to be important."

Emelina gave me a glance, so I knew she was trying to wind things up. Our whole afternoon had gone pretty much this way. Lydia, like everyone else, had no earthly notion of what to say to me, or I to them; I rarely even remembered who they were. But we were all polite, as if I were Emelina's lunatic maiden aunt.

I sat down on the wall in front of the courthouse and watched myself in the plate-glass window of Jonny's Breakfast, which was empty at this hour. My reflection stared back, looking more alone than anything I'd seen in my life. It occurred to me that I'd never drawn a breath here without Hallie. Not one I could be sure of. I was three when she was born. Before that I wasn't conscious of my place in the world, so it didn't matter.

Later, it mattered more than anything. Doc Homer drilled us

relentlessly on how we differed from our peers: in ambition, native ability, even physical constitution. The nearest thing to praise, from him, was "No one else in Grace knows *that!*" Or, "You are *Nolines*." We stood out like a pair of silos on a mid-western prairie. As far as I could see, being *Nolines* meant that we were impossibly long-limbed like our father and all the Noline relatives we never got to meet. He and mother came from a part of Illinois (this is a quote) where people were reasonable and tall.

The height, at least, wasn't lost on Hallie and me. We turned out to be six feet on average—Hallie one inch over, and I, one under. In high school they used to call us forty percent of a basketball team. We didn't play sports, but they still said that. Height isn't something you can have and just let be, like nice teeth or naturally curly hair. People have this idea you have to put it to use, playing basketball, for example, or observing the weather up there. If you are a girl, they feel a particular need to point your height out to you, as if you might not have noticed.

In fact, Hallie and I weren't forty percent of anything—we were all there was. The image in the mirror that proves you are still here. We had exactly one sister apiece. We grew up knowing the simple arithmetic of scarcity: A sister is more precious than an eye.

"You tell that daddy of yours I need a pill to get rid of my wrinkles," Lydia said loudly.

I made an effort to collect myself. "Okay."

I should have said, "You don't need any such thing," or something like that, but I didn't think fast enough. I wasn't managing this first day all that well. I had a lump in my throat and longed to get back to my cottage and draw the blinds. Grace was a memory minefield; just going into the Baptist Grocery with Emelina had charged me with emotions and a hopelessness I couldn't name. I'd finished my shopping in a few minutes, and while I waited for Emelina to provision her troops for the week I stood looking helplessly at the cans of vegetables and soup that all carried some secret mission. The grocery shelves seemed to have been stocked for the people of Grace with the care of a family fallout shelter. I was an outsider to this nurturing. When the cashier asked, "Do you need anything else?" I almost cried. I wanted to say, "I need everything you have."

▼▼▼

It was past midnight but a cold moon blazed in the window and I couldn't sleep. I lay on my back in the little painted bed in Emelina's cottage. I hated sleeping alone. As little as there was between Carlo and me, I'd adjusted to his breathing. All my life I'd shared a bed with somebody: first Hallie. Then in my first years at college I discovered an army of lovers who offered degrees of temporary insanity and short-term salvation. Then Carlo, who'd turned out to be more of the same. But companionable, still. Sleeping alone seemed unnatural to me, and pitiful, something done in hospitals or when you're contagious.

I'd finally reached that point of electric sleeplessness where I had to get up. I tucked my nightgown into my jeans and found my shoes out in the kitchen. I closed the door quietly and took a path that led away from the house, not down past other houses but straight out to the north, through Emelina's plum orchard and a grove of twisted, dead-looking apples. Every so often, peacocks called to each other across the valley. They had different cries: the shrill laugh, a guttural clucking—a whole animal language. Like roosters and children, on a full-moon night they would never settle down completely.

I wanted to find the road that led up the canyon to Doc Homer's. I wasn't ready to go there yet, but I had to make sure I knew the way. I couldn't ask Emelina for directions to my own childhood home; I didn't want her to know how badly dislocated I was. I'd always had trouble recalling certain specifics of childhood, but didn't realize until now that I couldn't even recognize them at point-blank range. The things I'd done with Hallie were clear, because we remembered so much for each other, I suppose, but why did I not know Mrs. Campbell in the grocery? Or Lydia Galvez, who rode our school bus and claimed to have loaned me her handkerchief after Simon Bolivar Jones chucked me on the head with his Etch-a-Sketch, on a dare. In fact, I felt like the victim of a head injury. I hoped that if I struck out now on faith I would feel my way to Doc Homer's, the way a water witcher closes her eyes and follows her dowsing rod to find a spring. But I didn't know. I could have lost the homing instinct completely.

I was on a road that looked promising, anyway. I could hear the river. (Why does sound travel farther at night?) I had my mother's death on my mind. One of my few plain childhood memories was of that day. I was not quite three, Hallie was newborn, and I'm told I couldn't possibly remember it because I wasn't there. The picture I have in my mind is nonetheless clear: two men in white pants handling the stretcher like a fragile, important package. The helicopter blade beating, sending out currents of air across the alfalfa field behind the hospital. This was up above the canyon, in the days when they grew crops up there. The flattened-down alfalfa plants showed their silvery undersides in patterns that looked like waves. The field became the ocean I'd seen in storybooks, here in the middle of the desert, like some miracle.

Then the rotor slowed and stopped, setting the people in the crowd to murmuring: What? Why? And then the door opened and the long white bundle of my mother came out again, carried differently now, no longer an urgent matter.

According to generally agreed-upon history, Hallie and I were home with a babysitter. This is my problem—I clearly remember things I haven't seen, sometimes things that never happened. And draw a blank on the things I've lived through. I told Doc Homer many times that I'd seen the helicopter, and I also once insisted, to the point of tears, that I remembered being on the ship with the nine Gracela sisters and their peacocks. For that one he forced me to sit in my room and read the *Encyclopaedia Britannica*. Novels were banned for a month; he said I needed to clear my mind of fictions. I made it to Volume 19, driven mostly by spite, but I still remembered that trip with the Gracelas. They were worried about whether the peacocks were getting enough air down in the hold of the ship.

I would concede now that all these things were fabrications based on stories I'd heard. Memory is a complicated thing, a relative to truth but not its twin. It was a fact that our mother had been terrified of flying. This part of our family history was well known in Grace. In her entire life she never left the ground. When her health deteriorated because of a failed kidney and a National Guard helicopter bore down from the sky to take her to Tucson, she'd explained to the men that she wasn't going to fly. When they ignored her, she just died before the helicopter could lift itself up out of the alfalfa. The big bird hovered for a minute, and went away hungry.

It wasn't her aversion to flight that was impressive; people in Grace didn't travel much by car, let alone by air. I think the moral of the tale, based on the way people told it, was the unsuspected force of my mother's will. "Who else would have married Doc Homer?" they seemed to be saying. And also, I suppose, "Who could have borne those unconforming girls?" People never said this directly, but when we were willful they would tell us, without fail: "You didn't suck that out of your thumb."

It made sense to me. I had no visual memory of a mother, and could not recall any events that included her, outside of the helicopter trip she declined to take. But I could remember a *sense* of her that was strong and ferociously loving. Almost a violence of love. It was the one thing I'd had, I suppose, that Hallie never knew. As the two of us grew up quietly in the dispassionate shadow of Doc Homer's care and feeding, I tried to preserve that motherly love as best I could, and pass it on. But I couldn't get it right. I was so young.

And somehow Hallie thrived anyway—the blossom of our family, like one of those miraculous fruit trees that taps into an invisible vein of nurture and bears radiant bushels of plums while the trees around it merely go on living. In Grace, in the old days, when people found one of those in their orchard they called it the *semilla besada*—the seed that got kissed. Sometimes you'd run across one that people had come to, and returned to, in hopes of a blessing. The branches would be festooned like a Christmas tree of family tokens: a baby sock, a pair of broken reading glasses, the window envelope of a pension check.

Hallie and I had a favorite *besada* in the old Domingos orchard, and one cold day on the way home from school we tucked wisps of our hair into its bark. Secretly. We'd hidden in the schoolyard to snip the ends off our braids and tie them up together with a pink thread unraveled from my coat button. If Doc Homer found out, he would construct some punishment to cure us of superstition. We agreed with him in principle—we were little scientists, born and bred. But children robbed of love will dwell on magic.

I stopped suddenly in the center of the road, in the moon's bright light, with shadow trickling downhill from my heels like the water witcher's wellspring finally struck open. I'd found the right path. The road angled up out of the orchards toward the top of the canyon. The steepness of the climb felt right. I would come back in daylight and go the rest of the way to Doc Homer's, past the old helicopter landing pad up in the alfalfa field. Those fields would surely be abandoned now, like half the cropland in Arizona, salted to death by years of bad irrigation. I didn't want to go up there now and see it all under moonlight, the white soil gleaming like a boneyard. It was too much.

I turned back down the road feeling the familiar, blunt pressure of old grief. Even the people who knew me well didn't know my years in Grace were peculiarly bracketed by death: I'd lost a mother and I'd lost a child.

6

THE MIRACLE

I was fifteen years old, two years younger than my own child would be now. I didn't think of it in those terms: losing a baby. At first it was nothing like a baby I held inside me, only a small impossible secret. Slowly it grew to a force as strong and untouchable as thunder. I would be loved absolutely. But even in the last months I never quite pictured the whole infant I might have someday held in my arms; that picture came later. The human fact of it was gone before I knew it. But evidently that word "lost" was somewhere in my mind because I've had thousands of dreams of losing—of literally misplacing—a baby.

In one of the dreams I run along the creek bank looking among the boulders. They are large and white, and the creek is flooded, just roaring, and I know I've left a baby out there. I thrash my way through mesquite thickets, stopping often to listen, hearing nothing but the roar of the water. I feel frantic until finally I see her in the middle of the water bobbing like a Cortland apple, little and red and bright. I wade in and pull her out and she lies naked there on the bank without so much as a surname, her umbilicus tied with a man's black shoelace such as my father might wear. I see her and think, "It's a miracle she's survived."

That thought is the truest part of the dream. Really there would be nothing new or surprising about a baby being born in secret and put into a creek. But to pull one out, that would be a surprise. A newborn has no fat yet; it wouldn't float. It would sink like a stone.

Loyd Peregrina was an Apache. He took me out four times. Our football team was called the Apaches, but Loyd was also a *real* Apache, and the kind of handsome you could see coming down the road like bad news. When he first asked me, I thought he'd made a mistake, or a joke, and I looked to see who was watching. Nobody was. Four Saturdays in a row, for exactly one lunar month: the odds of getting pregnant out of that were predictable, but I was unfathomably naïve. I was a motherless girl. I'd learned the words *puberty* and *menarche* from the *Encyclopaedia Britannica*. The rest I learned from girls in the schoolyard who weren't even talking to me when they said what they did.

Loyd wouldn't remember. For me it was the isolated remarkable event of a tenuous life but for Loyd—with his misspelled name and devil eyes—it was one in a hundred, he was a senior and ran around with everybody. Also he was such a drinker in those days that I was frankly surprised to hear he was still alive. He never knew what he'd spawned, much less when it died. Even Hallie didn't. It's the first time I understood that even with a sister I could be alone. At night I lay feeling my limbs, seeing what Hallie still saw, which was nothing near the truth, and I felt myself growing distant and stolid. I was the woman downtown buttoning her child's jacket, her teeth like a third hand clamped on a folded grocery list, as preoccupied as God. Someone important and similar to others. I was lured and terrified. I couldn't help but think sometimes of escape: the thing inside me turning to blood of its own accord, its bones liquefying, leaking out. And then one evening my savage wish was granted.

I never did tell Hallie. I kept quiet, first to protect her from the knowledge of terrible things, and later to protect myself from that rock-solid element she came to own. That moral advantage.

It divided me from the people I knew, then and later, but in broader human terms I don't pretend that it sets me apart in any great way. A miscarriage is a natural and common event. All told, probably more women have lost a child from this world than haven't. Most don't mention it, and they go on from day to day as if it hadn't happened, and so people imagine that a woman in this situation never really knew or loved what she had.

But ask her sometime: how old would your child be now? And she'll know.

7

POISON GROUND

Emelina was up with the chickens. I heard her out in the court-yard pulling honeysuckle vines away from the old brick barbecue pit. They came out with a peculiar zipping sound, like threads from a seam in rotten cloth. "You can see we haven't been festive for a while," she said. She was organizing what she called a "little fiesta" for the Saturday of Labor Day weekend. It was a family tradition; they roasted a whole goat. (Not John Tucker's.)

I found a broom and pitched in, sweeping up the pieces of a broken flowerpot I'd come to think of as part of the décor. Emelina asked, in the carefully offhand way a good mother would ask, if I'd been up to the school yet. I'd received numerous calls about a teacher's meeting.

"I know about the meeting, but I haven't gone up there yet," I confessed. School would begin the following Tuesday. I needed to get organized and see what kind of shape the labs were in, but I kept putting it off, on grounds of terror. I hadn't actually taught school before. When Emelina wrote me about the opening at Grace High School it had seemed sensible to apply. While Carlo slept I'd sat up in bed with my legal pad and a small reading light, feigning competence, attempting to organize the problem areas of my life into manageable categories: I had no real at-tachment to selling lottery tickets at 7-Eleven; Doc Homer was going off the deep end; Carlo was Carlo; Hallie would be leaving at summer's end, and without a destination for myself I'd be marooned. Grace was something. If I got this job I could spend ten months in Grace seeing about Doc Homer, possibly without his noticing. I reasoned that I wasn't qualified and didn't have a chance of being hired, and so I felt bold enough to apply.

They hired me. The state had some kind of emergency clause that in a pinch allowed people to teach without certification. And of course I did have a world of education in the life sciences. Also, I believe my last name had something to do with it. Nothing else I put down in my wobbly writing on that application could have impressed anyone too much.

I dumped the shards of the flowerpot into a plastic trash bag, making the satisfactory sound of demolition. I started in with Emelina on the honeysuckle vines. As we dragged them out she looped the long strands around her arm like strings of Christmas tree lights. "You excited about starting?" she asked.

"Nervous."

"Well hell, Codi, you're bound to be better than the last one. John Tucker says she was scared of her shadow. Some senior boys chased her into the teachers' lounge with a fetal pig."

Emelina's faith in me was heartening.

"Did I tell you J.T. called this morning?" she asked. "They're going to make it home for the fiesta. Him and Loyd. Do you remember Loyd?"

I yanked at a vine that was rooted right into the crumbling adobe. "Sure," I said.

"I didn't know if you would. I think you were the only girl in the whole high school that never fell for him."

It was humid and hot. I'd tied a bandana around my forehead and already it was soaking wet. The salt stung my eyes.

"I went out with Loyd a few times," I said.

"Did you? Him and J.T. are real good buddies. He's straightened out a lot. He's real sweet." She unburdened herself of the loops of vines, laying them in a pile, and stood up with her hands on her waist, arching her back. "Loyd, I mean." She laughed. "Not J.T. He's just the same as he always was."

I took off my bandana and wrung it out. The dark drops on

the hot brick dried up instantly, leaving behind a white lace of salt. Just like the irrigation water on the alfalfa. In just this way the fields get ruined, I thought to myself.

Emelina kicked tentatively at the brick barbecue pit. "You think this thing will stand up after we get the vines out of it?"

"I think they're what's holding it together," I said.

She cocked her head and looked at it thoughtfully. "Well, if it falls down we'll just have us a roasted-goat disaster. We'll just have to get extra beer."

▼▼▼

On the morning of the fiesta she sent John Tucker and me to town for last-minute supplies, including extra beer, although the barbecue pit showed every sign of standing through another Labor Day fiesta. I followed John Tucker down a path I didn't know, a short cut through a different orchard. "What kind of trees are those?" I asked John Tucker. The branches were heavy with what looked like small yellow-green pomegranates.

"Quince," he said, with a perfect short "i," not "queens." The Spanish-flavored accent of Old Grace was dying out, thanks to satellite TV, I suppose. I watched the back of his shorn head; the path was narrow and we walked single file. At thirteen he was my height, a head taller than Emelina. It must shift your liaison with a child when you have to look up to him.

I caught a glimpse of bright car windshield through the trees, and knew where we were. You could picture Grace as a house, with orchards for rooms. To map it of course you'd have to be a botanist. We left quince and entered pecan, where the ground was covered with tiny, immature nuts. "So what's happening with these orchards?" I asked, kicking at a slew of green pecans the size of peach pits. "I've been seeing this all over."

"Fruit drop."

John Tucker was already a man of few words.

The Baptist Grocery was nondenominational, but harked back to a time when everything in Grace, including grocery stores, was still segregated. This wasn't recent, but maybe a century ago. Here the Hispanic and Anglo bloodlines got very mixed up early on, starting with the arrival of the Gracela sisters. By the time people elsewhere were waking up to such ideas as busing, everyone in Grace had pretty much given up on claiming a superior pedigree. Nowadays the Baptist Grocery peddled frozen fish sticks to Protestant and Catholic alike.

John Tucker shopped like an automaton, counting out bags of chips and jars of salsa. Since he seemed interested in efficiency, not congeniality, I suggested we split up. I would go to the liquor store and meet him in front of the courthouse.

Drinking establishments had proliferated in Grace since my day. The mine had closed in the interim, of course; bars and economic duress are common fellow travelers. I passed the Horny Toad Saloon and the Little Dipper plus the one I remembered, the State Line, which was no more situated on the state line than the grocery was Baptist. New Mexico lay thirty miles to the east. I think the name referred to the days when Gracela County was dry and people had to drive to the border for beer.

Emelina had advised that I'd find the best price on beer at the Watering Hole, a package store. I located it on the corner of Main Street and the depot alley, which led down past the old movie theater to the railroad station. The theater had been remodeled into an exercise salon and video rental store called the Video Rodeo, with a huge hand-lettered sign in the window announcing "NINTENDOS NOWHERE." I stared for a good half minute before I made out that it meant "NOW HERE," not "NO-WHERE." The calligrapher got cramped.

The Watering Hole was closed, with a sign on the door saying "BACK IN TEN," so I waited. The placard was lettered in the same hand as the "NINTENDOS" sign. Maybe one person actually ran all the stores in Grace from behind the scenes, like the Wizard of Oz, powerfully manipulating people through hand-lettered signs. It was hot and my mind was fraying at the edges. I wiped the sweat out of my eyes and massaged my prickly scalp, thinking I must look like a drowned hen, but maybe nobody would recognize me today. Living without a lover was beginning to produce in me the odd sense that I was invisible.

A pretty, old carob tree stood near the door of the liquor

store, throwing dappled shade on the sidewalk. I knew that its twisted, woody-looking pods could be crunched between the teeth and tasted like cocoa. I sat on a concrete block and leaned my back against the trunk. Apparently this was a frequent waiting spot. Fallen carob pods lay all around my feet. I picked one up, polished it on my T-shirt and bit down: the first sensation was sawdust, but then the splinters turned strongly bittersweet on my tongue, a nostalgic tang. I looked up into the leathery leaves. Hallie had told me carobs were dioecious, which means that male and female parts are possessed by separate individuals. In plain English, they're like us; it takes two to tango. This one was loaded with fruit, but there wasn't another carob tree in sight. I looked all the way down the main street and down toward the depot. No male carobs. I patted the trunk sympathetically.

The door of the Watering Hole was opened by a proprietor who looked as if she might not be legal drinking age herself. In fact this must have been the case because after she bagged and rang up my purchase she asked if I'd mind waiting while she went next door to the Video Rodeo and got her dad. He arrived shortly to accept my money and put it in the register. I suppose they switched off, since she probably wasn't old enough to rent out porno movies either. I recognized neither father nor daughter, and they didn't make a point of knowing or not knowing me: a relief. The daily work of remeeting people was overwhelming, and Emelina's party was going to be a whole lot more of the same.

I took my paper bags and headed across the street. A red pickup truck beeped its horn and startled me—I'd charged right across without looking. I froze up, like one of those ridiculous squirrels that darts one way and then the other and is doomed to end up a road kill. Except my life was in no danger here; he'd stopped. It was Loyd Peregrina, looking exactly like himself. If anything he looked younger than fifteen years ago. His arm was out the window and I hurried out of his way thinking it was a turn signal, that he was trying to turn right. It didn't occur to me till he'd gone on down the street that he was waving at me.

▼▼▼

I stayed in the shower forever trying to rinse the salt out of my scalp and skin. I had fantasies of not going to this thing, but Emelina would be hurt, and also my house sat in the middle of the party like a floral centerpiece. It would be hard to pretend not to be home. I put on the most minimal thing I owned, a white cotton dress, and sneaked out my front door.

It was like a high-school reunion. Everyone was boisterously friendly and dying to be filled in on the last decade and a half, which in my case was not that pretty a picture, and of course they asked about Hallie. Children ran underfoot like rebel cockroaches. Emelina, my guardian angel, kept setting me up in conversations before running off to clean up some mess the kids had gotten into or check on the goat.

J.T. came over and gave me a hug that lifted me off the ground—but that's J.T., plus a few beers. It really was nice to see him. "I hear you wrecked a train," I said.

"Wrecked her good," he said. J.T. was broad-shouldered and dark, with the kind of face that's made more handsome, not less, by the scars of teenage acne. We'd known each other since we were babies. His older sister Pocha was at the party, and his brothers Cristobal, Gus, and Arturo, all of whom had been our neighbors when Hallie and I were small. I remembered playing Dutchman's tag with them at the graveyard on All Souls' Days— it was always a huge family picnic up there—until Doc Homer decided the graveyard was off limits. (Bird mites no doubt.)

People were jammed into the courtyard belly to elbow and it soon got too noisy to talk. I stood near the edge of things, in the shade of an olive that was probably planted when the house was built, middle-aged as olives go. A band called the Sting Rays, featuring one of J.T.'s formerly pigeon-toed cousins, was belting out "Rosa Lee." I spotted Loyd across the way, but would have had to step on a hundred toes to get to him. He was leaning against the wall with his arms crossed, paying attention to a small woman in a strapless dress. Loyd looked like someone in a cigarette ad, except he wasn't smoking: white T-shirt, white smile, those models are always the picture of health. His hair was mink black, in a ponytail. And he had terrific arms. I hate to admit things like this, but in a certain frame of mind I am a sucker for good muscle definition.

A woman approached me suddenly from behind and shouted, "Codi Noline! God, honey, you look like a rock 'n' roll star."

In my sundress and dimestore thongs I looked no more like a rock 'n' roll star than Mother Teresa. "I'll take that as a compliment," I said. "I take them where I can get them nowadays."

"Lord, I know what you mean," she said. It was Trish Garcia, who was a cheerleader and clandestine smoker when I'd last known her. Now she smoked openly, had a raspy cough, and looked like a cartwheel was out of the question. "I heard Hallie's in South Africa."

I laughed. "Nicaragua."

"Well, what in the world's she doing there?"

In high school, Hallie and I were beneath Trish's stratum of normal conversation. I remembered every day of those years, no lapses there. Once in the bathroom I'd heard her call us the bean-pole sisters, and speculate that we wore hand-me-down underwear. I wondered how the rules had changed. Had I come up in the world, or Trish down? Or perhaps growing up meant we put our knives away and feigned ignorance of the damage. "She's teaching people how to grow crops without wrecking the soil," I said. "She has her master's in integrated pest management."

Trish looked indifferent, but she was working hard at being unimpressed, whereas before it came naturally. I took this as a good sign. "Well, I guess it pays good," she said.

"No, they're not really paying her, just living expenses is about all, I think. She's doing it just to do it. She wants to be part of a new society."

Trish stared. I pretended Hallie was there at the party somewhere, about to walk up behind me. "Six or seven years ago they threw out the dictator and gave all his land to the poor people," I said. "But they need a lot of help in the farming department now, because these soldiers keep attacking the poor farmers from across the border and burning up their crops."

Hallie would laugh at "farming department." She'd laugh at the whole scene, the education of Trish the Cheerleader. She would love me.

"The Communists," Trish said knowingly. "I heard about that. I heard they're thinking about sending the Marines down there to stop them from doing that."

"No, it's the other way around," I said patiently. "The Marines aren't rooting for the new society. The U.S. is paying the contras, the guys that attack the farmers." Hallie would not laugh now, she would be inflamed. She said we were a nation in love with forgetting the facts. She saved clippings that proved it. When Castro released those prisoners from Mariel: One day the headlines said we'd gotten him to free all these wonderful political prisoners. A month later when they were burning down halfway houses in Miami the papers castigated Fidel for exporting his hooligans and junkies.

Trish fiddled with her bra strap. "Hallie always would just up and do anything under the blue sky," she said.

"You're right," I told Trish. "I wish I were that brave. I'd be scared to death to be where she is."

"Well, you know, we can't all be the hero," she said, jutting her lower jaw to blow smoke up toward the olive branches. If I could have drawn blood, if I'd known how to do that with words instead of a needle, I would have. I wasn't sure what Hallie craved but I knew it wasn't glory.

"How's Doc Homer?" she asked.

I hadn't yet found the valor to go see him. I feared seeing him in failing condition. And still disapproving of me, on top of it. "Hard to say," I said.

I felt a tap on my shoulder and turned to see Loyd, grinning broadly. "Too good to speak to an Indian boy on Main Street?"

The tingle of a blush started behind my ears, and I ignored it. I'd learned since high school that in an emergency shyness can be disguised with a completely fake bravado. "You tried to run me down, Loyd! I ought to turn you in for reckless driving." I ran my fingers through my hair. "Actually, I didn't think you'd know who I was."

"Are you kidding? How many beautiful six-foot-tall women you think we've got in this town?"

"Five eleven," I corrected. "I'm the shorter of the bean-pole sisters." I felt suddenly drunk, though I wasn't, chemically speaking. Trish drifted off toward the barbecue pit.

He looked at me for a long time, just looked. Grinning. His left hand was fingering the tip of an olive branch and I expected him to snap it off but he didn't, he only took in its texture as someone might eat chocolate or inhale a cigarette.

"You want another beer?" he asked.

So that was going to be it, no filling in the last fifteen years. No constructing ourselves for each other—otherwise known as falling in love. "Think you can get over to that ice chest and back before this party is over?" I knew he wouldn't.

"In case I don't, I've got your phone number." He winked.

"Don't you worry. You'll be hearing from my lawyer."

I felt adrift and disappointed, though I hadn't held any conscious expectations of Loyd. I looked around at other faces, wondering if they all held secret disappointments for me. Doña Althea, the ancient woman we used to call the "Peacock Lady," was holding court in a lawn chair under the fig tree. She was the one who used to collect the feathers for piñatas. She looked today like she always had, dressed in black, fierce and miniature like a frightening breed of small dog. Even with her braided crown of silver hair she wasn't five feet tall. J.T.'s mother, Viola Domingos, and several other women sat in a group with her, fanning themselves in time to the music and drinking beer. J.T. and Loyd had apparently been commandeered into serving them food; the goat had been pronounced done. People were beginning to move toward the makeshift table, which I'd helped Emelina improvise from the doors to Mason's and the twins' rooms, covered with embroidered tablecloths compliments of the Stitch and Bitch Club. There was enough food to save an African nation. Potato salad, deviled eggs, *menudo*, tortillas and refried beans and a thousand kinds of dessert. I heard somebody say in a high-pitched voice, "*Tomato soup* in that cake? I wouldn't have guessed that for love nor money."

I wasn't in any hurry. I moved out of the way of the principal rush and stood near the gate to the side yard, near my little house. I noticed a dog lying very still and alert, just on the other side of the gate. It looked like an oversized coyote but it was definitely a domestic creature. It had a green bandana tied around its neck. This dog didn't belong to Emelina's household—I was pretty sure I knew all the family animals. It sat with its mouth slightly open and its ears cocked, staring steadily through the wire gate at the people inside.

"You thinking about crashing this party?" I asked the dog.

It glanced up at me for a second, with a patient look, then fixed its gaze back on the crowd. Or maybe on the roast goat.

"I'll bring you some of that, if you're willing to wait awhile," I said. "Nobody's going to miss one little bite."

The dog didn't respond to this promise.

All the old men had served themselves first and were settling down into a huddle of folding chairs near the front door of my cottage, holding their plates carefully horizontal above their knees. I started to move away, out of deference, but I noticed they were talking about fruit drop. I plainly heard one of them say the words, "poison ground." I stood four feet away and invisible, I suppose because they were men, and women talked to women. They asked questions of each other, to which they apparently already knew the answers.

"Do you know how much sulfuric they put in the river? He said the EPA give Black Mountain thirty days to shut down that leaching operation."

"Damn, man, that's *veneno*. How long you think we been putting that on our trees?"

"When did anybody ever tell the Mountain what to do?" The man who said this had a remarkably wrinkled brown face, like an Indian mummy I'd once seen in a roadside museum. "They'll pull some kind of strings," he said.

A man who sat with his back to me spoke up. "They won't fight the EPA. It's not worth it. They been saying for ten years that mine is dead. They're not hardly getting anything from that leaching operation."

Another man nodded at this, pointing his fork toward the head of the canyon. "Just enough to pay the taxes. That's all. They'll shut her down."

"You think so?" asked the one who reminded me of a mummy. "They're getting gold and moly out of them tailing piles. If they wasn't, they wouldn't keep running the acid through them. You boys know that damn company. They're not going to stop no leaching operation on account of our pecan trees." His voice trailed off and he was quiet for a minute, his callused fingers fooling with an unlit cigarette. I heard women's voices rising randomly over the din of the party, calling out instructions, reining in their kids. The party seemed like something underwater, a lost continent, and I felt profoundly sad though it wasn't my continent. I would go get a bite to eat, say something grateful to Emelina, and slip back into my house.

The man with his back to me said, "It's in Ray Pilar's apples and quince." He pronounced it "queens."

Another man, younger than the others, said, "It's going to kill every damn tree in this canyon. If I'm wrong, my friend, you can shoot me."

The man with the wrinkled face said, "If you're right, my friend, you might as well shoot yourself."

8

PICTURES

The dead mountain range of tailings on the lip of the mine had sat for decades, washed by rain, and still was barren as the Sahara. From a distance you might guess these piles of dirt to be fragile, like a sandcastle, but up close you'd see the pinkish soil corrugated with vertical ridges and eroded to a sheen, like rock. It would take a pickaxe to dent it.

It was high noon and I knew where I was. I bypassed the old mine road at the top of the canyon and stayed on the un-marked lane that people called, for reasons unknown to me, the Old Pony Road. All Grace's streets went by odd names that had mostly to do with picturesque forms of transportation: the Old and New Pony roads, the Goatleg, Dog-Cart Road, and the inexplicable Tortoise Road. Amazingly, most or all of these also had official, normal-sounding names like West Street and San Francisco Lane, which were plainly marked on painted alumi-num street signs and totally ignored. Maybe somebody had just recently dreamed up these normal names and hammered up signs to improve the town's image.

From the canyon's crest I could see down into the isolated settlements at the north end of the valley, some abandoned, some buried in deep graves of mine tailings, through which, presumably, Black Mountain now ran quantities of sulfuric acid.

Far to the south lay open desert. The road I was on would pass through one more flock of little houses, all settled like hens into their gardens, before reaching Doc Homer's drafty two-story gray edifice.

I bypassed the main entrance of the hospital, the only one of the ghost town of Black Mountain buildings that was still in use. The hospital itself had finally closed—people had to leave Grace for a more equipped town if their problems were major—but Doc Homer's office in the basement could handle anything up to and including broken limbs. He wasn't working there today. I'd called him at home; I was expected.

"Cosima? *Cosima Noline!* I want you to look." A heavyset woman in a housedress and running shoes was standing at her mailbox, shouting at me. "Child, will you look. If you aren't the picture of your mother."

My mother was dead at my age. The woman put her arms around me. She was nobody I recognized.

"We've been so anxious to see you!" she said at a convincing decibel level. "Viola told us at sewing club you'd got in, and was staying down with her and J.T. and Emelina till you can help Doc get his place straightened out and move in up here with him. Oh, I know Doc's glad to have you back. He's been poorly, I don't expect he'd tell you but he is. They said when you was overseas you learned the cure they used on that actress in Paris, France. Bless your heart, you're a dear child." She paused, finally, taking in my face. "You don't remember me, do you?"

I waited, expecting help. It had been fourteen years, after all. But she offered no hints. "No, I'm sorry," I said. "I don't."

"Uda!" The woman said.

"Oh, Uda. I'm sorry." I still didn't have the foggiest idea who she was.

"I won't keep you, hon, but I want you to come for dinner soon as you can. I've baked Doc a squash pie I've been aiming to take up there. Hang on, I'll just run get it."

I waited while she hurried on her small feet up the path to the house and disappeared into the cave of honeysuckle that had swallowed her front porch. Uda returned directly with a covered pie tin that I accepted along with a bewildering kiss on both cheeks. I wondered how many people in Grace believed I'd flown in fresh from Paris with a cure for Alzheimer's.

▼▼▼

He'd told me two years ago. I had no idea if it was the confirmed truth or just his opinion, since Doc Homer made no distinction between the two. And if it was true, I still didn't know what to think. What we are talking about, basically, is self-diagnosed insanity and that gets complicated.

Carlo and I in fact weren't living in Paris (we never had), but in Minnesota; we'd already come back from Crete. Hallie had kept decently in touch with Doc Homer but I hadn't, and felt guilty, so I engineered a visit in Las Cruces. God knows how long he would have waited to tell me, otherwise. This meeting was not a plan he'd cooked up to give me the news, but my idea, sprung at the last minute. An accident of science, actually. Someone had recently spliced the glow gene from a glowworm into a tobacco plant, and the scientific world was buzzing over this useless but remarkable fact. All the top geneticists were meeting in New Mexico and my boss wanted me down there to take notes. I was working at a high-powered research lab; this was prior to my moving back to Tucson and falling into convenience-mart clerking. If I ever wrote down on paper my full employment history, I assure you it would look like the résumé of a schizophrenic.

And in my professional upswings I had more of what passes for confidence; it dawned on me that it's an easy bus ride over the state line from Grace to Las Cruces. I'd phone Doc Homer.

I was astonished when he agreed to come. "Barring unforeseen difficulties at the hospital," he'd said over the phone. I didn't know yet that the hospital had closed; that he sometimes forgot.

"You always say that." It was true, that was his standard disclaimer on every promise to Hallie or me, but it was uncharacteristic for me to tease him. Truthfully, after such an ice age, there was no such thing as characteristic. I tried out joking, more or less to see if it would work. "You'll say that at your own funeral, Pop," I'd said boldly into the receiver. Later, after he told me, I could have bitten my tongue off for that.

We met in the lobby of the Holiday Inn, just for a couple of drinks since he said he had to get back to Grace that night. The bar was done up in this madly cheerful south-of-the-border décor, with a blue tile fountain and silk bougainvillaeas climbing out of clay pots shaped like pigs. It was somebody's idea of what Old Mexico would look like if you didn't have to take poverty into account. The waitresses wore swishy miniskirts with ruffles in contrasting primary colors. In this setting my father told me he had a terminal disorder of the brain.

All I kept thinking was that he must be wrong. I doubted he'd had a CAT scan. The thing to do would be to check into the University Hospital in Tucson and get a neurological workup, to rule out other things, but I didn't try to talk him into it. The nature of my relationship with Doc Homer, which had eluded me over the phone, came back instantly when I saw him. There are all the small things you love and despise about a parent: the disappointed eyes, the mannerisms, the sound of the voice as much as the meaning of the words, that add up to that singular thing—the way you are both going to respond, whether you like it or not. It had settled heavily over our table and I could hardly breathe. I knew this man. He wouldn't seek out a second opinion to stack up against his own. He'd suffer his own doubts but never anyone else's. The waitress swished over and brought us fresh margaritas. The trickle of the fountain put me on edge, the way a running toilet will, or any sound of water going to waste. "What are you going to do?" I asked Doc Homer.

"I don't see a need to do anything special, for the time being. I'll make arrangements when the time comes."

My stomach was tight. I felt perversely annoyed with the smiling clay pigs. I touched my lips to the coarse salt on the rim of the margarita glass, and the crystals felt like sand in my mouth, or broken glass. I thought of walls I'd seen in Mexico—high brick *hacienda* walls topped with a crest of broken bottles imbedded in cement, to keep people on their correct sides of the fence. If they want to provide an authentic Mexican flavor they should have something like that in here, I thought.

"Nobody else knows," he said. "And I'd like for you not to mention it to your sister."

I stared at him. I knew it wouldn't matter what came next, whether I said "Okay," or "Why?" or "That's not fair," which is what I mainly felt. Dr. Homer Noline had stopped talking, there being nothing more to say, in his opinion. I imagined him going back to Grace on the bus and lying that night in his bed, tired but wide awake, recalling the events of his day and wondering what pathways of thought in his brain might be slipping off track. Trying to remember what vegetable he'd cooked for dinner or what tie he'd worn. He might be confronting these thoughts with fear, or only clinical interest. I really didn't know.

For the first time in my life then, and just for a few seconds, I was able to see Doc Homer as someone I felt sorry for. It was a turning point for me, one of those instants of freakishly clear sight when you understand that your parent might have taken entirely the wrong road in life, even if that road includes your own existence. I pitied Doc Homer for his slavish self-sufficiency. For standing Hallie and me in the kitchen and inspecting us like a general, not for crooked hems so much as for signs of the weakness of our age: the lipstick hidden in a book satchel, the smoldering wish to be like everyone else. Being like no one else, being alone, was the central ethic of his life. Mine too, to some extent, not by choice but by default. My father, the only real candidate for center of my universe, was content to sail his private sea and leave me on my own. I still held that against him. I hadn't thought before about how self-sufficiency could turn on you in old age or sickness. The captain was going down with his ship. He was just a man, becoming a child. It became possible for me to go back to Grace.

▼▼▼

I arrived at the house, nervous, ludicrously armed with Uda's squash pie. But he was in his darkroom. Not waiting. He called it his workroom, I think to try to legitimize his hobby to himself. Doc Homer made pictures. Specifically, he made photographs of things that didn't look like what they actually were. He had hundreds: clouds that looked like animals, landscapes that looked like clouds. They were pressed between slabs of card-board, in closets. Only one was framed. The matting and framing were my present to him one Christmas when I was in high school, after I'd started making my own money. It had cost me a lot, and was a mistake. His hobby was a private thing, too frivolous in his opinion to be put on public display. I should have foreseen this, but didn't.

Nevertheless, he'd hung it in the kitchen, God only knows why because the man was far from sentimental, and there it still hung. It was the first thing I noticed when I knocked on the screen door and walked in. The photo was my favorite, a hand on a white table. And of course it wasn't a hand, but a clump of five saguaro cacti, oddly curved and bumpy, shot against a clear sky. All turned sideways. Odd as it seemed, this thing he did, there was a great deal of art to it.

I put the pie in the refrigerator and nosed around a little, telling myself it's what a good daughter would do. I pictured these good daughters—wifely and practical, wearing perms and loafers and Peter Pan collars. I didn't remotely look the part. As I crept around the house it felt to me like a great, sad, recently disclosed secret. The kitchen seemed smaller than when I was a girl, standing on a bucket to reach the sink, but that's natural. It was also crowded with odds and ends you wouldn't expect in a kitchen: a pair of Piper forceps, for example, washed with the day's dishes and sitting amongst them on the drainboard. This didn't signify any new eccentricity on his part. He'd always had a bizarre sense of utility. I could picture him using the forceps to deliver a head of cabbage from a pot of boiling water. Holding it up. Not in a show-off way, but proud he'd thought of it, as if he were part of a very small club of people who had the brains to put obstetrical instruments to use in the kitchen.

The rooms were cool and stale although it was hot outside. I stepped through the living room, over the old Turkish carpet, which looked malnourished, its bare white threads exposed like ribs. Doc Homer could afford better, I heard somebody say in my mind, a voice I couldn't identify. "All the money he's got up there." Which of course wasn't true, we never had much, that was just what people thought because we were standoffish.

Beyond the living room was the parlor where he used to see patients who'd come to the house, embarrassed, it seems to me now, at night when the office was closed. At present the parlor was shockingly cramped. The door to the outside porch was blocked by furniture I didn't remember: two sofas and something that looked like a cobbler's bench. Folded on a sofa was one thing I remembered well, a black crocheted afghan with red flowers. Hallie and I used to drag that thing around everywhere, our totem against disaster. It looked cleaner now than I'd ever seen it.

Magazines and journals were everywhere. His *American Journal of Genetics* was still organized chronologically on the shelf. That was his pet interest; they'd once published his article on the greatly inbred gene pool of Grace, with its marble-eyed babies. (He'd even rigged up a system for photographing the newborns' eyes, for documentation.) The trait first began showing up in the fifties, when third-cousin descendants of the Gracela sisters started marrying each other. Emelina would have been one of his subjects. You needed to get the gene from both sides; it was recessive. That's about what I knew. For me it was enough to understand that everyone in Grace was somehow related except us Nolines, the fish out of water. Our gene pool was back in Illinois.

Other magazines, many in number, were piled on the floor. I picked up a *Lancet: 1977*, my first year of med school. There was an important article on diabetes I remembered. Underneath, a recent *National Geographic*. There was no order at all. Though if I mentioned it he'd come up with some elaborate rationale before he'd admit to disorganization. South Sea Islands and Islets of Langerhans, I could see him saying, and not meaning it as a joke. The smell of mold was making my eyes water. I was inclined toward the stairs, to go up and see what kind of shape the bedrooms were in, but I didn't have the heart. It wasn't my house. I forced my hand to knock on the darkroom door.

"Open. I'm about to start printing."

I closed the door behind me. There was only a dim red light bulb. "Hi, Pop," I said.

He looked at me, unsurprised and not very much changed,

I could see as my eyes adjusted. I was prepared for frailty and incoherence but he was lucid and familiar. The same substantial hands and wrist bones, the straight nose and low, broad mouth—things I also have, without noticing much. He motioned for me to sit.

"So how are you these days?" I asked.

He ignored the question. We hadn't been together since the Holiday Inn lounge, two years ago, but from Doc Homer you didn't expect hugs and kisses. He was legendary in this regard. Hallie and I used to play a game we called "orphans" when we were with him in a crowd: "Who in this room is our true father or mother? Which is the one grownup here that loves us?" We'd watch for a sign—a solicitous glance, a compliment, someone who might even kneel down and straighten Hallie's hair ribbon, which we'd tugged out of alignment as bait. That person would never be Doc Homer. Proving to us, of course, that he wasn't the one grownup there who loved us.

I sat carefully on a cool file cabinet. He was adjusting black knobs on the enlarger, preparing to make a print. When he switched on the bulb an image appeared against the wall, in reverse: white trees, black sky, mottled foreground. I'd learned how to look at negatives many years before I read my first X-ray. He shrank the frame into focus, shut it off while he slid a rectangle of paper into place and set the timer, and then projected the picture again, burning it into the paper. In the center were two old men hunched on a stone wall, backs to the camera.

"They look like rocks," I said. "It's hard to see where the wall ends and the men start."

"Men who look like stones," said Doc Homer. His speech was more formal than most people's writing. Who else who would really say "stones"?

"Except for the hat," I said. "That hat's a giveaway."

"I'm taking it out." He held a small steel spatula into the beam of light and waved little circles over the area of the man's hat, as if he were rubbing it out, which is exactly what he was doing. Photographers call this "dodging," and the spatula was a "dodging tool," though in all probability this one was something used in gall-bladder surgery. When I was little I called it the Magic Wand.

The timer rang and he shut the projector off. I looked at his face in profile in the faint red light. Deep lines ran from his nose to the corners of his mouth. He didn't look well, but maybe he never had. He picked up the print by its edges.

"You haven't heard anything from Hallie, have you?"

He shook his head.

"You're sure you don't want me to tell her you've got, that you're sick? I'm sorry to bring this up, but it's hard to be the only one. I think she'd want to know."

He appeared not to have heard me. I knew he had. Doc Homer never argued, he just didn't participate in conversation that didn't please him.

"So did the man's hat go away?" I asked.

He slipped the paper into a dishpan of clear liquid. "We'll see." He seemed suddenly happy now, almost friendly, as he often did in here. The darkroom was the nearest I'd ever come to feeling like I had a dad. We stood without talking and watched a gray image grow on the paper like some fungus with a mind of its own. I thought about the complex chemistry of vision, remembering from medical school the textbook diagrams of an image projected through the eyeball, temporarily inscribed on the retina.

"I never thought about how printing a photograph duplicates eyesight," I said. "It's the same exact process in slow motion."

He nodded appreciatively and my heart warmed. I'd pleased him. "Probably there is no real invention in the modern world," he said. "Just a good deal of elaboration on nature." He lifted out the slick print and slipped it into a second tray, the fixer.

"The stone has no head," he pronounced, correctly; it looked like a rock wall with two extra rocks balanced on top. You'd think it was just a simple snapshot of what it looked like. His finest art defeated itself. God only knows what was the point, but it made him smile. When the timer rang again he took the photograph out and slid it into its final bath. He fished out several other prints and attached them with small clothespins to a wire. Then he dried his hands on a towel, one finger at a time. These gestures made me think of all the years he'd spent alone, doing his own dishes, his laundry.

I felt our visit drawing to a close, like a scientifically predicted death. We would go out into the light, find a little more to say, and then I'd go.

"There's a pie for you in the kitchen," I said. "From Uda. Who is she?"

"Uda Ruth Dell," he said, as though that explained it.

"I mean, what is she to me? Did I use to know her?"

"Not especially," said Doc Homer, still studying the photographs. "No better than you knew anyone else."

"She knows all about me, and then some," I said. "She probably knows what I had for lunch."

"You're in Grace," he said.

"Well, I was embarrassed because I couldn't remember her. She wasn't very helpful. She just stood there waiting for me to rack my brain and come up with her name. She sure knew me right off the bat."

Doc Homer didn't care for expressions like "right off the bat." He switched off the red light before opening the darkroom door, passing us through a moment of absolute darkness. He knew, but refused to accept, that I was afraid of the dark. The click and blackness plunged me into panic and I grabbed his upper arm. Surprisingly, he touched my knuckles lightly with his fingertips.

"You're in Grace," he said again, as if nothing had happened. "There is only one of you for all these people to be watching for. And so many of them for you."

▼▼▼

I'd lived all my life with a recurring nightmare. It would come to me in that drowsy twilight where sleep pulls on your mind with tempting music but is still preventable. When I let down my guard the dream would spring again, sending me back into weeks of insomnia. It had to do with losing my eyesight. It wasn't a complicated dream, like a movie, but a single, paralyzing freeze frame: there's a shattering pop, like glass breaking, and then I am blind.

Once, years ago on Crete, Carlo and I were driving on a badly rutted gravel road to get to a beach on the south of the island. A truck loaded with blood oranges kicked up a rock that broke the windshield in front of my face. I wasn't hurt, the rock only pocked the glass and spun out a spiderweb of cracks, but I spent the rest of the day in mute hysteria. Carlo never did know what was wrong. Any explanation I could think of sounded like superstition. My dream was very much more than a dream. It had so much living weight to it, such prescience, it felt like something that was someday bound to happen.

The insomnia, on the other hand, wasn't such a big problem as you might imagine. I worked around it. I read a lot. In med school I did my best studying while my classmates were in the throes of rapid eye movement. I still considered my night-prowling habits to be a kind of secret advantage I had over other people. I had the extra hours in my day that they were always wishing for.

Emelina would not understand this. The night before school started, she brought me warm milk.

"Don't worry about it," I said. She'd also brought out a blue embroidered tablecloth, which she shook out like a little sail and spread efficiently over my table. She felt the place needed more homey touches.

"You've got to have your sleep. They had a special on Nova about it. This man in Italy died from not sleeping for around eight months. Before he died he went crazy. He'd salute the doctors like he was in the army."

"Em, I'll live. That's too pretty, that tablecloth. Don't you need that?"

"Are you kidding? Since Grammy joined Stitch and Bitch she's been embroidering borders on the dish rags. What happens if you just lie in bed and count backward from ninety-nine? That's what I tell the boys to do when they can't settle down."

"Insomnia's different," I said. It was hard to explain this to people. "You know the light that comes on when you open the refrigerator door? Just imagine it stays on all the time, even after you close the door. That's what it's like in my head. The light stays on."

Emelina made herself comfortable in my other living-room chair. "You're like that Thoreau guy that lived at Walden Pond. Remember when we read that in Senior English? He only had two chairs. We need to get you some more stuff in here."

I was surprised that Henry Thoreau entered into Emelina's world view. "If I want company I can always go over to your house," I pointed out.

"That's the God's truth. I'm about ready to move out. Tonight Glen and Grammy got into it, oh boy, she says he's *impudent*. That's her all-time favorite word. Whenever Mason gets mad at somebody he yells 'You're impotent!' And people laugh, so we'll never get him to stop now."

I drank the milk. I could stand some mothering. I wondered if I'd had this in the back of my mind when I moved in here.

Emelina scrutinized my clean, white walls. "Codi, I hope you'll take this the right way, but I don't see how you can live in a place and have it feel like nobody lives there."

"I have things in here. My clothes, look in the closet. And books. Some of those books are very personal." This was true. Besides my *Field Guide to the Invertebrates* there were things Hallie had sent me over the years, and an old volume of American poetry—incomprehensibly, a graduation gift from Doc Homer.

"Your room was like this when we were in high school. I had posters of Paul Revere and the Raiders and dead corsages stuck in the mirror, every kind of junk. And when we'd go over to your house it was like a room somebody'd just moved out of."

"I'm neat," I said.

"It's not neat. It's *hyper* neat."

"Can you imagine what Doc Homer would have said if Paul Revere and the Raiders turned up in his home? Without an appointment?"

She laughed.

"Emelina, who's Uda Ruth Dell?"

"Well, you know her, she lives up by Doc Homer. She used to take care of you sometimes, I think. Her and that other woman that's dead now, I think her name was Naomi."

"She used to take care of us?" I'd been trying all day to place her. I couldn't believe I'd draw a complete blank on someone who'd been a fixture of my childhood.

"Sure. Uda's husband Eddie saved you and Hallie's life that time when you got stranded in a storm down by the crick."

"I don't have any idea what you're talking about."

"Yes you do. When you and Hallie almost drowned in that flood. You were just little."

"Well, how do you remember it, then? I don't."

"Everybody knew about that. It was a famous incident. You hid down in a coyote burrow and wouldn't come out and Eddie Dell found you and drug you out. You all stayed at Uda's. Doc Homer must have been working at the hospital or something."

"I don't remember anything about that."

Emelina looked at me peculiarly, as if she thought I might be pulling her leg. "It was a real big deal. There was a picture in the paper of you two and Eddie the big hero, and his mule."

"I guess I do remember," I said, but I didn't, and it bothered me that my childhood was everyone's property but my own.

"You know what you are, Codi? I don't know if there's a word for it, but it's the opposite of 'homemaker.' "

I laughed. She was still distressed by my blank walls. "There's a word. Home wrecker. But I'm not one."

"No I don't mean in the sense of home wrecker. I mean in the sense of home ignorer."

"Oh, that way," I said. I was playing dumb. I knew what she meant. My first boyfriend in college was a Buddhist, and even he had had more pictures on his wall than I did. It wasn't anything noble; I couldn't claim a disdain for worldly things. Hallie had once pointed out that I had more shoes than you'd find in a Central American schoolroom with class in session. What I failed at was the activity people call "nesting." For me, it never seemed like nesting season had arrived yet. Or I wasn't that kind of bird.

After Emelina left for the night, I wrote Hallie. I had a general-delivery address for her in Managua and I asked, the way we did when we were kids leaving notes for each other in secret hiding places, "Are you there yet? Are you reading this now?" I told her about the dead alfalfa fields around Gracela Canyon, which I thought would interest her professionally, and I told her Doc Homer seemed pretty much the same as ever, which was the truth. And I asked if she remembered the time we almost drowned in a coyote den.

9

THE BONES IN GOD'S BACKYARD

Grace High School, backdrop of the worst four years of my life, was as familiar as one of my bad dreams. Walking toward it up Prosper Street filled me with dread. The building itself had a lot of charm, though, which surprised me. As a child I'd paid no mind to the façade. It was a WPA-era building made of Gracela Canyon's red granite, with ornate egg-and-dart moldings on the white-painted eaves and woodwork over the doors. The school was actually built by the mining company, in its boom years, and with minerly instincts (or possibly just the proper tools) it was built right into the steep side of the canyon, sunk into rock. It was in an old part of town where the cobbled streets wrapped up and around behind the buildings, occasionally breaking into flights of steps and elsewhere so steep as to make motor vehicles pointless. The principal form of exercise in Grace was just getting from your house to wherever you needed to go.

The school had four floors, and each one had a street-level entrance. I'm pretty sure the building was in some record book on account of this. The main entrance was on the side, halfway up the hill: floor three. Carved into its granite arch was a grammatically suspect motto in Latin, CAUSAM MEAM COGNOSCO, which boys used to quote like pig latin or the inane "Indian" talk we heard in movies.

I checked into the principal's office, where his secretary, Anita, gave me a set of keys and an armload of official-looking papers and cheered me on. "There's a million forms there: grade forms, class roster, some new thing from the DES, and your CTA. It all has to be filled out."

"What, you mean I have to work for a living here? Somebody told me teaching high school was easy money." I looked through the stack of forms. "What about DOA? I may need one of those."

Anita looked at me oddly for half a second, then laughed. "We'll just call the coroner when they bring you in."

I smiled. Doc Homer was the coroner of Grace, and had been for the entirety of my life and then some. Obviously Anita didn't know who I was; she looked like a recent graduate herself. Anyone in high school now would have been a toddler when I left Grace. This filled me with hope. Walking those wainscoted halls, still painted the exact same shade of toothpaste green, made me shrink into my skin, and I had to keep reminding myself: None of them knows you as Doc Homer's misfit child. No one here has seen you in orthopedic shoes.

"The kids'll just love you," Anita said, surprising me. "They're not used to anybody so . . ." she paused, tapping a complete set of maroon fingernails on her metal desk and presumably fishing for a tactful adjective . . . "so *contemporary.*"

I was wearing a dark green blazer, tight jeans, and purple cowboy boots. I ran a hand through my hair and wondered if I should have paid a call to the Hollywood Shop, after all. "Do you think I'm not enough of an authority figure? Will they revolt?" The teachers' meeting, two days prior, had been devoted primarily to theories of discipline.

Anita laughed. "No way. They know who turns in the grades."

I found the room where I would be teaching General Biology I and II, and made it through the homeroom period by taking attendance and appearing preoccupied. I'd finally paid my preparatory visit to the school a few days earlier, so I knew what to expect in the way of equipment: desks and chairs; some stone-topped lab benches with sinks and arched chrome faucets; an emergency shower; a long glass case containing butterflies and many other insects in ill repair; and a closet full of dissecting pans and arcane audiovisual aids. The quaint provisions led me to expect I'd be working in something like a museum, or a British movie. When the kids filled the room for first period, though, they gave it a different slant. So far in Grace I hadn't seen a lot of full-blown teenagers. I wasn't expecting skateboard haircuts.

The girls seemed to feel a little sorry for me as I stood up there brushing chalk dust off my blazer and explaining what I intended for us to do in the coming year. But the boys sat with their enormous high-top sneakers splayed out into the aisles, their arms crossed, and their bangs in their eyes, looking at me like exactly what I was—one of the last annoying things standing between them and certified adulthood.

"You can call me Codi," I said, though I'd been warned against this. "Ms. Noline sounds too weird. I went to this high school and had biology in this room, and I don't really feel that old. I guess to you that sounds like a joke. To you I'm the wicked old witch of Life Science."

This got a very slight rise out of the boys, not exactly a laugh. The girls looked embarrassed. A tall boy wearing a Motley Crüe T-shirt and what looked like a five-o'clock shadow on his scalp pulled a cigarette out of his pocket and thumped it against his knuckles.

"I was told we'd need an authority figure in the classroom, so I dug one up." I went to the closet and wheeled out a human skeleton. "This is Mrs. Josephine Nash."

I'd found her downstairs in a storage room filled with damaged field-hockey equipment and gym uniforms from the fifties. The skeleton was in pretty good shape; I'd only had to reattach one elbow with piano wire and duct tape (provided by the janitor). The name—along with an address in Franklin, Illinois—was written in fine, antique-looking letters on the flange of her pelvis. When I discovered her in the storage room I felt moved to dust her off and hang her up on the heavy cast-iron stand and wheel her up to my lab. I guess I was somewhat desperate for companionship.

"Miss," one of the boys said. "Miss Codi."

I tried not to smile. "Yes."

"That's Mr. Bad Bones." He enunciated the name in a way that made everybody laugh. "The seniors use him for the Halloween Dance."

"Well, not anymore," I said. Mrs. Nash was my compatriot from the Midwest; a possible relative, even. I could see her as somebody's mother, out pruning roses. "This isn't a toy," I said, my voice shaking slightly. "It's the articulated skeleton of a human being who was at one time, fairly recently, walking around alive. Her name was Josephine Nash and she lived in Illinois. And it's time she got some respect in her retirement."

I glared at them; teenagers are so attached to their immortality. "You never know where you're going to end up in this world, do you?" I asked.

Nineteen pairs of blank, mostly pale-blue eyes looked back at me. You could have heard a cigarette drop.

"Okay," I said. "Chapter one: Matter, Energy, Organization and Life."

▼▼▼

"I don't know if I'm going to live through this," I told Emelina, collapsing in her kitchen. Her kitchen chairs were *equipales* that took you in like a hug, which I needed. My first day had gone as smoothly as anybody could reasonably hope—no revolts, no crises major or minor. Still, I couldn't put a finger on what it was, but standing in front of a roomful of high school students seemed to use up a ferocious amount of energy. It made me think of those dancers in white boots and miniskirts who used to work bars in the sixties, trying desperately to entertain, flailing around like there was no tomorrow.

Emelina, Mason, the baby, and I were all exiled to the kitchen; Viola had taken over the living room with her friends for a special afternoon meeting of the Stitch and Bitch Club. They were preparing for their annual fundraising bazaar, and as a backdrop to our own conversation we could overhear the exchange of presumably vital information:

"Last year the Hospital Equipment Committee didn't make fifteen cents on them sachet cushions."

"Well, it's no wonder. They stunk."

"Lalo saw in a magazine where you can make airplanes out of cut beer cans. The propellers go around."

Emelina set a cup of tea in front of me. I picked it up and let the steam touch my eyelids, realizing that what I needed most at that moment was to lie in bed with someone who was fond of every inch of my skin.

"It must be weird, going back to that school," she said.

"Oh, sure. It is. I didn't let myself think too much about that part of the job. Till today."

Mason was on the floor, coloring, and Emelina was moving around the kitchen in an effortless frenzy, closing drawers with her hip, cooking dinner, and feeding the baby at the same time.

"Let me do that," I said, scooting myself over to the high chair and taking the cereal bowl from Emelina.

"Here, he makes a pretty fair mess, let me give you Grammy's apron," she said, tying around me a splendid example of Stitch and Bitch enterprise. The baby snapped up cereal as fast as I could spoon it in, wasting little on mess as far as I could see.

"You're having dinner with us tonight, right?"

"No, thanks," I said.

"Honestly, Codi, if you think one more mouth to feed is any trouble you're out of your mind. If I woke up one day and had six more kids I don't think I'd notice."

"No, Em, thanks, but I feel like resting in peace."

"You're not dead yet, hon."

From the living room we heard Viola raising her voice now in Spanish, saying something about peacocks: *pavones*. The other women answered in Spanish, and I could follow just enough to know that they'd moved rapidly onto the subject of fruit trees. Doña Althea sounded agitated. Her high-pitched voice was easy to recognize, exactly what you'd expect from a very small, strong-willed woman. Emelina raised her eyebrows as she looked under a pot lid. "Do you know the boys won't even speak Spanish to their Grammy?" she asked in a subdued voice.

I glanced at Mason, who was absorbed in his coloring book, though probably listening. "Is that a problem?"

"Oh, yeah. Viola's big on all the traditional stuff. She's real tight with Doña Althea. She wants us to raise the boys *puro*, speaking Spanish and knowing all the stories. Seems like it might be easier with girls, but these guys . . ." She shrugged her shoulders. "My parents were always so modern, you remember how Mom is, electric can openers all the way. I always felt like she wanted me to grow up *blonde,* you know? My dad told me she actually wanted to name me *Gidget!*"

I laughed. "No. He was pulling your leg."

"No, he wasn't. And poor Tucker was named after a car."

Tucker was a younger brother who'd died in infancy, before I ever knew the family. To tell the truth, I'd forgotten him, in spite of his name passed on to Emelina's first son.

The baby was sitting with his mouth opened unbelievably wide, waiting for my attention to return to his dinner. I poked in the next bite. A scattering of loud laughter like a rainstorm came from the other room, and all of us in the kitchen were quiet. This gang of old women staked out such a presence, we felt almost crowded out of the house. Mason actually gathered up his papers and started to go outside.

Emelina called him back. "Wait a minute, Mason, before you run off, come show Codi your hand. Codi, could you take a look at his hand? There's some kind of bump on it. Do you mind?"

"Why would I mind? Let's have a look." I felt uncomfortable, not because she'd asked, but with myself, playing doctor. I *was* a doctor, technically, which is to say I had the training, but it unnerved me to think people saw me in that role. Both Emelina and Mason were quiet while I examined his hand. I bent the wrist back and forth and felt the lump on the tendon. "It's a ganglion."

"Is that bad?" Emelina asked.

"No, it's not serious at all. Just a little bump. Usually they go away on their own. Does it hurt, Mason?"

He shook his head. "Only when he has chores to do," Emelina offered.

I put a kiss on my fingertips and rubbed it into his wrist. "There you go, Dr. Codi's special cure." As he ran off it occurred to me, with a certain self-punitive malice, that this was the extent of special curing I was licensed to dispense.

"So what's it like up there at the high school?" Emelina asked.

"Don't you keep feeling like Miss Lester's going to catch you smoking in the bathroom?"

"*I* never smoked in the bathroom," I said, scraping the bottom of the cereal bowl and wiping the baby's mouth with his bib. I'd never seen such efficient eating in my life.

"Oh that's right, Miss Goody Two-Shoes, I forgot. You didn't do things like that." Emelina smiled. She'd been at least as virtuous as I was in high school; the difference was she was popular. Virtue in a cheerleader is admirable, while in a wallflower it's gratuitous.

"Miss Goody Orthopedic-Shoes," I said.

She hooted. "*Why* on God's green earth did you and Hallie wear those shoes? I never did ask. I figured the polite thing was to just ignore them. Like when somebody has something hanging out of their nose."

"Thank you. We wore them because Doc Homer was obsessed with the bones of the foot."

"Kinky old Doc," she said, stabbing a wooden spoon into a pot of boiled potatoes.

"You have no idea. He used to sit us down and give us lectures on how women destroy their bodies through impractical footwear." I delivered his lecture, which Hallie and I used to ape behind his back: "Of the two hundred bones in the human body, more than a quarter are in the foot. It is a more complicated instrument that an automobile transmission, and it is treated with far less consideration."

Emelina was laughing. "Really, you have to give him credit. All my mom ever told me was 'Sit up straight! Don't get pregnant! And wear a slip!' "

"Doc Homer wasn't that great on pregnancy and underwear, but Lord knows the Noline girls were not going to have fallen arches."

"Where'd you get those god-awful things from? Not the Hollywood Shop, I know that."

"Mail order."

"No."

"Swear to God. Hallie and I used to burn the catalogues in the fireplace when they came but he'd still get those damn shoes.

For the sizing he'd draw around our feet on a piece of paper and then take all these different measurements. I expect I spent more time with Doc Homer getting my foot measured than any other thing."

Emelina found this hilarious. I know she thought I was exaggerating, but I wasn't. In a way we were grateful for the attention, but the shoes were so appalling. They affected our lives, the two of us differently. Hallie just gave up trying for image, while I went the route of caring too much. It was harder for me, being the first to break into junior high, then high school, in these shoes. I suffered first and therefore more.

"I'm positive that was the whole reason I hardly ever had any dates in high school," I told Emelina.

"That's ridiculous," she said. "The only reason boys didn't ask you out was because they thought you were too good for them. You were so smart, why would you want to run with a Grace boy? That's what they thought."

The meeting in the living room was beginning to break up. We lowered our voices automatically.

"No," I said solemnly. "It was the shoes. It's a known fact. The day I left Grace I bought a pair of gladiator sandals and my sex life picked right up."

▼▼▼

Emelina eventually remembered a letter for me she'd been carrying around a while. She'd stuck it in the diaper bag when she picked up the mail, and then forgotten it, so it suffered more in its last hundred yards of delivery than it had in its previous fifteen hundred miles. Of course, it was from Hallie.

I went home to read it, like a rat scurrying back to its hole with some edible prize. I settled into the living-room chair, polished my glasses, and scowled at the postmark: Chiapas, near Mexico's southern border, only days after she left. That was a disappointment, anything could have happened since then. I slit it open.

Codi dear,
    I've been driving the way you're supposed to here, like a bat out of hell, the *wrong way* out of hell whenever that's possible. I'm getting

the hang of outlawry. You'd be proud. I burned up the road till around La Cruz and then slowed down enough to enjoy the banana trees going by in a blur. The tropics are such a gaudy joke: people have to live with every other kind of poverty, but a fortune in *flowers*, growing out of every nook and cranny of anything. If you could just build an economy on flowers. I stayed in a house that had vanilla orchids growing out of the gutters and a banana tree coming up under the kitchen sink. I swear. There were some kind of little animals too, like mongooses. You would know what they are. I'm happy to be in a jungle again. You know me, I'm always cheered by the sight of houseplants growing wild and fifty feet tall. I keep thinking about 626-BUGS and all those sad ladies trying to grow zebrinas in an arid climate.

I wanted to take the coast highway as far as Nayarit, where it gets rugged, but I paid the price for that little adventure. (Doc Homer would say: I paid a dollar for my shiny dime.) I broke, not bent but flat out busted an axle in Tuxpan and spent two days waiting around while a man with a Fanta delivery truck and time on his hands brought in a new one from Guadalajara. The only hotel was a two-story pension with live band (euphemism) on weekends. I spent the time mostly sitting on my balcony watching pelicans dive-bomb the sea, and remembering our trip to San Blas. Remember those pelicans? If you'd been there, in Tuxpan, it would have been fun. I couldn't bring myself to do anything productive—there were people I could have talked to about crops and the refugee scene, but instead I spent one whole morning watching a man walk up the beach selling shrimp door to door. He had a pole over his shoulders, with the bucket of shrimp hung on one side and on the other side a plastic jug of water. Every time he sold a kilo of shrimp he'd pour out that much water and drink it, to balance the load. I watched him all the way down the bay and thought, *I want to be like that.* Not like the man selling shrimp. Like his *machine.* To give myself over to utility, with no waste.

But I was useless, lying around those two days. Saving my strength for what's ahead, I guess. I get more jumpy as I move south, like a compass needle or something. Saw an awful lot of dead cropland in the interior, and I know it will be worse in Nicaragua. War brings out the worst in production agriculture.

Tomorrow I cross the border, but it's hard to say where the border is, because this whole part of Chiapas where I am now is camps of

Guatemalans. This whole livelong day I drove horrible
roads in the rain and saw refugee camps, one after ano'
dream. They say the Guatemalan army is on a new scorc
campaign, so people come running across the border with th
on their backs and their hearts in their throats and on a g
the Mexican cops don't bother them. On a bad day, they ma.
wake up the kids, take down their hammocks, and move into
body else's district. It's a collective death. A whole land-based cu.
is being relocated out of its land—like a body trying to move out
its skin. Only the portable things survive. The women have thei
backstrap looms and woven clothes, like you see sometimes in import stores. All those brilliant colors in this hopeless place, it kills
you.

　　Right this minute I'm sitting in the rain, waiting for the mail
truck/water delivery (I keep expecting that same guy with his Fanta
truck) and watching four barefoot kids around a cook fire. The one
in charge is maybe six. She's sharpening cooking sticks while these
damp black chickens strut around shaking themselves and the toddlers pull logs out and roll them to make sparks. I'm just on edge.
You live your life in the States and you can't even picture something
like this. It's easy to get used to the privilege of a safe life.

　　I know you're worrying but you don't have to, since we've established that I'm the luckiest person alive. Even though I don't feel
like it. I'll write from Nica next. I'm sure I'll be happier once I'm put
to some use. I miss you, Codi, write and make me feel better.

　　Love from your faithful adoring slave-for-life,

　　　　　　　　　　　　　　　　　　　　　　　　　　Hallie

　　The ending was an old joke: in our letters we used to try to
outdo each other with ingratiating closures. The rest of the lette
was pure Hallie. Even in a lethargic mood she noticed ever
vanilla orchid, every agony and ecstasy. Especially agony. Sh
might as well not have had skin, where emotions were cor
cerned. Other people's hurt ran right over into her flesh. F
example: I'll flip through a newspaper and take note of the va
ious disasters, and then Hallie will read the same paper and cr
her eyes out. She'll feel like she has to *do* something about it.
And me, if I want to do anything, it's to run hell for leather i
the other direction. Maybe it's true what they say, that as lon

u're nursing your own pain, whatever it is, you'll turn your
on others in the same boat. You'll want to believe the fix
're in is their own damn fault.

The strangest thing is that where pain seemed to have
ssthetized me, it gave Hallie extra nerve endings. This haunts
e. What we suffered in our lives we went through together,
ut somehow we came out different doors, on different ground
levels.

▼▼▼

Friday night after the first week of school, the dog with the
green bandana showed up again at the gate. I saw it when I
came outside after my solitary supper to water the morning
glories and potted geraniums on my front step. The heat seemed
to wilt them right down to death's door, but water always
brought them back. I could only wish for such resilience.

"Hi, buddy," I said to the dog. "No barbecues today. You're
out of luck."

Thirty seconds later Loyd was standing at the door with a
bottle of beer. "I told you I'd get back to you with this," he said,
grinning. "I'm a man of my word."

"Well, okay," I said. "I guess you are." I wasn't sure how I
felt about seeing him in my doorway, other than surprised. I
pulled a couple of folding chairs onto the patio, where we could
see the sunset. The sky was a bright, artificial-looking orange,
a color you might expect to see in the Hollywood Shop. "Are
you going to have one too, or do I drink this alone?" I asked
him.

Loyd said he'd just take a soda because he was marked up
and five times out. I was mystified by this information.

"I'm marked up on the call board at the depot," he explained.
"To take a train out. Five times out means I'm fifth in line. I'll
probably get called late tonight or early tomorrow morning."

"Oh," I said. "It sounded like baseball scores. The count is
three and two and it's the bottom of the seventh."

Loyd laughed. "I guess it would sound like that. You get
used to talking railroad talk like it was plain English. Around
here that's about all everybody does, is railroad."

"That, and watch the fruit fall off their trees."

Loyd looked at me, surprised. "You know about that, do you?"

"Not very much," I said. I went into my house to get him a soda, picking my way over the rough bricks of the patio because I was barefoot. I will say this much for Doc Homer's career as a father: my arches are faultless.

When I came back out I sat down and handed over a Coke, letting Loyd fight with the easy-off twist cap himself. I had to use pliers on those things. It didn't give Loyd two seconds of trouble. He palmed it, then tipped his head back and drank about half the bottle. The things that aggravate me most in the world are the things men do without even knowing it.

"So is that your dog?" I asked.

"That's Jack. You met? Jack, this lady here is Codi Noline."

"We've met," I said. "I sneaked him some goat spare ribs the other day at the fiesta. I hope he's not on a special diet or anything."

"He's in love, is what he is, if you gave him a piece of that goat. That was one of Angel Pilar's yearling billy goats. Jack's had his eye on those spare ribs ever since last summer."

Jack looked at me, panting seriously. His tongue was purplish, and his eyes were very dark brown and lively. Sometimes when you look into an animal's eyes you see nothing, no sign of connection, just the flat stare of a wild creature. But Jack's eyes spoke worlds. I liked him.

"He looks like a coyote," I said.

"He is. Half. I'll tell you the story of his life sometime."

"I can't wait," I said, really meaning it, though it came out sounding a little sarcastic. Our chairs were close enough together so that I could have reached over and squeezed Loyd's hand, but I didn't do that.

"It was nice of you to come by," I said.

"So this was your first week of school, right? How's life with the juvenile delinquents of Grace?"

I was a little bit flattered that he knew about my job. But then everybody would. "I don't know," I said. "Pretty scary, I think. I'll keep you posted."

The sky had faded from orange to pale pink, and the courtyard was dusky under the fig trees. Every night as it got dark
the vegetation around the house seemed to draw itself in closer,
hugging the whitewashed walls, growing dense as a jungle.

Loyd touched my forearm lightly and pointed. On the cliff
above the courtyard wall, a pair of coyotes trotted along a narrow
animal path. Jack's ears stood up and rotated like tracking dishes
as we watched them pass.

"You know what the Navajos call coyotes? God's dogs," Loyd
said. His fingers were still resting on my forearm.

"Why's that?" I asked.

He took his hand back and cracked his knuckles behind his
head. He leaned back in his chair, stretching out his legs. "I
don't know. I guess because they run around burying bones in
God's backyard."

Jack got up and went to the courtyard wall. He stood as still
as a rock fence except for one back leg, which trembled, betraying
all the contained force of whatever it was he wanted to do just
then, but couldn't. After a minute he came back to Loyd's feet,
turned his body in a tight circle two or three times, and lay down
with a soft moan.

"Why do they do that? Turn in circles like that?" I asked. I'd
never lived with a dog and was slightly infatuated with Jack.

"Beating down the tall grass to make a nice little nest," Loyd
said. "Even if there's no tall grass."

"Well, I guess that make sense, from a dog's point of view."

"Sure it does." He bent forward to scratch Jack between the
ears. "We take these good, smart animals and put them in a
house and then wonder why they keep on doing the stuff that
made them happy for a million years. A dog can't think that
much about what he's doing, he just does what feels right."

We were both quiet for a while. "How do you know what
the Navajos call coyotes? I thought you were Apache." I felt
vaguely that it might be racist to discuss Loyd's breeding, but
he didn't seem offended.

"I'm a lot of stuff," he said. "I'm a mongrel, like Jack. I was
born up in Santa Rosalia Pueblo. My mama still lives up there.
You ever been up there to Pueblo country?"

"No," I said.

"It's pretty country. You ought to go sometime. I lived up there when I was a little kid, me and my brother Leander. God, we ran wild all over that place."

"You have a brother? I never knew that."

"Twin," Loyd said. "He's dead."

Everybody's got a secret, I thought, and for the first time that evening I remembered the child of Loyd's that was unknown to him. It felt furtive and strange to hold it in mind in his presence, as if I were truly holding it, and he might see it.

A dust-colored peafowl hopped onto the courtyard wall and then into the fig, rustling the leaves and warning us off with a throaty, chirruping sound. She was awkward and heavy-bodied, no more flight-worthy than a helicopter.

"So you're Pueblo, and Apache, and Navajo," I said.

"My dad's Apache. We boys left Mama and came down to White Mountain to live with him, but it didn't work out. I ended up in Grace with my mama's sister. You knew my *tía* Sonia, right?"

"I don't think so. Is she still around?"

"No. She's gone back to Santa Rosalia. I need to go up there and see her and Mama one of these days."

It sounded like a strangely scattered family. I still wasn't clear on the Navajo connection.

"Can I use your phone?" he asked suddenly.

"Sure. It might be in use, it's Emelina's and J.T.'s phone. They just ran an extension out for me."

He looked toward the main house as he ducked into my front door. Emelina and J.T. were both home tonight, and Loyd seemed a little guilty about not going over to say hello. It would have been easy for him to come by on the pretense of visiting them, but he hadn't. I wondered if Loyd still had a reputation as a ladies' man. Though it was nothing to me, one way or the other. Jack raised his head and peered at me through the darkness, then got up and moved slightly closer to me. I stretched my leg and rubbed his back with my bare foot. His coat was a strange blend of textures: wiry on top and soft, almost downy underneath.

Hallie and I almost had a dog once, back when our Tucson house was on the underground railroad. Hallie had come home one night with a refugee woman and child and a little cinnamon dog. The mother had been tortured and her eyes offered out that flatness, like a zoo animal. But I remember the girl, in a short pink dress and corduroy pants, following that puppy under the bathroom sink and all over the house. I had no reason to believe, now, that any of the three was still living. The woman and her daughter were eventually arrested and sent back to tropical, lethal San Salvador. And we'd decided realistically that we didn't have room for a dog, so it went to the Humane Society. Terms like that, "Humane Society," are devised with people like me in mind, who don't care to dwell on what happens to the innocent.

Loyd came back out, being careful not to slam the decrepit screen door. "I'm next in line," he said. "Three guys ahead of me laid off to watch the Padres game. I better get home." Jack got up instantly and went to his side.

"Well, thanks," I said, still thinking of the cinnamon dog. I held up my bottle. "It's nice to see you again, Loyd."

He stood there grinning, the fingers of his right hand playing with Jack's nape. I didn't know quite how to finish off the evening. Loyd hesitated and then said, "I've got to drive up to Whiteriver, a week from Saturday. To see about something."

"Well, that sounds mysterious," I said.

"To see about some game birds. Anyway I thought you might like to get out of here for some fresh air. You want to go?"

I took a deep breath. "Sure," I said. I wasn't sure at all, but my mind had apparently made itself up. "Okay. I could use some fresh air."

Loyd gave a funny little nod, and went out through the gate. Jack disappeared behind him into the cactus jungle.

10

THE MASK

He is lying on his own examining table, resting his eyes. The telephone buzzes quietly but Mrs. Quintana, his receptionist, has given up the battle with insurance forms and gone home.

He places his long hands over his face, the fingertips lightly touching his forehead, thumbs resting on the maxillary bones beneath his eyes. His office in the hospital basement is cool even in this late September heat, and pleasant in winter as well. As practical and comforting as a cave. The lack of windows has never been a problem; artificial lighting is adequate. He has just examined his last patient of the day, a sixteen-year-old with six small gold rings piercing the cartilage of her left ear. She is expecting twins. They will be born small, and in trouble. There was no reason to tell her everything.

He imagines the procedure by which the tiny gold wires were inserted through flesh and spongy bone. It would have to be painful. He is mystified. Children devote slavish attention to these things, but can't be bothered with prophylactics.

He drifts between wakefulness and sleep, thinking of Codi. Her eyes are downturned and secretive, her heart clearly hardened against him already, to have done this. Her hair is in her eyes. She flips it sideways, chewing the inside of her lip and looking out the window when he talks to her. She'd wanted

pierced ears at thirteen; he'd explained that self-mutilation was
preposterous and archaic. Now they discuss shoes. He wants to
ask, "Do you know what you have inside you? Does your sister
know?" Hallie is young to understand reproductive matters but
it's impossible that she wouldn't know, they're so much of a
single mind, and he is outside of it completely. He has no idea
what he can say.

She's in the fifth or sixth month, from the look of her, although Codi was always too thin and now is dangerously thin,
and so skillful at disguising it with her clothes he can only tell
by other signs. The deepened pigmentation under her eyes and
across the bridge of her nose, for one thing, is identical to the
mask of pregnancy Alice wore both times, first with Codi, then
with Hallie. It stuns him. He feels a sharp pain in his spleen
when he looks across the breakfast table each morning and sees
this: his wife's face. The ghost of their happiest time returned
to inhabit the miserable body of their child. He can't help feeling
he has damaged them all, just by linking them together. His
family is a web of women dead and alive, with himself at the
center like a spider, driven by different instincts. He lies mute,
hearing only in the tactile way that a spider hears, touching the
threads of the web with long extended fingertips and listening.
Listening for trapped life.

COSIMA

11

A RIVER ON THE MOON

Loyd and I didn't go to Whiteriver. He was called out on Friday for a seven-day stand on a switch engine in Lordsburg. He seemed disappointed and promised we'd go another time. Loyd didn't have much seniority on the railroad; he'd only moved back to Grace a few years earlier, and at Southern Pacific he was still getting what he called "bumped" a lot. It was hard to plan his time off.

I was somewhat relieved. I'd been unsure of what I was getting into, and had my doubts. Once I found out, I had more.

I'd asked J.T. what "game birds" were. He and I were out working in the old plum orchard one evening, pruning dead branches out of the trees. My job was mainly to stay out of the way of falling timber. It was a fair distance from the house, and Emelina had asked if I could go along to keep an eye on him. She wasn't the type to worry, but a man hanging from the tree-tops wielding a chainsaw is a nerve-racking sight, believe me. Even if he isn't your husband.

J.T. informed me that game birds were fighting cocks. He was taking a break just then, leaning on one hand against a tree trunk and drinking what seemed like gallons of water.

I was stunned. "You mean like cockfights."

J.T. smiled. "You been talking to Loyd?"

"He invited me to go with him up to Whiteriver. He said something about game birds, and . . ." I laughed at myself. "I don't know, I was thinking of something you'd eat. Cornish hens."

He laughed too. He offered me the jar of water and I drank from it before handing it back. I was surprised at the easy intimacy I felt with J.T. We hadn't been friends in high school—he was, after all, captain of the football team. Through no meanness on his part, but simply because of the natural laws of adolescent segregation, we might as well have gone to high school on different planets. Being neighbors again now brought back what we'd forgotten then: we had a relationship that dated back even before Emelina. We were next-door neighbors in toddlerhood. We'd played together before male and female had meaning.

He turned up the glass jar and drank it to the bottom, tensing the muscles in his jaw when he swallowed. J.T.'s whole body shone with sweat. I briefly imagined him naked, which disturbed me. I'd slept with someone's husband before—an Asian history professor in college—mistaking his marital status for something comforting and fatherly. But I was devoted to Emelina. No, that wouldn't happen.

It was early October, and still hot. Grace was supposed to have the perfect climate, like Camelot or Hawaii, and it's true that growing up here I could hardly remember an uncomfortable day, temperature-wise. Most of the homes had neither air-conditioning nor central heating, and didn't need them, but this fall had turned into hell warmed over. Down in the desert, in Tucson, every day was in the hundred-and-teens and the TV weathermen were reporting the string of broken records almost proudly, like scores in a new sport. In Grace no one kept track especially, but we suffered just the same.

J.T. knelt down to start the chainsaw again, but I spoke up before he could yank the cord. "I thought cockfighting was illegal."

"Most everywhere it is, but not in the state of Arizona. And up on the reservation they've got their own laws. Loyd's not a criminal, if that's what you're asking."

"I guess I don't know what I'm asking. I just can't see Loyd and cockfighting."

"His daddy was real big in the sport. He was kind of a legend up there in Apache country."

"So Loyd's got to keep up the tradition," I said, without sympathy. I knew Loyd's father was also a renowned drunk.

J.T. asked, "You an animal lover?"

"Not to extremes," I said. "I eat them." I thought of how unmoved I'd been watching Emelina chop off heads for our Sunday dinner, that first day in Grace. "But watching animals kill each other for sport," I said tentatively, "that's kind of an unsavory business, isn't it?" I looked toward the edge of the orchard. It was getting dark fast. Already I could see moonlight reflected in the irrigation ditches.

J.T. sat on his heels and looked straight up into the branches over our heads. "I don't know why I mess with these trees," he said. "They're sixty years old. They don't produce worth a damn anymore. I could cut them down and get a lot better out of this ground, not to mention the firewood. But my daddy gave me this orchard." He picked up the stone of a plum, weathered shiny white like a tooth, and rubbed it with his thumb. After a minute he raised his arm with a quick overhand snap and threw it toward the river. "Loyd's old man didn't have one damn thing to give him but cockfighting." J.T. looked at me. "I'm not crazy about it either, Codi. But you've got to know Loyd before you decide."

▼▼▼

I dropped the subject of cockfighting. Loyd had begun to come by fairly regularly in the evenings, which is to say regular for a railroad man: I'd see him three days in a row, and then not at all for a week. It reinforced the feeling that we were only casual acquaintances, meeting nearly by accident, and I tried to limit my expectations to the point where I paid no attention to how I looked in the evenings. Sometimes as I walked around the brick floors of my living room and bedroom I'd realize I was listening for the jingle of Jack's tags, and then I'd click on the radio.

When Loyd did show up we would drag our lawn chairs out for a view of the sun's parting shot at the canyon wall, and we'd talk about nothing in particular. For instance, he told me the story of Jack's life. Jack's mother was a coyote that Loyd took in when he was living up on the Apache reservation. She'd been crippled with buckshot in her shoulder, and had gone into heat. Loyd saw her one night skirting the arroyo behind his house, trying to get away from a pack of males. He got her attention with a low whistle, and then he left his front door open and went to bed; next morning, she was curled up under his cot.

I didn't question this. For one thing, he seemed to hold a power over females of all types. But truly Loyd had the most unself-conscious way of telling a story I'd ever heard, as if it didn't matter whether I was impressed or not, he was just going to give me the facts. It seemed as if he didn't care enough, one way or the other, to lie.

"I kept her shut up in the house for a week with my dad's old dog, Gunner. Gunner lost one of his back legs when he was a pup and he could get around real good, but he'd never in his life mounted a female. I thought she'd be safe with him."

This matter-of-fact talk about heat and mounting made me slightly edgy, or rather, edgy once-removed. I felt like I *ought* to be uneasy with Loyd, but I wasn't. To him it was life and death and dogs. Sometimes Loyd seemed about twelve.

"Well, Jack is here to tell the tale," I said. "So I guess she wasn't safe."

Loyd smiled. "Nope. Old Gunner had his one chance at love. He got into some poisoned coyote bait right after that. He died before the pups were born."

"How do you know they were his? She could have been pregnant already."

Loyd asked Jack, as politely as you'd ask a favor from a friend, to roll over. "See that?" Over Jack's heart was a white patch with a black crescent moon in its center. "That's Gunner's. There were seven pups, two black and five brown, and every one of them had that badge."

"How did you know which one to keep?"

He hesitated. "Dad decided," he said finally. "And Jack. Really I guess Jack's the one that decided."

They were nothing electrifying, these chats with Loyd in the dark, but they were a relief from my days at the high school, which were spent in a standoff just shy of open war. Occasionally Loyd took the tips of my fingers and rubbed them absentmindedly between his own, the way he would surely stroke Jack, if Jack had fingers. The night of the story of Jack, he also kissed me before he left, and I was surprised by how I responded. Kissing Loyd was delicious, like some drug I wanted more of in spite of the Surgeon General's warning. Later on, when I slept, I had dreams of coyotes in heat.

I also saw Hallie. Her hair moved around her like something alive. "I've kissed a man who kills birds," I confessed, but she looked past me as if she didn't have a sister. Her eyes were pale as marbles. I woke up confused, too shaken to get up and turn on a light.

I'd dreamt of Carlo, too, on several occasions, for no good reason I could see. He'd written me a letter that was fairly medical and devoid of passion. He did miss me, though, and that sentiment brought comfort as I lay in my empty bed. It meant I was lonely by choice, or by difficult circumstances such as an ailing father; these things are supposed to feel better than being lonely because nobody wants you. Lately I'd started thinking about Carlo with a kind of romantic wistfulness, which I knew was bogus. The truth is, we'd essentially promised each other from the beginning that we wouldn't stay together. "No strings," we said, proving that we were mature medical students without spare time. The odd thing is that we did stay together, physically, and so I suppose falling out of love was our hearts' way of keeping the bargain. The end was always curled up there between us, like a sleeping cat, present even in our lovemaking.

Especially there. Carlo and I had gone to bed together for the first time one early dawn during our rotation in pediatric intensive care, after we'd worked all night trying to save a Papago baby brought in too late from the reservation. We'd gone straight from the dead baby to my apartment, my bed. There was hardly any talk that I remembered, we just held on to each other, joined, for as long as our bodies could stand it. I wanted anything that would stop that pain, and Carlo was strong medicine. Not happiness, nothing joyful, only medicine.

There was one other time of desperate, feverish connection that I particularly remembered. This was much later, when Carlo and I were living abroad. Carlo had been granted the opportunity to spend a year in an unbelievably remote clinic, halfway up the tallest mountain in central Crete.

The work was rugged, but in December we took a trip away from the village, to Venice. The clinic closed for some combination of clan ritual and Greek Orthodox holiday that practically evacuated the village. We set off for Italy feeling like truant school kids, drinking wine in tin cups on the train and reeling with the heady sense of getting away with something. Before that he'd scarcely managed an afternoon off, much less a week. Then Carlo came down with a cold on the overnight ferry to Brindisi, and by the time we reached Venice we were both burning up, our skin hot to the touch, like furnaces. Our bodies' internal combustion gave rise to an unquenchable craving for carbohydrates, and for each other, so we checked into the *Penzione Meraviglioso* and for a week ate plates of pasta and made a kind of sweaty, delirious love previously unknown to either of us, in a bed that was memorably soft and huge.

The *Penzione* looked out onto the cold, damp Grand Canal and a dim little plaza ominously named the Piazza of the Distraught Widows. (Distraught or Inconvenienced, it could translate either way.) The origin of this name was unknown to the elderly matron, who was born and raised in the building. She brought food up to us and was alternately scandalized by our appetites and worried for our well-being. She was of the opinion that in damp weather any illness at all would find its way to the lungs. She ventured to tell us we ought to see a doctor.

Carlo spoke Italian. His father had come to America on a steamer carrying cured leather and Chianti. He explained in grammatically imperfect but polite terms that we were both doctors. We could not be in better hands, he said. For my benefit, later, he'd translated the double entendre. By the end of the week, Carlo and the matron were bosom friends. In spite of his notorious shyness, whenever she brought us hot tea he would sit up in bed with a shirt on and give opinions on the infertility of her eldest daughter and the lung ailment of her son-in-law who worked in the glassblowing trade. I lay beside him, meanwhile, with the sheets pulled around my neck, feeling sinful and out of place, like a whore taken home to meet Mother. The matron didn't ask for my opinions, probably because she didn't believe I was actually a doctor. Which I wasn't, technically. I did some work at the clinic—rural Crete was not overly concerned about licensure—but to be completely honest, I was Carlo's paramour. I did the shopping. I learned the Greek words for oil and soap and bread.

I know that a woman's ambitions aren't supposed to fall and rise and veer off course this way, like some poor bird caught in a storm. All I can say is, at one of the many junctures in my life when I had to sink or swim, Crete was an island, a place to head for, new and far away. I had just dropped out of medicine in my first year of residency, a few months shy of becoming a licensed M.D. I'd discovered there was something serious, mainly a matter of nerve and perhaps empathy, that stood in my way. I learned all this while a baby was trying to be born feet first. I couldn't think how I was going to tell Doc Homer, and I'll admit I was attracted just then to the idea of putting an ocean between myself and that obelisk of disapproval. It also helped that Carlo really wanted me to go with him. But I had no mission beyond personal survival; it was nothing like Hallie's going to Nicaragua. Our village had its own kind of bleakness, the bones and stones of poverty, but the landscape was breathtaking. Our classmates were treating intestinal parasites in Niger and Haiti, black lung in Appalachia, while Carlo and I set broken legs on the steep slope of Mount Ida, mythical birthplace of Zeus. Poverty in a beautiful place seemed not so much oppressive as sublime. Basically it's the stuff of the world's great religions, I told myself, although I knew better.

▼▼▼

It was 100 degrees in the shade, and the burgeoning minds of Biology I and II took a field trip to the river; our putative goal was to get some samples of water to examine under the microscope. We were learning about the plant and animal kingdoms, starting right down at the bottom of the ladder with the protozoans and the blue-green algae. I could easily have collected a gallon of river water myself and brought it in, but the school had no air-conditioning and I'm not completely without a heart. I'd played it tough with the kids long enough to prove my point, if there was one, and I was tired of it. We all were.

I knew the trip to the river would turn into a party. I didn't try too hard to go against nature. The tall kid with the skinhead haircut, whose name was Raymo, was the first one to get wet up to his T-shirt. It took about ninety seconds. I only drew the line when boys started throwing in girls against their will.

"Okay, knock it off, scientists, Marta says she doesn't want to get wet," I said. Marta shot me a lipstick-red pout when they put her down, but she'd shrieked "No" and I felt there was a lesson to be learned here, all the way around.

"I've got a ton of sample bottles here, so let's get going." I sat a safe distance up the riverbank under an ash tree, labeling full bottles as they were brought to me. I'd suggested that they collect shallow and deep water, moving and stagnant, but they went far beyond this, collecting anything that moved. It was enough to make you believe in the hunting instinct. There was a low, grassy island in the middle of the riffle, and several kids were out there on their knees catching bugs and frogs. Raymo actually caught a six-inch perch with a net fashioned from his T-shirt. "Sooner or later I figure we'll get around to fish," he said. "A fish is an animal, right?"

"Right," I said, and let him dump it, along with the frogs, into a mop bucket we'd cajoled from the janitor. I don't know what teaching in a big-city school is like, but at Grace High we were flexible about interdepartmental appropriations.

Back in the lab, we rounded up all the creatures visible to the naked eye and made a home for them in an aquarium that had once held blue and orange Ping-Pong balls used for some mystical experiment in physics. Marta and two other cheerleaders disposed of the Ping-Pong balls and took over the terrarium project. They made a pond on one side for the fish, and an admirable mossy island on the other side, complete with a beach, and a cave they called the Motel Frog. They refused to deal directly with the clients, though. Raymo transferred the fish and frogs (with his bare hands) from the mop bucket.

The next day we got out the microscopes. The kids groaned, preferring to do experiments on the frogs. It's hard to get people interested in animals that have no discernible heads, tails, fins, or the like—and plants, forget it. There's no drama. You just don't have the skulking and stalking and gobbling up of innocent prey in the plant world. They don't even eat, except in the most passive sense. In college I knew a botany professor who always went around saying, "It takes a superior mind to appreciate a plant." Hallie and I were a case in point, I guess. We divided the world in half, right from childhood. I was the one who went in for the instant gratification, catching bright, quick butterflies, chloroforming them in a Mason jar and pinning them onto typewritten tags with their Latin names. Hallie's tastes were quieter; she had time to watch things grow. She transplanted wildflowers and showed an aptitude for gardening. At age ten she took over the responsibility of the Burpee's catalogue.

But now I was on my own in the Garden of Eden. I was expected to teach the entire living world to these kids. I would write Hallie and ask her advice on how to turn adolescents on to organisms that have no appreciable sex life. In the meantime we were doing protozoans, which I could handle. I drew huge, fantastic pictures in colored chalk of what we could expect to see in this river water: strands of Nostoc like strings of blue pearls; multi-tentacled hydras; rotifers barreling into each other like hyperactive kids. I demonstrated the correct way to put a drop of water on a glass slide, coverslip it, and focus the scope. The lab grew quiet with concentration.

They couldn't see anything. At first I was irritated but bit my tongue and focused a scope myself, prepared to see the teeming microscopic world of a dirty river. I found they were right, there was nothing. It gave me a strange panic to see that stillness under powerful magnification. Our water was dead. It might as well have come from a river on the moon.

▼▼▼

For homework I assigned my classes the task of being spies. They were to find out from their parents what the hell was going on with this river. The pH, which we tested, from some areas came in just a hair higher than battery acid. I couldn't believe the poisoning from the mine had gone this far. Protozoans are the early-warning system in the life of a river, like a canary in a mine. And this canary was dead. We took a closer look at Raymo's perch (named Mr. Bad Fish) and the frogs in the terrarium, which seemed in reasonably good health. But then, they'd been awfully easy to catch.

"It can't be legal," I lamented to Viola as we sat on the front porch with three of the boys and four grocery bags of snap beans. Emelina and John Tucker were in the kitchen canning as fast as we could snap. When it came to childbearing and gardening, Emelina seemed unable to walk the path of moderation.

"It's not legal," Viola said grumpily. "What difference does it make?"

We worked in silence for a while. The aluminum bowl between us rang like a bell when we threw our hard green beans against its sides. Mason hadn't managed to master the art of snap beans and had fallen asleep in the glider. The twins elbowed each other like irritable birds on a wire. Viola had been overseeing the boys in the garden most of the morning, and for once seemed tired. She was wearing lavender stretch pants, an embroidered blouse, and a baseball cap with the insignia of the Steelworkers' Union. J.T.'s father had worked in the smelter for forty years, from age eighteen until he died of lung cancer. The cap sat forward on Viola's head because her long hair was pinned in a thick circle at the back. According to Emelina, Viola felt the boys were losing touch with their past, but looking at her now I couldn't get a fix on what that past might be. I thought of the Elvis whiskey bottle collection up in her room. I didn't really know Viola the way I knew Emelina and J.T. and the kids. She was always skirting around the edges of rooms with her hands full, just ready to go somewhere, too busy to sit down and talk.

"They'll have to pay a fine if they don't stop polluting the river," I said cheerfully. "The EPA will shut them down if they don't clean it up." At Emelina's urging, I'd gone down to the courthouse and filed an affidavit with local authorities on the pH and biotic death of the river. I used the most scientific language I could muster, such as "biotic death" and "oxygen load." I'd written Hallie about it.

Viola said without looking up, "They're just going to divert the river."

"What?"

She bent over with a soft groan and took another double handful of beans out of the grocery bag between her legs, and set them into her apron. Curtis and Glen had stopped hitting each other for the moment and were having a race. It took them forever to snap any beans because they had to stop every two minutes to count who had done the most.

"Dam up the river," Viola said. "That's all they have to do to meet with the EPA laws. Dam it up and send it out Tortoise Canyon instead of down through here. The EPA just says they can't put it down here where people live."

"But then there would be *no* water for the orchards. That would be worse than the way it is now."

"That's right. But it's okey-dokey with the EPA. The men all had a town meeting about it yesterday, with this hot-shot guy from Phoenix. They sat and talked for about nine or ten hours and finally what he told them is if Black Mountain dams up the river, it's out of the jurisdiction of the Environmental Protection Agency." Viola reeled out the long words scornfully, as if she were glad to get them out of her mouth.

"That's impossible," I said. "There are water rights."

"Nobody around here's got water rights. All these families sold the water rights to the company in 1939, for twenty-five cents an acre. We all thought we were getting money for nothing. We had us a *fiesta*."

I stared at her. "So do you know for sure that's what they're going to do? Divert the river?"

She shrugged. "Who knows what anybody is going to do for sure? We could all die tomorrow. Only the Lord knows."

I wanted to shake her. I wished she would look me in the eye. "But this is what you've *heard* is going to happen?"

She nodded once, never taking her eyes off the snap beans that flew through her hands and rang freshly broken into the aluminum bowl.

I still couldn't believe it. "How could they do that?"

"With bulldozers," Viola said.

▼▼▼

Loyd and I made another date for Whiteriver, this time on a Sunday in October. The evening before, I went with Emelina to hear Chicken Scratch music at the outdoor restaurant run by Doña Althea's four daughters. The same traveling Waila bands had been coming over from the Papago reservation for decades, substituting sons for fathers so gradually that the music never changed. Emelina's normal taste ran to Country—Merle Haggard and Dolly Parton; but Waila was something special, she said, she was crazy about it. Her boys, enlightened by MTV, rolled their eyes. She took Mason and the baby with us because, as Emelina put it, they were too little to have a choice.

The restaurant was outdoors, in a walled courtyard that was a larger, more baroque version of Emelina's. Flowers bloomed everywhere out of pots shaped like pigs and squatty roosters, some of which had lost body parts, and two enormous old olive trees sparkled with tiny Christmas lights that evidently knew no season. Carved out here and there in the thick adobe wall were rounded niches that were home to weather-worn saints the size of a G.I. Joe; some, in fact, looked suspiciously like dolls in saints' clothing. In a corner, near where the band was setting up, stood a four-foot-tall, almost comically thin St. Francis of Assisi. He looked venerable and tired (also hungry), and was surrounded by a postmodern assortment of glazed ceramic and plastic birds.

The tables and chairs were of every imaginable type, following the same theme, and the flatware too—like snowflakes, no two alike. The effect was completely festive, in spite of Doña Althea's daughters. All four of them (who each had *Althea* lodged somewhere in her name) were over sixty, as thin as St. Francis but without his animal magnetism. They moved through the crowd with efficient scowls, taking orders and bringing out heavenly food from the little kitchen, all the while acting as though they couldn't quite understand why they'd agreed to go to all this trouble. You would think they'd have figured it out by now. It had been the most popular restaurant in town for half a century.

With tender, paternal attention the Alvaro Brothers unwrapped their musical instruments, which traveled in comfort, nestled in bright-blocked quilts. The men appeared to be three generations, rather than actual brothers. The elder Alvaro, dressed in cowboy boots and a formal Western shirt, cradled a gunmetal saxophone that reminded me of World War II planes. A middle-aged Alvaro with shoulder-length hair played accordion, and two boys in T-shirts played bass guitar and drums. The old sax player stepped up to the microphone. "We are the Alvaro Brothers," he said. "If we make too much noise, let us know."

It was the last time any of them smiled. From the instant they began to play, they stood motionless with their mouths turned down in concentration. Everybody else was dancing in their seats. Chicken Scratch music is Mexican-spiced Native American polka. It sounds like a wild, very happy, and slightly drunken wedding party, and it moves you up and down; you can't keep still. A line of older women in dark skirts and blouses, possibly Alvaro Sisters or Alvaro Wives, stood near the kitchen, swaying a little and tapping their feet. Several couples began to dance, and I could tell Emelina was itching to join them, but she held herself back. Mason showed no such restraint. He was out of his seat in no time, front and center, jumping in circles and running into people's legs. The younger people moved aside when the Papago women moved out from the wall and began to do the traditional six-step dance. They moved in a loose line, slightly bent over, shuffling over the gravel and sounding—if not looking—exactly like the scratching hens that give the music its name.

The place was packed. It took forever to get served and there were some mixed-up orders, and nobody cared. The music was so buoyant. One of the Althea sisters actually cracked a smile. After forty-five minutes the bass player plucked his lit cigarette from the bridge of his guitar and the Alvaros took a break.

Emelina told me she and J.T. had come here on their first date. They were fourteen. Viola had come too, but fortunately she spent the whole time in the kitchen advising Doña Althea on the *menudo*, Viola's specialty. J.T. was thus able to eat his whole meal with one hand on Emelina's knee, under the table.

"Just think," I said. "If you'd come on another night, the soup of the day would have been something else and you and J.T. might never have gotten married."

She smiled an odd little smile. "I don't think there's anybody else in this town I could have married but J.T. It was like we had each other's names printed on us when we were born."

"Seems like there's a lot of that in this town."

"Oh, yeah. And people do what their parents did. The father's a hoghead, the son's a hoghead."

I smiled. "What's a hoghead?"

"Locomotive engineer. I don't know why they call them that." She pecked her fingertips on the tabletop, watching the Papago women talking to the musicians.

For a while I'd believed that Emelina and J.T., with their congenial partnership and all those miles between them, were like Carlo and me, parallel lines that never quite touched. I was wrong. Two nights before when J.T. came home at 3 A.M. they made love in the moonlit courtyard, urgently, with some of their clothes on. My house was dark but I was awake, invisible in my kitchen. I felt abandoned. Emelina was nothing like me.

"It's dangerous," she said suddenly. "Shit, you can't think about it but it's hell, the railroad. Did you know Fenton Lee, in high school?"

"Sure."

"He was in a head-on wreck two years ago. Bringing his train out of the yard in El Paso, at night, and somebody else was coming in, lined for the same track. Nobody knows why. Maybe a signal failed. Southern Pacific says no. But J.T. says it happens."

"So Fenton was killed?" I remembered him plainly, in horn-rim glasses. He had blond bangs and a loud laugh.

"Yeah, it was real bad. They heard the crash all over the yard. The one engine climbed up the other one and sheared off the top. There wasn't a whole lot left."

I felt numb. A train wreck and Fenton dead in it were beyond what I was willing to imagine.

"You can jump off, when you see that coming," Emelina told me. "Fenton's brakeman and conductor jumped off, and the other crew did, but Fenton stayed on. I guess he didn't really believe it. I told J.T., 'If you ever see a headlight coming at you, don't you dare save the train. You get your butt out of there.' "

The band started up again and Emelina's mood quickly lifted. Our food arrived and Mason snapped back to the table. Emelina resettled the baby in the rickety high chair. "So you're going up to the rez with Loyd tomorrow," she said, her eyes twinkling. "This is getting serious. If I was your mother I'd tell you to wear garlic around your neck." She dipped the tip of her spoon into her refried beans and fed it to the baby. He took the spicy brown mush like manna from heaven. "But since I'm not your mother," she said soberly, "I'd advise you to wear nice-looking under-wear."

She embarrassed me. "It's nothing serious," I said. "We're not exactly couple material, are we? Me and Loyd-with-one-L."

She looked up, surprised. "He can't help how his name's spelled." She paused a minute, studying me. "What, you think Loyd's dumb?"

Now I had embarrassed myself. "No, I don't think that. I just can't see myself with a guy that's into cockfighting."

I'm sure Emelina suspected this was nowhere near the whole truth. She was thinking I did hold Loyd's misspelled name against him, and a lot of other things. That I couldn't see myself with a roughneck Apache hoghead who was her husband's best friend. I felt myself blush. I was just like Doc Homer, raising himself and Hallie and me up to be untouched by Grace.

"I'll tell you something, honey," Emelina said, pausing her spoon midway enroute to the baby's open mouth. "Half the women in this town, and not just the single ones, would give up Sunday breakfast to go to Whiteriver in that little red truck."

"I know that," I said, paying attention to my enchiladas. I didn't know how to apologize to Emelina without owning up to something I wasn't sure I felt. Strictly speaking, I didn't think I was better than Loyd and half the women in Grace. I was amazed, in fact, by Loyd's interest in me. I also didn't think it would last very long.

Emelina directed her energies back to mothering. "Mason, honey, don't pull all that stuff out with your fingers," she shouted affectionately above the music, which had risen in pitch. "I know it's stringy. I'll cut it up for you." She reached across the table, expertly dissecting Mason's chicken burro.

For some reason I glanced up at the baby, whose eyes and mouth were wide. Something was severely wrong. He wasn't breathing. I knocked over my chair getting to him. I reached my finger into his throat and felt something, but couldn't dislodge it. He made a voiceless gag. I stood behind his chair and pulled him up by the armpits, folded him over my left arm, and gave him four quick whacks between the shoulder blades. Then I rolled him over so he was face up and wide-eyed but still head down; supporting his head with my right hand, I tucked two fingertips under his breastbone and poked hard. A small, hard, whole pinto bean shot out of his mouth like a bullet.

The whole operation took maybe thirty seconds. Emelina picked the bean up off the table and looked at me. Her face was ashen as the baby's.

"He was choking," I said dumbly, laying him carefully on the table. "That's the only way you can get something out of the windpipe when it's in that far."

He lay still for about half a minute, breathing but still looking gray, and then he coughed twice and began to scream. His face turned rosy purple. Several women from nearby tables had whipped the napkins off their laps and were crowding in close around us. The music stopped. Emelina stared at her son like he was something she hadn't ordered, set down on the table.

"It's okay to pick him up," I said. "He'll be sore in the ribs, but he's okay."

She held him against her shoulder. He was still shrieking,

and I don't think there was a person in the restaurant now who wasn't staring at us. At me, actually. Emelina looked up with enormous eyes, as if I were one of the saints in the wall: Our Lady of Blocked Windpipes. She wiped tears off her chin with the back of her hand.

"It's no big deal," I said.

It really wasn't. I'd just done what I knew how to do.

▼▼▼

Emelina begged me to sleep in the house with them that night, in case he stopped breathing again. There was no reason in the world for that to happen, and I told her so. But she was quietly beside herself. J.T. had left for El Paso that morning, for two weeks this time because of some mess about the derailment. Viola was out late at another so-called "emergency meeting" of her women's club. I think Emelina felt lonely, or vulnerable— afraid of the simple fact that life held possibilities she couldn't handle alone. It must have been a rare experience for Emelina, and I felt for her. While we were making up a bed for me in the baby's room, I stopped and hugged her. She held on to me like a child.

I knew better than to expect sleep. I lay curled on my side, listening in spite of myself to the baby's soft exhaled breaths, and I kept turning my mind away from the one thought that kept coming back to me, persistent as an unwanted lover's hand, that I'd saved a life.

I thought about Loyd instead. I knew nothing about where we were going tomorrow; I hadn't seen that country. My mind turned over various expectations, none of which I recognized as my own. Who did I think I was, and what did I want from an Apache cockfighter with a misspelled name? His body, yes. But I couldn't take that risk, and end up needing more.

At some time in my life I'd honestly hoped love would rescue me from the cold, drafty castle I lived in. But at another point, much earlier I think, I'd quietly begun to hope for nothing at all in the way of love, so as not to be disappointed. It works. It gets to be a habit.

A pack of coyotes set up a sudden racket near the house,

yipping and howling, so close by they sounded like they had us surrounded. When a hunting pack corners a rabbit they go into a blood frenzy, making human-sounding screams. The baby sighed and stirred in his crib. At seven months, he was just the size of a big jackrabbit—the same amount of meat. The back of my scalp and neck prickled. It's an involuntary muscle contraction that causes that, setting the hair follicles on edge; if we had manes they would bristle exactly like a growling dog's. We're animals. We're born like every other mammal and we live our whole lives around disguised animal thoughts. There's no sense pretending. Tomorrow, I thought, or the next day, or the day after that, I would have sex with Loyd Peregrina.

12

ANIMAL DREAMS

On Sunday morning I put on jeans, changed into a denim dress, then back into jeans again, feeling stupid. I can get into a mood where I annoy myself no end. At the moment when I got completely fed up and stopped caring, I had on jeans and a white cotton shirt and silver earrings, so that's what I wore. And yes, I'll admit it, nice underwear.

I waited on the porch and was relieved when Loyd pulled up before Emelina's household had roused. It was a little odd, living with a family that paid attention to my social life.

Jack stood up to greet me from the back of the pickup and I rubbed his ears. "I brought lunch," I told Loyd, sliding into the cab with a basket Emelina had helped pack the night before.

He smiled wonderfully. "That's mighty white of you."

I didn't know what to make of that. It was something people said, but usually when they said it both people were white.

I asked him to detour past the Post Office so I could check for mail. There was no regular mail delivery in Grace, probably on humanitarian grounds. A daily route up these stairstep streets would have put some postal employee into a cardiac high-risk category. Every family had a box at the P.O., which they could check daily or annually, as they pleased. Emelina leaned toward annual. I persuaded her to turn over the key to me; I was the only member of the household expecting mail.

The mailboxes were built right into the outside wall of the Post Office. I peeked through the little window of the Domingos family drawer and saw the striped margin of an airmail envelope.

"Hallie!" I called to Loyd, waving the envelope as I bounced back to the truck. He didn't seem to register. "My sister Hallie. In Nicaragua." I checked the postmark to make sure this was true, and it was. Mailed nearly three weeks ago. The stamps, two alike, were bright and beautiful, carrying across oceans and continents a childlike revolutionary hopefulness: a painting of a woman picking red coffee beans, and her baby strapped on her back. Hallie was in the fields of her dreams.

I ripped it open and read quickly. She'd arrived mid-September, was fine, got my letters, she spent a few days in Managua and then backtracked straight to the rural area near Chinandega. She'd expected (or feared) a little formality but they put her to work the day she arrived, wearing her one and only dress. "I'm in seventh heaven," she wrote, and I could see her hiking up that dress and striding across the plowed rows, leading a battery of stunned men. "This cotton's been getting sprayed to death and still eaten up with weevils. Cultivation practices are pitiful. I know exactly what to do. I think we'll get productivity up about 100 percent from last year. Can you imagine? You'd think it was Christmas, everybody's already talking about how the collective could use this prosperity: they could get a secondary-school teacher in here full time, or a good adult-ed program."

I got a vivid picture of Hallie's face and could hear her voice as I read. Her hair would be restrained in a red bandana, her face tense with concentration and her eyebrows knit at angles like accent marks. I could also recall her exact expression as she lay on our living-room sofa in Tucson with her long legs propped up, one hand pushing the hair up from her high forehead, while she calmly dispensed information over the Garden Hotline. I understood the full extent to which she'd been wasting her life on house plants.

The letter was short. She was living in a two-room house

with a widowed mother of four young children, who insisted that Hallie have one of the rooms to herself—a luxury that made Hallie uncomfortable. There was nothing to spare. The day she moved in, a request went out to the neighbors and somebody brought over a plate and a tin cup for her, and somebody else brought a fork. Both women had recently lost sons.

The territory she would have to cover, giving crop advice, was huge. She was issued a horse. There were problems with the roads, she said, that made jeeps a less desirable mode of transport for short trips: horses usually weren't heavy enough to trigger the land mines the Contras buried in the roads. The horse's name was *Sopa del Dia;* she was white with gray spots.

She signed it, "Your insane-with-love sister Hallie," with a P.S.:

Re your question about botany: tell your students plants do everything animals do—give birth, grow, travel around (how do you think palm trees got to Hawaii?), have sex, etc. They just do it a lot slower. Bear this in mind: flowers are the sex organs of plants. Tell the boys to consider that when they're buying their dates corsages for the prom.

And a P.P.S.:

Sure I remember when we almost drowned in a flood. Plain as day. God, Codi, don't you? We found those abandoned coyote pups, and the river was flooding, and you wanted to save them. You said we *had* to. I was chicken because Doc Homer would spank the shit out of us and I wanted to run for it, but you wouldn't let me.

"My sister's saving people's lives in Nicaragua," I told Loyd.

"She's a doctor? I thought she was a farmer."

"People can't live without crops. There's more than one way to skin a revolution."

He nodded.

I wanted him to know more than this about Hallie. That she was also a human being who did normal things. That she'd tried once, just as an example, to teach Carlo and me to break-dance.

She'd thrown her hair around like a prissy rock star and we died laughing. In wool socks on the hardwood floor she could moonwalk like Michael Jackson.

I kept folding and unfolding the letter. "She has to ride a horse, because there's land mines in the roads."

The cab of the truck shuddered every time we hit a pothole, but Loyd drove calmly, his mind far away, the way I imagined *he* might look riding a horse. I'd never seen him so relaxed. I looked back a few times to check on Jack, who seemed equally content. I presumed he'd walked around in circles a few times back there before curling up in his nest of imaginary tall grass.

"Is there anything you know of that you'd die for?" I asked Loyd.

He nodded without hesitation.

"What?"

He didn't answer right away. Then he said, "The land."

"What land?"

"Never mind. I can't explain it."

"The reservation? Like, defending your country?"

"No." He sounded disgusted. "Not property. I didn't say property."

"Oh."

We passed by another of Black Mountain's mines, abandoned for years, the buildings standing quiet as a shipwreck. The huge windows of the smelter were made of chicken-wire glass, but a lot of them were broken out anyway; inside loomed the dinosaur skeletons of old machinery. Next to the smelter were the concentrator and a hovel of shacks under rusting tin roofs. Beyond them lay more fallow alfalfa fields, their soil crusted white from all the years of slightly salty irrigation water. Hallie could have stayed right in Grace and done some good, but of course there was the question of relative desperation of need. Nobody was dying for lack of this alfalfa.

The edge of these fields was the southern border of the Apache reservation, just fifteen minutes north of Grace. I hadn't been there before, and was surprised it was that close.

"Are you kidding?" he asked. "Gracela Canyon used to be

in the reservation. The whites took that little section back after some guys hit gold down there."

"Is that true?"

"Look it up, Einstein. It's in the town records. They only gave the Apache this land in the first place because it looked like a piece of shit."

To some extent that must have been true: it was dead-looking country, though not as dead as the used-up cropland. It didn't look *murdered*. Here the gentle hills were pale brown grading to pink, sparsely covered with sage and fall-blooming wildflowers. Along the creekbeds were tall stands of cottonwoods. Their yellow leaves rained down. Every now and then we'd pass through clusters of homes that you couldn't exactly call towns, with long horse corrals strung between the houses. Red horses raised their heads and galloped along beside us for the short distance they'd been allotted, expertly turning aside just before they reached the ends of their corrals. Loyd waved at the people we passed, and they waved back.

"Do all those people know you?" I asked, incredulous.

"Nah. Just my truck."

Eventually we stopped in one of the settlements that was distinguished from the others by its size and the presence of a store. Rusting soft-drink signs nailed across the front porch marked it as a commercial establishment. Through the screen door I could see shadows of men in cowboy hats. Loyd pulled his parking brake, squeezed my hand, and held on to it for a second. "You want to come in?" he asked doubtfully. "It's only going to take me ten minutes."

"I know what this is about," I said. "J.T. told me you're into fighting cocks."

He nodded slightly.

"Well, is it okay for me to go in with you? Are women allowed?"

He laughed, then dropped my hand and flipped his index finger against my cheek. "Big old roosterfighting Indian boogeyman might get you."

"I'm a big girl," I said. I got out and followed him up the

wooden steps, but regretted it once we were inside. A short man leaning on the counter looked at Loyd and resettled his hat on his head, ignoring me completely. This wasn't going to be any of my business. I bought a lukewarm soft drink from the old guy behind the counter. He grasped it through his apron and screwed off the cap, leaving a broad asterisk of dust on the white cloth. The other men watched this gesture in silence.

"I'll be outside," I told Loyd.

I sat in a wooden rocker on the porch. Jack had lifted his head and cocked his ears but hadn't moved from the truck-bed.

Almost immediately I could hear Loyd raising his voice. "I told you I want Apodaca's line and not any of the others. I want gaffers. I'm not interested in knife birds."

The short man said, "Loyd, I'm telling you, you got to go up to Phoenix. They're getting goddamn tourists at those knife tourneys. It's a circus. You can get two hundred birds through there in a day."

"Don't tell me what I want. Do you have gaffers out there, or did I just waste a tank of gas?"

Their voices dropped lower again. I felt uncomfortable listening in, though I was fascinated and slightly appalled by the notion of "knife birds." It was encouraging that Loyd didn't want them, whatever they were. The words the men used were as mysterious as Loyd's railroad talk. He evidently spoke a lot of languages, not even counting Apache and Pueblo and Navajo.

Across the street from the store stood a substantial-looking whitewashed church—the only white building in an adobe town. It was shaped like the Alamo with a bell tower. The ground in front was planted with petunias, phlox, and marigolds: pink, purple, orange, in that order. One thing Hallie always said she loved about Indian reservations and Mexico was that there were no rules about color. She was right. It was really a splendid combination, now that I looked at it, but in some orderly country like Germany they'd probably arrest you for planting this in front of your house; in suburban Tucson they'd just avoid you. Keep their kids inside when you went out to weed.

People trailed out of the church in twos and threes, mostly

women, carrying out the same color scheme in their blouses and skirts. They all looked at me as they passed, not with hostility, but with the kind of curiosity you'd have if you noticed an odd plant had popped up in your garden: you wouldn't yank it out right away. You'd give it a few days to see what developed.

I could hear roosters cock-a-doodling somewhere, and I was curious. As I went down the steps an adobe-colored dog scooted out of my way and ran under the porch. The store, I discovered, had a deep back yard. The chain-link fence was overgrown with weedy vines, but I could still see in: it was a rooster garden in there. Roosters in small cubicles laid out in neat rows, one bird per cage. They strutted and turned in circles, eying each other as if each moment were new, as if they hadn't for all their natural lives been surrounded by these other birds. They had red faces and glossy black feathers that threw off iridescent flashes of color, like a hummingbird's throat. Beautiful. But the claustrophobic energy was tiring to watch.

I heard a door slam and I quickly went back around front. Loyd was ready to go, but not in the bad mood I expected. By the time we got to the edge of town he was smiling.

I offered him the last of my soda. "So, did you waste a tank of gas?"

He put his arm across the back of the seat, his thumb touching the nape of my neck, and shot me a sideways look. "No way."

We weren't headed back toward Grace. We drove north. There were no more towns, just reddish hills and a badly rutted road. "Was that Whiteriver?" I asked.

"No. This is what you'd call the Whiteriver metropolitan area."

"You used to live here? After you left your mother's pueblo?"

"Around here. We lived up at Ghost River. It's a little higher ground up there. It's nice, there's trees."

"You and your dad and . . ." I wanted to ask about his dead twin brother, but then again I didn't. Not today.

"And Jack," he said.

"Whatever happened to Jack's coyote mother?"

"After she had her litter, she left us. She went back to live in God's backyard."

I was quiet for a minute, taking in the hills. "And where are
we headed now?"

He smiled. "Who wants to know?"

"A hometown girl, looking for some adventure."

"Well, then, we're headed for some adventure."

Loyd kept both hands on the wheel in the washed-out
stretches, driving like a race-car driver—I don't mean fast, but
skillfully, with that generous kind of concentration that seems
easy as a reflex. We were gaining ground, getting higher, passing
through intermittent stands of evergreens. In between were
meadows, solidly carpeted in yellow flowers, punctuated by tall
white poppies with silver leaves and tissue-paper petals. In the
distance, the southern slopes of the mountainsides were dappled
with yellow. We passed through another tiny enclave of houses
and horse corrals. The people there would have been born into
that life; I couldn't imagine it. For some reason I thought of
Hallie's first letter—the babies playing around the cook fire, in
the refugee camps. But this wasn't like that; it didn't look desperate, just lonely. It was hard to understand why a person
would stay. Loyd hadn't. But then again, he wasn't born here.
And yet he seemed drawn back, for reasons beyond fighting
cocks.

The road smoothed out a bit and Loyd took his right hand
off the wheel and laid it on my leg. For a little while he and I
both pretended it wasn't there. Then I asked him, "What would
these people around here say if they knew you had your hand
on a white girl's thigh?"

He smiled. "They'd say I was a lucky son of a bitch."

He lifted the hand and ran his palm up the length of my arm,
from my wrist to my shoulder, lightly, just stroking the hairs
and not the skin. My nipples stood up and my scalp tingled and
my whole body wanted that hand on it, everywhere at once.
But he took it back and put it on the steering wheel, and I pitied
myself for envying a steering wheel.

"You still haven't told me where we're going," I said.

He nodded at the road. "That's where we're going. We're
almost there." After a minute he geared down into four-wheel
drive and turned off the dirt road onto a side path, not really a

road but a pair of tracks in the gravelly ground. If you hadn't known it was there, you'd never have seen it.

If we are going to see some more people about gaffers and knife birds, I thought, I'm going to have to sit and be still, be a white girl. No matter what, I'm going to have to stop thinking about kissing Loyd. I looked away from his face, out the window. There was nothing out there now but fields of yellow flowers, rocky red hills in the near distance, and off to the east very high mountains softly blackened around their tops by a pelt of pine forests. It would be cool up there now, even today. I pictured myself lying under the pines on a floor of brown needles. It was hard to keep Loyd out of the picture.

▼▼▼

"What *is* this?" I was out of the truck, entranced, before he'd even set the brake.

"Kinishba," Loyd said. "Prehistoric condos."

That's just about what it looked like. Out there in the middle of God's backyard, without a fence in sight, sat a long rectangular building made entirely of carefully set stone, no mortar. Dozens of small doors opened into it across the front.

"Can we go inside? Is it allowed?"

He hooked his elbow around my neck, like a friendly wrestler, as we walked toward the site. "It's allowed. I allow it."

"What, are you the landlord here?"

"Till somebody tells me I'm not."

He let me go and turned toward the truck, whistling once. Jack leaped in a high arc over the tailgate and streaked through the field of foot-tall grass, looking like the soul of happiness. He headed downhill toward what must have been a river; I could see cottonwoods. We were in higher country here, with more vegetation.

"That's a good dog," I said.

"Yep. That's a good dog."

The doors were no more than four feet high. I ducked through one into a small, rectangular room with a dust floor. It was cool as a cave, and quiet. The door was a square of bright light with the silhouette of Loyd coming through. Even inside the room, the ceiling was low, just inches above my head. I touched it. "People were short back then. Didn't eat their Wonder bread."

"They would've had to build a special room for you. You would have been their queen."

I laughed, though it struck me I'd been complimented. Was that how Loyd saw me? Not as a grain elevator on the prairie, but a queen? At the back of the room a door led into another room, which was darker, having no openings to the outside. Two more doors led out of that room—one to the side, and one up through the ceiling, which was made of thick, curved trunks of small trees. There was another whole set of rooms on top of this one.

"Can we go upstairs?"

He shook his head. "I wouldn't trust those beams. They're kind of old."

"How old?"

"Eight hundred years."

I looked at him. "Are you kidding?"

"Nope."

We went from room to room, changing directions in the dark until the compass points were entirely lost to me. It was a maze. Loyd said there were more than two hundred rooms—a village under one roof. The air smelled cold. I tried to imagine the place populated: stepping from room to room over sleeping couples, listening through all the noises of cooking and scolding and washing up for the sound of your own kids, who would know secret short cuts to their friends' apartments.

"The walls are thick," I observed.

"The walls are graveyards. When a baby died, they'd mortar its bones right into the wall. Or under the floor."

I shuddered. "Why?"

"So it would still be near the family," he said, seeming surprised I hadn't thought of this myself.

Without warning we came out into a bright courtyard in the center, surrounded by walls and doorways on all four sides. It was completely hidden from the outside—a little haven with a carpet of fine grass and an ancient ash tree. A treasure island. I was drawn to the shade. "We should've brought the picnic basket," I said, settling under the ash. The ground was cool. My brief vision of a living city was gone; it seemed ghostly again. For eight hundred years, those bones in the walls had been listening to nothing more than the dry skittering of lizards.

"We've got all day," Loyd said. He sat about two feet away from me, clasping his hands around his knees and looking at the toes of his boots.

"So who built this place, eight hundred years ago?"

"My mama's folks. The Pueblo. They had their act together back then, didn't they?"

They did. I couldn't stop running my eyes over the walls and the low, even roofline. The stones were mostly the same shape, rectangular, but all different sizes; there would be a row of large stones, and then two or three thinner rows, then a couple of middle-sized rows. There was something familiar about the way they fit together. In a minute it came to me. They looked just like cells under a microscope.

"It doesn't even look like it was built," I said. "It's too beautiful. It looks like something alive that just *grew* here."

"That's the idea." Loyd seemed as pleased as if he'd built it himself.

"Of what? The idea of Pueblo architecture?"

"Yep. Don't be some kind of a big hero. No Washington Monuments. Just build something nice that Mother Earth will want to hold in her arms."

It was a pleasant thought. I also didn't mind the thought of being held in Loyd's arms, but he was making no moves in that direction. He was explaining the water system—they evidently had some sort of running water—and how they'd grown squash and corn on the hillside facing the river.

I reached over and ran a finger from his knee to his ankle. He looked up. "I'm talking too much, right?"

I shook my head. "No, keep talking."

"You sure?"

I hesitated. I hadn't expected to have to make the suggestion, and my stomach felt tight. "Yeah. Just, could you move over here and talk?"

His eyes brightened. I'd taken him by surprise. He leaned

over and I took his head in my hands and gave him the kiss I'd been thinking about for the last two hours. It lasted a good long while. He twisted his fingers gently through the hair at the base of my skull and held on tight, and my breath stopped while he laid down a track of small kisses from my earlobe to my collarbone. We lay back on the grass and I rolled against him, looking down into his eyes. They were dark brown, a color with depth to it, like stained glass. It was a little surprising to look at brown eyes after all the pale blues of Grace.

Just being held felt unbelievably good, the long drink I'd been dying for. For a second I hugged back as tightly as I could. Something inside his buttoned shirt pocket made a crackling, cellophane sound. I raised up a little and poked it with my finger. "If you've got a condom in your pocket, Loyd Peregrina, this is my lucky day."

He did. It was.

▼▼▼

By late afternoon the shade had moved, and we also had rolled over a few times in the grass, I suppose, traveling from our original spot. Anyway we were in the sun. We disconnected and I lay on my back, feeling the forbidden touch of sun on my nipples and eyelids.

Loyd lay with his head propped on his elbow, just looking at me again, the way he had on the day of Emelina's party. With a finger he traced concentric circles around my breasts, and triangles on my abdomen, as if warpainting me for some ceremonial mission. Whatever it might be, I felt up to the job. I knew when reason returned I'd be scared to death of feeling that good with another person, but my body was renewed. I felt like a patch of dry ground that had been rained on.

Jack had come into the courtyard and was sleeping in the shade, a little distance away. "He found his way in here without any trouble," I said. "You boys must come here a lot."

Loyd kissed my cheek and sat up and pulled on his jeans. "Yep, kind of a lot. Not as much as I'd like to."

I thought of the condom in his pocket, the presumption, and felt irritated. "Well it's a good seduction spot. It worked on me."

I found the rest of my clothes and concentrated on getting my shirt buttoned up. I'd lost an earring somewhere.

Loyd stared at me for a full half minute, and then lay back down, his hands clasped behind his head, looking straight up. "I don't mean that I *bring* people here. Nobody but me and Jack's ever been here before." He glanced at me, and then away again. "But I guess that's just what you expect me to say." He didn't say anything more for another minute, and then he said, "Shit."

"I'm sorry. I guess I believe you. I do believe you."

He was wounded. I suppose some sharp thing in me wanted to sting him, for making me need him now. After he'd once cut me to the edge of what a soul will bear. But that was senseless. Anybody would say that baby was my own fault, and he didn't even know about it. I looked at this grown-up Loyd and tried to make sense of him, seeing clearly that he was too sweet to survive around me. I would go to my grave expecting the weapon in the empty hand.

"Codi, I couldn't believe it when you said you'd come up here with me. I couldn't even believe I asked."

I sat forward, letting the point of my chin dig into my knee. "I can see what it means to you. I'm sorry for thinking what I did."

He spoke slowly. "I've been looking forward to this ever since Labor Day. Not because I thought we'd . . . Not for any one reason. I just wanted to come here with you."

I looked at him. It was the truth. I could think of nothing at all to say.

"I don't blame you if you're still pissed off at me for when we were in high school."

My heart lost its rhythm for a second. "What for?"

"For being a jerk."

"You remember that?"

I suppose it was an insulting question. He said, "I have a lot of reasons in my mind for the way I was, but they don't make much difference. I hurt a lot of people."

I looked at him carefully. "In what way exactly do you think you hurt me?"

He shrugged. "Well, maybe I didn't. Maybe you didn't care. But still, I could have been a lot nicer. We went out those couple of times, and then so long sucker, that's it. Loyd's a good-time boy, he don't call the same girl twice."

I breathed out. Nobody knew, so Loyd couldn't, but for one minute I'd been afraid. I didn't want him to know how much of a mark his careless love had made on my life. It would oblige him to one of two mean possibilities: compulsory kindness or a vanishing act. I leaned over and kissed him. "You're forgiven," I said. "Plain Jane forgives Mr. High School Honcho for being a red-blooded boy."

"Plain Jane my ass," he said, rolling me over on top of him and grabbing mine. "I like you a lot. A real, whole lot. You buy that?"

"I'll buy it. Just don't try to sell me no knife birds."

He looked straight into my eyes. "I'm serious, Codi."

"Okay," I said. "Sold." I laid my head on his chest and nearly went to sleep while he gently stroked my spine. I felt like a baby being coaxed, reluctantly, into dreamland. A few yards away, Jack was already there. His legs jerked helplessly, making him look vulnerable.

"I've lost an earring. You see it?"

"No. I'll help you look in a minute."

"What's Jack dreaming about?"

"Chasing rabbits," Loyd said.

"That's what everybody says, but I don't think all dogs dream about that. You watch a city dog that's never even heard of a rabbit—it'll do that same thing."

"How do you know they really dream?"

"They do. All mammals that have been tested have REM sleep, except spiny anteaters." I cringed after I said this. I sounded like Codi Noline, brain of the seventh grade, despised by her peers.

"*Spiny anteaters?*"

"Well, I'm sorry, but it's the truth. I read it in the encyclopedia one time."

"You are an amazing person."

He meant it, he wasn't making fun of me. His hand stopped

moving and came to rest on the small of my back. He was actually thinking about all this. Carlo wouldn't have paid the slightest attention to a conversation like this; he'd be thinking about whatever men think about, how much gas is left in the tank. Loyd asked, "What do you think animals dream about?"

"I don't know. Animal heaven." I laughed.

"I think they dream about whatever they do when they're awake. Jack chases rabbits, and city dogs chase, I don't know what. Meter readers."

"But that's kind of sad. Couldn't a dog have an imagination, like a person?"

"It's the same with people. There's nothing sad about it. People dream about what they do when they're awake. God, when I used to work for *Tía* sorting the pecans I'd go to bed and dream about pecans, pecans, pecans."

I studied his face. "Didn't you ever dream you could fly?"

"Not when I was sorting pecans all day."

"Really, though. Didn't you ever fly in your dreams?" Even I had done that, though not often.

"Only when I was real close to flying in real life," he said. "Your dreams, what you hope for and all that, it's not separate from your life. It grows right up out of it."

"So you think we all just have animal dreams. We can't think of anything to dream about except our ordinary lives."

He gently moved a lock of hair out of my eyes. "Only if you have an ordinary life. If you want sweet dreams, you've got to live a sweet life."

"Okay," I said, feeling happy. I was sure no other man I'd ever known would have concerned himself with what animals dream about. "I'm going to sleep now, and I'll give you a report." I settled my head back down on his chest. His heartbeat moved faintly against my ear as I looked out across the ground. I saw my silver earring gleaming in the grass.

HOMERO

13

CRYBABIES

His name is gone. He understands that this is his own fault. He took a pen to paper and changed it, canceled his ancestors, and now his grandchild—Codi's child—has been erased like something in writing too, rather than flesh and blood. He knows she's no longer carrying it. He's aware of the signs.

The red darkroom light burns like a dying sun, very old: red dwarfs, they call them when they reach that stage. He sometimes reads astronomy now, when he can't sleep. But at this moment, outside this sealed room, it's daytime. He considers carefully the time of day and of year, and his daughters' ages, a ritual he performs a dozen times daily to keep himself rooted in time. That was nearly twenty years ago, when Codi lost the baby. He has photographed the eyes of so many babies. He gets lost among years now, the way he used to lose track when he sat in the dark movie theater for too many hours. He has always loved the dark.

The liquid feels cool on his hands, though it's a chemical bath, not particularly good for the elasticity of human skin. He should use the Piper forceps from the kitchen, but he has misplaced them. He moves the photograph into the fixative and stares at the lines. And frowns. They are a precise copy of what the real world offered his camera, and nothing more: the branched shadow of a cane cholla falling across a square of pale, cracked ground. He found the image while walking in the arroyo, and immediately saw the illusion he could draw out of it: a river in the desert. He'd seen exactly this sight, in aerial view. It was years ago, in wartime—they had taken him in a small plane over the bombing range near Yuma; a soldier lay wounded out there and couldn't be moved. They flew the quickest route, over the Algodones dunes, a dead ocean of undulating sand. The pilot said it was harder to fly over dunes on a hot day than through a tornado; the plane shuddered until its rivets creaked. Then suddenly they were over the Colorado River agricultural plain. He marveled, feeling lucky as a spaceman. Surely no one had ever seen this amazing sight, a complex river fretted with canals cutting an unearthly path through the bone-dry land.

He can't remember the wounded soldier. He closes his eyes and tries, but he can't. Possibly some chest wound, a punctured lung? No, he can't bring the soldier back. But he remembers the vision of that water. He gently agitates the photograph in its stop bath, lost in technical possibilities. He knows there must be a way to transfigure this cactus shadow into that other vision, which no longer exists outside his mind. All his photographs begin in his memory. That is the point. He might be the only man on earth who can photograph the past.

He stops suddenly, feeling a presence outside the door.

"Codi?" He listens. "I'm printing, it will be a few more minutes. Codi, are you there?" He hears nothing. It's a Monday morning, she can't be here. She's teaching school. He drops the print into the fixer, annoyed, and goes back to the enlarger to try again. He should lock that door to guard against accidents. What a shock that would be to the girls, a locked door. They have always had rules about this; a closed door is a sacred thing. Privacy is respected. There is no call for bolted doors in the Noline household. But she still locked him out—she was in the bathroom that night for more than four hours. When he walked by he could see that the upper bolt was turned. She'd gone in right after dinner. There are rules about this.

"Codi?"

He listens again, but there is no sound at all.

He knocks. "I just want to know that you're all right."

"I'm all right."

She is crying softly. "I can hear that you're crying," he says. "Your sister is concerned. You could just tell us what's wrong."

"Nothing's wrong. I'm just a crybaby. You're always telling me I'm a crybaby, so you're right."

That isn't true, he doesn't use that word. He tells them they should try to be grown-up girls. But he hasn't needed to tell them that for years.

In another minute she calls out quietly, "Is Hallie out there? I need to talk to her."

Hallie is in her room, reading. She doesn't seem especially concerned; Codi has been so moody of late that Hallie leaves her alone. They don't argue but there is a new distance between them. A gulf. Codi crossed over into adolescence, leaving Hallie behind for the time being. They both seem lost. All three of them, really: a marooned family, shipwrecked on three separate islands. Before, when the girls were close, he worried about what would happen when they lost each other. Now they have.

"Hallie." He stands in the doorway to their room and repeats her name quietly. "Hallie." She is reading in poor light, ruining her eyes. She looks up, her eyes nearly marble-white under the small, high-intensity lamp above her bed.

"Your sister has asked for you. Can you please find out what she needs?"

She puts her open book face down on the bed and gets up without a word. The two of them confer through the bathroom door. He tries to hear their whispers from the kitchen. He sees that Codi is not letting her in.

"The black one. That old one that was mother's."

Hallie is gone for only a minute, then comes back. "I can't find it. I got your green jacket."

"No!" Codi says something else that he can't hear. He washes the cast-iron skillet and sets it on the stove on low heat, to drive out the moisture. He goes into the living room, where he can't see but can hear better. Hallie glances up as he walks past her in the hall, and she lowers her voice.

"Why do you have to have that exact sweater, Codi? Are you going outside? It's not even cold."

"Just bring me the black sweater. I mean it, Hallie, find it. It's in the bottom of one of my drawers."

After a long while Hallie comes back with it. He hears the bolt slide back, then lock again; the door was not open even for a full second. Hallie returns to her reading.

In another fifteen minutes he hears scrubbing. She is cleaning the floor. The toilet has flushed more than two dozen times. There are rules concerning all of these things.

Much later he watches without lamplight from the living room. The house is dark. Her curtain of hair falls as she leans out, looking down toward the kitchen. She comes out. The small bundle in her arms she carries in the curl of her upper body, her spine hunched like a dowager's, as if this black sweater weighed as much as herself. When he understands what she has, he puts his knuckle to his mouth to keep from making a sound. Quiet as a cat she has slipped out the kitchen door.

He follows her down to the arroyo. She takes the animal path that cuts steeply down the bank. Round volcanic boulders flank her, their surfaces glowing like skin in the moonlight. She is going down to the same dry river where they nearly drowned ten years ago, in the flood. This tributary carved out Tortoise Canyon; it would be the Tortoise River if it had a name, but it never runs. It did years ago when he was a boy, hiking these banks to escape his mother's pot-black kitchen, but now it does not run except during storms. The land around Grace is drying up.

He stands a hundred yards away from Codi, above her, in the shadow of cottonwood trees. She has reached the spot where the rock bank gives over to the gravel and silt of riverbed. Even in the semi-dark there is a clear demarcation where the vegetation changes. She stoops down into the low acacias and he can see nothing but her back to him, her bent spine through the sleeveless cotton blouse. It is a small white square, like a handkerchief. In better light he could photograph it and make it into that, or into a sheet on a clothesline. It's shaking just exactly that way, like a forgotten sheet left out in a windstorm. She stays kneeling there for a long time being whipped like that.

Then her head pushes up through the fringe of acacias and she moves toward him, her face shining beautifully with its own privacy of tears. He sees how deeply it would hurt her if she understood what he knows: that his observations have stolen the secrets she chose not to tell. She is a child with the dignity of an old woman. He moves back up through the cottonwoods and into the house, into his workroom. He can't know who she has buried down there but he can mark the place for her. At least he can do that. To save it from animals. Before he goes to bed he'll cover it with a pile of stones, the heaviest he can move.

He pretends for a long time to be busy in his workroom, periodically coming out to feign a need in the kitchen. Where has he put the Piper forceps? Codi is emptied out and exhausted and still stays up half the night doing homework. Six volumes of the *Britannica* lie open on the kitchen table; she states that she is doing a report on the marsupial mammals.

So many times he comes close to speaking, but the sentences take absurd forms in his mind: "I notice that you've been pregnant for the last six months. I meant to talk with you about this earlier." He would sell his soul to back up the time, but even if he could do that, could begin where he chose, he can't locate the point where it would have been safe to start. Not ten weeks ago, or ten years. If he has failed his daughters he's failed them uniformly. For their whole lives, since Alice died, they've been too far away to touch. It's as if she pulled them with her through a knothole halfway into the other world, and then at the last minute left them behind, two babies stranded together in this stone cold canyon.

He can't think of anything more to do in the kitchen, and she's still working. There are dark depressions under her eyes, like thumbprints on her white face. She tells him she has a headache, asks for aspirin, and he goes immediately to the closet where he keeps the medications. He stands for a long time staring at the bottles and thinking. Aspirin would increase the bleeding, if she's still hemorrhaging, which is likely from the look of her. But he would know if she were in danger, he tells himself. It was probably uncomplicated as stillbirths go; it would have been extremely small even at six months. She is so malnourished, he could have predicted toxemia, even placenta abruptio. He continues to stare into the closet, tapping a finger against his chin. He can't even give her Percodan—it contains aspirin. Demerol. That, for the pain, and something else for the cramping. What? He wishes he could give her a shot of Pitocin, but doesn't see how he can.

He returns to the kitchen and hands her the pills with a glass of water. Four pills, two yellow and two blue, when she's only asked for aspirin, but she swallows them without comment, one after another, without looking up from her books. This much she'll take from him. This is the full measure of love he is qualified to dispense.

▼▼▼

He bends down again over the developer bath, his face so near the chemicals that his eyes water. The picture slowly gives up its soul to him as it lies in the pan, like someone drowned at the bottom of a pool. It's still the same: plain shadows on dust. Damn. What he is trying for is the luminous quality that water has, even dark water seen from a distance. There is a surface on it he just can't draw out of these dry shadows.

He straightens up, his eyes still running, and pats his pockets for his handkerchief. He locates it finally in the wrong pocket and blows his nose. He has manipulated this photograph in every possible way, and none of it has yielded what he wants. He sees now that the problem isn't in the development; the initial conception was a mistake. He fails in the darkroom so seldom that it's hard for him to give up, but he does. For once he lets go of the need to work his will. He clicks off the old red dwarf and turns on the bright overhead light, and the unfixed prints lying in the bath all darken to black. It doesn't matter. The truth of that image can't be corrected.

COSIMA
▲▲▲▲▲▲▲▲

14

DAY OF THE DEAD

On the last Monday of October Rita Cardenal made three announcements to the class: she was quitting school, this was her last day, and if anybody wanted her fetal pig they could have it, it was good as new.

We'd plowed right through the animal kingdom in record time, having had nothing to look at in the way of protozoans. We'd made a couple of trips back to the river and had given due attention to the amphibians and Mr. Bad Fish, whose glass home grew more elaborate with each field trip and was now called the Frog Club Med. There were fern palm trees and a mossy golf green, and the frogs obligingly did high-impact aerobics all over everything. Now we were up to exploring the inner mysteries of an unborn mammal, which had to be purchased mail order.

But Rita hadn't had the stomach to cut into hers, and I couldn't blame her, all things considered. She was expecting twins. She said she was dropping out because she felt too tired to get her homework done; I feared for these children's future.

Rita wore about half a dozen earrings in one ear and had a tough-cookie attitude, and I liked her. She'd been a good student. She seemed sorry to go but also resigned to her fate, in that uniquely teenage way of looking at life, as if the whole production were a thing inflicted on young people by some humorless committee of grownups with bad fashion sense. I was disappointed but unsurprised to lose Rita. I'd been watching her jeans get tight. The pregnancy dropout rate in Grace was way ahead of motor-vehicle accidents, as a teenage hazard. Rita was a statistic. On Tuesday I made my own announcement: we were doing an unscheduled unit on birth control.

The reaction in the ranks was equal parts embarrassment and amazement. You'd think I'd suggested orgies in study hall. There was some hysteria when I got to the visual aids. "Look, there's nothing funny about a condom," I said, pretending to be puzzled by their laughter. "It's a piece of equipment with a practical purpose, like a . . ." Only the most unfortunate analogies came to mind. Shower cap. Tea cozy. "Like a glove," I said, settling for the cliché. I turned from the blackboard and narrowed my eyes. "If you think this thing is funny, you should see the ridiculous-looking piece of equipment it fits over." The guys widened their eyes at each other but shut up. I was getting the hang of this.

"Miss," said Raymo. They'd never learned to call me Codi. "What is it?"

"You're gonna get busted for this."

I finished my diagram, which looked somewhat more obscene than I would have liked. I brushed my chalk-dusty hands on my jeans and hopped up to sit on the tall lab bench that served as my desk. "I know some of your parents might not be too thrilled about this field of study," I said, thinking it over. "I didn't get permission from the school board. But I think we'd better take a chance. It's important."

"Okay then, tell us something we don't know," said Connie Muñoz, who had even more holes punched in her left ear than Rita. I wondered if this was some kind of secret promiscuity index.

"Shut up, Connie!" said Marta. (Pearl studs, one per earlobe.) "My dad would kill me if he thought I knew this stuff."

"What you *do* is between you and your dad," I said. "Or not. Whatever. But what you *know* is my business. Obviously you don't need to put everything you know into practice, just like you don't have to go spraying the fire extinguisher around because you know how to use it. But if your house is already on fire, kiddos, I don't want you burning down with it just because nobody ever taught you what was what."

Raymo shook his head slowly and said again, "Bus-ted." He drew the laugh he wanted.

"You know what, Raymo?" I asked, tapping a pencil thoughtfully against my teeth.

"What?"

"It doesn't matter a whole lot what the school board thinks." This dawned on me forcefully as I said it. I understood this power: telling off my boss at the 7-Eleven, for example, two days before I left Tucson. The invulnerability of the transient. "There's nobody else to teach this course," I said. "And I only have a one-year contract, which I wasn't planning on renewing anyway. I'm not even a real teacher. I've just got this provisional certification deal. So that's the way it is. We're studying the reproductive system of higher mammals. If I'm offending anybody's religion or moral turpitude here, I apologize, but please take notes anyway because you never know."

They were completely quiet, but toward the end of the day you really can't tell what that means. It could be awe or brain death, the symptoms are identical.

"Miss?" It was Barbara, a tall, thin, shy student (ears unpierced), whose posture tried always to atone for her height. She'd latched onto me early in the semester, as if she'd immediately sniffed out my own high-school persona. "You aren't coming back next year?"

"Nope," I said. "I'm outta here, just like a senior. Only difference between you and me is I don't get a diploma." I gave them an apologetic smile, meant for Barbara especially. "It's nothing personal. That's just my *modus operandi*."

The kids blinked at this, no doubt wondering if it was a Latin name they needed to write down.

"Your *modus operandi* is the way you work," I said. "It's what you leave behind when you split the scene of a crime."

▼▼▼

At Grace High I taught Biology I, Biology II, two study halls, and I also pinch-hit an algebra class for a fellow teacher who was frequently absent on account of a tricky pregnancy. My favorite class was Biology II, my seniors—Raymo and Marta and Connie Muñoz and Barbara—but on that day I had a mission and didn't discriminate among souls. I gave everybody the lecture on baby prevention. Barbara, who was in my study hall and also in the algebra class, got to hear it three times, poor child, and I imagine she was the least in need.

It surprised me as much as the kids, this crusade, and I suspected my motives; what did I care if the whole class had twins? More likely I wanted to be sure of a terminal contract. After the last bell rang I erased the blackboard and stood for a minute sharing the quiet with the bones of my Illinois compatriot, Mrs. Josephine Nash. Our day was over. She gave me her silent, wide-jawed smile. Here was a resident of Grace who had never hurt me in childhood, didn't make me rack my memory for her name (she wore it on her pelvis), had thrown no spitballs at me nor asked for extra credit, and didn't suggest that I belonged in Paris, France, or a rock 'n' roll band.

From the back of the room I could hear the frogs clicking against the sides of their terrarium, constant as a clock: up and down, up and down, exposing soft white bellies. This time next year there would not even be fish or frogs in the river; these particular representatives of the animal kingdom were headed for extinction. Whoever taught this class would have to write Carolina Biological Supply and order those stiff preserved frogs that smell of formaldehyde, their little feet splayed like hands and their hearts exposed.

I stood over the terrarium and peered down into it from above, like a god. The fish hung motionless in its small lake. Droplets of condensation were forming on the underside of the glass top. Getting ready to rain in there. I'd grown fond of this miniature world, along with the kids, and had added my own touches: a clump of bright red toadstools that popped up in Emelina's courtyard, and a resurrection fern from the cliff behind my house. The terrarium was like a time capsule. I think everybody was trying to save little bits of Grace.

I slid the glass to one side, hating to disrupt the ecosystem but needing to feed the fish. The humid smells of mud and moss came up to meet my nose, and I thought of Hallie in the tropics. What would she do about these troubles if she were here? Well, stay, for one thing, whereas I wouldn't. I had come here with some sense of its being the end of the line, maybe in a positive way, but I found I had no claim on Grace. Seeing it as "home" was a hopeful construction, fake, like the terrarium. I'd deal with Doc Homer insofar as that was possible in one year, and then I'd rejoin Carlo, or think about another research job; I had no specifics in mind. My future was mapped in negatives. Next year I could be anywhere but here.

I'd told Hallie about my bold, ridiculous little deposition on the pH of the river, and a few days later I'd had to follow up with the news of the river's getting dammed—questions of pH being entirely academic. I felt humiliated. Eventually she wrote back to say: "Think of how we grew up. You can't live through something like that, and not take risks now. There's no getting around it." She was admonishing me, I guess. I should have more loyalty to my hometown. I wasn't brave; I was still trying to get around it. A good citizen of the nation in love with forgetting. I pelleted the surface of the water with goldfish flakes. In nature there are animals that fight and those that flee; I was a flighty beast. Hallie seemed to think I'd crossed over—she claimed I was the one who'd once wanted to dig in and fight to save the coyote pups. Emelina thought I'd been ringleader in campaigns to save stewing hens. In my years of clear recall there was no such picture. When Hallie and I lived in Tucson, in the time of the refugees, she would stay up all night rubbing the backs of people's hands and holding their shell-shocked babies. I couldn't. I would cross my arms over my chest and go to bed. Later, after my second year of med school, I'd been able to address their external wounds but no more than that.

The people of Grace would soon be refugees too, turned out from here like pennies from a pocket. Their history would dissolve as families made their separate ways to Tucson or Phoenix, where there were jobs. I tried to imagine Emelina's bunch in a tract house, her neighbors all keeping a nervous eye on the color coordination of her flowerbeds. And my wonderfully overconfident high-school kids being swallowed alive by city schools where they'd all learn to walk like Barbara, suffering for their small-town accents and inadequate toughness. It was easy to be tough enough in Grace.

Well, at least they'd know how to use condoms. I could give them that to carry through life. I settled the glass lid back over the terrarium and turned out the lights. I would be long gone before the ruination of Grace; I had a one-year contract. Now I'd made sure of it.

▼▼▼

Rita Cardenal called me up on the phone. She hesitated for a second before speaking. "I don't think your old man has all his tires on the road."

"It's possible." I sat down in my living-room chair and waited for her to go on.

"Did you tell him about me? About dropping out?"

"Rita, no. I wouldn't do that."

Silence. She didn't believe me. To Rita we were both authority figures—but at least she'd called. "My father and I aren't real close," I said. "I go up to see him every week, but we don't exactly talk." A pregnant teen could surely buy that.

"Well, then, he's got a slightly major problem."

"What did he do?"

"He just sorta went imbalanced. I went in for my five-month checkup? And he said the babies were too little, but he was all kind of normal and everything?" She paused. "And then all of a sudden he just loses it and gets all creeped and makes this major scenario. *Yelling* at me."

"What did he say?"

"Stuff. Like, that I had to eat better and he was going to make sure I did. He said he wasn't going to let me go *out of the house* till I shaped up. It was like he just totally went mental. He was using that tape measure thing to measure my stomach and then he just puts it down and there's tears in his eyes and he puts his hands on my shoulders and kind of pulls me against his chest. He goes, 'We have to talk about this. Do you have any idea what's inside of you?' I got creeped out."

I felt dizzy. There was a long pause.

"Miss? Codi?"

"Rita, I'm really sorry. What can I tell you? He's losing his mind. He's got a disease that makes him confused. I think he was really just trying to do his job, but he got mixed up about what was the appropriate way to talk to you."

"I heard that. That he had that disease where you go cuckoo and turn back into a baby."

"Well, that's not quite the way I'd put it, but it's true. Occasionally rumors are true."

"Is it true you're really a doctor?"

I looked out my east window at the wall of red rock that rose steeply behind the house. "No," I said. "That isn't true. Did he tell you that?"

"No." She paused. "Well, yeah. He said something a real long time ago, that you were in medical school or something. But not this last time. I heard it from somebody else, that you're a doctor and Doc Homer's dying and you're going to take over."

"Take over?"

"Take over being the doctor for Grace. They said you already saved that baby down at Doña Althea's restaurant."

"Oh, Jesus Christ."

"Look, people say stuff, okay?" Rita said. "This town is full of major mouths. It's just what I heard."

"I'm only here till the end of the school year, so you can tell whoever's spreading that gossip they're full of shit."

"Okay. Sor-ry."

I regretted snapping at Rita. "It's okay," I said. "It's not your fault. I'm not used to living in a place where everybody's into everybody else's business."

"It's the bottom level, isn't it? My mom found out I was pregnant from a lady that works at the bank. Mom goes, 'What is the date today?' and the lady goes, 'The fourteenth. Your daughter will be due around Valentine's Day, won't she? I had a baby on Valentine's Day.' " Rita paused for my opinion.

"Yeah," I said. "It's the bottom level."

"Uh-huh. Mom told me after that she had to tear up three checks in a row before she could make one out right. Like that was *my* fault."

▼▼▼

I set out to find Doc Homer the minute I hung up the phone, but it took me a long time to track him down, and my energy for drama kind of petered out. First I went to his office in the basement of the old hospital, up on the plateau—it was four o'clock on a Wednesday and he should have been there. But Mrs. Quintana said he'd gone downtown to check on old Mr. Moreno's oxygen machine because it was making a noise, and then he was going to stop at the grocery to pick up some pork chops. It had been half an hour so I figured I'd catch him if I skipped Mr. Moreno and went straight to the grocery, but I got there too late. The grocer, Mrs. Campbell, said he had come there *first*, having forgotten he needed to go to Mr. Moreno's. He'd stood for six or eight minutes in canned goods, as if lost, and then it came to him. Mrs. Campbell told me this with a sort of indulgent wink, as if he were Einstein or something and you could forgive it. He'd left for the Morenos' house, but first was going next door to the pharmacy to pick up Mr. Moreno's emphysema medication. I skipped the pharmacy and headed for the bright pink Moreno house, thinking I'd catch him as he came out and we could walk together back up the long hill, past the hospital, to his house. So the war on germs in Grace was being waged by a man who got lost in fruit cocktail. There was a clinic in Morse, just across the state line, and according to Mrs. Quintana a lot of people now drove over there. Disloyally, she had implied; she adored my father. She noted primly that they'd have problems with their state insurance forms.

On my way to the Morenos' I stopped at the P.O. There was a letter from Hallie, which I would save for later. I liked reading them alone, with time for filling in whatever she might leave out.

It turned out the Moreno visit had been unexpectedly brief, and he'd left already. The oxygen machine had stopped making noises all on its own. I walked back up the hill alone. By the time I finally did get to Doc Homer's kitchen his pork chops were cooked and he was just sitting down.

He looked surprised, almost pleased, his face turning up from the table, and he offered to put something on the stove for me but I told him I wasn't hungry. I sat down at my old place at the table where I'd passively refused food a thousand times before. But tonight it made me sad to watch him eat his solitary supper—he'd cooked one serving of an entire balanced meal, vegetables and everything. This amazed me. When Carlo went on his work binges at the hospital, I skipped meals notoriously; I was lucky if I hit all the food groups in four consecutive days. But I supposed Doc Homer had gotten the knack of solitude. For him it wasn't a waiting period, it was life.

"I hear you were kind of hard on Rita Cardenal," I said.

He flushed slightly. "Do you know her? She's expecting twins. She needs to take better care of herself."

"I know. She was one of my students till day before yesterday. She's a good kid."

"I'm sure she is," he said. "But she is rather hard to talk to. I wrote down a prescribed diet for her, which she wadded up and threw in the wastepaper basket before she left my office. She said she would eat what she pleased, since her life was already a totally creeped scenario. That is a quote."

I smiled. "Kids here have their own minds, I'm finding out. I hadn't really expected that."

"They do."

"My students talk like a cross between Huck Finn and a television set."

He seemed slightly amused. I knew I was avoiding the issue. I took a deep breath. "I think I've let things go too long. I should have talked to you a long time before now. I don't think you're doing too well, and I feel like I should be taking care of you, but I don't know how. We're the blind leading the blind here. All I know is it's up to me to do it."

"There is no problem, Codi. I'm taking an acridine derivative. Tacrine. It keeps the decline of mental functions in check."

"Tacrine *slows* the decline of mental functions, if you're lucky.

And it's experimental. I'm not stupid, I did a lot of reading in the medical library after you told me about this."

"No, you are not stupid. And I am fine."

"You always say you're fine."

"Because I always am."

"Look, I'm only here till next summer. We need to get things squared away. What are you going to do when you can't keep up your practice anymore? Do you think you're being fair?"

He cut up his cauliflower, running the knife between the tines of his fork. He dissected it into neat, identical-sized cubes, and did not answer me until he was completely finished. "I'll do what I've always planned to do. I'll retire."

"You're sixty-six," I said. "When do you plan to retire?"

"When I can no longer work carefully and capably."

"And who's going to be the judge of that?"

"I am."

I stared at him. "Well, I think there's some evidence that you're slipping in the careful and capable department." My heart was beating hard—I'd never come even close to saying something like that to him. I didn't wait for an answer. I got up and walked into the living room. It was the same, piles of junk everywhere. I was startled by something new: a dozen women's shoes from somewhere, arranged in a neat circle, toes pointed in. Superficial order imposed on chaos. It's exactly how I would have expected Doc Homer to lose his marbles. I felt dizzy and unsupported by my legs or Doc Homer's floor, and I sat down. I couldn't even tell Hallie this. She would come home.

The old red-and-black wool afghan, Hallie's and my comfort blanket in old times, was still folded tidily on the sofa. In the months I'd been here it hadn't been unfolded once, I was sure. I took the thick bundle of it into my arms and walked back into the kitchen and sat down, this time in Hallie's chair, the afghan pressed against my chest like a shield.

"I'm taking this, if you don't mind. I'll need it when it gets cooler."

"That's fine," he said.

I stared at him for another minute. "Do you know what people in Grace are saying?"

"That the moon is made of green cheese, I imagine." He got up and began to wash the dishes from his small meal. A large and a small skillet, a vegetable steamer, a saucepan, plate and glass, spoons and knives of various sizes, and the Piper forceps. Including the pot lids, around twenty separate utensils to cook and consume maybe eight ounces of food. I felt obsessive myself for counting it all up, but it seemed to be a symbol of something. The way he'd lived his life, doing everything in the manner he thought proper, whether it made sense or not.

"They're saying I'm a doctor," I said to his back. "That I've come here to save Grace." Hallie and I had already used up all the possible jokes on our town and Doc Homer: Saving Grace, Amazing Grace. Every one left a bitter taste in the mouth.

"And how do they propose that you're going to do that?"

"I don't know. However doctors usually perform their miracles."

"You know very well what doctors do. You finished four years of medical school and you nearly finished your internship. You were only two or three months away from being licensed to practice."

I touched my fingertip to some vagrant bread crumbs scattered across the table. Because his back was turned I had the courage to ask the question point blank. "How *severely* do you hold that against me? That I didn't make doctor?"

"Who is saying you didn't make it?"

"I'm saying it, right now. I don't have it in me, now or ever. Just the idea of me being a doctor is ridiculous. People depending on *me* in a life-or-death situation? Remember when I took Red Cross swimming lessons? I tried out the elbow-hold rescue on Ginny Galvez and we had a near-death experience."

He spoke without turning around. "How did you arrive at the conclusion that you could not be a doctor?"

For a minute I buried my face in the afghan, which smelled like a familiar animal. When I looked up again he was facing me, drying his hands on a dish towel, one finger at a time. "I would just like to know," he said.

"I couldn't make it through my rotation on OB-GYN. I was delivering a premature baby, which turned out also to be breach, and there was fetal distress, and the mother's pressure started to shoot up. I just walked away from it. I don't even remember exactly what I did, but I know I left her there. She could have died." I corrected myself. "They both could have died."

"You were only a first-year resident and it was a high-risk delivery. I'm sure there was someone on hand to back you up. Malpractice laws being what they are."

"That's not the point."

"You don't have to deliver babies to be a physician. I no longer deliver babies myself. There are a hundred specialties you could choose that have nothing to do with obstetrics."

"That *isn't* the point. People were looking to me for a decision, and I lost my nerve. You can't lose your nerve. You're the one that taught me that."

He looked me straight in the eye and said, "I lose my nerve a dozen times a day."

It was the last thing on earth I expected to hear. I felt as if I'd been robbed. I put my face back in the afghan and suddenly I started to cry. I have no idea where the tears came from, they just came from my eyes. I didn't want either one of us to admit helplessness here. I kept my face down for a long time, soaking the wool. When I finally glanced up he was putting something away in the refrigerator. In the dark kitchen, the brightly lit interior of the refrigerator was a whole, bright little foreign land of cheerful white boxes, stacked like condominiums. There must have been fifty tupperware containers in there: pies, cakes, casseroles. I thought of Uda's squash pie, and understood with surprise that all the women of Grace were taking care of Doc Homer. As a caretaker, I was superfluous.

He saw me looking at him. He stood with the refrigerator door half open, illuminating his face. "Codi, you could be a doctor if you wanted to do that. You learned the skills. Don't try to put the blame on something abstract like your nerve—you have to take responsibility. Is it something you want, or not?"

"I don't know."

He didn't move. I kept thinking he ought to close the refrigerator door. He'd always had a million rules about everything. Wasting electricity, for example.

"It's not," I finally said, for the first time.

"No?"

"No. I thought it would be an impressive thing to do. But I don't think it was a plan that really grew out of my life. I can't remember ever thinking it would be all that delightful to look down people's throats and into their nasty infected ears and their gall bladders."

"You're entitled to that opinion," he said. "That the human body is a temple of nastiness."

I held him steady in the eye and he smiled, ever so slightly. "You bet," I said. "People are a totally creeped scenario."

▼▼▼

The news from Hallie was brief and moderately alarming. There had been contra activity in her district, nobody hurt but four John Deere tractors burnt down to scorched metal hulls. She sounded sick about that. "A Deere is like a hunk of gold here. Because of the U.S. embargo we can't get parts, and the ones still running are Nicaragua's patron saints." She sounded completely, happily settled in, though, much more so than I was in Grace. She talked about waking up in the mornings: Roosters hopping up onto the windowsill. An army of little girls in polyester dresses out in the street with huge baskets on their heads, forging out on a hundred urgent missions. She was making good progress with some new cultivation methods; wished she knew more about diesel mechanics. A man named Julio, a literacy teacher from Matagalpa, had asked her out on a date. (She drew stars all around the word "date," making fun of herself.) They had busy schedules, so finally they met after work and rode together to a meeting in a church where Hallie delivered a lecture on pesticide safety. The church was full of gnats and kerosene smoke and little kids crawling around on a big piece of plastic, crying, impatient for their parents to take them home to bed. She and Julio had ridden over together on her horse, *Sopa del Dia*, and had a nice time going home.

▼▼▼

Sunday night was Halloween and Emelina's children took to the streets. Grace was at an interesting sociological moment: the teenagers inhaled MTV and all wanted to look like convicted felons, but at the same time, nobody here was worried yet about razor blades in apples.

Emelina volunteered me to go trick-or-treating with the four older boys while she stayed home to dispense bribes to the rest of the town's marauders; she felt a pagan holiday would do me good. I was only chaperone and crossing guard, not expected to go in costume. There was a state law against anyone over twelve wearing a mask or making direct requests at people's doors. The city fathers of Grace were independent to an extent: they ignored state law when they closed school on November 2 for the town's biggest holiday, the Day of All Souls. But to be on the safe side they were going along with the Halloween mask law. John Tucker was disappointed but tried not to show it. Emelina encouraged him to go with us anyway, more or less as a second chaperone. She was wonderful to watch. I guess I'd never really seen good mothering up close.

He agreed to go, dressed in J.T.'s black raincoat, with a quarter-inch of talcum powder on his face. Emelina ran deep eyeliner shadows under his eyes. It was convincing—he looked either sick or dead, depending on his position. Mason went as a bug, with grocery-bag wings and radio antennae strapped to his head with a yellow sweatband. He instructed Emelina to draw on bug fangs with her eyebrow pencil. I don't think Emelina ever actually wore makeup, she just kept it on hand for emergencies. The twins both were going as teenagers (i.e., convicted felons), but decided they needed fangs also.

We made a pretty good haul; in this fruit basket of a valley, I'd never seen such an orgy of sucrose. Jawbreakers and Gummi Bears multiplied in the kids' bags like the loaves and fishes. The twins pulled me along by both hands, and Mason gripped my leg when we crossed the street. We hit every house on the road that circled the canyon to the south—the longest possible route to the courthouse. John Tucker hung back in the shadows at the edges of yards, but I escorted the boys right up to the doorsteps, secretly enjoying these little peeks into people's bright living rooms. Our last stop was at the lemon-yellow home of Mrs. Nuñez, whom I knew to be an important figure in the Stitch and Bitch Club. I was beginning to learn my way around the matriarchy of Grace, a force unknown to me in childhood.

Old Mrs. Nuñez recognized the kids immediately, but for some reason mistook me for Emelina. I think she just didn't really look. She chattered at the boys as she dropped Hershey's kisses and bubble gum into their heavy grocery bags: "Oh, what an awful-looking bug you are. You get away from my house, you old *cucaracha*. And you ugly old twins, too. You're too scary." She kissed them all on the tops of their heads.

She stopped suddenly, holding her glasses and peering out at the pale apparition of John Tucker, who was hanging back around her shrubs as required by law. "*Cielo santo!*" she said, with real concern. "What's the matter with your brother?"

"He's thirteen," said Glen.

▼▼▼

All Souls' Day dawned cool, and the people of Grace put on their sweatshirts and gave thanks. The heat wave was broken. By half past eight the sun was well up and sweatshirts peeled off again, but it was still a perfect day. Every able-bodied person in Grace climbed the canyon roads to converge on the cemetery.

It was the bittersweet Mexican holiday, the Day of the Dead, democratic follow-up to the Catholic celebration of All Hallows. Some people had business with the saints on November 1, and so went to mass, but on November 2 *everybody* had business at the graveyard. The families traipsing slowly uphill resembled harvester ants, carrying every imaginable species of real and artificial flower: bulging grocery sacks of chrysanthemums and gladioli; tulips made from blue and pink Styrofoam egg cartons; long-stemmed silk roses bouncing in children's hands like magic wands; and unclassifiable creations out of fabric and colored paper and even the plastic rings from six-packs. The Stitch and Bitch Club had had four special meetings in a row.

When Hallie and I were very small we used to be allowed to

participate in this celebration, with J.T.'s family. I wondered if Viola remembered having us in tow. In my own mind it was all vague; what I remembered best was the marigolds. *Cempazu-chiles*, the flowers of the dead. I asked Viola about them.

"They come on the truck," she answered cryptically.

"Do you remember when Hallie and I used to come up here with you?"

"Sure I do. You always ran all over the graves and messed up everything." Viola didn't pull her punches.

"Well, we were little," I said defensively. "Doc Homer made us quit coming after a while. I remember that. I remember him saying, 'Those great-grandmothers aren't any of your business.' "

"Well, he was the boss."

"Right. He was the boss."

Emelina and the four older boys were marching ahead, but I was pushing the stroller over gravel and Viola was over sixty, so we both had an excuse to lag. We were a harvester-ant clan ourselves, burdened not only with flowers but with food and beer and soft drinks and sundry paraphernalia. John Tucker was carrying a new, largish St. Joseph for Viola's husband's grave. J.T. was still in El Paso, and Loyd was on a switch engine in Yuma, but we didn't seem to need them all that much. It looked like a female holiday, what with the egg-carton flowers. A festival of women and children and old people and dead ancestors.

Viola stopped for breath, holding the bosom of her shiny black dress and looking down at the canyon. I waited with her, adjusting the red handkerchief Emelina had tied over Nicholas's bald head to shield it from sun. As he vibrated over the corduroy road the kerchief kept slipping down over his eyes, and he looked like a drunken pirate. I bent over and looked into his face, upside-down. He enlightened me with a wicked pirate smile.

It was a spectacular day. The roadside was lined with bright yellow plumes of rabbitbrush, apparently too common a flower for anyone to take to a grave, but I liked them. I would try to remember to pick some on my way back down, to stick into the clay ollas around my house; I was determined to prove to Eme-lina that I wasn't completely bereft of domestic instincts.

From where we stood we could look down on the whole of Grace plus the many small settlements that lay a little apart from the town, strung out along the length of Gracela Canyon and its tributaries, often inhabited by just a few families, some with their own tiny graveyards. These settlements were mostly aban-doned now. A lot of them had been torn right up when Black Mountain chased a vein of copper under their floors; others had been buried; the company had an old habit of digging and dump-ing where it pleased. Grace's huge main cemetery was located on the opposite side of the canyon, as far as possible from the mine, for exactly that reason. Not even the graveyards were sacred.

At the upstream end of the canyon we could also see the beginnings of the dam that would divert the river out Tortoise Canyon. There had been a ridiculous photo in the local paper: the company president and a couple of managers at a ground-breaking ceremony, wearing ties, stepping delicately on shovels with their wing-tip shoes. These men had driven down from Phoenix for the morning, and would drive right back. They all had broad salesmen's smiles. They pretended the dam was some kind of community-improvement project, but from where Viola and I stood it looked like exactly what it was—a huge grave. Marigold-orange earth movers hunched guiltily on one corner of the scarred plot of ground.

"So what's going to happen?" I asked Viola.

"The Lord in heaven knows," she said.

I prodded. "Well, there was a meeting last night. Have you talked to anybody?"

"Oh, sure. The men on the council had another one of their big meetings about it and decided to have a lawsuit. A lawyer came up from Tucson to meet with Jimmy Soltovedas."

Jimmy was the mayor. The town council had nothing to do with Black Mountain anymore; Grace wasn't a company town in the classical sense, except for the fact that the company owned everything we walked on.

"What did the lawyer say?" In a moment of vanity I wondered if anyone had mentioned my affidavit. My line about "the approximate pH of battery acid" seemed like something a lawyer could gleefully quote.

"The lawyer said we might have grandfather rights to the water, and so we could have a class-action lawsuit to make the company give us back our river."

"How long will that take?"

She shrugged. "Maybe ten years."

"Ten *years?*"

"Right. In ten years we can all come back and water our dead trees."

"Did anybody go to the newspapers to get some publicity about this? It's ridiculous."

"Jimmy called the newspapers half a dozen times. I talked to Jimmy's wife. Nobody's interested in a dipshit little town like Grace. They could drop an atom bomb down on us here and it wouldn't make no news in the city. Unless it stirred up the weather over there and rained out a ball game or something."

"So it's a ten-year lawsuit." I didn't want to believe she was right, though her sources were always irreproachable. "Is that the only thing those guys can come up with against the Mountain?"

"Don't call that company the Mountain," she said curtly. "It makes it sound like something natural you can't ever move."

"I've heard the men call it that," I said.

Viola snorted like an old horse and started up the hill.

When we arrived, half a dozen elderly men were putting a fresh coat of white paint on the wrought-iron fence around the huge cemetery. Wrought iron was a theme here; there were iron crosses and wreaths, and over some of the graves there were actual little iron houses, with roofs. Through the ups and downs of Black Mountain's smelting plant, Grace had been home to a lot of out-of-work metalworkers.

Most families divided their time between the maternal and paternal lines, spending mornings on one set of graves and afternoons on the other. Emelina and the boys staked out the Domingos plot and set to work sweeping and straightening. One of the graves, a great-uncle of J.T.'s named Vigilancio Domingos, was completely bordered with ancient-looking tequila bottles, buried nose down. Mason and I spent half the morning gathering up the strays and resetting them all in the dirt, as straight as teeth. It was a remarkable aesthetic—I don't mean just Uncle Vigilancio, but the whole. Some graves had shrines with niches peopled by saints; some looked like botanical gardens of paper and silk; others had the initials of loved ones spelled out on the mound in white stones. The unifying principle was that the simplest thing was done with the greatest care. It was a comfort to see this attention lavished on the dead. In these families you would never stop being loved.

The marigold truck arrived at ten o'clock. Women swarmed down on it like bees, coming away with armloads of floral gold. There were many theories on the best way to put them to use, or to make them go farthest. Viola, who directed the Domingos family operations, was of the deconstructionist school. She had the boys tear the flowers up and lay the petals down over a grave, blanketing it like a monochrome mosaic.

John Tucker stayed at his work but the twins wandered and Mason disappeared altogether. Emelina.wasn't worried. "He's refining his begging skills he learned on Halloween," she said, and was probably right. Grandmothers everywhere, who at lunch had set out extra plates for the dead, were now indiscriminately passing out the sweet remains of their picnics.

By mid-afternoon Emelina felt we should send out a search party, "before he eats so many cookies he busts." Viola volunteered, and I went with her, more or less as a tourist. I wanted to see what else there was in the line of beautified graves. We skirted Gonzalez and Castiliano and Jones, each family with its own style. Some were devotees of color or form, while others went for bulk. One grave, a boy who'd died young, was decorated with the better part of a Chevrolet. There were hundreds of holes drilled into the fishtail fenders, to hold flowers. It was beautiful, like a float in a parade.

The cemetery covered acres. To the west of us were collections of small neglected mounds whose stones bore the names of families that had died out. "Trubee," I read aloud, wandering toward the desert of the forgotten. "Alice, Anna, Marcus. Lomas: Hector, Esperanza, José, Angel, Carmela."

"Honey, we better get back to where people are," Viola cautioned, but I wandered on, as distracted in my way as Mason must have been, wherever he was.

"Nolina," I shouted. "Look, here's my long-lost relatives."

Viola looked at me oddly from her distance across the graves.

"I'm kidding," I said. We came from Illinois, as she well knew. "Here's my Aunt Raquel, my aunt . . . something Maria." Most of the graves were illegible, or so crudely marked there was nothing to read. Then I found one that stopped me dead.

"Viola. Here's a *Homero* Nolina."

"So it is," she said, not really looking. "Son of a gun."

I eyed her. "Do you know something about this?"

"What do you want me to tell you?"

"Who were the Nolinas?"

"Come on back away from there and I'll tell you."

I stood my ground.

"Honey, come on, let's leave these dead folks alone. Nobody put any plates of food out for them for a long, long time. They're not feeling so happy today."

"Okay, but you have to tell me."

She told me the Nolinas used to live up around Tortoise River, in the northern end of Gracela Canyon. There was a little settlement there that dispersed when the area was covered by mine tailings. The Nolinas had dug up what they could of the family graveyard and carried the bones a few miles to bury them up here. It wasn't all that long ago, she said. Around 1950.

"I don't know any Nolinas in Grace now," I said.

"No, they're about gone. They never did settle too good into Grace. The most of them went to Texas or somewhere, after their houses got tore up. They weren't . . ." She stopped and took off her shoe, cocking her stockinged foot against her plump ankle while she examined the inside of it, then put it back on. "The Nolinas weren't real accepted. They were kind of different all the way back. There was one of the Gracela sisters had auburn hair and a bad temper, and she married Conrado Nolina. They say that family went downhill."

"They were trash, is what you're telling me."

"No. Just different."

I followed behind her as she plodded along, dodging headstones. She was as intransigent, in her way, as Doc Homer. "So how come one of them has practically the same name as my father?"

"You better ask him that," she said. "It's his name."

At that moment something hit me from behind like a torpedo, tackling me around the knees. It was Mason.

"Where have you been, *pachuco?* Your mama was worried to death about you," Viola said. Mason had an enormous sucker ballooning under one cheek. He laughed, recognizing Viola's scoldings as a bald-faced lie.

"I was at a birthday party," he lied back.

It took a while to coax him back to the fold. There were an infinity of distractions: *Calaveras*, little skull-shaped candies for children to crack between their teeth. The promise of a chicken leg for a kiss. Little girls and boys played "makeup," standing on tiptoe with their eyes closed and their arms at their sides, fingers splayed in anticipation, while a grownup used a marigold as a powder puff, patting cheeks and eyelids with gold pollen. Golden children ran wild over a field of dead great-grandmothers and great-grandfathers, and the bones must have wanted to rise up and knock together and rattle with joy. I have never seen a town that gave so much—so much of what *counts*—to its children.

More than anything else I wished I belonged to one of these living, celebrated families, lush as plants, with bones in the ground for roots. I wanted pollen on my cheeks and one of those calcium ancestors to decorate as my own. Before we left at sunset I borrowed a marigold from Emelina's great-aunt Pocha, who wouldn't miss it. I ran back to lay it on Homero Nolina, just in case.

HOMERO

15

MISTAKES

He has to look at her for a long time before he trusts himself to speak. Who is this girl? His daughter Codi, but which Codi? He thinks.

"You look surprised."

"You startled me. I wasn't expecting anyone." He was doing Mr. Garrison's lab work, waiting for the centrifuge to spin down Mr. Garrison's blood cells, and when he looked up she was standing in the doorway. He detests surprises.

"Pop, I called five minutes ago, to see if you were here. I told you I was coming. I came straight here. I spent the day up at the graveyard."

She is leaning against the doorsill holding a bouquet of rabbitbrush and roadside weeds, showering the air with pollen like an old feather duster. She has on purple cowboy boots, which even now are damaging her arches.

"And now you are here," he says carefully.

"I found a surprise in the graveyard, a headstone with a name on it you might recognize. Yours. Almost yours."

"Perhaps I am dead."

She stares. "Do we have relatives from here?"

Uda Dell gave those to her, to both girls, for Christmas: the boots and straw cowboy hats and holsters with cap guns, so that

169

they could run like banshees around the house pretending to fill each other with imaginary bullet holes. He took the guns away, for the preservation of their souls, and the boots on account of their arches. He let them keep the hats.

The minute hand on the wall clock jumps and the centrifuge slows to a stop, clicking suggestively, like the wheel of fortune. Without its mechanical whine the lab is very quiet. He looks up again and she is still there in her stocking feet and red straw cowboy hat, its dark cord knotted under her chin. She understands about the guns, but she wants the boots back. She has come on behalf of herself and her sister, she says. Her left foot in its white sock curls under. Why is it that only girls stand on the sides of their feet? As if they're afraid to plant themselves? Tears stream from her eyes.

He can't relinquish either the guns or the boots. He wishes he could do all these things differently, but he can't. He says, "I don't think we need to discuss this any further."

"Oh, come on, just tell me. Would it kill you to tell me?"

Startled, he looks again: she isn't in stockinged feet, she has boots on. She is much too tall. He is confused and becomes angry. He has a glass vial of blood in his hands. This is his office. She didn't need to sneak down here and startle him in his own doorway.

"I'm doing Mr. Garrison's hematocrit," he says. "I have a good bit more work to do."

She sighs loudly. She must be fourteen. In a year she will be sullen and furtively pregnant. Or has that passed too? He doesn't even look at her because there is too much there, and he's afraid. She is his first child, his favorite, every mistake he ever made.

COSIMA

16

BLEEDING HEARTS

At the first sign of winter the trees began to die. Leaves and aborted fruits fell in thick, brittle handfuls like the hair of a cancer patient. The abundance of sun and warmth, which we thought would never end, had led the trees on too, promising the impossible. But now the daylight grew thin and they showed no will to live. A dead sea of leaves drifted deep and undisturbed on the orchard floors. No children played there.

I spent a lot of time considering the mystery of my family tree. I didn't push the subject of the Nolinas, but I did ask people about my mother, whose leavings were scant. I'd grown up with only one sentence, repeated like a mantra: "It wasn't childbirth she died of, it was organ failure." I know this was meant to protect Hallie and me from guilt, but "organ failure," in its way, was equally unhelpful: a pronouncement that reminded me of those doubtfully groomed children in school whose report cards bore failing marks through every season, perennial as grass. "Organ failure" sounded like something our mother ought to be ashamed of, and us after her, *for* her, in death.

Viola dispensed with the organ-failure myth as easily as snapping a wishbone: "No, it was childbirth," she told me.

"But Hallie was born in June," I said. "She didn't die till later in the summer."

"It was a few weeks," Viola conceded. "Hallie gave her a real good round. She lost a lot of blood and after the birth she never got up again."

I was stunned by this news, and we walked in silence for a while. We were on our way to a special meeting of the Stitch and Bitch Club. To my surprise, I'd been invited as a guest scientist to talk about the pH of the river; needlework was not on the agenda.

Viola had on a brown cloth coat and what must have been her dead husband's hunting cap, earflaps down, the whole thing cocked forward to accommodate her thick, coiled bun. She stopped to pick up two stray peacock feathers, which she tucked into her coat pocket. One was perfect, with an iridescent blue eye bobbing at its tip. The other one had no eye.

"What did she look like?" I asked.

"Like you. Exactly like you, only smaller. She had real little hands and feet."

I looked down at my size 9's, defensively. "Not like Hallie?"

"Hallie always favored Doc more," Viola said.

I pondered this but couldn't see it—Hallie was so vital and Doc Homer looked drawn. But then what I saw really was their interiors, not their façades. Your own family resemblances are a frustrating code, most easily read by those who know you least.

"Well, I know she was pretty," I said. "Everybody says that. With a name like Alice how could you not be pretty?"

Viola made an odd sound, like unconsummated laughter.

"What?"

"He was the only one that ever called her Alice. Everybody else called her Althea. It means 'the truth.' "

"*Althea?* What, she was an honorary member of the Doña Althea family?"

Viola said nothing. I never knew what to make of her dark hints, but this one was wildly improbable. My impression was that she'd stayed an outsider, like the rest of us. Doc Homer had married my mother and come out here from Illinois after World War II, after he'd served in the army and finished his internship. Her maiden name was something like Carlisle. We never pressed him for more; when it came to our mother, Doc Homer seemed to be in an extended mourning period that lasted for our whole lives to date.

It made me curious, though. I had visions of trying again, of pinning his fragile shoulder blades against the wall of his basement office and forcing him to tell the whole truth about our family. As if Doc Homer's tongue could be forced.

Abruptly, Viola and I reached the American Legion hall. We walked into a noisy room bright with artificial light and I felt disoriented as to the decade. Women wearing cable-knit cardigans over thin housedresses crowded the hall with their talk, their large purses and imposing bosoms. When they saw Viola and me they began to come to some kind of order. Chairs were dragged, with much metallic howling, from conversational circles back into crooked rows. Many faces were familiar to me now from some encounter, such as old Mrs. Nuñez, who'd been so chatty when I took the boys to her house trick-or-treating, and others like Uda Dell I knew specifically. Doña Althea presided from an overstuffed chair at the front of the hall, but did not speak. Her face was as finely lined as the grain in maple wood, and about the same color. Her pale blue eyes blazed in the direction of the air over our heads. You could have taken her for a blind woman if you didn't know the truth, which was that Doña Althea's vision was sharp as a hawk's.

Norma Galvez, whose shellacked white hair was crowned with a navy bow that coordinated with her Steelworkers T-shirt, brought the meeting to order. It was a packed house. It took a while to achieve perfect quiet. Viola ushered me to a chair at the front table, hurried over to say hello to Doña Althea, and deposited the two feathers in a grocery bag of kindred feathers at the Doña's feet. Then she scurried back and took her seat by me.

"Viola brought a guest," announced Mrs. Galvez, accompanied by vigorous nodding from Viola. She'd removed her hunter's cap. "You all know Doc Homer's daughter Cosima. She's going to tell us about the contamination."

That was my introduction. I was expecting to hear all about myself and the situation, as is always done at meetings that go on too long. But she was through, and I was on. I stood a little shakily, thinking of Hallie, who felt at home giving a lecture in a church full of mosquitoes and kerosene smoke and squalling babies.

"I'm not an expert," I began. "Here's the chemistry of it. Black Mountain Mining has been running sulfuric acid, which is a clear, corrosive, water-miscible acid, through their tailing piles to recover extra copper. It combines to make copper sulfate, which is also known as 'blue vitriol.' People used to use it to kill rats and pond algae and about everything else you can name. There's a ton of it in your river. And there's straight sulfuric acid in there too. The EPA finally sent a report saying that kind of pollution is very dangerous, and they can't put it near people and orchards, so Black Mountain is building a dam to run the river out Tortoise Canyon. You know that part of the story. And the men on the town council are pushing for a lawsuit that will get some action in the twenty-first century." There was some snickering. I remembered my talk with Viola on the hill over-looking the dam construction site—her disgust. The Stitch and Bitch Club wasn't banking on the good old boys.

"I really don't know any way of helping out with your prob-lem. All I can tell you is that you have a problem, and why, which I guess is what scientists are mainly good for." I paused to swallow. The room was a silent garden of blinking faces, expecting something from me.

"My students and I looked at the river water under micro-scopes, and the usual things that live in a river aren't there. Then we tested the pH of the river and found out it's very acidic. The EPA has tested it too, and they agree. But your trees knew all this way before we did. Watering them from the river is just like acid rain falling on them, if you've heard of that. The acid-rain problem here in the West comes mostly from mine smelters. It's the same acid, one way or the other. Sulfuric acid." I feared I was losing my grasp of the subject, but they were still listening.

"I don't think I can tell you anything helpful. But Viola said I should come anyway. If you have questions I'll try to answer them." I sat down.

A thin woman in cat's-eye glasses and a red dress stood up

and demanded, "You mean the fish and stuff is all killed? My husband claims they was catching croppies out of there a month or two ago."

"Well, no, the fish . . ."

"Stand up, honey, we can't hear you," said Miss Lorraine Colder, my fourth-grade teacher. She and Miss Elva Dann, who sat next to her, had lived together forever and resembled each other although they were no relation.

"Not the fish," I said. "They're still alive, but the smaller things that live in the water . . ." I considered how to phrase this, and started again. "Usually there's a whole world of microscopic things living in a river, and in the dirt, and the air. If you were in an airplane and flew over a city and looked down and saw *nothing* was moving, you'd know something was up. That's how you can tell if a river is healthy or not. You can't see them, but they're supposed to be there."

The woman in the red dress hugged her sweater around her. "Like bugs?"

"Kind of," I said.

Another woman said in Spanish that if the river water killed bugs, she'd better take some and sprinkle it around her son's house. There was a good bit of laughter.

"It won't kill cockroaches," I said. "Too bad. You could sell it for a fundraiser." They laughed again, though there were some surprised looks, and I was secretly satisfied. All my life here, people had spoken Spanish around me the way grownups spell around children.

The woman in the red dress was still standing. "What we want to know is, *is* the river poisoned for good? Would we be better off to let them run it out Tortoise Canyon?"

Every person in the room was looking at me. It dawned on me that they weren't conceiving of their situation as hopeless. What they wanted was not sympathy or advice, but information. "Well, no," I said. "The river could recover. It doesn't *start* here, it starts up on the Apache reservation, in the mountains where the snow melts. As long as that's pure, the water coming down here will be okay."

"So if you could stop Black Mountain from running the acid

through the tailing piles, then after a while the junk would get washed out?" inquired Mrs. Galvez. "Like flushing the john?"

"Exactly like that," I said.

Fifty women started talking at once. You'd think I'd commuted a death sentence. After a minute Doña Althea carefully pushed herself up from the arms of her chair and stood, waiting for quiet. In her black dress she rustled like an old crow. She gave a short speech in Spanish, the gist of which was that I'd told them what they needed to know, and now they had to figure out how to get the company to stop building the dam and stop polluting the river and go to hell.

I sat down, a bit stunned. My Spanish was passably good, thanks to the years of Hallie's refugees sleeping on my couch, but some of Doña Althea's more idiomatic swear words were new ones on me. Also, she referred to me as *la huérfana*, the orphan. They always called Hallie and me that. It seemed unkind.

"My husband used to be a crane operator when the mine was running," shouted a woman in the back row. "He would know how to fix up them bulldozers from hell to breakfast."

"My husband was a dynamite man," volunteered another woman. "That would be quicker."

"Excuse me, but your husbands won't put Chinese arithmetic past no bulldozers," said Viola. Mrs. Crane Operator and Mrs. Dynamite seemed unperturbed, but Viola added thoughtfully, "No offense. Mine would be just as lazy, except he's dead."

Mrs. Galvez nodded. "Well, that's the truth. My husband says the same thing, 'The *lawyers* will fix it up, honey.' If the men were any use they'd be here tonight instead of home watching the football game."

"What are you talking about, *football?*" asked Mrs. Dynamite. "*Muchacha,* didn't you hear? The *Miss America Pageant* is on tonight." She stood up. "Whose husbands was watching the Broncos game when you walked out of the house?"

There was a show of hands.

"Okay, ten seconds and . . ." she leaned forward, dropped her jaw, and bugged her eyes wide like a pair of fried eggs . . . "if you got remote control, *three* seconds."

"Sure, why do you think they hurried us all out of the house tonight?" a woman added from the front row. " 'Why, yes, honey, go on to your club. I'll be okay. I'll just eat me a TV dinner here and watch football.' Like hell. Football in a bathing suit."

"Okay, girls," said Mrs. Galvez, adjusting her hair and rapping the table with her high-heeled pump. "Like Doña Althea says, we got some darn good thinking to do tonight."

"I say we were on the right track with the dynamite," said Viola. There was general nodding.

The woman in the red dress stood again. "We don't know how to use the dynamite, though. And the men, they might be good men but they wouldn't do it. They'd be scared to, I think. Or they don't see no need. These men don't see how we got to do something *right now*. They think the trees can die and we can just go somewhere else, and as long as we fry up the bacon for them in the same old pan, they think it would be . . ." she faltered, hugging her elbows in earnest . . . "that it would be *home*."

▼▼▼

On the way back Viola was quiet. She walked quickly, stopping only to pick up the feathers that littered the leafy orchard floor. The sudden cold snap that heralded the certainty of winter had caused the male peacocks to molt in unison. There being no hope of mating for months to come, they had shed their burdensome tails.

The meeting had ended in compromise: the Stitch and Bitch Club would officially sanction mass demonstrations against Black Mountain's leaching operation, to be held daily on the dam construction site, starting at 6 A.M. the following morning. Unofficially, the Stitch and Bitch Club would have no objection if a bulldozer met with premature demise.

Hallie wrote:

This morning I saw three children die. Pretty thirteen-year-old girls wearing dresses over their jeans. They were out in a woods near here, picking fruit, and a helicopter came over the trees and strafed them. We heard the shots. Fifteen minutes later an alert defense patrol shot the helicopter down, twenty miles north, and the pilot and another man in the helicopter were killed but one is alive. Codi, they're American citizens, active-duty National Guards. It's a helicopter from the U.S., guns, everything from Washington. Please watch the newspapers and tell me what they say about this. The girls were picking fruit. When they brought them into town, oh God. Do you know what it does to a human body to be cut apart from above, from the *sky?* We're defenseless from that direction, we aren't meant to have enemies attack us from above. The girls were alive, barely, and one of the mothers came running out and then turned away saying, "Thank you, Holy Mother, it's not my Alba." But it *was* Alba. Later when the families took the bodies into the church to wash them, I stayed with Alba's two younger sisters. They kept saying, "Alba braided our hair this morning. She can't be dead. See, she fixed our hair."

Codi, please tell me what you hear about this. I can't stand to think it could be the same amnesiac thing, big news for one day and then forgotten. Nobody here can eat or talk. There are dark stains all over the cement floor of the church. It's not a thing you forget.

She signed it, perversely, "The luckiest person alive."

I heard nothing. I listened to the radio, but there wasn't a word. Two days, nothing. Then, finally, there was one brief report about the American in the helicopter who was taken prisoner by the Nicaraguan government. He was an ex-mercenary running drugs, the radio said, no connection to us. He was shot down and taken prisoner, and that is all. No children had died in an orchard, no sisters, no mothers, no split skulls. And I'm sorry to say this, I knew it was a lie, but I was comforted.

▼▼▼

"Who came up with the idea that Indians are red?" I asked Loyd one morning. If I wasn't careful I could lose myself in this man. His color was like some wholesome form of bread, perfectly done. His forearm, which my head rested on, was sparsely covered with silky black hair.

He turned his head. His hair was perfectly straight, and touched his shoulders. "Old movies," he said. "Westerns."

We were in my bed very late on a Sunday morning. Loyd was a wonderful insomnia cure, good enough to bottle. That's what I'd written Hallie, whom I told everything now, even if my daily letters were comparatively trivial. "He's a cockfighter," I'd confessed, "but he's better than Sominex." When Loyd lay next to me I slept deep as a lake, untroubled by dreams. First I'd felt funny about his being here—exposing Emelina's children, and all that. But he didn't invite me to his place, saying mine was better. He liked to pull books down off my slim shelf and read parts aloud in bed, equally pleased with poetry or descriptions of dark-phase photosynthesis. It occurred to me that Emelina would have a good laugh over my delicacy concerning her children. She probably was daring them to look in the windows and bring back reports.

But the shades were drawn. "Old westerns were in black and white," I reminded him. "No red men."

"Well, there you go. If John Wayne had lived in the time of color TV, everybody would know what Indians look like."

"Right," I said, gently picking up Loyd's forearm and taking a taste. "Like that white guy in pancake makeup that played Tonto."

"Tonto who?"

"Tonto Schwarzenegger. Who do you think? Tonto. The Lone Ranger's secretary."

"I didn't grow up with a TV in the house." He withdrew his arm and rolled over on his stomach, forearms crossed under his chin. It looked like a defensive posture. "After we got plumbing in Santa Rosalia we all sat around and watched the toilet flush. Sounds like a joke, right? How many Indians does it take to flush a toilet."

"It's no big deal. Sorry. Forget it."

"No, it is a big deal." He stared at the painted headboard of my bed, rather than at me. "You think I'm a TV Indian. Tonto Schwarzenegger, dumb but cute."

I pulled up the covers. For a bedspread I'd been using the black-and-red crocheted afghan, Hallie's and my old comfort blanket. "And what is that supposed to mean?" I asked.

"Nothing. Forget it."

"If you said it, Loyd, you meant it."

"Okay, I did." He got up and began to put his clothes on. I reached over and caught his T-shirt when it was halfway over his head, and pulled him to me like a spider's breakfast. I kissed him through the T-shirt. He didn't kiss back. He pulled his head free of the shirt and looked at me, waiting.

"I don't know what you want from me," I said.

"I want more than I'm getting. More than sex."

"Well, maybe that's all I have to offer."

He still waited.

"Loyd, I'm just here till next June. You know that. I've never led you on."

"And where do you go after next June?"

"I don't know." I poked my fingers through the holes in the black-and-red afghan, a decades-old nervous habit. He held eye contact until I was uncomfortable.

"Who do you see yourself marrying, Codi?"

I could feel my pulse in my neck. It was a very odd question. "I don't."

"Yes, you do. But he'd have to be taller than you, smarter than you, more everything. A better job and more damn college degrees. You're like every other woman alive."

"Thanks very much," I said.

"Your height alone kind of limits the field."

"If that's supposed to be an insult, you're way off. I always wanted to be even taller than I am, taller than Hallie."

We sat not looking at each other for a minute. I took his hand and laid it, limp, against mine. It felt like a pancake or something. "This isn't about your deficiencies, Loyd. It's just me. I can't stay here. There's a poem by Robert Frost about this pitiful old hired hand who comes back home when he's run out of luck because he knows they won't kick him out. The poem says, 'Home is the place where, when you have to go there, They have to take you in.'" I stroked the tendons on the back of Loyd's hand. "I don't want to be seen as pitiful. I came here with a job to do, but I have places to go after this. I wish . . ." I turned my face toward the window so he wouldn't see tears.

"I'd like to find a place that feels like it *wants* to take me in. But this isn't it. At the end of the school year my time's up. If we get attached, you and me, then it's hard."

"That's your game, not mine, Codi." He got up and walked into the living-room to make his hourly call to the depot; he was expecting to be sent to El Paso soon. I was stunned that he would walk away from me when I needed to be taken in. Though I guess that's just what I'd asked him to do, walk away. His T-shirt was inside out, and he took it off and switched it around, still managing to keep the receiver cradled against his ear. He'd been put on hold. I watched him through the doorway and realized that the muscles in his back were taut with anger. I'd never seen Loyd mad, and was surprised he was capable of it.

I felt lost. I got up, throwing back the afghan and draping the flannel sheet around me like a sari, and went into the living room. The floor was cold. I shifted from one foot to the other, feeling vaguely like the Statue of Liberty. Jack on the front door-step was scratching his neck vigorously, jingling his tags. That dog had the patience of Job.

"What's going on?" I asked, when Loyd hung up the phone.

"I'm five times out. Plenty of time for a fuck."

"That's not what I meant. Loyd, I don't think you're dumb."

"Just not anything worth changing your plans for."

I laughed. "As if I had plans."

He looked at me, his eyes searching back and forth between my two pupils as if he were trying to decide which door con-cealed the prize. "What would happen if you stayed here, Codi?"

"I would have the wrong haircut. Everybody would remind me that I don't quite belong. 'Oh, honey,' they'd say, 'you're still here? I heard you were on your way to Rio de Janeiro to have tea with Princess Grace.' And I'd say, 'No, I've grown up to be the new Doc Homer. I've moved into his house and I'm taking over his practice so I can save the town.' "

"Save us from what, Great White Mother?"

"Oh, shit, you guys can all just go to hell." I laughed, since the other choice was to cry. He took me in his arms and I crum-pled against his chest like an armful of laundry. "This town was never kind to me," I said into his shirt. "I never even got asked out on dates. Except by you, and you were so drunk you didn't know better."

"You know what we used to call you in high school? Empress of the Universe."

"That's just what I mean! And you didn't care that the Empress of the Universe had to go home every night to a cold castle where the king stomped around saying hugs are for puppy dogs and we are housebroken."

Loyd seemed interested in this. "And then what?"

"Oh, nothing much. I'd hide in my room and cry because I had to wear orthopedic shoes and was unfit to live."

He turned my chin to face him. I hadn't noticed before that without shoes we were the same height. Proportioned differently—my legs were longer—but our chins punched in at the same altitude. "So, where you headed now, Empress?"

"God, Loyd, I don't know. I get lost a lot. I keep hoping some guy with 'Ron' or 'Andy' stitched on his pocket and a gas pump in his hand will step up and tell me where I'm headed."

His face developed slowly toward a grin. "I'll tell you. You're going with me to do something I'm real good at. The best."

I tried to figure this out. Behind his smile there was a look in his eyes that was profoundly earnest. It dawned on me. "Cockfights?"

There was no way I could say no.

▼▼▼

A fighting cock is an animal bred for strength and streamlined for combat. His wings are small, his legs strong, and when he's affronted his neck feathers puff into a fierce mane like a lion's. Individuality has been lost in the breeding lines; function is everything. To me each bird looked like any other. I couldn't tell them apart until they began dying differently.

The deaths are protracted. That was one thing I learned when I went to see Loyd excel in the profession to which he was born.

I'd had in mind that a cockfight would be an after-dark, furtive thing: men betting and drinking and sweating out the animal suspense under cover of night. But it was broad daylight. Loyd cut the wheel sharply, taking us off the road and up a gravel arroyo. He seemed to navigate the reservation by the same mysterious instincts that lead birds to Costa Rica and back home again unfailingly each year. We reached a thicket where a motley herd of pickup trucks were parked at odd angles, close together, like nervous horses ready to bolt. Loyd pulled his red truck into the herd. Beyond the trees was a dirt arena where roosters strutted around clearing their throats, barnyard-innocent.

Loyd steered me through the arena, his arm around my shoulders, greeting everybody. I saw no other women, but Loyd would have been welcome here if he'd shown up with a she-wolf. "Lot of people going to lose their shirts today," a man told him. "You got some damn good-looking birds." The man was handsome and thin, with a long ponytail tied up Navajo style. His name was Collie Bluestone. Loyd introduced us, seeming proud of me.

"Glad to meet you," I said. Collie's hand felt taut with energy. A chunk of turquoise on a leather thong rested on his collarbone, below the scar of an old tracheotomy.

"Collie's a cock mechanic," Loyd said. "We go back a ways."

I laughed. "You give them tune-ups before the fight?"

"No, after," Collie said. "I sew them up. So they live to fight another day."

"Oh. I thought it was to the death." I dragged a finger across my throat.

Collie smiled. "Out of every fight, one of them dies and one lives." He turned to Loyd. "How come the girls always forget about the one that lives?"

"Everybody loves a hero, I guess." Loyd winked at me.

"Nothing heroic about a dead bird," I pointed out.

The arena centered on a raked floor of reddish-brown dirt. Loyd maneuvered me through the men squatting and arguing at its perimeter to a dilapidated flank of wooden chairs where he deposited me. I felt nervous about being left alone, though the atmosphere was as innocuous as a picnic, minus women and food.

"I'll be back," he said, and vanished.

The place was thick with roosters but didn't smell like poultry, only of clean, sharp dust. I suppose the birds didn't stay around long enough to establish that kind of presence. Some

men took seats near me, jarring me slightly; the chairs were all
nailed together in long rows, the type used for parades. I spotted
Loyd through the crowd. Everybody wanted to talk to him,
cutting in like suitors at a dance. He was quite at home here,
and relaxed: an important man who's beyond self-importance.

He returned to me just as a short, dark man in deeply worn
plaid pants was marking out a chalk square in the dirt of the
center pit. Betting flared around the fringes. An old man stabbed
the stump of a missing forefinger at the crowd and shouted,
angrily, "Seventy! Somebody call seventy!"

Loyd took my hand. "This is a gaff tournament," he explained quietly. "That means the birds have a little steel spur
on the back of each leg. In the knife fights they get blades."

"So you have gaff birds and knife birds," I said. I'd been
turning over this question since our trip to Kinishba.

"Right. They fight different. A knife fight is a cutting fight
and it goes a lot faster. You never really get to see what a bird
could do. The really game birds are gaff birds."

"I'll take your word for it," I said.

The first two fighters, men named Gustavo and Scratch,
spoke to the man in plaid pants, who seemed in charge. Scratch
appeared to have only one functional eye. Loyd said they were
two of the best cockfighters on the reservation. The first position
was an honor.

"The roosters don't look honored," I said. Actually they
looked neither pleased nor displeased, but stalked in circles,
accustomed to life on one square yard of turf. Their tail feathers
ticked like weeds and one of them crowed nonstop, as if impatient. But impatience implies consciousness of time and a
chicken is existential. I know that much about birds.

"How come you're not down there playing with your
friends?" I asked Loyd.

"I've got people to train the birds, bring the birds, weigh in,
all that. I handle. You'll see."

"*Train* the birds? How do you teach a bird to fight?"

"You don't, it's all instinct and breeding. You just train them
not to freak out when they get in a crowd."

"I see. So you don't train, you handle," I said. "A handling man."

He pinched my thigh gently along the inside seam of my jeans. I'd been handled by Loyd quite a few times since Kinishba. The crowd quieted. Scratch and Gustavo squared off in the center of the pit, their charges cradled at thigh level, and they thrust their birds toward each other three times in a rhythm that was frankly sexual. Each time the men's hips rocked forward, the cocks dutifully bit each other's faces. Apparently the point was to contrive a fighting mood. Two minutes ago these birds were strutting around their own closed circuits, and if they looked away from each other even now they'd probably lose their train of thought and start scratching the dust for cracked corn.

But now they were primed, like cocked pistols. Their handlers set them down on opposite chalk lines and they shook themselves and inflated their pale ruffs. When the plaid-pants referee gave the word, the men let go. The birds ran at each other and jumped up, spurs aimed for the other bird's breast. They hopped over one another, fluttering their short wings, pecking each other's heads and drawing blood. After about thirty seconds the birds' spurs tangled and they lay helpless, literally locked in combat.

"Handle that!" the referee shouted.

The handlers moved in to pull them apart. They faced the birds off, waited for the count, and let them go at each other once more. Within another minute Scratch and Gustavo had to intervene again, this time because one bird had his spurs irretrievably embedded in the breast meat of his opponent. The handlers gently pulled them apart and started them again.

It takes a very long time for one bird or the other to die. Presumably they were dying of internal wounds and hemorrhage. Punctured lungs, for example, and literally bleeding hearts. Eventually they began to bleed from the mouths. At that point I could finally tell Scratch's bird from Gustavo's because it lay down in the dirt and wouldn't get up. Scratch had to place it on its feet and push it back in the direction of combat.

"Why don't they just declare the winner?" I whispered.

"There's rules."

It was a ridiculous answer, but correct. A death was required. It took thirty or forty minutes, and I guess the birds were showing their mettle, but it was hard to watch. The cocks were both exhausted and near death, no longer even faintly beautiful. Their blond breasts and ruffs were spotted with blood, stringy as unwashed hair. Collie Bluestone would have his work cut out for him here.

There seemed to be elaborate rules about how to keep things going after this point, when both birds really just wanted to sit with their beaks in the dirt. If one lay still, the other had no incentive to fight. I've studied a lot of biology; I quickly figured out that this industry was built around a bird's natural impulse for territorial defense, and that's where it broke down. No animal has reason to fight its own kind to the death. A rooster will defend his ground, but once that's established, he's done. After that he tends to walk around ignoring the bizarre surroundings and all the people who have next month's rent riding on him and he'll just act like a chicken—the animal that he is. The handlers had to keep taking the birds firmly in hand, squaring them off and trying to force the fight.

"This is making me sick," I told Loyd.

He looked at me with such surprise it angered me. Nobody could look at this picture and fail to see cruelty.

"I've seen little boys do this same exact thing," I said. "Take some pitiful animal and tease it and drag it back by the legs over and over again, trying to make it fight."

"The knife fights go a lot faster," he said.

"But you don't like knife fights. You like this. That's what you said."

He didn't answer. To avoid the birds I looked at the crowd, whose faces betrayed neither pain nor blood thirst but passive interest. It could have been any show at all, not two animals obliged to kill each other; it could have been TV. They were mostly old men in feed caps, or black felt cowboy hats if they were Apaches. I spotted a few families now, but knew if you asked these women about cockfighting they'd use the word *we*. "Oh, we love it," they'd say in cigarette-husky voices, meaning *he* does. A teenager in a black tank top, a greenish tattoo flowering across her broad back, hoisted a toddler onto her shoulder. She lit a cigarette and paid scant attention to the action in the pit, but her child took it in like a sponge.

Several people yelled loudly for Gustavo's bird. Then finally, without much warning, its opponent passed over from barely alive to dead. Without ceremony Scratch carried his limp loser out by its feet and tossed it into the back of a truck. Loyd Peregrina was called up next. A rooster was delivered into his arms, smooth as a loaf of bread, as he made his way down to the pit. This time I watched. I owed him that.

In the first fight I'd watched birds, but this time I watched Loyd, and soon understood that in this unapologetically brutal sport there was a vast tenderness between the handler and his bird. Loyd cradled his rooster in his arms, stroking and talking to it in a low, steady voice. At each handling call he caressed the bird's wings back into place, stroked its back, and licked the blood from its eyes. At the end, he blew his own breath into its mouth to inflate a punctured lung. He did this when the bird was nigh unto death and clearly unable to win. The physical relationship between Loyd and his rooster transcended winning or losing.

It lasted up to the moment of death, and not one second longer. I shivered as he tossed the feathered corpse, limp as cloth, into the back of the truck. The thought of Loyd's hands on me made the skin of my forearms recoil from my own touch.

▼▼▼

"What do they do with the dead birds?" I wanted to know.

"What?"

"What do they do with them? Does somebody eat them? *Arroz con pollo?*"

He laughed. "Not here. In Mexico I've heard they do."

I thought of Hallie and wondered if they had cockfights in Nicaragua. In the new, humane society that had already abolished capital punishment, I'd bet money they still had cockfights.

Loyd watched the road and executed a tricky turn. He was driving a little fast for gravel road and dusk, but driving well. I tried to picture Loyd driving a train, and came up with nothing.

No picture. No more than I could picture Fenton Lee in his head-on wreck.

"What do they do with them here?"

"Why, you hungry?"

"I'm asking a question."

"There's a dump, down that arroyo a ways. A big pit. They bury them in a mass grave. Tomb of the unknown chicken."

I ignored his joke. "I think I'd feel better about the whole thing if the chickens were getting eaten."

"The meat'd be tough," Loyd said, amused. He was in a good mood. He'd lost his first fight but had won four more after that—more than anyone else that day.

"It just seems like such a pathetic waste. All the time and effort that go into those chicken lives, from the hatched egg to the grave of the unknown chicken. Pretty pointless." I needed to make myself clear. "No, it's not pointless. It's pointed in a direction that makes me uncomfortable."

"Those roosters don't know what's happening to them. You think a fighting cock understands its life is pointless?"

"No, I think a fighting cock is stupider than a head of lettuce." I glanced at Loyd, hoping he'd be hurt by my assessment, but apparently he agreed. I wanted him to defend his roosters. It frightened me that he could connect so intensely with a bird and then, in a breath, disengage.

"It's a clean sport," he said. "It might be hard to understand, for an outsider, but it's something I grew up with. You don't see drunks, and the betting is just a very small part of it. The crowd is nicer than at a football game."

"I don't disagree with any of that."

"It's a skill you have in your hands. You can go anywhere, pick up any bird, even one that's not your own, a bird you've never seen before, and you can do this thing with it."

"Like playing the piano," I said.

"Like that," he said, without irony.

"I could see that you're good at it. Very good." I struggled to find my point, but could come up only with disturbing, disjointed images: A woman in the emergency room on my first night of residency, stabbed eighteen times by her lover. Curty and Glen sitting in the driveway dappled with rooster blood. Hallie in a jeep, hitting a land mine. Those three girls.

"Everything dies, Codi."

"Oh, great. Tell me something I don't know. My mother died when I was a three-year-old baby!" I had no idea where that came from. I looked out the window and wiped my eyes carefully with my sleeve. But the tears kept coming. For a long time I cried for those three teenage girls who were split apart from above while they picked fruit. For the first time I really believed in my heart it had happened. That someone could look down, aim a sight, pull a trigger. Feel nothing. Forget.

Loyd seemed at a loss. Finally he said gently, "I mean, animals die. They suffer in nature and they suffer in the barnyard. It's not like people. They weren't meant to live a good life and then go to heaven, or wherever we go."

As plainly as anything then, I remembered trying to save the coyotes from the flood. My ears filled with the roar of the flooded river and my nose with the strong stench of mud. I gripped the armrest of Loyd's truck to keep the memory from drowning my senses. I heard my own high voice commanding Hallie to stay with me. And then, later, asking Doc Homer, "Will they go to heaven?" I couldn't hear his answer, probably because he didn't have one. I hadn't wanted facts, I'd wanted salvation.

Carefully, so as not to lose anything, I brought myself back to the present and sat still, paying attention. "I'm not talking about chicken souls. I don't believe roosters have souls," I said slowly. "What I believe is that humans should have more heart than that. I can't feel good about people making a spectator sport out of puncture wounds and internal hemorrhage."

Loyd kept his eyes on the dark air above the road. Bugs swirled in the headlights like planets cut loose from their orbits, doomed to chaos. After a full half hour he said, "My brother Leander got killed by a drunk, about fifteen miles from here."

In another half hour he said, "I'll quit, Codi. I'm quitting right now."

17

PEACOCK LADIES AT
THE CAFÉ GERTRUDE STEIN

"He's giving up *cockfighting* for you?" Emelina's eyes were so wide I could only think of Mrs. Dynamite's husband watching Miss America.

"I guess. We'll see if he stays on the wagon."

"Codi, that's so romantic. I don't think J.T. ever gave up a thing for me except cracking his knuckles."

"Well, that's something," I said.

"No, it doesn't even count, because I terrorized him out of it. I told him it would give him arthritis or something."

Emelina and I were eating chili dogs at a roadside diner on I-10. Loyd's pickup, which we'd borrowed for the trip, was parked where we could keep an eye on it. Piled high in the back, individually wrapped in dry-cleaner bags, were fifty peacock piñatas with genuine peacock tail feathers. We were headed for Tucson, prepared to hit the streets with the biggest fund-raising enterprise in the history of the Stitch and Bitch Club.

The project was Viola's brainchild, although she shared credit with Doña Althea, who had opened up her storehouse of feathers. They'd held two all-night assembly lines to turn out these masterpieces, and really outdid themselves. These were not the likes of the ordinary piñata, destined to meet its maker at the end of a blindfolded ten-year-old's baseball bat. They had glass-button eyes and feather crests and carefully curled indigo crepe-paper wings. These birds were headed for the city, and so was the Stitch and Bitch Club, *en masse,* by Greyhound. Our plan was to meet at the bus station and take it from there.

I was surprised when Viola asked if I'd come. She said they needed me, I knew the city; you'd think it was a jail break. But Loyd was doing switch-engine time in Lordsburg and it was Christmas break, so I had time on my hands. I begged Emelina to come too, and spend a few days in Tucson. I needed to walk on flat sidewalks, risk my neck in traffic, go see a movie, that kind of thing. J.T. could stay with the kids. He was home on thirty days' probation from the railroad, for the derailment that was officially not his fault. The railroad moves in mysterious ways.

Emelina hadn't gone anywhere without a child in thirteen years. Out of habit she packed a roll of paper towels in her purse. As we drove out of Grace she gasped for air, wide-eyed, like a hooked fish. "I can't believe I'm doing this," she kept saying. "Turn the truck around. I can't go."

I drove westward, ignoring my hostage. "What, you think J.T. doesn't know how to take care of his own sons?"

"No," she said, staring at the center line. "I'm afraid I'll come back and find him dead on the kitchen floor with a Conquerers of the Castle arrow stuck on his head and a fistful of Hostess Ding Dongs."

By the time we hit the interstate she'd decided it would work out. The boys could go to college on J.T.'s life insurance.

"Oh, they won't pay if it's murder," I said gravely.

She brightened a little. "I always forget. He's the one that wanted so many kids."

It was mid-December, fourteen shopping days till Christmas, and by afternoon it was clear and cold. Twenty-two women in winter coats and support hose took the streets of downtown Tucson by storm, in pairs, each cradling a papier-mâché piñata in her arms. No one who witnessed the event would soon forget it.

Emelina and I and the truck were more or less set up as headquarters. We parked in front of a chichi restaurant called the Café Gertrude Stein, for the sole reason that it sported an enormous green plastic torso out front and the women felt they could find their way back to this landmark. As soon as they sold their birds, they were to head back for more. Emelina and I held the fort, perched carefully in the midst of our pyramid of paper birds.

A man in a black fedora and glen plaid scarf came out of the café and gave us a startled look. We'd not been there when he went in. "How much?" he asked.

This had been a much-debated question; apparently the Greyhound driver had threatened to stop the bus if the Stitch-and-Bitchers didn't quit yelling about it. Ultimately we'd been instructed to try and get what we could.

"How bad do you want it?" asked Emelina, saucily crossing her legs. Monogamous as a goose, and a natural-born flirt.

A small crowd of homeless people had gathered on the other side of the street from where our truck was parked. It seems we were by a good margin the best entertainment of their day.

"Fifty dollars?" the man in the scarf asked.

Emelina and I looked at each other, cool as cukes. "They're made by hand," I said.

"Sixty?"

"Okay."

He handed us three twenties and Emelina forked over a plastic-wrapped bird. Its tail bobbed gently behind him as he made his way down the street. I mouthed the words, "Sixty dollars!" and we collapsed against each other.

"They're made by hand," Emelina said, eyebrows arched, in perfect imitation of an Empress of the Universe.

Miss Lorraine Colder and Miss Elva Dann came back to the truck almost immediately. They'd enlisted a bag lady named Jessie, who owned her own shopping cart. When Miss Lorraine explained the threat to the homes of Grace, Jessie cried for a little while and then rallied her wits. They were able to pack half a dozen piñatas into her cart, and the trio of women set out to sell them all in a single foray.

Norma Galvez, in the meantime, lost her partner at a cross-walk and had to be escorted back to the big green naked lady by a bicycle policeman named Officer Metz. In a conversation that lasted only five blocks she'd acquired an amazing number of facts about this man: for example, he had twin daughters born on Christmas Day, and wore a hernia belt. She told Emelina and me these things when she introduced him. Officer Metz was sympathetic, but did ask if the ladies had a vendor's permit. Mrs. Galvez, a quick thinker, explained that we weren't selling anything. We were soliciting donations to save our town. Each and every donor got a free peacock piñata. In the interest of public relations she gave him one to take home to his twins.

By five o'clock we were out of birds. As it turned out, Emelina and I didn't make the best sale of the day. While too many peacocks went for only ten or fifteen, Doña Althea haggled one elderly gentleman up to seventy-five dollars. When the trans-action was completed, the Doña allowed him to kiss her hand.

By the time they were back in Grace on the last evening bus, I was later informed, the Stitch and Bitch Club had already laid plans to come back in ten days with five hundred peacock piñ-atas. There would be only two deviations from the original plan. First, each piñata would be accompanied by a written history of Grace and its heroic struggle against the Black Mountain Mining Company. To my shock I was elected, in absentia, to write this epic broadside and get it mimeographed at the school. (Miss Lorraine and Miss Elva had retired.) Second, the price would be fixed at sixty dollars. Some argued for seventy-five but the Doña overruled, pointing out that she couldn't be expected to kiss every damn cowboy in Tucson.

▼▼▼

Emelina and I let ourselves into my old house. Carlo was expecting us and had left the key under the usual brick. The neighborhood seemed even seedier than when I left. There was some demolition going on, with cheerfully nasty graffiti deco-rating the plywood construction barriers. Our old house with its bolted-down flowerpots stood eerily untouched, inside and out. Carlo had let all the plants finish dying, as expected, but beyond that he'd made no effort to make the place his own. He seemed to be living like a man in mourning, not wishing to disturb the traces of a deceased wife. Or wives.

"This is creepy, Carlo," I told him when he got home late that night from his ER shift. "Why haven't you moved things around? It looks like Hallie and I just walked out yesterday."

He shrugged. "What's to move around?"

Emelina had gone to bed, trying, I believe, to stay out of our way. She'd kept asking me if it wouldn't be awkward for us to stay with my "ex." It was hard for her to understand that Carlo and I were really "exes" right from the start. Having no claim on each other was the basis of our relationship.

I'd stayed up watching the news so I could see him when he got home. He slumped down next to me on the couch with a bag of potato chips.

"That your dinner?"

"You my mother?"

"I should hope not." On the news they were talking about an ordinance that banned charity Santas from collecting donations in shopping malls. The owner of a sporting-goods store was explaining that it took away business. Rows of hunting bows were lined up behind him like the delicately curved bones of a ribcage.

"You look exhausted," I told Carlo. He really did.

"I sewed a nose back on tonight. Cartilage and all."

"That'll take it out of you."

"So what's creepy about the way I'm living?" In his light-green hospital scrubs, Carlo looked paler and smaller than I remembered him. No visible muscles.

"It looks like you're living in limbo," I said. "Waiting for somebody else to move in here and cook a real meal for you and hang up pictures."

"You never did either of those things."

"I know. But it's different when there's *two* people living in a house with no pictures. It looks like you're just too busy having fun with each other to pay attention to the walls."

"I miss you. We did have fun."

"Not that much. You miss Hallie." Being here made me miss her too, more tangibly than in Grace. On these scarred wooden floors, Hallie had rolled up the rugs and attempted to teach us to moonwalk.

"How is she? Does she ever write you? I got one postcard, from Nogales."

"Yeah, we write. She's real busy." I didn't tell him we wrote a *lot*. We'd revived an intensity of correspondence we hadn't had since 1972, the year I escaped from Grace and Hallie came into a late puberty, both of us entirely on our own. This time she was over her head with joy and I with something like love or dread, but we still needed each other to make sure it was real. We had to live with an odd, two-week lag to our conversations. I'd be writing her about some small, thrilling victory at school, and she'd be addressing the blue funk I was in two weeks ago when I was getting my period. It didn't matter; we kept writing, knowing it would someday even out.

"How's your father?"

"Oh," I said, "deteriorating. Forgetting who I am. Maybe it's a blessing."

"Are you sleeping these days?"

"Yeah, I am, as a matter of fact," I said, evasively.

"You haven't had that eyeball dream?"

I'd never been able to explain this to Carlo's satisfaction. "It's not really an eyeball dream."

"What is it, then?"

"Just a sound, like popping glass, and then I'm blind. It's a very short dream. I'd rather not talk about it if you don't mind. I'm afraid I'll jinx myself."

"So you haven't been having it?"

"No, not for a while."

It was kind of him to be interested. He gently squeezed my shoulder in the palm of his hand, releasing the tightness in my deltoid muscle. Not that it applied to us anymore, but people who know a lot about anatomy make great lovers. "So you're getting along okay there?"

"As well as I get along anywhere," I said, and he laughed, probably believing I meant "As poorly as I get along anywhere."

"I've been giving some thought to Denver," he said. "Or Aspen."

"That would be a challenge. You could sew the faces back onto people who ski into trees."

"You want to come? We could ski into trees together."

"I don't know. I'm not really thinking too far ahead right now."

He took my feet into his lap and massaged my arches. He had the famous hands of a surgeon, there was no denying it, but I had no sexual interest in Carlo. I still had a slight hope he'd come up with the perfect plan for the two of us that would make me happy and fulfilled, but even that was fading.

"What else could a modern couple like ourselves do in Aspen?" I asked him. "Besides ski into trees, and try to spot movie stars snorting coke in hotel lounges? Aspen sounds kind of fast-lane."

"After Grace, it would be, yes."

"Don't make fun of my country of origin."

Carlo looked surprised. "I've never heard you defend it before."

"It was a joke."

"Well, what about Denver, then. Not so fast-lane."

"Denver's nice." I felt the familiar tug of a brand-new place that might, this time, turn out to be wonderful. And the familiar tug of Carlo wanting me to go with him. I'd seen Denver once. It had endless neighborhoods of sweet old brick houses with peaked roofs and lawns shaded by huge maples. It would be a heavenly place to walk a dog.

"Would you ever consider getting a dog, Carlo?"

"A dog?"

"They have four legs and say 'woof woof.' "

"Oh, right."

"I've met this wonderful dog, in Grace. He's half coyote and he'll sit for five hours in the back of a pickup truck waiting for you, just because he trusts you to come back."

"This sounds serious."

"He's a good dog." I realized I hadn't thought about Loyd all day, which I viewed as an accomplishment. This must be how it is to be alcoholic: setting little goals for yourself, proving you can live without it. When really, giving it all that thought only proves that you can't. My mood suddenly began to plummet; I'd felt elated all afternoon, but now I recognized the signs of a depression coming. If I timed it right, Hallie's letter addressing my *last* depression would arrive on target.

"Shoot, look at that!" Carlo dropped my feet and jumped to turn up the volume on the TV. "That's you!"

It was. I yelled for Emelina but the spot was over by the time she showed up in the doorway wearing one of J.T.'s shirts, looking stunned.

"You were on the news," Carlo explained excitedly. "They said something about the Peacock Ladies and then they said something about Southwestern folk art, and they showed you two standing up in the truck, and this old lady in a black dress . . ."

"Doña Althea," I said.

". . . holding up the piñata, and another lady and a cop . . ."

"Officer Metz."

". . . and I didn't hear anything else because we were yelling." He stopped suddenly, looking embarrassed by his enthusiasm. He and Emelina hadn't officially met.

"Oh. Carlo, Emelina. Emelina, Carlo. An old friend from a previous life."

I didn't say which one was the previous life, and which was the present. I didn't know.

Hallie, what I can never put a finger on is the *why* of you and me. Why did you turn out the way you did? You're my sister. We were baked in the same oven, with the same ingredients. Why does one cake rise and the other fall? I think about you on your horse, riding out to the fields in your gray wool socks and boots and your hair looking like the Breck Girl gone wild, setting off to make a new world. Life must be so easy when you have dreams.

I read in the paper that we'll be sending another 40 or 50 million to the contras, so they can strafe little girls and blow you up with your cotton crop. It hurts to know this; I could be a happier American if I didn't have a loved one sending me truth from the trenches. You're right, we're a nation of amnesiacs. I'm embarrassed. It's an inappropriately weak emotion. You risk everything, while I pay my taxes like everybody else and try not to recall the unpleasant odor of death.

My life is a pitiful, mechanical thing without a past, like a little wind-up car, ready to run in any direction somebody points me.

Today I thought I was a hero. We sold fifty peacock piñatas to raise money for the Stitch and Bitch Club, which will somehow save the town of Grace. But it's not my cause, I'm leaving. I have no idea how to save a town. I only came along today because it looked like a party and I was invited. Remember how we used to pray to get invited to birthday parties? And they only asked us because we were so grateful we'd do anything, stay late and help the mothers wash the cake pans. I'm still that girl, flattered to death if somebody wants me around.

Carlo asked me to go with him to Denver or possibly Aspen. Carlo's still Carlo. He wants to know why you haven't written. (I told him you're busy saving the world.) I almost think I *could* go to Denver. Carlo is safe because I don't really love him that much. If he stopped wanting me around one day, it wouldn't be so terrible. I wouldn't die.

Hallie, I realize how that sounds. I feel small and ridiculous and hemmed in on every side by the need to be safe. All I want is to be like you, to be brave, to walk into a country of chickens and land mines and call that home, and have it *be* home. How do you just charge ahead, always doing the right thing, even if you have to do it alone with people staring? I would have so many doubts—what if you lose that war? What then? If I had an ounce of your bravery I'd be set for life. You get up and look the world in the eye, shoo the livestock away from the windowsill, and decide what portion of the world needs to be saved today. You are like God. I get tired. Carlo says "Let's go to Denver," and what the heck, I'm ready to throw down the banner of the Stitch and Bitch Club and the republic for which it stands. Ready to go live in Denver and walk my dog.

I went out at dawn, alone, to mail my letter and prowl my old neighborhood. I kept trying to believe I felt good in this familiar haunt. I'd brought my city clothes: a short skirt and black tights and stiletto-heeled boots (the sight would have laid Doc Homer flat), and I walked downtown among strangers, smiling, anonymous as a goldfish. There was a newsstand four blocks down where I used to go for the *Times* or the Washington *Post*, which Hallie and Carlo would spread all over the living-room floor on Sunday mornings. Hallie would constantly ask us if she could interrupt for a second. "Listen to this," she'd say. She needed to read it all aloud, both the tragedies and the funnies.

I ducked into a coffee shop that had decent coffee and wonderful croissants. As I sat blowing into my cup I realized I was looking around to see who was there—a habit I must have picked up in Grace, where you looked at people because they were all identifiable.

A man at a table very close to my elbow kept looking at my legs. That's another thing you put up with when you're tall—men act like you've ordered those legs out of a catalogue. I crossed them finally and said, "See, look, I've got another one just like it."

He laughed. Amazingly, he wasn't embarrassed at all. I'd forgotten how the downtown scene could be—people cultivating weirdness like it was a disease or a career. He had a neatly trimmed beard and was extremely handsome. "How Emma Bovary," he said.

I smiled. "You seem to have lost your syntax. Perhaps you're in the wrong place. The Café Gertrude Stein is down the street."

"Well," he said. "Well well well. Perhaps you could provide me with some context. Do you have a name?"

"Cosima. It means Order in the Cosmos."

"Cosima, my love, I'm in desperate need of order. If you have the *New York Times* in your bag there, I'd be willing to marry you." I had the *New York Times*.

"I'm not in the habit of marrying strangers," I said. I was suddenly disgusted with what I was doing. I'd go anywhere Carlo wanted, I'd be a sport for my students in Grace, I'd even tried to be a doctor for Doc Homer, just as I'd humiliated myself in the old days to get invited to birthday parties. If I kept trying to be what everybody wanted, I'd soon be insipid enough to fit in everywhere. I grabbed my bag and stood up to go. I told the man, "You don't have the slightest idea who I am."

▼▼▼

The second night in Tucson I slept like a child, so drenched in sleep that when I woke up I didn't know where I was. For a minute I lay lost in the bed, trying slowly to attach the physical fact of myself to a name, a life, a room in a house within a larger place. It was a frightening moment, but nothing new to me, either. So rarely in my life did I truly surrender to sleep that it took an extra effort for me to pull myself out. It felt like slogging on my elbows up a riverbank.

Carlo wasn't in bed with me, of course; he'd skirted the awkward issue by saying he had a weird shift and might as well sleep on the sofa and not disturb anybody. But he'd had plenty of opportunities in the past to see me wake up confused. He always claimed there was something wrong with the electrical current in the temporal lobes of my brain. He said that explained why I couldn't remember parts of what I'd lived through, and remembered other parts that I hadn't. I was attracted to easy answers but mistrusted them too. Carlo's specialty was the nervous system; he tended to think all human difficulties were traceable to neural synapses gone haywire. And I feared—no, I knew—what was wrong with me was more complicated than what's wrong with a badly wired house.

Carlo was already gone but left a note, saying to think very seriously about Aspen. It sounded like a joke, put that way, but I folded the note and stuck it in my suitcase. Emelina was cheerful at breakfast. She'd sensed the previous day that my mood had turned black and blue, but she was intent on our having a vacation even if neither of our hearts was really in it. We'd gone to the movies and eaten at McDonald's, which by Grace standards is the high life. We ordered Happy Meals; she was collecting small plastic replicas of impossible-looking vehicles for her boys. We had enough now to go home.

On our way out of town she insisted that we stop at an obvious tourist trap called Colossal Cave. It was colossal by no means, but a cave. We stood a long time in the dim entry while the guide in a Smokey Bear hat made small talk, hoping for a bigger crowd. There were only seven or eight of us. It must be hard to give your whole spiel to a group that wouldn't even make a baseball team or a jury.

"So when's Loyd get home?"

"Friday," I said.

"That switch-engine deal gets long, doesn't it?"

"It never seems to bother you," I said, although I had an

acute memory of the night I'd glimpsed them making love in the courtyard.

"Mm," she said.

"Then again, Loyd might be making the whole thing up. He's probably got a sweetie in Lordsburg." Emelina looked startled. "I'm kidding," I said.

"Don't say stuff like that. Knock on wood." She thumped the side of her head.

"Well, it's occurred to me to wonder why Loyd wasn't married or anything when I came along. If he's such a hot item."

"He was."

"Married?"

"*No.* Seeing somebody, but not that serious. Definitely not married. He was once, awhile back, for a year or two, I think. No kids. He didn't tell you?"

"I never asked."

"Her name was Cissie. She didn't deserve him." Emelina peeled off her Dallas Cowboys sweatshirt (actually John Tucker's). It was cave temperature down there, only 55 degrees but much warmer than outside, where it was predicted to drop below freezing that night. A woman near us was wearing a mink coat.

"I wasn't about to leave it in the car," she said to us, without provocation.

Loyd had never mentioned even a large personal fact like a previous marriage, whereas this woman in mink felt compelled to explain herself to strangers. That's how it is: some people are content to wait till you ask, while others jump right in with the whole story. It must have to do with discomfort. Once while I was waiting to file off an airplane, a grandmother came down the aisle carrying a doll in one arm and a little boy in the other, and she actually took the time to explain to us all as she passed, "The doll is his sister's, she's up ahead." I could relate to the urge. I remembered all my tall tales to strangers on buses. I was explaining in my own way; making things up so there would be no discussion of what I was *really*.

At last our guide spoke some encouraging words and the little crowd followed him down into the cave. As he walked he told us about an outlaw who'd ducked in here to hide his loot, back in the days of Jesse James, and apparently had never come out. This was meant to give us a thrill of fear, but it seemed more likely that there was a back door somewhere and the bad guy got away with the money. That's how things go. I still believe Adolf Hitler is living in the South Pacific somewhere with sanded-off finger-prints and a new face, lying on a beach drinking mai-tais.

Emelina hadn't seen a cave before and was very impressed. There were delicate stalactites shaped like soda straws, and heavy, hooded stalagmites looming up from the cave floor. She kept pointing out formations that reminded her of a penis.

"You've only been away from home three days," I whispered.

"I didn't say it looked like J.T.'s," she whispered back.

The sound of trickling water was everywhere, even over our heads. I shivered to think how many tons of rock and dirt were up there above us. I'd forgotten that caves were not my favorite thing.

The highlight of the tour was the Drapery Room, which was admittedly impressive in size. The guide pointed with his flash-light to various formations, which had names like Chief Cochise and The Drapes. The walls and ceiling glittered with crystallized moisture.

Then, for just a minute—they always have to do this—he turned off the lights. The darkness was absolute. I grabbed for Emelina's arm as the ceilings and walls came rushing up to my face. I felt choked by my own tongue. As I held on to Emelina and waited for the lights to come back on, I breathed slowly and tried to visualize the size of the room, the distance between myself and the roof that I knew was there. Instead I saw random images that didn't help: Emelina collecting the little fast-food cars for her boys; the man in the café who'd suggested I marry him. And then while we all still waited I understood that the terror of my recurring dream was not about losing just vision, but the whole of myself, whatever that was. What you lose in blindness is the space around you, the place where you are, and without that you might not exist. You could be nowhere at all.

18

GROUND ORIENTATION

Loyd and I were going to spend Christmas at Santa Rosalia Pueblo. Snow fell steadily as we drove north through the Apache reservation. It enclosed translucent desert trees in spherical white envelopes, giving them form and substance. It was surprising to look out over a landscape that normally seemed empty, and see a forest.

When I closed my eyes I saw papier-mâché peacocks. I'd been helping out on the piñata assembly lines. I'd had nightmares again and wasn't sleeping well; I figured I could be useful. We didn't turn out five hundred piñatas in ten days—that was a little ambitious—but we passed the halfway mark. The last fifty or so were the best by folk-art standards. By then we'd already used up every scrap of blue crepe paper from the attics and bureau drawers of Grace, and so had to be enterprising. Some women cut up denim jeans. Mrs. Nuñez made peacock wings out of the indigo-colored flyleaves of all twelve volumes of the *Compton's Children's Encyclopedia*. To be sure, there were no two alike.

I also sweat blood over my mimeographed broadside. I wasn't a writer except by default. Viola refused to help, saying I was the one that went to college so quit whining. I tried to include all the things that made Grace what it was: the sisters coming over with their peacocks; their blue-eyed descendants planting an Eden of orchards in the idyllic days before Black Mountain; the confetti-colored houses and stairstep streets—everything that would be lost to a poisoned river. All in one page. Viola wouldn't let me go longer, claiming nobody would read it. There was some argument over whether to put the note *inside* the piñata, like a message in a bottle. I said city people didn't buy art just to crack it open; I was respected as an expert on city people. So my modest History of Grace was rolled, bound in ribbon like a diploma, and inserted into each peacock's beak.

The second Tucson excursion filled two chartered buses. Some husbands and kids got into the act, and also my students. I declared it a class project. I told Raymo if he sold ten peacocks I'd give him a C+. But I didn't go. Loyd had asked for a week's layoff and we set out on the trip he'd been planning forever.

"Don't you have to stop somewhere and check on your roosters?" I asked. We were near Whiteriver.

"I don't have any roosters."

"You don't?" I was incredulous. I thought he'd just stop going to fights himself. "What, you sold them?"

"Collie Bluestone kind of took over the business."

"So you could get back into it if you wanted to."

"Nope. He's moved over to the Colorado River reservation. He's fighting them over at Ehrenberg."

This was a good bit more frightening than if Loyd had presented me with a diamond ring. "But I'm not . . . What if you and I don't work out, Loyd?"

He downshifted for a rutted stretch in the road. "No offense, Codi, but I didn't give up cockfighting to impress you. I did it because you were right."

"I was *right*?"

"About what you said."

"What did I say?"

He didn't answer. I vaguely remembered saying something about puncture wounds and internal hemorrhage. Making that a spectator sport. "I can't believe you'd do this thing all your life and then just quit one day after something I said. Maybe you were ready to give it up anyway."

"Maybe I was." We were both quiet for a while, passing through winter-killed fields of grass and sage. Two black horses grazed on bristly shrubs in a field with no apparent fences.

"You and your brother were twins, right?" I asked, apropos of nothing.

He nodded. "Identical. Twins are bad luck."

I laughed. "For the mother."

"No, in the pueblo. When twins are born people say there'll be a poor rainy season or grasshoppers or some darn thing. In the old days you had to let twins die."

"Both? You couldn't pick one and let the other one go?"

"Nope."

"I can't imagine the mother who'd do it," I said, though of course I could. I had probably starved my own child to death *in utero*, rather than risk known disaster.

"There's a Tewa story about a mother sneaking her twins out of the pueblo and leaving them with Spider Grandmother to raise."

"Yeah? See, if there was a story like that, people knew it was wrong to let them die."

"Knew it was hard. Not wrong, necessarily. When Leander and I were bad, our mother said she was like poor old Spider Grandmother, got stuck with the War Twins."

"Were you bad a lot?"

"Just twice as bad as a regular boy." He laughed. "People called us 'Twice as Bad.' Our sisters talked about us like we were just one boy. They'd say 'he went out riding,' or whatever. I think *we* thought we were one person. One boy in two skins."

"Hallie and I feel that way sometimes."

I could see clear crescents of water collecting on Loyd's lower eyelids. "You don't have to talk about this," I said.

"I don't ever talk about him. Sometimes I'll go a day or two without even thinking about him, and then I get scared I might forget he ever was."

I laid a hand on his gearshift arm. "You want me to drive?"

He stopped and turned off the engine. We sat watching snowflakes hit the windshield and turn into identical dots of water. Then he got out. I pulled on my mittens and followed him.

Outside the cab it was impossibly quiet. We'd climbed a little now, and were in forest. Snowflakes hissed against pine needles. Jack sat in the truckbed watching Loyd carefully, exhaling voiceless clouds of steam.

"I ever tell you how I came to keep Jack?" Loyd asked.

I thought about it. "No. You told me how you took in his mother and she had pups. You didn't say how you picked Jack."

"He picked us." Loyd was leaning against the truck with his arms crossed over his chest. He looked cold. "Dad meant to drown the whole litter. He put them in an empty cement bag and tied the top real good and drove down to the river and pitched them in. He didn't know what he was doing; he was drunk as seven thousand dollars, I imagine. On the way back he picked me up from work and I said, 'Dad, here's one of the pups in the back of the truck.' He was hiding down in a box of pipe T-joints. Dad's old truck was a junkyard on wheels; you could find anything in the world back there. So I says to Dad, 'Where's the rest of them?' " Loyd's voice caught, and he waited a second, wiping his eyes. "I don't know what I'm getting all broke up for. God knows what I would have done with seven mongrel coyote pups."

God knows what I'd have done with a baby at sixteen, I thought. It's not the practical side of things that breaks us up. I leaned on the truck beside him and took his left hand between my mittened palms. It felt like a cold bottle. "So what happened? Why did you lose Leander?"

"Why?" He looked up at the sky. "Because we left the Pueblo. We were like the War Twins, I guess. A lot for our mother to handle. Our sisters were all older and having their own babies by that time. And people thought boys should go out in the world some. Be with our dad. He'd been down at Whiteriver more or less as long as we could remember. If we'd stayed up there in Santa Rosalia it would have worked out, but we came down here and Leander just ran into trouble. We didn't have anybody looking after us. Dad couldn't look after himself."

"Doesn't sound like it," I said.

"Everybody always talked like Leander died of drinking, but he wasn't but fifteen. Not old enough to sit down and order a beer. Everybody forgets that, that he was just a kid. We drank some, but I don't think he was drinking the night he died. There was a fight in a bar."

"What did he die of, then?"

"Puncture wounds. Internal hemorrhage."

▼▼▼

I drove through the pine forest, thinking off and on of Hallie, mindful of the slick road. Loyd was quiet, but took the wheel again when we descended into the Navajo reservation. He pointed out areas that were overgrazed. "It seems as big as the whole world, but it's still a reservation," he said. "There's fences, and a sheep can't cross them."

As dusk took us the landscape changed to an eerie, flat desert overseen by godheads of red sandstone. We were out of the snow now. The hills were striped with pinks and reds that deepened as we drove north and the sun drove west. It was dark when we left the highway and made our way down a bumpy road into the mouth of Canyon de Chelly. We passed several signs proclaiming the canyon bottom to be Navajo tribal land, where only authorized persons were admitted. The third sign, sternly luminous in the headlights, said, "Third and Final Warning."

"Are we *allowed* in here?" I asked.

"Stick with me. I can get you into all the best places."

Down in the canyon we bumped over rough road for an hour, following the course of a shallow river. There was no moon that I could see, and I lost any sense of direction I might have had while we still had sun. I was exhausted but also for the first time in weeks I felt sleepiness, that rare, delicious liqueur, soaking into my body like blotter paper. I almost fell asleep sitting up. My head bobbed as we crossed and recrossed the frozen river and climbed its uneven banks. Finally we stopped, and slept in the truckbed, cuddled like twin mummies inside a thick wrapping of blankets. We turned our bodies carefully and held each other to keep warm. Outside the blankets, our lips and noses were like chipped flint striking sparks in the frozen air.

"No fair, you've got Jack on your side," I murmured.

"Jack, other side, boy," Loyd commanded. Jack stood up and walked over the cocoon that contained us, stepping carefully on our chests. He turned around a few times in the wedge of space behind me, then dropped down with a groan and snuggled against my back. Within minutes I could feel the extra heat and I fell into heaven-sent unconsciousness.

In the morning, a sugar coating of snow had fallen, lightly covering the rocks. Ahead of us the canyon forked into two; from the riverbed a red rock spire rose a thousand feet into the air. Low clouds, or high fog, brushed its top. I held my breath. Looking up at a rock like that gave me the heady sensation of heights. He'd parked so this would be the first thing I saw: Spider Rock.

The canyon walls rose straight up on either side of us, ranging from sunset orange to deep rust, mottled with purple. The sandstone had been carved by ice ages and polished by desert eons of sandpaper winds. The place did not so much inspire religion as it seemed to be religion itself.

I was dressed in an instant and walking around awestruck like a kid, my head bent all the way back. "It doesn't look like a spider," I said, of the rock. "It looks like a steeple."

"It's named for Spider Woman. She lived up there a long time ago. One day she lassoed two Navajo ladies with her web and pulled them up there and taught them how to weave rugs."

The thought of standing on top of that rock, let alone trying to learn anything up there, made me shiver. "Is that the same Spider Grandmother who raised the twins?"

I expected Loyd to be impressed by my memory, but he just nodded. "That's a Pueblo story and this is a Navajo story, but it's the same Spider Woman. Everybody kind of agrees on the important stuff."

I shaded my eyes and looked up the canyon. Its narrows gave window views into its wider places. Giant buttresses of rock extended from the canyon walls, like ships, complete with knobbly figureheads standing on their prows. Some of the figureheads had been stranded, eroded away from the mother rock, and stood alone as sculptured spires. Where the canyon grew narrower the rock buttresses alternated like baffles, so the river had to run a slalom course around them. So did we. The truck crunched over icy shoals and passed through crystal tunnels of icy cottonwood branches. We passed a round hogan with a shingled roof and a line of smoke rising from its chimney pipe. A horse wandered nearby, nosing among the frozen leaves.

Several times Loyd stopped to point out ancient pictures cut in the rock. They tended to be in clusters, as if seeking refuge from loneliness in that great mineral expanse. There were antelope, snakes, and ducks in a line like a carnival shooting gallery. And humans: oddly turtle-shaped, with their arms out and fingers splayed as if in surrender or utter surprise. The petroglyphs added in recent centuries showed more svelte, self-assured men riding horses. The march of human progress seemed mainly a matter of getting over that initial shock of being here.

Eventually we stopped in a protected alcove of rock, where no snow had fallen. The walls sloped inward over our heads, and long dark marks like rust stains ran parallel down the cliff face at crazy angles. When I looked straight up I lost my sense of gravity. The ground under my boots was dry red sand, soft and fine, weathered down from the stone. If the river rose to here, the mud would be red. Loyd held my shoulders and directed my eyes to the opposite wall, a third of the way up. Facing the morning sun was a village built into the cliff. It was like Kinishba, the same multistory apartments and unbelievably careful masonry. The walls were shaped to fit the curved hole in the cliff, and the building blocks were cut from the same red rock that served as their foundation. I thought of what Loyd had told me about Pueblo architecture, whose object was to build a structure the earth could embrace. This looked more than embraced. It reminded me of cliff-swallow nests, or mud-dauber nests, or crystal gardens sprung from their own matrix: the perfect constructions of nature.

"Prehistoric condos," I said.

Loyd nodded. "Same people, but a lot older. They were here when Columbus's folks were still rubbing two sticks together."

"How in the world did they get *up* there?"

Loyd pointed out a crack that zigzagged up from the talus

slope to the ledge where the village perched. In places the crevice wasn't more than two inches deep. "They were pretty good rock climbers," he said. Loyd's forte was understatement.

There wasn't a sound except for the occasional, echoing pop of a small falling rock. "What were they scared of?" I asked quietly.

"I don't know. Maybe they weren't scared. Maybe they liked the view."

The doors were built so you'd have to step high to get out. Obviously, for the sake of the children. "Gives you the willies, doesn't it? The thought of raising kids in a place where the front yard ends in a two-hundred-foot drop?"

"No worse than raising up kids where the front yard ends in a freeway."

"You're right," I said. "No worse than that. And quieter. Less carbon monoxide."

"So you do think about that sometimes," Loyd said.

"About what?"

"Being a mother."

I glanced at him and considered several possible answers. "All the time," and "never" seemed equally true. Sometimes I wanted to say, "You had your chance, Loyd, we had our baby and it's dead." But I didn't. That was my past, not his.

"Sure, I think about it," I said, needing to relieve the pressure in my chest. "I think about hotwiring a Porsche and driving to Mexico, too."

He laughed. "Only one of the two is legal, I'm told."

I wanted to try and climb up into the cliff village, but Loyd explained that we'd crack our skulls, plus you weren't supposed to mess with the antiquities.

"I thought you broke all the rules," I said, as we climbed back into the truck and headed farther up the canyon.

He looked surprised. "What rules have I broken?"

"Authorized Navajo personnel only, for starters. We're not even supposed to be down here."

"We're authorized guests of Maxine Shorty of the Streams Come Together clan."

"Does she live here?"

"Not now. Almost everybody drives their sheep out and spends the winter up top, but the farms are down here. Leander and I spent almost every summer here till we were thirteen."

"You did? Doing what?"

"Working. I'll show you."

"Who's Maxine Shorty?"

"My aunt. I'd like you to meet her but she's down visiting at Window Rock for the holiday."

Loyd was full of surprises. "I'll never get your family straight. How'd you get a Navajo aunt? Are Navajos and Pueblos all one big tribe or something?"

Loyd laughed rather hysterically. It occurred to me that this redneck Apache former cockfighter must find me, at times, an outstanding bonehead. "The Pueblo people were always here," he explained patiently. "They're still building houses just like this—the Rio Grande Pueblos, Zuñi, Hopi Mesa. Not in the cliffs anymore, but otherwise just the same. They're about the only Indians that haven't been moved off their own place into somebody else's."

"And the Navajo?"

"Navajos and Apaches are a bunch that came down from Canada, not that long ago. A few hundred years, maybe. Looking for someplace warmer."

"And this is now Navajo tribal land, because?"

"Because the U.S. Government officially gave it to them. Wasn't that nice? Too bad they didn't give them the Golden Gate Bridge, too."

The truck crunched over frozen sand. "So the Pueblo are homebodies, and the Navajo and Apache are wanderers."

"You could look at it that way, I guess."

"What are you?"

"Pueblo." There was no hesitation. "What are you?"

"I have no idea. My mother came from someplace in Illinois, and Doc Homer won't own up to being from anywhere. I can't remember half of what happened to me before I was fifteen. I guess I'm nothing. The Nothing Tribe."

"Homebody tribe or wanderer tribe?"

I laughed. "Emelina called me a 'homewrecker' one time. Or no, what did she say? A 'home ignorer.' "

He didn't respond to that.

"So how'd you get a Navajo aunt?" I asked again.

"The usual way. My mother's brother married her. Pueblo men have to marry out of the clan, and sometimes they go off the pueblo. The land down here stays with the women. So my uncle came here."

Maxine Shorty's farm, which she inherited from her mother and would pass on to her daughters, was a triangle bordered by the river and the walls of a short side canyon. We parked by the line of cottonwoods near the river and walked over the icy stubble of a cornfield. A sad scarecrow stood guard. It occurred to me that the barrenness of a winter farm was deceptive; every-thing was there, it was still fertile, just as surely as trees held their identity in the shape and swell of their bare winter twigs.

"Has it changed much?"

I meant it as a joke, I saw nothing that *could* have changed, but Loyd looked around carefully. "Those little weedy cotton-woods have grown up along the stream. And there's a big boul-der on that slope, you see the one with dark stripes? That used to be up there." He pointed to a place in the canyon wall, visible only to himself, from which the boulder had fallen. Most men, I thought, aren't this familiar with the furniture in their homes.

"So what did you do here?"

"Worked our butts off. Weeded, picked corn, grew beans and watermelons. And had to carry a lot of water in the bad years."

"Were those peach trees here?" I asked. A weathered orchard occupied the steep upper section of land.

"They're older than my aunt. The peach trees go way back. They were planting orchards down here three hundred years ago."

"A canyon of fruit. Like Grace."

He inspected the trees carefully, one at a time: the bases of the branches, the trunks, the ends of twigs. I didn't know what he was looking for, and didn't ask. It seemed like family business. On this land Loyd seemed like a family man.

"And did the people that lived up in the cliffs grow corn and beans too?"

"That's right."

"So how come this canyon's stayed productive for a thousand and some-odd years, and we can't even live in Grace for one century without screwing it up?"

It was mostly a rhetorical question but Loyd considered it for a long time as he led me along a path up the talus slope to the back of the box canyon.

"I know the answer to that," he said finally. "But I can't put it in words. I'll have to show you. Not here. Later on."

I felt sadly let down, though it was closer to an actual promise of revelation than I'd gotten in nine years of watching Carlo's eyebrows. I could wait for "later on."

At the top of the slope was another ancient dwelling, this one mainly just ruined walls. The floor plan was clear. It interested me that the doors all lined up, I suppose to admit light to the interior.

"I found a whole clay pot in here one time," Loyd said. "It's in my mother's house." He lowered his voice. "Don't tell any Navajos, they'll throw Mama in jail."

"You brought it back to her at the end of one summer, right? As a present. And she still treasures it."

He smiled a little shyly. The image of a ten-year-old Loyd brought the threat of tears to my eyes. I'd spent my life watching mother-child rituals from outside the window.

"So you played in here when you were little?"

"Oh, yeah. This used to be me and Leander's fort."

"Cowboys and Indians?"

He laughed. "Good Indians and bad Indians."

"Which were you?"

"Nobody can be good all the time. Or bad all the time. We took turns."

He led me over a couple of tumbledown walls to the base of the cliff, and knelt down. I looked where he pointed. Set carefully among an assortment of old petroglyphs were two modern ones: the outlined left hands of two small boys, just touching, perfectly matched.

▼▼▼

We crossed the high desert from Chinle to Ship Rock, New Mexico, and on to the Jemez Mountains. Wind battered the windows and we warmed our hands at the heater vents and talked about everything under the sun. Loyd talked about his marriage to Cissie Ramon, which he said was noisy and short. Cissie was crazy about rooster fighting, men, and unusual colors of nail polish, like green. He'd thought she was exotic, but she was just wild; there was a difference. She ran out on him.

He was a good deal more interested in talking about working in his aunt's pecan orchards, in Grace. This aunt was his mother's sister, Sonia. She married a Pueblo man from her village but moved with him to Grace when Black Mountain drafted Native American men into the mines during World War II. Sonia and her husband planted fruit trees there, thinking the war would last at least twenty years, and when it didn't they felt they ought to stay on in Grace anyway, for the sake of the orchards.

It was a different story from farming in Canyon de Chelly, Loyd said. Sonia had started out as a tenant picker, before buying her own pecan orchard, and she learned harvesting the modern way. Usually the harvest started in October and ran till Thanksgiving. To get the nuts off the trees, they used a machine called a tree shaker.

"I remember guys hitting the branches with sticks, when I was a kid," I said.

"Nah, we were high-tech. After the tree shaker comes the harvester, which is this big thing with a vacuum-scooper that you drive along between the rows. It scoops up everything and blows the sticks and leaves out the back, and the pecans and rocks fall down into this cage at the bottom. More junk falls out the slots as it rolls around, and the hulls fall off, and the idea is you end up with mostly pecans. But really you end up with pecans and pecan-sized dirt clods and pecan-sized rocks."

"So did you get to drive the big machines?"

"Nope. Mostly I got to pick rocks and dirt clods off the conveyor. I think that was the best job I ever had. The hardest, but the best, because I grew up on it. Stopped thinking about myself all the time and started thinking about something else, even if it was just damn pecans."

I took it from Loyd's use of the singular pronoun that Leander was dead by this time. Slowly I was patching together Loyd's life, and it was not the poor little gypsy story I'd imagined. I suppose I'd wanted to see him as a fellow orphan. But everywhere he'd been, he'd been with family.

"How long will Grace last without the river?" I asked.

"Two or three years, maybe. The old orchards will go longer because their roots are deeper." He glanced at me. "You know I have an orchard?"

"No. In Grace?"

"Yep. Not the pecans, those belong to my cousins, but Tía Sonia's leaving me the peach orchard. The fruit trees were always my job, keeping the birds and squirrels off the fruit."

"How do you do that?"

"Well, the main way is by killing them."

I laughed.

"What's funny?"

"I don't know." I stared out the windshield. In the distance, Ship Rock floated like a ghost vessel on the snowy plain. "So you now have a dying orchard to call your own. Your Aunt Sonia's moved back to Santa Rosalia, right?"

"Right. But the orchard's not mine till I have kids."

"That doesn't seem fair."

"No, it makes sense. When you have a family, you need trees." He paused, carefully, it seemed to me, and redirected the conversation. "What job did you grow up on?"

I thought this over. "Maybe I haven't had it yet."

He smiled. "You went to medical school, right? And almost finished. That can't be too easy."

"When it stopped being easy, I quit."

"What were you doing in Tucson, then, before you came to Grace?"

"You don't want to know. Cashier in a 7-Eleven."

"Shoot. And I thought you were too good to go out with a locomotive engineer. What about before that?"

"You don't want to know."

"Yes, I do."

"Well, I did medical research at the Mayo Clinic in Minnesota."

"Damn! Really?"

"Yep. I was living up there two years ago when I first found out Doc Homer was sick."

"And before that?"

I rolled my head back and looked at the roof of the car. "You *really* don't want to know."

"You were President of the United States."

"Guess again."

"You hotwired Porsches."

I laughed. "The biggest thing I ever stole was a frozen lobster, for my boyfriend's birthday. I was working in frozen foods and I think I actually wanted to get fired. Doesn't that sound stupid?"

"Yes, it sounds stupid. So that came before Mayo Clinic?"

"That, and a bunch of different odd little things. A few piddly research jobs in between. Believe me, I never put everything on the same résumé."

"And what's the one you never mention? The one you're trying not to tell me about."

"For a few years in there I lived overseas."

"No kidding. Did you fly? Shoot, I'd love to go someplace in an airplane."

"Flying's okay," I said. In truth, flying terrified me. It's the one thing I knew I had in common with my mother, who'd flat-out refused, there at the end. In my own life I handled it by means of steadfast denial. I'd flown over the Atlantic Ocean twice without even checking to see if there really was a flotation device under my seat; flotation seemed beside the point. Oh, I flew like a bird.

"So, okay, what were you doing overseas?"

I glanced at him. "I was my boyfriend Carlo's girlfriend. On the island of Crete."

He seemed amused. "What, you mean you cleaned house and made cookies?"

"Kind of. Sometimes I'd help out in the clinic. One time I set the broken leg of a sheep. But mostly I was a housewife."

"So you'd, what, go shopping in a bikini?"

I laughed. "It really was not that kind of island. You know where it is, right? In between Greece and Egypt. The women wear black wool dresses and crucifixes the size of a hood ornament. Getting the picture?"

He nodded.

"The main baby present for a boy is a silver knife, which they present in this ceremony where the godparents list all the enemies of the family going back to around Adam and Eve."

"You liked it that much, huh?"

I took my coat off. It was finally warming up. "Well, it was interesting. It was someplace to go. It was like going to another century, actually. But I felt like a complete outsider." I closed my eyes, fighting an old ache.

"How do you mean?"

"I'm pretty good at languages but I never could get the hang of fitting in. Not anywhere, but especially not there."

"Why do you think you don't fit in? Give me an example."

It was plain that I'd always been an oddity in Grace, so he must have meant how was I an oddity in Crete. "Well, my first day there I marched into the bakery and asked for a *psoli*. The word for a loaf of bread is *psomi*. A *psoli* is a penis."

Loyd laughed. "Anybody could make a mistake like that."

"Not more than once, I promise you."

"Well, you were foreign. People expect you to say a few dumb things."

"Oh, every day I did something wrong. They had complicated rules about who could talk to who and what you could say and who said it first. Like, there were all these things you were supposed to do to avoid the Evil Eye."

"How do you do that?" he asked. Loyd was full of curiosity.

"You wear this little amulet that looks like a blue eyeball. But the main thing is, you never *ever* mention anything you're proud of. It's this horrible social error to give somebody a compliment, because you're attracting the attention of the Evil Eye. So you say everything backward. When two mothers pass each other on the road carrying their babies, one says to the other, 'Ugly baby!' And the other one says, 'Yours also!' "

Loyd laughed a wonderful, loud laugh that made me think of Fenton Lee, in high school. Who'd died in the train wreck.

"I swear to God it's true."

"I believe you. It's just funny how people are. People in Grace do that too, in a way. You give them a compliment and they'll say, 'Oh, no, that's just something I've had a long time.' We're all scared to be too happy about what we've got, for fear some-body'll notice and take it away." He reached over and stroked the underside of my arm, from the elbow up. "Like you, Codi. You're exactly like that. Scared to claim anything you love."

"Am I?" I was willing to believe whatever he said. Talking with Loyd was like talking to myself, only more honest. Emelina was always asking me what it was like to live overseas, and I knew she would love the penis story, but I'd never told her much about Crete. I was afraid of her seeing me as more of an outsider in Grace than I already was. But Loyd didn't make those judgments. I could have told Loyd I'd lived on Neptune, and he'd say, "Uh-huh? What was it like, was it cold?"

▼▼▼

In the Jemez Mountains we drove up the slope of what looked like a huge old volcano. A fluted core of granite jutted from its mouth, and twisted black ridges of old lava flows ran like var-icose veins down its sides. The snow was deep and the road icy. We crept along, then stopped. Loyd got out of the truck and started down the bank toward a frozen creek that cut between the road and the steep mountainside.

"Are you nuts?" I inquired.

"Come on." He waved energetically.

"Why should I follow you down there?" I demanded, fol-lowing as fast as I could.

"It's a surprise."

It was near sunset, near or below freezing, and Loyd wasn't

even wearing his jacket. I slipped several times behind him and then we both slid flat-out down the hill on our backs. We were sledding, not on snow but on an exposed hillside of bizarre, rounded gravel. I picked up a handful in my mitten and tossed it in the air. It was porous and weightless like Styrofoam popcorn. "What is this stuff?" I asked, but Loyd was already crossing a log over the frozen creek. I scrambled behind him up the forested slope on the other side. I picked my way between rocks, grabbing roots and tree trunks to pull myself up. Halfway up I had to stop, hugging a pine trunk and panting. The cold air cut my lungs, and I blinked hard against the sensation that the water in my eyes might freeze over.

"It's the altitude," I whined. Loyd grabbed my hand and pulled me gently uphill. Suddenly we were following the course of an odd unfrozen stream with lush plants thriving alongside it, their leaves glossy green against the snow. I'd never seen anything like this in nature, only in the sort of paintings that show improbable and dreamlike things. Loyd, who had gotten ahead of me again, was now taking off his shirt. I wondered if perhaps I was, after all, in one of my strange dreams, and whether I would soon be looking under the foliage beside the stream for my lost baby.

I climbed over the top of a boulder and there stood Loyd, naked, smiling, an apparition bathed in steam. He slid into the blue pool at the base of the boulder. I touched the steaming water and it blessedly scalded my fingertips. I undressed more quickly than I probably have in my life, before or since, and immersed myself up to my eyes.

The sun set. Venus opened her eye on the horizon. From where we sat we could see the Jemez range and the valley floor fifty miles to the south, its buttes and mesas still lit by a distant sun. When our bodies turned red we stood up briefly among the snow-covered boulders, shouting, and the steam rose off our uplifted arms like smokestacks.

Loyd asked, "So, am I nuts?"

I stretched my legs along the sandy bottom of the pool until my toes found his. The heat relaxed every muscle and sinew and reflex in my body, and most of the ones in my head. This kind of happiness was sure to attract the attention of the Evil Eye. "Have you got any more surprises?" I asked. "Or is this the last one?"

"I've got some more."

He scooted over and lifted me off the sand, supporting my floating body with both hands under the small of my back. "I don't give them away all at once, though," he said. "Only a half dozen a year."

I counted on my fingers: Kinishba. Spider Rock, the Cliff house, and Maxine Shorty's farm. And this, volcanic hot springs. I didn't know whether to count the cockfights or not. That he could give up cockfights, I'd have to count that. "So I've used up my half-dozen already," I said.

He lifted me slightly out of the water and kissed my ribs, one at a time. "If you're only staying around for a year. That's the rules."

"That's bribery."

"Whatever it takes." He kissed my navel and the damp hill over my pubic bone.

The front of my body was very cold and the back was very hot. Somewhere in the middle, near my heart, I was just right. I opened my eyes and saw constellations whose names were their own business. "Were you ever in love with my sister?" I asked.

He looked at me oddly.

"It's just a joke. Every man I've ever been with, it seems like, was really in love with Hallie."

"I can't picture your sister. She's shorter than you, right?"

I ducked my chin a little, immersing my smile. Right then I could have signed on for life.

▼▼▼

The day we left Grace, there had been four airmail letters in the P.O. box. Lately Hallie's letters sometimes came in bunches, owing to the accumulated pauses in postal service between Chinandega and Grace. But I saved them and read only one per day. It supported the pleasant, false notion that she was available to me all the time and would always be there tomorrow.

The fourth day of our trip was Christmas Eve. In the morning as we drove down from Jemez, before we arrived in Santa Rosalia, I laid out all four letters on the dash in order of postmark and spent one last hour with my sister.

I reread the old ones before opening the fourth one. Hallie's week had gone wildly up and down. On Tuesday she was nigh unto manic because the government had had a successful national meeting on the pesticide problem. Central America was becoming a toilet bowl of agricultural chemicals, she said, because of war-strained farming economies and dumping from the First World. In the seventies, when Nicaragua was run by the U.S. Marines and Somoza, it was the world's number-one consumer of DDT. But it seemed the new Nicaragua (*our* government, she called it) planned to take responsibility for its poisons. She also mentioned that her friend Julio was back in Chinandega after a stint of literacy work near the Atlantic coast. I couldn't read anything between the lines.

On Wednesday, a child was rushed in from the village of San Manuel to the Chinandega clinic in critical condition because someone had stored paraquat in a Coke bottle.

On Thursday she was grimly happy. Five contras were making a secret sabotage raid on a hydroelectric plant, somewhere to the east, and were surprised by some armed farmers who took them captive. The culprits had passed through town in the back of an open Jeep, slit-eyed with dishonor, on their way to trial in Managua. Wouldn't it be something, she mused, if that Jeep hit one of the contra road mines? But there was the driver to consider, and even if there hadn't been, it wasn't something she could wish for. She said, "You can't let your heart go bad like that, like sour milk. There's always the chance you'll want to use it later."

I wondered at what point I'd given up on later and let mine go sour. I didn't know, although Hallie might. I reread each of the three letters with fascination but also the same dissatisfaction I'd had on the morning I'd opened it. It was all just *things happening,* and selfishly, I wanted Hallie. Even if she didn't speak to me directly, I wanted her to speak.

I tore open the last envelope and was hit full in the face with what I wanted. It was four pages long, in a cursive enlarged by rage. When God wants to punish you, as Isak Dinesen declared, He answers your prayers.

I am like *God*, Codi? Like GOD? Give me a break. If I get another letter that mentions SAVING THE WORLD, I am sending you, by return mail, a letter bomb. Codi, please. I've got things to do.

You say you're not a moral person. What a copout. Sometime, when I wasn't looking, something happened to make you think you were bad. What, did Miss Colder give you a bad mark on your report card? You think you're no good, so you can't do good things. Jesus, Codi, how long are you going to keep limping around on that crutch? It's the other way around, it's what you *do* that makes you who you are.

I'm sorry to be blunt. I've had a bad week. I am trying to explain, and I wish you were here so I could tell you this right now, I am trying to explain to you that I'm not here to *save* anybody or any thing. It's not some perfect ideal we're working toward that keeps us going. You ask, what if we lose this war? Well, we could. By invasion, or even in the next election. People are very tired. I don't expect to see perfection before I die. Lord, if I did I would have stuck my head in the oven back in Tucson, after hearing the stories of some of those refugees. What keeps you going isn't some fine destination but just the road you're on, and the fact that you know how to drive. You keep your eyes open, you see this damned-to-hell world you got born into, and you ask yourself, "What life can I live that will let me breathe in & out and love somebody or something and not run off screaming into the woods?" I didn't look down from some high rock and choose cotton fields in Nicaragua. These cotton fields chose me.

The contras that were through here yesterday got sent to a prison farm where they'll plant vegetables, learn to read and write if they don't know how, learn to repair CB radios, and get a week-long vacation with their families every year. They'll probably get amnesty in five. There's hardly ever a repeat offender.

That kid from San Manuel died.

Your sister, Hallie

"What's new with Hallie?" Loyd asked.
"Nothing."

I folded the pages back into the envelope as neatly as I could, trying to leave its creases undisturbed, but my fingers had gone numb and blind. With tears in my eyes I watched whatever lay to the south of us, the land we were driving down into, but I have no memory of it. I was getting a dim comprehension of the difference between Hallie and me. It wasn't a matter of courage or dreams, but something a whole lot simpler. A pilot would call it ground orientation. I'd spent a long time circling above the clouds, looking for life, while Hallie was living it.

19

THE BREAD GIRL

Five miles outside of Santa Rosalia Pueblo, Loyd stopped the truck, pulled off his cowboy boots, and put on moccasins. Shortly we were going to have to get out and walk through snow.

"Saving your boots?" I asked.

He ignored me. Those particular boots looked as though they'd hitchhiked to hell and back without getting a single ride.

"Me and Leander used to come home at the end of the summer wearing cowboy boots and Mama would have a fit. And cowboy hats. She'd grab off our hats and swat us with them and say, 'Ahh! You look like Navajos!' "

I'd never seen Loyd wear a hat of any kind, now that I thought about it. His story brought back a memory, vague and incomplete, of cowboy boots and a hat I'd had myself, as a child. I could just recall the sheen of lacquered straw, and a terrible sadness.

"You see it yet?"

I squinted toward the south, but saw only snow-covered hills dotted with dark, spherical juniper bushes. The horizon was punctuated with bleak mesas whose rock shoulders stood exposed to the cold. "See what?"

"Where we're going to sleep tonight."

"I hope not."

A few minutes later he asked again. I saw mesas and scalped hills with rocky outcroppings on their tops. I saw juniper trees, and snow. "Is this an eye test?" I asked.

We were practically inside Santa Rosalia Pueblo before I saw it. The village was built on a mesa and blended perfectly with the landscape, constructed of the same stones as the outcroppings that topped all the other, empty mesas. Horses and broad-faced cattle looked up at us from their pens as Loyd's red truck, the newest-looking thing within a hundred miles, rolled up the dirt track into town.

It was a village of weathered rectangles, some stacked step-wise in twos and threes, the houses all blending into one another around a central plaza. The stone walls were covered with adobe plaster, smooth and appealing as mud pies: a beautiful brown town. The color brown, I realized, is anything but nondescript. It comes in as many hues as there are colors of earth, which is commonly presumed infinite.

We left the truck in the company of other pickups and station wagons at the edge of town, and walked up into the narrow streets. In his moccasins Loyd walked with a softer, less aggressive gait. Jack stayed close to his left knee. There wasn't a soul out, but lines of smoke drifted from chimneys and the big adobe beehive ovens that squatted in every third or fourth back-yard. A black dog pawed at the edge of a frozen puddle. The ladders that connected one rooftop to the next were drifted lightly with snow. One house had a basketball hoop nailed to the end beams. Front curtains everywhere glowed with warm interior light, though it was still early afternoon, and strings of bright red chilies hung by the front doors.

Loyd's mother's house had a green door. The front window was crowded with artificial flowers and ceramic animals. Loyd's oldest sister, Birdie, met us at the door. The two of them spoke rapidly in a language that sounded like song, as if the pitch might be as important as the syllable. Birdie had a perm, and wore a large turquoise necklace over her flowered blouse. She stopped talking to Loyd just long enough to touch my arm and say, "He still has that dog, don't he?" and "Come get warm." We followed her into the kitchen, where Loyd's mother enveloped him with a hug, then tugged his ponytail and lightly boxed his ears.

"What's she saying?" I asked Birdie.

"She's saying he looks like a Navajo."

The kitchen smelled of cedar smoke. Inez Peregrina was cooking a goose, among other things. She wore a large dress composed of about six different cotton fabrics, florals and plaids, somehow colorfully harmonic. The frames of her glasses were large and owlish. Her gray hair was trimmed in bangs and a pageboy over her ears, but long in back, twisted into a heavy, complicated coil and tied with red cloth. Her hands were noticeably large. I wanted her to hug me too, but she only smiled and touched my cheek when Loyd introduced us. She continued talking to him in a steady, musical downpour, to which he was attentive.

Birdie disappeared and soon returned at the head of a flock of women, and I was introduced, but the conversation between Inez and Loyd went on, uninterrupted. One at a time, each of the other women held out both hands to me, which I took, trying to appear gracious while I struggled to get their positions straight. They were Loyd's sisters; a niece; his Aunt Sonia, who had lived in Grace during the war and after; and someone Loyd called his "navel mother." I couldn't discern the generations. Aunt Sonia spoke to me in Spanish and poured cups of coffee for Loyd and me from a huge tin pot on the wood-fired stove. There were also a propane stove and the adobe oven in the backyard, and all three were in use.

I felt spectacularly out of place. For one thing, I stood a foot taller than any other woman in the room; we don't even have to get into matters of wardrobe. But I was also fascinated to watch Loyd being his mother's son, his sisters' brother, the apple of the family eye. The only remaining boy. The sisters asked him in calm, uninflected English about the drive and the length of our stay and whether he'd seen Aunt Maxine, who evidently had a heart condition. Aunt Sonia asked several specific questions about people in Grace, some of whom I knew better than Loyd because of my Stitch and Bitch association, but I was reluctant to speak. She and the sisters drifted away to other tasks, and Inez still hadn't stopped talking.

"Is it okay if I look around?" I asked Loyd.

"You can dance on the table if you want to, you're the guest," he said, grabbing me around the waist.

"I don't want to dance on the table."

He held on to me for just a minute, asking Inez in English what she thought of me. I passed a hand through my hair, thankful that it had had time to grow out from Billy Idol to a more or less regulation Mary Martin.

Inez smiled and said something, running the ladle in her right hand up and down an imaginary line. I looked at Loyd for translation.

"She says I'm lucky to have gotten such a big, strong girl. She thinks I'm lazy."

"Tell her I don't put up with lazy men. I make them pull their weight."

He told her and she laughed, giving me the hug I'd coveted.

The frosted windowpanes looked out onto the cold plain and dish-shaped, empty cornfields that lay to the south, but the kitchen was smoky and warm. The open pantry behind Inez was stocked with jars of dry yellow corn, cans of Spam, and fruit cocktail. (No orchards here, evidently.) And hominy. In Grace it was golden jars of home-canned peach halves that sat smug on kitchen shelves. Here it was puffy white hominy, jar after jar of it, hominy enough for an army.

The kitchen was at the end of a big room that contained a long wooden table, a sofa, numerous small chests, and many, many photos. A radio in another room played Hank Williams. I moved around the living room, idly looking out the windows and examining photographs. There was one of Inez and a man I presumed to be Loyd's father standing together in formal dress: he in silver-buttoned moccasins and a royal blue velvet shirt, Inez in turquoise bracelets and a silver squash-blossom necklace over her dark ceremonial dress. Her legs looked like white birch stumps in their buckskin leggings, and the woven blanket folded across her shoulders seemed to weigh her down. She looked much older than she must have actually been.

Most of the available tabletops were populated by little ceramic animals of the pastel, cute variety. Loyd had told me Inez made the best pottery in the Pueblo, but evidently it was made for Anglo collectors, not for home use. I did find in a china cabinet a display of extraordinary black-and-white pots, their glazed surfaces covered with microscopically fine geometric designs. Some of the pots were slightly less well made, maybe some of the proud early efforts of Inez's daughters. A crude, dark bowl with a chipped rim sat in the cabinet's central place of honor, and I stared at it, puzzled, until I realized this was Loyd's pot, the one he'd found in the ruins. Loyd's offering from Canyon de Chelly.

I peeked into the next room. Charlie Rich was singing from the radio now, and Birdie hummed "Behind Closed Doors" while she bent over an electric sewing machine. Its small light glowed on her face. A baby slept on a flat, fur-lined cradle board that hung like a swing on ropes from the ceiling. On every fifth arc of the swing, Birdie reached up without looking and gave it a push. She noticed me standing in the doorway and inclined her head toward the end of the room, where an iron bed stood behind a drawn-open curtain of blankets. "You can put things there. That's for you and Loyd."

"Thanks," I said. "Who's the little one?"

"My daughter's girl. Hester."

"How old?"

"Three weeks."

"Does your daughter live here too?"

Birdie pulled her cloth from the machine and shook her head slightly while she broke the thread with her teeth. "She goes to boarding school in Albuquerque."

I returned to exploring the living room. I was stunned to run across a small framed photo of two little Loyds, identical, sitting astride very different horses. Behind them was a backdrop of dry hills and a brown water tank. Loyd and Leander, nine years old, looking as if they owned the world. Until I saw that picture

I hadn't really heard a word he'd told me about losing his brother. You can't know somebody, I thought, till you've followed him home.

▼▼▼

That evening Inez's house filled with relatives for the feast. Cousins and uncles and aunts showed up, stamping the snow off their moccasins, bringing covered dishes and their own chairs. All the older women had their hair cut in the same style as Inez's, with short flaps over the ears and the heavy chignon in the back, and they wore silver necklaces and elaborate turquoise rings that shielded their knuckles. The teenage girls wore jeans and about everything else you'd expect on a teenage girl, except makeup. One of them nursed a baby at the table, under her T-shirt.

Loyd and I shared one chair; apparently we were the official lovebirds of this fiesta. He spent a lot of time telling me what I was eating. There were, just to begin with, five different kinds of *posole*, a hominy soup with duck or pork and chilies and coriander. Of the twenty or so different dishes I recognized only lime jello, cut into cubes. I gave up trying to classify things by species and just ate. To everyone's polite amusement, my favorite was the bread, which was cooked in enormous, nearly spherical loaves, two dozen at a time, in the adobe ovens outside. It had a hard brown crust and a heavenly, steaming interior, and tasted like love. I ate half a loaf by myself, believing no one would notice. Later, in bed, Loyd told me they were all calling me the Bread Girl.

Our bed was small, but after three nights in the truck it felt deliciously soft. I cuddled against Loyd. "What's a navel mother?" I asked, drowsy with warmth and a half loaf of bread.

"She's like a special aunt. She's the one that cuts the cord when you're born, and helps your mother get up out of bed when she's ready. They count that as your birthday—the day your mother gets up."

"Not the day you were born?"

"Not the day you came out. They count the mother getting better as all part of the birth."

"Hallie doesn't have a birthday, then," I said. "After she was born, our mother never got up. She got real sick, and then a helicopter tried to come get her and she died. All without ever putting her slippers on."

"Then Hallie never finished getting born," Loyd said. He kissed the top of my head.

I was aware of the sleeping sounds of Inez and Hester on the other side of the makeshift curtain. I asked, "Is it okay that we're sleeping together?"

Loyd quietly laughed at me. "It's okay with me. Is it okay with you?"

"I mean with your family."

"They're not hung up about it. Mama wanted to know if you're my woman."

"Meaning what?"

"As opposed to woman of the week, I guess."

"Woman of the year," I said.

In the morning snow had fallen, as deep as five or six quilts. The windows were round blue tunnels to the light, like the mouths of caves. Loyd got up and went outside, where, at dawn, Inez and Birdie were already involved with the day's industry. He was sent back to bed with a whole fresh loaf of bread.

▼▼▼

"How did your dad meet her?" I asked. Loyd and I were sitting on the roof of Inez's house now, facing south, waiting for ceremonies to begin in the plaza.

"At a dance over in Laguna. In the summertime. It was a corn dance. Everybody says she was a knockout when she was young. A real good dancer."

"I think she's a knockout now."

"He grew up over at Jicarilla."

"Where's that?"

"Not too far from here. It's another Apache reservation. Everybody goes to everybody's dances. We used to go over to the Navajo powwows in the fall."

Today, on Christmas Day in Santa Rosalia, there were supposed to be dances from morning till night. Half the town seemed to be preparing to dance, while the other half were busy getting good seats. I had no idea what to expect. Anxious-looking little boys clutching feather crowns and fox pelts ran across the corners of the plaza bent low, as if this would make them invisible. Earlier in the day these same little boys had run in boisterous gangs from house to house banging on doors and begging for warm crusts torn from the morning loaves. A wholesome version of trick-or-treat. Give these kids one Halloween in Grace, I thought, and they'd never be content with complex carbohydrates.

"So he married your mother," I said. "And came here."

"The women are kind of the center of things up here. The man goes to the wife's place."

"But he didn't stay."

"I never really knew Dad that well. He was already gone when he was still here, if you know what I mean. I don't know what it was that hurt him. I know he grew up at a boarding school and never had much family and he couldn't keep to the old ways. Or didn't know them. I don't know. It was real hard for him here."

I let the subject go. As the twig is bent, so grows the tree, Doc Homer used to say, referring mostly to the bone structure of the feet but it applied to moral life as well. And who knew how the kinks happened; they just did. I ought to know. As Hallie had bluntly pointed out in her letter, I'd marked myself early on as a bad risk, undeserving of love and incapable of benevolence. It wasn't because of a bad grade on a report card, as she'd supposed. It ran deeper than that. I'd lost what there was to lose: first my mother and then my baby. Nothing you love will stay. Hallie could call that attitude a crutch, but she didn't know, she hadn't loved and lost so deeply. As Loyd said, she'd never been born—not into life as I knew it. Hallie could still risk everything.

Loyd and I dangled our feet over the side of the roof, looking out over the plaza and beyond, to where the plaza ended suddenly, perforce, by the drop of a sheer cliff. I could only see this precipice as a threat, and wonder how toddlers lived to the age of reason without toddling over it, but many little feather-

bedecked children were running along its edge as if it were
nothing more than the end of a yard.

I heard a drum and a brief burst of what sounded like sleigh
bells. Then nothing. If anything ever did happen, we'd have a
good view. We'd climbed a ladder to get where we were. Jack
had given a long, dejected look up the rungs as if he might
consider the climb, if he weren't so dignified. Now he lay curled
at the bottom keeping watch. Old wooden ladders and alumi-
num extension ladders were propped everywhere; second- and
third-story roofs served as patios. All around the plaza, legs hung
like fringe over the sides of buildings. I spotted Inez and some
other relatives across the way. Inez's owlish glasses were the
type that turn dark outdoors; two huge black disks hid her round
face as she sat, hands folded, inscrutable as a lifeguard.

Not far from us in a sheltered corner of the roof was a wire
pen full of geese and turkeys muttering the subdued prayers of
the doomed. "Does your mama know you were a cockfighter?"
I asked Loyd.

"No." He hesitated. "She knew Dad did it, and that he took
Leander and me to the fights when we were little, but she didn't
care for him doing that. She never knew I went on with it. And
you better not tell her."

"I'm gonna tell," I said, poking him in the ribs. "I'm going
to look up in my *Keres*–English dictionary, 'Your son is a dirty
low-down rooster fighter.' "

Loyd looked pained. Pleasing his mother was nothing to joke
about. He'd given up cockfighting for Inez, not for me, I now
understood. I'd just been the cricket in his ear. But that wasn't
insignificant, I decided. I could settle for that. I looked down at
the plaza, whose quilt of fresh snow remained a virginal white,
unmarred by tracks. This seemed miraculous, considering the
huge number of people crowded around its edges—a good two
hundred or more. People must have come from outside the
Pueblo. Jicarilla Apaches looking for knockout wives.

"How come those houses over there near the edge of the cliff
are falling down?" I asked. Their adobe plaster had cracked off,
revealing the same artful masonry as Kinishba, in a state of
collapse.

"Because they're old," Loyd said.

"Thank you. I mean, why doesn't somebody fix them up? You guys are the experts, you've been building houses for nine hundred years."

"Not necessarily in the same place. This village was in seven other places before they built it up here."

"So when something gets old they just let it fall down?"

"Sometimes. Someday you'll get old and fall down."

"Thanks for reminding me." I shaded my eyes, looking to the east. Something was happening near the kiva, which was a building with a ladder poking out through a hatch in its roof. Loyd had suggested I shouldn't show too much interest in it.

"The greatest honor you can give a house is to let it fall back down into the ground," he said. "That's where everything comes from in the first place."

I looked at him, surprised. "But then you've lost your house."

"Not if you know how to build another one. All those great pueblos like at Kinishba—people lived in them awhile, and then they'd move on. Just leave them standing. Maybe go to a place with better water, or something."

"I thought they were homebodies."

Loyd rubbed his hand thoughtfully over my palm. Finally he said, "The important thing isn't the house. It's the ability to make it. You carry that in your brain and in your hands, wherever you go. Anglos are like turtles, if they go someplace they have to carry the whole house along in their damn Winnesotas."

I smiled. "Winnebagos. They're named after an Indian tribe." It occurred to me too late that Loyd already knew both these things. For months, I think, I'd been missing his jokes. Empress of the Universe, instructing the heathen.

"We're like coyotes," he said. "Get to a good place, turn around three times in the grass, and you're home. Once you know how, you can always do that, no matter what. You won't forget."

I thought of Inez's copious knickknacks and suspected Loyd was idealizing a bit. But I liked the ideal. The thought of Hallie's last letter still stung me but I tried to think abstractly about what she wanted to tell me: about keeping on the road because you know how to drive. That morality is not a large, constructed *thing* you have or have not, but simply a capacity. Something you carry with you in your brain and in your hands.

I'd come on this trip knowing I still had to leave Loyd in June, that Grace wouldn't keep me, but maybe I was just keeping to the road. I felt guilt slip out of me like a stone. "It's a nice thought," I told him. "I guess I'll probably carry something away with me when I leave Grace."

He looked at me carefully, started to speak, then stopped. And then did speak. "It's one thing to carry your life wherever you go. Another thing to always go looking for it somewhere else."

I didn't respond to that. I blinked hard and tried to look unconcerned, but the guilt nudged back along with the sharp glass edge of my own rationalization, recognized for what it was. I wasn't keeping to any road, I was running, forgetting what lay behind and always looking ahead for the perfect home, where trains never wrecked and hearts never broke, where no one you loved ever died. Loyd was a trap I could still walk out of.

I listened to the sad geese in their pen, and realized the crowd was quiet. The snowy plaza was marked with a single line of tracks: in the center of the white square stood a tall young woman in a black dress that hung from one shoulder. Her other shoulder was bare. Her waist, her upper arms and wrists, and her buck-skin moccasins were all decorated with garlands of colored yarn, fur, and sleigh bells; at the crest of her head was a tuft of white eagle down. The sun shone purposefully on her hair. It was cut like Inez's, but hung loose to her waist, swaying as she moved slightly from one leg to the other, her feet barely leaving the ground. She looked graceful and cold.

The sound of drums and then the drummers themselves emerged from the kiva. The four old men took their position at the edge of the plaza and propped their huge drums on their knees without missing a beat. They began a soft chant. A second line of men with blankets draped over their shoulders climbed down from the kiva, also singing, and took their places behind the old drummers.

Then deer arrived, from everywhere. They were men and

boys with black shirts and leggings, white kilts, and deer antlers. Their human features disappeared behind a horizontal band of black paint across the eyes. They moved like deer. They held long sticks in front of them, imitating the deer's cautious, long-legged grace, and they moved their heads anxiously to the side: listening, listening. Sniffing the wind. The woman in black stepped forward shaking her gourd rattle, and they followed her. They *became* deer. They looked exactly as deer would look if you surprised them in a secret rite in the forest, moving in unison, following the irresistible hiss of a maiden's gourd rattle.

I was entranced. More people climbed down out of the kiva. Some were dressed and armed as bow hunters who stalked the deer with patience. One man, who didn't seem to have any realistic function in the drama, was nearly naked and bizarrely painted. His body was ringed with black and white horizontal stripes, he had black rings painted around his eyes and mouth, and his hair was pulled up into a pair of corn-tassel horns. He bounced around like a hysteric, possibly in the interest of keeping warm.

"Who's the striped guy?" I asked Loyd.

"Koshari," he said. "A kachina. He has to do with fertility. His home's in the East."

This struck me as humorous. "The East, as in New York? Area Code 212?"

"The East as in where the sun rises."

"That's all part of his job description?"

"All the kachinas have whole histories and families and live in one of the important places."

"I thought a kachina was a little doll."

"That's right."

"And also a person dressed up?"

"Yep. And a spirit."

"A spirit with a family and a mailing address."

"That's right. When the person dresses up a certain way, the spirit comes into him. And into the doll, if it's made right."

"Okay," I said.

"What?"

"Nothing, just okay. I understand."

He smiled at me sideways. "You think it sounds voodoo?"

"All right, I'm narrow-minded. It sounds kind of voodoo."

We both paid attention to the dancers for a while. I needed to keep a little distance from Loyd.

"Anglos put little dolls of Santa Claus around their houses at Christmas," Loyd said without looking at me.

"Yeah, but it's just a little doll."

"And does it have a wife?"

"Yes," I conceded. "A wife and elves. And they live at the North Pole."

"And sometimes one guy will dress up like Santa Claus. And everybody acts a certain way when he comes around. All happy and generous."

I'd never been put in a position to defend Santa Claus. I'd never even *believed* in Santa Claus. "That's just because he stands for the spirit of Christmas," I said.

"Exactly." Loyd seemed very pleased with himself.

One of the hunters had drawn his bow and shot an invisible arrow into a deer. It gave an anguished shiver, and then the other hunters lifted its limp carcass onto their shoulders.

"I've seen Jesus kachinas too," Loyd said. "I've seen them hanging all over people's houses in Grace."

Now there was a thought to ponder.

Koshari must also have been the spirit of nuisance, or a good belly laugh. The other deer dancers still followed the maiden, ignoring the hunters and their own fallen brother, but Koshari clowned and cut between them, getting in their way and generally interfering with their solemnity. But when one of the youngest dancers lost his antlers, Koshari picked up the head-dress and carefully reattached it by its buckskin laces. The boy kept dancing, eyes front, paying no attention to the hobgoblin who was putting his costume back together.

At some later point, I noticed, Koshari had acquired a new-looking straw cowboy hat, which he cocked ridiculously on one of his horns. I had a feeling it wasn't the Navajo he was aping here. He walked duck-footed with a John Wayne swagger and was using a length of two-by-four as a gun. He knelt and fired repeatedly at the dancing deer, grandly falling over backward each time. Later he stalked them, trailing his gun in the snow and tripping over it with admirably practiced body comedy.

The deer eventually retreated to the cliff, and the plaza filled with two lines of new dancers—a row of black-clad women and a row of men in white kilts—whose bodies beat a loud rhythm as they walked. Their chests were crisscrossed with lines of seashell bells. The two rows of dancers faced one another and stamped their feet, shaking the bells, crowding the air above the plaza with a loud, hollow clicking like summer insects. The men wore crowns of eagle feathers and the women wore spectacular wooden headdresses painted with stylized clouds and slanting blue lines of rain and green blades of corn. This was the corn dance, officially a summer prayer but danced at every important occasion, Loyd said, because you couldn't pray it often enough.

"Most of the dances have to do with rain," he said. "Here, that's what everything hangs on."

Santa Claus kachinas and the beauty of the spectacle notwithstanding, I still felt outside of it. "So you make this deal with the gods. You do these dances and they'll send rain and good crops and the whole works? And nothing bad will ever happen. Right." Prayer had always struck me as more or less a glorified attempt at a business transaction. A rain dance even more so.

I thought I might finally have offended Loyd past the point of no return, like stealing the lobster from frozen foods that time, to get myself fired. But Loyd was just thinking. After a minute he said, "No, it's not like that. It's not making a deal, bad things can still happen, but you want to try not to *cause* them to happen. It has to do with keeping things in balance."

"In balance."

"Really, it's like the spirits have made a deal with *us*."

"And what is the deal?" I asked.

"We're on our own. The spirits have been good enough to let us live here and use the utilities, and we're saying: We know how nice you're being. We appreciate the rain, we appreciate the sun, we appreciate the deer we took. Sorry if we messed up anything. You've gone to a lot of trouble, and we'll try to be good guests."

"Like a note you'd send somebody after you stayed in their house?"

"Exactly like that. 'Thanks for letting me sleep on your couch. I took some beer out of the refrigerator, and I broke a coffee cup. Sorry, I hope it wasn't your favorite one.' "

I laughed because I understood "in balance." I would have called it "keeping the peace," or maybe "remembering your place," but I liked it. "It's a good idea," I said. "Especially since we're still here sleeping on God's couch. We're permanent houseguests."

"Yep, we are. Better remember how to put everything back how we found it."

It was a new angle on religion, for me. I felt a little embarrassed for my blunt interrogation. And the more I thought about it, even more embarrassed for my bluntly utilitarian culture. "The way they tell it to us Anglos, God put the earth here for us to use, westward-ho. Like a special little playground."

Loyd said, "Well, that explains a lot."

It explained a hell of a lot. I said quietly, because the dancers' bells were quieting down, "But where do you go when you've pissed in every corner of your playground?" I looked down at Koshari, who had ditched his cowboy hat and gun and seemed to be negotiating with Jack.

I remembered Loyd one time saying he'd die for the land. And I'd thought he meant patriotism. I'd had no idea. I wondered what he saw when he looked at the Black Mountain mine: the pile of dead tailings, a mountain cannibalizing its own guts and soon to destroy the living trees and home lives of Grace. It was such an American story, it was hardly even interesting. After showing me his secret hot springs, Loyd had told me the Jemez Mountains were being mined savagely for pumice, the odd Styrofoam-like gravel I'd thrown into the air in handfuls. Pumice was required for the manufacture of so-called distressed denim jeans.

To people who think of themselves as God's houseguests, American enterprise must seem arrogant beyond belief. Or stupid. A nation of amnesiacs, proceeding as if there were no other

day but today. Assuming the land could also forget what had
been done to it.

▼▼▼

Our Koshari friend had somehow bought off Jack and taken
away the ladder that was Loyd's and my only way down. He
was standing down there clowning now, pantomiming a
smooching couple and talking at great length, playing to the
crowd, which was laughing. At one point they all applauded.
Loyd was plainly embarrassed.

"What's he saying?" I asked.

"I'll tell you in a minute."

When Koshari had gone to another part of the plaza and
people had stopped staring, I pressed Loyd again.

"He said now we'll have to stay up here together a long
time."

"He talked for five minutes, Loyd. I know he said more than
that."

"Yeah. He said by the time the snow melts, we'll . . . Basically he said in the spring there'd have to be a wedding."

I made a face. "And people *liked* that idea? Of you marrying
me? They were clapping."

"You're not . . ."

He stopped, because a kind man in the crowd had come over
to replace our ladder.

"You're not the Ugly Duck, you know," Loyd said, once the
man had gone.

"They don't even know me. I'm an outsider."

"I'm an outsider too," he said. "They probably know my
mother likes you."

"How would they know that?"

"Word gets around."

"I mean, how does *she* know that? I can't even talk to her."

"Do you like her?"

"Yeah. I do."

"How do you know?"

"I like her hugs. She makes good bread."

"Well, maybe that's why she likes you. You like her bread."
It was hard to stay mad at Loyd.

▼▼▼

The corn dancers had remarkable stamina. Sometimes they
danced in two facing lines, their whole axis rotating around the
plaza like a wheel. At other times the women's line moved into
and through the men's and then they broke into pairs, the men
leading, practically prancing, while the women held their eyes
on the ground with such concentration as to render it fertile. I
would have believed a thunderclap just then, and a summer
rainstorm. They danced on and on. The women's moccasined
feet and thickly wrapped legs moved only a fraction of an inch
with each step, but the restrained action of that step must have
cost more effort than jumping jacks. They did it, and did it, and
did it until early afternoon.

The corn dance was followed by an eagle dance, which
seemed to involve all the young children in the village and a
few older, more skillful dancers. Each one was dressed in a dark
shirt and leggings, a white embroidered kilt, and a hood of white
eagle down, complete with eyes and a hooked beak. Running
from fingertip to fingertip across their backs, they had eagle-
feather wings. The youngsters trembled with concentration as
they crouched low, then rose in unison, raising their wings and
soaring in convincing eaglelike fashion.

It seemed slightly less reverent than the previous dances,
more akin to the childhood phenomenon of the dance recital,
but Loyd said this was also a prayer. Every dance is a prayer.
The eagle carries people's thoughts to the spirits in the sky.
Animal messengers for the small, human hope. As they danced,
the children's lips moved constantly in silent recitation.

"Watch," Loyd said. "One will go toward the east." One did.
It was one of the older, more reliable dancers. He glided with
outstretched wings to the edge of the plaza and past it, down
the central street toward the eastern end of the village. Loyd
explained that he was carrying the mothers' concerns for all the
boys in the armed service.

Koshari was now solemnly busy among the children, who

needed a good deal of prompting and putting-together of cos-tume parts. At several points he left the dancers and made his way around the crowd taking requests for special blessings, spe-cial worries. I asked Loyd to get his attention.

"For my sister," I said, and Loyd translated. "She's in the south. A long way to the south."

Near the end of the dance, one small eagle arched his wings and ran all the way to the southern end of the plaza. The wind lifted his feathers as he paused on the edge of the precipice and for just a second I was sure he would have to fall, or fly.

20

THE SCREAM

The kettle is about to boil, and the telephone rings. He dries his hands slowly and goes to answer it, expecting Mandy Navarrete's fourth child. Christmas Day, a long silent day, will end now with a long unpleasant night. There was a time when deliveries excited him; during the gene-pool study he looked forward to those infant eyes, and setting up his camera and lights. But there is nothing to study now. Mandy Navarrete is all muscles and resistance, a woman who delivers in her own time. Her grandmother Concepcion Navarrete was his first-grade teacher. She was similarly muscular, and disapproved of his family.

He lifts the receiver slowly on the fourth or fifth ring. The voice speaks in hurried Spanish but he answers in English because he knows they can understand. He hasn't spoken Spanish since the day he married Alice. "There is plenty of time," he says. "I know this process. We don't need to be in a panic."

He hears silence, static, several different voices and questions and then the same voice again, emphatically repeating its word: *Secuestrada*. Kidnapped.

"Who is this?"

He listens. The voice is very distant and often breaks. It is a woman, a friend of his daughter. He tries to understand which daughter they mean. *Secuestrada*. Codi has been away for several days but this voice is saying "Hollie." Someone is keeping her. She was in the field alone, with her horse, when they came to blow up the building where she has chemicals for the crop. He understands none of this and lets it sift past him like pollen, like his life. There are many more words in his life than he would like, most of the time.

Hollie, the woman insists, as if she is trying to wake him from sleep. Are you the father? *El padre de Hollie Nolina?* We are very much afraid.

We are very much afraid.

In the first grade she hit a boy and they kept her after school. The boy's name was Simon Bolivar Jones. He was angry at her and had called her vicious names because she climbed to the top of the tall slide the wrong way, up the slide and not the steps, and stood up there and danced, shouting, her hands outstretched. No boy could do it.

"You should let her come home. She hasn't done anything wrong. She's being punished for an act of bravery." He isn't sure whether he has just spoken in Spanish or English.

Sí, the voice answers after a moment. *Claro que sí.*

"Where is she?"

No estamos seguros. We think they must have taken her into Honduras, where they're camped. A large patrol has gone to look for her. Thirty people, more than half of them from the village where she lives. There were more who wanted to go. Even an eight-year-old boy. Hallie has many friends.

Even an eight-year-old boy. Thirty people.

The words are so much fine dust suspended in the air before him, in the long, trapezoidal block of sunlight from the window. He examines the dust. He sees the word "Hallie." It was Codi who stood up and danced on the slide.

"You should let her come home," he says again. He can remember precisely the muscular line of Mrs. Navarrete's disapproving jaw. "Let my daughter come home now."

The voice rejects this statement, says nothing.

He touches the corner of his eye and is surprised to find moisture on his fingertips. He stares at an iron coal bucket beside the fireplace, trying to recall its history, how it came to him. He thinks, for no reason, that this iron coal bucket could save his life, if only he could remember. He remembers instead that he no longer delivers babies, the telephone call could not possibly be Mandy Navarrete. It is a woman from another country, who knows his daughter. He is trying hard not to look at the dust in the air but the sun has illuminated each particle so that it glows. Each word burns.

"Is there something I can do?" he asks finally. "I know she has friends in the Ministry of Agriculture. Do they know?"

"Everyone knows. Our Ministry of Agriculture, your Ministry of Agriculture." There is a pause. "You understand that this occurs every day. We're a nation of bereaved families. The only difference this time is that it happens to be an American. It happens to be Hallie." The voice weakens again, and he waits, and it goes on. "We sent a telegram to your President and the NBC. We think if they are embarrassed enough by their contras, they could do something."

If they are embarrassed enough.

"Wait. Let me take down the number where you are. So I can call you tomorrow."

"I'm in the office of a church in Managua. Nobody here knows anything. You can call the Ministry of Agriculture if you want. Or your President. He is the responsible party."

He understands that she is being as helpful as she can. She is a kind, tired voice. He doesn't want her to hang up, because then his life will begin. There is a pause while she talks to someone else who is there with her, and then she returns to him and says, "I'm sorry."

"Is there anything more? Besides waiting?"

"I'm sorry. There is nothing."

Carefully he puts down the receiver and looks at the air in front of the window in this empty room. The dust. He listens inside himself for a long time before he understands that it's the teakettle that is screaming.

COSIMA

21

THE TISSUE OF HEARTS

Hallie was somebody's prisoner. Whether my eyes were open or closed, I saw her with a white cloth tied tightly over her mouth. That's the only image that would ever come.

If she couldn't scream, I did. I was in every way unreasonable, especially with the kids at school. Even at the time, I was lucid enough to be thankful that Rita had dropped out. One member of my family had already yelled at her; she didn't have to know that neither one of us had all our tires on the road.

The students had tried to be cooperative. They went to Tucson to assist the Stitch and Bitch Club, as I'd requested, and found the city to be a superb adventure. They discovered a video arcade; Raymo sweet-talked more than ten young women into buying piñatas; there were rumors that Connie Muñoz gave Hector Jones a hand job in the back seat of the bus on the way home. What did I expect? They were teenagers. I knew that, but still I screamed at them because Black Mountain was poisoning their mother's milk and all they cared about was sex and a passing grade.

I had rational intentions. I talked about evapotranspiration and rain forests and oxygen in the biosphere, how everything was connected. The last virgin timber cleared and milled to make way for a continent of landfills choking on old newspapers. It was a poetic lecture. Marta made the mistake of asking me how much of this poetry was going to be on the test.

I glowered. "Your life is the test. If you flunk this one, you die."

The whole front row looked stunned. Their pens stopped moving.

"What you people learn for a test you forget the next day. That's bullshit. That's a waste of your brains and my time. If I can't teach you something you'll remember, then I haven't even been here this year." I crossed my arms and glared at them. "You kids think this pollution shit is not your problem, right? Somebody will clean up the mess. It's not your fault. Well, your attitude stinks. You're as guilty as anybody. Do you, or do you not, think the world was put here for you to use?"

Nobody was fool enough to answer. I observed during the long silence that half the kids in the room were wearing stone-washed jeans. I yanked up Hector Jones by the arm and made an example of him. I have to admit I disliked Hector partially for unfair reasons: his father was a former hoodlum named Simon Bolivar Jones who'd been noticeably unkind to me in school.

"Stand up here," I said. "Show everybody your jeans. Nice, right? Turn around. Nice ass, Hector. Wonderful jeans. They were half worn out before you bought them, right?" I smacked Hector lightly on the butt and let him sit down.

"You know how they make those? They wash them in a big machine with this special kind of gravel they get out of volcanic mountains. The prettiest mountains you ever saw in your life. But they're fragile, like a big pile of sugar. Levi Strauss or whoever goes in there with bulldozers and chainsaws and cuts down the trees and rips the mountainside to hell, so that all us lucky Americans can wear jeans that look like somebody threw them in the garbage before we got them."

"Trees grow back," Raymo said. Raymo was a brave young man.

"Excuse me?"

He cupped his hands around his mouth and spoke as if I were his deaf grandmother: "Trees . . . grow . . . back."

I cupped my hands around my mouth and said, just as loudly, "Not if the whole . . . damn . . . mountain is gone, they don't."

"Well, there's other mountains."

"Sure, there's some other mountains," I said, feeling that I might explode if I weren't careful. "If you got hit by a truck, Raymo, I guess your ma would say, 'Well, I have some other kids.' "

About half the class thought that was funny. The other half was probably trying to figure out how to get out of my classroom alive.

I stared them down, ticking like a bomb. "Sure. Trees grow back. Even a whole rain forest could grow back, in a couple hundred years, maybe. But who's going to make it happen? If you had to pay the real price for those jeans—the cost and the time and the work of bringing that mountain back to life instead of leaving it dead—those pretty jeans would have cost you a hundred dollars."

I felt strangely high. Furious and articulate. "Think about the gas you put in a car," I said. "The real cost. Not just pumping it out of the ground and refining it and shipping it, but also cleaning up the oil spills and all the junk that goes into the air when it gets burned. That's part of what it costs, but you're not paying it. Gas ought to be twenty dollars a gallon, so you're getting a real good deal. But soon the bill comes due, and we pay it, or we eat dirt. The ultimate MasterCharge."

I can't swear they were listening, but they were watching me carefully. Thirty-six blue eyes ticked back and forth as I paced the floor in front of my desk.

"If Grace gets poisoned, if all these trees die and this land goes to hell, you'll just go somewhere else, right? Like the great pioneers, Lewis and Clark. Well, guess what, kiddos, the wilderness is used up." I walked around my little square of floor like a trapped cat. "People can forget, and forget, and forget, but the land has a memory. The lakes and the rivers are still hanging on to the DDT and every other insult we ever gave them. Lake Superior is a superior cesspool. The fish have cancer. The ocean is getting used up. The damn *air* is getting used up."

I pointed at the ceiling, meaning to indicate the sky. "You know what's up there? Ozone. It's this stuff in the atmosphere that acts like an umbrella."

I stopped and reconsidered this effete analogy. Teenagers who won't use condoms aren't impressed by the need for an umbrella. I surveyed the class thoughtfully and demanded, "Whose Dad or Mom ever worked in the smelter?"

About half the hands went up, reluctantly.

"You know what they did up there, right? One way or another they were around thousand-degree hot metal. You ever see them dressed for work? They wore coveralls like Mr. Neil Armstrong walking on the moon, and a big shield over their faces, right?"

They nodded, relieved, I suppose, that I wasn't going to single them out for humiliation. I sat on the desk and crossed my arms. "Imagine that's you, working up there with that hot metal in your face. Now, somebody rips that mask off you while you're working. Goodbye face. Goodbye nose and eyelids, beauty queens. You're dead."

They might well have been dead, for all the sound they made.

"That's what the ozone layer does for us, boys and girls, it's a big face shield in the sky." I was skipping a few steps here, but not really exaggerating the consequences. Not at all. I attempted to lower my voice and sound faintly reasonable. "And it's slipping away from us. There's a big hole in it over the South Pole. When you use a spray can you make that hole bigger. There's something in most aerosol cans and refrigerators and air conditioners, called chlorofluorocarbons, that neutralizes the ozone. Factories are still making tons of it, right now."

I suspect "chlorofluorocarbons" was the largest word ever spoken within the walls of Grace High, and I'm fairly sure also that nobody forgot it for at least the rest of the day.

After the bell rang, Connie Muñoz eyed me and said, "Miss, I seen you wear stone-washed jeans to school sometimes." The other kids were already out of there like bats out of hell.

"You're right," I said. "I didn't know about the mountains when I bought them. Just like Hector didn't, and you didn't."

"Yeah?" She chewed her gum and held me under a neutral,

military sort of gaze. I'd publicly humiliated her new boyfriend; this would require some diplomacy.

"I've been learning a lot of this stuff just lately," I told her. "I'm not saying I'm not part of the problem."

"So how come you're so mad at us, Miss?"

I felt conscious of my height, and embarrassed. "Connie, I don't really know. Because I'm guilty too, I guess. And now I'm trying to fix it all at once."

A hint of life came into her eyes. "Don't sweat it," she said. "I think it's cool that you cuss and stuff when you're mad. Everybody was paying attention. What you said was right, these guys just think when they use something up there's always going to be more."

"I shouldn't have cussed," I said. "I'm supposed to be setting an example. And I shouldn't have picked on Hector the way I did."

She laughed and cracked her gum. "Hector Jones is a dickhead."

▼▼▼

I had dinner at Doc Homer's house. I'd done so every night since I got back from Santa Rosalia and found out Hallie had been kidnapped. If I badgered him enough, I kept thinking, he would have something more to tell me. But he couldn't remember anything. If I'd ever doubted Hallie was his favorite, there was no question about it now—I'd never seen him so affected by any event in our lives. He still functioned, cooked for himself and went to work, but it was only an obstinate ritual; he was a mess. I'd found some of his medication bottles in a cache in the living room, inside an old iron coal bucket. There was no way to know whether he was taking them. Half the time he talked to me as if I were six years old.

"Who was the person you spoke with on the phone?" I asked again. "Was she somebody in the government? There's got to be somebody we can call." I cautiously eyed the plate he set down in front of me. Doc Homer had prepared liver with steamed apples and yellow squash. In certain restaurants things like this passed for *haute cuisine*, I knew, but here it passed for weird. It was getting to where he'd combine anything he found in his refrigerator. I'd started shopping for him, lest he get down to refried beans and ice cream.

"She suggested that we call the President of the United States," he said.

I set my fork down on the table. He'd said this quite a number of times before. "I think I *will* call the President." I moved my chair back from the table. It was an idle threat; I'd probably just get a polite recording. But I knew Doc Homer wouldn't want what he would consider an absurd long-distance call on his bill.

"I understand you have a boyfriend," he said, cutting his liver and apples into small pieces.

"What do they think will happen? Did this person you talked to sound real worried? Or did she say this was a routine kind of thing? Sometimes they'll just take a foreign hostage to get attention and then they'll let them go the next day. She's probably back at her house already." I knew this was unlikely. The contras, as I understood it, didn't need attention. They were fully supported by the richest sugar daddy in the modern world.

"He drinks, Codi. He will take advantage of you."

I stared at Doc Homer for a long time. "Not anymore," I said. "He doesn't drink anymore. And he couldn't take advantage of me if he wanted to. I'm as sweet and innocent as the Berlin Wall. Your concern is approximately two decades too late."

"My concern is for your welfare."

"Your concern." I picked up slices of apple and ate them with my fingers, to annoy him. "I'm going to have to go down there. I can get a bus to Tucson tonight and a plane to Managua and be there tomorrow." I doubted it was this easy.

The teakettle boiled and he jumped up. He seemed edgy. He got out the filter paper and slowly set up the drip machine for coffee, carefully positioning each part of the apparatus as if it were some important experiment in organic chemistry.

"I told you it wasn't a good idea," he said, pouring boiling water into the funnel. I waited for some further clue. He could be evaluating any mistake I'd made since age three.

"What idea is that?" I prompted, since he didn't go on.

"Loyd Peregrina."

We both watched the water pass through the dark grounds, absorbing their color and substance. He'd never mentioned Loyd's name before; I was surprised he knew it. I wondered whether Doc Homer had a whole other life in his head, in which he dispensed kind, fatherly advice. This gulf—between what Doc Homer believed himself to be and what he was—brought out the worst in me, or the most blunt. "Don't worry about Loyd Peregrina," I said. "I can't get hurt now. I'm leaving him this time. It's just a short-term thing."

"He won't elevate your life."

"Damn it, you don't know the first thing about my life. What's to elevate? I'm a medical-school dropout who works graveyard shifts in quick-marts."

"You left the profession by choice. We've established that."

"Okay, so I walked out the door with my eyes open. What did I choose instead? What am I good at? Name one thing."

He balked. I knew he would. Doc Homer wasn't fluent in the language of compliments.

"I have no career, no kids, not even a place I consider home. Basically I'm a bag lady with an education."

"That's a preposterous assessment."

"How would you know? You don't really see me, you just see what you want. You take pictures of people and turn them into rock walls."

"That is not what I do. I begin with a picture in my head, from the past. I try to duplicate it from the images I have at hand."

This was a new one. "I don't believe I give a damn about the images you have at hand." I lowered my voice. The quickest way to lose points with Doc Homer was to lose control. I said, "You always just wanted Hallie and me to be above everybody in Grace."

"You *were* above your peers."

I snorted at that. "I was as trashy as Connie Muñoz and Rita Cardenal, without half their guts or one-tenth of their sex appeal. I was ugly and embarrassed to be alive."

Doc Homer had a strange way of actually getting quieter when he raised his voice. "My daughters were not trash," he said.

I looked him square in the eye. "I got pregnant when I was fifteen."

"I know. I watched you bury the baby in the riverbed."

I felt an odd flush in my neck and face. For about a minute we both listened to the dripping of the coffeepot. Then I said, "Why do you lie about everything?"

"I've never told you anything but the truth."

"You've never told me anything, period. You said you and mother came from Illinois. But you came from here. You've got a whole family lying up there in the damn graveyard."

"We did come here from Illinois. I was stationed there, and went to medical school there. We moved back here after the war."

"What kind of war had people stationed in Illinois?" I asked absurdly, close to tears. "I'm sorry, but in history class they never told us about the Midwestern Front."

"Alice's family despised me."

I stopped, remembering how Viola had averted her eyes and said, "that family went downhill," the day I discovered Homero Nolina up in the cemetery. The red-haired Gracela sister with the temper, who married Conrado Nolina and produced a legacy of trash—that was my father's family. What he believed he came from, and what we still were. Auburn-haired and angry, living in exile in our own town. There wasn't enough air in the kitchen for me to breathe, and get all this in.

"So you, what, ran off to the army. Got yourself educated on the G.I. Bill, and then came back here as the mighty prodigal doctor with his beautiful new wife, and acted like nobody could touch you."

I watched him closely, but could read nothing. I couldn't even *see* him, really; I had no idea how he'd look to a stranger. Old? Sick? Mean-spirited? He poured coffee into two mugs and gave the larger one to me.

"Thank you," I said.

"You're welcome."

"Why did you come back here? If it was so important to you to start over, you could have gone anywhere. You could have stayed back there in Illinois."

Doc Homer sat down opposite me. He clenched and unclenched his left hand, then spread it flat on the table and examined it abstractly, as if it were a patient. I looked at the framed photograph on the wall over his head: his portrait of a hand that wasn't a hand, but five cacti with invisible spines.

"Why do you suppose the poets talk about hearts?" he asked me suddenly. "When they discuss emotional damage? The tissue of hearts is tough as a shoe. Did you ever sew up a heart?"

I shook my head. "No, but I've watched. I know what you mean." The walls of a heart are thick and strong, and the surgeons use heavy needles. It takes a good bit of strength, but it pulls together neatly. As much as anything it's like binding a book.

"The seat of human emotion should be the liver," Doc Homer said. "That would be an appropriate metaphor: we don't hold love in our hearts, we hold it in our livers."

I understand exactly. Once in ER I saw a woman who'd been stabbed everywhere, most severely in the liver. It's an organ with the consistency of layer upon layer of wet Kleenex. Every attempt at repair just opens new holes that tear and bleed. You try to close the wound with fresh wounds, and you try and you try and you don't give up until there's nothing left.

▼▼▼

For Christmas, Loyd had given me an Apache burden basket. It was exquisitely woven, striped with the colors of dried grass, and around its open mouth hung tin bells on leather thongs that made whispery, tinkling sounds. It wasn't much bigger than a teacup. The night he gave it to me in Santa Rosalia I felt it would easily hold all my burdens, forever. Now it hung on the wall over my bed, and at night I looked at it and wept for my own stupidity in trusting that life could be kind.

I apologized to my classes. I couldn't see trying to maintain the recommended authoritative distance; I told them my sister had been kidnapped and that I was scared to death. I told them everything seemed very serious to me now, including things like the ozone layer. The kids were extremely quiet. I don't think any adult had ever apologized to them before. From the store-room we got down a pre–World War II map that showed all the world's climatic zones, and we found Nicaragua, Honduras, Costa Rica, El Salvador. The shapes and names of many nations had changed during the lifetime of that map, but not the climatic zones. We talked more calmly about the rain forest and the manner in which fast-food chains were cutting it down to make hamburger farms. We talked about poor countries and rich coun-tries and DDT in the food chain, and the various ways our gar-bage comes home to us. The memory of the land. My students understood these things perfectly well. There is nothing boring about the prospect of extinction.

On Friday I took the day off to make phone calls. Hallie had left me a list of emergency telephone numbers, mostly specu-lative, and I called them all. It took the whole morning. I got nowhere with the State Department and the U.S. Department of Agriculture, and ended up with the Nicaraguan Ministry of Agriculture. Viola helped me contend with the impenetrable Spanish of international operators. Emelina sat on my other side holding my hand, wringing the fingers, apparently forgetting that it wasn't hers. Mason and the baby sat on the floor in front of us, silent, wondering as children always must wonder in a crisis what terrible thing they had done to wreck the world.

We learned nothing useful. They were sure now that Hallie had been taken across the border into Honduras, probably to a camp where many other prisoners were held. It was a well-outfitted camp; they had Sony radios and high-quality C-rations. It made me smile, a little, to think Hallie might be eating C-rations I'd dutifully paid for with my taxes. Dinner was on me. So were the land mines.

I spoke with a dozen secretaries of this and that and finally with the Minister of Agriculture himself. He knew Hallie. He talked for a long time about what an extraordinary person she was; it made me suspicious that she was dead, and I started crying. Viola took the phone and translated until I was fit to talk again. The Minister promised me she wasn't dead. He would call me the minute they knew anything at all. He was fairly sure the contras took her by mistake, not knowing she was an American citizen, and now were probably confused as to how to release her without generating too much bad publicity. He asked, had I called the President of the United States?

In the meantime, Hallie's letters still came to the Post Office box. I knew she had mailed them before she was kidnapped, but their appearance frightened me. They looked postmarked and cheerful and real, but they were ghosts, mocking what I'd believed was a solid connection between us. I'd staked my heart on that connection. If I could still get letters like this when Hallie was gone or in trouble, what had I ever really had?

I didn't read them. I saved them. I would open them all once I'd heard her voice on the phone. I wouldn't be fooled again.

▼▼▼

At some point between Christmas and mid-January, Grace became famous. The several hundred piñatas planted in Tucson had grown into great, branching trees of human interest, which bore fruit in the form of articles with names like "This Art's Not for Breaking" and "What Piñatas!" in slick magazines all over the Southwest. The Stitch and Bitch Club's efforts in papier-mâché became a hot decorator item in gentrified adobe neighborhoods like the one in Tucson that Hallie used to call Barrio Volvo.

It was the birds that caused the stir, but because it was there, people were also reading my urgent one-page plea for the life of Grace. Where Mayor Jimmy Soltovedas's repeated calls to the press had failed, Stitch and Bitch succeeded: our story became known. Hardly a day passed without some earnest reporter calling up to get a statement from Norma Galvez. The club designated her the media spokeswoman; Doña Althea was more colorful, but given to unprintable remarks. Ditto for Viola, who was even more unprintable because she spoke English.

But when a scout crew from CBS News came to town, they wanted the Doña. They sat in on a meeting at the American Legion hall and zeroed in on the Stitch and Bitch figurehead with her authority and charm and all she represented in the way of local color. They got some of the meeting on tape, but made an appointment to come back on Saturday with a crew to interview the Doña in her home. Norma Galvez would be (for safety's sake) her interpreter. By the time Saturday morning came, when CBS rolled into town in their equipment Jeeps like Jesus into Jerusalem on Palm Sunday, the whole town was anticipating the visit of what Viola had been calling "the B.S. News."

There were about fifty of us packed into Doña Althea's living room, just there to watch. The Doña looked as she always looked: tiny, imperious, dressed in black, with her long white braid pinned around her head like a crown. As a concession to the cameras she clutched an embroidered shawl around her shoulders.

She refused to close the restaurant, though, and it was lunchtime, so there were still comings and goings and much banging of pots. Cecil, the sound man, had to run his equipment off the outlet in the kitchen, since it was the only part of the house that had been wired in the twentieth century. "Ladies, we're just going to have to be cozy in here," he said, turning sideways and scooting between two Althea sisters to reach the plug.

"Son of a," he said, when one of the sisters tripped over his cord and unplugged it for the third or fourth time. The Althea in question stopped in her tracks and looked for a minute as if she might deck him, but decided to serve her customers instead. She was so burdened with plates it's lucky Cecil didn't get *menudo* in his amps.

The director of the crew had the Doña sit in a carved chair that normally stood in her bedroom and held the TV. Two men carried it out, sat her down in it, and arranged vases of peacock feathers at her feet. "Just cross your ankles," the director told her. Norma translated, and the Doña complied, scowling fiercely. She looked like a Frida Kahlo painting. "Okay," he said, wiping sweat off his forehead. He was a heavy man, dressed in Italian shoes and a Mexican wedding shirt, though his mood was not remotely festive. "Okay," he repeated. "Let's go."

There was a camera on the interviewer and two cameras were on Doña Althea: bright, hot lights everywhere. A crew member dabbed the interviewer's nose and forehead with a powder puff, eyed the Doña once, and backed off. The interviewer introduced himself as Malcolm Hunt. He seemed young and wore an outfit that suggested designer-label big-game hunting or possibly Central American revolutions. He probably meant well. He carefully explained to Doña Althea that they would edit the tape later, using only the best parts. If she wanted to go back and repeat anything, she could do that. He suggested that she ignore the cameras and just speak naturally to him. Norma Galvez translated all this. The Doña squinted at the lights, fixed her scornful gaze on a point just above the kitchen door, and shouted all her answers in that direction. Cecil took it personally and slinked around behind the steam table.

Mr. Hunt began. "Doña Althea, how long have you lived in this canyon?"

"Desde antes que tú cagabas en tus pañales!"

Norma Galvez shifted a little in her chair and said, "Ah, since before your mother was changing your diapers." The Doña scowled at Norma briefly, and one of the Altheas laughed from the kitchen.

Mr. Hunt smiled and looked concerned. "When did your family come to this country?"

The Doña said something to the effect that her family had been on this land before the Gringos took over and started calling it America. The prospectors came and mined out the damn gold, and the Black Mountain company mined out the damn copper, and then they fired all the men and sent them home to plant trees, and now, naturally, they were pissing in the river and poisoning the orchards.

Mrs. Galvez paused. "A long time ago," she said.

Mr. Hunt lost his composure for the first time. He made an odd, guttural noise and looked at Mrs. Galvez, who spread her hands.

"You want an exact translation?"

"Please."

She gave it to him.

It wasn't the afternoon anybody had expected. Malcolm Hunt

kept adjusting his posture and his eyebrows and appearing to start the whole interview over, framing new questions that sounded like opening lines.

"The Black Mountain Mining Company is polluting—and now actually diverting—the river that has been the lifeblood of this town for centuries. Why is this happening?"

"Because they're a greedy bunch of goat fuckers" (Mrs. Galvez said "so-and-sos") "and they got what they wanted from this canyon and now they have to squeeze it by the balls before they let go."

"They're actually damming the river to avoid paying fines to the Environmental Protection Agency, isn't that right? Because the river is so polluted with acid?"

The Doña waited for Norma's translation, then nodded sharply.

"What do you think could stop the dam from being built, at this point?"

"*Dinamita.*"

Mr. Hunt appeared reluctant to follow this line of questioning to its conclusion. "In a desperate attempt to save your town," he said, trying another new tack, "you and the other ladies of Grace have made hundreds of piñatas. Do you really think a piñata can stop a multinational corporation?"

"Probably not."

"Then why go to all the trouble?"

"What do you think we should do?"

She had him there; Malcolm Hunt looked stumped. He looked from Norma to the Doña and back to Norma. "Well," he said, "most people write their congressmen."

"*No sé.* We don't write such good letters. I don't think we have any congressman out here anyway, do we? We have a mayor, Jimmy Soltovedas. But I don't think we have any *congressman.*" She pronounced the word in English, making it stand out from the rest of her speech like a curse or a totally new concept. "*Si hay,*" she went on, "If we do, I haven't seen him. Probably he doesn't give a shit. And also we don't know how to use dynamite. What we know how to do is make nice things out of paper. Flowers, piñatas, *cascarones*. And we sew things. That's what we ladies here do."

I smiled, thinking of Jack following old habits, turning around three times on the kitchen floor and lying down to dream of a nest in the grass.

"But why peacocks, what's the history?" Malcolm persisted, after hearing the fully translated explanation. "Tell me about the peacocks."

"What do you want to know about peacocks?" the Doña asked, giving him a blank look. The full Spanish name for peacock is *pavo real*, "royal turkey," but Mrs. Galvez let that one slip by.

"How did they get here?"

Doña Althea lifted her head, adjusted her shawl, leaned back and put her hands on her knees, which were spread wide apart under her black skirt. *"Hace cien años,"* she began. "More than one hundred years ago, my mother and her eight sisters came to this valley from Spain to bring light and happiness to the poor miners, who had no wives. They were the nine Gracela sisters: Althea, Renata, Hilaria, Carina, Julietta, Ursolina, Violetta, Camila, and Estrella."

She pronounced the names musically and slowly, drawing out the syllables and rolling the r's. They were the names of fairy princesses, but the story, in her high, sustained voice, was Biblical. It was the Genesis of Grace. And of Hallie and me. Our father's own grandmother—mother of Homero Nolina up in the graveyard—was one of those princesses: the red-haired, feisty one. I could picture her barefoot, her hair curly like Hallie's and coming loose from its knot. I saw her standing in the open front door of her house, shaking a soup spoon at her sisters' arrogant children who came to tease her own. Perhaps she was Ursolina, the little bear.

When Hallie and I were little I used to make up endless stories of where we came from, to lull her to sleep. She would steal into my bed after Doc Homer was asleep, and I would hold her, trying to protect her from the wind that blows on the heads of orphans and isolates them from the living, shouting children who have inherited the earth. "We came from Zanzibar," I would whisper with my mouth against her hair. "We came from Ireland. Our mother was a queen. The Queen of Potatoes."

I could never know the truth of my mother, but there was another story now. Another side. I closed my eyes and listened to Doña Althea with the joy of a child. I don't know what they heard on the CBS news. I heard a bedtime story thirty years late.

22

ENDANGERED PLACES

It rained and rained in Gracela Canyon. February passed behind a mask of clouds. It seemed like either the end of the world or the beginning.

The orchards, whose black branch tips had been inspected throughout the winter for latent signs of life, suddenly bloomed, all at once: pears, plums, apples, quince, their normal staggered cycle compressed by the odd weather into a single nuptial burst. Through my classroom window I watched drenched blossoms falling like wet snow.

Water, in Grace, is an all-or-nothing proposition, like happiness. When you have rain you have more than enough, just as when you're happy and in love and content with your life you can't remember how you ever could have felt cheated by fate. And vice versa. I knew, abstractly, that I'd been happy, but now that I was in pain again, that happiness was untouchable. It was a garish color picture of a place I had not been. Memory runs along deep, fixed channels in the brain, like electricity along its conduits; only a cataclysm can make the electrons rear up in shock and slide over into another channel. The human mind seems doomed to believe, as simply as a rooster believes, that where we are *now* is the only possibility.

But it isn't. In spite of the promise of plenty that dripped from the rooftops and gushed down Gracela Canyon's ravines throughout February, the winter rains would soon dry up. Then there would not be another drop until July. During those brittle months the taste and smell of rain would be lost to us, beyond the recollection even of children and the deepest root tips of trees. That is the way of the seasons in a desert place. Only the river ran continuously. The river was Grace's memory of water.

▼▼▼

We heard nothing from Hallie. First I tried to tell myself she was already out of danger. In the past, the two-week delay of her letters had caused me to keep a distrustful eye on Hallie, like a star so many light years away it could have exploded long ago while we still watched its false shine. Now I tried the reverse psychology: we would hear, soon, that she'd been safe while we worried.

But we didn't, and I gave over to panic. I began to call Managua every week. The Minister of Agriculture, whose secretary now knew me by voice, said there wasn't any reason for me to fly down to Nicaragua; there was nothing I could do there but wait, which—he implied—I was doing badly enough where I was. He really was not unkind, just frustrated, like any of us. He pointed out that Hallie was an exceptional person, to those of us who loved her, but not an exceptional case—the contras made daily forays across the border to attack workers in their fields, sometimes even schoolchildren. Thousands of civilians had died. "If you came here," he said, "you would see." Every home had a framed photograph on a table that stood for a fresh empty space in the family, he said. Teachers and community workers were particularly at risk.

He said I might try making Hallie's status known to the general public in the United States. It could pressure her captors to show restraint; or, he warned me frankly, it could do the opposite.

I knew nothing else to do, so I wrote letters. Emelina helped. We papered her kitchen table with letters in progress. I drafted mine on stationery from the Grace High School principal's office, but the letterhead intimidated Emelina, who preferred lined paper from her kids' loose-leaf notebooks. Viola put a request to the Stitch and Bitch Club, and after that we had volunteers in Emelina's kitchen for nightly letter-writing sessions. I dictated the main ideas and then they all got the hang of it. I looked up who had voted for sending the guns, and who had voted against, and either way we tried to work it in. I expect we sent out more than a thousand letters. When we lost track of which congressmen we'd written, we wrote them again. We wrote radio stations and any other public entity we believed might be reading its mail. Sometimes I stopped and laid my head on my arms. Emelina would massage the back of my neck and say nothing, because we both suspected words were beside the point.

There may have been publicity we never knew about. We didn't get the *New York Times* in Grace. I do know there was a short piece in the Tucson morning paper, in the "Money" section, of all things, right next to an article about how to reduce your mortgage with twice-monthly payments. There was a small, smiling photo of Hallie, who was identified as a former employee of the University Extension Service. The reporter had called up the Minister of Agriculture as I'd suggested, and said that he "alleged" she had been kidnapped by agitators based in Honduras. This was followed by a much longer quote from a state senator who said the Nicaraguan civil war was a tragedy, and that the United States was doing its best to bring democracy to the region, and that no U.S. citizen could go there without expecting to be caught in crossfire.

The reporter, believing I would be pleased, sent me the clipping along with a note wishing my family all the best. The breadth of his ignorance made me feel hopeless, as I've sometimes felt in dreams, when the muscles dissolve and escape is impossible. I wept uncontrollably all day. At school I asked my students to read *Silent Spring* for an hour while I put my head down on my desk and cried. They were subdued. I suspected people in Grace of walking around me on tiptoe now, the way a town might avert its eyes when its resident crazy lady hikes up her skirt and scratches an itch and swears at the blackbirds watching from a telephone wire.

I stopped going to Doc Homer's for dinner. We were in the

worst position to comfort one another. I guessed he could go on about his routine—that had always been the core of his resilience—but I don't think I'd slept a single night since she'd been taken, and I was reaching an abnormal state of exhaustion. I fought off hallucinations. Late one night Hallie appeared in my bedroom doorway, very small, looking up at me. With those same eyes she used to ask without words to crawl into my bed.

"Hallie, I'm trying so hard. But I don't know how to save you."

She turned on stocking feet and walked back into the dark.

I got up and rifled my desk drawers till I found the newspaper clipping with her picture. I looked at it hard, trying to convince myself that Hallie wasn't a child. I had the black-and-red afghan bundled around me but I felt chilled and hard as a frozen branch. My hands shook. I tucked the clipping into an envelope and wrote a note to the President of the United States, begging him please just to look at her. "This is my only sister," I told him. "I'm coming to understand responsibility. You gave those men a righteous flag to wave and you gave them guns. If she dies, what will you tell me?" I licked the envelope and sealed it. I knew the address by heart.

We began to get letters back, to the effect that the matter would certainly bear investigation. They weren't form letters, each one was typed by a different secretary, but they all said the same thing. It surprised me to see how a meaningless phrase repeated again and again begins to resemble truth.

▼▼▼

In the middle of that gray month Emelina's youngest son learned to walk. I was alone with him when it happened. The sun had come out briefly as I walked home from school, and the baby and I were both anxious to be outdoors. Emelina asked if I could just not let him eat any real big bugs, and I promised to keep an eye out. I settled with a book in the courtyard, which was radiant with sudden sunlight. The flowers were beaten down, their bent-over heads bejeweled with diamond droplets like earrings on sad, rich widows.

For quite a while now Nicholas had been cruising the perimeters of his world, walking confidently from house to tree to lawn chair to wall, so long as he had something to hold on to. Sometimes what he touched was nothing more than apparent security. Today I watched the back of his red overalls with interest as he cruised along a patch of damp, tall four-o'clocks, lightly touching their leaves. He had no idea how little support they offered.

He spotted a hummingbird. It buzzed around the red tubes of a potted penstemon that stood by itself in the center of the courtyard. His eyes followed the bird as it darted up and down, a high-strung gem; Nicholas wanted it. For a long time he frowned at the brick path that lay between himself and the bird, and then he let go of the wall. He took one step and then more, buoyed up by some impossible anti-gravity. After two steps the hummingbird was gone, but Nicholas still headed for the air it had occupied, his hands grasping at vapor. It was as if an invisible balloon floated above him, tied to his overall strap, dragging him along from above. He swayed and swaggered, stabbing one toe at a time down at the ground, pivoting on the ball of one foot, and then suddenly the string was cut and down he bumped on his well-padded bottom. He looked at me and screamed.

"You're walking," I told Nicholas. "I promise you it gets easier. The rest of life doesn't, but this really does."

I stayed out there with my book for the rest of the afternoon, surreptitiously watching as he tried it over and over. He was completely undeterred by failure. The motivation packed in that small body was a miracle to see. I wished I could bottle that passion for accomplishment and squeeze out some of the elixir, a drop at a time, on my high school students. They would move mountains.

▾▾▾

The Stitch and Bitch Club was now wealthy beyond historic measure. On the heels of the blockbuster piñata sale came a steady flow of donations from the outside. Loulou Campbell, the treasurer, had always kept the club's funds in a coffee can in the back of the Baptist Grocery where she worked. But when the volume of cash filled twelve baby-formula cans she grew nervous. Loulou opened an account at the bank and turned the passbook over to Doña Althea, whose years as a top-notch restaurateur had made her somewhat more comfortable with affluence.

The cash languished in its vault while the women pondered its meaning. Having sent their peacocks out into the world like Noah's dove over the flood, they waited for the world to inspire their next move.

Inspiration came in the guise of an art dealer from Tucson. His name was Sean Rideheart, and he was a funny, charming little man who understood people as well as he understood beauty. The spectacular popularity of the Grace piñatas (some had been resold for as much as five hundred dollars) moved him to make a pilgrimage to the source. Mr. Rideheart was already an expert and he became a connoisseur; before he ever set foot in Grace he could already recognize the works of several individual piñata makers. Of particular value were those made by Mrs. Nuñez, who had been so resourceful with her *Compton's Children's Encyclopedia*. He wanted to know this town better.

I met him on his third visit, when he came to meet Viola. There was no school that day—I believe it was the birthday of a President—and I was staring at clouds. Emelina didn't bother me on my bad days; I was allowed to do nothing, not even pretend to feel better, which I recognized as a rare act of human kindness and I appreciated. I spent the morning sitting on Emelina's front porch, watching our neighbor, whose roof was on the same level with our floorboards. We were having another brief break in the rain, as if the clouds had called a time-out to muster their resources. Our neighbor Mr. Pye was taking advantage of the moment to climb up and inspect his roof.

"Got a few leaks," he called out in a friendly way. I waved back, unsure of how to answer. I watched the top of his engineer's cap bob down the ladder out of sight, and shortly thereafter, appear again. Mr. Pye negotiated the ladder with one hand while balancing a small, old-looking cardboard box against his hip. It made me think of the surprises coming out of the kiva at Santa Rosalia Pueblo. Mr. Pye knelt near his chimney pipe and opened the box like a birthday present, carefully lifting out some shingles. They were green, and shaped like the ace of spades— an exact match to the ones on his roof, only a little brighter. Grass-green rather than the green of old bronze. I remembered once, months ago, looking at that roof of antique shingles and assuming them to be irreplaceable.

Curiosity overcame my lassitude. "How'd you match those shingles?" I called out.

He looked at me, puzzled.

"Where'd you get the new shingles? They're a perfect match."

He examined the shingles in his hands, as if noticing this for the first time, and then called back, "Well, they ought to be, they're all from the same lot. I bought two hundred extras when I put this roof on."

"When was that?" I asked.

He looked up at the clouds. I don't know whether he was divining the weather or the past. "Right after the war," he said. "That would have been forty-six."

Just then Mr. Rideheart came walking up the road under a navy blue umbrella. Maybe it was still raining down the way, where he'd just come from. He walked directly to the front porch where I sat, jauntily hopped up the steps, stomped his feet delicately a few times as if to knock off mud (though his shoes were immaculate), and extended his hand to me. I'd expected to spend the day in numb, depressed solitude, and now I felt uncomfortably honored to sit at the end of Mr. Rideheart's long line of effort—like a princess in a tale of impossible tasks. Although I was fairly sure he hadn't come all this way looking for me.

"Sean Rideheart," he said. He had white eyebrows and bright green eyes; an appealing face.

"Codi Noline." I shook his hand. "I've heard about you. You're the piñata collector."

He laughed. "I've been called many things in my time, but that's a first. I'm looking for Viola Domingos." At my invitation he sat down in the only other chair on the porch, wicker, of doubtful character.

"She's not here," I said. "Nobody's home today. Viola and the kids have gone down to the church. They're having some kind of a big party down there today, painting the saints."

"Painting the saints?" Mr. Rideheart extracted a largish blue handkerchief from the pocket of his tweed jacket and cleaned his wire-rimmed glasses with extraordinary care. I watched for a long time, mesmerized, until he glanced up at me.

"The statues of saints, in the church," I explained. "I guess they have to get freshened up every so often, like anybody else. The women paint the saints and the kids paint each other."

He replaced his glasses and observed the rooftops and tree-tops that led stepwise down the hill. Mr. Pye had his back to us now. He was industriously tacking down shingles he'd secured for this purpose ten years before Hallie was born.

"Quite a place," Mr. Rideheart said, finally. "How long have you lived here?"

It wasn't an easy question to answer. "I was born here," I said slowly. "But right now I'm just on an extended visit. My time's up soon."

He sighed, looking out over the white path of blossoming treetops that led up toward the dam. "Ah, well, yes," he said, "isn't everybody's. More's the pity."

▼▼▼

At first the Stitch and Bitch was divided in its opinion of Mr. Rideheart. While he was graciously received into the kitchens of half the club members, where he drank tea and stroked his white mustache and listened in earnest while the piñata artists discussed their methodologies, the other half (led by Doña Althea) suspected him of being the southwestern equivalent of a carpetbagger.

But for once the Doña judged wrong. His intentions were noble, and ultimately providential. When the club assembled in March for its monthly meeting in the American Legion hall, Mr. Rideheart was the guest speaker. He was supposed to lecture on folk art, which he did, but mostly he talked about Grace. He told these women what they had always known: that their town had a spirit and disposition completely apart from its economic identity as an outpost of the Black Mountain Mining Company. During the last century while men labored underground to rob the canyon of its wealth, the women up above had been paying it back in kind. They'd paid with embroidery and peacocks and fruit trees and piñatas and children. Mr. Rideheart suggested that he had never known of a place quite like Gracela Canyon, and that it could, and *should*, be declared a historic preserve. There existed a thing called the National Register of Historic Places. The landmarks on this list, he said, were protected from the onslaught of industry, as if they were endangered species. He allowed that it wasn't perfect; listing on the register would provide "a measure of protection from demolition or other negative impact," he said. "In other words, a man can still shoot an elephant, even though it has been declared endangered, and the elephant will still be dead. But the man will come out looking like a very nasty guy."

"But really it's not our houses that are going to get endangered by the poison and the dam," Norma Galvez pointed out. "It's the trees."

Mr. Rideheart replied, "Your trees are also historic."

He knew all the ins and outs of becoming a historic place. He explained where to begin, and where to go after that, to see that the river would run clean and unobstructed. There was a fair amount of bureaucracy involved, but the process was reasonably speedy. "Considering the amount of publicity that has already been brought to bear," he said, gesturing toward the window, or possibly the invisible airwaves of CBS, "I think it could be done in less than two years."

He said we would need to document everything, to prove the age and architectural character of the community. "All the photocopying, photography, and so forth can be expensive. Sometimes communities apply for block grants."

After a brief silence Viola said, succinctly, "We don't need any block grants. We're rich." And that was that.

▼▼▼

At some point during the spring I got a letter from Carlo. He'd finally made plans: he was going to Telluride. The clutch had gone out on our old Renault and he'd junked it—he hoped I wasn't attached. He was thinking of getting a motorcycle, unless I was coming to Telluride, in which case we'd get another car.

I was in such a state, running on so little sleep and such dead nerve endings, I didn't know what to think. I knew I'd have to make plans soon. And I was touched that he still took me into account when he made his move, as if we were family. But I felt nothing when I read his words; maybe it was just the same nothing there had always been between us. The words seemed to be coming from a very great distance, with the same strange, compressed tone as a satellite phone call. I looked carefully at each sentence and then waited for it to register. All I could really get clearly was the name of the town, with its resonant syllables: Telluride. It sounded like a command.

▼▼▼

I'd become estranged from Loyd after our trip. Of course, because of Hallie. I felt guilty for being away when the call came. Loyd and I had been laughing and making love for all those days while the news was laid out like a corpse in Doc Homer's house. I didn't even call him the night we got back into town. We hadn't wanted the vacation to end, so we just went straight to Loyd's house and spent the night. Surprisingly, I'd never slept in his bed. Loyd's house was entirely his own: a mobile home set up against the cliff of upper Gracela Canyon on a masonry foundation he'd built slowly himself, over the years. Through his efforts the stonework had gradually grown up over the metal shell, so that now it was pretty much a rectangular stone house, overgrown with honeysuckle vines.

Leafless for winter, the honeysuckles made a lace curtain over the bedroom window. Their shadows left faint tracings on the walls, which I watched all through the bright, moonlit hours of that first night home. Loyd held on to me tightly in his sleep. I couldn't find sleep myself, but I was happy.

The next morning he left at dawn for a seven-day stand in Yuma, and I walked down to have breakfast at Emelina's. But of course as things turned out I didn't eat—not that day or the next. By the time Loyd got back from Yuma I was too far gone to be touched.

▼▼▼

It was Uda Dell on the phone, telling me Doc Homer had gone to Tucson for a CAT scan. She called it a "skin the cat."

I sat up in bed, cradling the phone and pulling the red-and-black afghan around me; school was out for the spring break, so my life had lost what little sense of order daily work could still impose. "When did he go?" I asked. "Just this morning?" What I wanted to ask her was "Why did he tell you, and not me?" But I guess I knew the answer to that.

"No, honey, he went yesterday. He took the bus." Uda seemed industrious on her end of the phone, even as she spoke. Every few seconds she paused and I could hear a high ascending sound like cloth ripping.

"Did he tell you how long he'd be gone?"

There was another rip, then Uda's voice. "Honey, he didn't tell me a thing about it. I don't think he wanted anybody to know. You know Doc. He don't want anybody to make a fuss. [Rip . . .] But he come over and asked me to look after the house. If you or anybody was to come looking for him, he said just tell them he'd gone to Tucson for the weekend to get some medical supplies. [Rip . . .] Now, I knew that didn't sound right. I never heard of him doing that before, and you'd think whatever we all got along without for forty years we could get along without till the Judgment, don't you think? [Rip . . .] So I said, 'Doc, are you pulling my sleeve, there's something up, ain't it,' and he said there was more to it, he was going to get tested for his Alsizer's and get a Cat Skin Test done on him."

"Oh, well, that's good," I said. It was a challenge to follow this trail of reason. I could perfectly picture Uda: her large face, the cheeks tightly packed and shiny like a plum. I rubbed the top of my head and looked at the clock, with astonishment. I'd fallen asleep around 4 A.M. and slept an unprecedented seven hours.

"So, honey, what I'm calling you for is [Rip . . .] I've been itching to get into that house and clean. I know he hasn't been up to it, and I don't mean any offense, Lord knows I think the world of Doc, but I expect he needs somebody to get up there and clean. And I was thinking now'd be a good time but I didn't feel right about just going in. I've had the key all this time, ever since I used to keep you girls. He never did want the key back." She paused. "But I thought I better call and see what you said."

The key was more or less a symbolic matter. He didn't lock his front door. Nobody in Grace did. "I think the cleaning's a good idea. But I also think he'd be mad." I hesitated, uncertain of my loyalties. Outside my window I could see John Tucker in the courtyard with a tape measure. He appeared to be measuring the hundred-year-old beams that supported the roof of the back porch. I knew what it was about—the Historic Register. I had a brainstorm.

"Uda, let me go up there with you. I've got to go through the attic and dig up some old documents on the house and the land for the historic preserve thing. I've been meaning to do it, and you could help me. We could tell him you were helping me look through stuff, and that we just got carried away and beat the rugs and mopped the bathroom while we were at it. If he even notices."

Uda undertook the conspiracy with the relish of a criminal. I agreed to meet her at Doc Homer's in half an hour.

▼▼▼

The attic was pleasantly chilly and smelled of pine. Decades of summer heat had forced droplets of resin out of the rough floorboards, which in cooler weather hardened to little amber marbles that scattered in all directions as we shifted trunks and cardboard boxes. The afternoon is fixed in my memory with the sharp smell of resin and that particular amber rattle, like the sound of ball bearings rolling around in a box. It's surprising how much of memory is built around things unnoticed at the time.

I was amazed by what we found. Doc Homer's disease had manifested itself mostly downstairs; up here, our past was untouched by chaos. Stacked boxes of Hallie's and my old clothes, school papers, photo albums, and all kinds of other detritus stood in neat rows, labeled chronologically and by content. I felt overwhelmed by so much material evidence of our family's past. I couldn't think why he'd kept it. He was so practical. What conceivable use did he foresee for a box marked "ALICE, MATERNITY," for example? But you don't ask questions of an attic. Museums are their own justification.

"Look," I said to Uda, tipping up a cardboard box so she could see inside: some thirty pairs of black orthopedic shoes stacked from small to large, toes up, neat as eggs in a crate. There was a little more variety than I'd remembered. Two pairs were rather dapper little saddle oxfords, black and maroon. Another year—I vaguely did remember this—we'd been allowed to order them in charcoal suède.

Uda had a full-front apron over her old trousers and a print blouse, and she looked prepared for anything. Her lavender hoop earrings matched her wedgies, and she'd tied a red handkerchief over her hair. I was tempted to ask what she'd been ripping up this morning. She bent over beside me and picked out one of the smallest shoes, cradling it like an orphaned bird. "Law, he was so careful about you girls and your feet. I remember thinking, Oh, mercy, when those girls get big enough to want heels there's going to be the Devil to pay."

I laughed. "He wasn't just careful. He was obsessed."

Uda looked down at me. "He just wanted awful bad for you kids to be good girls," she said. "It's hard for a man by himself, honey. You don't know how hard. He worried himself to death. A lot of people, you know, would just let their kids run ever which way."

She stopped, cocking her head a little, staring at the shoe in her hand. "One year for Christmas I gave the two of you little cowboy outfits, with guns, and you just loved them, but he had to take away the guns. He didn't want you killing, even pretend. I felt awful that I'd done that, once I thought about it. He was right."

As she talked, I remembered the whole story: the cowboy outfits and the guns. Hallie and I had tried to claim moral high ground, saying he was taking away what belonged to us. He stood in front of the window, his thin face turned to the light, speaking to the world outside: "I will not have the neighbors arming my children like mercenaries." I'd looked up "mercenaries" in the dictionary, later, and felt ashamed. I explained the ethics of armament to Hallie.

"How long did you take care of us?" I asked Uda.

"Oh, I expect close to ten years all in all. Till you was about fourteen and Hallie was eleven. You remember that. You'd come up after school and we'd play Old Maid or you'd play swinging statues out in the yard. We had us a time. And I'd come up here at night when he had to go tend a baby or something. Sometimes of an evening you'd run off with the Domingos kids without telling me where you'd gone to." She laughed. "I liked to skinned you alive a couple of times. You girls was a couple of live potatoes. She was bad and you was worse."

I remembered her arms when they were thinner; a younger Uda. And I remembered standing at a kitchen counter, on a stool, patting out my own handprints in floured dough while she wove strips of piecrust, pale and thin as flayed skin, over and under to make a perfect pie top. I was experiencing a flash flood of memories. I feared I might drown in them. My skull was so crowded with images it hurt.

"He raised you to be good girls," she said again. She reached over and squeezed my upper arm before returning the shoe to its box.

I didn't know what to tell her we were looking for, for the historical project—anything documenting the age of the house would be helpful, and more generally, old photographs of any kind. Uda seemed content to poke into boxes at random, but I tried to ground myself by reading labels: "CROCKERY AND FLATWARE." "GARDEN RECORDS." One bore the mystic title "ELECTRICITY." I looked inside: socket hardware, lamp cord, the reflector from a heat lamp, a pair of rubber gloves.

I couldn't resist getting sidetracked by one marked, "ARTWORK, H., AGE 3–6." The subjects of Hallie's crayon drawings were mainly the two of us, stick sisters holding hands, or else just me, my orangeish hair radiating from my head like a storm of solar flares. There was not one figure anywhere representing Doc Homer. I wondered if he'd noticed. But he must have. He was the one who'd picked up each drawing, rescued it from destruction, and finally labeled the box. The invisible archivist of our lives.

Out of curiosity I tracked down the corresponding box called "ARTWORK, C." As I'd expected, it was full of family portraits. Big sister, little sister, father, mother, a cockeyed roof over our heads and above that an omnipresent yellow sun. It didn't resemble anyone's reality but mine, but there it was. Or maybe it wasn't so much a matter of reality as of expectation—what I felt the world owed me. I held two of our drawings side by side and concluded that there was no puzzle as to why we were different. Hallie and I had grown up in different families.

"Here's pictures," Uda reported suddenly. There was a whole aisle of boxes marked "PHOTOGRAPHS," with inscrutable suffixes. I picked up one marked "PHOTOGRAPHS, AM JOUR GEN" and found it surprisingly light, so I carried it over to the east window and sat down on a steamer trunk, settling the box on my lap before opening it. Inside were stacks of ancient eight-by-tens, their brown edges curled like autumn leaves. Each one was a photograph of a newborn baby with a startled-looking face and marble-white eyes. I leafed through them, one after another, awestruck by the oddity of these children. Of course I knew about the eyes, an anomaly of pigmentation that was genetic proof of Gracela heritage on both sides. But I'd never seen them. They tended to darken just hours after birth, and in modern times a person can easily go through life, in Grace or anywhere, without seeing a newborn.

On top of the stack of photos was a handwritten page with the heading: "Notes on Methodology." The ink had faded to brown. This would all be for his genetics paper: Doc Homer's careful notations on how he'd set up the camera, the distance, the amount of light. Apparently he'd rigged some set-up that used powerful flashbulbs, the old-fashioned kind that popped once and then were used up. It was before the days of modern electronics.

All those babies. How they must have screamed, one second

after he shot them in the name of science. Or in the name of his own desire to set himself apart. What could be more arrogant than to come back and do a scientific study of your own towns-people, like so many natives in Borneo? I looked through the photos again and kept coming back to one that had an arresting familiarity. The eyes looked back as if they knew me. I stared at the baby for a long time.

It was *me*.

"You were a doll baby," Uda said. She was looking down over my shoulder.

"That's me? Are you sure?"

She took the stack and shuffled through it like a card trick. She produced another photo. "There's Hallie. You didn't look a thing alike when you were born." To her the eyes were com-monplace, not a feature to connect us, but they were the only feature I could see. To me, we looked identical.

I held the two photographs up to the light, mystified. The eyes were unearthly. We were two babies not of this world. Just like every other one in the stack of photos; two more babies of Grace. He was doing exactly the opposite of setting himself apart. He was proving we belonged here, were as pure as anybody in Grace. Both sides. *Our mother's name was Althea. Her family despised him.*

"We're *puro*," I said out loud. And then I dropped the photographs because I heard the broken-glass pop of the flash and went blind. I heard myself make an odd little whimper.

Then Uda appeared in my field of vision, moving away. "Codi, hon, I'm going on downstairs and beat the rugs or some-thing. I'll try not to scare up too much dust."

23

THE SOULS OF BEASTS

"Hallie, I'm going to die."

"I'm Codi."

"I'm dying."

"Well, I know. We all are, more or less." After a lifetime on the emotional austerity plan, my father and I were caving in to melodrama. When I put my hand on his hand it lay dead on the sheet. It was the diagnosis that killed him. Sometimes that's how it happens.

"Where is Hallie?"

"Please don't ask me that again. We don't know where she is. Don't worry about her right now, okay? We can't do anything."

He looked at me accusingly. "You shouldn't have stood on the slide. I defended you on principle, but it was dangerous."

How do people live with loved ones after their minds have fallen into anarchy? I rejected his ruined monologues every day, still expecting order to emerge victorious in Doc Homer's universe. I can remember once seeing a monument somewhere in the desert north of Tucson, commemorating a dedicated but ill-informed platoon of men who died in a Civil War battle six months after Lee had surrendered at Appomattox. That's exactly who I was—a soldier of the lost cause, still rooting for my father's recovery. Pain reaches the heart with electrical speed, but *truth* moves to the heart as slowly as a glacier.

He'd gone off the Tacrine, his experimental drug; the doctors in Tucson found his liver was wrecked from it. Now his mind scuttled around like a crab, heading always for the dark corners. People with this disease can linger on for six or seven years, I'd read, and on average they do. But Doc Homer wouldn't.

"Do you want something to eat? Uda brought over this thing made out of crackers and walnuts and apples. It looks like one of your concoctions."

"No, thank you."

His bedroom was the largest upstairs room, with dark green walls and a high white ceiling and dormer windows across the west side. As children, Hallie and I rarely came into this room; it held an aura of importance and secrecy, the two things that most attract and frighten children. But for two days now I'd been taking care of Doc Homer here, and when I stopped to notice, I found myself the most commanding presence in the room. I felt long-legged and entitled, and strode around in my boots, adjusting curtains and moving furniture to suit myself. I'd tried to close the blinds, but he wanted them open. He insisted on the light, so I let it be.

I'd been keeping a restless vigil by his bed throughout the late afternoon, watching for signs of a lucid moment. I'd about decided it wasn't coming. I pulled my chair closer and squeezed his hand hard in an effort to make him pay attention. "Pop, I want to talk to you about Mother."

"Her kidneys were weak, and we knew it was a possibility. She had already had one episode of renal failure with the first pregnancy. She knew the risk."

I didn't really try to absorb this information. "Her name was Althea. How was she related to Doña Althea?"

"No relation." The answer, quick and firm.

"*What* relation? I know she came from here. I found some things in the attic. What was she, a great-niece?"

"What things in the attic?"

"Cousin?" I crossed my arms like the obstinate child I was.

No answer.

"Granddaughter?"

His face changed. *"Malcriado."*

"Doña Althea's family didn't want you to marry her, right?"

He let out a short, bitter little laugh unlike any sound I'd ever heard him make. "We were *Nolinas.*" Just the way he said it told me plenty.

"And you married her anyway. You eloped." I leaned forward and touched his forehead, something I'd never done. It felt cool and thin-skinned, like a vegetable. "That's so romantic. Don't you know that's what all of us would like to think our parents did? You didn't have to hide something like that from us."

"You understand nothing." He seemed very lucid. At times I suspected him of feigning his confusion, or at least using it to his advantage.

"That's probably true," I said, withdrawing my hand.

"We were a bad family. Try to understand. We learned it in school along with the multiplication tables and the fact that beasts have no souls. I could accept the verdict, or I could prove it wrong."

"You did that. You proved it wrong."

In the slanted afternoon light his eyes were a cloudy blue and his skin was translucent. He looked up at the ceiling and I had a disturbing view of his eyes in profile. "I proved nothing," he said. "I became a man with no history. No guardian angels. I turned out to be a brute beast after all. I didn't redeem my family, I buried it and then I built my grand house on top of the grave. I changed my name."

"You still have plenty of guardian angels."

"I don't think anybody in this town remembers that I'm a Nolina."

"No, you're wrong about that, they do remember. I think people are sorry. And they love you. Look at your refrigerator."

He gave me an odd, embittered look. How could he not know this was true? "Refrigerators don't preserve love," he said.

"The hell they don't. Yours does. The women in this town

bake you casseroles and pies like the world was going to end."

He made a slight sound by breathing out of his nose. He seemed strangely like a child.

"They probably can't forgive themselves for the past," I said. "Mother died before they could get everything straightened out. And then you kind of took your phone off the hook, emotion-wise."

He looked away from me again. "We aren't from here, we came from the outside. That is our myth and every person in Grace believes it, because they want to. They don't want to see a Nolina when they look at me. They want a man they can trust with their children's ear infections. And I am that man. If you change the present enough, history will bend to accommodate it."

"No. I'm pretty sure you're wrong about that. What's true is true, no matter how many ways you deny it."

He closed his eyes for a while. I'd never seen him frail or impaired. All the time I'd been his daughter, he'd never been sick.

"How long are you going to stay in bed?" I asked softly, in case he was falling asleep.

"I'm exhausted."

"I know. But after you rest, you might want to get up for a while. I can warm up some soup."

He didn't open his eyes. "Do you think Hallie is coming back?"

"I don't know what to think. We have to think yes, don't we?"

"You're the advocate of ordained truth. Are you telling me now that we can *will* Hallie back to safety?"

"No. I don't guess we can. We just have to wait."

It was the first honest conversation we'd had about Hallie. It took us both by surprise. We were quiet for a long time then, but I knew he wasn't sleeping. I could see his eyes working back and forth under his eyelids, as if he were reading his own thoughts. I wondered what his thoughts looked like, in his clear moments and in his confusion. I very much wished to know him.

"Pop?"

He slowly opened his eyes and looked at the ceiling.

"Did you really see me bury the baby?"

He looked at me.

"Why didn't we ever talk?"

He sighed. "You get beyond a point."

"You could have just given me a hug or something."

He turned away from me. His short, gray hair stood up in whorls on the back of his head. He said, "It's Friday, isn't it? Mrs. Nuñez's lab work is due back today. Can you pull her chart?"

"Okay, sleep now," I said, reaching over to pat his shoulder. "But after a while I want you to get up and get dressed. Today or tomorrow, whenever you're feeling up to it."

"I feel fine."

"Okay. When you're feeling better, I want you to take me to the place where I buried it. I can remember a lot of that night. Cleaning up the bathroom, and that old black sweater of Mother's, some things like that. But I can't remember the place."

He didn't promise. I think he'd forgotten again who I was. We were comically out of synchrony—a family vaudeville routine. Whatever one of us found, the other lost.

▼▼▼

I received a letter from the school board. It was early April, a long time after I'd stopped my hopeful excursions to the Post Office box and had given the key back to Emelina, so this letter appeared on my table among the breakfast dishes while I was at school. I saw it the minute I walked in, but tried to ignore it for the longest time. I carefully went around to the other side of the table and dropped a heavy pile of tests and began to grade them, trying not to see it. "A predator is a big guy that eats little guys," wrote Raymo. "A herbivore is your wussy vegetarian. In other words, lunch meat." She'd wedged it between the coffee cup and a bottle of aspirin. Did she think it would be bad news? I gave in and tore it open.

I can't really say what sort of news it was. Surprising news. It was notification that my contract was going to be renewed for the next year. The term wasn't over, but the school board recognized my circumstances as unusual and wanted to give me ample notice; they were eager for me to return in the fall. My temporary teaching certificate could easily be extended, especially if I had intentions of working toward certification. It was a personal letter written on behalf of the entire board and signed by someone I knew of but had never met, a Mr. Leacock. His letter cited my popularity with the students and commended me for my "innovative presentation" and "spirited development of a relevant curriculum." It didn't mention contraception or Mrs. Josephine Nash or the ozone layer. I wondered how much they really knew; it made me nervous. I kept looking sideways at that word "spirited." After knocking myself out to be accepted, I'd finally flown off the handle in a seditious direction, and won a gold star. "We are all aware of the difficulties of engaging teenagers in a vital course of academic instruction," wrote Mr. Leacock. Someone apparently felt I'd succeeded in this endeavor. I was going to be named something like teacher of the year. Teachers and kids all voted, secret ballot.

I was stunned. I stuck the letter into the pocket of my corduroy jumper and went out for a walk. I tramped quickly down the hill past Mr. Pye's green roof and Mrs. Nuñez, who sat in a rocker on her front porch, leaning precariously forward out of her chair, trying to nail a fast-moving spider with the rubber tip of her cane. She lifted the cane and stabbed the air sociably as I passed by; I waved back. I wondered about the lab work Doc Homer had mentioned in his delirium. Was she really waiting for someone far away to examine her cells or her blood and pronounce a verdict? Or was this history, a sentence she was already serving?

In town, the 4-H Club had set up a display of rabbits and fancy chickens in cages in front of the courthouse. A little county fair was planned for Easter weekend. The rabbits were of an odd-looking breed but all exactly alike, fancily marked with black-tipped ears and paws and a gorget under the throat, and it occurred to me how much simpler life would be if people were like that, all identically marked. If I were not the wrong breed. I corrected an old habit of thought: both my parents were born in Grace, and their parents before them. Possibly Doc Homer was right—I'd believed otherwise for so long it had become true; I was an outsider not only by belief but by flesh and bone.

Children knelt by the cages and talked to the rabbits in high voices, poking in sprigs of new grass from the courthouse lawn. Some shoppers had strayed over from their errands across the street. Mary Lopez, a middle-aged woman I knew from Stitch and Bitch, waved at me. She was there with her mother, a very short, broad woman with a long black braid down her back. The old woman leaned over the rabbit cages like a child. Mary rested a hand on the back of her mother's neck, a slight gesture that twisted my heart. I turned up the road toward Loyd's house. I knew he was home, or would be shortly. He was on a fairly regular schedule these days, running the Amtrak to Tucson and back. We stayed in touch.

The air had a fresh muddy edge, the smell of spring. I had several choices of route, and on a whim I took a less familiar road. I found myself walking through a neighborhood that wanted to pull me into it: the dirt shade of salt cedars, the dogs that barked without getting up. A woman and her husband argued congenially while they picked grapefruits off the tree in their back yard. The fruits rustled solidly into grocery bags while the woman talked in a low, steady voice and the man answered, on and on, a cycle of gentle irritation and love that would never be finished.

"Gee, you're pretty. Are you the new schoolteacher?"

I turned around, startled by a man on a moped. I'd never laid eyes on him before, but I was completely charmed by his line. I felt like Miss Kitty in *Gunsmoke*.

"Well, yes," I said.

"You want a ride? There's a wicked pair of brindle bulldogs up at the corner."

"Okay." I gathered my skirt and straddled the back of his bike. We buzzed smoothly uphill past the putative wicked bulldogs, who lay with their manifold chins on their paws.

"My son Ricky's in one of your classes. He says you give them a pretty good round."

"They give me one, too," I said.

He laughed. "You're Doc Homer's girl, aren't you?"

"That's right. Homer Nolina of the white trash Nolinas. He married his second cousin for mad love." I'd been lying to strangers all my life, and no wonder. Here was the truth and it sounded like a B-grade fairy tale. But I wanted to know if Doc Homer was right—if everyone had forgotten.

"I never heard that," my driver said. "I just heard she was dead."

"She's dead all right. But she was born and grew up right here. You're around the same age I am, you wouldn't remember her, but it's the truth. Her family thought unkindly of my daddy, so they ran off for a while and he put on an attitude."

He laughed at that, but said, "You oughtn't to talk bad about a man like him."

"Oh, I know. Doc Homer's inclined to be useful. But I swear it looks to me like he's been running his whole life on vengeful spite."

"I got me an old Ford that runs on something like that."

Ten seconds later he let me off at the base of the path up to Loyd's house. Loyd was sitting outside, drinking coffee under the huge mesquite that shaded his front yard. He was just out of the shower, wearing only a pair of soft gray sweatpants. His damp hair lay loose on his shoulders. He looked very happy to see me but also unsurprised; typical, maddening Loyd. Jack betrayed excitement in his thumping tail, but Loyd made no sudden movements. He let me come to him, bend over to kiss him, sit down in the chair beside him. I was oddly conscious of his skill with animals.

"You want coffee?"

"No thanks."

He sat looking at me, smiling, waiting.

"Guess what," I said finally, handing him the letter. He read it, grinning broadly.

"It doesn't mean anything," I said. "I still can't stay."

"It does mean something. It means they want you, whether you stay or not. It means you're real good at what you do."

I took the letter back and looked at it, not at the words but the object itself. "I guess you're right," I said. "I don't think anybody ever told me that before. Not in a letter. I guess that's something."

"Sure it is."

"I was thinking of it as just one more choice I'd have to make. A complication."

"Life's a complication."

"Sure," I said. "Death is probably a piece of cake by comparison."

We looked at each other for a while. "So tell me about your day, honey," I finally said. We both laughed at that.

"Another buck in the bank, doll."

"Is that it? Do you like driving trains? You never talk about it."

"You really want to hear about it?"

"I think so."

"Okay. Yeah, I like driving trains. Today I went out on a dog catch."

"Not the Amtrak?"

"No. A special mission."

"You had to catch a dog?"

"A dog catch is when you go out to bring in a train after the crew's died on the main line."

"The whole crew died?" I was visited by the unwelcome thought of Fenton Lee in his sheared-off engine, after the head-on collision. I knew this couldn't be what Loyd meant.

He smiled. "Died on the hours-of-service law. They'd worked a full twelve hours but there were holdups somewhere and they still hadn't gotten to a tie-up point. You can't work more than twelve hours straight because you'd be tired and it would be dangerous; it's federal law. So you just stop where you are, and wait for a relief crew."

"Good thing airline pilots don't do that," I said.

"I bet they go to sleep at the wheel more than we do, too," Loyd said.

"So you went out and caught the dog."

"Me and another engineer and a conductor and a brakeman all deadheaded out to Dragoon to pick up the train. The dead crew came back to Grace in a car."

"And you, what, took the train on into Tucson?"

"Yep."

"So what does that mean, what do you do exactly? Is there a steering wheel?"

He laughed. "No. You adjust throttles, you set brakes, you watch signals. You use your head. Today I had to use my head. I was the lead engineer and it was a real heavy train, over ten thousand tons. There were two helper engines coupled at the rear of the train."

"Ten thousand tons?"

He nodded. "A little better than a mile and a half long."

"And you're in the front engine, and there's two engines pushing on the back?"

"Yep. The hard part was topping over Dragoon. That's a real long hill, a long descending grade from Dragoon to the Benson bridge, and there's a siding you sometimes have to pull into there, at twenty-five miles an hour. But the train is so damn heavy it wants to take off on you down that hill. I've messed up on that hill a bunch of times before. Just between you and me, one time I went flying through there at sixty, hoping to God there was nobody coming on the main line. I never could have gotten into the siding track."

"I guess there was nobody coming."

"No. But today there was, and I got us in safe and sound. Today I did it exactly right." He smiled at me over his coffee cup.

"So tell me about it."

"Well, we topped over the hill way below the speed limit, and when I got about half the train over the hill I set a minimum amount of air brakes. Then I waited for it to take hold. The brakes take hold all along the train, in every car, front to back. And then I just watched the speedometer keep coming up."

"You're still speeding up? Even after you've set the brake?"

"You've got six thousand tons and a mile of train coming down the hill behind you. What do you think it's going to do?"

Doc Homer used to pose puzzles like this to Hallie and me, to develop our cognitive skills. "But you've also got some-odd thousand tons still coming *up* the hill behind you."

"That's right. A little less coming up, and a little more coming down, every minute. That's the tricky part. That's the Zen of Southern Pacific."

I was extremely impressed.

"On a normal train you'd be real leery of setting the brake while half your train's still coming up the hill. The rear would start pulling backward and you'd break in two."

"Oh," I said. "So then you'd have two trains."

"Then you'd have a nice long vacation without a paycheck."

"Oh."

"But I had helper engines that could push on me from the back, so I was pretty sure we wouldn't break in two. I radioed my helper engineer back there to keep pushing up the hill at full throttle, that's throttle eight, and then cut it back to throttle one when he topped over."

"So he was pushing and you were braking at the same time."

"Yep. Setting the brake early enough, that was the part I never got before. It kind of goes against what you think's right."

"Nobody can just tell you how to do that hill?"

"No, because every train's different on every hill. Every single run is a brand-new job. You have to learn the feel of it."

"So you can't necessarily do the same thing next time?"

"Not exactly the same thing, no. But on this train the minimum set worked perfect. And then I worked the throttle to maintain forty miles an hour. I came down the hill through Sybil and Fenner, the last siding before the Benson bridge. I got a flashing yellow after Sybil so I knew we'd probably have to go into Fenner. Then we went by a yellow, and the next signal was a diverging approach, a red over yellow, and I had to be down to twenty-five at that signal so we could get into the siding. Sure enough, there was a train on the main line headed east."

"What if you'd been going sixty, like last time?"

He winked. "I wouldn't be getting any nice letters telling me how good I am at my job."

"Seriously. What if you saw a headlight coming at you in the dark?"

"You heard about Fenton Lee, then, did you?"

"What would you do?"

Loyd looked at me. "Jump off."

"Yeah?"

"Oh, yeah. I did it one time already, when I was a fireman. The engineer hit a siding too fast and that sucker looked like it was going off the track. I was out of there like buckshot. I got a big old bruise on my butt, and the guys laughed at me because they didn't derail. I don't care. There's things worth risking your life for, but a hunk of metal's not one of them."

I watched him drink his coffee. In the hot sun his hair had dried to its normal glossy, animal black. The mesquite leaves cast feathery shadows all over his face and the muscular slope of his chest. The sight of his bare feet stirred me oddly. I badly wanted to take him inside to bed.

"Well. But you *are* real good at your job," I said.

"I'm getting there."

"I guess I never knew there was so much to it."

He set down his cup and crossed his arms. "Pretty good for an Injun boy, huh?"

"You could have told me more about it."

He smiled. "Codi, did anybody ever tell you a damn thing you didn't want to know?"

I stalled, avoiding the question. "If I told you I wanted to go to bed with you right now, would you think I only loved you for your mind?"

His eyes sparkled. "I think I could overlook it."

▼▼▼

That night I lay in Loyd's arms and cried. Since the day I spent with Uda in the attic, wishes and anger had backed up in me, and now they rushed out, rocketing my mind around on a wild track toward emptiness. I told Loyd about the photographs and unrelated things, old things, like making pies with Uda Dell. "I have all these memories I couldn't get hold of before, but it doesn't make me feel any better," I said.

"What kind of memories?"

"Everything. Really, my whole childhood. Most of it I had no idea was there. And most of it's happy. But Loyd, it's like the tape broke when I was fifteen, and my life started over then.

The life I'd been living before that was so different—I don't know how to say this, but I just couldn't touch that happiness anymore, I'd changed so much. That was some other little bright-eyed, righteous girl parading around trying to rescue drowning coyotes and save chickens from the stewpot. A dumb little kid who thought the sun had a smiley face on it."

"And what happened when she was fifteen?"

I withdrew from Loyd's arms. Had I set him up to ask? I lay looking at the wall, considering whether I could tell him. If I only had two more months in Grace, it wasn't long enough. "I can't explain it," I said. "I guess it finally hit me that nobody was going to take care of me."

"In high school you were doing a pretty good job of taking care of yourself."

"That's what it looked like. It probably looks like that now, too."

Loyd took me back onto his shoulder, which felt hard like a cradleboard under my head. He stroked my cheek. "You still have all the family you grew up with. Hallie's somewhere out there. She'll come back. And Doc's still here."

"Neither one of them is *here*."

"Codi, for everybody that's gone away, there's somebody that's come to you. Emelina thinks you're her long-lost sister. You know what she told me? She wants you there in that little house forever. She said if I let you leave Grace she'll bust my butt. She loves you to death."

"So this is all a conspiracy, I said."

"Yeah. Emelina bribed me to fall in love with you." He laughed and kissed my hair. "Honey, there's not that much money in the world."

I didn't wish to be comforted. "You can't replace people you love with other people." I said. "They're not like old shoes or something."

"No. But you can trust that you're not going to run out of people to love."

"I don't think I can trust life that far. I lost my mother. You don't know what that's like."

"No, I don't."

"You don't have any idea what the whole story is, Loyd. You don't know everybody I've lost."

He gathered me into his arms and we didn't talk anymore, but in my chest I could still feel a small, hard knot of anger and I held on to it. It was my wings. My exit to safety.

▼▼▼

Finally I read all of Hallie's letters. There were half a dozen I'd never opened, the ones that came after. I knew she'd mailed them before she was kidnapped—I could read the postmarks— but I still held the hope that there might be some clue in there that would help bring her back. Once I opened the letters that hope would be gone.

But I was past a certain point now, like Loyd's train going over the hill. The momentum of wanting to hear Hallie, even for a few minutes, was growing heavier than anything I might have had to lose. More than ever in my life I needed to ask her what to do, how to live without guarantees, without safety.

So I read the letters, and there were no clues. Only the ordinary, heartbreaking details of war and rural life and the slow progress of hope.

I'd forgotten that her last letter, which I'd read on the trip to Santa Rosalia, was a tirade. I had to get it out and read it again to remember, and the sting was gone. "If I get another letter that mentions SAVING THE WORLD, I am sending you, by return mail, a letter bomb." (Had I really used those words? But I knew I had, more than once.) "I don't expect to see perfection before I die. What keeps you going isn't some fine destination but just the road you're on, and the fact that you know how to drive." Two hours after she'd mailed that, she had written a pained apology that reached me now, a lifetime later. Any one moment could be like this, I thought. A continental divide.

Codi [she wrote], I'm sorry, I didn't say it right. I'm touchy about being worshiped. I'm afraid of becoming Doc Homer Junior, standing on a monument of charity and handing down my blessings, making sure everybody knows where we all stand. I don't *feel* like I'm doing that, but it's the thing you fear most that walks beside you all the time. I don't want you of all people to see me that way. I'm not Saving Nicaragua, I'm doing the only thing I can live with under the circumstances. The circumstances being that in Tucson I was dying among the garden pests. Working with refugees, and also subsidizing the war that was killing them. I had to get out.

By virtue of our citizenship we're on one side of this war or the other. I chose sides. And I know that we could lose. I've never seen people suffer so much for an ideal. They're sick to death of the embargo and the war. They could say Uncle, vote for something else, just to stop this bludgeoning. And you know what? I don't even consider that, it's not the point.

You're thinking of revolution as a great all-or-nothing. I think of it as one more morning in a muggy cotton field, checking the undersides of leaves to see what's been there, figuring out what to do that won't clear a path for worse problems next week. Right now that's what I do. You ask why I'm not afraid of loving and losing, and that's my answer. Wars and elections are both too big and too small to matter in the long run. The daily work—that goes on, it adds up. It goes into the ground, into crops, into children's bellies and their bright eyes. Good things don't get lost.

Codi, here's what I've decided: the very least you can do in your life is to figure out what you hope for. And the most you can do is live inside that hope. Not admire it from a distance but live right in it, under its roof. What I want is so simple I almost can't say it: elementary kindness. Enough to eat, enough to go around. The possibility that kids might one day grow up to be neither the destroyers nor the destroyed. That's about it. Right now I'm living in that hope, running down its hallway and touching the walls on both sides.

I can't tell you how good it feels. I wish you knew. I wish you'd stop beating yourself up for being selfish, and really *be* selfish, Codi. You're like a mother or something. I wish you knew how to squander yourself.

I sat with this letter for a long time trying to understand what peace she was asking me to make.

The others were impersonal, full of description and the usual manic-depressive mélange of experience. The weather had been too dry. A shipment of Yugoslav tractors had come in and they were working out well. "The Deeres were better," she lamented, "but you have to run them like glass hammers, they can be dry-docked for lack of a bolt. The U.S. refuses to trade with us and then makes secret, niggling lists of what we get from the Eastern bloc. The embargo having slipped their minds, apparently."

In another letter she said they heard gunfire almost every night. "People talk about the second reconstruction. They mean after the U.S. invades. We get up every day and scan the horizon for holocaust." In this same letter she talked about her young trainees and the joy of seeing a new idea take root in a mind; I knew the moment. When Raymo grasped DNA, his countenance was touched with light. We'd shared something.

I stayed up most of the night rereading letters, all the way back to the first one from the Guatemalan border, where she saw women running from the army carrying babies and back-strap looms. And earlier, on the beach, where she'd watched a man sell shrimp from a bucket that was counterweighted with a plastic jug of drinking water. He drank as he went along, to keep the load balanced. The purity of direct necessity.

But the letters ended, finite as a book or a life, and I had no choice but to keep coming back to the last one, scrutinizing it for a sign of goodbye. It wasn't there. It was a description of the children's Christmas Eve pageant, three or four words about Julio, and a self-effacing story of how she'd broken her plate that morning at breakfast. Of course it was a disaster; there was only one anything per person in the house. She was mad at herself for being careless, but the neighbor women rounded up a new plate. They made a joke of its being tin, unbreakable.

Nothing else. The closest thing to prescience had come a few days earlier, in a pensive pared-down note that said: "Sometimes I still have American dreams. I mean literally. I see microwave ovens and exercise machines and grocery-store shelves with thirty brands of shampoo, and I look at these things oddly, in my dream. I stand and I think, 'What is all this for? What is the hunger that drives this need?' I think it's fear. Codi, I hope you won't be hurt by this but I don't think I'll ever be going back. I don't think I can."

▼▼▼

I had my own nightmare again, but this time I understood that it wasn't blindness. It was a flash bulb in my father's camera. Even from inside the dream I knew that, and I didn't wake myself when I heard the glass pop. I took the risk of staying where I was, and went on dreaming. What I saw next was an infant face that wasn't my own but my child's, lit in the flash. Then I saw her whole body in moonlight. She was a seventeen-year-old girl, naked and long-limbed, walking up the path toward our house. I stood in the kitchen and watched her through the screen door as she came up the path from the river. For a second she disappeared in the inky shadows under the cottonwoods and I felt completely afraid, but then she emerged again in the light. Her skin glowed white.

I thought: "If she tries to walk through this screen door into Doc Homer's kitchen, she'll evaporate. She can't come in here." So I ran outside and gathered her up, a ridiculous bundle of long arms and legs. I carried her back through the cottonwood grove and down the path, away from the house. Over our heads was a chalky full moon with cloud rubbed across it, like something incompletely erased. I was hunched over and stumbling and I started to run along the dry riverbed, absurdly burdened with this long-legged child as big as myself. I didn't talk or look at her, I just carried her along.

Hallie followed me down the path. I didn't see her come, but I heard her voice right behind me.

"Codi, stop. She's too heavy. You can put her down now."

I clamped her weight against my chest. "No I can't, she'll fall."

"Let her go. She won't fall."

"I can't."

Hallie urged gently, "Let her go. Let go. She'll rise."

And then I woke up with empty arms.

24

THE LUCKIEST PERSON ALIVE

The call came sometime before dawn.

While I brushed my teeth I watched the mirror closely and became aware of my skull: of the fact that my teeth were rooted in bone, and that my jawbones and all the other bones lay just under the surface of what I could see. I wondered how I could have missed noticing, before, all those bones. I was a skeleton with flesh and clothes and thoughts. We believe there is such a safe distance between the living and the dead. I recalled how I'd used Mrs. Josephine Nash to shock my students into paying attention, on the first day of school. I'd thought I understood something they didn't, about death. That it was understandable.

I was still at the mirror when Loyd came. I saw him appear behind me. First he wasn't there, and then he was. He was going to drive me to Tucson. I had to go to the Mexican consulate to get a registered letter and some papers, and then I would sign some other papers from the Nicaraguan government. Of course, there was no Nicaraguan consulate. It was the Minister of Agriculture who called. We had become something like friends, though we would probably not speak again now. Or perhaps we would. I'd heard of people united by disaster keeping track for years afterward, holding reunions. I thought of boat people.

Business executives stranded overnight in elevators. How would they celebrate? What specific moments would they recall for each other? My thoughts kept straying onto random paths like these, hoping to get lost in a thicket.

The Minister said there would be a package coming later. Not her body, but a parcel of personal things, some books and journals. Her plate and cup, her clothes, those items were distributed to neighbors. The body would stay there. She had requested of somebody, at some point, that she be buried in Nicaragua if that ever had to happen. She said Nicaragua could use the fertilizer.

What was the last thing she said to me in person? How did she look? Why can't I remember?

"Loyd," the face in the mirror said. "What do I do now?"

"Put on your shoes."

"Okay."

The sun was just coming up as we drove away from Grace. The world looked inhospitable.

"I should have gone down there," I said.

"And done what?"

We drove past an old junkyard outside of town. I'd never noticed it before, though it must have been there since before I was born. A man stood on the bonnet of a rusted car, shading his eyes, looking down into the ravine.

"On the phone they said her hands were tied," I told Loyd. "He said they found her that way. But I can't believe that. It doesn't sound right to me that she would let anybody just tie her up and then shoot her in the head."

"Maybe they made a mistake," he said. "Maybe it didn't happen exactly that way."

"I know my sister. I think she would get away somehow," I said.

"Wait for the letter. That'll tell everything."

"Maybe they made a mistake," I repeated. "Maybe so."

Within an hour the daylight had overcome its early bleakness. Now it looked like any normal, slightly overcast day. The normalcy made me angry, but it was a weak kind of anger that held no pleasure.

"If I'd told her about Doc Homer back in December, how bad he was, she would have come home."

"You can't make this your fault."

"But she would have come home"

"Codi," Loyd said, looking at me and not finishing. His face held such pain I didn't want to see it. Finally he said, "You could probably think of a hundred little things that would have made this turn out different. But you'd be wrong. A life like your sister's isn't some little pony you can turn around any way you want. It's a train. Once it gets going it's heavier than heaven and hell put together and it runs on its own track."

I didn't say anything to that. Loyd barely even remembered meeting my sister. How could he know what her life meant?

On the interstate we passed the site of a bad accident. You could see it coming: the cop cars and ambulances all huddled around, lights flashing importantly, making their scene. As we came closer we had to slow down; one lane was blocked by a trailer rig with a smashed front end. Out in the median, at an angle that bore no relation to the direction of traffic, sat a white convertible with its frame bent violently into a V-shape.

When we passed it I saw that it wasn't a convertible after all; the top had been sheared off, and lay on the other side of the road. An arc of glass and chrome crossed the highway like a glittering river littered with flotsam and jetsam: a pair of sun-glasses, a bright vinyl bag, a paperback book. At the trail's end was the pile of steel. I'd never seen such a badly wrecked car.

"Doesn't look like anybody walked away from that one," Loyd said.

I thought of Hallie walking out of the library that time, years ago, then remembering her sunglasses and turning back just before the marble façade fell down. She could just as well have died then. It made no difference now.

The luckiest person alive.

The ambulance pulled out right behind us, its warning lights alternating like crazy winking eyes. We quickly left it behind, though, and we weren't speeding by any means. Loyd saw me watching the ambulance and glanced up at the rear-view mirror. "They're not in much of a rush, are they?"

Just then, while we watched, the lights stopped flashing. I understood that I had just seen someone die. No reason to hurry anymore. My limbs flooded with despair and I didn't see how I was going to survive. I kept imagining what that little white car must have looked like half an hour ago, and the driver, some young woman listening to the radio, checking her hair in the mirror, preoccupied with this afternoon or tonight or whatever small errand had taken her out.

"Why does a person even get up in the morning?" I asked Loyd. "You have breakfast, you floss your teeth so you'll have healthy gums in your old age, and then you get in your car and drive down I-10 and die. Life is so stupid I can't stand it."

"Hallie knew exactly what she was doing. There wasn't anything stupid about her life."

I practically shouted at Loyd, "I'm not crying about Hallie right now. I'm crying about that person that just died in the ambulance."

He was quiet.

"Loyd, I don't know what I'm going to do." I was afraid the muscles in my chest might tear themselves apart. I thought senselessly of Doc Homer's discussion of liver tissue and heart tissue. As if it mattered what part of your body was the seat of emotion, all of it could be torn up, it was just flesh. Doc Homer didn't even know about this yet. I'd called, and we talked, and it was clear he didn't know what I was telling him. He talked about Hallie being kept after school. Maybe he never would understand, maybe his mind would just keep wandering down other happy trails. Loyd handed me his handkerchief and I tried to blow my nose.

"What would she want you to do?"

"*She* would be crying for a person in a damn ambulance that she didn't even know. Not *me*."

I saw lightning erupt in the dark clouds behind the Catalina Mountains. It was an impossible time of year for a lightning storm. I'd seen photographs of lightning frozen in its terrible splendor, ripping like a knife down the curtains of the sky. They say that to take those pictures you just open your camera on a dark night, in a storm, and if you're lucky you get a wonderful picture. You have no control.

"Hallie isn't dead," I said. "This is a dream." I laid my head back against the headrest and cried with my knucklebones against my mouth. Tears ran down to my collarbone and soaked my shirt and still I didn't wake up.

25

FLIGHT

Getting on the bus was the easiest thing in the world. I only took what I could carry. Emelina would send my trunk to Telluride.

I noticed the junkyard again on the way out of town. They should have had a sign there: Welcome to Grace. Farewell to Grace. Dead grass poked up through the rusted husks of big old cars that hunched on the ground like elephants, the great dying beasts of the African plain. It was early June, soon after the end of school. The land was matchstick-dry and I felt the same way, just that brittle, as if no amount of rain could saturate my outer layers and touch my core. I was a hard seed beyond germination. I would do fine in Telluride. Carlo had lined up a job for me as a model in a summer fine-arts school. I would sit still for solid hours while people tried for my skin tones.

Uda Dell and Mrs. Quintana, Doc's assistant for twenty-one years, were going to take shifts with Doc Homer. His office was closed for good, and everybody now drove over to New Mexico to be healed. There were no thunderclaps when it happened; all this time we'd thought he was indispensable. Uda and Mrs. Quintana revered him. I couldn't picture them feeding him, buttoning up his shirt, but I knew they would do those things. Somehow reverence can fashion itself into kindness, in a way that love sometimes can't. When I went up there to tell him goodbye, he was eating a soft-boiled egg and said he couldn't tarry, he was in a hurry to get to the hospital.

I bobbed along with the motion of the Greyhound bus, leaning with the curves. When I relaxed enough I could feel like a small chunk of rock in outer space, perceiving no gravitational pull from any direction: not from where I was going, nor where I had been. Not Carlo, not Loyd, not Doc Homer. Not Hallie, who did not exist.

"Where do you think people go when they die?" Loyd asked, the day before I left. He was on his way out to take a westbound into Tucson; the next day he would fetch home the Amtrak. We stood in my front door, unwilling to go in or out, like awkward beginners trying to end a date. Except it wasn't a beginners' conversation.

"Nowhere," I said. "I think when people die they're just dead."

"Not heaven?"

I looked up at the sky. It looked quite empty. "No."

"The Pueblo story is that everybody started out underground. People and animals, everything. And then the badger dug a hole and let everybody out. They climbed out the hole and from then on they lived on top of the ground. When they die they go back under."

I thought of the kivas, the ladders, and the thousand mud walls of Santa Rosalia. I could hear the dry rattle of the corn dancers' shell bells: the exact sound of locusts rising up from the grass. I understood that Loyd was one of the most blessed people I knew.

"I always try to think of it that way," he said, after a minute. "He had a big adventure up here, and then went home."

Leander, he would mean. My spleen started to ache when I thought of Hallie fertilizing the tropics. Thinking about how much she loved stupid banana trees and orchids. I said, "I have this idea that if I don't stay here and cry for Hallie, then there's no family to absorb the loss. Nobody that remembers."

"And that's what you want? For Hallie to be forgotten?"

I couldn't have said what I meant. "No. I just don't want to be the one that's left behind to hurt this much. I want to be gone already. If you're dead when somebody stabs you, you don't feel it."

"Leaving won't make you dead. You'll just be alive in a different place."

"This place has Hallie in it. When I lived here, I was half her and half me."

"Going away won't change how you feel."

"I won't know that till I'm gone, will I?"

He picked up my hand and examined it as if it were a foreign object, which was just how it looked to me. He was wearing a green corduroy shirt with the sleeves rolled to the elbows, and I felt I could look at that shirt for as long as Loyd might choose to stand in my door. There were all those small ridges, the greenness, the nap of the cloth. If I kept my focus minute enough I could remain in the world, knowledgeable and serene.

"Anyway you're wrong," he said. "There's family here to absorb the loss."

"Doc Homer, Loyd, he's . . . I don't think he understands she's gone."

"I wasn't talking about Doc Homer."

I shifted my field of vision to include the lower part of Loyd's face and the blunt dark ends of his hair. A whole person seemed an impossible thing to take in all at once. How had I lived so long and presumed so much?

"I'm sorry about everything, Loyd."

"Listen, I know how this is. You don't think you'll live past it. And you don't, really. The person you were is gone. But the half of you that's still alive wakes up one day and takes over again."

"Why should I look forward to that?"

He turned my hand over. "I can't answer that."

"Well, I'm sorry, Loyd."

"I'm sorry too."

"Well. You've got to go to work." I avoided his eyes.

Loyd took my face in one hand and put the other hand on

the small of my back and he kissed me for a long time. His mouth felt cool as green corduroy, a simple thing I could understand. We began the kiss standing up, and when we finished we were sitting on the step.

"You have to go," I said again. That was the last thing, my last words for Loyd.

When he and Jack were gone I stood for a long time looking out at the rambling jungle of the courtyard. A hummingbird, possibly the same one that had inspired Nicholas to learn to walk, was hovering at the red funnels of the trumpet vine climbing my wall. I watched the bird move stiffly up and down over an invisible path, pausing, then moving left, then up again and back, covering the vertical plane with such purpose it might have been following a map.

I felt Emelina's presence. She stood in her kitchen door, shading her eyes, watching me. I waved, but she didn't wave back. Her face was drawn tight with mute, unarmed rage; it must have been the worst thing she was capable of aiming at a friend. She didn't know my tricks, that you could just buckle up your tough old heart and hit the road. My course must have been as indecipherable to her as the hummingbird's. We are all just here, Emelina, I wanted to say. Following our maps, surviving as we know how.

The kitchen door closed quietly and I understood that it was her kindest goodbye. The sun was strangely bright on the whitewashed wall and the hummingbird hung in the air, frozen inside its moment. A photograph of the present tense.

▼▼▼

All morning on my last day people came pecking softly at my door like mice. A legion of mice bearing gifts. It was mostly women from the Stitch and Bitch. No one else was as succinct as Emelina. They wanted to know what I would be doing, where I would live. I mentioned the art school, but wasn't specific.

"We sure do love you, hon," said Uda Dell. "I packed you a lunch. There's yellow banana peppers in there from the garden. They're not as big as some years but they've got a right smart bite. Stay another year," she added.

"Do you have a good winter coat?" Norma Galvez asked me. "It snows up there. You'd just as well stay here."

In their eyes my life should have been simple, purely a matter of love and the right wardrobe. It was as if I had fifty mothers.

In the last hour before I left I had to go through Emelina's kitchen to retrieve a pair of jeans from the laundry room. John Tucker was folding laundry. He told me Emelina was lying down upstairs with a bad headache.

"You got a baseball game today?" I asked.

"Yeah."

"Sorry I won't be around to see you win."

He smiled. In a year I'd watched him grow into his elbows and lose the better part of his shyness. His voice was beginning to crack. "Mom's really going to miss you. She'll be a witch for the next month. She'll make us clean out the chicken pens and stuff."

"It's all my fault," I said, grabbing a runaway corner of a sheet and helping him fold it. "You guys can send me hate mail in Telluride."

He laughed. "Okay."

"If it gets too bad you can run away from home. Come up and see me. We'll go skiing."

He hoisted his laundry basket and headed for the stairs.

When I came back out through the kitchen Viola was there at the table, lying in wait like a predator.

"Sit down," she said. "Save your shoes."

I was lunch meat. I sat down.

"Boy oh boy, kiddo," she said.

"What does that mean? That I should stay here?"

"Sure you should."

"Well," I said.

"But nobody ever could tell you a darn thing."

"That's what I hear."

"I been wanting to tell you something."

"I know Emelina's pissed off at me."

She snorted. "If you don't know that already you're not going to hear it from me."

"Oh." I thought about what else she might have to reveal to

me. "I know about my mother," I said. "I know she came from here, that she was a cousin or something to Doña Althea. And that she and Doc Homer ran off."

Viola smiled a little. "Son of a gun. He told you?"

"More or less."

She adjusted the coil of hair on the back of her head, reclaiming its territory with the planting of a few long bobby pins. "Well, that's not what I was wanting to tell you."

We sat looking at each other for a good while. Her T-shirt said I WAS DEEP DISHED AT MAMA LENARDA'S. I had no idea where it might have come from.

"I'm not supposed to tell you," she added.

"Says who?"

"Says me. Doc Homer would shoot me if he found out."

"I don't think there's much danger, Viola."

"Well, but it's the principles."

Now I was curious. "So, did you sit me down here to tell me something or not?"

She hesitated, shifting her weight forward onto her elbows on the table. "I was looking after you girls the day your mama died."

"You kept us at home?"

She nodded. "I was supposed to."

"But you didn't."

"I thought you had the right to say bye to your mama, like anybody else. To tell her, *'Vaya con Dios.'* Anybody else had no business up there, they just went to watch the show, but you had business and you was not allowed to go. Hallie was just born, she didn't know anything anyway so I left her with Uda Dell."

"And you took me up to the field to see the helicopter come down."

Viola leaned back in her chair. "I'm not saying I did, and I'm not saying I didn't."

"What are you saying?"

"Just that you had a right. That's all. Now, skedaddle. *Que le vaya bien.*"

▼▼▼

The Greyhound was mostly empty, a dry gourd rolling across the desert, occasionally spilling out a seed or two in an inhospitable outpost: Bowie, Willcox, Benson. It was 110 degrees down there, not something people would travel through unless they were desperate to be elsewhere.

As things had turned out, Grace was not going to dry up. The women of the Stitch and Bitch had won back the river. A vice-president of the Black Mountain Mining Company called a press conference in Phoenix to announce that after seventy years of productive and congenial relations with the people of Gracela Canyon, the mine operation there was closing up shop. It was a matter of the leaching operation's being no longer profitable, he said. The dam would be deconstructed. Naturally, if any harm had been incurred, all necessary reparations would be made to the people of Grace. He made no mention of the historic registry petition that had been filed one week earlier. So mountains could be moved. Now I knew.

When my bus paused in Willcox a woman climbed aboard and chose to sit by me, rather than take her chances on something worse that might come along, I guess. She wore an ample white jogging suit and had an odd, metallic hair color. I spent the next fifty miles in fear of a conversation I wasn't in the mood for, but she just kept scowling at a gardening magazine.

Then suddenly she held out her magazine as if it had offended her. "That kills me, how people can grow four o'clocks like that," she said, whacking the page with the back of her plump hand.

I glanced over at the unbelievable floral displays in her magazine. I could relate to her frustration. You just knew they trucked in those flowers from a climate-controlled greenhouse somewhere and arranged them on the lawn, right before snapping the photo.

"I'm Alice Kimball," the woman explained. "I get the worst slugs."

Alice. Would my mother be wearing tepid jogging suits now,

if her organs had not failed her? I tried to smile. "Where do you get them?"

"In my four o'clocks. That's what I'm trying to tell you, I can't grow a four o'clock to save my life. The leaves get so full of holes they just look pitiful. And they get in the lawn, too. My husband says he hears them out there eating up his grass. What can you do?"

"I'm not the right person to ask," I said. "My sister could sure tell you, though. She got a degree in Integrated Pest Management. She used to answer the Garden Hotline in Tucson, 626-BUGS."

Mrs. Kimball brightened as if I'd offered her a peppermint. "I've called that before. They have the nicest little girl on that line, she'll tell you anything you want to know."

"That was my sister you talked to. Hallie Noline." I was amazed by the coincidence, but then again probably half of Tucson had turned to Hallie for advice. And half of Nicaragua. "That was part of her job," I said. "She did that for six years."

Mrs. Kimball looked around at the neighboring seats as if Hallie might turn up for consultation. "Well, do you mean she's quit? I just thought the world of her."

"Yep, she quit. She left the country."

"Left the *country?*"

"She went to Nicaragua." Everybody in this country should know her name, I thought. During the Iran hostage crisis they had a special symbol on the newscasts: a blindfolded man, and the number of days. A schoolchild glancing up from a comic book would know that this story was about *them*. But a nation gloats on the hostility of its enemies, whereas Hallie had proved the malevolence of some men we supplied with machine guns. Hallie was a skeleton in the civic closet.

Some people knew. I'd gotten a card from a nun in Minneapolis who had known Hallie. She was one of several thousand people who had gone down to Nicaragua for just a week or two, she said. They helped pick coffee, or if they had training they did other helpful things. The idea was just to be there in the danger zone, so that if the U.S. should attack, it would have to attack some of its own citizens. This nun, Sister Sabina Martin, had helped give vaccinations. She met Hallie at the clinic in Chinandega the day Hallie brought in a child who'd drunk paraquat from a Coke bottle. Sister Martin and Hallie sat with the child the whole day, and she said that although I might not think it possible, she felt she'd come to know Hallie well during that time. In some circumstances, she said, an afternoon can be a whole life.

"Oh, well," Mrs. Kimball said, after quite a while. "You must miss her."

"I will, when it really sinks in. She hasn't been gone that long."

"I know what you're going through," said Mrs. Kimball. "I lost my sister in 1965."

I hadn't told her Hallie was dead. Mrs. Kimball had seized the subject of death all on her own. "I'm sorry," I said, not really wanting to be encouraging, but you couldn't just ignore it, either.

"She's been dead all this time of an aneurysm and there are still days when I think, 'Oh, wait till I tell Phoebe about that!' Before I realize. I always think it's harder to believe they're gone when it's sudden."

"My sister," I said, and then stopped, afraid of the lie I was about to tell. I was going to say, "isn't dead." I heard an old voice in my head, the teller of tales: I am a cello player running away from home. We are from Zanzibar, we're from Ireland, our mother is the Queen of Potatoes. I was through constructing myself for other people. I didn't say anything.

Several seats ahead of us, a teenage couple had begun necking enthusiastically. You couldn't blame these kids, the scenery was boring and would drive you to anything, but they made me feel hopelessly alone.

"Well," Alice said, apparently remembering it was garden pests we'd agreed to talk about. "What would *you* do for the slugs?"

"I really don't know, I'm not that good with plants." I considered the problem for a while. "I think what Hallie used to do was put out beer for them, in little tin cans. The slugs are attracted to it and they fall in, or something. I know that sounds crazy but I'm pretty sure it's right."

"Well." She stared at me thoughtfully. "My husband and I aren't drinkers, but I guess I could go out and get some beer for the slugs. Do you know what brand?"

"I don't think it matters. I'd get whatever's on sale."

"All right, I'll do that," said Mrs. Kimball. She opened her magazine again to the incendiary four o'clocks, but then closed it right back up, holding the place with her finger. "You ought to try to keep in touch with your sister," she told me. "Young people think nothing will ever happen. You should treasure your family while you have it."

"Well, really I don't have it," I said, resentful of her assumptions. "It's gone. My mother died when I was little and my father will probably be dead before the year's out, and my baby died, and now my sister is dead too. Maybe I'm not as young as you think."

Mrs. Kimball looked stunned. "Your sister? The one on the phone?"

"She got killed by the contras. The ones down there that we send all the money to. I think you probably heard about it."

She looked uneasy. "I don't know. I might have."

"It made the news in Tucson, at least for a day. You just forgot. That's the great American disease, we forget. We watch the disasters parade by on TV, and every time we say: 'Forget it. This is somebody else's problem.' "

I suppose I was going, as Rita Cardenal would say, mental. I didn't look at Mrs. Kimball but I could see her magazine drift slowly to her lap. I looked at the bright garden on the magazine cover and felt strangely calm. "They kidnapped her one morning in a cotton field," I said. "They kept her as a prisoner for weeks and weeks, and we kept hoping, but then they moved everybody to another camp and some of the prisoners they shot. Eight of them. Hallie and seven men. All of the men were teachers. They tied their hands behind them and shot them in the head and left their bodies all sitting in a line at the side of a road, in a forest, right near the border. All facing south."

I felt a hard knot in my chest because this was the one image I saw most clearly. I still do. My voice sounded like a voice that would come from some other person's throat, someone who had a dead sister and could speak of such things. "The man that found them was driving up from Estelí, coming along the road, and at first when he saw them all sitting there he thought, 'Oh, that's too many. I can't give them all a ride, they won't fit in my truck.' "

Mrs. Kimball and I didn't speak again after that. I looked out the window. Far to the south, low cone shapes pushed up against the flat, bright sky. Those distant mountains were probably in Mexico, I knew, though borders in this barren land seemed beside the point. I heard Mrs. Kimball turn a page of her magazine. We'd been silent for over an hour before she first spoke up about the four o'clocks, but the silence was much more noticeable now, after we'd broken it with our little conversation. Awareness is everything. Hallie once pointed out to me that people worry a lot more about the eternity *after* their deaths than the eternity that happened before they were born. But it's the same amount of infinity, rolling out in all directions from where we stand.

▼▼▼

My airplane was said to be bound for Denver, but it sat on the runway for a very long time. I had a window seat and could watch other planes lift their noses one after another and plow their way up an invisible road into the sky. I wasn't impatient. Normally at this point in a flight my heart would pound and my mouth would go to cotton, but today my viscera were still. It didn't matter especially if we burned in a fiery crash.

I thought maybe the air traffic controllers were trying to decide whether we were worth the trouble; we were only a small, twin-engine plane, incompletely filled. A few seats ahead of me a mother coached her preschooler, who was already crying because he knew his ears would hurt when we went up. This was not the first leg of their trip.

"You swallow, honey. Just remember to swallow, that makes your ears feel better. And yawn."

"I can't yawn."

"Sure you can." She demonstrated, her voice stretching wide over the yawn: "Think about being real, real sleepy." People yawned all the way back to the smoking section, so strong was the power of motherly suggestion. I felt overcome with sadness.

The aisle seat of my row was occupied by a teenager, and the empty seat between us was filling up with her overflow paraphernalia. She threw down a hairbrush and a curling iron—whack! whack!—and pulled a substantial mirror out of a makeup case the size of my carry-on luggage. She began applying careful stripes of pastel eye shadow. When she blinked, her eyelids waved like a pair of foreign flags.

"Give it a rest, Brenda," said the man sitting across the aisle. "You're not going to see your boyfriend for ten whole days. Why not take this wonderful opportunity to let your face get some fresh air?"

Brenda ignored this advice, staring with deep absorption into her makeup mirror while her parents in B and C beamed her the Evil Eye. The mother was wearing a polka-dot jumpsuit with coordinated polka-dot earrings, all a little too eager-looking even for the first day of vacation. The man had on sunny golf pants that clashed with his disposition. It was hard to ignore them, but Brenda was practiced. She glanced serenely at her left wrist, which bore three separate watches with plastic bands in the same three shades as her eye shadow. Her hair looked as if each strand had been individually lacquered and tortured into position. No matter how you might feel about the aesthetic, you had to admire the effort. Most people put less into their jobs.

"Brenda, honey, please pay attention when your father is talking to you," said the woman in the polka dots. "Could you please just try? Listening to you and your father bicker for a week and a half is not my idea of a vacation."

"You should have left me at home," Brenda said quietly, staring directly ahead. " 'Honey, I think we forgot something. Did I leave the iron on? No, we forgot Brenda.' " She shot me a glance, and I think I smiled a little. I couldn't help being on Brenda's side here. In my term as a schoolteacher I'd gained sympathy for adolescence. If I had to take a trip with those two I'd probably paint my face blue for spite.

The plane jerked a little and then began to roll creakily down the runway, gathering speed. We were taking off without a warning announcement of any kind. "Flight attendants prepare for takeoff" came out in a single scrambled burst over the intercom, and the women in pumps and dark suits ran as if from an air-raid siren. I closed my eyes and laid my head back, trying to hold on to my visceral indifference, but it fell right away. My heart had caught up with me. I heard the little boy chattering to his mother and I yawned nervously. So much of life is animal instinct: desire and yawning and fear and the will to live. We left the earth and climbed steeply into the void.

My habit was to count seconds during the lift-off, with my mind on news stories that ran along the lines of "crashed into a meadow only seconds after takeoff . . ." Somewhere I'd gotten the idea it took seven minutes to get past imminent peril. I counted to sixty, and started over. We'd been airborne for maybe three or four minutes when our pilot's deep Texan voice came over the intercom. "Folks, I apologize for the delay in taking off today. We had trouble getting one of these cantankerous old engines started up."

The announcement startled my eyes open. I looked at Brenda, who widened her eyes comically. "Great," she said.

"It's nice to know you're riding the friendly skies in a bucket of bolts."

Brenda laughed. "Like my boyfriend's car."

"I think we'd be safer in your boyfriend's car."

"Not in their opinion," she said, inclining her head across the aisle.

I closed my eyes again. I tried to relax, but couldn't help listening to every change of pitch in the engine noise. They sounded wrong. Suddenly I confided in Brenda, "I hate to fly. You know? It scares me to death."

I hadn't admitted this aloud before, and was surprised to hear it come out so naturally. The truth needs so little rehearsal. Brenda reached over and patted my hand.

"Folks, this is Captain Sampson. I'm sorry to report that we've lost that engine again."

Against my will I glanced out at the wing to see if anything had actually fallen off. My heart beat hard and out of synch with itself and I felt I might die of fright. I let the fingertips of my right hand lie across my left wrist, tracking the off-rhythm of my aimless heart. If I were really dying, I wanted to be the first to know.

After another minute, during which I imagined Captain Sampson and his copilot trying everything, his paternal drawl crackled on again. "We could probably make it to Stapleton on one engine," he said, "but we'll play it safe. We're going to turn around and head back into Tucson to see if they'll let us have some new equipment."

I hated the sound of the word "equipment." I had visions of men in coveralls running out to strap a spare engine onto the wing. If we made it back to the airport at all. Suddenly we banked so steeply my stomach turned. I must have looked pale, because Brenda reached over and squeezed my hand again.

"Try to think about something relaxing," she said. "Think about kissing your boyfriend."

"That's *relaxing?*"

She smiled. "No. But it takes your mind off."

She was right; it did, for a second or two. I thought of Loyd's last kiss on my doorstep in Grace. But it also made my chest ache, further distracting my heart from the task at hand. Nausea pressed on the back of my throat. I closed my eyes, but vertigo is an internal distress; shutting out the world does nothing to help. The plane took another steep bank.

We were in an unnatural position, vertical in the air and slipping down, with nothing to support us.

When we finally leveled out again I opened my eyes. We were skimming low over Tucson and I was comforted—irrationally I know—by the nearness of things. Clusters of houses huddled together as if for reassurance, and in between them lay broad spans of flesh-colored desert. The freckled ground was threaded with thin, branched lines of creeks, like veins in the back of a hand. It looked as if there were water in the creeks, although I knew better. At this time of year they were bone-dry rivers of sand.

The rush of adrenalin had rinsed me clean. I looked hard out the window and understood suddenly that what I saw was full of color. A watercolor wash of summer light lay on the Catalina

Mountains. The end of a depression is that clear: it's as if you have been living underwater, but never realized it until you came up for air. I hadn't seen color since I lost Hallie. I thought hard, trying to remember; it seemed unbelievable, but there was none. Almost none. Loyd's green corduroy shirt, and the red flowers and the hummingbird against the brightly lit wall, the moment Emelina said goodbye. And that was all. Before that, the last thing I clearly remembered in color was Santa Rosalia in its infinite shades of brown.

I laughed at myself for carrying my mother's phobic blood in my veins. And for telling Alice Kimball how to cure slugs. Practicing all this family business without a license. It seemed extraordinary and accidental that I was alive. I felt crowded with all the sensory messages that make up life, as opposed to survival, and I recognized this as something close to joy. As we slipped down over the city every building and back lot was beautifully distinct. I forgot about my heart, left it to look after itself. We passed south of downtown, over the railyard, where the boxcars stood in line looking sweet and mismatched like a child's toy put together with no eye for color coordination. Just past the railyard was a school where a double row of corn-colored school buses were parked in a ring, exactly like one of those cheap Indian necklaces made for tourists. Bright backyard swimming pools gleamed like turquoise nuggets. The land stretched out under me the way a lover would, hiding nothing, offering up every endearing southwestern cliché, and I wanted to get down there and kiss the dirt.

I made a bargain with my mother. If I got to the ground in one piece, I wasn't leaving it again.

▼▼▼

The Amtrak didn't depart until three-thirty; I made it with time to spare. The station clerk wouldn't sell me a ticket to my destination, saying it wasn't a passenger stop. I argued. I knew the train stopped there for a crew change. Finally I realized he could sell me a ticket for anywhere at all on the eastbound line, it didn't matter. I knew where I was getting off.

We pulled out of the station and I hugged myself, cradled in the wide reclining seat, letting the rails rock me like a baby. The car smelled like smoke and old leather. I lay sideways in the seat, facing the window, my legs curled under me. Tucson, Arizona, passed slowly enough to nod at, take notice of, and then let go. At a steady, measured pace these things were revealed to me: the backs of brickyards, the backs of barrios, a large outdoor factory where Mexican women painted tiles. We passed buildings whose high walls, empty of windows, were spray-painted with huge secrets seen by no one but the travelers of the Southern Pacific. And then came the broad, open desert— mile after mile of it. I understood the appeal of train travel. You couldn't help knowing where you'd been.

At some point I fell asleep, and at some point I woke up again. I felt I'd been on that train for the whole of my life. We approached Grace from a direction that was new to me. We didn't go by the junkyard. There was a tunnel through the granite cliffs and we entered it fast—the dark rock wall magnifying the rocketing clamor of tons of forward motion—and then, quiet and sudden, out into the bright light again. I blinked against the overexposed world. By the time my eyes adjusted we were right downtown behind the old jailhouse, pulling the sighing brakes, slowing down. We came gliding under the long wooden porch of the depot. The sun glinted on its pleated tin roof, and I noticed a carob tree there with a trunk the size of a rain barrel. It must be the male—the mate to the one up by the liquor store. The one I'd been looking for.

The conductor looked a little surprised when I pulled my bag off the rack and hopped down onto the concrete apron of the depot.

"This isn't anywhere, sweetheart," he said, looking down at me from the doorway. He was a very old, very dark-skinned man whose uniform looked as if it could hold up its shoulders without him.

"I know," I said.

"You can't get back on," he warned. "Ten minutes for a crew change, and then we're headed out for El Paso."

"I know. I don't want to get back on. I live here."

"Well, how do you do," he said. He stepped back into the

car and waved at me through the window. His gloved hand fluttered like a dove.

A hundred yards up the line I saw the fireman climb down the ladder from the engine. It was someone I'd gone to school with—Roger Bristol. Loyd tossed down Roger's grip and his own, one at a time, and then swung himself easily down the ladder as if he were born for this work. He talked briefly with two other men—the oncoming crew, I guessed. They would speak in their magical language of dog catchers and sun kinks and the ones that had died on the line, picking up trains from the dead and moving on. They parted ways and the new crew climbed into the engine. The other two men walked toward the depot carrying their grips and lunch buckets: one short and stocky, the other taller, broad-shouldered, with his hair in a ponytail. The people you love always look perfectly proportioned from a distance.

Shortly the train began to move again, very slowly, the speed of a living creature. You could still run and catch it. Loyd and Roger kept walking toward me without seeing me. Standing there watching him, knowing what he didn't, I had so much power and none at all. I was on the outside, in a different dimension. I'd lived there always.

Then he stopped dead, just for a second. I'll remember that. The train moved and Roger moved but Loyd stood still.

He caught up to me in an instant, with a twinkle in his eye and his bag slung over his shoulder like a ready traveler.

"Thanks for the ride," I said.

He put one arm around my neck and gave me the kind of kiss no fool would walk away from twice.

26

THE FIFTY MOTHERS

For several days I kept coming back to this: we had no body. I wanted to have a funeral for Hallie, but I was at a loss. I knew the remains should not have been important, but in a funeral the body gives the grieving a place to focus their eyes. We sit facing it, bear it on our shoulders, follow it down the road in procession and finally long to follow it into the ground. The body would have provided an agenda and told me what to do, in lieu of Hallie, who was gone.

I went to look for something else that in my mind stood for her: the *semilla besada*, one of the supernaturally blessed trees that in the old days were festooned like Christmas trees with the symbols of people's hopes. We could hold a funeral there, outside, under the leaves. I wanted to find the exact plum tree where we'd hidden a lock of our intertwined hair. I knew the orchard but couldn't find the tree. Either it was gone, or it was no longer exceptional. Maybe the trees all around it had stretched their taproots and found the same nurturing vein.

It was June, a week before Hallie's thirtieth birthday. The canopies were in full green, each one as brilliant as a halo. The blossoms had dropped and left behind incipient fruits swelling three and four to a cluster, not yet pruned by nature or by hand. Every tree in every orchard looked blessed. So we had the funeral there, in the old Domingos plum orchard.

I'd asked people to bring something that reminded them of Hallie. I spread the black-and-red afghan on the ground and we stood around that. Instead of decorating a tree with our hopes for the future, we decorated a blanket with icons from the past. All the women from Stitch and Bitch were there. And J.T. and Emelina, of course, and Loyd. All of my students, as well. Doc Homer didn't make it. He didn't go very far out of his house these days, or very far out of his head.

It was awkward getting started. I remembered the last time I'd hugged her, thinking I could hold on and stop our lives right there. I took some breaths. "Hallie asked to be buried in Nicaragua," I said. "She wanted that. To enrich the soil of a jungle. But I wanted something here too." I stopped, because it sounded to me like small talk. Words only cover the experience of living. I looked around at the unpretentious faces like slices of bread, all the black dresses, the dark shoes, and I looked up at the bright leaves lit from above. It was a brilliant, hot day and I didn't feel at all like crying. The black dresses made me think of Greece. Nothing seemed quite real.

Several peacocks had gathered in the trees behind our heads, keeping their distance, but curious, probably hoping for food. A peacock wouldn't know the difference between a picnic and a funeral. The outward signs were similar.

"Do you think we should sing?" I asked.

"Yes," said Emelina. "We ought to sing."

"What?" I couldn't think of any particular song that Hallie liked, except some silly things from our teenage years. "Mother and Child Reunion" and "Maggie May." I thought of Hallie moonwalking to "Thriller," and then I thought abstractly about never seeing her again, what that really meant. In the back of my mind I was still wondering when she would come home. I couldn't concentrate. Someone suggested "Let the Circle Be Unbroken," so we sang that, and then we sang "De Colores" because everybody knew it. Norma Galvez's husband Cassandro played the guitar.

Then it was quiet again. People shifted slightly on their feet, the same motion repeated many times throughout the crowd, like the dancers at Santa Rosalia. Except unconscious, and unrehearsed. I pulled some letters out of my pocket and read parts of them that Emelina had helped me pick out. I read what Hallie said about not wanting to save the world, that you didn't choose your road for the reward at the end, but for the way it felt as you went along. And I read some things she'd said about nations forgetting. Refusing to sell tractor parts, then wondering why people would turn to Yugoslavia for tractors. I was aware that my reading might seem a little rambling, but I felt there was some logic to it, and people were tolerant. Truly, I think they would have listened to me all day. It occurred to me that such patience might be the better part of love.

I read a quote she'd written me that seemed important, a thing said by Father Fernando Cardenal, who was in charge of the literacy crusade: "You learn to read so you can identify the reality in which you live, so that you can become a protagonist of history rather than a spectator." I waited a minute, while a peacock screamed. Then I read some words of Hallie's: "The very least you can do in your life is to figure out what you hope for. And the most . . ."

Another peacock suddenly howled nearby. I saw Emelina's twins craning their necks, trying to spot it. I went on:

"And the most you can do is live inside that hope. What I want is so simple I almost can't say it: elementary kindness. Enough to eat, enough to go around. The possibility that kids might one day grow up to be neither the destroyers nor the destroyed."

I finished by reading the letter from Sister Sabina Martin. She said thousands of people joined us in mourning Hallie. "I know that doesn't make your grief any smaller," she wrote. "But I believe it makes Hallie's presence larger. Certainly, she won't be forgotten."

Several peafowl had hopped to the ground and were making insistent, guttural noises, impatient for food. I saw Glen and Curtis sneak off into the trees in pursuit of a peacock they'd never catch.

"This is what I brought." I knelt by the afghan and set down a pair of Hallie's small black shoes, about second-grade size. They could have been mine, it was impossible to tell, but I said they were Hallie's. I put them in the center of the red-and-black crocheted blanket. "I brought these because they just reminded me of growing up with Hallie. We had to wear these ugly shoes. It was just one of the important things we did together. I don't know. We felt kind of alone sometimes." I stood up and looked at the trees through the curtain of water in my eyes.

Viola laid down some marigolds. She had on her polyester, the funeral dress for all seasons, and she was perspiring; broad damp spots underlined her bosom. "Whenever I think of you kids I think of the *cempazuchiles* and being up at the graveyard for All Souls'. You were always a very big help."

I looked at Viola. She stared back, rubbing the bridge of her nose. There was the faintest light of a smile.

Several women had things they claimed we'd left in their houses when we played there as children: a doll with unpleasant glass eyes and a gruesomely pockmarked head where its hair had come out; a largish plastic horse; a metal hen that, when you pushed her down on her feet, made a metallic cluck and laid a small marble egg. Also a pink sweater, size 6X. Mrs. Nuñez swore it was Hallie's. "It was behind the refrigerator. I didn't find it till last year when the refrigerator give out and we had to call the man to move it out and get us a new one in there. The dust, I hate to tell you! And there was this little sweater of Halimeda Noline's. She used to set up there on top of the refrigerator, because I told her she couldn't drink beer till she was as tall as her daddy."

This was the truth, dead center. I remembered her up there huddled among the Mason jars and bright cracker boxes. I stared at the freshly laundered pink sweater lying with outstretched arms and thought about how small Hallie had been at one time. Miss Colder and Miss Dann were just then displaying an ancient-looking picture book, but there was a roaring in my ears and I lost track of what they were saying. I believe it was the physical manifestation of unbearable grief. But you learn in these situations that all griefs are bearable. Loyd was standing on one side of me, and Emelina on the other, and whenever I thought I might fall or just cease to exist, the pressure of their shoulders held me there.

I could hear people's words, but my vision was jarred by showers of blue sparks. Or the world went out of focus. And at other times I could see but couldn't hear. Doña Althea clumped forward with her cane and set down a miniature, perfectly made peacock piñata. It perched there on the pile of childhood things, its small eyes glittering and its tail feathers perfectly trimmed. It was an exquisite piece of art that could have made it into Mr. Rideheart's gallery, but it was for Hallie. I tried to listen to what she was saying. She said, "I made one like this for both of you girls, for your *cumpleaños* when you were ten."

To my surprise, this was also true. I remembered every toy, every birthday party, each one of these fifty mothers who'd been standing at the edges of my childhood, ready to make whatever contribution was needed at the time.

"*Gracias, Abuelita,*" I said softly to Doña Althea as she clumped away.

She didn't look at me, but she heard me say it and she didn't deny that she was my relative. Her small head crowned with its great white braid nodded a little. No hugs or confessions of love. We were all a little stiff, I understood that. Family constellations are fixed things. They don't change just because you've learned the names of the stars.

Uda Dell went last. "I brought this bouquet of zinnias because every spring Hallie helped me dig my zinnia bed." She laid down the homely, particolored bouquet, and added, "I crocheted that afghan, too."

"You did?"

She looked at me, surprised. "Right after your mommy died. Well, I don't guess you'd remember."

"This blanket got us through a lot of tough times," I said. I was feeling a little more steady on my feet. I folded in the corners and drew it all up into a bundle against my chest. About everything Hallie and I had ever done was with us there in the Domingos orchard. Everything we'd been I was now.

"Thank you," I said, to everybody.

I turned my back and headed alone with my bundle up the Old Pony Road to Doc Homer's house.

HOMERO

27

HUMAN REMAINS

There are women in every room of this house, he thinks: Mrs. Quintana upstairs, and now there is Codi, standing in the kitchen with her baby. Her arms and chest clutch the black wool bundle and it weighs her down like something old, made of stone. The weight makes him want to turn away. He thinks, This is the fossil record of our lives.

"I'm going to bury this. Do you want to help me?" She looks up at him and tears stream down. The grief on her face is fresh as pollen.

"You already buried it."

"No, no, no!" she screams, and slams the screen door behind her. He follows her down the path but she doesn't go down to the riverbed this time, she turns and goes right around the house into the backyard. When he catches up, a little breathless, she is standing with her boots on the ground like rooted stalks. Standing beside the old plot where Hallie used to grow a garden. A few old artichoke bushes have gone thistly and wild around its perimeter. Codi drops the knotted bundle and goes to the tool shed to retrieve a shovel. She comes back and digs hard into the ground. It hasn't been disturbed for many years.

"Are you sure this is a good place?" he asks.

Without speaking, she steps on the shovel and its tip bites

into the sandy soil again and again, lifting, digging, and lifting out a deep, square hole.

"You might want to have a garden here again someday. When this house is yours."

The shovel stops suddenly. "Did you know I'm staying?" She looks at him.

He looks back, waiting.

"I told Loyd about the baby. Yesterday I took him down there to the riverbed where you showed me. I can remember every minute of that night. You gave me some pills, didn't you? You really did want to help." She looks up at the sky, using gravity and the small, twin dams of her eyelids to hold in tears. "So Loyd knows about that now. He's sad. I didn't think about that part—that he would be sad. I was thinking the baby was just mine."

"It wasn't just yours."

"I know." She wipes her cheeks with the back of her hand, leaving a faint dark smudge under each eye. She looks at him very oddly. "We might have another one. Loyd and I. I don't know. There's time to see."

"Yes."

"Did you know I'm a good science teacher? The kids and the teachers all voted. They say I'm spirited. How do you like that?"

"It's what I would expect."

"I'm teaching them how to have a cultural memory." She looks at her hands, and laughs, but looks sad. "I want them to be custodians of the earth," she says.

He also looks at her hands. They remind him of something. Whose hands?

"You really can't approve of me staying, can you?" she demands, suddenly angry. "You raised me to turn my back on this place. That worked for you, but the difference is you *knew* it was really your home. You knew you had one. So you had a choice."

"That's all very well and good," he says, "but you still might want a garden. These artichoke bushes still produce. Every summer they bloom as if their hearts depended on it. Never mind that there was nobody taking in the harvest." He takes the tip of a silvery leaf between his fingers. It looks knifelike, but is yielding and soft.

She looks at him for quite a long time, smiling, and then she looks down at the bundle. "It's all right to bury this here," she says. "There are no human remains."

No human remains. No. Human. Remains. The three words chime in his head like large, old bells, three descending notes that ring and ring, speeding up in tempo until they clang against one another.

"How true," he says finally.

She shaves out the edges of the hole so it is neat and square, and then drops the bundle in. She throws a handful of dirt on top of it and stands there looking down.

"We're a pair of scarred old souls, aren't we, Codi?"

"I don't know what we are. I'm trying to figure out what I hope for."

"It's a most dangerous thing, hope."

Her eyes flash with something bright. Love or anger. But she doesn't speak.

"Hope involves giving a great deal of yourself away," he tells her.

"That's a pitiful excuse."

"Oh, it's pitiful all right, but there you have it. It's hard to give much away when you're the subject of widespread disapproval and your heart is leaking from puncture wounds."

"That's true. We got punctured pretty bad. But we still gave the world a lot, Pop. We gave it Hallie."

"We did. We surely did."

She begins shoveling dirt back into the grave. He thinks about the fact that all these particles of dirt have now been rearranged. No fixed strata. Alice was the gardener. When she has finished she moves to his side and he takes her elbow. They stand side by side in their small garden of sand and buried children. The bones in his wife's arm are as thin as whistles. "Do you have any idea how much I love you?" he asks her.

She stares at him, then squeezes his hand. "Hallie was a protagonist of history," she says.

"She wanted to save the world."

"No, Pop, that's not true. She wanted to save herself. Just like we all do."

He looks at the tall, living daughter his wife has suddenly become. He is no longer angry about these changes. "Save herself from what?"

"From despair. From the feeling of being useless. I've about decided that's the main thing that separates happy people from the other people: the feeling that you're a practical item, with a use, like a sweater or a socket wrench."

He asks, "Are we the other people?" He is curious.

"You're not useless. You gave yourself to this town for forty years. Scarred soul or not."

"Yes. But I gave for the wrong reasons. As you have pointed out."

She laughs. "I did, didn't I? Damn!" She pulls at the end of a silver artichoke leaf. "I was scared to death I was going to grow up to be just like you." She looks at him, and laughs again. She says: "God, I could never be just like you."

They are standing in the garden, in a dwarf forest of artichokes. She has just dug a hole and buried God knows what and now has made a confession of either contempt or admiration. He waits to see what will happen next.

"Maybe the reason you gave yourself to this town doesn't matter that much. Maybe what matters is just that you did it. Maybe that makes you a good man. You know what Loyd told me one time?"

"No."

"He thinks people's dreams are made out of what they do all day. The same way a dog that runs after rabbits will dream of rabbits. It's what you do that makes your soul, not the other way around."

It's what you do that makes your soul. Standing opposite him, staring down into the grave, he sees two sad little girls in cowboy hats. Is this what he has done? "I don't think you should be here," he says to them.

The elder daughter looks up, her pale eyes steady. "But we are here, Papa."

"Yes, you are."

"Why don't you want us?"

"Oh, God, I do." He kneels down and takes them both in his arms and pulls them against his chest. He understands for the first time in his life that love weighs nothing. Oh God, his girls are as light as birds.

COSIMA

28

DAY OF ALL SOULS

Gracela Canyon, if you strip it down to the enduring things, is a great, granite bowl of air. It's a wonderful echo chamber. Voices of women and children in the cemetery reached Viola and me from all the way across the canyon, rising on invisible air currents with the ravens and the spirits of all those old bones being tended by their children. It was getting on toward late afternoon, and we walked slowly. Viola had spent the morning supervising family operations, and said she was tired. But she'd promised that any day I asked her she would take me to the place where we watched my mother go. I chose that particular day in 1989, the end of a decade, the Day of All Souls, when we were all up decorating the graves. I don't know why.

I'd finished sweeping off my father and the other Nolinas and had decked them out with little bunches of marigolds at their heads and feet. It was something like tucking children into bed. I was their historian and their guardian angel. I never found Ursolina, the little bear. I imagine she's somewhere closer to the mine, where the earth has been shifted too many times to bear witness to what it has buried in it. The rest of the family, for all the times they'd had to be exhumed, had stayed together surprisingly well.

I knelt all morning in the dirt, laying out a border of creek rocks around Doc Homer. He'd been gone more than two years, but it took me awhile to decide on this. Emelina's boys had hauled the rocks up there for me. When we took them out of the water and piled them into the wheelbarrow they lost their luster, all drying to the same whitish color of dust, and I was afraid after all that work they would be the wrong thing, but they were fine. Uniform and shipshape, washed smooth by the abrasion of natural forces. I laid them end to end around the dirt mound, knocking them together and working them back and forth a little to find a natural fit. As I worked I thought of the masonry walls of Kinishba, with the bones of children inside.

When I stood back finally and dusted my chapped hands against my jeans, I saw I'd achieved nothing so fine as Kinishba, but had marked out a clear boundary, anyway. He would like it. I'd brought some order to his cosmos finally.

I squinted into the sun. Across the tops of about a hundred gravestones and many people I saw Viola in her black dress, standing on a little rise, her gray hair wandering from its knot. She pressed one hand to the small of her back while Mason and Nicholas danced in front of her with their hands full of candy, begging for something, wearing her out. Nicholas was three and a half; John Tucker was talking about quitting school to be a hoghead for Southern Pacific. I thought: "I can't wait forever." So I went and asked her right then and she said fine, after lunch we would go. "I'm about done here," she'd said, cracking the sugar skull of a *calavera* between her molars. "They can figure out which end of the flowers to put in water without me."

We took the quickest road down into town, then cut across the hill behind the high school and through the splendid canopies hung with fruit that the Stitch and Bitch Club had won back from Black Mountain Mining. From there we headed up the Old Pony Road toward the abandoned mine. The tops of the flat tailing mounds were dimpled with rain-catching basins and I'd noticed that sprigs of rabbitbrush were starting to grow up there.

The road was steep. No route out of Grace was an easy climb. Twice I had to ask Viola to let me catch my breath. I held a fist to my breastbone, panting hard, a little embarrassed by my infirmity but also a little pleased by the external proof of what was still mostly an internal condition. I was pregnant.

"I feel like I don't have any energy. I come home from school and sleep till Loyd wakes me up for dinner, and then I go back to bed." This new relationship with sleep was a miracle to me.

"Oh, yeah," she said. "All your get-up-and-do-it goes to the baby. Right from the start you know who's gonna be the boss."

Those first few weeks are an unearthly season. From the outside you remain so ordinary, no one can tell from looking that you have experienced an earthquake of the soul. You've been torn asunder, invested with an ancient, incomprehensible magic. It's the one thing we never quite get over: that we contain our own future.

I'd written this to Hallie in the pages of a bound notebook that would never be torn out or mailed. These letters stayed with me. I told her: it feels like somebody's moved in. It's a shock. You find you're not the center of the universe, suddenly it's all flipped over, you have it in you to be a parent. You're not all that concerned any more with being someone's child. It helps you forgive things.

We reached the crest of the canyon where the white salt crust of the old alfalfa fields began. Dead for two decades, the earth was long and white and cracked, like a huge porcelain platter dropped from the heavens. But now the rabbitbrush was beginning to grow here too, topped with brushy gold flowers, growing like a renegade crop in the long, straight troughs of the old irrigation ditches.

A wind was picking up from the south, and Viola and I could smell rain. High storm clouds with full sails and a cargo of hail made their way in a hurry across the sky. Viola's hair blew around her face as she walked. I asked, "Did you know her kidneys had failed her once before, when she was pregnant with me?"

"Sure," Viola said. "She was real sick both times."

"But she went ahead and had Hallie anyway."

"You don't think about it that much. You just go on and have your kids."

I wanted to believe my mother had thought about it. That

Hallie was her last considered act of love—an act with unforeseen consequences, some of them just now coming into flower in the soil of another country. I said, "I always knew I was up here that day. I can remember seeing the helicopter."

"You remember that?"

"I thought I did. But people told me I hadn't, so I'd about decided I'd made it up."

Viola took my hand. I could feel the soft flesh and the hard wedding band in her grip. "No, if you remember something, then it's true," she said. "In the long run, that's what you've got."

I knew the place when we came to it. We were right there already.

This is what I remember: Viola is holding my hand. We're at the edge of the field, far from other people. We stand looking out into the middle of that ocean of alfalfa. I can see my mother there, a small white bundle with nothing left, and I can see that it isn't a tragedy we're watching, really. Just a finished life. The helicopter is already in the air and it stays where it is, a clear round bubble with no destination, sending out circular waves of wind that beat down the alfalfa. People duck down, afraid, as if they're being visited by a plague or a god. Their hair is blowing. Then the helicopter tilts a little and the glass body catches the sun. For an instant it hangs above us, empty and bright, and then it rises like a soul.